WILLIAM
SHAKESPEARE

JOHN DAVENANT'S PAINTED CHAMBER

WILLIAM SHAKESPEARE

A STUDY OF FACTS AND PROBLEMS

BY

E. K. CHAMBERS

VOL. II

Ὁ κόσμος σκηνή· ὁ βίος πάροδος·
ἦλθες, εἶδες, ἀπῆλθες

FRAGM. DEMOCRITI

OXFORD
AT THE CLARENDON PRESS
1930

OXFORD UNIVERSITY PRESS
AMEN HOUSE, E.C. 4
LONDON EDINBURGH GLASGOW
LEIPZIG NEW YORK TORONTO
MELBOURNE CAPETOWN BOMBAY
CALCUTTA MADRAS SHANGHAI
HUMPHREY MILFORD
PUBLISHER TO THE
UNIVERSITY

Printed in Great Britain

CONTENTS

vi CONTENTS

APPENDIX B. CONTEMPORARY ALLUSIONS—*cont.*

APPENDIX C. THE SHAKESPEARE-MYTHOS—*cont.*

LIST OF ILLUSTRATIONS
VOLUME II

NOTE ON RECORDS

As far as possible, I have used originals, or published facsimiles, or photographs specially taken. But in the interests of intelligibility, I have often supplemented the inadequate punctuation and varied the irregular capitalization of manuscripts. Contractions are generally extended. If of sufficient importance, cancelled passages are printed with lines through them, and interlineations in thick type. Occasionally I have used the symbol ⟨ following a date, to indicate an uncertain date not earlier than that named, and the symbol ⟩ followed by a date, to indicate an uncertain date not later than that named. In registration entries and pedigrees, n. stands for birth, ob. for death, C. or c. for christening, M, m (or =) for marriage, B. or b. for burial.

PRINCIPAL DATES

1556, November 24.	Will of Robert Arden.
1558, November 17.	Accession of Queen Elizabeth.
1561, February 10.	Administration of Richard Shakespeare.
1564, April 26.	Christening of Shakespeare.
1568, September 4.	Election of John Shakespeare as Bailiff.
1582, November 27.	Licence for Marriage of Shakespeare.
1583, May 26.	Christening of Susanna Shakespeare.
1585, February 2.	Christening of Hamnet and Judith Shakespeare.
1592, March 3.	Production of *1 Henry VI*.
1592, September 3.	Death of Robert Greene.
1593, April 18.	Registration of *Venus and Adonis*.
1593, May 30.	Death of Christopher Marlowe.
1593, September 25.	Succession of Ferdinando Lord Strange as Earl of Derby.
1594, April 16.	Death of Earl of Derby.
1594, May 9.	Registration of *Lucrece*.
1596, July 22.	Death of Henry Lord Hunsdon.
1596, August 11.	Burial of Hamnet Shakespeare.
1596, October 20.	Grant of Arms to John Shakespeare.
1596, November 9.	Burial of George Peele.
1597, March 17.	Appointment of George Lord Hunsdon as Lord Chamberlain.
1597, May 4.	Fine on Purchase of New Place.
1598, September 7.	Registration of *Palladis Tamia*.
1599.	Opening of Globe Theatre.
1601, February 8.	Revolt of Robert, Earl of Essex.
1601, September 8.	Burial of John Shakespeare.
1602, May 1.	Conveyance of Land in Old Stratford.
1602, September 28.	Copy for Cottage in Chapel Lane.
1603, March 24.	Death of Queen Elizabeth.
1603, May 19.	Patent for King's men.
1605, July 24.	Conveyance of Tithes in Stratford.
1607, June 5.	Marriage of Susanna Shakespeare to John Hall.
1608, February 21.	Christening of Elizabeth Hall.
1608, September 9.	Burial of Mary Shakespeare.
1608–9.	Acquisition of Blackfriars Theatre by King's men.
1609, May 20.	Registration of *Sonnets*.
1610.	Probable Migration of Shakespeare to Stratford.

1613, February 14.	Marriage of Princess Elizabeth to Frederick Elector Palatine.
1613, March 10.	Conveyance of Blackfriars Gate-House.
1613, June 29.	Fire at Globe Theatre.
1616, February 10.	Marriage of Judith Shakespeare to Thomas Quiney.
1616, March 6.	Death of Francis Beaumont.
1616, March 25.	Will of Shakespeare.
1616, April 23.	Death of Shakespeare.
1619.	Printing of Jaggard's Quartos.
1623, August 6.	Death of Anne Shakespeare.
1623, November 8.	Registration of First Folio.
1626, April 22.	Marriage of Elizabeth Hall to Thomas Nash.
1635, November 25.	Death of John Hall.
1647, April 4.	Death of Thomas Nash.
1649, June 5.	Marriage of Elizabeth Nash to John Bernard.
1649, July 11.	Death of Susanna Hall.
1662, February 9.	Burial of Judith Quiney.
1670, February 17.	Burial of Elizabeth Bernard.

PEDIGREE OF SHAKESPEARE AND ARDEN

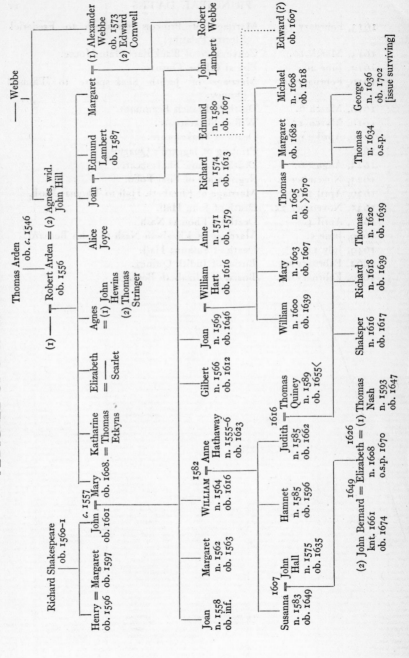

APPENDIX A
RECORDS

I. CHRISTENINGS, MARRIAGES, AND BURIALS

(a) Stratford-on-Avon.

[From *Register*, printed in full by R. Savage (*Parish Register Society*); extracts in *Var*. ii. 610, H. P. ii. 51. The Register begins in 1558, but the entries to Sept. 1600 are a transcript in a single hand, probably that of the Vicar Richard Byfield, made in accordance with a provincial constitution of 25 Oct. 1597 (Savage, *Baptisms*, vii).]

1558, Sept. 15. C. Jone Shakspere daughter to John Shakspere.

1562, Dec. 2. C. Margareta filia Johannis Shakspere.

1563, Apr. 30. B. Margareta filia Johannis Shakspere.

1564, Apr. 26. C. Gulielmus filius Johannes Shakspere.

[There is no record of the actual birthday, which is most fully discussed by B. Corney, *Argument on the Assumed Birthday of Sh.* (1864); Ingleby, i. 21; Elton 22. All that can be inferred from the present entry and the words of the monumental inscription (no. xxv) *'obiit anno . . . aetatis 53'* is that the birth was on a day not earlier than 24 Apr. 1563 or later than 23 Apr. 1564, since otherwise Shakespeare would have died either in his 54th or his 52nd year. This of course rests on two assumptions. One is that the draftsman of the inscription understood by an *annus aetatis* a current and not a completed year. He probably did in this case, as an interval of a year is not likely between birth and baptism, although the practice is by no means uniform in old datings. The other is that he followed the present legal convention by which a new year of life is treated as beginning at the first moment of the anniversary of the day of birth, without regard to the time of day at which the birth took place. The statement that the birthday was April 23 seems to have been first made by Oldys (*c.* 1743 ⟨ ⟩ 50) in a note on Langbaine (App. C, no. xxxiv), where he also gave the year as 1563. Presumably he took '*anno aetatis*' as meaning 'aged', and made an incorrect use of the result, since, if Shakespeare had in fact been 53 on 23 Apr. 1616, he might have been born on any day not earlier than 24 Apr. 1562 and not later than 23 Apr.

1563. Joseph Greene, Master of the Stratford Grammar School, also stated in the *Gentleman's Magazine* (1759, xxix. 257) that 'Shakespeare died at the age of 53', and gave Steevens through James West an extract from the *Register* with the note 'Born April 23, 1564'. The date was adopted in Steevens's edition of 1773 and by later editors, although Malone expressed doubt whether Greene had any authority beyond the monument.[1] Halliwell, *1848*, 32 was sceptical, thinking that the coincidence of the days of birth and death would have been noticed in the 17th century. Incidentally he said that 'three days was often the period which elapsed between birth and baptism'. So far as I know, there is no evidence that any special importance was ever attached to this interval; Halliwell's observation of it in the cases of two out of four children of John Dee does not, as he admitted, prove much; and later he adopted a suggestion of De Quincey that the marriage of Elizabeth Hall on 22 April may indicate her grandfather's birthday.[2] The *Prayer Book* of 1559 directed baptism not later than the Sunday or other holy day next after birth. If therefore the birth was on April 23, itself a Sunday, the baptism should have been not on April 26, but on St. Mark's Day, April 25. Elton suggests that this day would be avoided, as 'unlucky' in popular belief. Halliwell's abandoned suggestion is adopted by Lee 8 in a confident assertion that baptism on the third day was 'a common practice at the time'; and this, with De Quincey's sentiment, probably accounts for the statement that Shakespeare 'was born on April 22 or 23, 1564'. Adams 21 follows suit, but leaves April 21 open as 'possible', and adds that 'the day ⟨Apr. 23⟩ of St. George, the patron saint of England, would be especially appropriate'. But Eileithuia cares little for St. George. There does not seem to me to be enough material for an opinion as to the exact birth-date.]

1566, Oct. 13. C. Gilbertus filius Johannis Shakspere.
1569, Apr. 15. C. Jone the daughter of John Shakspere.

[It must be inferred that the elder Joan had died.]

1571, Sept. 28. C. Anna filia magistri Shakspere.
1574, Mar. 11. C. Richard sonne to Mr John Shakspeer.
1579, Apr. 4. B. Anne daughter to Mr John Shakspere.
1580, May 3. C. Edmund sonne to Mr John Shakspere.
1583, May 26. C. Susanna daughter to William Shakespeare.

---

[1] *Var.* ii. 63, 610.   [2] H.P. ii. 332.

1584, Feb. 10.   C.   Elizabeth daughter to Anthony Shaksper of Hamton.

1584, Nov. 25.   M.   John   Shakspere   &   Margery Roberts.

[This John Shakspere was evidently not the Alderman, who is 'M^r' in the *Register* from 1571 onwards, but a second John as to whom facts are recorded in *Var.* ii. 51; Hunter, i. 14; H.P. ii. 137; *M.A.* iii. 155. Probably he was a son named in the will (1577) of Thomas Shaxper, corvizer or shoemaker of Warwick (cf. App. E), succeeded to the business on the drowning in the Avon of a brother William in 1579, married Joan Webbe on 17 July 1579 at St. Nicholas, Warwick, as Saxper *alias* Demayles, and is traceable in the Market Place there in Feb. 1582. If so, Margery Roberts, widow of Thomas Roberts, corvizer, of Back Bridge Street, Stratford, was his second wife. He took out his freedom as a foreigner to Stratford in 1586 on joining the Gild of Shoemakers, filled some minor corporation offices, was Master of his gild in 1592, then disappears from the records and had probably left Stratford by 1595. He is probably a John Shakespeare buried at St. Mary's, Warwick, on 7 Feb. 1624. It must be presumed that he married a third wife after Margery's death in 1587, and that the Ursula, Humphrey, and Phillip of the *Register* are his children. The addition of these to the eight children of the Alderman and a failure to distinguish between the two Joans will account for Rowe's statement (App. C, no. xxv) that Shakespeare was one of a family of ten.]

1585, Feb. 2.   C.   Hamnet & Judeth sonne and daughter to William Shakspere.

[It is idle to guess at the origin of common names, such as William. But the conjunction of unusual names here suggests that the god-parents were Shakespeare's legatee, Hamnet Sadler, a baker of High Street, and his wife Judith Staunton of Longbridge. C. W. Bardsley shows that Hamonet—Hamnet and Hamolet or Hamelet—Hamlet were distinct derivatives of the Norman Hamon; that both are fairly common in medieval documents; that Hamnet prevailed in the north and Hamlet in the south; but that the forms were often confused.[1] Sadler in fact appears in Stratford documents as Hamnet, Hambnet, and Hamlet. The *Register* also gives a Hassall, who is Hamonetus in 1561 and Hamoletius in 1564, and a Hamlet Holdar in 1576. And the name was also used as a surname. An inquisition was taken on 11 Feb. 1580 upon the body of Katherine Hamlett of

[1] 5 *N.Q.* v. 461.

Tiddington, spinster, who was drowned in the Avon while fetching water in a pail.[1] The resemblance of the name to that of the hero of Shakespeare's tragedy, which has a different Scandinavian origin, can hardly be more than a coincidence.]

1587, Oct. 29. B. Margery wife to John Shakspere.
1589, Feb. 26. C. Thomas sonne to Richard Queeny.

[For the Quineys, cf. no. xiii.]

1589, Mar. 11. C. Vrsula daughter to John Shakspere.
1590, Mar. 6. B. Thomas Green alias Shakspere.

[For the Greenes, cf. no. xix.]

1590, May 24. C. Humphrey sonne to John Shakspere.
1591, Sept. 21. C. Phillippus filius Johannis Shakspere.
1593, June 20. C. Thomas filius Anthonij Nash generosi.
1596, Aug. 11. B. Hamnet filius William Shakspere.
1600, Aug. 28. C. Wilhelmus filius Wilhelmi Hart.

[The marriage of Joan Shakespeare to William Hart is not recorded in the *Register*, but can be inferred from later entries and the mention in Shakespeare's will of 'my sister Johane Harte'. Nothing is known of Hart, except that he was a hatter and had some cases in the Court of Record. Possibly he only came to Stratford on his marriage. But he may have been a son, unrecorded in the *Register*, of a John and Margaret Hart or Hert, who both died in 1564. If so, he was presumably a good deal older than Joan.]

1601, Sept. 8. B. Mr Johannes Shakspeare.
1603, June 5. C. Maria filia Wilhelmi Hart.
1605, July 24. C. Thomas fil. Wilhelmus Hart Hatter.
1607, June 5. M. John Hall gentleman & Susanna Shaxspere.

[The researches of Hunter, i. 94, H.P. i. 219, ii. 320, French 386, Lee 463, and *D.N.B.*, Stopes 92 and *Cont.* 173, A. Ransford in *N.Q.* clii. 438, have left the origin of John Hall obscure. His monument shows him a gentleman of coat-armour, bearing *Three talbots' heads erased*, and aged 60 at his death on 25 Nov. 1635. His own record (cf. p. 11) gives him as *circa etatis annum 57 Die August 27 anno Salutis 1632*. We may take it that he was born in

[1] *M.A.* iii. 50.

the summer or autumn of 1575. The editor of the *Observations* says that he had been a traveller and knew French. Very possibly he took a foreign medical degree. But he is also described as *generosus in Artibus Magister* in a Stratford document of 1632,[1] and this fact, with the coincidence of age, bears out Fripp's identification of him with the John Haule of Worcestershire, *generosi filius*, who matriculated from Balliol, Oxford, aged 16, on 4 Feb. 1592, and took his B.A. in 1595 and his M.A. from St. Edmund Hall in 1598.[2] It is therefore primarily in Worcestershire, rather than Warwickshire, that we must look for him, and very possibly among the Halls of Henwick and Esbury in the parish of Hallow.[3]

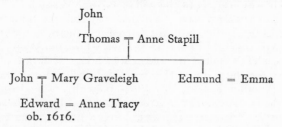

John
|
Thomas ⊤ Anne Stapill
|

John ⊤ Mary Graveleigh   Edmund = Emma
|
Edward = Anne Tracy
ob. 1616.

The younger John took a lease of Henwick in 1575. His brother Edmund is probably the Edmund Hall of Grimley, close to Hallow, at whose house took place an irregular marriage of 1576.[4] He had then himself a wife, and the not very common combination of names suggests that these were the Edmund and Emma Hall from whom John Shakespeare bought his Stratford houses (cf. no. iii) in 1575. It is possible that Dr. John Hall was their son. The Halls of Hallow bore *Argent three talbots' heads erased sable, between nine crosses crosslet azure.* John Hall's monument shows no tinctures, and there are no crosses. He might use a younger son's variant. But it must be added that the talbots' heads, variously combined, are in the arms of many Hall families in different parts of the country. Edmund Hall does not appear again in Stratford, although Richard Quiney had business with Mr. Hall of Esbury in 1601.[5] Nothing obvious connects John with other Halls who do appear from an early date. A Richard of Stratford broke the park of the Lady of Bergavenny at Snitterfield in 1427 [6] and is in a list of Warwickshire

[1] Fripp, *S.S.* 57.
[2] *Register*, ii. 2. 187; 3. 190.
[3] *Harl. Soc. Visitations*, xxvii. 64; *V. H. Worc.* iii. 368; T. Habington, *Survey of Worc.* i. 160, 403, 542; ii.

106; Stopes 94.
[4] Gray 215.
[5] Fripp, *Quyny*, 173.
[6] *Cal. Pat. Rolls*, 5 *Hen. VI*, p. 2, m. 19ᵈ.

gentry for 1433 (French 386). A Christiana of Stratford is in the Gild *Register* in 1504–5 and a John and his wife in 1506–7.[1] A John who made his will in 1519 left a house in the town.[2] He was of Hook Norton, and may belong to a group of Oxfordshire and Warwickshire Halls who bore *Argent an eagle displayed gules*. Among these were the Halls of Idlicote, to whom belonged a Richard Hall, who buried a wife Isabel at Stratford in 1559, and christened children, by Joyce, widow of Hugh Reynolds (p. 137), there in 1560 and 1562. He may be the 'Mr Hall' fined for not keeping his gutter clean in 1559. In 1583 his house at Idlicote was searched, when the priest Hugh Hall was concerned in a Catholic plot. He was overseer of the will of George Whateley of Stratford in 1593. Attempts have been made to connect John Hall with the Idlicote family, but are barred by their use of the eagle arms. Moreover Idlicote is in Warwickshire, not Worcestershire.[3] A Robert Hall rented the old school house at Stratford and did masonry for the town.[4] He married Isabella Wood and died in 1578. Another Robert, also a mason, with a wife Joan, both of whom died in 1609, may have been his son. These were apparently not gentry. Yeatman 146, 233, citing a fine of 1622 for land in Rowington sold by John and Joyce Hall in 1598–9 to Thomas Shakespeare, says that Joyce Blunt (cf. no. xviii) married 'one Hall' of Stratford after the death of Hugh Reynolds, her first husband, and supposes Dr. Hall derived from these. But Hunter's *Addl. MS.* 24500, f. 55 gives the Rowington vendors as John and Joyce Hill. It may be added, for any one not satisfied with the Hallow origin, that a John Hall succeeded Richard Shakespeare as bailiff of Wroxall in 1535,[5] and that an Edmund and an Anthony Hall were gentlemen or freeholders at Prior's Marston, Warwickshire, in 1580.[6] The name, indeed, is too common to make any conclusion more than tentative.

Dr. Hall must have had some connexion with Acton in Middlesex, since his will[7] and his daughter Elizabeth's settlement[8] show that he owned a house there, as well as another in London. A John Hall of Acton christened a daughter in 1575.[9] This seems to exclude him as our John's father; if he had had twins, they would

---

[1] Bloom 201, 208.
[2] Bloom, *Top. Notes*, i. 12.
[3] *M.A.* i. 93; iii. 53; Stopes 93, 179, and *Cont.* 174; A. Ransford in *N.Q.* clii. 438; Fripp, *S.S.* 57; Barnard 105.
[4] *M.A.* ii. 8, 116.

[5] Yeatman 134.
[6] *M.A.* iii. 57.
[7] H.P. ii. 61.
[8] H.P. *1848*, 309.
[9] H.P. ii. 320.

have been christened together. The arms given for Hall, without
mention of Acton, in *Middlesex Pedigrees (Harl. Soc.* lxv. 181) are
not the doctor's. Nor can any connexion be traced with another
doctor, John Hall of Maidstone, who died in 1566. The Bagley
and Welles cousins of Lady Bernard's will (cf. no. xxiv) may have
been on the Hall side.]

1607, Dec. 17. B. Mary dawghter to Willyam Hart.
1608, Feb. 21. C. Elizabeth dawghter to John Hall
    gentleman.
1608, Sept. 9. B. Mayry Shaxspere, wydowe.
1608, Sept. 23. C. Mychaell sonne to Willyam Hart.
1612, Feb. 3. B. Gilbert Shakspere, adolescens.

[Little is known of Gilbert. H.P. ii. 298 thought that he had
found him in a *Coram Rege* roll (1597) described as a haberdasher
of St. Bride's, London, and standing bail for a Stratford clockmaker,
but the records of the Haberdashers' Company do not reveal him,
and do reveal a Gilbert Shepheard, whose name was probably misread.[1] He took delivery for his brother of the conveyance of land
at Old Stratford in May 1602 (no. xiv), and appended a well-
written 'Gilbart Shakespere' as witness to a Stratford lease on
5 Mar. 1610.[2] Malone thought that the *adolescens* of this entry
was a son, and says that the elder Gilbert 'certainly' died before
him.[3] Lee 505 thinks that he survived and is the brother said by
Oldys (App. C, no. xxxiv) to have reported a performance by the
poet as an actor. But Capell's version (App. C, no. xliv) of the
same tradition only makes the narrator 'related to Shakespeare', and
it is safer to assume that there was only one Gilbert, who died in
1612. Gilbert is not in the poet's will. The term *adolescens*, applied
to a man of 45, need not trouble us. *Adolescens, adolocentulus,
adolocentula* appear several times in the *Register* during 1603–11.[4]
My impression is that they mean no more than 'bachelor' and
'spinster'. I hope that Mrs. Stopes is jesting when she suggests
that they may be malapropisms for 'deeply regretted'.]

1613, Feb. 4. B. Rich: Shakspeare.
1616, Feb. 10. M. Tho Queeny tow Judith Shakspere.

[Gray's transcript of proceedings in the Worcester Consistory Court

[1] Stopes, *Env.* 64.   [3] *Var.* ii. 615.
[2] *B.P. Cat.* 58, with facs.   [4] Stopes, *Env.* 65, 332.

on a date before 11 May 1616 is wrong.[1] I emend with the kind help of Dr. Greg and Dr. H. H. E. Craster.

Stratford.

viis et modis	Officium domini contra Thomam Quynie et ejus vxorem. Excommunicatio emanatur.	Quod nupti fuerunt absque licencia vir citatus per Nixon non comparuit in consistorio et ⟨?⟩ non comparuit vxor.

Presumably a licence should have been obtained for the marriage because it took place in the prohibited season between Septuagesima and the Octave of Easter. 'Viis et modis' is a formula of citation. The reasons for the irregularity and for the compliance of the Vicar of Stratford remain obscure. Possibly the event may have left some trace in the provisions of Shakespeare's will (no. xxiv). Thomas Quiney, on whose family cf. no. xiii, was a vintner at The Cage in Stratford from 1616 to about 1652, when he may have left the town. He was a man of some education and a competent chamberlain to the corporation. But in 1633 he was in financial difficulties, and John Hall and Thomas Nash acted as trustees for his wife and children. He was alive in 1655; the date and place of his death are unknown.[2] The mark of Judith Quiney is facsimiled in H.P. i. 169, 254 and B.P. Cat. 60.]

1616, Apr. 17. B. Will. Hartt, hatter.

1616, Apr. 25. B. Will. Shakspere, gent.

1616, Nov. 23. C. Shaksper fillius Thomas Quyny gent.

1617, May 8. B. Shakspere fillius Tho. Quyny, gent.

1618, Feb. 9. C. Richard fillius Thomas Quinee.

1618, Nov. 1. B. Micael filius to Jone Harte, widowe.

1620, Jan. 23. C. Thomas filius to Thomas Queeney.

1623, Aug. 8. B. {Mrs Shakspeare. / Anna uxor Richardi James.

[W. Harness[3] started a theory that the bracket in this entry[4] implies that Anne Shakespeare had remarried with Richard James,

[1] Gray 67, 248.
[2] H.P. i. 257, 272; ii. 305; Fripp, Quyny, 205; B.P. Cat. 66.
[3] Sh. Soc. P. ii. 107.
[4] Facs. in H.P. ii. 372.

and this has been revived by Appleton Morgan, who suggests that James made haste on his widow's death to sell manuscripts of Shakespeare's unpublished plays to Heminges and Condell for F1.[1] It is quite untenable. Events of even date are usually recorded in the *Register*, not with a bracket, but with a repeated date or with the abbreviation 'eod⟨em die⟩'. But in the years 1622 and 1623, several baptisms, of members of different families, are exceptionally bracketed, just like these deaths. Moreover H.P. ii. 372 cites 'a contemporary transcript of the original notes that were made on the occasion' in the form—

> August 8.   Mrs Ann Shakespeare.
> 8.   Ann, wyfe to Richard James.

Dowdall (App. C, no. xviii) records a tradition that Anne desired to be laid in her husband's grave, but that the sexton feared the poet's curse. Her grave is in fact to the left of his in the chancel of Stratford church, below his monument. On the stone is a brass with the inscription:

HEERE LYETH INTERRED THE BODY OF ANNE WIFE
OF WILLIAM SHAKESPEARE WHO DEPARTED THIS LIFE THE
6TH DAY OF AVGVST : 1623 · BEING OF THE AGE OF · 67 · YEARES

> Vbera, tu mater, tu lac, vitamque dedisti.
> Vae mihi: pro tanto munere saxa dabo?
> Quam mallem, amoueat lapidem, bonus ang^elus orem
>   Exeat^vt, christi corpus, imago tua ⁓
> Sed nil vota valent. venias citò Christe; resurget
> Clausa licet tumulo mater et astra petet.

Lee 506 prints this incorrectly, missing the *m* in *orem*, although the circumflex abbreviation is clear.]

1626, Apr. 22.   M.   Mr Thomas Nash to Mrs Elizabeth Hall.

[The Oxfordshire *Visitation* of 1574 (*Harl. Soc.* v, 218, 320) and Warwickshire *Visitation* of 1619 (*Harl. Soc.* xii. 147), with the Stratford *Registers* and the notes of Hunter, i. 101; French 384, 412; Lee 491, enable the following Nash pedigree—

---

[1] *Mrs. Shakespeare's Second Marriage* (1926).

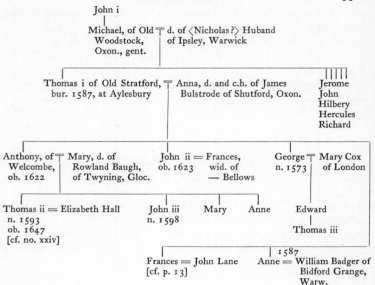

John i
|
Michael, of Old ⊤ d. of ⟨Nicholas?⟩ Huband
Woodstock, | of Ipsley, Warwick
Oxon., gent.

Thomas i of Old Stratford, ⊤ Anna, d. and c.h. of James   Jerome
bur. 1587, at Aylesbury | Bulstrode of Shutford, Oxon.   John
                                                                Hilbery
                                                                Hercules
                                                                Richard

Anthony, of ⊤ Mary, d. of   John ii = Frances,   George ⊤ Mary Cox
Welcombe, | Rowland Baugh,   ob. 1623   wid. of   n. 1573 | of London
ob. 1622 | of Twyning, Gloc.   — Bellows

Thomas ii = Elizabeth Hall   John iii   Mary   Anne   Edward
n. 1593   n. 1598 |
ob. 1647   Thomas iii
[cf. no. xxiv]

                                                    1587
Frances = John Lane   Anne = William Badger of
[cf. p. 13]   Bidford Grange,
                                        Warw.

Thomas i seems to have come to Stratford by 1575–6. He made
payments in that and subsequent years to the Corporation in
respect of tithes, as agent or farmer for his cousin Sir John Huband,
as his son Anthony (cf. no. xvii) did for Shakespeare afterwards.
Interrogatories for Huband's executors in a dispute with the
Corporation in or about 1591 include one as to their knowledge of Thomas Nash, sometime servant to Huband.[2] The *Harl.
MS.* 1167 copy of the *Visitation* contains a certificate showing
that he came from Woodstock,[3] and here I find Jerome and Richard
Nash, presumably his brothers, concerned with Sir Henry Lee in
1609.[4] Anthony and John, sons of Thomas, are legatees in Shake-
speare's will (no. xxiv), and Anthony, who farmed at Welcombe,
was concerned in the Welcombe enclosure controversy (no. xix).
Thomas ii, of the present entry, was his son, and was admitted at
Lincoln's Inn on 15 May 1616.[5] He owned in 1642 the house next
New Place in Chapel St., but it is not clear that he ever lived in it.[6]]

1634, Apr. 13. C. Thomas filius Thomæ Hart.

[1] *M.A.* ii. 114.   [4] *2 Genealogist,* ix. 21; xiii. 29.
[2] *Misc. Docts.* v. 159; ix. 10.   [5] *Admissions,* i. 173.
[3] Hunter, i. 101.   [6] H.P. ii. 91.

1635, Nov. 26. B. Johannes Hall, medicus peritissimus.

[His gravestone, the second to the right of Shakespeare's in the chancel at Stratford, bears the arms of Hall, *Three talbots' heads erased*, impaling Shakespeare, and the inscription:

HEERE LYETH Y^E BODY OF IOHN HALL
GENT: HEE MARR: SVSANNA, Y^E DAUGH
    & coheire
TER, OF WILL: SHAKESPEARE, GENT. HEE
DECEASED NOVE^R 25 . A^O . 1635, AGED 60.

Hallius hic situs est medica celeberrimus arte;
    Expectans regni Gaudia laeta Dei;
Dignus erat meritis, qui nestora vinceret annis;
    In terris omnes, sed rapit aequa dies.
Ne tumulo, quid desit adest fidessima coniux,
    Et vitae comitem nunc quo*que* mortis habet.

Hall left a selection from his case-books, which was translated from the Latin and published by James Cooke, a Warwick surgeon, as *Select Observations on English Bodies* (1657). Hall's manuscript, used by Malone and Halliwell-Phillipps, is now *Egerton MS*. 2065, entitled *Curationum Historicarum et Empjrjcarum, in certis locis et notis personis expertarum et probatarum libellus*. Hall notes illnesses of his wife (f. 10) and daughter (f. 18^v), and his own (f. 76^v) in 1632. There is no mention of Shakespeare. Malone suggested one in error.[2] The earliest dated case (f. 30^v) is of 1617; many are undated, but the dates of others point to compilation late in Hall's life. Other details, extracted from Cooke by J. H. Fennell[3]; Hunter, i. 94; Elton 239, 264; Lee 463, 507; Stopes 98 and *Cont.* 173 show that Hall had a wide practice, not only at Stratford, but among families of position in Warwickshire and the neighbouring counties. One of his patients (f. 10^v) was Mr. Drayton, 'an excellent poet', whom he cured of a tertian fever by an infusion of violets. Hall writes like a Protestant, and Yeatman 164, 192, 221 is clearly wrong in asserting that he was a Catholic; but we are told in the prefatory matter to the *Observations* that even 'such as hated his religion' were glad to use him as a doctor. He lived in a house in Old Stratford, but moved to New Place upon Shakespeare's death.[4]]

1636, Sept. 18. C. Georgius filius Tho: Hart.
1639, Jan. 28. B. Thomas filius Thomæ Quiney.
1639, Feb. 26. B. Richardus filius Tho: Quiney.
1639, Mar. 29. B. Willielmus Hart.

[1] *Var.* ii. 506, 617.   [2] H.P. *1848*, 285; Malone, *Davenport*, 51, 53.
[3] 1853, *Shakespeare Repository*, 9.   [4] H. P. i. 220; ii. 321.

1646, Nov. 4. B. Joan Hart, widow.

1647, Apr. 5. B. Thomas Nash, Gent.

[His stone, to the right of Shakespeare's in the chancel, has under the arms of Nash (⟨*Az.*⟩ *on a chevron between three ravens' heads erased* ⟨*arg.*⟩ *a pellet between four crosses crosslet* ⟨*sa.*⟩), quartered with Bulstrode, and impaling Hall quartered with Shakespeare:

> HEERE RESTETH Yᴱ BODY OF THOMAS
> NASHE, ESQ. HE MAR. ELIZABETH, THE
> DAVG: & HEIRE OF IOHN HALLE, GENT.
> HE DIED APRILL 4. A. 1647, AGED 53.

> Fata manent omnes, hunc non virtute carentem
> vt ncque diuitiis, abstulit atra dies;
> Abstulit, at referet lux ultima; siste viator,
> si peritura paras per male parta peris.]

1649, July 16. B. Mʳˢ Sussanna Hall, widow.

[Her stone, to the right of her husband's in the chancel, has under the arms of Hall impaling Shakespeare in a lozenge:

> HEERE LYETH Ỿᴱ. BODY OF SVSANNA
> WIFE TO IOHN HALL, GENT: Ỿᴱ. DAVGH
> TER OF WILLIAM SHAKESPEARE, GENT:
> SHEE DECEASED Ỿᴱ. 1Jᵗʰ OF IVLY. Aᵒ.
> 1649, AGED 66.

> Witty above her sexe, but that's not all,
> Wise to salvation was good Mistris Hall,
> Something of Shakespeare was in that, but this
> Wholy of him with whom she's now in blisse.
> Then, Passenger, hast nere a teare,
> To weepe with her that wept with all;
> That wept, yet set her self to chere
> Them up with comforts cordiall.
> Her love shall live, her mercy spread,
> When thou has't ner'e a teare to shed.

This, however, was erased for another interment in the 18th century and has been recut from a copy in Dugdale's *Warwickshire*.[1]

Susanna's reputation did not escape calumny. In July 1613 she brought an action for slander in the Consistory Court at Worcester[2] against John Lane, junior, of Stratford, who had reported that she 'had the runninge of the raynes & had bin naught with Rafe Smith

---

[1] Lee 512.   [2] H.P. i. 242, with facs.; ii. 394; Gray 167.

at John Palmer'. Lee 464 says 'and John Palmer' in error. Robert
Whatcott, afterwards a witness to Shakespeare's will (no. xxiv),
appeared for the plaintiff. The defendant did not appear and was
excommunicated. Ralph Smith was a hatter of Stratford. The
Lanes were gentry of Alveston manor, near Bridgetown,[1] and the
culprit was a first cousin of Thomas Nash (cf. p. 10).

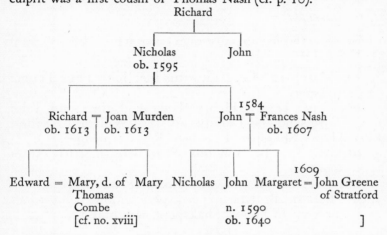

1662, Feb. 9. B. Judith, vxor Thomas Quiney Gent.

[Judith's grave is unknown. All her children had predeceased her,
presumably unmarried; and with the death of the childless Elizabeth
Hall, remarried to John, later (1661) Sir John, Bernard, of Abington, Northants, at Billesley on 5 June 1649, and buried at Abington
on 17 Feb. 1670, the descent from Shakespeare was extinct.[2]]

(b) Budbrooke.

[From *Register* begun 1539, extracted by Savage at B.P.]

1573, Nov. 14. M. Antony Shaxspere Jonne Whetrefe
        were maried.

1575, March 24. C. Henrie Shackespere the sonne of
        Shackespere and Jone his wif.

[A hamlet of Budbrooke is Hampton Corley or Curlew, and here
a Subsidy Roll for 1524–5, but not one for 1523,[3] places a Richard

---

[1] Fripp, *Haunts*, 148; *Harl. Soc.*   [3] Yeatman 142, 164; Stopes 13 from
xxi. 307.   Joseph Hunter's *Addl. MS.* 24500.
[2] French 386.

'Shakyspere'. It is not inconceivable, although it certainly cannot be taken for granted, that this was Shakespeare's grandfather, who is first traceable at Snitterfield (cf. no. ii) in 1528 or 1529. For Anthony, cf. *infra*, s.v. Clifford Chambers. There was still a Nicolas Shakespeare, a recusant, at Budbrooke in 1640–1.[1]]

(c) *Snitterfield.*

[From *Register* begun 1561, extracted by Savage at B.P; Halliwell (1848) 8; H.P. ii. 211.]

1581, March 10. C. Baptizatus fuet John filius Thome Shaxper.

1586, Sept. 4. C. Henry Townsend the sonn John Townsend and Darrity, his wyff, William Meaydes, Henry Shexsper, Elizabeth Perkes, pledges.

1596, Jan. 5. B. Johanna Shaxspere mortua est et sepulta.

1596, Dec. 29. B. Henrey Sakspere was Bureyed.

1597, Feb. 9. B. Margret Sakspere widow, being times the wyff of Henry Shakspere, was bured.

[Records of which most and probably all refer to this Henry Shakespeare are collected by H.P. ii. 209, 241, 407 and Stopes, *Env.* 66. They show him a tenant from 1574 to his death in 1596, on the Hales manor in Snitterfield (cf. no. ii). Here he was fined at leets, as 'Shakespere' in 1574 for default of suit and for an affray with Edward Cornwaile; as 'Shackesper' in 1583 for default of suit and for not wearing caps to church; as 'Shaxper' on 22 Oct. 1596 for default of suit 'being resiaunt within the precinct of this leete', for not labouring with teams on the Queen's highway, and for having a ditch between Burman and Red Hill in want of repair. In 1580–2 he had to answer, as 'Saxspere' and 'Shagspere', in an ecclesiastical suit for failure to pay tithes on crops in Snitterfield and was excommunicated as contumacious. Other records bring him into relation with John Shakespeare. In 1573 he witnessed, as 'Shaxspere', the will of Alexander Webbe, of which John was overseer, and as 'Shakspere' prised the goods with John. In 1582 both 'Hary Shakspere' and John appear in lists of witnesses for a law-suit which concerned a farm on the Warwick College manor in Snitterfield once occupied by Richard Shakespeare (cf. no. iv). In 1587

---

[1] Yeatman 192.

John Shakespeare was sued in the Court of Record by Nicholas Lane in respect of £10, which was part of a debt of £22 due to Lane from 'Henricus Shakspere frater dicti Johannis' and for which Lane alleged that John had made himself responsible. There are other evidences of debt. The will of Christopher Smith, *alias* Court, of Stratford in 1586 specifies £5 9s. 0d. due from 'Henry Shaxspere of Snytterfild'; and there were actions by other creditors in the Court of Record in 1591 and 1596. After his death, Bartholomew Hales and others were commissioned by the Court of Requests to inquire into an allegation by John Blythe of Allesley that he had sold Henry Shakespeare of Snitterfield two oxen for £6 13s. 4d., which had not been paid; that the money was in Henry's house when he died; and that William Meades of Coleshall, who dwelt near him, broke open his coffers on pretence of recovering a debt, took away not only money, but also a mare, the corn and hay from the barn, and all the goods and household stuff, and would not pay Blythe. Meades, however, said that he only went to the house to ask the widow Margaret about £4 6s. 8d. due to him, and went away quietly; and that William Rounde of Allesley, who was Henry's surety for the £6 13s. 4d., had removed the oxen while Henry was in prison for debt, and had given them back to Blythe. It seems reasonable to infer from these records that Henry, like John Shakespeare, was a son of Richard Shakespeare of Snitterfield. Possibly he carried on Richard's copyhold farm on the Hales manor. Halliwell-Phillipps, however, if I understand him rightly, locates the fields which still retain the names of Burman and Red Hill in a different part of Snitterfield from Dawkins Close, near which Richard's farm seems to have been. It is possible that the Henry Shakespeare whose children appear (p. 16) in the Hampton Lucy registers may be the same.

Thomas Shakespeare, of whom notices are in H.P. ii. 212, was perhaps a freeholder on the Hales manor, as a rental of 1563 records a rent from him of £4. He was juror at leets of 1581 and 1583, and *decennarius* or tithingman in 1581. Nevertheless he was presented as a forestaller and engrosser of barley as 'Shakespeare' in 1575, and fined as 'Shaxper' in 1581, for engrossing and forestalling, for exceeding his rights of common, and for default of bows and arrows; and as 'Shackesper' in 1583, for not wearing caps on Sundays, and for having unringed swine on the common. Anthony 'Shaxpere' was a billman of Snitterfield in 1569.[1] He was almost certainly a brother of Thomas.[2] It is not possible to relate Johanna;

---

[1] H.P. ii. 213.   [2] Cf. *infra*, s.v. Clifford Chambers.

she might be the wife of Thomas or a daughter of either Thomas or Henry. That a William 'Shakspere' prised the goods of John Pardu of Snitterfield in 1569 does not prove him of Snitterfield.[1]]

(d) Hampton Lucy.

[From *Register* begun 1556, extracted by Savage at B. P., H.P.ii. 253, 373.]

1582, June 10. C. Lettyce the Daughter of Henrye Shakespere.

1585, Oct. 16. C. Jeames the sonne of Henrye Shakespere.

1589, Sept. 25. B. Jeames Shakespere of Yngon.

[H.P. gave 'Joannes' for the last entry in error. Ingon is a hamlet in Hampton Lucy, formerly known as Bishop's Hampton. *Close Rolls* cited in *Var.* ii. 94 show that on 11 Dec. 1570, but not on 30 May 1568, John 'Shaxpere' or his assigns occupied a 14-acre freehold belonging to William Clopton called 'Ingon *alias* Ington meadowe' and rented at £8; and the will of John Combe in 1613 (cf. no. xviii) leaves to his brother George closes known as 'Parsons Close *alias* Shakesperes Close' in Hampton. This John Shakespeare might be either the poet's father or John of Clifford Chambers. If the former, perhaps his brother Henry was his assign.]

(e) Clifford Chambers.

[From *Register* begun 1538. The marriages are printed in W. P. W. Phillimore, *Gloucestershire Registers*, v. 133: the burials are from extracts by Savage at B.P.; H.P. ii. 253, 373.]

1554, Oct. 7. M. John Hobbyns and Julyan Brown.

1560, Oct. 15. M. John Shaxspere to Julyan Hobbyns, widow.

1579, Feb. 4. M. Charles Malary to Alice Shaxspere.

1583, June 10. B. Henry sonne vnto Antony Shaxspere.

1587, Oct. 18. B. Katheryn Morres, servunt vnto John Shaxspere.

1608, July 22. B. Julian Shakespeare.

1610, Oct. 29. B. John Shaxspere.

[A few notices of John Shakespeare of Clifford Chambers have been collected.[2] He was a Rainsford tenant on the manor in 1571, let ('Shaxver') property at Stratford as one of the proctors for the

---

[1] Yeatman 174, 179.
[2] A. Ransford in *N.Q.* clii. 291; Bloom, *Top. Notes*, i. 41; Stopes 119.

parish in 1572, and had debts in 1572 and 1583. A plate on a bier
in St. Helen's Clifford records 'Will of John Shakespear of Clifford
Chambers. To the Church Here. The Beere that is now in the
Church, which I have caused to be made upon myne own cost and
charges, 1608. Julian Shakespeare was buried ye 20th of June same
year.' This date does not quite agree with the register. Mr. E. I.
Fripp has kindly given me the following extracts from the will at
Gloucester:

'To my cousin John Shakespeare, son to my brother Thomas Shakespeare 45^s, to my brother Anthony Shakespeare 10^s . . . to my son-in-law
⟨step-son⟩ John Hobbins yearly during the life of my sister Alice Mallory
to ear plough and sow the land of my said sister.'

This makes it possible to link John of Clifford Chambers with
Thomas of Snitterfield, who had a son John, and probably also
with Anthony of Snitterfield. Nor do I see any reason to suppose
that the Anthony of Budbrooke, who appears also as Anthony of
Hampton ⟨Corley⟩ in the Stratford register, is distinct. Anthony
is not a common name. If so, we get

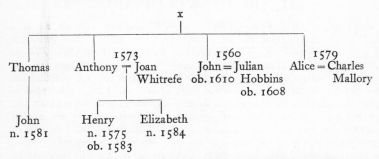

Can we trace a further link between this family and that of the poet?
The common connexion with Snitterfield suggests it. Jordan
(App. C, no. xlvi) had no ground for giving William a cousin
Anthony, beyond the occurrence of the name in the Stratford
register. Thomas might be the same who occasionally appears in
Stratford records during 1578–86,[1] and might be the Thomas Green
alias Shakspere buried at Stratford in 1590. And the poet had a cousin
Thomas Greene (cf. no. xix) of a Warwick family. We cannot arrive
at any certainty. It is possible that John of Clifford and his brothers
might derive from the Anthony who disappears after 1530 from

[1] H.P. ii. 213.

Wroxall (cf. App. E) with his mother Ellen Cockes. The name Cox, Cockes, Cokes, or Cookes is found at Budbrooke, Snitterfield, and Clifford Chambers,[1] but is too widespread to be indicative.]

(f) *London*.

(i) [From *Register* of St. Giles's, Cripplegate, extracted Collier, *Actors*, xv; Hunter. *Addl. MS.* 24589, f. 24; G. E. Bentley in *P.M.L.A.* xliv. 819.]

1607, Aug. 12. B. Edward sonne of Edward Shack-speere, Player: base-borne.

(ii) [From *Register* of St. Saviour's, Southwark, extracted Collier, *Actors*, xiv; H.P. ii 343.]

1607, Dec. 31. B. Edmond Shakespeare, a player: in the Church.

[A fee-book adds 'with a forenoone knell of the great bell, xxˢ' Cf. *Eliz. Stage*, ii. 338.]

II. THE GRANTS OF ARMS

(a) [1596, 20 Oct. From *College of Arms Vincent MS.* 157, art. 24, facs. S. Tucker (*2 Misc. Gen. et Her.* i. 109); pr. J. G. Nichols (*Her. and Gen.* i. 492) and French 514. There is another draft (pr. H.P. ii. 56) in *Vincent MS.* 157, art. 23. This is almost certainly the earlier. Both have erasures and interlineations, but these are more numerous in art. 23, and the corrections of this often appear in the body of art. 24. I have attempted to give the final intention of this, indicating any variants of the slightest importance shown by either draft in my note. Unfortunately art. 24 has *lacunae* due to mutilation. I have supplied these in angular brackets, in nearly all cases from the words of art. 23. No doubt a few more verbal corrections would have been made in the actual grant. The note at the end, which seems to be in the same hand as the draft itself, is not in art. 23. Here the final bracketed words are from *Var.* ii. 89. Halliwell, *1848*, 77 says they were 'now decayed and lost from the MS.', although this is not apparent in the facsimile.]

Shakespere

non sanz droict
[Trick of coat
and crest]

To all and singuler Noble and Gentilmen: of what Estate, degree, baring Arms to whom these presentes shall come. William Dethick Garter principall king of Arms sendethe greetinges. Knowe yee that whereas, by the

---

[1] Yeatman 153, 174, 178, 188, 190; Fripp, *Haunts*, 90.

authorite and auncyent pryveleges perteyning to my office
from the Queenes most excellent Maiestie and by her
highnesse most noble & victorious progenitours, I am to
take generall notice & record and to make declaration
& testemonie for all causes of Arms and matters of
Gentrie thorough all her maiesties kingdoms, dominions,
principalites, Isles and provinces, To the'nd that, as
manie gentillmen by theyr auncyent names of families,
kyndredes, & descentes have & enioye certeyne enseignes
& cottes of arms, So it is v⟨erie⟩ expedient in all Ages
that some men for theyr valeant factes, magnanimite,
vertu, dignites & des⟨ertes⟩ maye vse & beare suche
tokens of honour and worthinesse, Whereby theyr name
& good fame may be the better knowen & divulged and
theyr children & posterite (in all vertue to the service
of theyr prynce & contrie) encouraged. Wherefore being
solicited and by credible report ⟨info⟩rmed, That John
Shakespeare of Stratford vppon Avon, ⟨in⟩ the count⟨e of⟩
Warwike, ⟨whose⟩ parentes ⟨& late⟩ grandfather for his
faithfull & va⟨leant service was advanced & rewar⟩ded ⟨by
the most prudent⟩ prince King Henry the seventh of
⟨famous memorie, sithence which tyme they have⟩ continewed in those partes being of good reputacon ⟨& credit,
and that the s⟩aid John hath maryed the daughter ⟨&
one of the heyres of Robert Arden of Wilmcoote in the
said⟩ Counte esquire, and for the encouragement of his
posterite to whom ⟨these achivmentes by the a⟩uncyent
custome of the Lawes of Arms maye descend. I the
Said G⟨arter king⟩ of Arms have assigned, graunted, and
by these presentes confirmed: This sh⟨ield⟩ or ⟨cote of⟩
Arms, viz. Gould, on a Bend Sables, a Speare of the first
steeled argent. And for his creast or cognizaunce a falcon
his winges displayed Argent standing on a wrethe of his
coullers: suppo⟨rting⟩ a Speare Gould steeled as aforesaid sett vppon a helmett with mantelles & tasselles as
hath ben accustomed and doth more playnely appeare
depicted on this margent: Signefieing hereby & by the
authorite of my office aforesaid ratefieing that it shalbe
lawfull for the said John Shakespeare gentilman and for

his children yssue & posterite (at all tymes & places convenient) to beare and make demonstracon of the same Blazon or Atchevment vppon theyre Shieldes, Targetes, escucheons, Cotes of Arms, pennons, Guydons, Seales, Ringes, edefices, Buyldinges, vtensiles, Lyveries, Tombes, or monumentes or otherwise for all lawfull warlyke factes or ciuile vse or exercises, according to the Lawes of Arms, and customes that to gentillmen belongethe without let or interruption of any other person or persons for vse or bearing the same. In wittnesse & perpetuall remembrance hereof I have herevnto subscribed my name & fastened the Seale of my office endorzed with the signett of my Arms. At the office of Arms London the xx daye of October the xxxviii^th yeare of the reigne of our Soueraigne Lady Elizabeth by the grace of God Quene of England, France and Ireland Defender of the Fayth etc. 1596.

> This John shoeth A patierne herof vnder Clarent Cookes hand.
> —paper. xx years past.
> A Justice of peace And was Baylyue The Q officer & cheff of the towne of Stratford vppon Avon xv or xvi years past.
> That he hath Landes & tenementes of good wealth, & substance 500^li.
> That he ma⟨rried a daughter and heyre of Arden, a gent. of worship⟩.

(b) [1599, Nov. 17–1600, March 24. From draft in *College of Arms MS.* R. 21 (formerly G. 13), p. 347, facs. S. Tucker (2 *Misc. Gen. et Her.* i. 109); pr. H.P. ii. 60. There are a few erasures and interlineations; I have given the draft as these left it. The bracketed insertions at the end are given from an old transcript by H.P. who says that a corner of the paper is now lost.]

[Tricks of coats for Shakespeare and Arden.] To all and Singuller Noble and Gentelmen of all estates & degrees bearing arms To whom the presentes shall come. William Dethick Garter, principall king of Arms of England and William Camden alias Clarentieulx, king of Arms for the Sowthe, East and weste partes of this Realme Sendethe greetinges. Know yee that in all nations and kingdoms the Record & remembrances of the valeant factes & verteous dispositions of worthie men have ben made knowen and divulged by certeyne shieldes of Arms & tokens of cheualrie, The grant & testemonie wherof apperteynethe vnto vs by vertu of our offices from the Quenes most excellent maiestie, & her highenes most noble & victorious progenitours. Wherfore being solicited and by credible report informed, That John Shakespere, nowe of Stratford vppon Avon in the Counte of Warwik Gentleman, Whose parent great Grandfather and late Antecessor, for his faithefull & approved service to the late most prudent prince king H 7 of famous memorie, was advaunced & rewarded with Landes & Tenementes geven to him in those partes of Warwikeshere where they have continewed bie some descentes in good reputacon & credit. And for that the said John Shakespere, having maryed the daughter & one of the heyrs of Robert Arden of Wellingcote in the said countie, And also produced this his Auncient cote of Arms heretofore Assigned to him whilest he was her maiesties officer & Baylife of that Towne. In consideration of the premisses, And for the encouragement of his posterite vnto whom suche Blazon of Arms & atchevementes of inheritance from theyre said mother, by the auncyent Custome & Lawes of Arms maye Lawfullie descend, We the said Garter and Clarentieulx have Assigned, graunted, & confirmed & by these presentes exemplefied Vnto the said John Shakespere, and to his posterite that Shield & cote of Arms viz. In a field of Gould vppon a Bend Sables A Speare of the first the poynt vpward hedded Argent, And for his creast or cognizance A Falcon, with his wynges displayed, standing on a wrethe of his coullers Supporting a Speare Armed hedded or & steeled sylvor fixed vppon a helmet with mantelles & tasselles as more playnely maye appeare depicted on this Margent. And we have lykewise vppon an other escucheone impaled the same with the Auncyent Arms of the said Arden of Wellingcote, Signefeing thereby that it maye & shalbe Lawefull for the said John Shakespere gentleman to beare & vse the same Shieldes of Arms Single or impaled as aforesaid during his natural Lyfe, And that it shalbe Lawfull for his children yssue & posterite (Lawfully begotten) to beare vse & quarter & shewe forthe the same with theyre dewe differences in all Lawfull warlyke factes, and ciuile vse or exercises, according to the Lawes of Arms & Custome that to Gentelmen belongethe without let or Interruption of any person or persons for vse or persons bearing the same. In wyttnesse & testemonye wherof we hav⟨e⟩ subscribed our Names & fastened the Seales of our offices yeven at the office of Arms London the

in the xlij^te yeare of the reigne of our Most gratious Soveraigne Elizabeth, by the grace of God ⟨Quene of Ingland⟩ France and Ireland defender of the fayth etc. 1599.

(*c*) [1602, March 21. From *Ashm. MS.* 846, f. 50 (no. ix, originally a separate paper, endorsed with date). Two other drafts in *College of Arms MS. W.Z.*, pp. 274, 276 do not differ materially as regards this passage. P. 276 (facs. S. Tucker in *2 Misc. Gen. et Her.* i. 109) is also for both Dethick and Camden; fuller extracts are in *Var.* ii. 90. P. 274 is for Dethick only, and its heading in *Var.* ii. 89 shows that he was called upon to answer on 10 May 1602 a case heard by Lord Henry Howard, Sir Robert Sidney, and Sir Edward Dyer on 1 May.]

The answeres of Garter and Clarencieux Kings of Arms to the Scrowle of Arms exhibited by Raffe Brokesmouth caled York Herauld . . . . .

It maye as well be said That Harley who bearethe Gould a bend 2 Cotizes [Tricks of Sable, or Ferrers etc., or any other that coats. beare Silver, or Gould a bend charged in Mauley like manner, Vsurpe the Coate of the Lo: (*a bend, sa.*) Harley. [Trick of Mauley. As for the Speare on the Bend, Ferrers coat] is a patible difference. And the man was (*or, on a* Shakespere bend sa. 3 A magestrat in Stratford vpon Avon. A horseshoes Justice of peace he maryed A daughter arg.).] and heyre of Ardern, and was of good substance and habelité.

[The grants are discussed by J. G. Nichols in *Herald and Genea-logist*, i. 492; French 416, 514; S. A. Tannenbaum, *The Sh. Coat of Arms* (1908). Additional material is described by Lee 285 and in *Nineteenth Century* (May 1906).

There can be little doubt that the 1596 grant was actually made. The arms were used on the Stratford monuments (nos. i, xxv) and on Susanna Hall's seal.[1] They are noted as granted by Dethick in an *Index* at the College of Arms, in a collection of grants by W. Segar,[2] in the 4th ed. of J. Guillim, *Display of Heraldry* (1660), as well as in the 18th-century *Stowe MS.* 676, f. 116ᵛ. Against this it can hardly weigh that John Shakespeare is described as 'yoman' in a conveyance not executed until 26 Jan. 1597.[3] More-over, the draft of 1599, so far as the Shakespeare arms are con-cerned, only contemplates an exemplification of an earlier grant. It is true that it speaks by error of the coat as assigned to John when he was bailiff of Stratford, but if this had been so, the application of 1596 would have been superfluous, and it is clear from the office notes then made that John only received from Robert Cook a 'patierne' or trick of arms as a suggestion for a possible grant. No record of this transaction has been found among Cook's papers. He had made a *Visitation* of Warwickshire as a deputy in 1563, before he became Clarencieux King-at-Arms in 1567. But John may of course have opened negotiations at the Heralds' office when he was bailiff in 1568–9 or later. The interval of 15 or 16 years named in the notes endorsed on the 1596 grant is incorrect.

The draft of 1599, on the other hand, probably did not issue in a grant. The only object of this was to authorize the impalement of bearings for Arden, called by an obvious error 'of Wellingcote', with those already granted. There is no evidence for the actual use of Arden arms by the Shakespeares or their heirs. Possibly the transaction with the heralds was not complete before John's death in September 1601. Indeed, Sir William Dethick's enemies alleged that it was his practice to take fees and delay the issue of the grant until the applicant was dead.[4] Shakespeare could of course have made a fresh application in his own name, which would have been irregular during his father's lifetime.

The words 'non sanz droict' above the coat in the second draft of 1596 are generally taken to represent a motto. It may be so, as no heraldic critic has claimed that they only represent an heraldic certificate of correctness. In the first draft they were originally

---

[1] Facs. H.P. ii. 109.   [3] H.P. ii. 13.

[2] *Harl. MS.* 6140, f. 45.   [4] Lee 287.

written above the coat as 'non, sanz droict', erased there and replaced by 'Non, Sanz Droict', and also written as 'NON SANZ DROICT' at the head of the document. They do not appear in the draft of 1599. No motto is assigned in the text of any of the drafts. Guillim's *Display* (1610), 271 says that a motto was 'the Invention or Conceit of the Bearer', and J. Woodward, *A Treatise on Heraldry*, ii. 378, that a motto 'has no inherent hereditary character, and may be changed at pleasure'. If so, presumably no allowance by the heralds was called for. There is no evidence that Shakespeare or his heirs in fact used this or any other motto, unless it is to be found in the jesting allusion of Ben Jonson in *E.M.O.* (1599) 2045 (cf. App. B, no. xxii), where the rustic Sogliardo is chaffed for the purchase of arms. One of the charges is a boar's head, and Puntarvolo says, 'Let the word be, *Not without mustard'*. Sogliardo is not an actor, and his arms have no resemblance to Shakespeare's. But in *Poetaster* (1602), i. 2, Tucca says of the players, 'They forget they are i' the Statute, the Rascals, they are blazond there, there they are trickt, they and their *Pedigrees*: they neede no other *Heralds* Iwisse'.

A more serious charge against Dethick's grant was brought by his own profession. Under Elizabeth and James, the Heralds' College was honeycombed with controversies, and in particular the arrogance and greed of Dethick seem to have estranged most of his colleagues. In 1602 Ralph Broke, or Brooke, *alias* Brokesmouth, York Herald, brought a formal complaint against him and Camden, which was heard by the commissioners for the office of Earl Marshal. He alleged that grants had been made to base persons, and arms assigned which already belonged to others. The actual terms of this complaint are unknown, but a MS. described by Lee 286 evidently contains notes made in preparation for it. A list of 23 cases upon which Broke relied includes the name Shakespeare, but of this case, unfortunately, no details are given in the manuscript. They are, however, easily inferred and adequately answered in the reply quoted by Malone, the full text of which also deals with 23 cases. This reply seems to be based upon the office notes to the second draft of the 1596 grant. If, as I suppose, the grant of 1599 was never issued, Camden, appointed Clarencieux King-at-arms in 1597, would not have been concerned in this particular case, although he may have been in others. On the merits, it is clear that the Shakespeare arms were, as Dethick claimed, sufficiently differentiated from those of Mauley, and also that John was perfectly entitled to claim a grant. As bailiff of Stratford he is properly described as the queen's officer. This has been questioned,

but under the charter of 1553 the bailiff of Stratford not only held
the Court of Record, which was a court of the Crown, but also
executed the *officia* of Escheator, Coroner, Almoner, and Clerk of
the Market in the borough. Moreover, J. Ferne, *Blazon of Gentrie*
(1586), 60, says, 'In the ciuill or polliticall estate, diuers offices
of dignitie and worship, doe merite coats of Armes, to the possessour
of the same offices: ... as Maiors, Prouosts, Vicounts, and Bailiffes,
of Cities, and auncient Boroughes, or incorporated Townes.' Presumably Broke's complaint failed, for Dethick continued to hold
office, and was knighted by James in 1603. Later in the year he
got into trouble on another matter, was suspended, pardoned, and
reinstated, and finally deprived for irregular conduct on an embassy.
A *Remembrance* of these transactions tells us that Broke had
renewed the charge of granting arms to base persons under James.[1]
It may be added that his list of cases for the 1602 hearing also
contains, without details, the name Cowley. Lee says that the person
concerned was the actor Richard Cowley. But the reply relates
to a Walter Cowley, claiming descent from a Staffordshire family.[2]
It would be hazardous to assume that he was Richard's father.
Another manuscript cited by Lee and now owned by Mr. W. A.
White really deals with another matter. It was written by William
Smith, Rouge Dragon pursuivant, in or after 1604, and describes
the abuses of heraldic painters and their clients, including the actors
Phillips and Pope, who used arms to which they had no title.[3]
Shakespeare is not named, and was not open to this charge; he went
quite regularly to the heralds.

The chief interest of the heraldic documents is in such light as
they may throw upon Shakespeare's pedigree. Unfortunately this
is but dim. The grant of 1596, as originally drafted, recited that
John's 'antecessors' were 'for their valiant and faithful services
advanced and rewarded' by Henry VII, and had continued 'in good
reputation and credit'. It was amended by turning 'antecessors' into
'parents and late antecessors', and specifying the continuance as 'at
those parts', that is, in the county of Warwick aforenamed. The
only substantial change disclosed by the second draft of 1596 is the
substitution of 'grandfather' for 'antecessors', but the document is
mutilated at the critical point. The draft of 1599 had originally
'parent and antecessor', which was altered by interlineations to
'parent, great grandfather, and late antecessor'. It is more detailed
as to the nature of the royal reward, which consisted of 'lands and

[1] Pr. *Sh. Soc. Papers*, iv. 57 from
Bodl. Ashm. MS. 857, f. 493.

[2] Quoted *Var.* ii. 91.

[3] Cf. *Eliz. Stage*, i. 350.

tenements given to him in those parts of Warwickshire, where they have continued by some descents in good reputation and credit'. No such grant to a Shakespeare appears on the Patent Rolls, or has been traced elsewhere. The landed *status* of the early Warwickshire Shakespeares, so far as discoverable, was that of manorial copyholders, or at the most freeholders or leaseholders. There is an exception at Baddesley Clinton, where Shakespeares seem to have held land by knight's service, but from a date at least a century earlier than the reign of Henry VII. The heraldic clue, therefore, has so far led to nothing. It is conceivable that the grant may have been to an ancestor who was not himself a Shakespeare. Certainly some pains seem to have been taken to state a precise degree of relationship. But Harrison, ii. 5 warns us that 'whosoeuer can liue without manuell labour, and thereto is able and will beare the port, charge and countenance of a gentleman, he shall for monie haue a cote and arms bestowed upon him by heralds (who in the charter of the same doo of custome pretend antiquitie and seruice, and manie gaie things)'.

Actually we cannot trace John's paternal descent beyond his father. It would be unreasonable not to accept him as the 'Johannes Shakespere de Snytterfyld agricola', who with 'Thomas Nycols de Snytterfyld agricola' sealed a bond on 10 Feb. 1561 to the diocesan authorities of Worcester for the proper administration of the estate of 'Richard Shakespere deceased late whiles he lyved of the parishe of Snytterfyld', and to whom a grant of administration on the same day as son of 'Ricardus Shackespere' is recorded in the Probate *Register*.[1] There are several notices of Richard at Snitterfield. Here there were—a point which has been generally overlooked—at least two distinct manors. The principal one was held in dower from 1411 by Joan Beauchamp, Lady of Bergavenny,[2] and on her death in 1435 reverted to Richard Beauchamp, Earl of Warwick. Under his will,[3] it passed to his daughter Anne, and became part of the vast estates of her husband, Richard Neville, Earl of Warwick, the 'king-maker'. After Neville's fall, the 'Warwikeslands and Spencerslands' came by the end of the 15th century, in a complicated fashion,[4] to the Crown, and Snitterfield remained a Crown manor to 1545, when it was granted to Sir Richard Morison, who had licence in 1546 to alienate it to John Hales, for a regrant in trust for Lucy Harper and her children.[5] One of these, Mary, mar-

<hr>

[1] *Index*, i. 32, 181, printed Halliwell-Phillipps, *Visits*, 44, and Gray 259, with date, by a slip, 1601.

[2] *C.P.R. 5 Hen. VI*, p. 2, m. 19d.

[3] Pr. F. E. Greville, *Warwick Castle and its Earls*, ii. 830.

[4] Cf. *Monastic Estates*, xvi.

[5] Brewer, xx. ii. p. 123; xxi. ii. p. 99.

ried Bartholomew Hales, brother of John, who held the manor from 1570 to his death in 1599.[1] Rolls of this manor used by H.P. ii. 207 show Richard 'Shakespere' fined at leets on 1 Oct. 1535 for overloading the common pasture with cattle, and on 3 Oct. 1560 for keeping beasts on the leys; and on the latter date the tenants were ordered to make a hedge and ditch before 18 October 'inter finem venelle Ricardi Shakespere et sepem vocatam Dawkyns hedge'.[2] H.p. traced a Dawkins Close near a farm called the Wold on the north of a lane from Snitterfield to Warwick, and here Richard's holding may have been. John 'Shakespere' and others were fined for a breach of this order at the leet of 1 Oct. 1561. Richard had died in the interval and presumably John held as his administrator. A Thomas and a Henry Shakespeare are found on the manor later, and a Stratford suit showing a John and a Henry Shakespeare as brothers (cf. no. i) helps to identify John of Stratford with John of Snitterfield. The holding may have been either freehold or copyhold, but a Shakespeare is not one of a considerable group of freeholders with whom Bartholomew Hales exchanged lands, probably for the purposes of an inclosure, in 1575.[3] The second Snitterfield manor was a member of a manor at Warwick belonging to the College of St. Mary there. On the dissolution it passed to the Crown, and two sets of rolls, covering, but not quite continuously, the years 1528–51, are at the P.R.O.[4] Extracts from these [5] again reveal Richard. He first appears in 1528 or 1529, and thenceforward to 1550 was frequently fined or excused for default of 'suit of court', that is, attendance at meetings of the leet. On 9 May 1538 he was also ordered to mend hedges between his land and that of Thomas Palmer. In these records he is 'Shakspere', 'Shakespere', 'Shakkespere', 'Shaxpere', but also, curiously enough, 'Shakstaff' (1533) and 'Shakeschafte' (1541–2). I do not think it is possible to doubt, on a small manor, that these are the same Richard. In 1550 and 1560 Richard and his widow occupied (no. iv) a freehold on this manor belonging to Robert Arden, whose father Thomas had bought it in 1501 or 1504, and as John of Stratford married Robert Arden's daughter Mary, this is another link between John and Richard of Snitterfield. I suppose, although I am not sure, that for this holding suit of court would be owed by

---

[1] *Harl. Soc.* xii. 210; *M.A.* iii. 59.
[2] The rolls were (1887) in the hands of R. N. Philips of Welcombe.
[3] Stopes, *Env.* 19.
[4] *Court Rolls*, Pfo. 207, nos. 88, 89; *Exchequer Augmentation Court Rolls*,

Pfo. 28, nos. 39, 40.
[5] R. Savage, *Edward Pudsey's Book*, 81; Yeatman 172; Stopes, *Env.* 16; N. Hone, *Manor and Manorial Records*, 308.

the freeholder and not by his leasehold tenant; and if so, Richard's suit must have been for another holding than the one he leased. Robert Arden was in fact also fined for default of suit, sometimes on the same day as Richard, and for ruinous hedges bordering not on Thomas Palmer but on John. He had another holding on the manor, but this also was on lease by 1550. If Richard had a holding of his own, it was a copyhold and not a freehold, since there were only four freeholders on the manor in 1546–7 and he was not one.[1] In any case, we have him clearly farming at Snitterfield from 1528 or 1529 to his death in 1560 or 1561, and occupying land, as holder or tenant, on both its manors. A series of wills and inventories[2] also show him as of Snitterfield, or as concerned with the estates of Snitterfield men in 1543, 1557, 1558, and 1560 (1 June). In one of these he is Richard 'Shakesper'.

It does not at present seem possible to take Richard back beyond 1528–9, or to connect him with earlier Shakespeares elsewhere. It is merely by guess-work that Jordan (App. C, no. xlvi) arrives at a John for the poet's great-great-grandfather, and a William for his grandfather.

The numerous Shakespeares of Rowington (App. E) yield no obvious link. Here there were Richards, but they are accountable for in Rowington itself. Yeatman 131, 171 confidently identifies Richard of Snitterfield with Richard of Wroxall, who ceased to be bailiff of the manor there in 1535 and had a wife Alice, whom Yeatman 239, 266 equally confidently identifies with the sister 'Alys Shakespere' named in the will (1546) of Francis Griffin of Braybrook in Northants. But the facts are against him. The ex-bailiff was at Wroxall (App. E) long after his namesake appears at Snitterfield, and retired to a farm at Haseley which he had rented since 1523, and at which he seems to have died about 1559. Some connexion with Wroxall or Rowington is not in itself unlikely, and may some day emerge. But perhaps the most hopeful line of research would be through the Richard Shakespeare who was at Hampton Corley in Budbrooke (p. 13) in 1524–5, a little before the Snitterfield occupation begins.

The heralds recite the marriage of John Shakespeare with a daughter and heir, called Mary in the first draft of 1596 but unnamed thereafter, of Robert Arden of Wilmcote (1596) or Wellingcote (1599), and appear in 1599 to have been in some doubt as to what were the correct arms of that house. Indeed, had there been no doubt, John would have been entitled to impale them without

---

[1] *Monastic Estates*, 92.   [2] H.P. ii. 207 and *Visits*, 46; Yeatman 151.

any empowering grant. Full *data* as to the main branch of the
Ardens of Warwickshire, whose seat was at Park Hall in Curd-
worth, are collected by French 416 and Stopes 162. From French's
pedigrees and the Visitations I adapt the following:

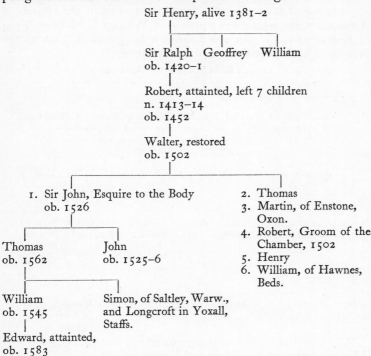

Sir Henry, alive 1381–2

Sir Ralph   Geoffrey   William
ob. 1420–1

Robert, attainted, left 7 children
n. 1413–14
ob. 1452

Walter, restored
ob. 1502

1. Sir John, Esquire to the Body
   ob. 1526

Thomas   John
ob. 1562   ob. 1525–6

William   Simon, of Saltley, Warw.,
ob. 1545   and Longcroft in Yoxall,
                    Staffs.
Edward, attainted,
ob. 1583

2. Thomas
3. Martin, of Enstone,
   Oxon.
4. Robert, Groom of the
   Chamber, 1502
5. Henry
6. William, of Hawnes,
   Beds.

The Ardens of Park Hall bore the arms *Ermine, a fesse checquy
or and azure*, a coat derived from that of the Beauchamps, Earls of
Warwick, *Checquy or and azure, a chevron ermine*. This coat the
heralds began to delineate in the margin of the draft of 1599, but
scratched it out, and substituted *Gules, three cross crosslets fitchées
and a chief or, with a martlet for difference*. This was declared by J. G.
Nichols [1] to have been irregular, on the ground that the coat belonged to the Ardens of Alvanley, Cheshire, who were only
remotely related to the Park Hall house. But French shows
that this criticism was misconceived, and that the coat is ascribed,
with the differentiating martlet, to Ardens of Warwick and Beds
in the *Ordinary* of Robert Glover (ob. 1588), and was borne, with-

---

[1] *Herald and Genealogist*, i. 492.

out the martlet, by Simon Arden of Saltley.[1] It appears to have been used by various cadet branches of the Ardens, and to have been derived, like their main coat, from the Beauchamps, one of whose branches, Beauchamp of Bergavenny, bore *Gules, a fesse between six cross crosslets or*. Dugdale found these arms in the church of Aston Cantlow, which was a manor of William Lord Beauchamp of Bergavenny, and descended through his grand-daughter to the Nevilles. Again a pedigree will be useful:

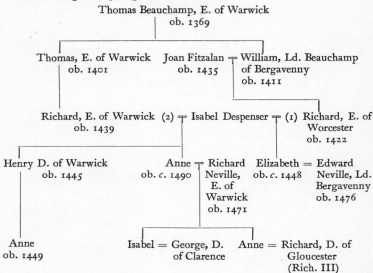

Thomas Beauchamp, E. of Warwick
ob. 1369

Thomas, E. of Warwick
ob. 1401

Joan Fitzalan
ob. 1435

William, Ld. Beauchamp
of Bergavenny
ob. 1411

Richard, E. of Warwick (2)
ob. 1439

Isabel Despenser

(1) Richard, E. of
Worcester
ob. 1422

Henry D. of Warwick
ob. 1445

Anne
ob. c. 1490

Richard
Neville,
E. of
Warwick
ob. 1471

Elizabeth
ob. c. 1448

Edward
Neville, Ld.
Bergavenny
ob. 1476

Anne
ob. 1449

Isabel = George, D.
of Clarence

Anne = Richard, D. of
Gloucester
(Rich. III)

Wilmcote is a hamlet in Aston Cantlow, and in 1501 we find Thomas Arden of Wilmcote and Robert his son taking a conveyance of property in Snitterfield (cf. no. iv). Robert was the father of Mary Arden, and it was his coat which it was proposed in 1599 to impale with John Shakespeare's. The *Subsidy Rolls* assess Thomas and Robert of Wilmcote on £10 in goods each in 1523–4. On 10 March 1546 Robert has the same assessment for Aston Cantlow, and Thomas is put down at 40s. in land.[2] Possibly he died about that date, as Robert had, by 1547, two freeholds at Snitterfield, of which one had been his father's (no. iv). It is necessary to distinguish Thomas of Wilmcote from the contemporary Thomas of Park Hall (1526–62). Stopes, *Env.* 38, misdescribes a *Fine* of 1526.[3] This confirms a life annuity settled upon Robert Arden

[1] Fuller, *Worthies,* s.v. *Warwick.*
[2] Hunter, i. 33, 37.
[3] *Feet of Fines,* Warr. Trin. 18 *Hen. VIII.*

'armiger' by Sir Antonio Fitzherbert. It is charged upon the manor of 'Warde Barnes *iuxta* Wilemcote', and is payable in the church of Yoxall, Staffs. Fitzherbert, in right of his wife Matilda Cotton, who joined in the fine, held Ridware Hampstall, Staffs. Robert Arden joined the Gild of Stratford in 1517–18.[1] He must have held land on the manor of Balsall, since he was excused attendance at a leet of 15 Oct. 1547, and on 21 Apr. 1548, Agnes Hill, widow, paid a fine of 5s. for the lord's licence to marry him.[2] She was widow of John Hill of Bearley.[3] Bearley lies between Aston Cantlow and Snitterfield, but may have been a member of Balsall manor. Robert Arden died in 1556, and probably all his children were by an earlier wife, whose name is unknown. He may have left other relatives in Aston Cantlow, for a Christopher Arden was buried there in 1581 and an Elizabeth in 1588.[4] The after-history of his possessions in Wilmcote and Snitterfield is dealt with in no. iv.

French thought that Thomas Arden of Wilmcote was probably Thomas the son of Walter of Park Hall. The manuscripts of the Warwick *Visitation* of 1619 differ as to whether he was the second or the third son. Walter's will, in which Thomas is named first among the younger brothers and gets ten marks as against five or the equivalent allotted to the others, suggests that he was the second. The will is witnessed by Thomas Arden 'Squire'.[5] Usage was not so lax at the beginning of the 16th century as it became later. According to Camden a gentleman was not *armiger* unless he had a special grant, or was elder son of a knight or his lineal representative through elder sonship, or elder son of the younger son of a peer, or held high office in the Household or the public service.[6] This might cover a justice of peace. Thomas of Wilmcote is not described as esquire in the Snitterfield documents. Nor is Robert. The heraldic drafts of 1596 so designate him, although in the second draft 'gent' was first written and then altered, and the notes call him a 'gentleman of worship'. Thomas son of Walter was still alive when his brother John's will was made in 1526. His age would fit in with that of Thomas of Wilmcote, and he has not been located as living elsewhere. Nevertheless I much doubt whether French's conjecture is sound. The name of Arden is traceable in the neighbourhood of Stratford long before the time of Walter of Park Hall. Robert Ardern of Snitterfield and his wife joined the Gild of Stratford in 1440–1.[7] Presumably the same Robert was

[1] Bloom, *Register*, 219.
[2] Ryland, *Wroxall*, 230.
[3] Will in H.P. ii. 368.
[4] Halliwell, *1848*, 12.
[5] Pr. French 452.
[6] *Britannia* (1607), 127.
[7] Bloom, *Register*, 86.

bailiff of a manor in Snitterfield in the middle of the 15th century and a recent farmer of the demesne in 1461.[1] It is reasonable to suppose that he was an ancestor of Thomas. Dugdale 678 says that Sir Henry Arden had 'a special relation to Thomas de Beauchamp' Earl of Warwick, and his grandson Robert was placed in the custody of Joan Beauchamp, Lady of Bergavenny, as a minor in 1420.[2] She had Snitterfield in dower from 1411 to 1435, and conceivably this bailiff was a *cadet* of Arden placed in Snitterfield during her time or her husband's, perhaps a son of one of the younger sons of Sir Henry. In any case, although the coat selected by the heralds of 1599 seems good evidence for a derivation of the Ardens of Wilmcote from the Ardens of Park Hall, I think that they must have split off earlier than French's conjecture entails. The fine of 1526 relates Robert to Yoxall, where were Ardens in the 14th century.[3]]

III. HENLEY ST.

[1611, Oct. 5. Extract from *Inventory* of goods of Robert Johnson, late of Stratford-on-Avon, given by R. Savage in *Athenæum*, 29 Aug. 1908.]

A lease of a barne that he holdeth of Mr Shaxper, xx^{li}.

[This is the only known record, other than the will (no. xxiv), during Shakespeare's lifetime, of his property in Henley St. Lady Bernard's will of 1670 [4] mentions the barn as 'belonging to' one of her two houses there, not that which she calls the Maidenhead. It was then in the occupation of Michael Johnson, son of Robert and his successor in the White Lion inn. Later documents show that it stood on the backside, in the Gild Pits.

The *data* for the present note are all, unless otherwise specified, in H.P. i. 377. No will or administration of John Shakespeare has been found, but Shakespeare doubtless inherited the houses from him in 1601, probably subject before her death in 1608 to Mary Shakespeare's dower of a third and right of residence. They can be identified in the i.p.m. of Ambrose Earl of Warwick in 1590 as standing next each other in a row of tenements, which H.P. has satisfactorily located from a number of conveyances as running from east to west on the north side of Henley St., and themselves backed on the north by the parallel way known as the Gild Pits. John held them *libere* of the manor of Stratford, i.e. on a 'burgage' tenure, practically equivalent to a freehold, at a chief rent and suit of court. For the eastern house the rent was 6*d.*, for the western 13*d.* It is not quite so easy to say how and when he acquired them. He was

---

[1] H.P. ii. 366.
[2] *C.P.R. 8 Hen. V*, m. 10.
[3] Stopes 186.
[4] Halliwell, *1848*, 318.

living in Henley St. on 29 Apr. 1552, when he was fined 1s. at a leet for making a *sterquinarium* there.[1] We do not know whether he was then an owner or merely an occupying tenant. On 2 Oct. 1556, the property in two houses was transferred to him at a leet; one in Greenhill St. by George Turnor, the other in Henley St. by Edward West. Each bore a chief rent of 6d.[2] The Henley St. house was therefore the eastern one. In April 1564 his son William was born. In Michaelmas term 1575 a fine was levied on his purchase for £40 of two houses in Stratford from Edmund Hall and his wife Emma. We do not know where they were situated, or whether they were held of the manor. No further history is recorded of the Greenhill St. house or of any house property of John's outside Henley St. But of course sales may have been made by John or William which have escaped us. About 1582 John let a house in Stratford to William Burbage.[3] There was a dispute and an arbitration in London. It was decided that the bargain should be cancelled, and that John should repay Burbage £7 at a house called the Maidenhead. Such payments were very often on neutral ground, and probably this assignation was not at John's eastern house later called the Maidenhead, but at another of which there is mention in 1597.[4] John did not pay, and Burbage brought actions in the Common Pleas for recovery in 1588–92. John is described in an order of 1592 as 'senior' and 'glover'. In 1597 he sold a strip of 84 by 1½ feet, described as a 'toft', at the end of his western tenement to his neighbour on that side, George Badger, for 50s. The conveyance shows that he was then occupying this tenement. The chief rent was apportioned, and he thereafter paid 12d. About 1598 he sold 17 square feet on his eastern boundary to his neighbour on that side, Edward Willis.

Where, then, was Shakespeare born? So far as the records go, it may have been in Greenhill St., and it may have been in Henley St.; and if in Henley St., it may certainly have been in the eastern house, bought in 1556. Can it have been in the western house? Conceivably John may have bought this before 1552, but it is also possible that in that year he was merely tenant of the eastern house. Conceivably the western house may have been one of those bought in 1575, or indeed the only house then bought, if it is the case, which seems probable, that fines sometimes exaggerated the number of houses, as well as acreage, for security against omissions. We do not get much guidance. Modern Stratford belief regards the western

[1] H.P. ii. 215; *M.A.* i. xxii.
[2] *M.A.* i. 57.
[3] J. L. Hotson in *Times*, 29 Dec. 1926.
[4] H.P. i. 383.

house in Henley St. as the 'Birthplace', and calls the eastern house, after a designation invented by H. P., the 'Woolshop', although there is little evidence that it was ever put to that use. A plan of 1759 and a view of 1769 couple the two buildings as the house in which the poet was born. And at the Jubilee of 1769, a precise 'Birthroom' was indicated by a painting hung before its windows, 'representing the sun breaking through the clouds'. The eastern first-floor room of the western house is now called the 'Birthroom'. But we need not trouble about it, and when Lee 9 says that it 'has been claimed for two centuries and more', we may venture to doubt his arithmetic. Obviously the influx of visitors in 1769 would require precise specification, rather than historical accuracy, from the mouths of local guides. Nor can it be certain that even a birthplace in Henley St. itself, still less the identification of it as the western rather than the eastern tenement, rests on any continuous local tradition.

At the time of Shakespeare's will one of the Henley St. houses was occupied by his sister Joan Hart. Both were included in the entailed estate (no. xxiv), subject to a life-interest which was left to Mrs. Hart in her dwelling—not in both houses, as Lee 9 states—at a rent of 1s. This was doubtless the western house and the 1s. its chief rent. The eastern house was probably already an inn, as Lewis Hiccox was licensed for an inn in Henley St. in 1603, and in the same year there was a scuffle between his wife Alice and the wife of Robert Brookes, who then lived next door to the eastern house in the Bell inn. In 1639 it was occupied by Jane Hiccox, widow, and in 1647 it was certainly an inn, known as the Maidenhead. Thomas Hart, presumably holding from Susanna Hall, had then succeeded his mother in the western house. To his sons Thomas and George and their heirs successively Lady Bernard left both houses in 1670. The family of George long continued to occupy the western house and to show it to visitors, and to let the eastern house. In 1806 they sold the property, and fell into poverty. The western house became a butcher's shop. But in 1847 both houses were purchased as a public trust. Their present condition and the traces of pre-Elizabethan construction are fully described in *B.P. Cat.* p. 13.]

IV. THE ARDEN INHERITANCE

[1588, Michaelmas Term. From Bill of complainant in Queen's Bench case of *Shakespeare v. Lambert*, recited in Order for trial of 9 Oct. 1589 (*Coram Rege Roll* 1311, f. 516), printed in full, H.P. ii. 11.]

Warr. Johannes Shackespere queritur de Johanne Lamberte, filio et herede Edmundi Lamberte nuper de Barton Henmarshe in comitatu predicto yoman, in custodia marescalli Marescallie domine regine, coram ipsa regina existente, pro eo, videlicet, quod cum idem Edmundus in vita sua, scilicet, decimo quarto die Nouembris anno regni domine Elizabethe nunc regine Anglie vicesimo ⟨1578⟩, per quandam indenturam gerentem datum die et anno predictis, emisset sibi et heredibus suis de prefato Johanne Shackespere et Maria vxore eius vnum mesuagium siue tenementum, vnam virgatam terre et quatuor acras terre arrabilis cum pertinenciis in Wilmecote in dicto comitatu Warr. Habendum et tenendum mesuagium siue tenementum predictum, et alia premissa cum pertinenciis, prefato Edmundo, heredibus et assignatis suis, imperpetuum, Proviso semper quod si dictus Johannes Shackespere, heredes, executores, administratores vel assignati sui soluerent seu solui causarent prefato Edmundo quadraginta libras legalis monete Anglie in die festi Sancti Michaelis Archangeli, quod tunc esset in anno Domini millesimo quingentesimo et octogesimo ⟨29 Sept. 1580⟩ quod tunc deinceps indentura predicta, et omnia in eadem contenta, vacua forent, Virtute cuius idem Edmundus in tenementa predicta, cum pertinenciis, intrauit, et fuit inde seisitus in dominico suo vt de feodo, et sic inde seisitus existens, postea, scilicet primo die Marcii anno regni dicte domine regine nunc vicesimo nono ⟨1587⟩, apud Barton Henmarshe predictam obiit, post cuius mortem mesuagium predictum et cetera premissa, cum pertinenciis, discendebant prefato Johanni Lamberte, vt filio et heredi dicti Edmundi, Dictusque Johannes Lamberte, dubitans statum et interesse sua de et in tenementis predictis, cum pertinenciis, esse vacua, et noticiam habens quod predictus Johannes Shackespere eum implacitare vellet et intendisset pro premissis, in consideracione quod predictus Johannes Shackespere adtunc imposterum non implacitaret dictum Johannem Lamberte pro mesuagio predicto et ceteris premissis, cum pertinenciis, et quod dictus Johannes Shackespere et Maria vxor eius, simulcum Willielmo Shackespere filio suo, cum inde requisiti essent, assurarent mesuagium predictum et cetera premissa, cum pertinenciis, prefato Johanni Lamberte, et deliberarent omnia scripta et evidencias premissa predicta concernentia, predictus Johannes Lamberte, vicesimo sexto die Septembris anno dicte domine regine vicesimo nono ⟨1587⟩, apud Stratford super Avon in comitatu predicto, in consideracione inde super se assumpsit et prefato Johanni Shackespere adtunc et ibidem fideliter promisit, quod ipse, idem Johannes Lambert, viginti libras legalis monete Anglie prefato Johanni Shackespere modo et forma sequentibus, videlicet, in et super decimum octavum diem Nouembris tunc proxime sequentem viginti solidos, et in et super vicesimum tercium diem eiusdem mensis tres libras, et in et super quartum diem Decembris tunc proxime sequentem sexdecim libras, predictarum viginti librarum residuas, apud domum mancionalem cuiusdam Anthonii Ingram generosi, scituatam et existentem in Walford Parva in comitatu predicto, bene et fideliter soluere et contentare vellet, Et predictus Johannes Shackespere in facto dicit quod ipse hucusque non implacitauit dictum Johannem Lambert pro premissis, nec aliqua inde parcella, et insuper quod ipse, idem Johannes Shackespere, et Maria vxor eius, simulcum Willielmo Shackespere filio suo, semper hactenus parati fuerunt tam ad assurandum premissa predicta quam ad deliberandum eidem Johanni Lamberte omnia scripta et evidencias eadem premissa concernentia, Predictus tamen Johannes Lamberte, promissionem et assumpcionem suas predictas minime curans, set machinans et fraudulenter intendens ipsum Johannem Shackspere de predictis viginti libris callide et subdole decipere et defraudare, easdem viginti libras prefato Johanni Shackespere, iuxta promissionem et assumpcionem suas, hucusque non soluit, nec aliqualiter pro eisdem contentauit, licet ad hoc per eundem Johannem Shackespere postea, scilicet primo die Septembris anno regni dicte domine regine nunc tricesimo ⟨1588⟩, apud Barton Henmarshe predictam in comitatu predicto, sepius requisitus fuit, per quod idem Johannes Shackspere totum lucrum, commodum et proficuum, que ipse, cum predictis viginti libris emendo et barganizando, habere et lucrari potuisset, totaliter perdidit et amisit, ad dampnum ipsius Johannis Shackspeare triginta librarum. Et inde producit sectam.

[This is the only reference to Shakespeare in the litigation conducted by his parents about the property concerned. Up to a point the story is clear; the *data* are collected by H.P. ii. 11, 14, 199, 370. On 14 Nov. 1578 the Shakespeares mortgaged a house and land, the inheritance of Mary, at Wilmcote in Aston Cantlow, to Edmund Lambert of Barton, a brother-in-law of Mary, as security for a loan of £40 to be repaid by Michaelmas 1580. The mortgage was confirmed by a fine in the Easter term of 1579. For whatever reason, the loan was not repaid, and the property was held by Lambert to his death, on 1 Mar. 1587 according to the Bill, but about 23 April according to the burial register of Barton. It passed to his son John, but the Shakespeares put forward a claim to recover it, and the Bill alleges that this was compromised by an arrangement for an absolute transfer to Lambert in consideration of a further payment of £20. William, probably in respect of some right of inheritance, was to be a party to this, but the negotiation was apparently oral, and would not necessarily entail his presence at Stratford in 1587. The £20 was not paid. The Shakespeares brought a Queen's Bench action for £30 damages, and Lambert denied the alleged arrangement. The decision of the court is not recorded, but must have been in Lambert's favour, since in 1597 the Shakespeares brought a Chancery suit against him, presumably on the lines of the abandoned claim of 1587, for the recovery of the property. They said no more about the proposed compromise, but alleged that repayment of the loan of £40 had been tendered to Edmund Lambert, and later to John, but refused by Edmund on the ground that other debts to him were still outstanding. There is some confirmation of this in the will of Roger Sadler of Stratford, dated 14 Nov. 1578, which claims £5 of Lambert and another 'for the debt of Mr John Shacksper'.[1] John Lambert denied the alleged tender, and said that

---

[1] *Var.* ii. 87; H.P., *1848*, 52.

the action was brought because a lease made by the Shakespeares was nearly expired and the value of the property would be raised. Again the decision of the court is lost. The property had passed by 1699 to the family of Etkyns, which was connected by marriage (cf. *infra*) with both the Shakespeares and the Lamberts.

The subject-matter of these suits is taken by Lee 14 and Fripp [1] to be 'my lande in Willmecote cawlid Asbyes', which Robert Arden left to his daughter Mary by his will of 24 Nov. 1556.[2] But this seems to me more than doubtful. By a second fine of Easter Term, 1579, initiated on 12 Nov. 1578, two days before the mortgage, John and Mary Shakespeare and George Gibbes surrendered to Thomas Webbe and Humphrey Hooper, for the benefit of Webbe and his heirs, property in Wilmcote, subject to a lease to be granted to Gibbes for twenty-one years from Michaelmas 1580, at a rent of half a quarter of wheat and half a quarter of barley, and with a reversion to John and Mary. The 'pepper-corn' rent suggests that Gibbes had paid a sum down for his interest. This second fine is ignored by Lee and treated as relating to the mortgaged property, both by Fripp and by C. E. Phelps, who thinks that a 'double fine' was levied to bar an entail.[3] Arden's will had not entailed Asbies. There may have been a marriage settlement. But there is a discrepancy in the accounts of the parcels. The mortgaged property is described in the litigation as consisting of a messuage, a virgate (about forty-four acres in Aston Cantlow, according to H.P. ii. 367) and four acres of arable, and appurtenances, which may include some meadow and pasture. The Etkyns holding of 1699 was of the same extent. The fine consequent on the mortgage describes two messuages, fifty acres of arable and six of meadow and pasture. This, except for an exaggeration in the number of messuages, is substantially equivalent. But the fine of 12 Nov. 1578 was for a property of seventy acres, with sixteen of meadow and pasture and appurtenances. No messuage is specified. The two holdings can hardly be the same. Asbies is not named in any of these documents, but as no messuage is referred to in Arden's bequest, it is probable that this was the land conveyed to the Webbes. John and Mary may have sold their reversion. At any rate it is not traceable in the poet's hands. In the 18th century the name Asbies was attached in error to a house which had belonged to George Gibbes long before 1578, as part of a property which included the manor of Great Wilmcote, bought from the Fyndernes. Up to 1575 he had held this property in common with

[1] *M.A.* iii. xxxvi.   [2] Pr. H.P. ii. 53.   [3] *8 N.Q.* v. 127.

Adam Palmer and they then divided it. It was 'adjoining to the close of John Shakesperes'.

It is probable, then, that the subject of the mortgage to Lambert was some part of Mary Arden's inheritance other than Asbies; and if so she must have acquired it under an instrument distinct from the will, which yields no evidence of any land possessed by Robert Arden in Wilmcote, other than Asbies, presumably a freehold, and a copyhold, which his widow Agnes, Mary's step-mother, was entitled to occupy during her widowhood. Such an instrument is quite possible, since Arden also had properties in Snitterfield, which did not pass under his will, but under settlements made during his lifetime. In these the Shakespeare interest was small, but I give their story because it has been confusedly told. The documents, some of which have found their way into the Stratford archives,[1] can be studied in H.P. ii. 173, 236, 366, and *New Boke*, 14; Stopes, *Env.* 11; Yeatman 172; N. J. Hone, *The Manor and Manorial Records*, 308; *Monastic Estates*, 92. There were two freeholds, not on the principal manor of Snitterfield, but on land once belonging to the College of St. Mary at Warwick, and treated as a parcel of its manor at Warwick, which passed to the Crown at the dissolution. One of these had been conveyed by William son of Richard Mayowe to his brother John in 1440, and probably by a younger John to a body of trustees, including Thomas Arden of Wilmcote and his son Robert, in 1501. The possession of it was confirmed to Thomas by John Mayowe in 1504. It consisted of a messuage with eighty acres. The other once belonged to William Harvey and was divided between his daughters Agnes wife of Richard Rushby and Elizabeth wife of John Palmer. Robert Arden bought the Rushby share in 1519 and the Palmer share in 1529, and I think it is clear that the two purchases were again treated thereafter as a single holding. Thomas Arden is traceable as a tenant on the Warwick manor in 1525 and Robert in 1533. In 1546–7 there were only two Arden freeholds on the Warwick estate, and each was held by Robert, at a chief rent of 4s. and a cock and two hens. In 1550 he settled both properties upon his daughters, subject to his own life interest and that of his wife Agnes. One, proved by later events to be the Mayowe property, was to go in thirds to Agnes, wife of Thomas Stringer, Johanna, wife of Edward ⟨Edmund⟩ Lambert of Barton super lez Hethe, and Katerine, wife of Thomas Etkyns of Wilmcote. It consisted of a messuage with land attached and was then in the tenure of Richard 'Shakespere'.

---

[1] *Misc. Docts.* vol. ii.

The other was to go to Margaret wife of Alexander Webbe of Bearley, Jocosa Arden, and Alice Arden. Some trace of the earlier partition survived, for it consisted partly of a messuage and three 'quartronas' of land in the tenure of Richard Henley, and partly of a cottage in the tenure of Hugh Porter. After Robert's death, his widow Agnes leased the properties as a whole on 21 May 1560 for forty years from 25 Mar. 1561 to Alexander Webbe at 40s. The total extent is given as a yard and a half of arable land with appurtenances, and the tenants as Richard 'Shakespere', John Henley, and John Hargreve. The Shakespeare occupation probably terminated on Richard's death in 1560 or 1561, since Webbe was himself occupying in 1569. A new lease at £4 was granted to his son Robert by Agnes Arden shortly before her death in 1580. By 1582 a long series of conveyances had also brought all the reversionary rights of both holdings into Robert Webbe's hands. One of these [1] was a sale to him on 15 Oct. 1579 by 'John Shackspere and Marye his wyeffe' of their moiety of two messuages in Snitterfield for a sum of £4. It was confirmed by a fine in Easter Term, 1580. This states the interest as a sixth part of two parts of two messuages, gardens, and orchards, with sixty acres of land, ten of meadow, and thirty 'jampnorum et bruere'. Evidently, therefore, it was in the 'Harvey' holding, not therefore that once occupied by Richard Shakespeare. Mary is not named in the settlements, but her acquisition of an interest is intelligible on the assumption that Jocosa and Alice Arden had died unmarried, and that Mary and another sister, Elizabeth Scarlet of Newnham in Aston Cantlow, also not named in the settlements, had divided the inheritance of their shares with the Stringer, Lambert, Etkyns, and Webbe families. The fine gives the sale price as £40. I do not know why Lee 14 says that this 'is the correct sum'. A deed is more likely to be exact than a fine, and the interest was a small one. The Scarlets, however, got £13 6s. 8d. for theirs.

In 1580 Thomas Mayowe, a descendant of William, the grantor of 1440, brought a Chancery action against Robert Webbe and others whom he supposed in possession, for the recovery of the property then alienated, on the ground that it was entailed and that William had no right to dispose of it. The case was at least partly tried in 1582, and among the expected witnesses were John and Henry Shakespeare. Unfortunately their depositions, if taken, have not been found, and the decision of the court, if arrived at, is unknown. There is practically nothing in such evidence as has been

[1] *B.P. Cat.* 27.

preserved to support Mayowe's claim. Adam Palmer, aged 60, John Henley, aged 80, and John Wager, aged 60, spoke to possession by Robert Arden and his father Thomas before him and to occupation by 'one Rushby' and Richard 'Shaxpere'. The tenement abutted upon Snitterfield High St.]

V. SHAKESPEARE'S MARRIAGE

(*a*) [1582, Nov. 27. Entry of Licence. A facsimile from the Bishop of Worcester's *Register*, vol. xxxii, f. 43ᵛ, is in Gray 21.]

Item eodem die similis emanavit licencia inter Willelmum Shaxpere et Annam Whateley de Temple Grafton.

(*b*) [1582, Nov. 28. Bond of Sureties. A facsimile from the Bishop of Worcester's registry is in Gray 9. In the lower margin are two marks, apparently a cross and an English capital S. There is no attestation. When the bond was discovered in 1836 a strip of this margin bore two seals, figured in H.P. ii. 184, which have since crumbled. One showed a tree device, the other initials, already imperfect. They have been taken for R. H. and ascribed to Richard Hathaway. According to Gray 33, they are R. K. and both seals were in common use at the registry, and not proper to any of the parties to the marriage.]

Noverint vniversi per presentes nos Fulconem Sandells de Stratford in comitatu Warwicensi agricolam et Johannem Rychardson ibidem agricolam teneri et firmiter obligari Ricardo Cosin generoso et Roberto Warmstry notario publico in quadraginta libris bone et legalis monete Anglie Soluendis eisdem Ricardo et Roberto, heredibus executoribus vel assignatis suis, ad quam quidem solucionem bene et fideliter faciendam obligamus nos et vtrumque nostrum per se pro toto et in solidum, heredes executores et administratores nostros, firmiter per presentes sigillis nostris sigillatas. Datum 28 die novembris Anno Regni Domine nostre Elizabethe Dei gratia Anglie Francie et Hibernie Regine fidei defensoris etc., 25° ⟨1582⟩.

The condicion of this obligacion ys suche that if herafter there shall not appere any Lawfull Lett or impediment by reason of any precontract consanguinitie affinitie or by any other lawfull meanes whatsoeuer but that William Shagspere on thone partie, and Anne Hathwey of Stratford in the Dioces of Worcester maiden may lawfully solennize matrimony together and in the same afterwardes remaine and continew like man and wiffe according vnto the lawes in that behalf prouided, and moreouer if there be not at this present time any action sute quarrell or demaund moved or depending before any iudge ecclesi- asticall or temporall for and concerning any such lawfull lett or impediment, And moreouer if the said William Shagspere do not proceed to solennizacion of mariadg with the said Anne Hathwey without the consent of hir frindes, And also if the said William do vpon his owne proper costes and expenses defend & save harmles the right Reverend father in god Lord John bushop of Worcester and his offycers for Licencing them the said William and Anne to be maried togither with once asking of the bannes of matrimony betwene them and for all other causes which may ensue by reason or occasion therof, That then the said obligacion to be voyd and of none effect or els to stand & abide in full force and vertue.

(*c*) [1601, Mar. 25. Extracts from Will of Thomas Whittington of Shottery, husbandman. Sir T. Phillipps (1847, *Archaeologia*, xxxii. 444) prints the full text of the will from Worcester Probate Registry (*Index*, ii. 1). Gray 28 adds the extracts from the schedule of debts.]

Item I geve and bequeth unto the poore people of Strat- ford 40ˢ. that is in the hand of Anne Shaxspere, wyf unto Mʳ Wyllyam Shaxspere, and is due debt unto me, beyng payd to myne Executor by the sayd Wyllyam Shaxspere or his assigns, accordyng to the true meanyng of this my wyll . . . Item I geve to Thomas, sonne to Edward Cottrell, my godson, 12ᵈ . . . Item I geve and bequeth unto John Pace, of Shottre, the elder, with whom I sojorne, 20ˢ . . . Item, I geve to Thomas Hathaway, sonne to the late decessed Margret Hathway, late of Old Stratford, 12ᵈ. [*Schedule*.] Imprimis John Hathway and Wylliam Hathway executours unto the late decessed Jone Hathway theyr mother do owe me that is due to me by her last will iiij marks iijˢ viijᵈ: Item the sayd John and Wyllyam Hathway owe me more lvˢ vijᵈ. Item the foresayd John Hathway oweth me more iijˢ iiijᵈ. Item the sayd Wyllyam

Hathway oweth me iij^s. Item I owe the sayd John and Wyllyam Hathway for a quarter of an yeares bord.

[The best account of the Worcester documents is in J. W. Gray, *Shakespeare's Marriage* (1905); that in Lee 27 is slight and in some points misleading. Gray has made a careful analysis of the procedure which may reasonably be taken to have prevailed in the diocesan consistory court under Bishop Whitgift, a disciplinarian and reformer of ecclesiastical abuses, in 1582; although for certain details he has had to rely upon the recorded practice of a slightly later date, and sometimes upon analogies from Canterbury or London practice. Ordinarily a marriage could only be solemnized after thrice asking of the banns on previous Sundays and holidays and in the residential parish of one of the parties, which was by usual custom that of the bride. Moreover, although the English canon law is rather obscure on the point, there were certain prohibited seasons, during which banns could not be asked, or probably marriages solemnized.[1] These included Advent Sunday (Dec. 2 in 1582) to the octave of the Epiphany (Jan. 13) and Septuagesima Sunday to the Quinzaine (a week after the octave) of Easter. The consistory court, at the head of which was the bishop's chancellor (Richard Cosin in 1582), with the registrar (Robert Warmstry) as his executive officer, had power to license dispensations from some of the ordinary conditions. The stages of the procedure were as follows:

(*a*) A sworn *Allegation* by the applicant for a licence, probably setting out the names, residences, and occupations of the parties and their parents or guardians, and the reasons for desiring a dispensation. No 16th-century Worcester allegations are preserved.

(*b*) A *Fee*, varying from about 3*s*. 8*d*. to 10*s*. 4*d*., according to the nature of the dispensation.

(*c*) A *Bond*, such as we here have, by the applicant or other surety. Usually the bridegroom was a surety, but Shakespeare as a minor was ineligible. For alternative sureties Worcester practice seems to have preferred persons other than the father or a relative of the bridegroom.[2] The bond would be safe from forfeit if certain conditions expressed in it were satisfied. These in the Shakespeare case were four. There must be no legal impediment to the marriage. No suit alleging an impediment must exist. The bridegroom must not proceed to marriage without the consent of the bride's 'friends'. The bridegroom must guarantee the bishop and his officers against

---

[1] Gray 66, 246; Elton 32.   [2] Gray 57.

any penalty resulting from the issue of the licence. Had the bride had living parents or guardians, the consent expressed would probably have been theirs, rather than that of 'friends'. It was not usual in Worcester bonds of this date to express the consent of the bridegroom's parents, but the absence of such consent in the case of a minor would be a legal impediment, and it is probable that evidence of John's consent was obtained in the allegation or by certificate. The chancellor had, however, power to override an unreasonable refusal of consent.[1]

(*d*) A *Certificate* giving further assurance of required consents and of the absence of impediments, either from parents or guardians, or from an intermediary known to the bishop or his officials, and sometimes on oath.

(*e*) The *Licence* itself, addressed by the officials to the officiating minister, and presumably retained by him. No actual licences of this date are preserved.

(*f*) An *Entry*, such as we have here, in the Bishop's *Register*. These entries, with the bonds, are the chief source of information as to the nature of the dispensations given. Some of the earlier Worcester ones are fairly full, but those for 1579–85 are summary. Shakespeare's licence is described as 'similis' to one already entered. Gray does not say what the terms of the earlier entry were, but the full formula may have been no more than 'licentia solemnizandi matrimonium', to which possibly was added 'cum una edicione bannorum'. The bond shows that this was the actual nature of the dispensation. It may be taken to have been what is known as a 'common' licence, such as was often issued to persons of no higher social status than Shakespeare's, husbandmen or craftsmen, who could pay the fee and produce the necessary security. Common licences normally required some publication of banns, and probably on a day previous to that of marriage, and they named one church, not necessarily that of residence, although this was often the case, to the minister of which they were addressed. 'Special' licences, dispensing with banns altogether, or permitting banns on the day of marriage, or giving a wider choice of places of solemnization, were occasionally issued, at a higher fee, and normally to clerical bridegrooms or to persons of more exalted rank than Shakespeare. I think it must be taken for granted, although the Worcester documents and entries say nothing about it, that both special and common licences, expressly or by implication, also gave dispensation from the seasonal prohibitions against marriages, if not those against banns.[2]

[1] Gray 61.   [2] Gray 247.

The entries in the Worcester *Register* are carelessly made. They contain obvious mistakes in names. Some bonds exist, for which there are no corresponding entries. Often, as here, the date of the bond is later than the date of the entry. Occasionally, indeed, it is later than the date of the marriage as disclosed in a parish register. Indeed, the bond came in time to be regarded as little more than a formality. But Gray makes the reasonable conjecture that the entries were made up from the allegations and bear their dates.

So far as the form of the documents is concerned, there is nothing to bear out the suggestions of Lee that they show 'irregularity', or that the clergyman, who acted upon an official licence, was 'obviously of easy temper', or that the wedding 'took place without the consent of the bridegroom's parents—it may be without their knowledge', or that the sureties 'secured the deed'—I suppose he means the licence—'on their own initiative'. It is true that Sandells and Richardson appear as supervisor and witness respectively in the will of Richard Hathaway, who is supposed to have been the bride's father, and may be taken to represent her family. But the whole Worcester procedure seems to have laid stress on the bride's interests; which is natural, as marriage abuses were often concerned with heiresses. The initials with which the bond was sealed have been taken to be Hathaway's, but Gray has shown that they were probably R. K. and not R. H. and impressed by a seal in common use at the registry.

The real *crux* of the documents is that the bond names the bride as Anne Hathwey of Stratford, maiden, and the entry names her as Anne Whateley of Temple Grafton. I do not feel able to accept Lee's conjecture that the bridegroom of the entry was another William Shakespeare. Broadly speaking, the series of bonds and the series of entries at Worcester agree. Occasionally one or other is missing, but it would be an odd coincidence that one should be missing for a William Shakespeare on 27 November and the other for a William Shakespeare on 28 November. Nor is it a plausible theory that Sandells and Richardson cut in with a *caveat* on the ground of pre-contract against a licence issued the day before. I think we must assume that only one licence was issued or contemplated. And if so, the authority of the bond, as an original document, confirmed by the tradition as to the name of Shakespeare's wife known to Rowe in 1709 (App. C. no. xxv) before the bond was discovered, must prevail. No doubt Shakespeare might easily have married a Whateley. Several of this name were leading citizens of Stratford, and others, or the same, were of Henley-in-Arden, which seems to have been their place of origin. In particular a George Whateley of Stratford, who made his will in 1593, had one brother John, once vicar of Crowle, where a William Whateley had followed him, and another brother Robert, who haunted Henley as a massing priest.[1] But there is nothing, outside the licence, to suggest any close link between Whateleys and Shakespeares.

The question, then, reduces itself to one of the reason for an erroneous name in the entry, and carelessness on the part of the entry clerk, perhaps in copying names from an allegation, is the probable solution. The name Whateley bears a slight general resemblance to that of Hathwey, and Gray thinks that the clerk may have been bemused by the fact that a long-standing tithe dispute to which William Whateley of Crowle was a party had been before the consistory court on 27 November. This, however, does not account for the name Temple Grafton, which probably occurred somewhere in the allegation, but was not the residence of either surety, or, so far as we know, of any Shakespeare or any Hathaway. Was it given as the parish in which the marriage was to take place? If so, it should not have got into the entry. Gray has shown that, while one parish and one only appears regularly at the end of Worcester entries, this was practically always that of the bride's residence, but in many of the cases traced not also the parish of marriage. But here again an error is quite possible, and on the whole I think it probable that the marriage did take place at Temple Grafton, about five miles from Stratford, for which no register covering the period is extant. It has been sought in vain elsewhere from the time of Malone onwards. It is not in the register of Stratford church, or in that of St. Michael's, Worcester, hard by the registry. Conceivably it might have been in that of St. Martin's, from which two leaves covering 1582 had been cut out not long before 1905.[2] Other places without early registers have been suggested. Malone thought Weston possible, which is in Gloucestershire, outside the episcopal jurisdiction of Worcester; and Billesley, because it was near Mary Arden's home at Wilmcote, and Shakespeare's granddaughter was married there, for no known reason, to John Bernard in 1649.[3] And there were two available chapelries in Stratford parish itself. The register for St. Peter's Bishopton only begins in 1591. That for All Saints' Luddington is only represented by 17th-century returns to the bishop. The chapel itself was burnt down before 1782. But S. W. Fullom, *History of William*

---

[1] *M.A.* I. xxi. 6, 28, 62, 101, 108, 116, 123, 131; iii. 58, 63; F. C. Wellstood, *Records of Henley*; Bloom, *Top.*

Notes, i. 12; Fripp, *S.S.* 15, *Haunts*, 62; *Worcester Wills*, i. 356, 388.

[2] Gray 235.   [3] *Var.* ii. 117

Shakespeare (1862), 202, tells a story of the survival of the register:

'The [former parsonage] house is occupied by a family named Dyke, respected for miles round, and here the report of the marriage can be traced back directly for a hundred and fifty years. Mrs. Dyke received it from Martha Casebrooke, who died at the age of ninety, after residing her whole life in the village, and not only declared that she was told in her childhood that the marriage was solemnized at Luddington, but had seen the ancient tome in which it was registered. This, indeed, we found, on visiting the neighbouring cottages, was remembered by persons still living, when it was in the possession of a Mrs. Pickering, who had been housekeeper to Mr. Coles, the last curate; and one cold day burnt the register to boil her kettle.'

This is very circumstantial, and although Fullom was not a critical writer, it does not read like sheer invention. H.P. ii. 183, 364 could find no knowledge of the tradition among Stratford writers, Jordan *c*. 1780 or R. B. Wheler up to 1821, who would naturally have taken notice of it. But Gray 236 had heard from Mr. Edgar Flower that it was accepted at Stratford early in the 19th century. Even if it existed, however, it was not necessarily veridical.

The question of the place of marriage is closely related to that of the identity of the bride. If she was an Anne Hathaway, of what Hathaways did she come? The name was widely spread, both in Gloucestershire, where Hathaways were people of some importance in the Forest of Dean, far from Stratford, and in Warwickshire. Most of the *data* are collected in *Var.* ii. 87, 114; H.P. ii. 183, 362; French 375; Elton 26; Gray 28, 221; Stopes 53, 62, 87, 106, 117, 224; *M.A.* iii. 86; Fripp, *Haunts*, 4. There were many Hathaways in Stratford itself, and it is not possible to affiliate with safety all who appear in the registers. No importance attaches to the statement of an 18th-century adapter of Rowe's life that Shakespeare's father-in-law was a John.[1] A family of William and Sibylla of Bishopton seems to have died out in 1569. The sureties to the bond are traceable as of Shottery. But even here there was more than one family of Hathaways. A survey of 1556, burnt among the *Longbridge MSS.*, gives as manorial tenants a George, who held a copyhold with Richard Hobbyns, and a John who held another copyhold, consisting of two messuages, one called Hewland, and two virgates of land, at a rent of 33*s*. 4*d*. Both tenures dated from 1543. A George Hathaway of Billesley is in a muster roll of 1569. A George was buried at Stratford in 1573.

---

[1] *Sloane MS.* 4225, f. 33.

Several names in the registers may be of this branch; the affiliations suggested in Fripp, *Haunts*, 24, seem to me very dubious. One may have been an Anne of Shottery, but she married William Wilson in 1579 and is not therefore our Anne. The family of John of Shottery is more clearly traceable, by means of the wills of his presumed son Richard and grandson Bartholomew; together with the devolution of Hewland, which appears as held by Richard's widow Johanna in the i.p.m. of Ambrose Earl of Warwick in 1590, and the freehold of which was bought by Bartholomew in 1610. It remained in the hands of Hathaways to 1746, and is the farm-house now known as Anne Hathaway's Cottage. These particular Hathaways were distinguished by the *alias* of Gardiner, Gardener, Gardner, or Garner. The following pedigree can be constructed:

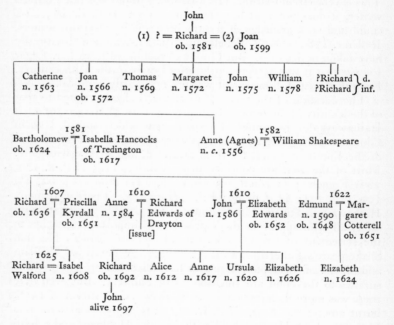

A John Gardyner of Shottery and his wife Alice joined the Stratford Gild in 1482–3. John Hathaways or Gardners are traceable on rolls of the manor court for Old Stratford, Shottery, and Welcombe in many years from 1520 to 1548. A John was constable in 1520 and a John in 1548. Johns are on Subsidy Rolls for 1524–5 and 1549–50. Probably more than one generation is involved, and the last John died before the registers begin in 1558. Richard is on the Subsidy Roll for 1566–7. His will of 1 Sept. 1581 names his wife Joan, eldest son Bartholomew, younger sons Thomas, John, and William, and daughters Agnes, Catherine, and Margaret.[1] Legacies of £6 13s. 4d. each to Agnes and Catherine are payable on the days of their marriages. Careful provisions for the financial relations of Bartholomew to Joan may suggest that she was a second wife. A sheep each is left to Agnes and Elizabeth, daughters of a Thomas Hathaway, clearly not the testator's son. Fowlke Sandells is a supervisor and John Richardson a witness. These are the sureties to Shakespeare's marriage bond. A schedule of debts includes £4 6s. 8d. to 'Thomas Whittington my shepherd'. Richard was buried on 7 Sept. 1581 and his will proved on 9 July 1582. His daughter Agnes seems, so far as one can tell from the registers, to be the only 'Anne Hathwey of Stratford maiden' available to marry William Shakespeare in 1582. Her marriage was contemplated at the date of the will. The difference of nomenclature need cause no perturbation. It is true that legal decisions, both before and after 1582, declared Agnes and Anne to be distinct names,[2] but the very need for these shows that they were often treated as convertible; and of this there is abundant confirmation.[3] Mrs. Shakespeare's gravestone (no. i) shows her born in 1555 or 1556. If, therefore, she was Richard's daughter and Richard had two families, she presumably belonged to the elder, and was full sister of Bartholomew, whose baptism, like hers, is not in the register. Whether any of Richard's other children were her full brothers and sisters we cannot say. No burial of a first wife or marriage to Joan is recorded at Stratford. Joan presumably held Hewland to her death in 1599, and kept her sons John and William with her. It may be this John who appears on the Subsidy Roll for 1593. John and William, as executors of Joan, are in the 1601 will of Thomas Whittington, Richard's former shepherd. Here, too, is Mrs. Anne Shakespeare. The son Thomas has not been traced in Stratford. Bartholomew, who was of Tysoe in Worcestershire in 1583, presumably succeeded in 1599 to the Hewland copyhold. His will of 16 Sept. 1621 names John Hall as overseer.[4] Here, and in Whittington's will, and in the bond sureties, we have some confirmation of a connexion between Shakespeare and the family of Richard Hathaway. It is, however, curious,

---

[1] Pr. H.P. ii. 195; Gray 221; *M.A.* iii. 86.

[2] Elton 29.

[3] H.P. ii. 184; Gray 29; Ryland,

Wroxall, 92, 113; *10 N.Q.* ii. 389, 429, 473; *M.A.* iii. 87; cf. App. E, s.v. Bishop's Tachbrook.

[4] Pr. H.P. ii. 196.

not only that Shakespeare's will makes no mention of Hathaways,
but that, while Hathaways appear in the dispositions of his grand-
daughter's property, these are not descendants of Bartholomew, and
not certainly of the 'Gardner' family at all. Possibly the explanation
is in a difference of religion. Bartholomew's will is Protestant, and
both he and his son Richard, who was a baker in Stratford, were
churchwardens. But a John of Old Stratford is in a list of Catholic
recusants for 1640–1,[1] and the description is probably wide enough to
cover Bartholomew's son John of Hewland in Shottery. However
this may be, the facts (cf. no. xxiv) are as follows. Thomas Nash's
codicil of 1647 leaves legacies to Elizabeth, Thomas, and Judith
Hathaway. The settlement of 1647 appoints as trustees 'William
Hathaway of Weston upon Avon in the county of Gloucester,
yeoman, and Thomas Hathway of Stratford upon Avon, joiner'.
Lady Barnard's will of 1670 leaves legacies to Judith, Joan, Rose,
Elizabeth, and Susanna, all being daughters of 'my kinsman Thomas
Hathaway late of Stratford'. Thomas the joiner was not a native of
Stratford, since he took out his freedom there in 1636. The baptisms
of his five daughters are in the registers, and he left a widow Jane.
Quite possibly Thomas came from Weston and was brother of
William of that place. An elaborate series of conjectures attempts to
establish for him a pedigree from George the copyholder of Shottery
in 1556, through the possible kinsman Thomas of Richard's will in
1581.[2] This Thomas had a wife Margaret and a son Thomas both
of whom appear in Whittington's will of 1601. It is suggested that
this second Thomas went to Weston, and became the father of a
third who was the joiner. Even if all these steps could be proved,
the kinsmanship with Lady Bernard would be very remote. Conjecture for conjecture, a descent of the joiner from Thomas the son
of Richard would bring it much nearer. But it must not be forgotten that Malone asserts that Hathaways were tenants of Sir
John Conway at Luddington 'early in the reign of Elizabeth', and
adds that 'one of them is said to have had a little patrimony of his
own, probably at Weston'.[3] Here, therefore, he thinks that Shakespeare may have found his wife. The 'probably' looks as if it were
based on the settlement of 1647 itself, and the Elizabethan tenancy
at Luddington has not been verified, although Hathaways were
certainly there in the 18th century, and this seems to have led
Joseph Greene, in drafting about 1750 an adaptation of Rowe's life,
to place Shakespeare's father-in-law there. In later versions he

[1] Yeatman 192. [2] M.A. iii. 89.
[3] Var. ii. 117.

accepted Shottery.[1] I suspect, however, that for Malone's Weston we ought to substitute Loxley, somewhat farther than Weston from Luddington.   The Subsidy Rolls show a Richard Hathaway at either Loxley, Alveston, or Luddington itself in 1540–1, and a Simon and a John at Loxley in 1549–50 and 1592–3 respectively.[2] But the Loxley registers give no available Anne, and the balance of evidence seems to point to Anne, daughter of Richard Hathaway *alias* Gardner, of Hewland, Shottery, as Shakespeare's wife.

It is perhaps hardly profitable to speculate why Shakespeare should have been married by licence instead of banns, or why the ceremony should have taken place at Luddington, if it was at Luddington, or at Temple Grafton, if it was at Temple Grafton, and not in the parish church of Stratford. Obviously, if Anne's father farmed at Luddington, a marriage there would be natural enough. Fripp conjectures that Anne's mother came from Temple Grafton and that Anne went to live there after her father's death.[3] But she is 'of Stratford' in the bond. Mr. S. O. Addy conjectures that John Shakespeare farmed at Temple Grafton, for which there is no evidence whatever.[4] A memorandum of *c.* 1597 in defence of the system of licences against contemporary criticism justifies them, partly on the convenience of determining questions of impediment and consent in advance, rather than by a forbidding of the banns, partly on the occasional need for expedition where there has been previous cohabitation, and partly in the interests of reasonable secrecy, where there is disparity of condition or the parties desire to avoid expense.[5] There may have been need for expedition in Shakespeare's case, since the baptism of Susanna on 26 May 1583 shows that Anne was already with child, and if a sudden decision to marry had been arrived at, there was only time for one reading of the banns on St. Andrew's day, November 30, before the prohibited season of Advent began on December 2. Marriages by licence were by no means always secret, being often celebrated in the bride's parish. But Anne's bashfulness or John Shakespeare's financial straits may have motived secrecy. It has been suggested that William was under an apprenticeship covenant against marriage. Such covenants are invalid in modern law; it is not clear that this was so in the 16th century. But presumably the absence of such an impediment, like the absence of parental objection, would have been safeguarded by the licensing procedure. A kindly sentiment for an honoured poet has led to a belief that William and

[1] H.P. ii. 189.
[2] H.P. *Subsidies.*
[3] *M.A.* iii. 88, 112.
[4] *N.Q.* cli. 291, 309.
[5] Gray 243 from Strype, *Whitgift,* iii. 380.

Anne had been living together under a contract amounting to a valid legal marriage, and this has been glossed by T. Le M. Douse with a suggestion that a church marriage was only necessitated because the validity of the contract stopped short of enabling Anne to claim the paternal legacy payable on her marriage.[1] No doubt canon law recognized a contract *per verba de praesenti*, or a contract *per verba de futuro* followed by cohabitation, as constituting a marriage.[2] But this does not seem to have been accepted by English secular law. Nor does contemporary moral sentiment appear to have approved the anticipation of the fuller ceremony.]

VI. THE CLAYTON SUIT

[H.P. i. 185 says that in 1600 Shakespeare brought an action against John Clayton and recovered a debt of £7. Stopes, *Ind.* 259, 262 found the record of the case in *Coram Rege Roll*, Easter 42 Eliz. 1361, m. 293. I agree with Lee 321 that there is no ground for identifying the Willelmus Shackspere of this with the dramatist. The debt was acknowledged in Cheapside on 22 May 1592. No local description is given by which the habitation of the plaintiff can be fixed. The defendant was of Willington in Bedfordshire.]

VII. SHAKESPEARE'S INTERESTS IN THE GLOBE AND BLACKFRIARS

(*a*) [1619, April 28. From *Answer* of John Heminges and Henry Condell in suit of *Witter v. Heminges and Condell* (Court of Requests), pr. in full C. W. Wallace (1910, *Nebraska Univ. Studies*, x. 261).]

The said defendantes . . . do say & either of them for himself saith, that he thincketh it to be true that the said Augustine Phillipps in the said bill of complaint named was in his life time lawfully possessed of such terme of yeeres of & in a fiveth parte of the moitie of the said galleryes of the said playhowse called the Globe in the said bill mencioned and of divers gardens therevnto belonging & adioyning, and that the said Nicholas Brend in the said bill named was thereof seised in his demesne as of fee as in the said bill is alledged. But the said defendantes say that they do not thincke that the said

[1] *T.L.S.* 21 Apr. 1905.

[2] Gray 195; F. J. Furnivall, *Child Marriages in the Diocese of Chester*, xiii.

Augustine Phillips was so possessed of the said terme of yeeres by force of a demise or lease to him the said Augustine Phillipps made of all the same by the said Nicholas Brend ymediatly, for the said gardens and groundes wherevpon the said playhowse & galleryes were afterwardes builded were demised & letten by the said Nicholas Brend by his indenture of lease tripartite bearing date in or about the xxj^{th} day of February in the xlj^{th} yeere of the raigne of the late Queene Elizabeth ⟨1599⟩ vnto Cuthbert Burbadge, Richard Burbadge, William Shakespeare, the said Augustine Phillipps, Thomas Pope, the said John Heminges one of the said defendantes, and William Kempe, to have and to hould the one moitie of the said garden plottes and ground to the said Cuthbert Burbadge and Richard Burbadge, their executours, administratours & assignes, from the feast of the birth of our Lord God last past before the date of the said indenture vnto thend & terme of xxxj yeeres from thence next ensuing for the yeerely rent of seaven poundes & five shillinges, and to haue & to hould thother moitie of the said garden plottes & groundes vnto the said William Shakespeare, Augustine Phillipps, Thomas Pope, the said John Heminges one of the said defendantes, & William Kempe, their executours, administratours & assignes, from the said feast of the birth of our Lord God then last past before the date of the said indenture vnto the said full end & terme of xxxj yeeres from thence next ensuing for the like yeerely rent of seaven poundes & five shillinges. Which said William Shakespeare, Augustine Phillipps, Thomas Pope, John Heminges & William Kempe did shortlie after graunte & assigne all the said moitie of & in the said gardens & groundes vnto William Levison and Thomas Savage, who regraunted & reassigned to euerye of them seuerally a fift parte of the said moitie of the said gardens & groundes, vpon which premisses or some parte thereof there was shortly after built the said then playhowse. So as the said Augustine Phillipps had a fiveth parte of the moitie of the said gardens & groundes, & after the said playhowse was built he had a fiveth parte

of the said galleryes of the said playhowse, in ioynt
tenancie with the said William Shakespeare, Thomas Pope,
the said John Heminges, & William Kempe, & as tenant
in common during the said terme of yeeres demised by
the said Nicholas Brend as aforesaid, as the said defendantes do take it. But the said defendantes do say that
about the time of the building of the said playhowse &
galleryes or shortlie after a third parte of the fiveth parte
of the said moitie of the said playhowse, galleryes, gardens
& ground, which was the fiveth parte of the said William
Kempe, did come vnto the said Augustine Phillipps by
a graunte or assignement of the said fiveth parte made by
the said William Kempe to the said William Shakespeare,
the said John Heminges one of the said defendantes, and
the said Augustine Phillipps. Which said last mencioned
fiveth parte did shortlie after come to Thomas Cressey by
the graunte & assignement of the said William Shakespeare, the said John Heminges and Augustine Phillipps,
which said Cressey did shortlie after regraunte and
reassigne the said fiveth parte to the said William Shakespeare, John Heminges, Augustine Phillipps & Thomas
Pope, as the said defendantes do take it. So as the said
Augustine Phillipps then had a fiveth parte and the fourth
parte of another fiveth parte of the said moitie of the said
playhowse, galleryes, gardens and groundes, as the said
defendantes do verily beleeve, for & during the same terme
of yeeres. And the said defendant John Heminges doth
also say that he thincketh it to be true that the said
Augustine Phillipps . . . in or about the time in the said
bill mencioned ⟨May, 1605⟩ made his last will & testament in writing & thereby made his then wife Anne his
executrix of his said last will & testament & shortlie after
died. . . . And the said defendant John Heminges doth
say that he likewise thincketh it to be true that by vertue
of her the said Annes being executrix of the said will shee
into the said partes of the moitie of the said galleryes,
ground & playhowse late of the said Augustine Phillipps
as aforesaid did enter & was thereof possessed accordingly
and did receive & take the yssues, profittes and com-

modities thereof. . . . And this defendant John Heminges
doth also say that, although the said testatour Augustine
Phillips in & by his said last will and testament did ordeyne
& make the said Anne his wife executrix of his said last
will & testament, yet the same was not absolutely but
onely with proviso or vpon condicion in the said will
expressed that, if the said Anne his wife should at any
time marrie after his decease, that then & from thenceforth shee should cease to be any more or longer executrix
of his said last will or any wayes intermedle with the same,
and that then and from thenceforth this defendant John
Heminges, the said Richard Burbadge, William Slye &
Tymothie Whitehorn should be fully & wholie his
executours of his said last will and testament, as though
the same Anne had never byn named. . . . And this
defendant John Heminges further saith that the said
complainant in or about the moneth of November in the
fourth yeere of the kinges Maiesties raigne of England
⟨1606⟩ did come to this defendant, and making shewe and
affirming that the said Anne and himself then stood in
greate nede of money did make offer to procure the said
Anne to mortgage her said terme of and in the said fiveth
parte of the said playhowse, galleryes, gardens and
groundes . . . for the somme of fiftie poundes or thereaboutes . . . and therevpon both the said complainant & the
said Anne, then confessing themselues to be maried, ioyned
in the said mortgage. . . . And this defendant saith that,
after the said intermariage of the said complainant with
the said Anne, he the said complainant did ioyne in the
graunting of two sixth partes of the said moitie of & in
the said playhowse, galleryes, gardens and groundes with
this defendant & the rest then interessed therein vnto
William Slye and the said other defendant Henry Condell.
. . . And this defendant further saith that by meanes that
the said complainant & the said Anne were intermaryed,
whereby the said condicion in the said will of the said
Augustine Phillipps was broken, . . . the administracion of
the goodes and chattells of the said Augustine Phillipps
in or about the moneth of Maie in the fiveth yeere of his

maiesties said raigne ⟨1607⟩ was committed to this
defendant in the prerogative court of Canterbury as
executour of the said last will & testament of the said
Augustine Phillipps, by virtue whereof he this defendant
did enter into the said fiveth parte of the said moitie of the
said playhowse, galleryes, gardens and groundes, and did
take the rentes, yssues and profittes thereof, as well &
lawfull it was as he hopeth for him to doe. . . . And this
defendant further saith that . . . the said complainant &
his said wife did take a lease of this defendant by indenture
bearing date the xiiij^th day of the said moneth of February
⟨1611⟩ . . . of a sixth parte of the said moitie of the said
playhowse, garden plottes and premisses for the terme
of eighteene yeeres from the birth of our Lord God then
last past, . . . provided alwayes that . . . if the said complainant, his executours, administratours or assignes should
not within one yeere then next comeing pay and discharge
the said legacie of five poundes geven & bequeathed by
the last will & testament aforesaid vnto the poore of the
parish of Mortlack . . . that then the demise & graunte
aforesaid of the premisses should be void & of none effect.
. . . And this defendant further saith that, about the said
terme of five yeeres last past mencioned in the said
bill of complaint or about six monethes before, the said
playhowse and galleryes were casually burnt downe &
consumed with fier. Shortlie after which this defendant
and his partners in the said playhowse resolued to reedifie
the same, & this rather because they were by covenante
on their parte in the said originall lease conteyned to
mainteyne & repaire all such buildinges as should be
built or erected vpon the said gardens or ground during
the said terme, as by the said originall lease may appeare.
And therevpon this defendant did write his lettres to the
said complainant signifieing the same vnto him, & therein
required him to come & bring or send 50^li or 60^li by a
day therein mencioned for & towardes the reedifieing of
a howse in regard of his the complainantes parte of the
said ground, which this defendant had so demised vnto
him and his said wife by the said lease, if he would

adventure so much (he the said complainant having latly before ioyned with the said defendantes & the rest then interessed in the said moitie of the said playhowse, gardens & ground ⟨in the graunting?⟩ to William Ostler of a seaventh parte of the said moitie). But the said complainant neither brought or sent any money towardes the reedifieing of the said playhowse, . . . the said complainant had broken the said condicion of the said lease by not paying the said legacie of five poundes. . . . And therevpon this defendant did enter into the said parte so demised as aforesaid for the said condicion broken, and because he found that the reedifieing of the said playhowse would be a verie greate charge & doubted what benefitt would arise thereby, & for that the said originall lease had then but a fewe yeeres to come, he this defendant did geve away his said terme of yeeres & interest of & in the one moitie of the said parte of the said moitie of the said garden plottes & ground to the said other defendant Henry Condell gratis. The reedifieing of which parte hath sithence cost the said defendantes about the somme of cxx^{li}, and yet one other sixth parte of the said moitie of the said playhowse, galleryes, gardens & ground, before the said playhowse was burned & consumed with fier, was absolutely sould for lesse money then the half of the said charges of the said defendantes in the newe building thereof, when there were more yeeres to come therein then there were at the time of the said burning thereof. . . . Without that the said defendantes haue made or contrived to themselues or to any other person or persons any estate or estates of the said parte, other then is aboue mencioned & one eight parte of the said moitie of the said playhowse, galleryes, gardens & groundes graunted by the said defendantes & other their partners in the said moitie to Nathan Field, and one other estate made to John Atkins gentleman in trust for the said defendant John Heminges of two litle parcells of the said ground by the said defendant John Heminges & the rest of the partners in the said playhowse & premisses, vpon parte whereof the said John Heminges hath built a howse.

(*b*) [1615, Oct. 9? From *Plea* of Thomasina Ostler in suit of *Ostler v. Heminges* (*Coram Rege Roll* 1454, 13 Jac. 1, Hilary Term, m. 692), pr. C. W. Wallace, *Advance Sheets from Shakespeare, the Globe, and Black-friars* (1909), and *Jahrbuch*, xlvi (1910), 235.]

(1) [*As to the Globe.*]

Cumque per quandam aliam indenturam inter Basilium Nicholl, Will*elmu*m Shakespeare, Johannem Witter, Johannem Hemynges, Henricum Condall, & Johannem Edmondes & Mariam vxorem eius ex vna parte & prefatum Willelmum Osteler ex altera parte, apud Londoniam predictam in predicta parochia beate Marie de Arcubus in Warda de Cheape Londonie factam, gerentem datum vicesimo die Februarii anno regni dicti domini Regis nunc Anglie nono supradicto ⟨1612⟩, recitando quod,

> Cum quidam Nicholaus Brend de West Moulsey in Comitatu Surria armiger per indenturam suam tripartitam, gerentem datum vicesimo primo die Februarii anno regni domine Elizabeth nuper Regine Anglie quadragesimo primo ⟨1599⟩, pro consideracionibus in eadem indentura tripartita mencionatis & expressatis, dimisisset, concessisset & ad firmam tradidisset quibusdam Cuthberto Burbadge & Ricardo Burbadge de Londonia generosis, prefato Will*elm*o Shakespeare, & Augustino Phillips & Thome Pope de Londonia generosis defunctis, predicto Johanni Hemynges, & Willelmo Kempe nuper de Londonia generoso defuncto, totam illam parcellam fundi nuper preantea inclusam & factam in quatuor separalia gardina, nuper in tenuris & occupacionibus Thomae Burt & Isbrand Morris diers & Lactantii Roper salter civis Londonie, continentem in longitudine ab oriente vsque occidentem ducentos & viginti pedes assise vel eo circiter, iacentem & adiungentem vie sive venelle ibidem ex vno latere, & abbuttantem super peciam terre vocatam the Parke super boream, & super gardinum tunc vel nuper in tenura sive occupacione cuiusdam Johannis Cornishe versus occidentem, & super aliud gardinum tunc vel nuper in tenura sive occupacione cuiusdam Johannis

Knowles versus orientem, cum omnibus domibus,
edificiis, structuris, viis, easiamentis, commoditatibus
& pertinentiis adinde spectantibus vel aliquo modo
pertinentibus, que dicta premissa sunt scituata,
iacentia & existentia infra parochiam sancti Salvatoris
in Southwarke in Comitatu Surria; aceciam totam
illam parcellam terre nuper preantea inclusam &
factam in tria separalia gardina, vnde duo eorumdem
nuper in tenura sive occupacione cuiusdam Johannis
Robertes carpenter ac aliud nuper in occupacione
cuiusdam Thomae Ditcher civis & mercatoris scissoris
Londonie, scituatam, iacentem & existentem in parochia
predicta in predicto Comitatu Surria, continentem in
longitudine ab oriente ad occidentem per estimacionem
centum quinquaginta & sex pedes assise vel eo circiter,
& in latitudine a borea ad austrum centum pedes assise
per estimacionem vel eo circiter, iacentem & adiun-
gentem super alio latere vie sive venelle predicte, &
abbuttantem super gardinum ibidem tunc vel nuper
preantea in occupacione Willelmi Sellers versus
orientem, & super vnum aliud gardinum ibidem tunc
vel nuper preantea in tenura Johannis Burgram sadler
versus occidentem, & super venellam ibidem vocatam
Mayden lane versus austrum, cum omnibus domibus,
edificiis, structuris, viis, easiamentis, commoditatibus,
& pertinentiis ultimus recitatis premissis seu alicui
parti vel parcelle inde spectantibus seu aliquo modo
pertinentibus, simulcum libero ingressu, egressu &
regressu & passagio ad & pro prefatis Cuthberto
Burbadge & Ricardo Burbadge & prefatis Will*elm*o
Shakespeare, Augustino Phillipps, Thome Pope,
Johanne Hemynges & Willelmo Kempe, executoribus,
administratoribus & assignatis suis, & omnibus &
quibuslibet aliis persone & personis habentibus occa-
sionem ad veniendum ad eos per & trans predictam
viam sive venellam, iacentem & existentem inter
premissa predicta dimitti mencionanda vt supradictum est, ad & a predictis premissis dimitti men-
cionandis vt predicitur, ac ad omnia tempus & tempora

durante dicto termino subscripto; Habendam & tenendam vnam medietatem sive dimidiam partem dictorum separalium gardinorum, anglice garden plottes, ac omnia & singularia alia premencionata & dimissa premissa, cum omnibus & singulariis pertinentiis, prefatis Cuthberto Burbadge & Ricardo Burbadge, executoribus, administratoribus & assignatis suis, a festo Natalis Domini vltimo preterito ante datum dicte indenture ⟨25 Dec. 1598⟩ vsque plenum finem & terminum triginta vnius annorum extunc proxime sequentium & plenarie complendorum & finiendorum ⟨25 Dec. 1629⟩, pro annuali redditu septem librarum & quinque solidorum; ac habendam & tenendam predictam aliam medietatem sive dimidiam partem predictorum separalium gardinorum, anglice garden plottes, ac omnia & singularia alia premissa dimitti mencionanda, vt supradictum est, cum omnibus & singulariis suis pertinentiis, prefatis Will*elm*o Shakespeare, Augustino Phillips, Thome Pope, Johanni Hemynges & Willelmo Kempe, executoribus, administratoribus & assignatis suis, a festo Natalis Domini vltimo preterito ante datum dicte indenture ⟨1598⟩ vsque plenum finem & terminum triginta vnius annorum extunc proxime sequentium & plenarie complendorum & finiendorum ⟨1629⟩, pro annuali redditu septem librarum & quinque solidorum; qui quidem separales redditus solubiles extiterunt super quatuor festa sive terminos in anno, videlicet ad festum Annunciacionis beate Marie virginis, Natiuitatis sancti Johannis Baptiste, sancti Michaelis Archangeli, & Natalis Domini, vel infra sexdecim dies proxime post quodlibet festum festorum predictorum per equales porciones, prout per predictam recitatam indenturam inter alia plenius liquet & apparet;

de quibus quidem premissis vel desuper aliqua parcella inde, anglice vpon somme parte therof quedam domus lusoria apta pro ostencione & actione comediarum & tragediarum existebat;

quorum quidem domus lusorie, gardinorum anglice

garden plottes, & premissorum vnam medietatem sive
dimidiam in sex equales partes & porciones dividen-
dam predicti Basilius Nicoll, Will*elm*us Shakespeare,
Johannes Witter, Johannes Hemynges, Henricus
Condell, Johannes Edmondes & Maria vxor eius,
tempore confeccionis predicte indenture prefato
Willelmo Osteler facte, habuerunt & gavisi fuerunt;
videlicet predicti Basilius Nicoll, Johannes Edmondes
& Maria uxor eius habuerunt vnam equalem sextam
partem inde, predictus Will*elm*us Shakespeare habuit
vnam aliam equalem sextam partem inde, predictus
Johannes Witter habuit vnam aliam equalem sextam
partem inde, & predicti Johannes Hemynges &
Henricus Condell habuerunt tres equales sextas partes
inde, prout per separales conveiancias inde factas
plenius apparet;
predicti Basilius Nicoll, Will*elm*us Shakespeare, Johannes
Witter, Johannes Hemynges, Henricus Condell, Johannes
Edmondes & Maria vxor eius, pro & in consideracione
cuiusdam competentis pecunie summe eisdem Basilio,
Will*elm*o, Johanni, Johanni, Henrico, Johanni & Marie
per predictum Willelmum Osteler ante sigillacionem
dicte indenture pre manibus solute, vnde iidem Basilius,
Will*elm*us, Johannes, Johannes, Henricus, Johannes &
Maria cognoverunt receptionem apud Londoniam predictam in predicta parochia beate Marie de Arcubus
in Warda de Cheape Londonie predicte, dimiserunt,
barganizauerunt, vendiderunt, assignaverunt & trans-
posuerunt prefato Willelmo Osteler vnam equalem
septimam partem & porcionem predicte medietatis &
dimidie partis & porcionis predictorum gardinorum,
anglice garden plottes, domus lusorie & premissorum
in & per predictam recitatam indenturam dimissionis
dimissorum (eadem medietate & dimidia parte predictorum gardinorum, anglice garden plottes, domus lusorie
& premissorum in septem partes & porciones dividenda),
habendam & tenendam predictam septimam partem &
porcionem predicte medietatis sive dimidie partis
predictorum gardinorum, anglice garden plottes, domus

lusorie & premissorum, per predictam indenturam
prefato Willelmo Osteler concedi, barganizari, vendi,
assignari, & transponi mencionatorum, prefato Willelmo
Osteler, executoribus, administratoribus & assignatis suis,
a tempore confeccionis indenture illius pro & durante
residuo adtunc venturo predicti termini triginta vnius
annorum per predictam indenturam dimissionis concessi,
in tam amplis modo & forma quam predicti Basilius
Nicoll, Willelmus Shakespeare, Johannes Witter, Johannes
Hemynges, Henricus Condell, Johannes Edmondes &
Maria vxor eius, seu eorum aliquis, premissa predicta
habuerunt seu gavisi fuerunt . . .

(2) [*As to the Blackfriars.*]

Cum per quandam indenturam inter Ricardum Burbadge
de Londonia generosum ex vna parte & prefatum Willelmum Osteler de Londonia generosum, in vita sua nuper
virum prefate Thomasine, ex altera parte, apud Londoniam predictam in parochia beate Marie de Arcubus
in Warda de Cheape Londonie factam, gerentem datum
vicesimo die Maii anno regni domini Jacobi nunc Regis
Anglie nono ⟨20 May, 1611⟩, recitando per eandem
indenturam quod,

Cum predictus Ricardus Burbadge per quandam
aliam indenturam dimissionis, gerentem datum nono die
Augusti anno Domini millesimo sexcentesimo octavo
⟨9 August, 1608⟩ annoque regni dicti domini Regis
nunc Anglie sexto, pro consideracionibus in eadem
vltima recitata indentura dimissionis specificatis, dimisisset & ad firmam tradidisset cuidam Willelmo Slye
nuper de Londonia generoso defuncto vnam plenam
septimam partem tocius illius domus lusorie, vocate
a playehouse, & diuersarum aliarum rerum ipsius
Ricardi Burbadge, particulariter specificatarum, tam
in predicta recitata indentura dimissionis, quam in
quinque aliis separalibus indenturis dimissionis de
eodem dato separatim concessis de parcellis predicte
domus lusorie & premissorum (exceptis prout per
predictas separales indenturas excipitur) per & a pre-

dicto Ricardo Burbadge prefato Johanni Hemynges
& quibusdam Willelmo Shakespeare, Cuthberto Burbadge, Henrico Condell, Thome Evans, de Londonia
predicta generosis, scituatorum in precinctu de le
Blackfryers Londonie, pro termino viginti vnius
annorum ⟨to 1629⟩, ac pro & subter annualem red-
ditum quinque librarum quatuordecim solidorum &
quatuor denariorum,

Quam quidem primam recitatam indenturam dimissionis sic vt prefertur prefato Willelmo Slye
factam & concessam, vt supradictum est, quedam
Cecilia Browne executrix testamenti & vltime volun-
tatis eiusdem Willelmi Slye, pro bonis consideracionibus ipsam adinde moventibus, virtute executriciati
sui predicti sursumreddidit & illi prefato Ricardo
Burbadge deliberauit cancellandam & vacuam faciendam
simulcum toto iure & interesse suo de & in predicta
septima parte eiusdem domus lusorie & premissorum,
prout per predictam indenturam dimissionis &
sursumreddicionis inde indorsate plenius apparere
potest,

Et que quidem septima pars euisdem domus lusorie
& premissorum sic prefato Willelmo Slye dimissa
& sursumreddita, vt supradictum est, postea divisa,
dimissa & reservata fuit per predictum Ricardum
Burbadge prefato Johanni Hemynges, Henrico Condell, prefato Ricardo Burbadge et aliis per separales
indenturas dimissionis,

Omnes que quidem indenture dimissionis sursum-
reddite & deliberate fuerunt prefato Ricardo Burbadge
cancellande & frustrande;
predictus Ricardus Burbadge, pro diuersis bonis & racio-
nalibus consideracionibus ipsum prefatum Ricardum
adinde moventibus, dimisisset & ad firmam tradidisset
prefato Willelmo Osteler totam predictam septimam
partem predicte domus lusorie & premissorum, sic vt
prefertur prefato Willelmo Slye & aliis dimissorum, sursum
redditam vt supradictum est (exceptis prout in predicta
prima recitata indentura dimissionis & predictis quinque

aliis indenturis dimissionis primo mencionatis excipitur), habendam & tenendam predictam septimam partem predicte domus lusorie & premissorum, superius per predictam indenturam prefato Willelmo Osteler ⟨Slye⟩ modo dimissam, (exceptis preexceptis) prefato Willelmo Osteler, executoribus, administratoribus & assignatis suis, a festo Annunciacionis beate Marie Virginis vltimo preterito ante datum dicte indenture ⟨25 March, 1611⟩ vsque finem & terminum octodecim annorum & vnius quarterii anni tunc proxime sequentium plenarie complendorum & finiendorum ⟨25 June, 1629⟩ . . .

(c) [1610, Feb. 8. From suit of *Keysar v. Burbadge and Others* (Court of Requests), pr. in full C. W. Wallace (1910, *Nebraska Univ. Studies*, x. 336). The action is only against the Burbadges, Heminges, Condell, and Evans, although Keysar speaks of 'others' as their partners; and Evans, although still alive, made no reply. Apparently the suit was never completed.]

(1) [1610, Feb. 8. From *Bill* of Robert Keysar.]

[*Recitals*, without dates, of lease of Blackfriars by Richard Burbadge to Henry Evans; of conveyances by Evans to John Marston and by Marston to Keysar of one-sixth interest in the premises and in the apparel, properties, and play-books of the Children of the Queen's Revels; and of an alleged promise by the Burbadges, Heminges, Condell, and their partners to make no arrangement with Evans without satisfaction of Keysar's interest].

Yet notwithstandinge and by the giveinge of some small peece of monye to the said Henrye Evans to the end that he would surrendour vp the originall lease to the said Richard Burbage, which he the said Burbage had made formerlye to the said Henrye Evans of the said Hall & Roomes in the Blackfryers as afforesaid, he the saide Evans did surrendour the same, by meanes wheirof they the said Richard Burbage, Cuthbert Burbage, John Heminges, Henrye Condell and others, have entred in and vpon the said playe howse, and all the said goodes, apparell and premisses and have soe continewed in the possession for a longe tyme and made proffitt theirof to themselves to the full valewe at the leaste of fifteene hundred poundes, a full sixt parte wheirof in all equitye and conscyence doth of right belonge vnto your suppliant.

(2) [1610, Feb. 12. From *Answer* of Richard Burbadge, Cuthbert Burbadge, John Heminges, and Henry Condell.]

[*Recitals* of the fact that the premises had long been 'voyde and without vse for playes'; of the failure of Evans to fulfil his covenants for repairs; and of the consequent forfeit of his bond for £400.]

He the said Evans began to treate with the said Richard Burbage about a surrender of the said Evans his said lease, which fynally for and in regarde of some competent consideracion giuen him in recompence of his the said Evans his charge formerly bestowed in buildinges in & about the premissed was accomplished, and the said Evans his whole estate of in & to the premisses was surrendred by the said Evans vnto the said Burbage who accepted the same surrender accordingly (without knowinge of or intendinge to preiudice the estate of the said Marston or the complaynant or eyther of them,) as he hopeth it lawfull was for him to doe, especially the premisses beinge in such decay for want of reparacions as then they were, & the said defendantes confesse that true it is that sithens the said surrender made by the said Evans to the said Richard Burbage as aforesaid, which was about the tenth of August last past ⟨1609⟩, they the said defendantes have entred into occupied & enioyed the said great hall or play house & taken the benefytt & profytt thereof ... without that ... these defendantes haue made fifteene hundred poundes profitt of and by the premisses at any time since the said surrender made as aforesaid.

(*d*) [1635, *c*. Aug. 1. From *Answer* of Cuthbert Burbadge, Winifred Robinson, and William Burbadge to *Petition* of Robert Benfield and Heliard Swanston to the Lord Chamberlain (*R.O. Lord Chamberlain's Books*, v. 133, p. 44) pr. H.P. i. 312.]

The father of vs Cutbert and Richard Burbage was the first builder of Playhowses, and was himselfe in his younger yeeres a Player. The Theater hee built with many Hundred poundes taken vp at interest. The players that liued in those first times had onely the profitts arising from the dores, but now the players receaue all the commings in at the dores to themselues and halfe the Galleries from the Houskepers. Hee built this house vpon leased ground, by which meanes the landlord and Hee had a great suite in law, and by his death, the like troubles fell on vs, his sonnes; wee then bethought vs of altering from thence, and at like expence built the Globe with more summes of money taken vp at interest, which lay heauy on vs many yeeres, and to our selues wee ioyned those deserueing men, Shakspere, Hemings, Condall, Philips and others partners in the profittes of that they call the House, but makeing the leases for twenty-one yeeres hath beene the destruction of our selues and others, for they dyeing at the expiration of three or four yeeres of their lease, the subsequent yeeres became dissolued to strangers, as by marrying with their widdowes, and the like by their Children. Thus, Right Honorable, as concerning the Globe, where wee our selues are but lessees. Now for the Blackfriers that is our inheritance, our father purchased it at extreame rates and made it into a playhouse with great charge and troble, which after was leased out to one Euans that first sett up the Boyes commonly called the Queenes Majesties Children of the Chappell. In processe of time the boyes growing vp to bee men, which were Vnderwood, Field, Ostler, and were taken to strengthen the Kings service, and the more to strengthen the service, the boyes dayly wearing out, it was considered that house would bee as fitt for our selues, and soe purchased the lease remaining from Evans with our money, and placed men Players, which were Hemings, Condall, Shakspeare, &c.

[The evidence of these suits for the general history of the Globe and the Blackfriars is discussed in *Eliz. Stage*, ii. 57, 414, 509. A correction is, however, necessary. I there (ii. 417) followed C. W. Wallace [1] in accepting what appears on the face of it to be the statement of (*a*) that the holding of the actors in a moiety of the Globe after the conveyances to and from Levison and Savage was

---

[1] *Century Magazine*, lxxx (1910), 508.

a joint tenancy, the shares in which were inalienable by will and passed to the survivors of the joint tenants; and I pointed out that, in spite of this, shares appear in fact to have passed to heirs of the tenants. It is now clear to me that the words 'ioynt tenancie', which some one has underlined in the MS. of (a), are a draftsman's error, and that the object of the conveyances was to convert an original joint tenancy into a tenancy in common. The law as to co-ownership is set out in Holdsworth, *Land Law*, 69 and *H.E.L.* iii. 126; H. W. Challis, *Real Property*, 368; Halsbury, *Laws of England*, xxiv. 200. Rights in a joint tenancy pass in survivorship; those in a tenancy in common as if the shares were separate estates. A conveyance to two or more persons creates a joint tenancy unless there are 'words of severance' in it; if there are, it creates a tenancy in common. The joint tenancy, therefore, which (a) ascribes to Augustine Phillips and his fellows, cannot have existed after the regrant by Levison and Savage to each of them 'severally'.

The extracts here given show the extent of Shakespeare's interests. He held one-fifth of a moiety, i.e. one-tenth of the Globe, as the shares were originally constituted by the lease of 21 Feb. 1599; one-eighth of the whole after Kempe dropped out a little later, one-twelfth after Condell and Sly were brought in during 1605–8, one-fourteenth after Ostler was brought in on 20 Feb. 1612. In the Blackfriars he held one-seventh under the original lease of 9 Aug. 1608, one-sixth after the death of Sly in the same year, one-seventh again after Ostler was brought in on 25 March 1611. Whether he held his shares to the end of his life, and if not, when he parted with them, is not clear. They are not mentioned specifically in his will, although the residuary bequest of 'leases' to the Halls would cover them; and they do not appear in any of the recorded transactions of his heirs (no. xxiv). The share in the Globe noted in (a) as sold before the fire of 1613 was doubtless Sly's, as Heminges and Condell already held three shares between them on 20 Feb. 1612. Shakespeare was then still holding, as (b) shows. The original lease was due to expire in 1629, but was extended to 1635 and then again to 1644,[1] and the papers in the suit of 1635 show that at some date earlier than 1633 the whole of the actor-housekeepers' moiety was held as to four shares by the Heminges family, and as to the other four by the Condell family. They must at some time have acquired the Shakespeare interest, from himself or his representatives. It is possible

---

[1] C. W. Wallace, *Times* for 30 Apr. and 1 May, 1914; Adams, *Playhouses*, 256, 262.

that Shakespeare sold in 1613, rather than pay the levy of £50 or £60 needed for rebuilding after the fire. If so, he might have taken occasion to sell his Blackfriars share at the same time, but it should be noted that he is not a defendant in Keysar's *Bill* of 8 Feb. 1610, and he may therefore have ceased to hold before that date.

What was the value of Shakespeare's interests? Lee 308 estimates that, as a 'housekeeper', he received £150 a year from the Globe and £150 from the Blackfriars, 'while the two were in active work'. This rests upon the incorrect or arbitrary assumptions, that the daily takings in the early years of the Globe 'were not likely on a reasonable system of accountancy to exceed £15 nor the receipts in gross to reach more than £3,000 a year'; that the working expenses 'might well absorb half the total receipts'; that the net profit of £1,500 was divisible among the five original housekeepers; that as their number increased, the profits of the Globe increased proportionately; that the profits of the Blackfriars were half those of the Globe; that each house was open for 200 days in the year, and therefore to some extent concurrently with the other; and that 'a lower valuation of Shakespeare's holdings than the one which is here suggested' would be inconsistent with the affluence imputed to sharers and disclosed by their wills, and with the value attached in *Ham.* iii. 2. 288 to 'a fellowship in a cry of players'. Lee then adds £180 as an actor's salary, £15 as a share of court rewards, £2 to £3 and perquisites as a groom of the chamber, indefinite premiums for taking apprentices, £40 for writing plays and £20 for 'benefits and other supplementary dues of authorship'; and finally concludes that Shakespeare, during fourteen or fifteen years of his life, 'must have been earning at the theatre a sum well exceeding £700 a year in money of the time'. Apart from the mathematics of this, it is obvious that Lee has failed to understand the finance of the King's company or the respective positions of Shakespeare as at once a 'housekeeper', interested in a proportion of takings assigned as quasirent to the owners of a theatre, and an actor-sharer receiving no salary at all, but making his profit with his fellows, after outgoings had been paid, out of the rest of the takings.[1] The basis of Lee's estimate may be disregarded; its amount more than trebles any earnings with which we can possibly credit Shakespeare. A. Thaler, *Sh.'s Income*, would halve it.[2] But I doubt whether even his calculation is quite sound. The available evidence is minutely analysed by Baldwin 162, 332, and I think his results are approximately correct, although expressed with a greater appearance of precision than the

---

[1] *Eliz. Stage*, i. 352–8.   [2] 1918, *S.P.* xv. 82.

elements of conjecture involved leave quite justifiable. Statements in the suit of 1635, from which (d) is taken, make it possible to determine pretty exactly the financial position of the King's men during a year extending from 26 May 1634 to 18 May 1635. This seems to have been a full year of playing, and it may reasonably be assumed that the Globe was open for about 150 days in the summer, and the Blackfriars for about 150 days in the winter. Each of the actor-sharers made a net profit of about £90. The Blackfriars 'house' was nearly twice as profitable as the Globe. Each of sixteen housekeeper's shares in the Globe made about £25; each of eight such shares in the Blackfriars about £90. I differ from Professor Baldwin in that I take these figures to include a sum of £220 received for court performances during a year ending on 27 Apr. 1634, for which a warrant was issued on 28 April, and which was probably paid after some little delay.[1] Clearly the argument in which the figures are used would be understated if so important an annual receipt were not taken into account. If, then, Shakespeare had still been in 1635 an actor-sharer in the King's men and a housekeeper both at the Globe and the Blackfriars, his total profits would have been about £205, hardly more than two-thirds of what Lee gives him. But in fact nearly twenty years had elapsed in 1635 since his death. We have very little material for determining how far financial conditions had remained stable in the interval. Probably there had not been much change at the Globe, in spite of the rebuilding in 1614. Witter in suit (a) claims to have received £30 or £40 from a seventh share in the house before the fire. He is not likely to have understated his claim, and it is fairly consistent with the £25 derived from an eighth share in 1635. But it may be that the value of the Blackfriars had appreciated. For the earlier period we are again dependent upon *ex parte* statements made by litigant shareholders of the Revels companies which had preceded the King's men in the occupation of the house.[2] Keysar, in suit (c), said that the Burbadges and their partners had gained £1,500 at the Blackfriars between August 1609 and February 1610. But this was denied, and Keysar is not likely to have had accounts to go upon. In any case he probably included the profits of actor-sharers as well as of housekeepers, since the distinction did not exist in the Revels company, on the basis of his interest in which he was making a claim. Edward Kirkham similarly claimed in 1612 that the King's 'gott & as yet dothe, more in one Winter in the said great Hall by a thousand powndes than they

[1] *Lord Chamberlain's Bks.* v. 134, p. 2; *A.O. Declared Accounts*, Bundle 394, no. 72.   [2] *Eliz. Stage*, ii. 57.

were used to gett in the Banckside'.[1] Kirkham's figure, even if not exaggerated, probably refers to takings, rather than profits. I think that Baldwin 347 makes a fair case for putting the Blackfriars takings in 1635 at from £2,000 to £2,200. Kirkham also gives an estimate of the profits of the 'house', when he had himself an interest during the occupation of the Revels company.[2] It is not clear, and of no use for comparison, as the Revels boys do not appear to have played daily.[3] On the other hand, Shakespeare's shares were rather larger than the eighths of the Blackfriars and the sixteenths of the Globe in 1635. So far as the earnings of an actor-sharer go, we can only say, I think, that while the number of court performances and consequent rewards had certainly grown by 1635, the Caroline methods of presenting plays were probably more costly than the Jacobean. On the whole it seems safe to say that the returns of 1634–5 for a full year's playing must give an outside figure for anything which Shakespeare can be supposed to have enjoyed. Moreover, he can have had very few full years. The records of 1603–16 show that the company travelled in most of these years, and that there were long periods of inhibition, chiefly for plague, during which the meagre profits of provincial performances and the royal allowances for private practice (cf. App. D) would be a poor compensation for the closure of the London houses. We cannot, I think, accept any of the subsidiary sources of professional income which Lee supposes Shakespeare to have enjoyed. The 'boys' employed by players were an expense and not a source of profit, as they did not pay premiums (cf. no. viii). The King's men were no doubt grooms of the chamber, but 'without fee'.[4] This cannot possibly mean that they had to pay no fee for their places. Such a gratuity as the King's men received, when they were employed as ordinary grooms of the chamber in 1604, must have been quite exceptional. No doubt the Admiral's company paid for plays written by its own actor-sharers, just as it did for those written by outsiders. But Shakespeare not improbably gave up acting at an early date, and I think we must assume that, if he continued to be an actor-sharer, his plays were thereafter his contribution to the enterprise, and did not bring him any additional remuneration. This view is perhaps confirmed by Ward's story (App. C, no. ix) that he 'supplied the stage with 2 plays every year, and for that had an allowance so large, that hee spent att the rate of 1000¹ a year', although the figure is even more absurd than Lee's. Oldys (App. C,

---

[1] Fleay, *C.H.*, 248.
[2] *Ibid.* 225, 249.
[3] *Eliz. Stage*, ii. 556.
[4] *Ibid.* i. 313.

no. xxxiv) had heard that he received £5 for *Hamlet*, but, if so, that may have been while he still acted. At his possible earnings in the 16th century, it is hardly worth guessing.

Nor can we form much opinion as to the capital value of his shares in the Globe and the Blackfriars when he parted with them. Thomasina Ostler in suit (*b*) estimated the values of her terms in her Blackfriars and Globe shares at £300 each. This can only have been a rough estimate. The term was about fifteen years in each case, and the Blackfriars share was certainly far more productive than the Globe. A third of a Blackfriars share was sold for £20 about 1633, a share in each for £156 in that year, one Blackfriars and two Globe shares for £350 in 1634. It is difficult to reconcile the fluctuating prices for short terms and perhaps with varying prospects of renewal. These seem to have been purchases in the open market 'surreptitiously' from needy owners. But the suit of 1635 makes it clear that when shares passed regularly from one actor to another by seniority, it was at 'usuall and accustomed rates'.[1] And we do not know what these rates were. Similarly it may be assumed that, when an actor-sharer retired, he received a sum representing his interest in the common stock of apparel, properties, and 'books'. There would be a corresponding investment on admission. The sum may not have been a fixed one. Hotson 31 shows from a Chancery suit that about 1635 a particular incoming actor had paid £200 towards a stock valued at over £3,000, and complained that some other sharers had paid no more than £50. Shakespeare would have had to contribute to the original stock of the Chamberlain's in 1594, and possibly also, as a housekeeper, to the building of the Globe in 1599.]

VIII. SHAKESPEARE AND HIS FELLOWS

(*a*) [1598, before 20 Sept. Note after text of *Every Man In his Humour* in *First Folio* of Ben Jonson's *Workes* (1616). A contemporary letter shows that *E.M.I.* was 'a new play' shortly before 20 Sept. (*Eliz. Stage*, iii. 359).]

This Comoedie was first Acted, in the yeere 1598. By the then L. Chamberlayne his Seruants. The principall Comœdians were.

Will. Shakespeare.	Ric. Burbadge.
Aug. Philips.	Ioh. Hemings.
Hen. Condel.	Tho. Pope.
Will. Slye.	Chr. Beeston.
Will. Kempe.	Ioh. Duke.

[1] H.P. i. 313.

(*b*) [1599, Autumn. Note after text of *Every Man Out of his Humour* in *First Folio* of Ben Jonson's *Workes* (1616). On the date, cf. *Eliz. Stage*, iii. 362.]

This Comicall Satyre was first acted in the yeere 1599. By the then Lord Chamberlaine his Seruants. The principall Comœdians were,

Ric. Burbadge.	Ioh. Hemings.
Aug. Philips.	Hen. Condel.
Wil. Sly.	Tho. Pope.

(*c*) [1603, May 19. From Licence for King's men (*Patent Roll, I Jac. I*, p. 2, m. 4), pr. in full *M.S.C.* i. 264; *Eliz. Stage*, ii. 208.]

Wee . . doe licence and aucthorize theise our Servauntes Lawrence Fletcher, William Shakespeare, Richard Burbage, Augustyne Phillippes, Iohn Heninges, Henrie Condell, William Sly, Robert Armyn, Richard Cowly, and the rest of theire Assosiates freely to vse and exercise the Arte and faculty of playing Comedies, Tragedies, histories, Enterludes, moralls, pastoralls, Stageplaies and Suche others like as theie haue alreadie studied or here-after shall vse or studie aswell for the recreation of our lovinge Subjectes as for our Solace and pleasure when wee shall thincke good to see them duringe our pleasure.

(*d*) [1603, July 22. Extract from *Will* of Thomas Pope (*P.C.C.* 12 Harte), proved 13 Feb. 1604, printed in full in *Variorum*, iii. 506; Collier, iii. 360.]

Item, I give and bequeath to Robert Gough and John Edmans all my wearing apparel, and all my arms, to be equally divided between them.

(*e*) [1603, *c.* Christmas. Note after text of *Sejanus* in *First Folio* of Ben Jonson's *Workes* (1616). On the date, cf. *Eliz. Stage*, iii. 367.]

This Tragœdie was first acted, in the yeere 1603. By the Kings Maiesties Seruants. The principall Tragœdians were,

Ric. Burbadge.	Will. Shake-Speare.
Aug. Philips.	Ioh. Hemings.
Will. Sly.	Hen. Condel.
Ioh. Lowin.	Alex. Cooke.

(*f*) [1604, *c.* Mar. 15. From *Account* of Sir George Home, Master of the Great Wardrobe, for the Proceeding of King James through London on 15 Mar. 1604 (*R.O. Lord Chamberlain's Books*, II. 4 (5)), pr. *N.S.S. Trans.* (1877–9) 15*.]

Red Clothe bought of sondrie persons and giuen by his Maiestie to diuerse persons against his Maiesties sayd royall proceeding through the Citie of London, viz :— . . .

The Chamber . . .	
Fawkeners &c. &c.	Red cloth
William Shakespeare	iiij yardes di.
Augustine Phillipps	,,
Lawrence Fletcher	,,
John Hemminges	,,
Richard Burbidge	,,
William Slye	,,
Robert Armyn	,,
Henry Cundell	,,
Richard Cowley	,,

(*g*) [1605, May 4. Extract from *Will* of Augustine Phillips (*P.C.C.* 31 Hayes, proved 16 May 1605), pr. Chalmers, *Apology*, 431; Collier, iii. 327.]

Item I geve and bequeathe unto and amongste the hyred men of the Company which I am of, which shalbe at the tyme of my decease, the some of fyve pounds of lawfull money of England to be equally distributed amongeste them, Item I geve and bequeathe to my Fellowe William Shakespeare a thirty shillings peece in gould, To my Fellowe Henry Condell one other thirty shillinge peece in gould, To my Servaunte Christopher Beeston thirty shillings in gould, To my Fellowe Lawrence Fletcher twenty shillings in gould, To my Fellowe Robert Armyne twenty shillings in gould, To my fellowe Richard Coweley twenty shillings in gould, To my fellowe Alexander Cook twenty shillings in gould, To my fellowe Nicholas Tooley twenty shillings in gould. . . . Item, I geve to Samuell Gilborne my late apprentice, the some of fortye shillings, and my mouse colloured velvit hose, and a white taffety dublet, a blacke taffety sute, my purple cloke, sword and dagger, and my base viall. Item I geve to James Sands my Apprentice the some of fortye shillings and a citterne a bandore and a lute, to be paid and delivered unto him at the expiracion of his terme of yeres in his indenture of apprenticehood. [Robert Goffe is a witness.]

(*h*) [1605 ? Note after text of *Volpone* in *First Folio* of Ben Jonson's *Workes* (1616). On the date, cf. *Eliz. Stage*, iii. 368; *4 Libr*. vi. 345.]

This Comoedie was first acted, in the yeere 1605. By the Kings Maiesties Seruants. The principall Comœdians were,

Ric. Burbadge.	Ioh. Hemings.
Hen. Condel.	Ioh. Lowin.
Will. Sly.	Alex. Cooke.

(*i*) [1610, Jan.–July. Note after the text of *The Alchemist* in *First Folio* of Ben Jonson's *Workes* (1616). On the date, cf. *Eliz. Stage*, iii. 371.]

This Comoedie was first acted, in the yeere 1610. By the Kings Maiesties Seruants. The principall Comœdians were,

Ric. Burbadge.	Ioh. Hemings.
Ioh. Lowin.	Will. Ostler.
Hen. Condel.	Ioh. Vnderwood.
Alex. Cooke.	Nic. Tooley.
Rob. Armin.	Will. Eglestone.

(*k*) [1611. Note after *Catiline his Conspiracy* in *First Folio* of Ben Jonson's *Workes* (1616).]

This Tragoedie was first Acted, in the yeere 1611. By the Kings Maiesties Seruants. The principall Tragœdians were,

Ric. Burbadge.	Ioh. Hemings.
Alex. Cooke.	Hen. Condel.
Ioh. Lowin.	Ioh. Underwood.
Wil. Ostler.	Nic. Tooly.
Ric. Robinson.	Wil. Eglestone.

(*l*) [1608–13. Note before text of *The Captain* in *Second Folio* of the *Works* of Beaumont and Fletcher (1679). The play was given at Court in

1612–13, and Ostler is present. The absence of Heminges may indicate a date not earlier than 1611, but the list is too short to make an inference safe.]

The principal Actors were,

Richard Burbadge. ⎱   ⎰ William Ostler.
Henry Condel.   ⎰   ⎱ Alexander Cooke.

(*m*) [1611 or 1613–14. Note before text of *Bonduca* in *Second Folio* of the *Works* of Beaumont and Fletcher (1679). Only in 1611 and 1613–14 could Ecclestone and Ostler have played together. The absence of Heminges makes a year before 1611 unlikely.]

The Principal Actors were

Richard Burbadge, ⎫   ⎧ William Ostler,
Henry Condel,   ⎪   ⎪ John Lowin,
William Eglestone, ⎬   ⎨ John Underwood,
Nich. Toolie,   ⎭   ⎩ Richard Robinson.

(*n*) [1611–14. Note before *Valentinian* in *Second Folio* of the *Works* of Beaumont and Fletcher (1679). The source (cf. *Eliz. Stage*, iii. 229) was published in 1610. Heminges is absent, Ostler present.]

The principal Actors were,

Richard Burbadge. ⎫   ⎧ William Ostler.
Henry Condel.   ⎬   ⎨ John Underwood.
John Lowin.   ⎭   ⎩

(*o*) [1619, Mar. 27. From Licence for King's men (*Exchequer, Treasury of the Receipt, Privy Seals*, 17 *Jac. I*, Bundle ix, no. 2), pr. in full *M.S.C.* i. 280; cf. *Eliz. Stage*, ii. 218. Burbadge died on 13 Mar. 1619, while the patent was going through its stages.]

Wee . . . do license and authorize theis our welbeloved servantes Iohn Heminges, Richard Burbadge, Henry Condall, John Lowen, Nicholas Tooley, Iohn Vnderwood, Nathan Field, Robert Benfield, Robert Gough, William Ecclestone, Richard Robinson and Iohn Shanckes and the rest of their associates freely to use and exercise the Art and facultie of playing Comedies, Tragedies, Histories, Enterludes, Morralles, Pastoralles, Stage plaies, and such other like as they have already studied, or hereafter shall vse or studie, aswell for the recreacion of our loving Subiectes, as for our solace and pleasure when wee shall thinke good to see them, during our pleasure.

(*p*) [1619, May 19. Abstract of Lord Chamberlain's *Warrant* for liveries (*Hist. MSS*. iv. 299, from MS. of Earl De La Warr). This and (*q*) came, no doubt, from Sir Lionel Cranfield, afterwards Earl of Middlesex, who was Master of the Great Wardrobe.]

Order signed by the Earl of Pembroke for delivery to the bearer, John Hemminges, on behalf of himself and the rest of his followers ⟨fellows⟩, His Majesty's servants, the players whose names are underwritten, such allowance for their liveries as hath been heretofore accustomed.

John Hemminges, Henry Condell, John Lowen, Nathan Field, John Underwood, Nicholas Tooley, Robert Goffe, Robert Benfield, William Eccleston, John Shanke, Richard Robinson, Joseph Taylor.

(*q*) [1621, Apr. 7. Note of Lord Chamberlain's *Warrant* for liveries (*Hist. MSS*. iv. 299, from MS. of Earl De La Warr); cf. (*p*) *supra*.]

The like—except that John Rice is there, and Nathan Field is absent; and the names of Condell, Goffe, and Benfield are here spelt Cundale, Gough, and Bennefield.

(*r*) [1613⟨⟩14; 1619⟨⟩23. From note before text of Webster's *Duchess of Malfi* (1623). The full cast must represent a revival, but three of the original performers are also given. For the dates, cf. *Eliz. Stage*, iii. 510.]

Bosola, I. Lowin.
Ferdinand, 1 R. Burbidge.　2 I. Taylor.
Cardinall, 1 H. Cundaile.　2 R. Robinson.
Antonio, 1 W. Ostler.　2 R. Benfeild.
Delio, I. Vnderwood.
Forobosco, N. Towley.
The Marquesse of Pescara, I. Rice.
Siluio, T. Pollard.
The seuerall madmen, N. Towley, I. Vnderwood, etc.
The Dutchesse, R. Sharpe.
The Cardinals M^{i}s, I. Tomson.
The Doctor,　⎫
Cariola,　　 ⎬ R. Pallant.
Court officers, ⎭

(*s*) [1623. From ninth preliminary leaf to F1.]

The Names of the Principall Actors in all these Playes.

William Shakespeare.	Samuel Gilburne.
Richard Burbadge.	Robert Armin.
John Hemmings.	William Ostler.
Augustine Phillips.	Nathan Field.
William Kempt.	John Vnderwood.
Thomas Poope.	Nicholas Tooley.
George Bryan.	William Ecclestone.
Henry Condell.	Joseph Taylor.
William Slye.	Robert Benfield.
Richard Cowly.	Robert Goughe.
John Lowine.	Richard Robinson.
Samuell Crosse.	Iohn Shancke.
Alexander Cooke.	Iohn Rice.

[A narrative account of the Chamberlain-King's men is given in *Eliz. Stage*, ii. 192, and supplemented (ii. 295) by biographical details for the individual actors. A few new facts have since come to light, and a comprehensive survey, covering a much longer period than this book is concerned with, has appeared in T. W. Baldwin, *The Organisation and Personnel of the Shakespearean Company* (1927). Some of the views there advanced, I find it difficult to accept. It is necessary to distinguish between (i) the actor-sharers, some of whom were also (ii) 'housekeepers' interested as part-landlords in the theatres used by the company, (iii) the hired men, (iv) the boys.[1]

We have a good deal of material for determining a list of sharers, at any rate from 1603 onwards. There are the official lists in patents and livery warrants. There are lists of actors in individual plays, mainly those of Jonson and those of Beaumont and Fletcher. The latter did not appear in the Folio of 1647, but were added in 1679. They presumably came from some theatrical record, and are only intelligible on the assumption that the great majority relate to the first productions of the plays concerned. As a rule they are too late to be of value as evidence for the period before 1616, and indeed many of the plays are only datable with their help. The Jonson dates are more secure. There is the more comprehensive list in F1 itself. There are (cf. App. D) the names of responsible sharers who

---

[1] Cf. *Eliz. Stage*, i. 352, 362 ; ii. 416, 509.

acted on behalf of the company as payees for court rewards. There are dates of death or burial, and occasionally wills. E. M. Denkinger has recently traced the burial of Robert Armin on 30 Nov. 1615,[1] and F. Brinkley the death of Nathan Field between 19 May 1619 and 2 Aug. 1620.[2] We have older information for Thomas Pope (ob. 22 July 1603 ⟨ ⟩ 13 Feb. 1604), Augustine Phillips (ob. 4 ⟨ ⟩ 13 May 1605), William Sly (bur. 16 Aug. 1608), Lawrence Fletcher (bur. 12 Sept. 1608), Alexander Cooke (bur. 25 Feb. 1614), William Ostler (ob. 16 Dec. 1614), William Shakespeare (ob. 23 Apr. 1616), Richard Cowley (bur. 12 Mar. 1619), Richard Burbadge (ob. 13 Mar. 1619). One can assume that vacancies were not long left unfilled. From these and some miscellaneous sources the order of succession given in ch. iii is derived. The fundamental document is the F1 list. It professes to give the 'Principall Actors' in Shakespeare's plays, and I take it to be in effect a complete list of sharers from the establishment of the company in 1594 to the date at which it was prepared. This may have been in 1621 rather than 1623. The last name given is that of John Rice, who became a groom between 19 May 1619 and 7 Apr. 1621. The history of the next few years is rather obscure, but Gough seems to have become a messenger of the chamber in October 1621,[3] and his successor, probably George Birch, is not in the list. This, however, cannot be taken as fixing the order of seniority. That the official lists diverge from it on this point might be explained on the assumption that they follow the order of swearing in as grooms of the chamber and the F1 list that of joining the business associateship. The two things are of course technically distinct. Normally the same persons were sharers and grooms, but not invariably. It seems probable that Lawrence Fletcher was made a groom because he had already been 'comediane sserviture to his maiestie' in Scotland,[4] and that he was never a business associate of the King's men, although Phillips calls him his 'Fellowe' in 1605. I have a suspicion that the honorific designation 'Mr', applied to leading actors in theatrical documents, may really indicate the *status* of groom or lord's servant, rather than, as usually supposed, that of sharer.[5] But the official lists do not themselves follow a consistent order, and on the other hand we cannot suppose that Armin, who is in the 1603 patent, was really as junior as his place in F1 suggests. Some element of conjecture as to the actual succession of new recruits is

[1] *P.M.L.A.* xli. 95.

[2] *M.L.N.* xlii. 12.

[3] R. C. Bald, *Middleton's Game at Chesse*, 22, from *Inner Temple Petyt*

MS. 515. 7.

[4] *Eliz. Stage*, ii. 269; A. J. Mill, *Mediaeval Plays in Scotland*, 306.

[5] Cf. *Eliz. Stage*, ii. 125.

therefore necessary. It is reasonable to suppose that the clown Shank replaced the clown Armin, and that the playwright Field was looked to as a substitute for Shakespeare. My order does not differ materially from Baldwin's, although he, believing the Chamberlain's company to be continuous with Lord Strange's, would antedate (81) the beginning of the F1 list to 1588, when he thinks that Shakespeare began writing. I do not, of course, believe that he did, and if the F1 list covered 1588–94, one would certainly expect to find in it the names of Alleyn and other members of his combination, who never became Chamberlain's men. It seems clear that an increase in the number of the company took place shortly after the patent of 1603. But Baldwin cannot be right in placing it (49) on 'Whitsun Monday, June 13, 1603, the beginning of the company's financial year'. There are nine grooms in the patent of May 1603 and nine still in the livery list of March 1604. The increase to twelve must have taken place between this last date and the attendance upon the Spanish ambassador (vol. i, p. 77) in August 1604. The fact that the company followed a Whitsun financial year, not in 1603 but in 1634–5, is surely irrelevant. It is true that Lowin and Cooke, who were almost certainly two of the added members, are in *Sejanus* (1603), but unless there was a very long interval between their enrolment as sharers and their appointment as grooms, they must at first have been hired men. The playlists are not so limited in their scope as the official lists. Those for Beaumont and Fletcher and Webster include some hired men and even boys. For the same reason, one cannot be certain that Beeston and Duke, who are in the list for *E.M.I.* (1598) were sharers. I do not think that the F1 list itself contains any others than sharers, and here again I differ from Baldwin (68), who treats it as including 'the apprentice actors of the chief women's parts', and thus explains the appearance of Samuel Crosse and Samuel Gilburne. I take him to mean that these were the only important boy actors who did not become sharers by 1623. This seems to me unlikely. Thomas Pollard, Thomas Holcombe, Richard Sharpe, and John Thompson all probably played leading ladies in Shakespeare's plays by 1623, or even by 1621. On the whole, since twenty-four of the twenty-six men named in F1 were certainly sharers, it seems safest to assume that they all were. My chronicle, therefore, includes Crosse and Gilburne, and I suppose them both to have died early. Premature deaths must be expected in plague-time. I do not now much think [1] that Crosse was the old actor only known to Heywood [2] by repute,

---

[1] Cf. *Eliz. Stage*, ii. 200, 313.   [2] *Ibid*. iv. 252.

although it is just conceivable that this Crosse survived long enough to be with the Chamberlain's for a short time before Heywood came to London. It is more likely that Samuel was of a younger generation. I therefore differ from Baldwin (49) by taking him, rather than Tooley, to have been the third added sharer of 1604, and Tooley to have succeeded him before Phillips's will of 4 May 1605. Similarly, I think that Gilburne, and not with Baldwin (49) Gough, must have succeeded Phillips in 1605, and that he left a vacancy for Gough at some date before August 1611, when Gough is designated 'M^r' in *2 Maiden's Tragedy*. Gough's name comes low down both in F1 and in the patent of 1619. I take it that he had for some time been a hireling of the company. Pope left him a legacy in 1603. He cannot have been a very important actor, as he is in none of the play-lists.

The position of hired men is discussed in A. Thaler, *Minor Actors and Employees in the Elizabethan Theatre*,[1] and very fully by Baldwin. It is impossible to recover the names of most of those attached to Shakespeare's company during his career. No doubt Gough was not the only sharer who had been promoted from this class, which may also have included John Duke and Christopher Beeston. Phillips in his will speaks of Beeston as his 'servant'. Similarly Tooley, in his, speaks of Burbadge as his 'late M^r'. But in both cases the relationship implied may be that (cf. *infra*) of a boy. For any further indications we are dependent upon names casually preserved (cf. vol. i, p. 237) in stage directions. And when they are directions of F1, they may only date from late revivals. Such are the Tawyer of *Mid. N. Dr.*, the musician Jack Wilson of *Much Ado*, and the 'G.' and 'E.' of *All's Well*, who have been rather hazardously identified with Gough and Ecclestone. Similarly the 'T. Tucke' and 'Curtis' of *Two Noble Kinsmen*, probably Thomas Tuckfield and Curtis Greville, are only in a late text of 1634. On the other hand, I think that the Gabriel, Humphrey, John Holland, and Bevis of *2, 3 Hen. VI*, although they also come in F1, are more likely to belong to a performance by an earlier company than to a revival by the Chamberlain's. Wilson, in his turn, ascribes to the Pembroke's men of 1592–3 *The Shrew*, which I regard as an early Chamberlain's play. It has a 'Nicke', a 'Par', a 'Fel', a 'Peter', which may be actor names, although other explanations are possible for some of them. Wilson supposes that Petruchio's servants, Gabriel and Curtis, also bear actor names. But if the directions date from 1592–4 or thereabouts, he can hardly be safe in making

---

[1] 1922, *M.P.* xx. 49.

Curtis into Curtis Greville, who was married on 23 Dec. 1615,[1] and of whom there is no certain notice of earlier date. *The Shrew*, however, is again a F1 text. I do not now think that the 'Harvey' and 'Rossill' of *1 Hen. IV* were actors; they are almost certainly, like 'Oldcastle', survivals of a discarded nomenclature.[2] Of one hired man, however, we can be pretty sure. This is John Sincler or Sincklo, a relic (cf. vol. i, p. 50) of the Alleyn company, who is found, not only in *The Shrew* and *3 Hen. VI*, but also in *2 Hen. IV* and the induction to *The Malcontent*. This would bring him on to at least 1604. A. Gaw, *John Sincklo as One of Sh.'s Actors*, has some speculations on his physique and parts.[3] Many names must have been lost. On 27 Dec. 1624 Sir Henry Herbert issued a protection from arrest during the service of the Revels for twenty-one 'musitions and other necessary attendantes' of the King's men.[4] The names are given. Either Edward or Anthony Knight we know to have been the book-keeper, a functionary of whom I have said enough in ch. iv. John Rhodes (vol. i, p. 107) was wardrobe-keeper, William Gascoigne (vol. i, p. 121) a stage-hand. Henry Wilson (App. D, *s.a.* 1631) and William Toyer were musicians. Toyer must be the Tawyer of *Mid. N. Dr.*, buried in 1625 as 'William Tawier, M[r] Heminges man'. But the list certainly includes actors as well. George Vernon seems to have become a sharer, although Baldwin (119) puts him in a special class of hired men entitled to wear royal livery, for the existence of which I see no sufficient evidence, except in so far as it is possible that a man, who had been sworn as a groom while in another company, may have retained the right during hired service with the King's. Robert Pallant (p. 76), Thomas Tuckfield (*supra*), Henry Clay (*P.M.L.A.* xliv. 799), and William Patrick and William Mago are also traceable as actors. Nicholas Underhill may be the 'Nich' of *Barnavelt*. I do not know why Baldwin (120) adds Edward Ashborne. There is a residue in 1624 of nine, as to whom we cannot say whether they were actors, musicians, or stage-hands. Probably all the staff, except the book-keeper, who was also prompter, were available for minor parts on occasion. A later protection of 1637 for attendants also yields player names.[5] If, then, the King's had twenty-one hirelings in 1624, of whom at least six were players, we have no reason to suppose that they were very differently

---

[1] *Bodl. MS. Eng. Hist. e.* 1, f. 403, from *Register* of St. Andrew's Wardrobe.

[2] *Eliz. Stage*, iii. 196; cf. vol. i, p. 382.

[3] 1926, *Anglia*, xlix. 289.

[4] *Herbert*, 74.

[5] *Lord Chamberlain's Books*, v. 134, p. 142.

staffed in Shakespeare's time. Some elaboration of the provision for
music there probably was, after the Blackfriars was taken over in
1608 or 1609. It was not necessarily all in the hands of hirelings.
Phillips's will (cf. *infra*) suggests that he was a musician. Richard
Cowley had taken a musician's part in *Seven Deadly Sins*, and as
he never appears in the actor lists, music may have been his chief
function throughout. Jack Wilson was a singer for the company
before 1623 (cf. vol. i, p. 386). It is uncertain whether he is to
be identified with the court musician John Wilson (1595–1674).[1]
Probably it would be safe to assume that the King's had normally
some six or more regular hired men available, and could draw upon
temporary help from outside if need be. London parish registers
show a large number of players who were certainly never sharers
in any known company. E. M. Denkinger's list for St. Botolph's
Aldgate [2] and G. E. Bentley's for St. Saviour's Southwark and
St. Giles's Cripplegate [3] give many names hitherto unrecorded.

The wages of hired men and boys were a charge upon the common funds of the sharers in 1635. The facts (*supra*) for Beeston,
Gough, and Tawyer suggest that the hiring of the men was as
'servants' to individual sharers. Those of the Admiral's in 1597
seem to have been engaged by Henslowe, the company's financier,
as covenant servants to himself personally for short terms of two
years, and to have been required to give bonds of £40 for service
during the full period.[4] The boys may have been upon a rather
different footing. It is here, however, that I differ most funda-
mentally from Baldwin. He tells us (32) that the boys were 'taken
under the provision of the apprentice law'; that 'according to this law
(5 *Eliz.* c. 4) the apprentice must serve a minimum of seven years
and must be at least twenty-four at the end of his apprenticeship'.
He knows that this principle was often varied in the practice of the
London gilds, and that apprenticeship sometimes ended at twenty-
one. He supposes this to have been the case with actors, and that
for them it usually began at ten. This he rests largely upon the
histories of Salathiel Pavy and Nathan Field. Here his facts are not
quite correct. Pavy, no doubt, had acted for three years before he
died at the age of thirteen; but Field, born in 1587, began his career
with the establishment of the Chapel at Blackfriars, which was in
1600, not, as Baldwin thinks, in 1597. In any case there was no
question of apprenticeship at the Chapel; it was recruited under

---

[1] Cf. *D.N.B.* and Grove, *Dict. of Music and Musicians*, iv. 727.
[2] *P.M.L.A.* xli. 91.
[3] *T.L.S.* for 15 Nov. 1928; *P.M.L.A.* xliv. 789.
[4] *Eliz. Stage*, ii. 151.

the prerogative of impressment for the royal service.[1] I dare say, however, that boys often began to act at an early age. At twenty-one Baldwin (35) supposes that 'an apprentice might take up his freedom and become a member of the organisation'. He knows that there was no gild of actors in London. But he asserts (37) that 'each patent company was incorporated by the crown as a brother-hood, a temporary method of attaining the same thing', and that 'the actors could secure boy labor only through the apprentice law, and they could admit as "masters" in their legal corporation only those who had conformed to that law'. Most of all this is com-pletely misconceived. The *Statute of Artificers* of 1563 [2] had very little application to London, and still less to the playing companies. It was an attempt at the regulation of industrial labour. So far as relevant, its objects were, (a) to impose an obligation to accept service for hire upon all young or unmarried tradesmen, subject to various exceptions, of which one was for persons lawfully retained in household or office with noblemen, gentlemen, or others, and would cover players; and (b) to establish for the country in general a system of industrial apprenticeship on the model of that already existing in London. The age for apprenticeship, as given by Bald-win, is set out in § 19, and by § 24 the exercise of crafts by persons who had not undergone apprenticeship is prohibited. But the application of the Act to London itself is barred by a special pro-vision (§ 33) saving the liberties of the city 'for having of appren-tices'. And in any case it did not cover actors. This is clear from a decision of the King's Bench in 1615 known as 'Tolley's Case'.[3] Tolley had been apprenticed as a woolpacker, but followed the trade of an upholsterer. The court decided that he was not barred, because (a) he was following the custom of London, and (b) upholstering did not fall within the statute. It was not one of the sixty-one trades specifically mentioned therein, and if it had been thought to be 'such a trade that required art and skill for the exercising of it', it would have been mentioned. What applies to upholstering clearly applies to acting also. The *Statute of Artificers* is in fact only con-cerned with artisan occupations. It is equally certain that no custom of London regulated the practice of acting, and that no apprentice-ship was necessary before entering upon it. No actor, as such, ever 'took up his freedom' in the sense of that phrase as used in civic documents, which implies at once the licence to follow a trade and

[1] *Eliz. Stage*, ii. 33, 42.
[2] 5 *Eliz*. c. 4; *Statutes of the Realm*, IV. i. 414.
[3] R. H. Tawney and E. Power, *Tudor Economic Documents*, i. 378, from H. Calthrop, *Reports of Special Cases Touching Several Customes and Liberties of the City of London* (1670), 9.

enrolment as a London citizen. We never hear of a 'citizen and player of London'. What Baldwin says of the incorporation of the companies by the Crown as quasi-gilds is entirely baseless. All that he has to go upon is a loose statement by J. Cocke, not,[1] as he says, John Stephens, in 1615, that the actor 'incorporates himselfe by the title of a brotherhood'. Even Cocke does not say that the Crown incorporated him. We have the patents, and of course they do nothing of the kind. Nor could swearing in before the Lord Chamberlain have such an effect.

The actual *data* bearing upon the conditions under which boys were employed are rather scanty. Henslowe 'bought' his boy James Bristow from a player for £8 in 1597, and recovered 3s. a week for his services from the company.[2] John Shank, who joined the King's about 1615, asserted in 1635,[3] that he had

'still of his owne purse supplyed the company for the service of his Majesty with boyes as Thomas Pollard, John Thompson deceased (for whome hee payed 40l[i]) your suppliant haveing payd his part of 200l[i] for other boyes since his comming to the company, John Honiman, Thomas Holcome and diuerse others, and at this time maintaines three more for the sayd service'.

In 1527 Thomas Arthur agreed to serve George Mayler of the King's interluders for a year, and paid a sum down, on condition that Mayler would maintain him and give him 4d. a day, would teach him 'in playinge of interludes and plaies', and would bring him into the King's company.[4] This is of course rather too early evidence to be of much value here. The agreement for the conduct of the King's Revels in 1608 provides that the children shall all be bound to one sharer for three years, and that he shall give a bond to his associates against his 'partinge with, or puttinge awaye' any of them to other persons without general consent, 'excepte the tearme of his or their apprenticeshipp be fully expired'.[5] On 14 Nov. 1606 Thomas Kendall, then manager of the Queen's Revels, took Abel Cooke as one of the children 'to be practized and exercised in the sayde qualitye of playinge', and his mother gave a bond that he would 'abide with and searve' Kendall for three years.[6] These last two records relate to boy companies, although in a period after the system of recruiting by impressment had been brought to an end.[7] But I see no reason to suppose that the conditions in the adult

[1] Cf. *Eliz. Stage*, iv. 255.
[2] *Eliz. Stage*, ii. 153, 155.
[3] H.P. i. 316.
[4] *Eliz. Stage*, ii. 81; *N.S.S. Trans.* 1877–9, 425.
[5] *Eliz. Stage*, ii. 65; *N.S.S. Trans.* 1887–92, 276.
[6] H. N. Hildebrand, *The Child Actors*, 197.
[7] *Eliz. Stage*, ii. 52.

companies were materially different, and should take the engage-
ments to have been for terms of two or three years, rather than of
seven years or longer, and not under formal indentures of apprenticeship, but, as in the case of men, ordinary contracts of service with
individual sharers, backed by bonds. Evidently a partly trained boy
had a value, and if his services were transferred to a new master,
a premium could be obtained. There is an ambiguous jest on it in
Chapman, *May-Day*, iii. 3. 228. A phrase in *Eliz. Stage*, i. 371,
might imply that premiums were paid to parents. I do not see any
evidence of this. 'Apprenticeship' is no doubt a convenient term to
use, but it seems likely to be misleading. Actually we generally hear
of a 'boy', or of the 'boy of' an individual. The record of 1608
cited above, however, does speak of apprenticeship. And I have
come across one other case, which raises a complication. Augustine
Phillips, in his will, leaves legacies to Samuel Gilburne, his 'late
apprentice', and to James Sands, his 'apprentice'. Baldwin, rather
inconsistently with his theory of incorporation, suggests (37) that
some actors, who were also members of trade gilds, might have
apprenticed the boys to their own trades. I cannot conceive this to
be possible as regards the majority of trades. The courts of the gilds
would have a responsibility for seeing to it that the training was in
their own craft. But I do think it possible that Phillips, who leaves
Gilburne a bass viol, and Sands a cithern, a bandore, and a lute, was
a member of the Company of Minstrels or Musicians, and that his
boys had exceptionally gone through a regular apprenticeship to
music, with which a training in acting would not have been incom-
patible. The Ordinances made by the Company in 1606 under
their charter of 1604, as set out in *The Worshipful Company of
Musicians* (1905), issued by the Livery Club, provide for a system
of apprenticeship. Its pre-Jacobean history has not been written.
But some earlier ordinances of 16 Mar. 1500,[1] of which I owe
a copy to the kindness of Mr. A. H. Thomas, show that a system
then already existed, and I think it is likely that a good many
musicians took up the 'quality' of acting. 'Musician' and 'player'
seem convertible terms in the records of St. Saviour's, Southwark,
as given by G. E. Bentley in *T.L.S.* (15 Nov. 1928). Both seem
to be applied to Robert Gough, and to others, such as Thomas
Downton and Thomas Heywood, not of the King's men, whom
we know as players. Phillips himself is not here called 'musician',
but he is called in 1594 'histrio', perhaps still in the old sense of
'minstrel', rather than 'actor'. The ordinances of 1500 give the

---

[1] City *Letter Book*, M, f. 22.

period of apprenticeship as seven years. No period is specified in those of 1606, and no age limit in either set. The company acquired in 1500 a monopoly of minstrelsy in London, subject to a saving clause for royal minstrels and those of nobles. This it retained in 1606, with an added power to license others not of the fellowship. The ordinances claim no control over acting. In view of what has been said, I will not go into a detailed analysis of Baldwin's attempt (417) to plot out the succession of apprentices or supposed apprentices in the Shakespearean company on the basis of eleven-year terms. I do not think with him (288) that 'the evidence would strongly indicate' that Shakespeare, who was already twenty-three, became an apprentice among Leicester's men in 1587; still less that this may have been to Heminges in the grocery trade. He mercifully refrains from citing *Wint. Tale*, iv. 3. 38–52 in support of this.

Shakespeare's plays have been examined by J. Engelen, *Die Schauspieler-Ökonomie in Shakespeares Dramen*,[1] and some of them also by M. Sack, *Darstellerzahl und Rollenvertheilung bei Shakespeare* (1928), with a view to determining the number of actors required, after taking into account the possibilities of 'doubling', for their performance. Both investigators arrive at a maximum of fifteen, which would only be reached in a few plays. It is obvious that a company of twelve, with six or more hired men, in addition to boys, would be ample. Some special arrangement probably had to be made for the spectacular fairies in *Mid. N. Dr.* and perhaps *Merry Wives of W.* It may be noted that the second Lord Hunsdon had a musical establishment, and that boys from this might be available. As Sir George Carey, he took Robert Johnson as a 'allowes or covenaunt servaunt' on 29 Mar. 1596, and engaged to teach him the art of music. Johnson was a royal lutenist from 1604 to 1633 and set songs for *Temp.*[2] W. J. Lawrence has an interesting chapter on *The Practice of Doubling*,[3] although I do not accept the view that this was limited to minor actors, which is inconsistent with the cast of the *Duchess of Malfi*. It is not, of course, necessary to assume that doubling was carried to its full theoretical extent, or on the other hand that all the company appeared in every play. Some tragedies, for example, would not accommodate a clown. It is pretty clear, indeed, that some of the sharers ceased to act some time before they left the company. Shakespeare is only in two early

---

[1] *Jahrbuch*, lxii. 36; lxiii. 75.
[2] I. H. Jeayes, *Berkeley Castle Muniments*, 239; Grove, *Dict. of*
Music, ii. 783.
[3] *Pre-Restoration Stage Studies*, 43.

play-lists. Heminges is in all up to *Catiline* (1611) and in none thereafter. By 1613 he stuttered.[1] Condell similarly drops out about 1620. Much of Baldwin's book is devoted to an attempt to establish the 'lines' or types of part appropriate to each of the principal actors and boys, and on the basis of this to arrive at the actual parts played by each in Shakespearean plays. I find this too speculative to invite criticism here.]

IX. SHAKESPEARE'S LONDON RESIDENCES

(*a*) [1597, Nov. 15. From *Certificate* of London Commissioners for second instalment of third subsidy granted by Parliament of 1593 (*R.O. Subsidy Rolls*, 146/354) pr. J. W. Hales (*Ath.* 26 Mar. 1904).]

The petty collectors . . . within the warde of Byshopsgate . . . upon their corporall othes upon the holye Evangelists of Allmighty God . . . dyd saye and affirme that the persons hereunder named are all ether dead, departed, and gone out of the sayde warde or their goodes soe eloigned or conveyd out of the same or in suche a pryvate or coverte manner kept, whereby the severall sommes of money on them severallye taxed and assessed towards the sayde secound payment of the sayde last subsydye nether mighte nor coulde by anye meanes by them the sayde petty collectors, or ether of them, be levyed of them, or anye of them, to her Majesties use.
St Ellen's parishe.
. . . William Shackspere v^{li}–v^s.

(*b*) [1598, Oct. 1. From *Indenture* between London Commissioners for first subsidy granted by Parliament of 1597–8 and petty collectors for Bishopsgate ward, with list of persons assessed for payment (*R.O. Exchequer Lay Subsidies, City of London*, 146/369), pr. Hunter, i. 77; facs. Giuseppi 3.]
St: Hellens parishe.
Affid.   William Shakespeare—v^l.—xiii^s. iiij^d.

(*c*) [1598–9. From list (*Exchequer L.T.R. Enrolled Accounts of Subsidies*, no. 56) furnished for Bishopsgate and five other wards, showing defaulters for the first subsidy granted by Parliament in 1597–8, who had no goods or chattels, lands or tenements within the limits of the collection on

[1] *Eliz. Stage*, ii. 421.

which the collector could distrain, and for whom answer will be due in the *Pipe Roll* for 1598-9 in *Residuum London*; facs. Giuseppi 4.]

In Warda de Bishopsgate . . . In parochia Sancte Helene . . . Willelmus Shakespeare ibidem xiij.^{s}. iiij^d.

(*d*) [1599, Oct. 6. From list of persons owing sums to the Exchequer in membrane *Residuum London* of *Pipe Roll* for 1598-9; facs. Giuseppi 5.]

Surr R

Willelmus Shakspeare in parochia sancte Helene in Warda predicta debet xiij.^{s} iiij.^{d} de eodem subsidio ibidem. [*Added*] Respondebit in rotulo sequente in Residuum Sussex.

(*e*) [1600, Oct. 6. From list of persons owing sums to the Exchequer in membrane *Residuum Sussex* of *Pipe Roll* for 1599-1600; facs. Giuseppi 6.]

London R:
o n^i Episcopo
Wintonensi T

Willelmus Shakspeare in parochia sancte Helene xiij.^{s} iiij^d de primo integro subsidio predicto Anno xxxix^{no} concesso Qui requiritur super eundem ibidem.

(*f*) [1596, 1608. From Malone, *Inquiry* (1796), 215.]

From a paper now before me, which formerly belonged to Edward Alleyn, the player, our poet appears to have lived in Southwark near the Bear-Garden, in 1596. Another curious document in my possession, which will be produced in the History of his Life, affords the strongest presumptive evidence that he continued to reside in Southwark to the year 1608.

[The facts as to Shakespeare's subsidies are incorrectly summarized by Lee 274 and *Contemporary Review*, civ (1913), 348. They are given by Hunter, i. 76, J. W. Hales in *Athenæum* for 26 Mar. 1904, and most precisely by M. S. Giuseppi in *Trans. London and Middlesex Arch. Soc.* (1925). I am indebted to Mr. Giuseppi for some explanations. The history of subsidies and of the older 'fifteenths and tenths', to which they were supplementary, is given in S. Dowell, *History of Taxation and Taxes* (1888), which requires some correction from J. Tait, *Taxation in Salford Hundred* (1924, *Chetham Soc.*), xx. They were imposed from time to time by statute, at the alternative rates of 4*s.* on the annual value of lands or 2*s.* 8*d.* on the value of personal property. The valuations were low and there was much evasion. The collection was entrusted to local commissioners with collectors under them. Defaulters were reported to the Exchequer, who instructed the sheriffs of counties to recover arrears and answer for them at the annual view of their accounts on the octave of Michaelmas in each year. The transactions were recorded in supplementary membranes on the *Pipe Rolls* of sheriffs' accounts. Two payments by Shakespeare as a resident in St. Helen's Bishopsgate were not forthcoming. The first was a sum of 5s. due as a second instalment of the last of three subsidies granted by the parliament of 1593. The assessment was made in October 1596 and payment should have been made by February 1597. But the collectors reported in the following November (a) that they had been unable to collect it. Giuseppi 8 found an Exchequer statement that the amount was set down for answer in the London section of the *Pipe Roll* of 1613–14, but the reference was not sufficiently exact to enable the membrane to be traced in the bulky rolls. A new subsidy was granted by the parliament of 1597. Shakespeare was assessed, again in St. Helen's, on 1 Oct. 1598 (b) at 13s. 4d. on goods valued £5, and should have paid in the following winter. 'Affid⟨avit⟩' was subsequently written in the margin of the assessment against his name, which indicates that again the collectors swore to their inability to collect. The arrear was reported to the Exchequer (c) and entered on the *Pipe Roll* for 1598–9, with the marginal notes 'Surr⟨ey⟩' and 'R', probably for 'R⟨espondebit⟩'. These were intended for reference at the sitting of the Court of Exchequer in October 1599, and at this sitting a note seems to have been added to the main entry, directing the sheriff for Surrey and Sussex, which were combined for fiscal purposes, to answer for the amount on the *Roll* for 1599–1600. The marginal 'R' was then cancelled. Accordingly the amount appears on the Sussex membrane of the *Roll* for 1599–1600. And here there are three marginal notes, (i) London R, (ii) o⟨neratur⟩ n⟨is⟩i, (iii) Episcopo Wintonensi, (iv) T⟨ot⟩. Presumably (i) indicates the origin of the entry as an amount to be answered from the London membrane for 1598–9; (ii) that the sheriff for Surrey and Sussex was to be charged with the amount unless he showed cause to the contrary; (iii) that the amount was referred for collection to the Bishop of Winchester, who had a liberty, the Clink, in Surrey, outside the sheriff's jurisdiction; and (iv), probably a later addition, that the amount was collected and would be accounted for. And in fact the Bishop of Winchester did account in the *Roll* of 1600–1 for a lump sum received from various persons referred to him by the sheriff. This probably includes Shakespeare's 13s. 4d., although names are not given. Shakespeare has not so far been traced in any other subsidy rolls, either for London or Surrey or

Stratford, where his name certainly does not appear,[1] or for the Royal Household, of which he became an officer in 1603.

So far as his residence is concerned, the inference is that at some date before October 1596 he had lived in St. Helen's, Bishopsgate; that by 1599, and possibly by the winter of 1596–7, he had ceased to do so, and that by October 1599 he was resident in the Clink on the Surrey Bankside. This is not inconsistent with Malone's statements (*f*) of 1796. But unfortunately Malone left his *Life* incomplete before he reached the evidence for these, and Boswell, who completed the *Life* for the *Variorum* of 1821, did not give it. Collier (cf. App. F) attempted to supply the gap by two forged documents, which he ascribed to 1596 and 1609 respectively. The *Belott v. Mountjoy* papers (no. x) make it improbable that Shakespeare was continuously resident in Southwark up to as late a date as 1608.]

X. THE BELOTT-MOUNTJOY SUIT

[1612, 11 May, 19 June. From *Depositions* in suit of *Belott v. Mountjoy* (Court of Requests), pr. C. W. Wallace (1910, *Nebraska Univ. Studies*, x. 263).]

(*a*) [11 May 1612. *Depositions to Interrogatories on behalf of Belott.*]

[(1) *Deposition of Johane Johnsone.*]

3 To the thirde interrogatory this deponent sayth . . . there was a shewe of goodwill betweene the plaintiff and defendantes daughter Marye, which the defendantes wyffe did geue countenaunce vnto and thinke well of. And as she remembereth the defendant did send and perswade one Mr Shakespeare that laye in the house to perswade the plaintiff to the same marriadge.

[(2) *Deposition of Daniell Nicholas.*]

3 To the thirde interrogatory this deponent sayth he herd one W^m: Shakespeare saye that the defendant did beare a good opinion of the plaintiff and affected him well when he served him, and did move the plaintiff by him the said Shakespeare to haue ⟨a⟩ marriadge betweene his daughter Marye Mountioye ⟨and⟩ the plaintiff, and for that purpose sent him the said Sh⟨akespeare⟩ to the plaintiff to perswade the plaintiff to the same, as Shakespere tould him

[1] Cf. H.P. *Subsidies.*

this deponent, which was effected and solempnized vppon promise of a porcion with her. And more he cannott depose.

4 To the iiij^th interrogatory this deponent sayth that the plaintiff did requeste him this deponent to goe with his wyffe to Shakespe⟨are⟩ to vnderstande the truthe howe muche and what the defendant did promise ⟨to⟩ bestowe on his daughter in marriadge with him the plaintiff, who did soe. And askinge Shakespeare therof, he answered that he promissed yf the plaintiff would marrye with Marye his the defendantes onlye daughter, he the defendant would by his promise as he remembered geue the plaintiff with her in marriadge about the some of ffyftye poundes in money and certayne houshould stuffe.

(3) [*Deposition of William Shakespeare*; cf. Plate XII, Fig. (1).]

William Shakespeare of Stratford vpon Aven in the Countye of Warwicke gentleman of the age of xlviij yeres or thereaboutes sworne and examined the daye and yere abouesaid deposethe & sayethe

1 To the first interrogatory this deponent sayethe he knowethe the partyes plaintiff and deffendant and hathe know⟨ne⟩ them bothe as he now remembrethe for the space of tenne yeres or thereaboutes.

2 To the second interrogatory this deponent sayeth he did know the complainant when he was servant with the deffendant, and that duringe the tyme of his the complainantes service with the said deffendant he the said complainant to this deponentes knowledge did well and honestly behaue himselfe, but to this deponentes remembrance he hath not heard the deffendant confesse that he had gott any great profitt and comodytye by the service of the said complainant, but this deponent saithe he verely thinkethe that the said complainant was a very good and industrious servant in the said service. And more he canott depose to the said interrogatory.

3 To the third interrogatory this deponent sayethe that it did evydentlye appeare that the said deffendant did all the tyme of the said complainantes service with him beare

and shew great good will and affeccion towardes the said
complainant, and that he hath hard the deffendant and
his wyefe diuerse and sundry tymes saye and reporte that
the said complainant was a very honest·fellow: And this
deponent sayethe that the said deffendant did make a
mocion vnto the complainant of marriadge with the said
Mary in the bill mencioned beinge the said deffendantes
sole chyld and daughter, and willinglye offered to performe the same yf the said complainant shold seeme to be
content and well like thereof: And further this deponent
sayethe that the said deffendantes wyeffe did sollicitt and
entreat this deponent to move and perswade the said
complainant to effect the said marriadge, and accordingly
this deponent did moue and perswade the complainant thervnto: And more to this interrogatorye he cannott depose.

4 To the ffourth interrogatory this deponent sayth that the
defendant promised to geue the said complainant a
porcion ~~of monie and goodes~~ in marriadg⟨e⟩ with Marye
his daughter, but what certayne ~~some~~ **porcion** he remem-
berethe not, nor when to be payed ~~yf any some weare
promissed,~~ nor knoweth that the defendant promissed the
~~defendant~~ **plaintiff** twoe hundered poundes with his daughter Marye at the tyme of his decease. But sayth that the
plaintiff was dwellinge with the defendant in his house, and
they had amongeste them selues manye conferences about
there marriadge which ⟨afterwardes⟩ was consumated and
solempnized. And more he cann⟨ott depose.⟩

5 To the vth interrogatory this deponent sayth he can saye
noth⟨inge⟩ touchinge any parte or poynte of the same
interrogatory, for he knoweth not what implementes and
necessaries of houshould stuffe the defendant gaue the
plaintiff in marriadge with his daughter Marye.

                                            Wiłłm Shakp

(*b*) [19 June 1612. *Depositions to further Interrogatories on behalf of
Belott.*]

(1) [*Deposition of Daniell Nicholas.*]

4 To the iiij[th] interrogatory this deponent sayth that the
defendant did never send him this deponent vnto the

complainant to make mocion of marriadge betwixte the complainant and the said Marye Mountioye beinge the defendantes sole daughter and childe, but M^r: William Shakespeare tould him this deponent that the defendant sent him the said Mr Shakespeare to the plaintiff about suche a marriadge to be hadd betweene them, and Shakespeare tould this deponent that the defendant tould him that yf the plaintiff would marrye the said Marye his daughter he would geue him the plaintiff a some of monney with her for a porcion in marriadge with her. And that yf he the plaintiff did not marry with her the said Marye and shee with the plaintiff shee should never coste him the defendant her ffather a groat. Wherevppon, and in regard Mr Shakespeare hadd tould them that they should haue a some of monney for a porcion from the father, they weare made suer by Mr Shakespeare by geuinge there consent, and **agreed to marrye**, ~~geuinge eache others hand to the hande~~ and did marrye. But what some yt was that M^r ~~Shake~~ Mountyoye promised to geue them he the said Mr Shakespeare could not remember, but said yt was ffyftye poundes or theraboutes to his best rememberaunce. And as he rememberith Mr Shakespeare said he promised to geue them a porcion of his goodes: but what, or to what valewe he rememberithe not. And more he cannott depose.

(2) [*Deposition of William Eaton.*]

4 To the iiijth interrogatory this deponent sayth he hath herd one Mr Shakspeare saye that he was sent by the defendant to the plaintiff to move the plaintiff to haue a marriadge betweene them the plaintiff and the defendentes daughter Marye Mountioye, and herd Mr Shakespeare saye that he was wished by the defendant to make proffer of a certayne some that the defendant said he would geue the plaintiff with his daughter Marye Mountioye in marriadge, but he had forgott the some. And ~~Mr Shakespeare tould the plaintiff~~ more he cannott depose touchinge the same interrogatory.

(3) [*Deposition of Nowell Mountjoy.*]

4 To the iiijth interrogatory this deponent sayth he was

never sent by the defendant vnto the complainant to make
a mocion to him of a marriadge to be hadd betwixte the
complainant and Mary Mountioy the defendantes sole
child and daughter, nor knoweth of any other that was
by the defendant sent vnto the plaintiff vppon that
messiage: but the plaintiff tould this deponent that one
Mr Shakespeare was imployed by the defendant about
that buysnes: in what manner: or to what effecte he
knoweth not: ...

[Shakespeare was not a party to this suit, which was discovered
with other related documents by Professor Wallace. Christopher
Mountjoy was a French Huguenot, who had apparently been resident in London for some years before 1600, when he was of
St. Olave's parish. Probably then, and certainly in 1612, he occupied a house at the corner of Silver and Monkwell Sts., close to
St. Olave's church, in Cripplegate ward, within the NW. corner
of the city walls. His business was that of a tire-maker, and he had
an apprentice, Stephen Belott, also of French extraction. On
19 Nov. 1604 Belott married Mountjoy's daughter Mary. Some
years later he quarrelled with his father-in-law, and brought the
suit of 1612, in which he alleged that Mountjoy had broken promises to pay a portion of £60 with his daughter and to make a will
leaving her a further £200. The claims were disputed, and evidence
as to the negotiations leading to the marriage became relevant. Joan
Johnson, once a servant in Mountjoy's house, deposed that Shakespeare 'that laye in the house' had been his agent to persuade Belott
to the marriage, and this was confirmed on hearsay from Shakespeare himself, but whether in 1604 or later is not clear, by one
Daniel Nicholas, who further said that Shakespeare had named the
portion to him as about £50 and some household stuff. Obviously
Shakespeare's own evidence was crucial. Unfortunately his memory
failed him when he was examined on 11 May 1612. He had known
the plaintiff and defendant for ten years and could speak to the
plaintiff's good behaviour as an apprentice and the defendant's goodwill towards him. He had persuaded Belott to the marriage at the
instigation of Mountjoy's wife. A portion had been promised, but
he could not remember how much, or when it was to be paid, and
knew nothing as to the alleged promise of a legacy or as to what
goods had been given to Belott. Shakespeare's name appears in the
margin of a set of interrogatories for a second hearing on 19 June,
and presumably it was intended to press his memory further; but

there is no second deposition by him. Nicholas repeated his hearsay and added that Belott and Mary Mountjoy were 'made sure', i.e. betrothed, by Shakespeare. Some slight confirmation, still at second-hand, was obtained as to Shakespeare's part in the matter from William Eaton, now an apprentice to Mountjoy, and Mountjoy's brother Nowell, and the court, after hearing other evidence, referred the case for arbitration to the overseers and elders of the French church in London. They awarded Belott 20 nobles which Mountjoy had not paid a year later. Incidentally they noted 'tous 2 pere & gendre desbauchéz', and later notes also record Mountjoy as of licentious life.

What we learn of Shakespeare is that he had known the Mount-joy household since 1602, had been a lodger in it, but perhaps only temporarily, in 1604, was described as of Stratford-on-Avon in 1612 and therefore presumably had no London residence, was present at Westminster on 11 May 1612, and, perhaps, was then of failing memory. It is quite a pleasing fancy of Adams 380 that Mary Mountjoy taught him broken French for *Hen. V*.]

XI. NEW PLACE

(*a*) [1597, 4 May. Extract from *Exemplification of Fine* (*B.P. Cat.* 30 from *Wheler MSS.*), facs. H.P. ii. 106. The *Foot of Fine* (*R.O.*) is pr. H.P. ii. 104.]

Inter Willielmum Shakespeare querentem et Willielmum Underhill generosum deforciantem, de vno mesuagio duobus horreis et duobus gardinis cum pertinenciis in Stratford super Avon, vnde placitum conuencionis sum-monitum fuit inter eos in eadem curia, Scilicet quod pre-dictus Willielmus Underhill recognovit predictum tene-mentum cum pertinenciis esse jus ipsius Willielmi Shake-speare, ut illa que idem Willielmus habet de dono predicti Willielmi Underhill, et illa remisit et quietumclamavit de se et heredibus suis predicto Willielmo Shakespeare et heredibus suis imperpetuum, Et preterea idem Willi-elmus Underhill concessit pro se et heredibus suis, quod ipsi warantizabunt predicto Willielmo Shakespeare et heredibus suis predictum tenementum cum pertinenciis imperpetuum, Et pro hac recognicione, remissione, quieta clamancia, warantia, fine et concordia idem Willielmus

Shakespeare dedit predicto Willielmo Underhill sexaginta libras sterlingorum.

(*b*) [1598. Extract from *Chamber Account* (Xmas) of Stratford (*B.P. Cat.* 42).]

pd to m^r Shaxspere for on lod of ston x^d.

(*c*) [1602, Michaelmas term. Extract from *Foot of Fine* (*R.O.*), pr. H.P. ii. 105. The purchaser's and vendor's exemplifications were found (1886) among papers of the Severne family of Wallop, Shropshire (*Ath.* 13 Feb., 20 Mar., 1886; H. P. *Rarities*, 140.]

Inter Willielmum Shakespeare generosum querentem et Herculem Underhill generosum deforciantem, de uno mesuagio duobus horreis duobus gardinis et duobus pomariis cum pertinenciis in Stretford-super-Avon [*Rest follows* (*a*) *with* Hercules *for* Willielmus Underhill.]

(*d*) [1609, Sept. 9. Extract from *Memorandum* of Thomas Greene on delay in delivery to him of a house by George Browne (*Misc. Doct.* xii. 103), given by H.P. ii. 378.]

He doubted whether he might sowe his garden, untill about my goinge to the Terme. (seeing I could gett noe carryages to help me here with tymber) I was content to permytt yt without contradiccion & the rather because I perceyued I mighte stay another yere at newe place.

(*e*) [*c*. 1603–16. Extract from endorsement on lease of property east of New Place, given by H.P. ii. 127.]

The barne on the west sid bounds by Mr William Shaxpeare of Pynley Holt, and on the est sid on the Kinges land.

[H.P.'s full *Historical Account of New Place* (1864) is supplemented in *Illustrations* (1874), 124, and abridged and revised in *Outlines*, ii. 101, 277, 373. It renders J. C. M. Bellew, *Shakespere's Home at New Place* (1863) obsolete, but some material on the Cloptons and Underhills is to be found here and in Dugdale 524; *Harl. Soc.* xii. 108; W. Underhill in *8 N.Q.* v. 478; Stopes, *Cont.* 214, 226; Bloom, *Top. Notes*, i. 5; Fripp, *Haunts*, 127.

Sir Hugh Clopton, a younger son of the Cloptons of Clopton manor in Stratford parish, and Lord Mayor of London in 1491, acquired before 1483 a 12*d.* burgage at the angle of Chapel St. and Chapel Lane, also called Dead Lane and Walcastret or Walker St., and opposite the Gild Chapel, which, with the bridge over the Avon, he rebuilt for the town. On this burgage he built New Place, and left 'my grete house in Stratford upon Avon' to his great-nephew William in 1496, subject to a life lease to Roger Paget, Master of the Gild, who died in 1504. The name 'the Newe Place' first appears in a document of 1532. About 1540 Leland [1] describes it as 'a praty howse of brike and tymbar'.

A pedigree of the Cloptons will be useful, although I fear its first three descents are uncertain:

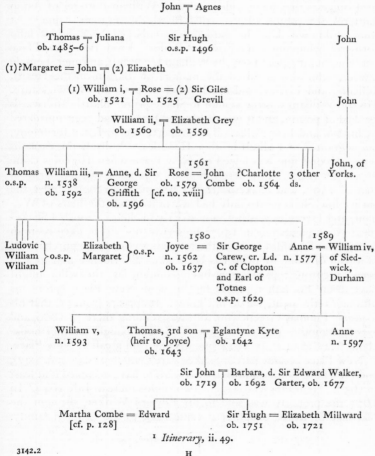

John = Agnes

Thomas = Juliana   Sir Hugh   John
ob. 1485–6   o.s.p. 1496

(1)?Margaret = John = (2) Elizabeth

(1) William i, = Rose = (2) Sir Giles   John
ob. 1521   ob. 1525   Grevill

William ii, = Elizabeth Grey
ob. 1560   ob. 1559

           1561
Thomas   William iii, = Anne, d. Sir   Rose = John   ?Charlotte   3 other   John, of
o.s.p.   n. 1538   George   ob. 1579 Combe ob. 1564   ds.   Yorks.
       ob. 1592   Griffith   [cf. no. xviii]
              ob. 1596

                      1580   1589
Ludovic ⎫   Elizabeth ⎫   Joyce =   Sir George   Anne = William iv,
William ⎬ o.s.p.   Margaret ⎬ o.s.p.   n. 1562   Carew, cr. Ld.   n. 1577   of Sled-
William ⎭   ob. 1637   C. of Clopton   wick,
                                  and Earl of   Durham
                                  Totnes
                                  o.s.p. 1629

William v,   Thomas, 3rd son = Eglantyne Kyte   Anne
n. 1593   (heir to Joyce)   ob. 1642   n. 1597
           ob. 1643

Sir John = Barbara, d. Sir Edward Walker,
ob. 1719   ob. 1692   Garter, ob. 1677

Martha Combe = Edward   Sir Hugh = Elizabeth Millward
[cf. p. 128]   ob. 1751   ob. 1721

[1] *Itinerary,* ii. 49.

From William i New Place passed to William ii, who let it in 1543–5
to Thomas Bentley, physician to Henry VIII and President of the
College of Physicians, and his wife Anne. Bentley died in 1549
and his widow remarried with Richard Charnocke. The house had
been left 'in great ruyne and decay', and litigation followed, in
which Clopton claimed that the lease was forfeit. Here New Place
is described as a 'mannour place'. This it was not, by origin or in
Shakespeare's time, but Clopton seems to have treated it as part of
his neighbouring manor of Ryen Clifford. From William iii the
house passed in 1563, possibly as a result of some sharp practice, to
William Bott, who seems to have been already its tenant. A. Ransford suggests that he was identical with William Botterel of Aston
Botterel, Shropshire, who married Bentley's daughter Anne.[1] At
some unknown date the garden was enlarged by a bit of land
formerly belonging to the Priory of Pinley. From Bott New Place
was bought for £40 in 1567, by William Underhill, an Inner Temple
lawyer, who also acquired the manors of Barton-on-the-Heath,
Idlicote, and Loxley, and much other property in Warwickshire.
His son William was the vendor to Shakespeare. Shortly afterwards
he died of poison, and it was discovered that he had been murdered
by his son and heir Fulke. The property was forfeited for felony,
but regranted to Fulke's brother Hercules. Probably this explains
why a second fine was levied on New Place when Hercules came
of age in 1602. The description in this adds two orchards to
that of 1597, and Shakespeare has become *generosus*. Under the
earlier fine Shakespeare only had warranty from the heirs of William, and Hercules was not now strictly his heir. Probably Shakespeare took possession in 1597; he seems (no. xii) to have been an
occupier in Stratford early in the following year. The purchase (*b*)
of a load of stone in 1598 has been taken as evidence that he had
been executing repairs; it is likely enough, but the seller might
have been his father. How far he used New Place before his
ultimate retirement, we do not know. It appears from (*d*) that his
'cousin' Thomas Greene (no. xix) was residing there in 1609, and
expected another year's occupation. Greene bought another house
about May 1611.[2] In 1614 (no. xix) he paid a call at New Place.

New Place became part of Shakespeare's entailed estate (no. xxiv),
and the Halls, Nashs, and Bernards seem to have occupied it at least
to 1653. Henrietta Maria spent two nights there in July 1643. In
1675 the property was sold to Sir Edward Walker, through the
marriage of whose daughter it came back to the Clopton family.

[1] *N.Q.* clii. 419.   [2] *Misc. Doct.* vii. 125.

His grandson Edward transferred it to his father Sir John, and Sir John rebuilt the house and settled it upon his younger son Hugh in 1702. The Great Garden was for a time detached, and later restored to the house. After Sir Hugh Clopton's death New Place was sold to the Rev. Francis Gastrell, who pulled the house down in a fit of pique with Stratford in 1759. After passing through various hands the site was bought for public uses in 1827 and 1861, and is now held by the Birthplace Trust.

A description of the pre-1702 house was given to Joseph Greene by Richard Grimmitt, formerly a shoemaker in Stratford, born in 1683: [1]

'This Rich^d the younger, Said He in his youth had been a playfellow with Edwd Clopton Senr eldest son of Sr John Clopton Kn^t. & had been often with him in ye Great House near ye chapel in Stratford, call'd New-place: that to ye best of his remembrance there was a brick Wall next ye Street, with a kind of porch at that end of it near ye chapel; when they cross'd a small kind of Green Court before they enter'd ye House which was bearing to ye left, & fronted with brick, with plain windows, consisting of common panes of Glass set in lead, as at this time.'

The engravings in *Var.* ii. 319 and S. Ireland, *Picturesque Views on the Avon*, 197, derive with an improbable history from Jordan. Malone added the Shakespeare arms over the door. H.P.'s investigation of the foundations shows that the house had a frontage of 60 feet, a depth of *c.* 70 feet, and a height of *c.* 28 feet. In 1663 it had ten hearths.]

XII. SHAKESPEARE AS MALTSTER

[1598, Feb. 4. Extract from *S.A. Misc. Doct.* i. 106; pr. H.P. ii. 58: facs. *B.P. Cat.* 41. The full return is in H.P. (*1848*) 167. Presumably the holdings, such as Shakespeare's, not specified as corn, were in malt.]

Stratforde Burrowghe, Warrwicke. The noate of corne & malte Taken the iiijth of ffebruarij 1597 in the xlth yeare of the raigne of our moste gracious Soveraigne Ladie Queen Elizabethe etc. . . .
Chapple street warde . . . W^m. Shackespere. x quarters.

[This return is related to economic conditions, which are most fully described in Cheyney, ii. 3. Three wet summers in 1594, 1595, and 1596 had produced, not only *Mid. N. Dr.* (cf. vol. i, p. 360),

---

[1] H.P. ii. 134.

but also a serious dearth of corn, leading to high prices, poverty, and discontent. The position was aggravated by the engrossing and forestalling of corn—that is, holding supplies in bulk for a rise of price and purchasing direct from farmers, instead of in open market; and by the excessive use of barley for malt. The Privy Council attempted to remedy these abuses by reissuing in 1594[1] a set of *Orders* to Justices of the Peace originally framed in 1586.[2] These were revised in *A New Charge* of 1595,[3] and enforced by letters from the Council to the Justices on 26 Oct. 1595.[4] The export of grain was forbidden. The Justices were required to form local committees of constables and other substantial inhabitants, to obtain returns from them as to the number of cornholders, the size of their households, their stocks and bargains; and also as to the number of maltsters and their other occupations. On the basis of these the Justices were to regulate the trade, requiring excessive stocks to be sold in open market and limiting the amount of malting. Stratford maltsters were bound over not to make malt on 4 November, and a return of cornholders was made on 7 December.[5] Shakespeare's name does not appear; he was not yet a householder in Stratford. But Abraham Sturley and Richard Quiney (cf. no. xiii) are noted amongst other townsmen as 'great corn-buyers' and incidentally as evading the subsidies. Quiney held as much as 47 quarters of barley and 32 quarters of malt of his own, as well as stocks belonging to other men. The Council's remedies, which told against the interests of many Justices and other well-to-do men, were not altogether effective, in spite of proclamations in their support of 31 July and 2 Nov. 1596[6] and another letter to Justices of 3 Aug. 1596.[7] The matter was still occupying Lord Burghley in preparation for the parliament of 1597,[8] and a Council letter of 22 August called upon the Justices for a fresh inquisition upon the engrossers, 'a nomber of wycked people in condicions more lyke to wolves or cormerants than to naturall men', and including, as the Council regretfully note, 'men which are of good lyvelyhoode and in estymacion of worshipp'.[9] The dearth appears to have been particularly felt in south-west Warwickshire, which was in part dependent for its supply upon the neighbouring corn-growing districts of Worcestershire. Sturley reports to Quiney on 24 Jan. 1598,[10] that the people were growing 'malcontent', and were approaching neighbouring Justices

[1] *S.T.C.* 9201.
[2] *Ibid.* 9194.
[3] *Ibid.* 9202.
[4] Dasent, xxv. 25.
[5] Fripp, *Quyny*, 103.

[6] *Procl.* 884, 888.
[7] Dasent, xxvi. 80.
[8] *Hatfield MSS.* vii. 497.
[9] *Ibid.* vii. 410; Dasent, xxvii, 359.
[10] *Var.* ii. 566; Fripp, *Quyny*, 125.

with complaints against 'our maltsters'. There was wild hope of leading them in a halter, and 'if God send my Lord of Essex down shortly, to see them hanged on gibbets at their own doors'. It was in these circumstances that the return of 4 February was made. There was not now much engrossed wheat in the town; only 44 quarters of wheat and practically no barley. The amount of malt was still considerable, 438 quarters belonging to townsmen and 251 to strangers. But the individual holdings were less than in 1595. The largest was 18 quarters; only a dozen men had more than Shakespeare's 10. The appeal to the Justices led them to write to the Council on 28 January 1598, setting out the special needs of the Stratford and Alcester districts, and asking the Council to fix a price for malt. This the Council reply of 19 February refused to do.[1] The Justices were blamed for not carrying out the *Charge* and restraining malting. But a letter was written to Worcestershire to give what help was possible to Warwickshire. The Stratford petition for relief from the taxes imposed by the parliament of 1597–8 lays stress on the hardships imposed by the inability to malt, 'in that our towne hath no other especiall trade, havinge therbye onlye tyme beyownde mans memorye lyved by excersyseng the same, our howses fytted to no other vses, manye servantes amonge vs hyered onlye to that purpose'.[2] It asks that the neighbouring farmers and husbandmen may be forbidden to malt their own barley. The *Charge* of 1595 was again enforced on 23 Aug. 1598.[3] A better harvest in 1599 led to some temporary relaxation of the prohibition against the export of grain, and by 2 June 1600, 'There is no lack of corn'.[4]]

XIII. THE QUINEY CORRESPONDENCE

(*a*) [1598, Jan. 24. Extract from letter of Abraham Sturley ⟨to Richard Quiney⟩ (*S.A. Misc. Doct.* i. 135; *B.P. Cat.* 43), pr. *Var.* ii. 566; H.P. ii. 57; *1848*, 172.]

This is one speciall remembrance from v[r] fathers motion. It semeth bj him that our countriman, M[r] Shaksper, is willinge to disburse some monei vpon some od yardeland or other att Shottri or neare about vs; he thinketh it a verj fitt patterne to move him to deale in the matter of our tithes. Bj the instruccions v can geve him theareof, and bj the frendes he can make therefore, we thinke it a

---

[1] *Dasent*, xxviii. 314.
[2] *B.P. Cat.* 61; cf. no. xiii.
[3] *Procl.* 898.
[4] *Ibid.* 909.

faire marke for him to shoote att, and not unpossible to
hitt. It obtained would advance him in deede, and would
do vs muche good. Hoc movere, et quantum in te est
permouere, ne necligas, hoc enim et sibi et nobis maximi
erit momenti. Hic labor, hoc opus esset eximiae et gloriae
et laudis sibi . . . . Stretfordia, Januarii 24. Abrah. Strl.

(*b*) [1598, Oct. 25. Richard Quiney to Shakespeare, pr. *Var.* ii.
485; H.P.i. 167; *B.P. Cat.* 45; both with facs. (cf. Plate XVII). Malone
describes the discovery in letters of 21 Sept. 1793 to Bp. Percy (*Bodl. Mal.
MS.* 26, f. 22) and 15 Nov. 1793 to Ld. Charlemont (*H.M.C. Charlemont
MSS.* ii. 220). It was then in a bundle of letters to and from Quiney in
the Stratford archives, but is now among the *Wheler MSS.*]

Loveinge Contreyman, I am bolde of yowe as of a ffrende,
craveinge yowre helpe with xxx^{ll} vppon Mr Bushells &
my securytee or Mr Myttons with me. Mr Rosswell is
nott come to London as yeate & I have especiall cawse.
Yowe shall ffrende me muche in helpeinge me out of all
the debettes I owe in London, I thancke god, & muche
quiet my mynde which wolde nott be indebeted. I am
nowe towardes the Cowrte in hope of answer for the
dispatche of my Buysenes. Yowe shall neither loase
creddytt nor monney by me, the Lorde wyllinge, & nowe
butt perswade yowre selfe soe as I hope & yowe shall nott
need to feare butt with all hartie thanckefullenes I will
holde my tyme & content yowre ffrende, & yf we Bar-
gaine farther yowe shalbe the paiemaster yowre self. My
tyme biddes me hasten to an ende & soe I committ thys
⟨to⟩ yowre care & hope of yowre helpe. I feare I shall
nott be backe thys night ffrom the Cowrte. Haste. The
Lorde be with yowe & with vs all Amen. ffrom the
Bell in Carter Lane the 25 October 1598. Yowres in all
kyndenes Ryc. Quyney. [*Addressed*] H⟨aste⟩ To my Loveinge good ffrend & contreymann M^r W^m. Shackespere
deliver thees. [*Seal*] On a bend three trefoils slipped.

(*c*) [n.d. ⟨1598, *c*. 30 Oct.⟩. Extract from letter of Adrian Quiney to
Richard Quiney (*S.A. Misc. Doct.* i. 131; *B.P. Cat.* 46), pr. H.P.
ii. 58; *1848, 175.*]

Yow shalle, God wylling, receve from your wyfe by
y^e baylye, thys brynger, aswrance of x^s. . . . Yff yow

PLATE XVII

RICHARD QUINEY'S LETTER TO SHAKESPEARE

bargen with Mr Sha. . or receve money therfor, brynge your money home yf yow maye, I see howe knite stockynges be sold, ther ys gret byinge of them at Evysshome. Edward Wheat and Harrye, your brother man, were both at Evyshome thys daye senet, and, as I harde, bestow 20^{ll}. ther in knyt hosseyngs, wherefore I thynke yow maye doo good, yff yow can have money. . . . [*Addressed*] To my lovynge sonne Rycharde Qwyney at the Belle in Carter Leyne deliver thesse in London.

(*d*) [1598, Nov. 4. Extract from letter of Abraham Sturley to Richard Quiney (*S.A. Misc. Doct.* i. 136; *B.P. Cat.* 44), pr. *Var.* ii. 569; H.P. ii. 59; *1848*, 175.]

V^r letter of the 25 of October came to mj handes the laste of the same att night per Grenwaj, which imported . . . that our countriman M^r Wm. Shak. would procure vs monej, which I will like of as I shall heare when, and wheare, and howe; and I praj let not go that occasion if it may sort to any indifferent condicions. Allso that if monej might be had for 30 or 40^l, a lease, &c., might be procured. Oh howe can v make dowbt of monej, who will not beare xxx^{tie} or xl^l towardes sutch a match? . . . Now to v^r other letter of the 1° of November receved the 3^d of the same. . . . For present advise and encouragmente v have bj this time Mr Bailj . . . Mr Parsons supposeth that Wenlock came the same daj with Mr Bailj that v writt v^r letter . . . From Stretford Novem. 4th 1598 . . . Abrah. Sturlej. [*Addressed*] To his most lovinge brother, Mr Richard Quinej, att the Bell in Carterlane att London, geve these.

(*e*) [1598, Nov. 24. Extract from letter of Daniel Baker to Richard Quiney (*S.A. Misc. Doct.* i. 124), quoted Fripp, *Quyny*, 157.]

My aunt Quyny telleth me that you are to receive £20 or £30 in London, and that you will pay some money for me if need be; and in that respect I have lent her some money already to serve her occasions.

[The correspondence of which these letters form part is fully described, with much valuable illustration, by E. I. Fripp, *Master*

Richard Quyny (1924). It consists mainly of letters received by Richard during visits to London (Oct. 1597–Feb. 1598; Oct. 1598–Feb. 1599; Nov.–June 1600; Jan.–Nov. 1601). A few others are from the papers of Thomas Greene. Richard was the son and partner of Adrian Quiney a mercer, bailiff of Stratford in 1559, 1571, and 1582. He was himself bailiff in 1592 and 1601. His son Thomas married Judith Shakespeare. The family bore arms, *Or, on a bend sable, three trefoils slipped argent*, said by French 389 to be those of Quiney of Staffordshire, from whom they may have come. But they were settled in Stratford by 1497, and several appear in the Gild register,[1] some of whom cannot be worked into the following pedigree, the first two steps of which are, as it stands, rather conjectural:

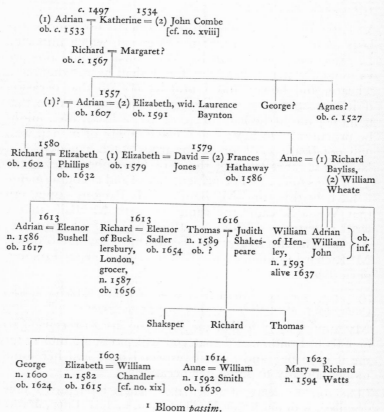

¹ Bloom *passim*.

Richard's chief correspondent was Abraham Sturley, who often writes himself Strelley. He was from Worcester, a student of Queens', Cambridge, and for some time in the service of Sir Thomas Lucy at Charlecote. He came to Stratford about 1580 and was bailiff in 1596. In his letters he refers to Richard and his wife as his 'brother' and 'sister'. Malone believed him to be Richard's brother-in-law through a wife Susanna,[1] but it is clear from Fripp's investigations that Malone misread the 'Elisā.' of a letter as 'Susā.' Sturley's letters are religious in tone, and Fripp supposes that he and Richard were members of a Puritan brotherhood. On the other hand, they may have been 'brothers' as fellow members of the Corporation. Daniel Baker, whom Sturley also calls 'brother', was so in fact, since his wife Joan Taylor was step-sister of Sturley's wife Anne Hill. Baker, who came from Henley in Arden, also calls Richard Quiney's wife Elizabeth 'aunt'. Probably his mother was her sister Mary who is named in the will (1556) of Thomas Phillips. Mr. Fripp tells me that *B.P. Cat.* 60 is wrong in calling Elizabeth the 'daughter and sole heir'. Daniel is probably the 'cousin' Baker named by Thomas Greene (no. xix), although Greene's marriage with William Chandler's mother gives a very distant connexion.

Of the references to Shakespeare (*a*) belongs to Richard's London visit of 1597–8 and (*b*), (*c*), and (*d*) to that of 1598–9. There is no date in (*c*), but it came with the bailiff, whose visit is also referred to in (*d*). The only occasion on which a bailiff joined Richard in London seems to have been in 1598–9. He was John Smith, and another letter [2] shows that he was 'coming' on 27 October. Adrian Quiney had written to Richard on 29 October [3] and probably this undated letter immediately followed.

Richard's London visits seem to have been partly occupied with the private affairs of himself, his father, their associate Sturley, and other relatives and friends, and partly with public business entrusted to him by the Corporation. Stratford, at the end of the 16th century, was a 'decaying' town. Its trade had diminished. It had suffered from the long dearth of corn and the restrictions on malting (no. xii). There had been disastrous fires in 1594 and 1595. It is clear from the correspondence that Sturley and probably also the Quineys were in financial straits. The Corporation was endeavouring to secure an enlarged charter with additional fairs, and to obtain relief from the tenths and fifteenths and subsidies granted by the Parliament of 1597–8. Richard was charged to negotiate with the Privy Council, and to enlist the support of Sir Edward Greville,

---

[1] *Var.* ii. 563.   [2] Fripp, *Quyny*, 143.   [3] *Ibid.* 144.

then lord of the manor of Stratford. A new charter was not granted until 23 July 1610,[1] but Richard did in fact succeed in securing relief from the taxes by a royal warrant of 27 Jan. 1599.[2] Lee 292 says that 'it was on Shakespeare that he was counselled to place his chief reliance', and that he and his friends 'were sanguine of benefiting by Shakespeare's influence and prosperity'. So far as public affairs are concerned, I find no warrant for this in the terms of the letters, and it is difficult to see what influence Shakespeare could be supposed to have with the Privy Council. Richard's relations with his 'contreyman' were, so far as we know the facts, limited to his private concerns. He wanted a loan on reaching London in October 1598, and either applied to Shakespeare or thought of applying to him. The fact that the letter was found with Richard's own correspondence suggests that it was never delivered. This loan was apparently to be spent on London debts. On the other hand, the later letters show an expectation of money to come from Shakespeare, which might be available for an investment. Was this to be the proceeds of a loan or of the bargain in tithes proposed by Adrian Quiney in the preceding January? We can hardly say. Nor is it clear what tithes were in question. Lee 293 and others assume that they were those of Old Stratford, ultimately bought by Shakespeare, but not until 1605. It is possible. Richard seems to have been one of the farmers for those tithes in 1596 (no. xvii). But one Quiney and Abraham Sturley were farmers for the Clopton tithe-hay in 1590,[3] and it may have been this parcel which Sturley referred to as 'our tithes'.

The Rosswell of (b) may be Peter Roswell, gentleman, of Welcombe, who appears in several early 17th-century records,[4] and the Bushell an Edward Bushell, worsted weaver, who was surety with John Shakespeare the corvizer in 1587.[5] Richard Quiney's son Adrian married a Bushell. I cannot identify Mytton. The 'Grenwaj' of (d) was William Greenway, carrier (ob. 1601).]

[1] H.P. *Cal.* 446.
[2] B.P. *Cat.* 61, from *Wheler Papers*, i. 44.
[3] H.P. ii. 340.

[4] e.g. B.P. *Cat.* 59; H.P. *Vestry Book*, 88.
[5] H.P. *1848*, 83.

XIV. THE OLD STRATFORD FREEHOLD

(*a*) [1602, May 1. Conveyance by William and John Combe to Shakespeare (*B.P. Cat.* 31), pr. in full H.P. ii. 17; *1848*, 198. An unexecuted counterpart, with a seal attached, is in Wheler (1806) 139.]

This Indenture made the firste daie of Maye, in the fowre and fortieth yeare of the raigne of our Soueraigne Ladie Elizabeth, by the grace of God of England, Fraunce and Ireland Queene, defendresse of the faithe, &c., Betweene William Combe of Warrwicke, in the countie of Warrwick, Esquier, and John Combe of Olde Stretford, in the countie aforesaide, gentleman, on the one partie, And William Shakespere of Stretford vppon Avon, in the countie aforesaide, gentleman, on thother partye, Witnesseth that the saide William Combe and John Combe, for and in consideracion of the somme of three hundred and twentie poundes of currant Englishe money to them in hande at and before the ensealinge and deliuerie of theis presentes well and trulie satisfied, contented and paide, wherof and wherwith they acknowledge themselues fullie satisfied, contented and paide, and therof and of euerie parte and parcell therof doe clearlie exonerate, acquite and discharge the saide William Shakespere, his heires, executors, administrators and assignes, for euer by theis presentes, have aliened, bargayned, solde, geven, graunted and confirmed, and by theis presentes doe fullye, clearlie and absolutelie alien, bargayne, sell, give, graunte and confirme vnto the saide William Shakespere, All and singuler those errable landes, with thappurtenaunces, conteyninge by estymacion fowre yarde lande of errable lande, scytuate, lyinge and beinge within the parrishe, feildes or towne of Olde Stretford aforesaide, in the saide countie of Warrwick, conteyninge by estimacion one hundred and seaven acres, be they more or lesse, And also all the common of pasture for sheepe, horse, kyne or other cattle in the feildes of Olde Stretford aforesaide, to the said fowre yarde lande belonginge or in any wise apperteyninge, And also all hades, leys, tyinges, proffittes, advantages and commodities whatsoeuer, with their and euerie of their appurtenaunces, to the saide bargayned premisses belonging or apperteyninge, or hertofore reputed, taken, knowne or occupied as parte, parcell or member of the same, And the reuercion and reuercions of all and singuler the same bargayned premisses, and of euerie parte and parcell therof, nowe or late in the seuerall tenures or occupacions of Thomas Hiccoxe and Lewes Hiccoxe, or of either of them, or of their assignes or any of them, Together also with all charters, deedes, writinges, escriptes and mynumentes whatsoeuer, touchinge or concerninge the same premisses onlie or only any parte or parcell therof, And also the true copies of all other deedes, evidences, charters, writinges, escriptes and mynumentes, which doe touche and concerne the saide premisses before bargayned and solde or any parte or parcell therof, which the saide William Combe or John Combe nowe haue in their custodie, or herafter may haue, or which they may lawfullye gett or come by without suite in lawe, To haue and to holde the said fowre yarde of errable lande, conteyninge by estymacion one hundred and seaven acres, be they more or lesse, and all and singuler other the premisses before by theis presentes aliened and solde, or mencioned or entended to be aliened and solde, and euerie parte and parcell therof, and all deedes, charters, writinges, escriptes and mynumentes before by theis presentes bargayned and solde vnto the saide William Shakespere, his heires and assignes, for euer, to the onlie proper vse and behoofe of the saide William Shakespere, his heires and assignes, for euer. [*Covenants* by the vendors, assuring their 'estate in fee simple' in the premises and their power to alienate in the form of the conveyance; for indemnity by John Combe against any encumbrances, 'the rentes and services herafter to be due, in respect of the premisses before mencioned or entended to be bargayned and solde, to the cheife lorde or lordes of the fee or fees onlie excepted and foreprized'; for additional legal assurance 'bye fyne or fynes with proclamacion' or otherwise, if required within five years; and for quiet occupation.] In wytnes

wherof the parties to theis presentes have enterchangeably
sette their handes and seales, the daie and yeare first aboue
written, 1602. W. Combe. Jo. Combe. [*Endorsed*]
Sealed and deliuered to Gilbert Shakespere, to the vse of
the within named William Shakespere, in the presence of
Anthony Nasshe, William Sheldon, Humfrey Maynwaringe, Rychard Mason, Jhon Nashe.

(*b*) [1610. From *Finalis Concordia* in Common Pleas (*P.R.O. Pedes
Finium Warwick,* Trin. 8 Jac. 1, m. 15), pr. H.P. ii. 25; *1848,* 231.]

Inter Willielmum Shakespere generosum querentem et
Willielmum Combe armigerum et Johannem Combe
generosum deforciantes, de centum et septem acris terre
et viginti acris pasture cum pertinenciis in Old Stratford
et Stratford super Avon, Vnde placitum conuencionis
summonitum fuit inter eos in eadem curia, scilicet, quod
predicti Willielmus Combe et Johannes recognouerunt predicta tenementa cum pertinenciis esse ius ipsius Willielmi
Shakespere, vt illa que idem Willielmus habet de dono
predictorum Willielmi Combe et Johannis, et illa remi-
serunt et quietumclamaverunt de ipsis Willielmo Combe
et Johanne, et heredibus suis, predicto Willielmo Shakespere et heredibus suis imperpetuum, Et preterea idem
Willielmus Combe concessit, pro se et heredibus suis,
quod ipsi warantizabunt predicto Willielmo Shakespere
et heredibus suis predicta tenementa cum pertinenciis
contra predictum Willielmum Combe et heredes suos imperpetuum, Et vlterius idem Johannes concessit, pro se
et heredibus suis, quod ipsi warantizabunt predicto
Willielmo Shakespere et heredibus suis predicta tenementa cum pertinenciis contra predictum Johannem et
heredes suos imperpetuum. Et pro hac recognicione . . .
idem Willielmus Shakespere dedit predictis Willielmo
Combe et Johanni centum libras sterlingorum.

[The property here bought by Shakespeare was freehold land with
rights of common within that part of the manor of Old Stratford
which lay outside the borough. A note of its limits at the time of
the enclosure controversy of 1614 (no. xix (*a*)) shows that it was
not affected thereby, and most of it was therefore probably in the

field of Old Stratford proper, to the west of the hamlet of Welcombe. Shakespeare's will established an entail of all his property within 'Stratford upon Avon, Oldstratford, Bushopton and Welcombe, or in anie of them', and this holding in particular is similarly described in later documents dealing with the estate down to Lady Bernard's death (no. xxiv). Parts, therefore, may have been in Welcombe and also in Bishopton. Most of Bishopton, however, formed a separate manor. It is possible to trace some pre-history of the land. It seems to have been once property of the Cloptons (no. xi). Sir Edward Griffin of Dingley, by his will of 1569, left £5,000 to purchase lands for his younger son Rice, with remainder to his elder son Edward and his heirs.[1] In 1571 a fine was levied on the purchase by Rice Griffin from William and Ann Clopton of a considerable property in and about Stratford, subject to a similar remainder.[2] In 1593 there was another fine on the purchase by William Combe from Rice and Margaret Griffin of 107 acres of land and 20 acres of pasture in Old Stratford, with warranty against Edward Griffin and his heirs.[3] This is clearly, from its measurements, the holding bought by Shakespeare, but as John Combe is the principal guarantor to him, William must have associated his nephew (no. xviii) by entail or otherwise in the estate. I think Lee 319 is wrong in suggesting that the 20 acres of pasture specified in (b) but not in (a) formed a supplementary purchase by Shakespeare. They may well be the 'hades, leys, tyinges' of (a). Strictly speaking, 'hades' are bits of unploughed land left between the ploughed strips in arable common fields, and 'leys' are bits of grass-land dispersed among arable. The O.E.D. does not recognize the word 'tying', but a 'tye' is a close, and there was a meadow at Rowington (App. E) called Les Tyings. Nor do I suppose that the £100 of (b) was an additional payment. It was probably a fictitious sum named in a fictitious transaction. A fine (finalis concordia) was a conveyance in the form of an action brought in a court of law, and there was compromised by leave of the court. Its object was sometimes to bar an entail, but sometimes only to get the result enrolled and prevent subsequent litigation.[4] It was in fact such a further 'assurance' as a covenant of (a) contemplated. But this fine was not completed, although it may have been claimed, within the five years specified.

No messuage was included in the purchase, and the land was occupied by Thomas and Lewis Hiccox. They may, or may not, have continued to till it under Shakespeare. Probably they had

---

[1] Yeatman 252.
[2] Ibid. 278.
[3] Ibid. 237.
[4] Holdsworth, Land Law, 58, 116.

other land in the manor. Thomas Hiccocks 'junior' was admitted as a tenant in 1552.[1] Lewis, son of Thomas of Welcombe, was christened at Stratford on 12 Feb. 1565. A Thomas 'agricolus', whose will is at Stratford,[2] was buried on 18 Nov. 1606, a Lewis in 1627, and another in 1637. But Hiccox, in many variant forms, of which I think Hitchcock is one, was a common name in Stratford. At Welcombe itself there was a William, whose son, again a Lewis, was christened and buried in 1585. Possibly it was Shakespeare's tenant Lewis, who took one of his Henley St. houses as an inn in 1603 (no. iii). If he was the Lewis Hiccox who figures in the Welcombe enclosure affair (no. xix), he seems to have been also a tenant of Mrs. Reynolds.

Of the witnesses to (a) Anthony and John Nashe were of Welcombe (no. i). William Sheldon may be of the Beoley family (no. xviii). Humphrey Mainwaring is not demonstrably connected with the Arthur of the enclosures. Of Richard Mason I know nothing.]

XV. THE CHAPEL LANE COTTAGE

(a) [1602, Sept. 28. From *Copy* of entry in *Court Roll* of Rowington Manor (*B.P. Cat.* 32), pr. H.P. ii. 19. A facs. is in H.P. *Folio*, i. 8.]

Rowington. Visus franci plegii cum curia baronis prenobilis domine Anne Comitisse Warwici ibidem tentus xxviij° die Septembris anno regni domine nostre Elizabethe Dei gracia Anglie Francie et Hibernie regine fidei defensoris etc. quadragesimo quarto coram Henrico Michell generoso deputato senescallo Johannis Huggeford armigeri capitalis senescalli ibidem. . . . Ad hanc curiam venit Walterus Getley, per Thomam Tibbottes iuniorem attornatum suum unum customariorum tenencium manerii predicti (predicto Thoma Tibbottes iurato pro veritate inde) et sursumreddidit in manus domine manerii predicti vnum cotagium cum pertinenciis scituatum iacens et existens in Stratford super Avon, in quodam vico ibidem vocato Walkers Streete alias Dead Lane, ad opus et vsum Willielmi Shackespere et heredum suorum imperpetuum, secundum consuetudinem manerii predicti, Et sic remanet in manibus domine manerii predicti, quousque predictus Willielmus Shakespere venerit ad capiendum

[1] *M.A.* i. xxiii.   [2] H.P. *Cal.* 64.

premissa predicta. In cujus rei testimonium predictus
Henricus Michell huic presenti copie sigillum suum
apposuit die et anno supradictis. Per me Henricum
Michell.

(*b*) [1604, Oct. 24. Extract from *Survey* of Rowington Manor (*R.O.
Exchequer Special Commissions*, 4661), pr. H.P. ii. 355.]

William Shakespere lykewise holdeth there one cottage
and one garden, by estimation a quarter of one acre, and
payeth rent yeerlye ij^s, vj^d.

(*c*) [1606, Aug. 1. Extract from *Survey* of Rowington Manor (*R.O. Land
Revenue Rentals and Surveys*, ccxxviii, ff. 149–208), pr. H.P. ii. 355.]

                        Tenentes Custumarii.
Stratford-⎫ Willielmus Shakespere tenet ⎫ ij^s.
super-   ⎬ per copiam datam ——— anno ⎪ finis.
Avon.   ⎭ ——— videlicet   ⎬ heriettum.
             Domum mansionalem.   ⎪ annualis valor.
               Reddendo per annum   ⎪ dimittenda.
             Habendum.   ⎭

(*d*) [1617, Apr. 18. From *Estreats* of Rowington *Court Rolls* (*R.O. Land
Revenue Records*, Bundle 50, no. 720), pr. Stopes, *Ind.* 269.]

Item of John Haule gen. and Susan his wief for the Fyne
of admyttance of the said Susan unto one cottage in
Stratford after the decease of Wm. Shakespere, gen. late
father of the said Susan ii^s vj^d.

[A short account of Rowington is in Elton 129 and many documents in J. W. Ryland, *Records of Rowington* (1896, 1922). Many
Shakespeares dwelt there (App. E), but this fact seems unrelated to
Shakespeare's acquisition of 1602. The manor had belonged to the
abbey of Reading, and various outlying properties, including this
and another small copyhold in Church St., Stratford, were treated
as parcels of it. It was granted by Elizabeth to Ambrose, Earl of
Warwick, and continued to be held by his widow until her death
in 1604, when it reverted to the Crown. The other copyhold
had been held at 2*s.* by Henry Sadler in 1561.[1] It was surrendered
to the manor in 1586[2] by Hamnet Sadler and granted to Stephen
Burman. Shakespeare's was transferred to him from Walter Getley.

_____
[1] Ryland, i. 159.   [2] *Bodl. Warwick. Rolls*, 1.

It stood in Chapel Lane, otherwise called Dead Lane and Walker's St. According to H.P. ii. 143 and *New Place*, 40, it was on the south or Chapel side of the Lane, opposite to the garden of New Place. One may conjecture that Shakespeare used it for a servant's dwelling. Under the will (no. xxiv) provision was made for surrender by Judith of any interest she might have in it to Susanna. This is not quite intelligible, as the normal custom of the manor provided for inheritance by elder sons or daughters.[1] H.P. i. 205 suggests that Shakespeare may have settled the cottage on himself and his daughters. It is more likely that the custom did not extend to the outlying members.[2] The *Survey* of 1606 must be in error as to the rent. It seems to have been 2s. in 1555, but is 2s. 6d. in various minor documents from 1582, which also show tenure by the Halls to 1638, and frequent fines of 6d. or 1s. for default of suit of court.[3] On Susanna's death in 1649, the holding may have been surrendered to the manor. The cottage was rebuilt about 1690[4] and there is a drawing of it[5] as it stood before it was pulled down in the middle of the 19th century.]

XVI. COURT OF RECORD SUITS

(*a*)　*Shakespeare v. Rogers.*

[*c.* 1604. Note of hearing in Court of Record (*B.P. Cat.* 48, from *Wheler MSS.*), pr. H.P. ii. 77; (*1848*), 208. A facs. is in H.P. *Folio*, i. 171.]

Stretford Burgus. R. Willielmus Shexpere per attornatum
　　　　　　　　suum Willielmum Tetherton versus
　　　　　　　　Phillipum Rogers de placito debiti.

Phillipus Rogers summonitus fuit per servientes ad clavam ibidem ad respondendum Willielmo Shexpere de placito quod reddat ei triginta et quinque solidos decem denarios quos ei debet et injuste detinet, et sunt plegii de prosequendo Johannes Doe et Ricardus Roe, &c., Et vnde idem Willielmus per Willielmum Tetherton attornatum suum dicit, quod cum predictus Phillipus Rogers vicesimo septimo die Marcii, anno regni domini nostri

[1] H.P. ii. 356.　　　　　　　*Times*, 8 May 1915.
[2] Elton 131.　　　　　　　　[4] H.P. i. 205.
[3] H.P. ii. 356; Stopes, *Ind.* 267;　　[5] H.P. *1848*, 201.
Ryland, i. 190, 193; C. W. Wallace in

Jacobi regis nunc Anglie, Francie et Hibernie primo ⟨sic⟩
et Scocie tricesimo septimo ⟨1604⟩ et hic apud Stretford predictum ac infra iurisdiccionem huius curie
emisset de eodem Willielmo tres modoras brasii pro sex
solidis de predictis triginta et quinque solidis decem
denariis, ac etiam quod [further purchases of malt on 10
and 24 April, 3, 16, and 30 May 'anno secundo' recited]
Ac etiam quod cum predictus Phillipus vicesimo quinto
die Junii, anno dicti domini regis nunc Anglie &c., hic
apud Stretford predictum ac infra iurisdiccionem huius
⟨curie⟩ mutuatus fuisset duos solidos legalis monete &c.
de predictis 35° solidis 10° denariis residuis solvendis
eidem Willielmo cum inde requisitus fuisset, Que
omnia ⟨sic⟩ separales sommae attingunt se in toto ad
quadraginta et unum solidos decem denarios, Et predictus Phillipus Rogers de sex solidis inde eidem Willielmo postea satisfecisset, Predictus tamen Phillipus,
licet saepius requisitus, predictos triginta et quinque
solidos decem denarios residuos eidem Willielmo nondum
reddidit, sed illos ei huc usque reddere contradixit et
adhuc contradicit, vnde dicit quod deterioratus est et
dampna habet ad valenciam decem solidorum, Et inde
producit sectam, &c.

(b) *Shakespeare v. Addenbrooke.*

[1608, Dec. 17–1609, June 7. Abstract of Stratford Court of Record
documents (*S.A. Misc. Docts.* v. 139, 127, 115, 116, and *Wheler MSS.*;
B.P. Cat. 49–55), pr. H.P. ii. 78; *1848*, 229.]

(1) 1608, Dec. 17. Bailiff's precept to serjeants at the
mace to arrest 'Johannem Addenbrooke generosum' and
produce him 'ad respondendum Willielmo Shackspeare
generoso, de placito debiti', signed 'Greene' and endorsed
by Gilbert Charnock, Serjeant, with note of arrest and
bail by Thomas Hornebye 'manucaptor'.

(2) 1608, Dec. 21. Precept to empanel jury for the
case, signed 'Greene' and endorsed by Charnock with note
of return (3).

(3) Panel of twenty-four 'iuratores'.

(4) 1609, Feb. 15. Precept to bind 'iuratores' to appear

at next sitting of court, signed 'Greene' and endorsed by
Francis Boyce, serjeant, with note of return (5).

(5) Panel, as in (3), with twelve names marked 'iura-
tus', and note, 'Quilibet iuratorum predictorum, per se
separatim, attachiatus est per plegios, Johannem Doo et
Ricardum Roo. Exitus cujuslibet eorum per se, vj^s viij^d.
Juratores dicunt pro querente; misas iiij^d; dampna ij^d.'

(6) 1609, March 15. Precept to arrest and produce
Addenbrooke at next sitting, 'ad satisfaciendum Willielmo
Shackspere generoso, tam de sex libris debiti quas predictus Willielmus in eadem curia versus eum recuperavit
quam de viginti et quatuor solidis qui ei adiudicati fuerunt
pro dampnis et custagiis suis quos sustinuit occacione
detencionis debiti predicti,' signed 'Greene' and endorsed
by Boyce, 'Infranominatus Johannes non est inventus
infra libertatem hujus burgi.'

(7) 1609, June 7. Stratford Burgus. Preceptum est
servientibus ad clavam ibidem quod cum quidam Willielmus Shackspeare, generosus, nuper in curia domini
Jacobi, nunc regis Anglie, burgi predicti, ibidem tenta
virtute literarum patentium domini Edwardi, nuper regis
Anglie, sexti, levavit quandam querelam suam versus
quendam Johannem Addenbrooke de placito debiti,
cumque eciam quidam Thomas Horneby de burgo predicto in eadem querela devenit plegius et manucaptor
predicto Johanni, scilicet quod, si predictus Johannes in
querela illa legitimo modo convincaretur ⟨sic⟩, quod idem
Johannes satisfaceret prefato Willielmo Shackspeare tam
debitum in querela illa per prefatum Willielmum versus
predictum Johannem in curia predicta recuperandum
quam misas et custagia que eidem Willielmo in querela
illa per eandem curiam adiudicata forent versus eundem
Johannem, vel idem se redderet prisone dicti domini regis
Jacobi nunc, burgi predicti, ad satisfaciendum eidem
Willielmo eadem debitum misas et custagia, Et ulterius
quod, si idem Johannes non satisfaceret eidem Willielmo
debitum et misas et custagia, nec se redderet predicte
prisone dicti domini regis nunc ad satisfaciendum eidem
Willielmo in forma predicta, quod tunc ipse idem Thomas

Horneby debitum sic recuperandum et misas et custagia sic adiudicata eidem Willielmo satisfacere vellet, Cumque eciam in querela illa taliter processum fuit in eadem curia quod predictus Willielmus in loquela illa, per iudicium eiusdem curie, recuperabat versus predictum Johannem tam sex libras de debito quam viginti et quatuor solidos pro decremento misarum et custagiorum ipsius Willielmi in secta querela illius appertinentes ⟨?⟩, Super quo preceptum fuit servientibus ad clavam ibidem quod capiant, seu etc., predictum Johannem, si etc., et eum salvo etc., ita quod habeant corpus eius coram ballivo burgi predicti, ad proximam curiam de recordo ibidem tenendam, ad satisfaciendum predicto Willielmo ⟨tam⟩ de debito predicto sic recuperato, quam de viginti et quatuor solidis pro predictis dampnis et custagiis adiudicatis, Vnde Franciscus Boyce tunc et nunc serviens ad clavam, ad diem retorni inde mandavit quod predictus Johannes non est inventus in balliva sua, Vnde idem Willielmus, ad predictam curiam dicti domini regis, supplicaverit sibi de remedio congruo versus predictum manucaptorem in hac parte provideri, Super quod preceptum est servientibus ad clavam ibidem quod per probos et legales homines de burgo predicto scire faciant, seu etc., prefatum Thomam quod sit coram ballivo burgi predicti, ad proximam curiam de recordo in burgo predicto tenendam, ostensurus si quid de se habeat vel dicere sciat quare predictus Willielmus execucionem suam versus eundem Thomam de debito et misis et custagiis illis habere non debeat, iuxta vim, formam et effectum manucapcionis predicti, si sibi viderit expedire, et ulterius facturus et recepturus quod predicta curia dicti domini regis consideret in ea parte, Et habeant ibi tunc hoc preceptum. Teste Francisco Smyth Juniore, generoso, ballivo ibidem, septimo die Junii, annis regni domini nostri Jacobi, Dei gracia regis Anglie, Francie et Hibernie, septimo, et Scotie xlijº. Greene. [*Endorsed*] Virtute istius precepti mihi directi, per Johannem Hemynges et Gilbertum Chadwell, probos et legales homines burgi infrascripti, scire feci infranominatum Thomam Hornebye, prout interius mihi precipitur. Franciscus Boyce, serviens.

[The Stratford Court of Record was established by the charter of 1553.[1] It was to sit fortnightly under the bailiff, with a civil jurisdiction over cases of debt, trespass, and the like arising within the borough, up to a limit of £30. The borough was to have the profits, and the serjeants at the mace were to be the officers. By an order of the Corporation they were also appointed common attorneys for litigants, with fees of 4d. for each day of action. If they refused to act, the bailiff might admit substitutes.[2] The leave of the court seems also to have been required for the bringing of an action by one who was not a townsman; in any case the liability must have arisen within the borough. The court seems to have taken over the debt jurisdiction of the leet and also the duty of fining for breaches of assize or by-laws. The steward of the borough acted as clerk to the court, and it is in this capacity that the name of Thomas Greene (no. xix) is attached to the precepts in (b), which invoke the 'teste' of the bailiff as the authority for issue. Lee 322 must be wrong in supposing Greene to sign as Shakespeare's attorney, and Stopes 121 in suggesting that the Shakespeare of (a) cannot have been the poet, because he was not there the attorney. There is nothing to show that he ever acted for Shakespeare in a legal capacity. He did not make his will. The *Register* of the court is extant for the years 1553–70 and 1584–1601, and is used in H.P., *Selected Extracts from . . . the Court of Record* (1867). But many scattered documents for other years are in the town archives[3] and the *Wheler MSS*. The procedure in debt cases seems to have been as follows. On the issue of a summons the alleged debtor was arrested by precept of the court and released on finding a surety (*manucaptor*) in case of his subsequent default. A jury was, in some if not all cases, empanelled for the trial. On proof of debt, and failing payment, the plaintiff was entitled to a writ of distraint (*distringas*) directing the serjeants to attach his goods and chattels. There is no record of this stage in (b), but there is an example in a case of debt by John Shakespeare in 1586.[4] Here the serjeants reported 'quod predictus Johannes Shackspere nihil habet unde distringi potest'. H.P. thinks that the writ and return were mere formalities to give the debtor time. However this may be, the next stage was a writ of arrest (*capias*), with a view to imprisonment. In (b) arrest was also impossible, because the debtor was outside the very limited jurisdiction of the court, and the plaintiff became entitled to bring a fresh action against the surety.

---

[1] *M.A.* i. 11.
[2] *Ibid.* i. 125.

[3] H.P. *Cal.* 180 and *Misc. Docts.* passim.
[4] H.P. ii. 238.

Some of the technical terms used in (*b*) are puzzling. 'Misae', 'custagia', and 'exitus' should all mean 'costs',[1] and 'dampna' 'damages'. But in (7) 'misae et custagia' seem to mean 'damages and costs', and in any case it is difficult to relate the 24*s*. of (6) and (7) to the amounts of (5). The abbreviation 'seu, etc' seems to stand for 'seu unus eorum capiat' or 'scire faciat'; the 'si, etc' and the 'salvo etc' for the 'si inventus fuerit in balliva sua' and 'salvo custodiant' of the writ of *capias*.

Phillip Rogers was an apothecary of Stratford.[2] C. W. Wallace[3] and Stopes 121 suggest that the action may have been brought by some William Shakespeare other than the poet, perhaps of Rowington or Knowle (App. E), and perhaps the William, papers about whose transactions in malt were once at Warwick Castle. But these seem to be of 1620 or later; the action must have arisen in Stratford; and we know (no. xii) that the poet had a stock of malt in 1598. It does not seem very material that he is not described as *generosus* in the record.

As to Addenbrooke I only know that 'one Addenbrooke' had issued licences for starch in Warwickshire about 1600.[4] Thomas Horneby succeeded his father Richard in 1606, as a blacksmith in Henley St.[5]]

XVII. THE STRATFORD TITHES

(*a*) [1553, June 28. Extract from Incorporation *Charter* of Stratford; pr. in full in *M.A.* i. 1.]

Ac ulterius de ampliori gratia nostra dedimus et concessimus ac ex certa sciencia et mero motu nostris per presentes damus et concedimus prefatis Balliuo & Burgensibus dicti Burgi de Stratford super Avon et successoribus suis omnes et omnimodas decimas granorum et feni prouenientes crescentes seu renouantes in Villis et Campis de Olde Stratforde Welcombe et Busshopeston in dicto Comitatu nostro Warr modo vel nuper in tenura Johannis Barker ac nuper Collegio de Stratford super Avon in dicto Comitatu nostro Warr' dudum spectantes et pertinentes ac parcellas possessionum inde existentes Aceciam omnes et omnimodas decimas lane agnellorum et alias minutas et priuatas decimas ac oblaciones et

---

[1] Martin, *Record Interpreter*, s.vv.
[2] Lee 322.
[3] *Times*, 15 May 1915.
[4] *Hatfield MSS*. xiv. 150.
[5] H.P. i. 378; Lee 323.

alteragia quecumque prouenientia crescentia seu reno-
uantia infra totam Parochiam de Stratford super Avon
predicta et dicto nuper Collegio de Stratford super Avon
dudum spectantia et pertinentia ac modo vel nuper in
tenura Willelmi Barker Generosi vel assignatorum suorum
existentia Ac reuersionem et reuersiones quascumque
predictarum decimarum et cuiuslibet inde parcelle Ac
redditus reuenciones et alia annalia proficua quecumque
reseruata super quibuscumque dimissionibus seu con-
cessionibus de predictis decimis seu de aliqua inde parcella
factis reseruata Quequidem decime oblaciones et alteragia
modo extenduntur ad clarum annuum valorem triginta
quatuor librarum Habendum tenendum et gaudendum
predictas decimas oblaciones et alteragia cum eorum
pertinentijs vniuersis prefato Balliuo et Burgensibus dicti
Burgi de Stratford super Avon et successoribus suis
imperpetuum Tenendum de nobis heredibus et successoribus nostris vt de manerio nostro de Estgrenewich in
comitatu Kancie in libero et communi socagio per fideli-
tatem tantum et non in capite pro omnibus alijs redditibus
seruicijs et demandis quibuscumque proinde nobis heredibus vel successoribus nostris quoquo modo reddendis
soluendis vel faciendis.

(*b*) [1605, July 24. Abstract of assignment of an interest in a lease of tithes
from Ralph Huband to Shakespeare (*B.P. Cat.* 33, from *Wheler MSS.*)
in hand of Francis Collins; pr. in full by H.P. ii. 19; *1848*, 210; with
Bond of Huband of even date in £800 for observance of indenture (*Misc.
Doct.* ii. 3. The lease of 1544 (*S.A. Expired Leases, Tithes*, 361) was
really on Oct. 2. Sh. owed Huband's estate £20 in Jan. 1606 (Barnard 61.).]

Indenture between 'Raphe Hubande of Ippesley in the
countye of Warr. Esquier, on thone parte, and William
Shakespear of Stratforde vpon Avon in the sayed countye
of Warr., gent., on thother parte'.—*Recitals* of (i) *Lease* of
7 Sept. 1544 by Anthony Barker, warden, and College of
Stratford to William Barker of Sonning, Berks, for ninety-
two years from Michaelmas 1543, at an annual rent of £122
18*s*. 9*d*. of all 'tythes of corne, grayne, blade and heye' in
'Stratforde vpon Avon, Olde Stratforde, Welcombe and
Bushopton', and of all 'tythes of wooll, lambe and other

small and pryvie tythes, oblacions, obvencions, alterages, mynumentes and offeringes' in 'the parishe of Stratforde vpon Avon aforesayed', and of all other tithes and other property of the College in Warwickshire and Worcestershire, except the mansion and its site; (ii) *Seisin* of reversion by the Crown under Act of *1 Edw. VI* ⟨1547–8⟩ for 'the dissolucion of chauntries, colledges, and free chappels'; (iii) *Grant* by royal patent of 28 June 1553 to Corporation of Stratford of corn and hay tithes in Old Stratford, Welcombe, and Bishopton and small tithes in the parish; (iv) *Conveyance* of the interest in the whole property to John Barker of Hurst, Berks, together with 'the interest of certein copieholds in Shotterie'; (v) *Assignment* of 24 June 1580 by John Barker of his interest to Sir John Huband, subject to the chief rent and a further annual rent of £27 13s. 4d. to Barker, with right of re-entry in default of the payment of this rent 'in parte or in all'; (vi) *Bequests* by will of Sir John Huband ⟨1583⟩ to his executors for purposes specified of 'the moytie or one half 'of the tithes 'before mencioned to bee graunted to the sayed baylyffe and burgesses of Stratford' and of the other moiety, subject to a payment of £5 towards Barker's rent, to his brother Ralph Huband.[1] —*Declaration* that—

'This indenture nowe witnesseth that the sayed Raphe Hubande, for and in consideracion of the somme of foure hundred and fourtye poundes of lawfull Englishe money to him by the sayed William Shakespear, before then-sealinge and deliuerye of thees presentes well and truelye contented and payed, whereof and of everye parte and parcell whereof hee, the sayed Raphe Hubande, dothe by thees presentes acknowledge the receipt, and thereof and of euerye parte and parcell thereof dothe clerelye acquite, exonerate and discharge the sayed William Shakespear, his executours and administratours, for ever by thees presentes, hathe demised, graunted, assigned and sett over, and by thees presentes dothe demise, graunte, assigne and

---

[1] H.P. prints a comma after 'men-cioned', which makes the passage read as if the moiety of the leasehold was bequeathed to the Corporation.

sett over vnto the sayed William Shakespear, his executours and assignes, the moytie or one half of all and singuler the sayed tythes of corne, grayne, blade and heye, yearelye and from tyme to tyme cominge, encreasinge, reneweinge, arrysinge, groweinge, issueinge or happenynge, or to bee had, receyved, perceyved or taken out, of, vpon or in the townes, villages, hamlettes, groundes and fyeldes of Stratforde, Olde Stratforde, Welcombe and Bushopton aforesayed in the sayed countye of Warr., and alsoe the moytie or one half of all and singuler the sayed tythes of wooll, lambe, and other smalle and pryvie tythes, herbage, oblacions, obvencions, alterages, mynumentes and offeringes whatsoeuer, yearelye and from tyme to tyme cominge, encreasinge, reneweinge or happeninge, or to bee had, receyved, perceyved or taken, within the parishe of Stratforde vpon Avon aforesayed.' Words follow to cover a moiety of any conceivable interest of Huband in Stratford tithes, and a reservation, 'the pryvie tythes of Luddington and suche parte of the tythe heye and pryvie tythes of Bushopton, as of right doe belonge to the vicar, curate or minister there for the tyme beinge, always excepted and foreprised'. Shakespeare is to hold 'from the date of the daye hereof, for and duringe the residewe of the sayed terme of fourescore and twelve yeares in the sayed first recyted indenture mencioned, and for suche and soe longe terme and tyme, and in as large, ample and benefyciall manner as the sayed Raphe Hubande should or ought enjoye the same, yeldinge and payeinge therefore yearely duringe the residewe of the sayed terme of fourescore and twelve yeares which bee yet to come and unexpired the rentes hereafter mencioned, in manner and forme followeinge, that is to saye, vnto the baylyffe and burgesses of Stratford aforesaied, and their successors, the yearelye rent of seaventeen poundes att the feastes of St Michaell tharchangell and the Anunciacion of blessed Marye the Virgin by equall porcions, and vnto the sayed John Barker, his executours, administratours or assignes, the annuall or yearelye rente of fyve poundes at the feaste dayes and place lymitted, appointed and mencioned in the sayed recyted indenture of assignement made by the sayed John Barker, or within fortye dayes after the sayed feaste dayes by even porcions, as parcell of the sayed annuall rent of twentye seaven poundes thirteene shillinges foure pence in the sayed assignement mencioned'.

Covenants by Huband assuring his right to grant the interest and for quiet occupation by Shakespeare as against Huband or any claimant under him or under Sir John Huband and against John Barker or any claimant under him, subject to the payment of the rent, 'thestate and interest of the Lorde Carewe of, in and to the tythes of Bridgtowne and Ryen Clyfforde, and the interest of Sir Edwarde Grevill, knight, of and in the moytie of the tythe hey, woolle, lambe, and other smalle and pryvie tythes, oblacions, obvencions, offeringes and profittes before by thees presentes graunted and assigned vnto the sayed William Shakespear, which is to endure untill the feast of St Michaell tharchangell next ensueinge the date hereof, and noe longer, onelye excepted and foreprised'. Further *Covenants* by Huband assuring the freedom of the interest from encumbrances and for additional legal assurance, if required. *Covenant* by 'Shakespeare' for payment of reserved rents. *Signature* of 'Raffe Huband', in presence of 'William Huband, Anthony Nasshe, Fra: Collyns'.

(*c*) [1611 ? Abstract of Draft Bill of Complaint for Chancery suit of *Richard Lane et al. v. Dominus Carewe et al.* (*S.A. Misc. Doct.* ii. 11); pr. in full by H.P. ii. 25; *1848*, 258.]

Recitals by the 'dayly oratours' of Lord Chancellor Ellesmere, 'Richard Lane of Awston in the county of Warwicke, esquire, Thomas Greene, of Stratford uppon Avon in the said county of Warwicke, esquire, and William Shackspeare, of Stratford uppon Avon aforesaid in the said countye of Warwicke, gentleman', of (i) College lease of 1544 to W. Barker, (ii) Transfer to J. Barker; (iii) Assignment of 1580 to J. Huband. *Allegation* of claim of Henry Barker, as executor, administrator or assignee of J. Barker, to re-entry in default of any part of the rent of £27 13s. 4d. payable at 'the parishe church of Stratford aforesaid'. *Enumeration* of present estates held 'by divers and sundry severall sufficiente meane assignementes and under estates deryved under the said assureance and conveyance soe made unto the said Sir John Huband', both by the orators and by other persons.

'Your oratour William Shackspeare hath an estate and interest of and in the moyty or one half of all tythes of corne and grayne aryseing within the townes villages and fieldes of Old Stratford, Byshopton and Welcombe, being of and in the said parishe of Stratford, and of and in the moity or half of all tythes of wooll and lambe, and of all small and pryvy tythes, oblaciones, and alterages arisynge or increasyng in or within the wholl parishe of Stratford-upon-Avon aforesayd, for and duringe all the residue of the said terme, being of the yearely value of threescore powndes.'

The other moiety of these, also valued at £60, is held by 'Mary Combe, widowe, and William Combe, gent., and John Combe, gent., or some or one of them', for 'the terme of six yeares or thereaboutes yet to come', and the reversion 'after the feast day of thanunciacion of our blessed lady Ste Mary the Virgin which shal be in the yeare of our Lord God 1613' by the orator Greene. The corn, grain, and hay tithes of Rien Clifford are held by the same Combes; those of Bridgetown by Lord Carewe of Clopton for nineteen years yet to come, with a reversion to the orator Lane; those of the barony of Clopton and village of Shottery, worth £80 a year, by Lane; those of Luddington by Sir Edward Conway; those of Drayton by John Nashe, gent.; those of Shottery meadow and Broad meadow by Daniel Baker, gent. All these places are in the parish of Stratford, and the aggregate annual value of the tithe estates is £293 6s. 8d. There are also messuages, shops, and lands held by Lane, Greene, William Combe and his mother Mary, and many others, in various parts of the parish. Most of these are worth about £3 a year. Their aggregate value is about £180.

Allegation that all the holders of these estates 'ought in all right, equity, reason and good conscience . . . to

pay . . . a ratable and proporcionable part and porcion'
of the rent of £27 13s. 4d. reserved by John Barker; but
that, while amounts of £5 are to be paid respectively by
Shakespeare and by the holders of the corresponding
moiety of tithes, the holders of other estates are not
'directed or appoynted' under their deeds, nor are any
covenants made 'whereby yt might appeare howe much
of the same rente of xxvij.[li]. xiij[s]. iiij[d]. ought to be paid
for every of the said severall premisses'; that they 'could
never yet be drawen to agree howe to paye the residue of
the said rente, or be brought to pay anie precise parte or
porcion at all towardes the same'; that divers of them
refuse to pay anything and others who would do so are
deterred by fear of forfeit through the negligence or
wilfulness of the rest; so that 'your oratours Richard
Lane and William Shackspeare, and some fewe others
of the said parties, are wholly, and against all equity and
good conscience, usually dryven to pay the same for
preservacion of their estates'. *Prayer* for letters to Lord
Carew and subpoenas to the other parties, and to Henry
Barker, to appear in Chancery, answer to the complaint,
and show cause why a commission should not be issued
for valuing, assessing, taxing, and rating the several estates,
and an order made fixing the amount which each party
ought to pay towardes the residue of the rent, and Henry
Barker bound 'to accept the rentes ratablye to be assessed
as aforesaid, and to enter onely into the tenement and
estate onely of such persons which shall refuse or neglecte
to pay such parte of the said rente, as by your most
honorable order there shal be sett downe and rated uppon
them severally to paie'. [*Endorsement*] Lane, Greene et
Shakspeare contra W. Combe et alios respondentes.

(*c*) [1611. Abstract of Answer to (*b*) by William Combe (*S.A. Misc. Doct.*
x. 9), undated, but sworn to in Chancery on 13 Feb. 1611.]

Defendant admits that he holds as executor to his late
father Thomas Combe a moiety of the tithes of corn and
grain in Old Stratford, Bishopton, and Welcombe and of
other tithes, for which he pays £5 annually. Is willing

to pay for yet other tithes 6s. 8d. annually, which he thinks the complainants are willing to accept. Asks that, if an order is made on him accordingly, the other parties may also be ordered to contribute rateably to the rent of £27 13s. 4d.

[The facts are given with some inaccuracy by Lee 320, and rather less by Adams 388. T. Brooke, *Sh.'s Moiety of the Stratford Tithes*,[1] supplies, and needs, corrections. Shakespeare's purchase in 1605 was the half of a leasehold interest in a parcel of tithes, consisting of the corn and hay tithes of three hamlets in Stratford, i.e. Old Stratford, Welcombe, and Bishopton, together with the small tithes of the whole parish. It was subject to certain small reservations for earlier interests, such as that of the minister of Luddington chapel to the small tithes of that hamlet, which is noted in a certificate of 1546 in connexion with the dissolution of the College of Stratford.[2] The purchase did not make Shakespeare the principal tithe-owner in Stratford. There were several other parcels of corn and hay tithes. Shakespeare's interest was valued in 1611 at £60 annually. But an equal moiety of the same parcel was held by the Combes, and a larger parcel, valued at £80, by Richard Lane. The aggregate value of the whole tithes was just over £293, so that Shakespeare's interest was about a fifth. A little confusion is due to the reference to 'Stratforde', as well as 'Olde Stratforde, Welcombe and Bushopton' in the operative words of the conveyance of 1605. This possibly slipped in from the lease of 1544, recited in the conveyance, which had covered all the tithes. But it is clear from the documents as a whole that Shakespeare's corn and hay tithes were limited to the three hamlets named. The lease of 1544 also covered some houses and land, worth in 1611 about £190 a year; in fact the whole property of the College in Warwickshire and Worcestershire, except the mansion house (cf. p. 135). It was given by the College before the dissolution to William Barker, probably a relative of the Warden, Anthony Barker, whose will he executed in 1553.[3] The reserved rent of £122 18s. 9d. agrees approximately with a valuation of £128 9s. 1d. about 1546.[4] By 1611 the value had appreciated to about £480. From William Barker the lease passed to John Barker who in 1580 gave a sub-lease, at a mean rent of £27 13s. 4d., to Sir John Huband of Ipsley,[5] who seems[6] in fact to have held the tithes irregularly from 1575. Meanwhile the *corpus*

[1] 1925, *M.L.N.* xl. 462.
[2] Leach, *English Schools*, ii. 232.
[3] *M.A.* i. 14.
[4] Leach, *ut supra*.
[5] *M.A.* iii. 59.
[6] *S.A. Expired Leases, Tithes*, 406.

of the College estate, with the reserved rent of £122 18s. 9d., had been appropriated by the Crown at the Dissolution; and out of this the particular parcel of tithes of which Shakespeare acquired a moiety, and that only, was granted to the Corporation by the charter of 1553. The share of the reserved rent allocated to this parcel was £34, and the Corporation can be traced as receiving this amount from successive farmers of the tithes.[1] Sir John Huband, dying on 24 Dec. 1583, left a moiety of his leasehold interest in this parcel to his brother Ralph Huband. An awkward punctuation in (b) by H.P., corrected above, has given the impression that he left the other half to the Corporation.[2] This was not so. He left it to his executors towards the general purposes of his will, one of which was a bequest of 100 marks to the Corporation for charitable purposes.[3] This moiety was acquired by Abigail Lady Digby, and from her a sub-lease for twenty-one years from Lady Day 1596 was taken by William Combe.[4] He was apparently acting for his nephew Thomas Combe i (no. xviii), since (c) shows the latter's estate as still with a term of about six years to run. The reversion was given by Lady Digby to her son Sir John, assigned by him to Humphrey Colles, and by Colles to Thomas Greene on 1 Mar. 1609. Apparently, however, this last transaction was only finally completed on 1 Sept. 1614.[5] Ralph Huband's moiety was assigned to Shakespeare by (b) on 24 July 1605 for £440. It is possible (cf. no. xiii) that an earlier purchase had been suggested to him in 1598 by Richard Quiney, who was farming the tithes for Huband in 1596.[6] Shakespeare was bound to pay half of the reserved rent of £34 to the Corporation and £5 of the mean rent to Barker. It seems that Anthony Nash, whose father had farmed the tithes for the Hubands, was farming Shakespeare's in 1606 and 1614.[7] The interest of the Corporation in the Stratford tithes was long limited to the rent and reversion of the single parcel given by the charter. In 1598 they were contemplating the possibility of securing 'the rest of the tithes and the College houses and lands you speak of', or at least a moiety of them.[8] This was the freehold of the bulk of the property, still vested in the Crown. In 1625 they acquired Shakespeare's interest from his heirs for £400, less the tithes of two closes, which had been leased to William Combe for 20s. The annual value was then £90.[9]

The bearing of the Complaint is also clear. Shakespeare and his

[1] M.A. i. 86 and passim; H.P. 1848, 101.
[2] M.A. iii. 59.
[3] Extract from Will in M.A. iii. 124.
[4] S.A. Expired Leases, Tithes, 397.
[5] H.P. Cal. 153, 154, 157, 159; Misc. Docts. xii. 99, 120.
[6] H.P. 1848, 101.
[7] Ibid. 103, 105.
[8] Fripp, Quyny, 147.
[9] H.P. ii. 348.

fellow complainants were in risk of a re-entry by the Barkers, if the mean rent of £27 13s. 4d. was not all paid, through the default of other tenants, whose ill-drawn leases had not defined their responsibility. They very reasonably desired an equitable relief. Evidently the Combes were willing to assent. The Bill is undated; Halliwell-Phillipps put it in 1612, but it must have been earlier. Combe had replied by Feb. 1611. Brooke points out that the Bill must be later than the death of Thomas Combe, buried on 11 Jan. 1609, as his widow is named. This is so, but it leaves the difficulty that the Combes are said to have still an interest for 'six yeares or thereaboutes yet to come', and Greene to have a reversion of the same interest from Lady Day 1613. John Barker, pretty clearly dead at the time of the Bill, was signing deeds in May 1610.[1] Moreover, the Digby-Combe lease ran to Lady Day 1617, and the Combes were in fact still paying half the reserved rent of £34 in 1614.[2] I am driven to conclude that the '1613' of the Bill, which seems to have been altered from 1603 in the manuscript, must be an error for '1617', and that the document was prepared early in 1611. Brooke's attempt to treat 1609 to 1613 as six years obviously does not hold water. The Bill is a draft only, but the Chancery notes on the answer point to an actual suit. In 1626 the Corporation 'agreed that a bill in Chauncery shal be exhibited, and subpens taken forthe against and served on such as have not payde theire partes towardes Barkers Rente'.[3]]

XVIII. THE COMBE FAMILY

[1613, Jan. 28. Extract from *Will* of John Combe (*P.C.C.* 118 Wood; official copy in *Misc. Doct.* vii. 254), pr. H.P. *1848*, 234.]

Item, I give . . . to M[r] William Shackspere five pounds.

[Notices of Shakespeare after his return to Stratford more often relate him to the Combes than to any other local family (cf. nos. xiv, xvii, xix, xxiv), and some account of them is desirable. The material collected by Lee 318, 469; Stopes, *Cont.* 219; Fripp, *S.S.* 61 can be supplemented from various sources. The pedigrees in J. C. M. Bellew, *Shakespeare's Home* (1863), and Yeatman 234 are unsatisfactory, and I attempt a new one, based on the 1619 *Visitation of Warwickshire*.[4] This is from a transcript in *Harl. MS.* 1167; a College of Arms *Vincent MS.* 126, f. 109, was used, but not printed, by Bellew and Hunter, i. 89.

[1] *Misc. Docts.* x. 8, 10.   [3] H.P. ii. 348.
[2] H.P. *1848*, 105.   [4] *Harl. Soc.* xii. 291.

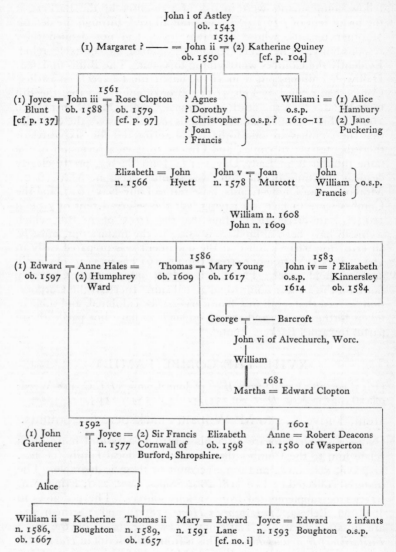

I know practically nothing of John i, except that he was of
Astley, Worcestershire, although it is possible that some of the
earlier notices here ascribed to John ii may really belong to him.

Combe (Combes, a Combe, a Combes) is a widespread name. Stopes, *Cont.* 219 has no ground for connecting the Astley family with one which held land of the manor of Swanscombe, Kent, until the time of Edward IV.[1] There were already Combes on the Priory manor of Wroxall by the middle of the 14th century,[2] and to these probably belonged a John Combe and his wife who joined the Gild of Knowle in 1460. It is only by conjecture that Yeatman 235 relates them to Astley. On the other hand, the arms *Ermine, three lions passant in pale gules* granted in 1584 (*infra*) suggest some connexion with a family bearing the same coat at Stoke Newington in Middlesex and afterwards at Hemel Hempstead in Herts, where they long survived.[3] No early link is, however, traceable.

I do not know to what family a Thomas Combes, employed in 1536 as a commissioner for the suppression of monasteries in Hunts, Derbyshire, and probably Cheshire,[4] belonged, but John ii, the son of John i, was engaged on similar work. Of him, or probably of him, we have the following notices. On 30 Apr. 1534 a licence from the Bishop of Worcester was issued for a marriage at Stratford between 'Johannem Combe Juniorem de Astley Wigorniensis dioc. et Katherinam Quynye de Stratford'.[5] On 17 July 1534 John Combe was chosen an alderman of the Stratford gild and during 1534–5 payment was made to the gild for the soul of his daughter Dorothy.[6] On 30 Nov. 1534 John a Combes and Elmor Hickmons took a lease of a house in Eport St., Worcester, from Worcester Priory.[7] From 1535 to 1539 Hugh Latimer was Bishop of Worcester, and appears to have found Combe a useful agent. In August 1536 John a Combe 'servant to the bishop of Worcester' and William Lucy of Charlecote imprisoned John Wetwood, President of Warwick College, for ringing bells on St. Laurence's day.[8] In December Latimer and John Combes were taking depositions at Hartlebury about the Aske rebellion.[9] In March 1537 Mr. Combes had, on behalf of Thomas Cromwell, imputed slackness to the Abbot of Evesham about the cell of Alcester.[10] In July John Combes, Lucy, and John Greville of Milcote were appointed commissioners to consider disputes arising out of allegations of heresy against Sir Edward Large, parson of Hampton Lucy. They committed Richard Coton, who had abused Large, to the custody

[1] Hasted, *Kent*, i. 262.
[2] Rylands, *Wroxall*, 41 and *passim*.
[3] *V.H. Herts.* ii. 219; J. E. Cussans, *Herts.* iii. 1. 153; *Harl. Soc. Visitations*, xxii. 6, 44.
[4] Brewer, x. 499; xi. 94, 265.
[5] Gray 224.
[6] Bloom 239–40.
[7] Bloom, *Worcester Charters*, 47.
[8] Brewer, xi. 172, 173.
[9] *Ibid.* xi. 522.
[10] *Ibid.* xii. 1. 280.

of the bailiff of Stratford. This appears to have been Combe himself. Coton was supported by William Clopton (cf. no. xi), who taunted one Richard Lightfoot, 'you will not displease Master Combes, for that he will make you this year master of the guild'. Lightfoot did become master of the Stratford gild in 1544.[1] In March 1539 the same commissioners examined Sir Robert Maude, parson of Whatcote, on a charge of railing at the king.[2] After Latimer's fall, Combe was concerned, to his profit, with Sir Richard Morison, and this is perhaps further evidence of a connexion with Herts. John Bell, master of St. Wulstan's hospital at Worcester, and formerly warden of the college at Stratford, became Bishop of Worcester in 1539. He was succeeded at St. Wulstan's by Morison, with the result that on 20 May 1540 the hospital was surrendered to Combe and Lucy as commissioners for the Crown. Morison got his reward out of grants from the hospital property, and in his turn sold the manor of Commanders in Crowle, Worcestershire, with the rectory of Crowle and Huddington, to Combe in 1544. Other property of the hospital went to a Richard Combes, possibly a relative, and the same who made his will, as of Northwick, Worcestershire, in 1546.[3] John Combe also acquired land at Kyre Parva and Coston Hacket in Worcestershire and a reversion of the manor of Clifford Chambers in Gloucestershire, but of all this he or John iii seems to have disposed.[4] He is on subsidy lists for various years from 1540 to 1550, but apparently not for 1524–5, generally as of the borough, but in 1548–9 as of Old Stratford and Welcombe.[5] In 1546 he held the post of *Senecallus* of the Stratford gild for life, at a fee of 20s.[6] In 1550 he died.[7]

It is possible that John ii did not come direct from Astley to Stratford. The only Combes recorded as admitted to the gild are 'John Combe of Meculton' and his wife in 1506–7, and in the same year there was a payment for 'John Coome of Mykelton & Margaret his wife & for the soul of Agnes Come'.[8] This seems rather early, although not impossible, for a man who died in 1550. The register is fairly complete, but there are no entries for 1509–11, 1513–14, and 1516–17, and possibly individual entries may have

[1] *Athenæum* for 18 Apr. 1857; Brewer, xii. 2. 93, 124, 190, 318; Fripp, *Haunts*, 108.

[2] Brewer, xiv. 1. 211.

[3] *Ibid.* xv. 324, 409; xvi. 327; xix. 1. 285, 2. 418; *V.H. Worc.* ii. 176; iii. 332, 410, 412; iv. 411; Nash, *Worc.* i. 280; *Worc. Wills*, i. 13.

[4] *V.H. Worc.* iii. 56; iv. 351; *Bristol and Glouc. Arch. Soc.* xiv. 63.

[5] H.P. *Subsidies.*

[6] Leach, *English Schools*, 232.

[7] *V.H. Worc.* iii. 332, from i.p.m. in 2 *Chancery Series*, xciv. 98.

[8] Bloom 206, 210.

been overlooked in other years. If John ii was ever of Mickleton in Gloucestershire, he may have left progeny there. A Walter Combe of that place made his will in 1557 and a John Combe in 1632. There were also Combes of Cheltenham and of Berkeley in the same county.[1] A. R. Ransford says that a John Comber or Comb built the church of Sevenhampton in Gloucestershire, where there is a brass to him, and that he was apparently of Worcester City and made his will in 1461.[2] But the brass gives the name as Camber and the date as '1497', and this is confirmed by the date of the will of a John Combre.[3] Etymologically, however, Comber may be the equivalent of 'a Combe'.[4]

Whether John ii was John of Mickleton or not, it is very likely that he had an earlier wife than Katherine Quiney. She was the widow of Adrian Quiney, and Adrian Quiney and a wife Katherine entered the Stratford gild in 1498.[5] Unless, therefore, she was another Katherine, she was no longer young in 1534. Probably she was the mother of William i (*infra*), and if so, she seems to have been by birth a Sheldon. The mother of John iii is uncertain. We do not know the parentage of a Francis, buried at Stratford on 8 Apr. 1575, or whether a Christopher, son of John, buried on 15 May 1561, and a Joan, daughter of John, buried on 4 Apr. 1573, were children of John ii or John iii.

John iii had livery of his father's Crowle manor in 1553,[6] and on April 22, being then of Stratford, presented to the living as his father's executor. But a right was claimed by George Whateley of Stratford, who presented John Whateley, and a William Whateley held the living in 1582 (cf. no. v). There were other manors at Crowle and the position as to the advowson remains obscure, since William Combe ii presented in 1610.[7] In 1553–5 Adrian Quiney (cf. no. xiii) brought an action against John Combes, 'sometimes written John A'Combes', of Stratford, gentleman, for retaining his title-deeds of Barland House in Stratford and attempting to convey it.[8] In 1555 John was amerced for irregular running of sheep on the Bancroft.[9] In 1557 he was called upon to repair three ruinous tenements in Church St. leased from the Corporation. In 1561 there were two of these and in 1567 the rent of these 'late

[1] *Gloucestershire Wills*; *Harl. Soc.* xxi. 156; lxv. 118.   [2] *N.Q.* clii. 330.
[3] C. T. Davis, *Monumental Brasses of Gloucestershire*, 95 ; *Glouc. Wills.*
[4] A. Mawer, *Problems of Place-name Study*, 68.
[5] Fripp, *Quyny*, 13; Bloom 193.

[6] *V.H. Worc.* iii. 332 from *Fine Roll* 7 Ed. VI, no. 18.
[7] Nash, *Worc.* i. 282.
[8] *Athenæum* for 22 Sept. 1906; Stopes, *Cont.* 219 from *R.O. Early Chancery Proc.* Bundle 1373.
[9] *M.A.* i. 42.

in his occupacion or his assignes' was unpaid.[1] This is not evidence
of his death, as Fripp suggests. In 1559 his man Morres was
amerced for a fray on a man of William Clopton.[2] He was fined
for non-suit as a freeholder at a leet of 5 Oct. 1560,[3] and in 1565
sold with his wife a house in Stratford to John Sadler.[4] Probably
he was steward or bailiff to the Earl of Warwick, as the Corporation paid their chief rent for some land at Shottery to him from
1567 to 1582.[5] And by 1562 he occupied the College mansion
(v. *infra*), where the Earl's leet was held in 1577–8.[6] He is
described as of Old Stratford in the *Visitation* and is on the Subsidy
Roll for Shottery, Bishopston, and Welcombe in 1566–7.[7] John
ii's relations to Latimer and Cromwell suggest Protestant sym-
pathies, but John iii is noted as an 'adversary of true religion'
in 1564.[8] The *Visitation* gives John iii sons Edward, Thomas,
John, and George and a daughter Elizabeth by a 'Blount' wife,
whom Yeatman 231 makes Joyce, daughter of Edward Blunt of
Kidderminster. This is plausible, since the Blunts of Kidderminster
seem to have had near kin (cf. p. 137) at Astley. Some burials at
Stratford (*supra*) may represent other children of this marriage. On
27 Aug. 1561 John iii took at Stratford a second wife, Rose,
daughter of William Clopton (cf. no. xi), by whom he had John
(c. and b. 10 Mar. 1563), William (c. 8 Nov. 1564, b. 2 Feb.
1585), Elizabeth (c. 26 May 1566), Francis (c. 8 Apr. 1575, b.
11 June 1576), John (c. 29 Jan. 1578). Rose Combe was buried
on 14 Oct. 1579. All these entries are at Stratford, except the
baptism of William, which is at Budbrooke.[9] It was perhaps through
Rose that John iii acquired the Clopton manor of Ryen Clifford,
although it did not descend to her son. There must be some error
in Yeatman's statement that a John Combe, with a wife Ellis,
fined for land there in 1570.[10] It is conceivable that John iii
married a third wife, Elizabeth Kinnersley of Stratford, at Crowle
on 23 June 1583,[11] but it is more likely that this was John iv (*infra*).
She was buried at Stratford on 24 May 1584. John iii obtained
his grant of arms (*supra*) in 1584 and died in 1588.[12]

William i is described as the second son of 'John Combes late of
Stratford on Avon Esq deceased' on his admission to the Middle
Temple on 19 Oct. 1571. He was called to the bar on 9 Feb.

[1] *M.A.* i. 75, 109; ii. 10.
[2] *Ibid.* i. 94.   [3] *Ibid.* i. 105.
[4] Yeatman 236.
[5] *M.A.* ii. 21; iii. 123 and *passim*.
[6] *Ibid.* iii. 29.
[7] H.P. *1848*, 327.

[8] *Camden Miscellany*, ix. 3, 8.
[9] Yeatman 190.
[10] Dugdale 529; Yeatman 236.
[11] Gray 227.
[12] *V.H. Worc.* iii. 332 from i.p.m.
2 *Chancery Series*, ccxix. 79.

1578.[1] Evidently he did not share his brother's religious views. A very hostile account of him is given in an account of the 'martyr-dom' of William Freeman, a Catholic priest, on 13 Aug. 1595.[2] According to this he was 'alied by mariage of their parentes unto Mistres Sheldon, with whom Mr. Freeman now conversed'. Having been 'in his childhood bereft both of father and mother', he was educated by Mrs. Dorothy Heath. He was in favour with Whitgift, Burghley, and Sir John Puckering, and 'of some counte-nance and accounte in the countrey'. He got a farm for his life and his wife's from Mrs. Sheldon at Alvechurch, and then practised to get the adjoining park from Mrs. Heath by spoil during her recusancy. This must have been about 1589, since some five or six years later he kept the Christmas of 1594 at Stratford, and there acted as justice of peace on a commission for the arrest of Mrs. Heath and Freeman. It is possible to find traces of the persons concerned. Alvechurch Park was and long remained the property of the see of Worcester, but Bishop Nicholas Heath (1543–51; 1553–5) may have leased it to a relative. Mrs. Heath of Alve-church is in a recusancy list of 1577.[3] Mary, wife of Thomas Sheldon, and Jane Sheldon, widow, are in another list of 1596.[4] Jane Lewknor, wife of Anthony Sheldon of Broadway, inherited some chantry land in Alvechurch.[5] She was clearly William i's Mrs. Sheldon, and Katherine Combe, his mother, may be con-jectured to have been a sister or daughter of the first Ralph Sheldon in the following pedigree : [6]

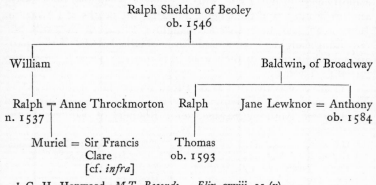

Ralph Sheldon of Beoley
ob. 1546

William   Baldwin, of Broadway

Ralph ⊤ Anne Throckmorton   Ralph   Jane Lewknor = Anthony
n. 1537   ob. 1584

    Muriel = Sir Francis   Thomas
             Clare   ob. 1593
             [cf. infra]

[1] C. H. Hopwood, *M.T. Records*, i. 181, 224.

[2] J. H. Pollen in *Catholic Record Soc. Publ.* v. 345, from *Engl. Coll. at Rome Collectanea*, F, f. 90.

[3] *V.H. Warw.* ii. 35, from *S.P.D.*

Eliz. cxviii. 11 (v).

[4] *Hatfield MSS.* vi. 266.

[5] *V.H. Worc.* iii. 257.

[6] *Harl. Soc.* xii. 3, xxvii. 38; Nash, *Worc.* i. 145; *V.H. Worc.* iv. 38.

William practised as a lawyer in London. He was reader at his Inn in 1595, but defaulted with his readings.[1] He sat in Parliament for Warwick in 1592 and for the county in 1597. In 1608 he was High Sheriff. He seems to have been of Warwick, where he held a lease of tithes, and gave counsel to the town, in which he was held 'an honest gentleman their neighbour, well known to them all'.[2] But he also kept up a close connexion with Stratford, advised the Corporation in their business of 1597 (no. xiii), and took part in other local affairs.[3] In 1593 he bought the land which he afterwards, with his nephew John iv, sold to Shakespeare (no. xiv). He is, I suppose, the William Combe on a subsidy list of 1605–6 for land at Old Stratford.[4] In 1599 he had the wardship of his great-grand-nieces, the children of John Gardener.[5] He married Alice, daughter of Richard Hambury, a London goldsmith, before the time of the Freeman affair.[6] On her death in 1606 he promptly married the widow of Sir John Puckering (ob. 1596), the Lord Keeper, who owned St. Sepulchre's Priory, at Warwick, and to her, having no children, he left his property on his death in 1610.[7] John iv and William ii were his executors.

Edward was the eldest son of John iii and inherited Crowle in 1588.[8] He married Anne, daughter of Stephen Hales of Newland, Coventry, and a daughter Anne was baptized at Tachbrook in 1580.[9] He dwelt at Wasperton, Warwickshire, and seems to have got into financial difficulties. In 1590 John Blunt fined with him for Crowle, Huddington, and Ryen Clifford.[10] Presumably this was a mortgage and not a sale, since Crowle was entailed on Edward and his brothers and their heirs, and after the deaths of Edward in June 1597 and an unmarried daughter Elizabeth in 1598, the remaining daughters Anne and Joyce obtained seisin of two parts and sold their rights to their uncle Thomas i.[11] Ryen Clifford also passed to Thomas.

Thomas i was married at Stratford on 10 Jan. 1586 to Mary Young, widow of William Young of Caynton, Shropshire, and daughter of Anthony Savage, *alias* Bonner, of Elmley Castle,

[1] Hopwood, i. 345, 356.
[2] Kemp, *Black Book*, 404.
[3] Fripp, *Quyny*, 193, 196; *Hatfield MSS*. vii. 429.
[4] H.P. *Subsidies*.
[5] *Hatfield MSS*. ix. 222.
[6] *Harl. Soc.* xxvii (*Worc.*), 68.
[7] *P.C.C.* 52, Wood, prob. 1 June 1611; Fripp, *S.S.* 61.

[8] *V.H. Worc.* iii. 332, from i.p.m. *2 Chancery Series*, ccxix. 79.
[9] Yeatman 288.
[10] *Ibid.* 237.
[11] *V.H. Worc.* iii. 332, from i.p.ms. *2 Chancery Series*, cclii. 54; cclix. 43; cclxi. 30; *Fine Roll, 43 Eliz.* pt. ii, no. 29; Yeatman 237.

Worcestershire, and Broad Campden, Gloucestershire.[1] He bought land in Old Stratford in 1584 [2] and the manor of Edgiock, Worcestershire, in 1587.[3] He had a sub-lease (cf. p. 126) of a moiety of the tithes of which Shakespeare afterwards acquired the other moiety (no. xvii), had a household of fourteen in 1595,[4] and is on a subsidy list for Old Stratford in 1596–7.[5] Fripp credits him with 'a book intituled The Theatre of Fine Devices, containing An Hundred Moral Emblems translated out of French by Thomas Combe', which was registered on 9 May 1593, but of which no example is known. The translator is perhaps more likely to be another Thomas Combe, a follower of Sir John Harington of Kelston, who describes him as 'apprentice in poetry, practiser in music, professor of painting', and to whose *Metamorphosis of Ajax* (1596) he appears to have contributed something. At his death about 11 Jan. 1609, Thomas i left his elder son William, besides the manors of Crowle and Ryen Clifford,[6] a leasehold estate. His will of 22 Dec. 1608 [7] disposes of 'the house I dwell in called the College House and the ortyards and appurtenances therewith, to me by our late Sovereign Queen Elizabeth demised'. It is left for thirty years to his widow, should she live so long, with successive remainders to William and his other children for periods terminating in September 1644. This was the old mansion of the College of Stratford. The Stratford archives contain a seventy years' lease of it, distinct from that of the rest of the College property (no. xvii), by the College to William Barker on 5 Oct. 1544.[8] Malone says that it was granted with the manor of Stratford to John Dudley, Earl of Warwick, from whom it escheated, and in 1562, being then occupied by John Combes, to Ambrose Dudley, Earl of Warwick, and also that it was leased by the Crown to Richard Coningsby for twenty-one years in 1574–5.[9] This is puzzling, because Barker is still tenant in the Earl's i.p.m. of 1590.[10] But in any case Fripp, *S.S.* 63, can hardly be right in saying that Thomas Combe purchased the house in 1596. It is pretty clear from the will that he only had a lease to 1644. The ownership reverted to the Crown in 1589 and was sold to Francis Morice and Francis Phelips in 1609.[11] Another provision for the widow is interesting from its

---

[1] *Harl. Soc.* xii. 291; xxi. 144; xxvii. 124; xxix. 519; Brewer, xix. 2. 419, 420; Rudder, *Gloc.* 322.

[2] Yeatman 236.

[3] *V.H. Worc.* iii. 425.

[4] Fripp, *S.S.* 63.

[5] H.P. *Subsidies.*

[6] I.p.m. in *2 Chancery Series*, cccxi. 91.

[7] *P.C.C. Dorset*, 13; cf. Lee 470.

[8] *Misc. Doct.* ix. 2.

[9] *Var.* ii. 44, 46, from *P.R. 4 Eliz.* p. 4 and *18 Eliz.* p. 12.

[10] *M.A.* iv. 92.

[11] *Misc. Doct.* xii. 104.

analogy to Shakespeare's. She is to have the use and occupation of all 'tables bedsteads and other standerdes except the best Bedsteads which I will giue and bequeath vnto my sayed sonne William with the best Bedd and best furniture thervnto belonging to haue to his owne vse'. The reversion of a copyhold of Byttell in Alvechurch and a leasehold house there are left to the younger son Thomas, and there is mention of the testator's unmarried daughters Mary and Joyce, brothers John, George, and John the younger, uncle William, godson Henry Rainsford, and servant James, who appears in the Welcombe enclosure controversy (no. xix). The widow died in 1617.

The *Visitation* makes John iv the third son of John iii. It is probable that he and not his father married Elizabeth Kinnersley in 1583. If so, he does not seem to have remarried after her early death. In 1590 he had had a fee of 53s. 4d. for gathering the Earl of Warwick's rents, and held property from the manor by various tenures.[1] His will mentions one John Davies as his 'landlord'. He purchased land at Stratford-on-Avon, Old Stratford, and Bishop's Hampton in 1594, at Ingon and Bishop's Hampton in 1603, and at Tiddington and Alveston in 1604.[2] He is on a subsidy list for land at Old Stratford in 1596–7.[3] But tradition (*infra*) makes him a money-lender, rather than a landholder, and he is presumably the 'Dominus Combe', a 'cognatus' of Richard Quiney, who in 1598 held the Corporation plate in pawn.[4] He seems to have shared his brother's interest in the tithes (no. xvii), and in 1602 was a party with William i in selling to Shakespeare the land bought by William in 1593 (no. xiv). He died, according to his monument, on 10 July 1614 and was buried at Stratford on 12 July. His will of 28 Jan. 1613,[5] proved[6] on 10 Nov. 1615, is printed in H.P. *1848*, 234. It helps to fix the family relationships. He entailed a house at Warwick, perhaps that of his uncle William i, whose apparel he mentions, but now occupied by William Cawdrey, *alias* Cooke, on his brother John v and his heirs, with remainders to his nephews William ii and Thomas ii and his brother George, who had a son John, and their heirs. Plots of land went to William, Thomas, and George, who got (cf. p. 16) Shakespere's Close in Hampton Lucy, and to his cousin Margaret wife of Thomas Reynolds, and another to Thomas Combe in trust for a sermon at Stratford and gowns for the poor. But most of his property was evidently in money. Besides the legacy to Shake-

---

[1] *M.A.* iv. 92. *sqq.*
[2] Yeatman 237.
[3] H.P. *Subsidies.*

[4] Fripp, *Quyny*, 122.
[5] *P.C.C.* 118, Rudd.
[6] Lee 471.

speare (*supra*), there were others to various members of the Combe
and Reynolds families, to his sister Hyett and her children, to his
cousin Anne Dickins (Deacons), to his Garden grand-nieces, to
his cousin Sir Henry Clare and his daughter Frances Combe, to his
uncle John Blunt, and to Francis Collins (cf. no. xxiv). Executors
and overseers or their kin, godchildren, and servants were also
remembered. Debts were forgiven or reduced. There was another
£20 for the poor of Stratford, smaller sums for those of Warwick
and Alcester, and £100 for loans to Stratford tradesmen. A tomb
worth £60 is to be erected. Over £1,500 can thus be accounted
for. The residuary legatee for 'goods, chattels, leases, credits, and
rights' was Thomas ii, who was executor with Sir Richard Verney
and Bartholomew Hales, and Sir Edward Blunt, Sir Henry Rainsford, Sir Francis Smith, and John Palmer of Compton. Evidently
a liberal man, at least posthumously, and with wide connexions.
The following pedigree shows the kinship of Blunt, Clare, and
Reynolds.[1] The Blunt descents are, however, very uncertain :

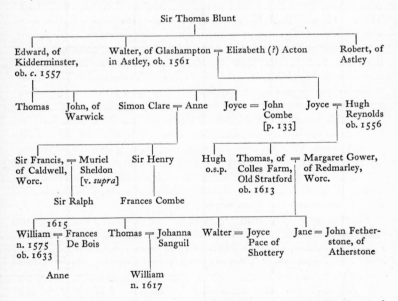

The *Visitation* gives George as the fourth son of John iii. Beyond

---

[1] *Harl. Soc.* xii. 243; xxvii. 19, 37; xxviii. 53; W. C. Metcalfe, *Worc. Visitation*,
106; *V.H. Worc.* iii. 168, 376; iv. 233; Habington, *Survey of Worc.* ii. 14;
A. Croke, *Family of Croke*, i. 157; Yeatman 230; Lee 491; Fripp, *S.S.* 31, 41.

the indications in John iv's will, I only know that in 1648, during the Commonwealth, parliamentary trustees sold the manor of Alvechurch to a William Combe and the mansion and park to John Combe and Richard Quiney. The bishops recovered at the Restoration. A Thomas Combe held land of the manor *c.* 1650–60.[1] Thomas ii in 1657 left his personalty to William, eldest son of John vi of Alvechurch.[2] George may have inherited his uncle William i's land at Alvechurch. Bellew's pedigree, followed in mine, is possibly right for this branch. I suspect that the Frances Combe of John iv's will was John vi's wife.

The children of John iii's second marriage are not in the *Visitation*. John v is in John iv's will; his wife and children are given by Yeatman 234. I suppose the sister Hyett of John iv's will to be the Elizabeth born in 1566.

The children of Thomas i are clear enough from the *Visitation* and the Stratford *Registers*. The heir, William ii, figures in the tithes complaint (no. xvii) and is the protagonist of the enclosure controversy (no. xix). He entered the Middle Temple on 17 Oct. 1602.[3] He was High Sheriff in 1616, and seems to have lived amicably with the Corporation in later life. He dwelt at the College and perhaps also at Welcombe. There is a monument at Stratford to his daughter Judith, who died in 1649 shortly before her intended marriage to Richard Combe of Hemel Hempstead. This confirms the theory (p. 129) of kinship between the Combes of that place and those of Astley. Thomas ii, the legatee of Shakespeare's sword (no. xxiv), entered the Middle Temple on 14 Nov. 1608. The brothers succeeded to the chamber of their uncle William on 10 Feb. 1609.[4] Both William and Thomas, described as of Old Stratford, are in a recusancy list of 1640–1.[5] William seems to have avoided taking an active part in the Civil War. Richard Symonds notes in 1645, 'R. Justice Combes, of Stratford-upon-Avon, sitts at home'.[6] He left a son and nine daughters.[7]

Finally something must be said of the alleged Shakespearean epigrams on John iv and Thomas i (App. C, nos. ii, vi, xi, xiii, xxv, xxxii, xxxiii, xlvi). A study of these is in J. Q. Adams, *Sh. as a Writer of Epitaphs.*[8] That on John iv first appeared, shortly after his death, in an addition (L2ᵛ) to Richard Brathwaite, *Remains after Death* (1618), as reissued with P. Hannay, *A Happy Husband*

[1] Nash, *Worc.* i. 25; *V.H. Worc.* iii. 252.

[2] *Var.* ii. 604.

[3] Hopwood, i. 425.

[4] *Ibid.* i. 498, 503.

[5] Yeatman 192.

[6] *Diary*, 192.

[7] Stopes, *Cont.* 225.

[8] 1923, *Manly Studies*, 83.

(1619). It is not, I think, like some others in the book, Brathwaite's own.

An Epitaph vpon one Iohn Combe of Stratford vpon Auen, a notable Vsurer, fastened vpon a Tombe that he had caused to be built in his life time.

> Ten in the hundred must lie in his graue,
> But a hundred to ten whether God will him haue ?
> Who then must be interr'd in this Tombe ?
> Oh (quoth the Diuell) my *John a Combe*.

There is no mention of Shakespeare here. The epigram is first ascribed to him by Hammond (1634) as on 'a bachelor, Mr Combe'; but he gives no copy. A two-line version is in *Ashm. MS.* 38 (*c.* 1650) as by Shakespeare on John Combe 'at his request, while he was yet living', and is accompanied by a palinode, also ascribed to Shakespeare, on Combe's charitable will. H.P. had another Caroline manuscript with verses by 'Shakespeare on Sir John Coome'.[1] Dobyns (1673), Aubrey (1681), and Rowe (1709) give versions which vary slightly in wording from each other and from Brathwaite. They are independent. Dobyns alone claims to have seen it himself at Stratford, 'upon the monument of a noted usurer', and he adds that, since he was at Stratford, 'the heirs of Mr Combe have caused these verses to be razed, so that now they are not legible'. Aubrey says that the composition was 'extemporary' at the tavern at Stratford, and Rowe that it was at Combe's own invitation 'in a laughing manner', but that 'the sharpness of the satyr is said to have stung the man so severely, that he never forgave it'. Peck (1740) adds a second 'sour' epigram, as written by Shakespeare on '*Tom a Combe*, alias *Thin-Beard*, brother of the said *John*'. It was known to Jordan, but he probably got it from Peck, and where Peck got it from is unknown. Macklin gave Malone, as derived from Sir Hugh Clopton in 1742, a couplet, which has nothing to do with usury, but which at one time Malone understood to have been another Shakespearean gibe at John Combe. But when Malone printed it in 1790, it was as an impromptu against a drunken blacksmith. It seems to have been a traditional jest of Tarlton, and can be disregarded in this connexion. On the other hand, the usury lines had clearly been applied to John Combe at an early date, and ascribed to Shakespeare soon after. It must be added that they too are of early origin, and continued to be applied to other usurers. Camden places his version among a group of 'conceited, merry, and laughing Epitaphes, the most of them composed by Master *Iohn Hoskins* ⟨1566–1638⟩ when he was young'. Here is a *catena* :

---

[1] *Rarities*, 754.

(*a*) H.P., *The More the Merrier* (1608).

Feneratoris Epitaphium

Ten in the hundred lies under this stone,
And a hundred to ten to the devil he's gone.

(*b*) W. Camden, *Remaines concerning Britaine* (1614), 383.

Heere lyes ten in the hundred
In the ground fast ramd.
T''is an hundred to ten,
But his soule is damnd.

(*c*) *Addl. MS.* 15227 (*c.* 1630), f. 11ᵛ.

In Dominum Edw Stanhop foenerat⟨orem⟩

Ten in the hundred lies under this stone,
An hundred to ten, to the deuil he's gone.

(*d*) *Ashm. MS.* 38 (*c.* 1650), p. 186.

Another on hym ⟨Sir John Spencer⟩
Ten In the hundred lies vnder this stone
yttes a hundred to ten to deuill he 's gone.

(*e*) John Cotgrave, *Wit's Interpreter* (1655), sign. Cc.

Here lies at least ten in the hundred,
Shackled up both hands and feet,
That at such as lent mony gratis wondred,
The gain of usury was so sweet:
But thus now being of life bereav'n,
Tis a hundred to ten he 's scarce gone to heav'n.

(*f*) *Sloane MS.* 1489, f. 11.

(i) Heere lyes 10 ith 100 under this stone
A 100 to one but to th' divel hees gone.

(ii) Who is this lyes under this hearse:
Bo. ho. quoth the divel, tis my Dʳ pearse.

If there is anything in the story, Shakespeare can at most, jesting at the Bear, or in the parlour of the College, have adapted verses which he knew from Hoskins or another. Rowe's notion of Combe's resentment is negatived by the legacy in Combe's will. What is rather puzzling is the double reference of Brathwaite and Dobyns to the lines as on Combe's tomb. It is absurd to suppose that Shakespeare put them there, but some enemy might have recalled them and done so. Brathwaite merely says that they were 'fastened upon' the tomb, but the account of Dobyns implies that they were cut or scratched there, were still there in his time, and were erased by the Combe family, half a century after John's death, and after the deaths of his long-lived nephews, William and Thomas. There is the tomb, in the chancel, close to Shakespeare's own and according to Dugdale by the same artist, Gerard Johnson or Janssen.[1] It was not, as Brathwaite says, built in Combe's lifetime, unless he altered the intention of his will. It is an altar-tomb with a recumbent effigy, above which are Combe's arms and a slab with his name, the date of his death, and an account of his charitable bequests. Bloom, *Church*, 185, says that the inscription was unfinished, and Lee 474 that the last word 'pounds' has been erased. But there is a small superscript 'li', and the words 'Virtus post funera vivit' complete the record.]

XIX. THE WELCOMBE ENCLOSURE

(*a*) [1614, Sept. 5. Extract from *The Particulers of Olde Stratforde*; *also Landes of Freeholders & where they lye* (*S.A. Misc. Doct.* i. 94), pr. Halliwell, *1848*, 267; *B.P. Cat.* 35, with facs.; facs. in H.P. i. 248; in hand of Thomas Greene.]

5 Septembris. 1614.

Auncient ffreeholders in the ffieldes of Oldstratford and
   Welcombe.

Mr Shakspeare. 4. yard Land. noe common nor ground beyond gospell bushe, noe grownd in Sandfield, nor none in slowe hill field beyond Bishopton nor none in the enclosure beyond Bishopton.

(*b*) [1614, Oct. 28. Contemporary extract from Articles between Shakespeare and William Replingham (*Wheler Papers*, i. 64; *B.P. Cat.* 36), facs. H.P. ii. 38.]

Vicesimo octavo die Octobris, anno Domini 1614. Articles of agreement indented made betweene William Shackespeare, of Stretford in the county of Warwicke, gent., on the one partye, and William Replingham, of Greete Harborowe in the countie of Warwicke, gent., on the other partie, the daye and yeare abouesaid. Inter alia Item, the said William Replingham, for him, his heires, executours

---

[1] *Life*, 99.

and assignes, doth covenaunte and agree to and with the said William Shackespeare, his heires and assignes, That he, the said William Replingham, his heires or assignes, shall, uppon reasonable request, satisfie, content and make recompence unto him, the said William Shackespeare or his assignes, for all such losse, detriment and hinderance as he, the said William Shackespeare, his heires and assignes, and one Thomas Greene, gent., shall or maye be thought, in the viewe and judgement of foure indifferent persons, to be indifferentlie elected by the said William and William, and their heires, and in default of the said William Replingham, by the said William Shackespeare or his heires onely, to survey and judge the same, to sustayne or incurre for or in respecte of the increasinge ⟨decreasinge⟩ of the yearelie value of the tythes they the said William Shackespeare and Thomas doe joyntlie or seuerallie hold and enioy in the said fieldes, or anie of them, by reason of anie inclosure or decaye of tyllage there ment and intended by the said William Replingham; and that the said William Replingham and his heires shall procure such sufficient securitie vnto the said William Shackespeare and his heires, for the performance of theis covenauntes, as shalbee devised by learned counsell. In witnes whereof the parties abouesaid to theis presentes interchangeablie their handes and seales have put, the daye and yeare first aboue wrytten. Sealed and deliuered in the presence of us, Tho: Lucas; Jo: Rog⁊rs; Anthonie Nasshe; Mich: Olney. [*Endorsed.*] Coppy of the articles with Mr Shakspeare.

(*c*) [1614, Nov. 17 to 1615, Sept. 5. Extracts from memoranda of Thomas Greene, pr. in facs. and transcript by E. J. L. Scott in C. M. Ingleby, *Shakespeare and the Enclosure of Common Fields at Welcombe* (1885). Of the four original leaves f. 1 is now among the *Wheler MSS*. and ff. 2–4 in *Misc. Doct.* xiii. 27: all are at the B.P. (*Cat.* 37). Stopes, *Env.* 86, points out that pp. 6 and 7 are transposed by error in the facs. and transcript, disordering the entries for 1615.]

(1) [1614.] Jovis 17 No. At my Cosen Shakspeare commyng yesterday to towne I went to see him howe he did he told me that they assured him they ment to inclose

PLATE XVIII

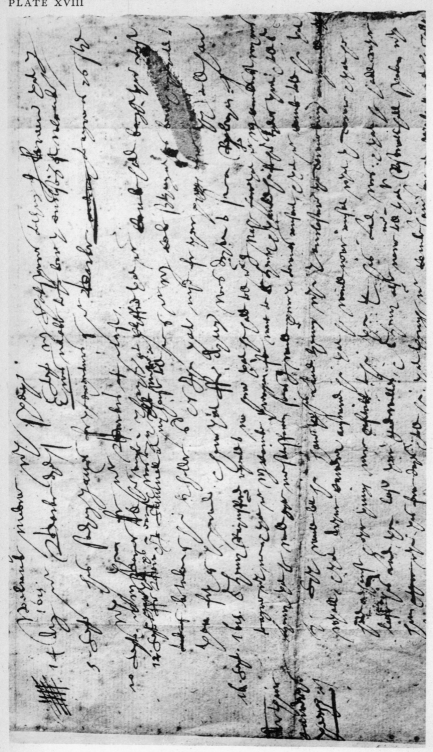

MEMORANDA OF THOMAS GREENE

noe further then to gospell bushe & so vpp straight
(leavyng out part of the dyngles to the ffield) to the gate
in Clopton hedge & take in Salisburyes peece: and that
they meane in Aprill to servey the Land & then to gyve
satisfaccion & not before & he & Mʳ Hall say they think
there will be nothyng done at all. . . .

(2) ⟨*In margin*⟩ 10 Dec. that the survey there was
past, & I came from Wilson to look Mʳ Replingham
at the beare & at new place but myssed him & on the
narowe sid but he was not to be spoken with: . . .

(3) 23 Dec. 1614. A Hall. L⟨ett⟩res wrytten one
to Mʳ Manneryng another to Mʳ Shakspeare with almost all the com⟨panyes⟩ hands to eyther: I alsoe wrytte
of myself to my Cosen Shakespeare the Coppyes of all
our oathes m⟨a⟩de then alsoe a not of the Inconvenyences
wold gr⟨ow⟩ by the Inclosure. . . .

(4) r⟨emember⟩ . . . 9 Jan. 1614. Mʳ Replyngham
28 Octbris articled w⟨i⟩th Mʳ Shakspeare & then I was
putt in by T. Lucas. . . .

(5) [11 Jan. 1615] On Wednesday, being the xjᵗʰ
day. . . At night Mʳ Replingham supped w⟨i⟩th me and
Mʳ Barnes was to beare him Company, where he assured
me before Mʳ Barnes that I should be well dealt w⟨i⟩thall,
confessyng former promisses by himself Mʳ Manneryng
& his agreement for me w⟨i⟩th my cosen Shak-
peare. . . .

(6) 7. Apr. being goodfryday Mʳ Barb⟨e⟩r commyng
to the colledge to Mʳ T C⟨ombe⟩ about a debt he stood
surety for M⟨ist⟩ris Quyney W C⟨ombe⟩ willed his
brother to shewe Mʳ Barb⟨e⟩r noe favour & threatned
him that he should be served vpp to London within a
ffortnight. (and so yt fell out:). . . .

(7) 14 Aug. 1615. Mʳ Barb⟨e⟩r dyed.

(8) [*Inserted later*] Sept. W Shakspeares tellyng J
Greene that J was not able to beare the encloseinge of
Welcombe.

(9) 5 Sept. his sendyng James for the executours of
Mʳ Barb⟨e⟩r to agree as ys sayd w⟨i⟩th them for Mʳ
Barb⟨e⟩rs interest.

[Several illustrative documents are printed by Ingleby and in H.P., *Council Bk.*, but it is clear from H.P., *Calendar*, that there is still much unprinted material in the Stratford archives. It is not likely that this would throw any fresh light on Shakespeare's concern in the affair, but it might afford an interesting study for an economist desiring to trace in detail the progress of a 17th-century enclosure. There are various misapprehensions in Lee 474, Adams 454, and Stopes, *Env.* 81, 336, although this last has some useful facts.

So far as one can judge from published material, the history is as follows. The notion of an enclosure was first mooted about September 1614 when (*a*) was prepared. The Corporation took alarm, and those members of the council who had land in Welcombe agreed, in at least one case reluctantly, to oppose. In November Thomas Greene, the town clerk, was in London, negotiating unsuccessfully with the promoters, Arthur Mainwaring and William Replingham, and drafting a petition to the Privy Council. He failed to see William Combe, a large landholder in Welcombe. But he saw Shakespeare and his son-in-law Hall, who happened to come to town, and (*c* 1) records the interview. Shakespeare's interest and Greene's own, as tithe-holders in Welcombe, had already been safeguarded by the agreement (*b*). Early in December Greene was back in Stratford and was sent (Dec. 9) with a deputation of protest from the council to Combe, who said that the enclosure would not hurt the town, and that he would not intervene. It was Mainwaring's affair, not his, although he might get some profit by it. Meanwhile the land had been surveyed, earlier than Shakespeare had anticipated, and on December 10 Greene notes (*c* 2) a fruitless attempt to see Replingham at New Place. On December 20 Combe committed himself to Mainwaring's side. The council attempted to secure support from landholders outside their own body. On December 23 they wrote (*c* 3) to Shakespeare and to Mainwaring. The correspondence with Shakespeare is lost. The letter to Mainwaring [1] dwelt on the losses of the town from fire and the risk from the enclosure to over seven hundred benefiting by alms out of Edward VI's grant. Mainwaring's reply (Dec. 30) is unprinted.[2] Early in January 1615 a ditch was dug by Combe's men, including one Stephen Sly. Members of the Corporation who interfered were assaulted and Combe called them 'puritan knaves and underlings in their colour'. A stay of proceedings was proposed pending an action at the Assizes, but while it was under discussion, the ditch was filled in by women and children from Stratford and Bishopton. On

---

[1] Ingleby 15, from *Wheler MS.* i. 109.   [2] *Misc. Doct.* vii. 17.

March 27 a staying order was made at the Warwick Assizes, until good cause could be shown for the enclosure. Then followed a year of delay during which Combe maintained his right to enclose his own land, attempted to buy up other interests in Welcombe, and bullied the smaller tenants. But the order of the Judges was confirmed at the Lent Assizes of 1616, and Sir Edward Coke, then Chief Justice of the King's Bench, bade Combe 'sett his heart at rest: he should neyther enclose nor laye downe any earrable nor plowe any ancient greensward'. In April Combe was 'out of hope ever to enclose'. But in June he opened a fresh negotiation with the Corporation, and made proposals which do not appear unreasonable.[1] He needed grass land in place of tillage for 'mainteynance of hospetallitie & good husbandrie'. But he would reduce the area originally intended for enclosure. If the council would obtain the agreement of the freeholders interested, he would secure them against loss of tithe by a conveyance of land or a yearly rent-charge, or by giving them the tithes of Drayton in exchange for those of the enclosure. He would also satisfy through an arbitration those who had present interest in the tithes. He would keep at least a third of the enclosed land in tillage. He would abate his own right to run beasts on the common greensward, beyond the proportion represented by the area cut off by the enclosure. Sand might still be dug by the 'better sorte' of the town. The Corporation, however, remained obdurate. Greene's notes fail us early in 1617, but the controversy evidently dragged on. There was another confirmatory order against Combe, this time by Sir Henry Hobart, Chief Justice of the Common Pleas, at the Lent Assizes of 1617. The Corporation complained that Combe disregarded it, and apparently brought or contemplated an action in the Court of Common Pleas itself.[2] But in February 1619 their petition was before the Privy Council who referred it to Coke and Sir Julius Caesar, the Master of the Rolls, and in March issued a letter to Combe directing him to plough the land as before, and replace the greensward until further order should be made by the judges of assize.[3]

The best accounts of enclosures under the Tudors and Stuarts are in I. S. Leadam, *Domesday of Inclosures*,[4] E. M. Leonard, *The Inclosure of Common Fields in the Seventeenth Century*,[5] R. H. Tawney, *The Agrarian Problem in the Sixteenth Century* (1912).

[1] Ingleby, 16 from *Misc. Doct.* i. 107.
[2] Stopes, *Env.* 341, from *Misc. Doct.* vii. 1.
[3] *P.C. Acts* (1617–19), 370, 394.
[4] 1897, R. Hist. Soc.
[5] 1905, 2 R. Hist. Soc. Trans. xix. 101.

They made for more profitable husbandry, since the communal tillage of open fields was not conducted on scientific lines, and obviously no one would spend capital on improving his scattered and unenclosed plots for the benefit of his neighbours. But in so far as they involved the restriction of communal grazing over waste and fallow, they were naturally objected to by those who did not themselves benefit; and in so far as they involved the conversion of tillage into grassland they had serious political consequences in the reduced amount of employment available and the reduced production and consequent increased price of grain. There were statutes against them, which were no doubt the basis of the orders at assizes in the Welcombe case. But the extent to which these were enforced varied at different periods, becoming less rigid when the price of grain was low. Arrangements for the exchange of plots and the enclosure of the concentrated holdings thus formed were often carried out by agreement between freeholders. They required the approval of Chancery or the Exchequer and the consent of the lord of the manor, although Chancery would sometimes overrule a lord whose consent was unreasonably withheld. This seems to have been the method of enclosure contemplated at Welcombe. Possibly the enterprise was prompted by a knowledge that Lord Ellesmere, the Lord Chancellor of 1614, had expressed an opinion that enclosures were to the public advantage.[1] The original promoter, Arthur Mainwaring, was Lord Ellesmere's steward.[2] He was a son of Sir George Mainwaring of Ightfield, Shropshire, by Anne daughter of Sir William More of Loseley, whose other daughter Elizabeth had been Ellesmere's second wife.[3] I have not traced any connexion with the Humfrey Maynwaringe who witnessed the conveyance of Old Stratford land to Shakespeare in 1602 (no. xiv). Arthur's cousin Alicia married William Replingham, the William of Great Harborough associated with him in the enclosure. This evidently began as a speculation by the cousins. Land in Welcombe had been conveyed to Mainwaring,[4] and he approached the matter as an expert. On 24 Nov. 1614 he said that 'yf he might not doe yt well &c. he cared not for inclosyng and cared not howe little he did meddle therein'. William Combe's connexion with the matter was therefore at first subsidiary, and it was not until December that he agreed to take over the interest of 'the contractours'. He was already a considerable landholder in Welcombe by inheri-

---

[1] Elton 148.
[2] *Wheler MS.* i. 109; *Egerton Papers*, 342, 472, 481.
[3] *Harl. Soc.* xxix. 349.
[4] *Wheler MS.* i. 109.

tance from his father Thomas. Lee 474 and Stopes, *Env.* 336, are clearly wrong in relating the enclosure to the death of his uncle John on 10 July 1614. John's land, such as it was, lay in another part of Stratford, and his heir was William's brother Thomas (no. xviii). As I read the documents, Mainwaring and Replingham dropped out of the enterprise after the assizes order of March 1615, and thereafter it was wholly in Combe's hands. There is a mention of some bill by Combe against Replingham in the spring of 1616. Combe acquired interests from Sir Henry Rainsford and from Lord Carew of Clopton. Other landholders were Sir Francis Smythe of Wootton Wawen and Shottery, who farmed the demesne, Combe's cousin Margaret Reynolds and her son William, Sir Simon Archer, Peter Roswell, William Parsons, Richard Smith, Arthur Cawdrey, Thomas Barber, William Walford, William Chandler, Anthony Nash, John Sheffield, Richard Hiccox, a Lane, a Mace, and Vicar Wright of Bishopton. Some were freeholders and the interests of some copyholders and leaseholders seem to have been overridden.[1] The area concerned is given as 400 acres of arable in the Privy Council letter of Feb. 1619. It had been more, since Combe reduced his scheme later than January 1615, when the value of the enclosure was estimated at £250 per annum. The locality can be approximately traced from a rough contemporary plan in H.P. i. 250, a Welcombe estate map of 1832 in Ingleby, and the modern ordnance map.[2] It was 'the north part of the field of Oldstratford, Welcombe and Bushopton', lying mainly in Welcombe hamlet, north of the road from Stratford to Warwick, and west of the present Welcombe Lodge. As finally planned, the western ditch was to run north-west from the Warwick road, by Gospel Bush to the Dingles, and then west by a highway still extant from Welcombe to the gate of Clopton. The ditch thrown down in 1615 would have gone nearer Stratford to the west.

It does not appear that the lord of the manor had any part in the initiation of the proposals for an enclosure. The passage of the lordship (cf. ch. i) is traced by Dugdale, 516, and Malone[3] from the Bishop of Worcester to John Dudley,[4] to the Crown,[5] back to Dudley,[6] to Dudley's widow after his attainder,[7] to the hospital of Savoy after her death and back to the Crown,[8] to Ambrose Dudley.[9] It reverted to the Crown

[1] *Misc. Doct.* vii. 10.
[2] H.P. i. 22.
[3] *Var.* ii. 42.
[4] *S.P.D. Ed. VI.* iii. 1; *P.R. 3 Ed. VI,* p. 3.

[5] *P.R. 3 Ed. VI,* p. 9, m. 4.
[6] *P.R. 7 Ed. VI,* p. 8.
[7] *P.R. 1 Mary,* p. 5.
[8] *P.R. 3, 4 P. and M.,* p. 12.
[9] *P.R. 4 Eliz.,* p. 4.

on Dudley's death without heirs in 1590,[1] and was granted on 27 Jan. 1591 [2] to Henry Best and John Wells, who sold it to Ludovic Greville of Milcote. His heir, Sir Edward Greville, was alive in 1614, but in embarrassed circumstances, and the manor must have been surrendered to the Crown at some date before 4 Mar. 1610, when it was sold to William Whitmore of London and John Randoll of Preston Bagot, Warwickshire.[3] This was at the suit of John Eldred and others, contractors, and must be related to an agreement made on 12 Oct. 1610 between the Commissioners for the Sale of Lands and John Eldred, Arthur Ingram, Martin Freeman, and William Whitmore, for the allocation to the latter of lands worth £50,000 in discharge of a Crown debt to them as late contractors for the customs.[4] Presumably the manor fell in some way to the share of Sir Arthur Ingram, who married Greville's daughter Mary. John Chamberlain, writing on 20 July 1615, says that Ingram had contracted to give £22,000 for the best of Greville's lands. He may have been acting for Lionel Cranfield, Earl of Middlesex, to whom, according to other accounts, some or all of the Greville estate passed.[5] Ultimately Cranfield acquired the Stratford manor itself. But in February and July 1615 the promoters of the enclosure were attempting to buy the 'royalty' of Ingram and using Greville's interest with him for this purpose, although evidently without success. The Corporation, on their side, were attempting in December 1614 to stir up opposition through John Randoll. Clearly, therefore, Lee 475 and others are wrong in suggesting that Lord Ellesmere was himself interested in the enclosure as 'ex-officio lord of the manor of Stratford on behalf of the Crown'. It was not a Crown manor at the time, and indeed, if it had been, its administration would not have fallen to the Lord Chancellor.

The direct interest of the Corporation in the matter was limited to their reversion in the tithes of the enclosed lands, which might fall if arable was converted to grass land. Shakespeare, too, was only concerned for his lease of the tithes (no. xvii). It is clear from (a) that he had no land or common rights within the area affected. He was therefore secured from loss by his agreement (b) with Replingham, later confirmed by Combe's offer of 1616, which included a provision that 'those that have presente intereste of tythes within

---

[1] I.p.m. in 2 Chancery Series, ccxxix. 138.

[2] P.R. 33 Eliz., p. 3.

[3] Docquet in Cal. S.P.D. 1603–10, p. 590; cf. B.P. Cat. 59.

[4] S.P.D. Jac. I. lvii. 97.

[5] Birch, James, i. 367; H. Spelman, History of Sacrilege, 128; J. Edmondson, House of Greville, 11.

this place shall haue reasonable satisfaccion for them if this inclosier goe one, as ffower indifferente men shall judge to be worth eyther in yearelye rente or a sume of mony'.   Much has been written as to what may have been his sentimental attitude.   If he shared Combe's view that there would be no hurt to the town, he may, so far as we know, have been right.   Nor do I think we can safely identify with his tenant of 1602 (no. xiv) and regard as entitled to his protection the Lewis Hiccox, a tenant of Mrs. Reynolds, whom Combe abused for ploughing his land within the enclosure, and who is probably also the 'poore blynd Hiccox' to whom he refused a replevin to recover his milch cattle when they were found in other men's corn and impounded by the heyward.   A tendency to see Shakespeare everywhere is perhaps responsible for some misinterpretations of Greene's memoranda of August and September 1615 (c 7–9).   It has been supposed that it was he who 'was not able to beare the encloseinge of Welcombe'.   The phrase is a little cryptic in itself.   'Beare' may mean 'endure' or 'justify'; it may even be a slip for 'bar'.   But in any case Greene wrote 'I' not 'he', and although he sometimes wrote 'I' for 'he' elsewhere, and did not always correct it, there is no ground for assuming that he did so here.   It has also been supposed by Stopes, *Env.* 88, followed by Lee 481, that it was Shakespeare who wanted to buy an interest from Mr. Barber's executors, because he was 'benevolently desirous of relieving Barber's estate from the pressure which Combe was placing upon it' (cf. c 6).   Scott and Ingleby read 'Barker' for 'Barber', but the facsimile (Plate XVIII) certainly gives 'Barbr', and Mrs. Stopes points out that Thomas Barbor was buried at Stratford on 15 Aug. 1615.   But in fact (c 7 and 9) have nothing to do with (c 8).   It seems to me clear from the facsimile that (8) was a later insertion in a blank space left by the short (7) and that the two Barber entries were at first continuous.   And if so the 'his' of (9) does not refer to Shakespeare but to Combe, who is several times indicated merely as 'he' in Greene's notes, and who naturally took the opportunity of Barber's death to try to acquire his interest in Welcombe.   The James whom he sent to negotiate was presumably the James of his father's will (no. xviii).   Once more, Shakespeare's sentiments elude us.

About Thomas Greene a good deal is known, but unfortunately it does not include an explanation of how he came to be Shakespeare's cousin.   It is natural to look for a clue in the Thomas Green, *alias* Shakspere, who was buried at Stratford on 6 Mar. 1590 (no. i), but so far it has led to nothing.   Lee 476 says that the '*alias*' implies that Shakespeare was the maiden name of this Thomas

Greene's mother, and H.P. ii. 213 that it 'almost invariably originated with a bride, the first being her maiden and the second her husband's name'. These contradictory statements are alike in being too sweeping. An '*alias*' may surely also indicate a definite change of name, bastardy, a place of origin,[1] a nickname,[2] an abbreviation, as in Broke *alias* Brokesmouth (cf. p. 24), and, I think, an occupation, as perhaps in Hathaway *alias* Gardner (no. v). The town clerk came from Warwick. His father, also Thomas, was an Assistant Burgess there, and Master of the Company of Mercers, Grocers, and Haberdashers in 1586,[3] and his will of 22 July 1590 names sons Thomas, John, to whom he left a house in Northampton, and Richard, a daughter Margaret Weale, a brother John, who was a tanner at Tanworth, where a Henry Greene was a freeholder in 1580,[4] and a cousin John of Warwick. This was no doubt John of the Crown Inn, Warwick, a Principal Burgess,[5] whose own will of 16 Jan. 1606 names a wife Joan and leaves land in Hampton Budbrooke. The town clerk himself mentions in his *Diary* a 'cosen Graves' and a 'cosen Baker'. I owe my knowledge of the wills to the kindness of Mr. E. I. Fripp, who suggests [6] the following pedigree:

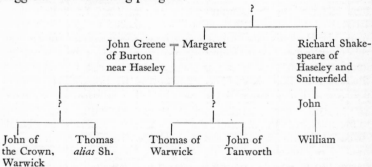

But there is no justification (cf. no. ii) for identifying the Richard Shakespeares of Haseley and Snitterfield, and although John and Margaret Greene of Burton held land late of Wroxall priory in 1547,[7] there is nothing to show that Margaret had been a Shakespeare. Moreover, the affiliation of Greene *alias* Shakespeare to the Warwick Greenes is conjectural. The name Greene was

---

[1] *Var.* ii. 146.

[2] *Ibid.*

[3] T. Kemp, *Book of John Fisher*, 159, 385.

[4] *M.A.* iii. 55.

[5] T. Kemp, *Black Book of Warwick*, 206.

[6] *Quyny*, 154.

[7] *Monastic Estates*, 20.

common in Warwickshire, as elsewhere. Two Thomas Greenes, father and son, of Bishopton, are to be distinguished. For the same reason, it is hazardous to identify the town clerk with the Thomas Greene, gentleman, of Worcester diocese, who was a recusant in 1596.[1] The Warwick Greenes were Protestants and supporters of the puritan Job Throgmorton.[2] What we do know of the early days of the town clerk is that he was fined with his father at Warwick in 1586 for not wearing a statute cap on Sundays,[3] inherited £80 and a grey mare, and on 20 Nov. 1595 entered the Middle Temple from Staple's Inn as son and heir of Thomas Greene of Warwick, gentleman. John Marston of Coventry and his son John, later the dramatist, were his sureties. He was called to the Bar in 1602.[4] There are several references to him in the Quiney correspondence (cf. no. xiii). The first is an obscure one to 'Thomas Greene's band of Marston' in 1598. In 1601 and 1602 he was acting as 'solicitor' for the Stratford Corporation in London.[5] On 31 Aug. 1603 he was appointed steward of the borough; [6] the post became that of town clerk under the Jacobean charter of 1610. In 1609 he was living at New Place, and expected (no. xi) to remain there for a year, but in 1611 at a house by the churchyard. By 1611 he had a wife Lettice who witnessed a deed with him and Judith Shakespeare.[7] I had thought it conceivable that she might be the Lettice, daughter of Henry Shakespeare, baptized at Hampton Lucy on 10 June 1582 (no. i). But Mr. Fripp tells me that she was the widow of one Chandler of Leicester, and this is confirmed by a letter of 26 Jan. 1615 from William Chandler of Stratford addressed to Greene as his 'father' and mentioning his 'mother Greene'.[8] In 1609 Greene had obtained a reversionary interest in a moiety of the Welcombe tithes, of which Shakespeare held the other moiety (no. xvii), and this made his position in the enclosure controversy a delicate one. He was included in the safeguarding agreement (b), apparently (c 4) through the good offices of Thomas Lucas of Tanworth [9] who afterwards himself became town clerk of Stratford,[10] and may have been acting in 1614 as Replingham's lawyer. Presumably Shakespeare assented, but I do not know why Lee 478 says that it was at his suggestion. On 12 Dec. 1614 the Corporation questioned Greene's whole-hearted-

---

[1] *Hatfield MSS.* vi. 266.
[2] *M.A.* iii. 55.
[3] Kemp, *Fisher*, 155.
[4] Hopwood, i. 357, 426.
[5] Fripp, *Quyny*, 153, 175, 179, 183, 185, 186, 196.
[6] H.P. *Cal.* 102.
[7] *B.P. Cat.* 60.
[8] *Misc. Doct.* v. 151.
[9] *M.A.* iii. 55.
[10] H.P. *Cal.* 104.

ness as their agent, and he pledged himself to withstand the enclosure as their steward and counsellor. This he seems to have done, in spite of an offer of £10 to buy a gelding if he would get a friendly suit arranged with a view to a compromise. He was still acting for the Corporation in the matter during March 1615, but thereafter seems to have dropped out, although he continued to note events in his diary up to the beginning of 1617. On 8 Apr. 1616, however, Francis Collins (no. xxiv) replaced him as steward. He advertised his house for sale and with his wife Lettice sold his lease of tithes to the Corporation,[1] and went to live in Bristol. Many of his private papers seem to have been left in the Corporation archives. Fripp, *S.S.* 60, cites a letter of 22 May 1617 to the Stratford Corporation[2] in which he speaks of his 'golden days' in their service, and adds 'we cannot doubt that it was the Poet's friendship and kinship which made these days of strenuous labour "golden" and his death which turned sunshine into night'. I am not sure that in the mouth of a practising lawyer 'golden days' means quite what Fripp thinks. Later Greene was a successful barrister in London, becoming reader at the Middle Temple in 1621, master of the bench by 1623, and treasurer in 1629.[3] Here, too, his son William was admitted at the age of thirteen in 1621. He died in 1640. His brother John Greene (*c* 8) was appointed solicitor to the Stratford Corporation on 22 Oct. 1612 and a deputy town clerk on 23 Apr. 1613, being then one of the Principal Burgesses.[4] In 1617 Lord Carew recommended him for the town-clerkship, but Collins was already appointed.[5] On 29 Mar. 1609 he married Margaret Lane (p. 13). He is presumably the John Greene of Clement's Inn, who became a trustee of Shakespeare's Blackfriars property in 1618 (no. xxiii).]

XX. THE HIGHWAYS BILL

[1611, Sept. 11. Extract from contribution list (*S.A. Misc. Doct.* i. 4), facs. *B.P. Cat.* 47.]

Wednesdaye the xj[th] of September, 1611.

Colected towardes the charge of prosecutyng the Bill in parliament for the better Repayre of the highe waies and amendinge diuers defectes in the Statutes alredy made.

[1] Lee 476; *Misc. Docts.* vii. 125, 128; x. 23.
[2] *Misc. Doct.* i. 1.
[3] Hopwood, ii. 655, 684, 753.
[4] H.P. *Cal.* 102, 104.
[5] *H.M. Comm.* ix. 1. 292.

List of seventy-one names follows; in margin is added
Mr William Shackspere.

[Bills dealing with highways were before the House of Commons
during the sessions of 9 Feb.–23 July 1610 and 5 Apr.–7 June
1614, but did not get beyond the Committee stage.[1]]

XXI. A PREACHER'S THIRST

[1614. From *Account* (Xmas) of Chamberlains, given in H.P. *Accounts*,
1609–19, 31.]

Item for one quart of sack and one quart of clarrett winne
geuen to a precher at the newe place. xxd.

[Such a gift was a common courtesy to a neighbouring justice or
other distinguished visitor at his inn or lodging in the town. H.P.,
New Place, 27, notes other preachers so refreshed between 1619
and 1630. Lee 466 says that the preacher was 'of Puritan pro-
clivities'. It may be so, but there is no evidence. There were three
official foundation sermons each year before the Bailiff and Corporation;[2] the Oken on election day in September, the Hamlet Smith
at Easter, the Perrott at Whitsuntide. John Combe left a legacy
for another in 1614.]

XXII. LORD RUTLAND'S IMPRESA

[1613, Mar. 31. From *Account* of Thomas Screvin, steward to Francis
Manners, 6th Earl of Rutland (*H.M.C. Rutland MSS.* iv. 494.)]

Item, 31 Martii, to Mr Shakspeare in gold about my
Lorde's impreso, xliiijs; to Richard Burbage for paynting
and making yt, in gold xliiijs.—iiijli. viijs.

[This was for the tilt upon the King's Accession day, 24 Mar. 1613.[3]
There is no reason to doubt that the payment was to the poet, as
the association with Burbadge, known to have been a painter, suggests. Stopes, *Env.* 229, thinks that it might have been to John
Shakespeare, the royal bitmaker (cf. App. E), but the *imprese* were
not trappings for horses, but painted shields of paper, with emblems
and mottoes.[4] Of the tilt in 1613, Wotton, *Letters*, ii. 17, records
'bare *imprese*, whereof some were so dark, so that their meaning is not
yet understood, unless perchance that were their meaning, not to
be understood'. Burbadge was paid again on 25 Mar. 1616 'for
my Lorde's shelde and for the embleance, 4l: 18s'.[5]]

---

[1] *Commons Journals*, i. 408, 416,
441, 465, 476, 494, &c.
[2] *M.A.* iii. li.

[3] Cf. *Eliz. Stage*, i. 148.
[4] *Ibid.* i. 143.
[5] *Rutland MSS.* iv. 508.

XXIII. THE BLACKFRIARS GATE-HOUSE

(*a*) [1613, Mar. 10. From *Conveyance* (in Guildhall Library, London), facs. Library Committee (1896). This is the counterpart held by the vendor; it was found in 1796 among the title-deeds of the Fetherstonhaugh family (Malone, *Inquiry*, 119) and bought by the Corporation in 1843. The deed held by the purchasers (pr. H.P. ii. 31) was formerly in H.P.'s collection (*Rarities*, 148) and is now in that of H. C. Folger. It was enrolled (*Close Roll, 11 Jac.*, p. 31) on 23 Apr. 1613.]

This Indenture made the tenthe day of Marche, in the yeare of our Lord God, according to the computacion of the church of England, one thowsand six hundred and twelve, and in the yeares of the reigne of our Sovereigne Lord James, by the grace of God king of England, Scotland, Fraunce and Ireland defender of the faith &c (that is to saie) of England, Fraunce and Ireland the tenth, and of Scotland the six and fortith; Between Henry Walker citizein and Minstrell of London of th'one partie; And William Shakespeare of Stratford Vpon Avon in the countie of Warwick gentleman, William Johnson, citizein and Vintener of London, John Jackson and John Hemmyng of London gentlemen, of th'other partie; Witnesseth that the said Henry Walker (for and in consideracion of the somme of one hundred and fortie poundes of lawfull money of England to him in hande before th'ensealing hereof by the said William Shakespeare well & trulie paid, whereof and wherewith hee the said Henry Walker doth acknowledge himselfe fullie satisfied and contented, and thereof, and of every part and parcell thereof doth cleerlie acquite and discharge the saide William Shakespeare, his heires, executours, administratours and assignes, and every of them by theis presentes) hath bargayned and soulde and by theis presentes doth fullie, cleerlie, and absolutlie bargayne and sell vnto the said William Shakespeare, William Johnson, John Jackson, and John Hemming, their heires, and assignes forever; All that dwelling house or Tenement with th'appurtenaunces situate and being within the Precinct, circuit and compasse of the late black Fryers London, sometymes in the tenure of James Gardyner Esquiour,

and since that in the tenure of John Fortescue gent, and
now or late being in the tenure or occupacion of one
William Ireland or of his assignee or assignes; abutting
vpon a streete leading downe to Pudle wharffe on the
east part, right against the Kinges Maiesties Wardrobe;
part of which said Tenement is erected over a great gate
leading to a capitall Mesuage which sometyme was in the
tenure of William Blackwell Esquiour deceased, and
since that in the tenure or occupacion of the right Honorable Henry now Earle of Northumberland; And also all
that plott of ground on the west side of the same Tenement which was lately inclosed with boordes on two
sides thereof by Anne Bacon widowe, soe farre and in such
sorte as the same was inclosed by the said Anne Bacon,
and not otherwise, and being on the thirde side inclosed
with an olde Brick wall; Which said plott of ground was
sometyme parcell and taken out of a great peece of voide
ground lately vsed for a garden; And also the soyle wherevppon the said Tenement standeth; And also the said Brick
wall and boordes which do inclose the said plott of ground;
With free entrie, accesse, ingresse, egresse, and regresse
in, by and through the said greate gate and yarde there vnto
the vsuall dore of the said Tenement; And also all and
singuler cellours, sollers, romes, lightes, easiamentes,
profittes, commodities and hereditamentes whatsoever to
the said dwelling house or Tenement belonging, or in any
wise apperteyning; And the reversion and reversions whatsoever of all and singuler the premisses, and of every parcell
thereof; And also all rentes, and yearlie profittes whatsoever reserved and from hensforth to growe due and
paiable vpon whatsoever lease, dimise, or graunt, leases,
dimises or grauntes made of the premisses, or of any
parcell thereof; And also all thestate, right, title, interest,
propertie, vse, possession, clayme and demaund whatsoever which hee the said Henry Walker now hath, or of
right may, might, should, or ought to have of, in, or to the
premisses, or any parcell thereof; And also all and every
the deedes, evidences, charters, escriptes, minimentes, &
writinges whatsoever which hee the said Henry Walker

now hath, or any other person or persons to his vse have, or hath, or which hee may lawfullie come by without suite in the lawe, which touch or concerne the premisses onlie or onlie any part or parcell thereof; Togeither with the true coppies of all such deedes, evidences and writinges as concerne the premisses (amounges other thinges) to bee written and taken out at the onlie costes and charges of the said William Shakespeare his heires, or assignes. Which said dwelling house or Tenement, and other the premisses above by theis presentes mencioned to bee bargayned and soulde the said Henry Walker late purchased and had to him, his heires and assignes forever, of Mathie Bacon of Graies Inne in the countie of Middlesex gentleman, by Indenture bearing date the fifteenth day of October, in the yeare of our Lord God one thowsand six hundred and fower, and in the yeares of the reigne of our said Sovereigne Lord king James of his Realmes of England, Fraunce and Ireland the second, and of Scotland the eight & thirtithe; To haue and to holde the said dwelling house or Tenement, shopps, cellours, sollers, plott of ground and all and singuler other the premisses above by theis presentes mencioned to bee bargayned and soulde, and every part and parcell thereof with th'appurtenaunces, vnto the said William Shakespeare, William Johnson, John Jackson and John Hemmyng their heires, and assignes forever; To th'onlie & proper vse and behoofe of the said William Shakespeare, William Johnson, John Jackson and John Hemmyng their heires, and assignes forever. [*Vendor's covenants*] to Shakespeare for (i) freedom from encumbrances, 'Except the rentes and services to the cheefe lord or lordes of the fee or fees of the premisses from hensforth for or in respecte of his or their seigniorie or seigniories onlie to bee due and donne', to which a cancelled passage, not in the counterpart, added an exception for a lease granted by Henry Walker to William Irelaund, citizen and haberdasher of London, on 12 December 1604 for twenty-five years from the following Christmas at a rent of £7; (ii) quiet enjoyment; (iii) further assurance, on request within three years, 'And further

that all and every fyne and fynes to bee levyed, recoveryes
to bee suffered, estates and assurances at any tyme
or tymes hereafter to bee had, made, executed, or passed
by, or betweene the said parties of the premisses, or of
any parcell thereof, shalbee, and shalbee esteemed,
adiudged, deemed, and taken to bee to th'onlie and
proper vse and behoofe of the said William Shakespeare his heires, and assignes forever, and to none other
vse, intent or purpose.' In witnesse whereof the said
parties to theis Indentures interchaungablie have sett their
seales. Yeoven the day and yeares first above written.
William Shakspẽ   Wᵐ Johnsonn   Jo: Jacksonn.
[*Endorsed*.] Sealed and delivered by the said William
Shakespeare, William Johnson, and John Jackson, in the
presence of Will: Atkinson; Ed. Ouery; Robert Andrewes, scr.; Henry Lawrence, servant to the same scr.

(*b*) [1613, Mar. 11. From Mortgage (*Egerton MS.* 1787), facs. B.M.;
pr. in full, *Var*. ii. 591; H.P. ii. 34. It was found in 1768 among the
Fetherstonhaugh title-deeds. It was given to Garrick, but was missing in
1796 (Malone, *Inquiry*, 119) and had apparently returned to the family
solicitors. It was bought by the B.M. from one of the firm in 1858.
Ingleby, ii. 145, has confused it with the Guildhall purchase deed.]

This Indenture made the eleaventh day of March in the
yeares of the reigne of our Sovereigne Lord James, by
the grace of God, king of England, Scotland, Fraunce
and Ireland, defender of the faith, &c (that is to saie) of
England, Fraunce and Ireland the tenth, and of Scotland
the six and fortith; Betweene William Shakespeare, of
Stratford vpon Avon in the countie of Warwick, gentleman, William Johnson, citizein and Vintener of London,
John Jackson and John Hemmyng, of London, gentlemen, of th'one partie, and Henry Walker, citizein and
Minstrell of London, of th'other partie: Witnesseth that
the said William Shakespeare, William Johnson, John
Jackson and John Hemmyng, have dimised, graunted
and to ferme letten, and by theis presentes doe dimise,
graunt and to ferme lett vnto the said Henry Walker, All
that dwelling house or Tenement, with th'appurtenaunces,
situate and being within the precinct, circuit and compasse

of the late Black Fryers, London [*Description as in (a)*]
to haue and to holde the said dwelling house or Tenement,
cellers, sollers, romes, plott of ground, and all and singuler
other the premisses above by theis presentes mencioned
to bee dimised, and every part and parcell thereof, with
th'appurtenaunces, vnto the said Henrye Walker, his
executours, administratours and assignes, from the feast
of th'annunciation of the blessed Virgin Marye next
comming after the date hereof, unto th'ende and terme of
one hundred yeares from thence next ensuing and fullie
to bee compleat and ended, without ympeachment of or
for any manner of waste, Yeelding and paying therefore
yearlie during the said terme unto the said William
Shakespeare, William Johnson, John Jackson and John
Hemmyng, their heires and assignes, a pepper corne at
the feast of Easter yearlie, if the same bee lawfullie
demaunded, and noe more. Prouided alwayes that if the
said William Shakespeare, his heires, executours, administratours or assignes, or any of them, doe well and
trulie paie or cause to bee paid to the said Henry Walker,
his executours, administratours or assignes, the some of
threescore poundes of lawfull money of England in and
vpon the nyne and twentith day of September next
comming after the date hereof, at or in the nowe dwelling
house of the said Henry Walker, situate and being in the
parish of Saint Martyn neere Ludgate of London, at
one entier payment without delaie; That then and from
thensforth this presente lease, dimise and graunt, and all
and every matter and thing herein conteyned (other than
this provisoe) shall cease, determyne, and bee vtterlie
voyde, frustrate, and of none effect, as though the same
had never beene had ne made, theis presentes, or any
thing therein conteyned to the contrary thereof, in any
wise notwithstanding. [*Covenant* by Shakespeare to Walker
for freedom from encumbrances.] In witnesse whereof
the said parties to theis Indentures interchaungablie
have sett their seales. Yeoven the day and yeares first
above written. 1612. Wᵐ Shakspē, Wᵐ Johnson, Jo:
Jackson.

[Endorsed] Sealed and delivered by the said William Shakespeare, William Johnson, and John Jackson, in the presence of Will: Atkinson; Ed: Ouery; Robert Andrewes scr.; Henry Lawrence, servant to the same scr.

(*c*) [1615, Apr. 26–May 22. *Bill, Answer,* and *Decree* in suit of *Bendishe, et al. v. Bacon* (*R.O. Chancery Proceedings, Bills and Answers, Jac. 1,* Bundle B 11, No. 9; *Decrees and Orders,* vol. 1614ᴬ, p. 1074), pr. C. W. Wallace (1905, *Nebraska Univ. Studies,* v. 347; *E.S.* xxxvi. 56.]

(1) *Bill of Complaint.*

xxvjᵗᵒ die
Aprilis, 1615.
Saunders.

To the Right Honorable Sir Thomas Egerton Knight, Lord Ellesmere and Lord Chancellour of England.

Humblie complayninge sheweth vnto your Honorable Lordship your daylie oratoures Sir Thomas Bendishe Baronet, Edward Newport and Willyam Thoresbie Esquiours, Robert Dormer Esquiour **and Marie his wife, Willyam Shakespere, gent.,** and Richard Bacon Citezen of London, That wheareas your oratours be and are seuerallye lawfullie seised in there demesne as of fee of and in one capitall messuage or dwellinge howse with there appurtenaunces with two court yardes, and one void plot of grownd sometymes vsed for a garden on the east parte of the said dwellinge howse, and so much of one edifice as now or sometymes served for two stables and two haye loftes over the said stables and one litle colehowse adioyninge to the said stables, lyinge on the south side of the said dwellinge howse, and of another messuage or tenemente with thappurtenaunces now in the occupacion of Anthony Thompson and Thomas Perckes **and of there assignes, & of a void peece of grownd whervppon a stable is builded to the said meassuage belonginge,** and of seuerall othere howses devided into seuerall lodginges or dwellinge howses, toginther with all and singuler sellours, sollers, chambers, halls, parlours, yardes, backsides, easementes, profites and comodityes hervnto seuerallie belonginge, and of certaine void plotes of grownd adioyninge to the said messuages and premisses aforesaid or vnto some of them, and of a well howse,

All which messuages, tenementes and premisses aforesaid be lyinge within the precinct of Black Friers in the Cittye of London or Countye of Middlesex, late the messuages, tenementes and enheritances of Willyam Blackwell thelder, Henrie Blackwell and Willyam Blackwell the younger, and of Ann Bacon, or some or one of them, Vnto which foresaid capitall messuages, tenementes and premisses aforesaid seuerall deedes, charteres, letters patentes, evidences, munimentes and wrightinges be and are belonginge and apperteyninge and do belonge vnto your oratours, and doe serve for the provinge of your oratours lawfull right, title, interest and estate in, to and vnto the foresaid messuages and premisses, All which foresaid letters patentes, deedes, evidences, charteres, munimentes and wrightinges aforesaid were left in trust with Ann Bacon deceassed for and vnto the vse and behooffe of your orators; Now so yt is, may yt please your Honorable Lordship, that the said Ann Bacon beinge latelie dead and Mathy Bacon being her sole executour the foresaid letters patentes, deedes, charteres, and evidences, muniments and wrightinges aforesaid be since her death come vnto and now be in the handes and possession of the foresaid Mathy Bacon, who doth not clayme any right, estate or interest at all in or vnto the foresaid messuages or tenementes, Yet neuertheles the said Mathy Bacon, knowinge the messuages, tenementes, letters patentes, deedes, evidences, charteres, munimentes and wrightinges aforesaid to be belonging and onelie to belonge to your oratours, doth neuertheles withhould, keepe and deteyne awaye from your oratours the foresaid letters patentes and other deedes, evidences, charteres, munimentes and wrightinges aforesaid and will not deliuer the same vnto your oratours, wherby your oratours be in great danger for to loose and be disinherited of the messuages, tenementes and premisses aforesaid; In tender consideracon wherof and forasmuch as your oratours have no remoudye at and by the course of the common lawes of this realme for to have the said letters patentes, deedes, charteres, munimentes, evidences and wrightinges deliuered vnto

your oratours, for that your oratours doo not knowe the
certaine dates nor particuler contentes of them, nor
whither they be in box, bag or chist sealed or locked,
Therfore, that the said Mathy Bacon maye make
direct answere vnto the premisses and maye set downe
expresslie what letters patentes, deedes, evidences, charteres, munimentes or wrightinges he hath in his handes
or knoweth where they be, which concerne your oratours
or the messuages and premisses aforesaid or any of them,
and the same maye bringe into this honorable court to be
deliuered vnto your oratours, May yt please your Lordship to grant to your oratours his maiesties most gracious
writt of Subpena and also of Ducens tecum vnto him the
said Mathew Bacon to be directed commandinge him
therby, at a certaine daye and vnder a certaine payne
therin to be lymited, personallie to be and appeare before
your Lordship in his maiesties high court of Chancerie,
then and there for to make answere vnto the premisses,
and also to bring with him the said letters patentes, deedes,
evidences, charteres and wrightinges into this honorable
court, and to stand to and abide such further order therin
as to your Honorable Lordship shalbe thought fitt; And
your Lordships daylie oratours shalbe in all dewtye bownd
to pray for your good Lordship in all health and happines
long to contynue.

Lock.

(2) *Answer.*

Jur. 5 Maij 1615.   The answeare of Mathye Bacon
  Mat. Carew   gent. defendant to the bill of
  Pennyman   complaynte of Sir Thomas Bendishe
                       Baronett, Edward Newport esquier,
                       William Thoresbye esquier, Robert
                       Dormer esquier and Mary his
                       wife, William Shakespeare gent.
                       and Richard Bacon citizen of Lon-
                       don, complaynantes.

The said defendant, savinge to himselfe nowe and all
tymes hereafter all advantage and benefit of excepcion to
all and every the incertenties & insufficiencies of the said

bill of complaynte, saieth that hee thinketh it to be true
that the said complaynantes are lawfullye severally seised
in theire demesne as of fee of and in one capitall messuage
or dwellinge house with thappurtenances and other the tenementes, stables, edefices and voide groundes mencioned
in the said bill of complaynte, and likewise thinketh it to
be true that the same were late the messuages, tenementes
and inheritances of William Blackwell the elder deceased,
Henry Blakwell and William Blakwell the yonger, and
of Anne Bacon deceased mother of the said defendant,
or of some of them. And this Defendant further saieth
that hee doth not nowe clayme to haue any estate, right,
title or interest of, in or to the said premisses or any parte
or parcell thereof. And hee alsoe saith that one letteres
patentes and certeyne deedes, evidences, writinges and
mynumentes concernynge the said messuages, tenementes and other the premisses mencioned in the said
bill of complaynte or some of them are come to the
custodie & possession of this defendant as executor vnto
the said Anne Bacon his mother. But this defendant
denieth that the said letteres patentes, evidences, writinges
and mynumentes or any of them were left in trust with
the said Anne Bacon for and to the vse and behoofe of the
said complaynantes, or any of them, to the knowledge of
this defendant in any such manner as in the said complaynantes bill is sett forth and alledged. And this
defendant further saieth that hee doth not certeynelie
knowe whether the said letteres patentes, evidences,
writinges and mynumentes doe onlie belonge vnto the
said complaynantes or any of them or to any other person
or persons aswell as to the said complaynantes. And
therefore hee this defendant hath deteyned the same vntill
such tyme as hee may be lawfully and orderlie discharged
thereof vpon his deliuerie of the same. And soe as hee
may be discharged and saved harmles from all further
trouble, charge and damage, which maie hereafter happen
vnto him for or concernynge his possession of the said
letteres patentes, deedes, evidences, writinges and mynumentes, hee this defendant is and wilbe readie to deliver

all such letteres patentes, evidences, writinges and mynumentes concernynge the premisses, as came to the custodie
and possession of this defendant to his knowledge and
doe of right belonge vnto the said complaynantes or any
of them, vnto such person or persons and in such sorte
as this honorable court shall order and thinke meete,
without that anie other matter or thinge in the said
bill of complaynte mencioned materiall or effectuall in
lawe to be answeared vnto and herein before not sufficiently
answeared vnto, confessed and avoyded, traversed or
denied, is true. All which this defendante is and wilbe
readie to averre, maynteyne and prooue as this most
honorable court shall awarde, and humblie prayeth to be
dismissed forth of the same with his reasonable costes and
charges in this behalfe most wrongfully susteyned.

Blakwell.

(3) *Decree.*

xxij^do die Maij [1615].

Thomas Bendishe, Knight & Baronet, Edward Newporte et alii plaintiffes, Mathias Bacon gentleman defendant.

Whereas this corte was this presente daie informed by Mr Richard Moore, being of the plaintiffes counsell, that the said plaintiffes beinge seised in fee of and in one cappitall messuage with the appurtennces scituate in Black-fryers and that divers the letters patentes, deedes, evidences, charteres, mynumentes and writinges concerninge the same did heretofore come vnto the custodye of Anne Bacon, the defendants mother, as executrix to her mother, who latelie dyed and made the defendant her executor, and that by meanes hereof the said letters patentes, deedes, evidences and charters, mynumentes & writinges are nowe come vnto his handes, for obteyninge whereof the said plaintiffes have exhibited there bill into this corte, wherevnto the defendant havinge answered doth by his said aunswere confesse that one letters patentes and certeyne deedes, evidences & writinges & mynumentes concerninge the said messuages and premisses in the bill mencioned are come into his handes and possession, the said defendant not makeinge any title therevnto, but desiringe that hee maye be orderlie dischardged thereof vpon delivery of the same as this corte should thincke fitt, and therefore it was desired that the said letters pattentes and other the deedes, evidences and writinges soe confessed might be brought into this corte vppon the defendants oath. It is therevppon ordered that the said defendant shall bringe into this corte all the said letters patentes, deedes, evidences, writinges & mynumentes soe by him confessed to be in his custodye or possession vpon his oath, here to remayne to bee disposed of as shalbe meate, and for that purpose the plaintiffes maye take proces against the defendant if they will.

[The property was conveyed by (*a*) in joint ownership to Shakespeare, John Hemmyng, William Johnson, and John Jackson. There is no reason to suppose that Hemmyng, who did not sign either the conveyance or the mortgage deed, was any other than Heminges of the King's men. The commonness of the name makes it hazardous to identify Johnson with Queen Elizabeth's man.[1] Of Jackson nothing is known. Clearly these three were only trustees for Shakespeare, who paid the purchase-money and to whose use any further assurance was to be made. And in fact it was 'in performance of the confidence and trust in them reposed by William Shakespeare' that on 10 Feb. 1618 the three conveyed the property to John Greene of Clement's Inn (no. xix) and Mathew Morrys of Stratford, upon trusts agreeing with the terms of the entail in Shakespeare's will.[2] Elton suggested [3] that the object of the procedure of 1613 was to bar Shakespeare's widow from a right to dower on the property, and this would certainly have been the effect, as Chancery did not recognize a right to dower out of an equitable estate.[4] Presumably the mortgage was temporary, as security for a balance of the purchase-money. The property followed the fortunes of the entail down to about 1647 when means seem to have been found to sell it, probably to Edward Bagley, who conveyed it in 1667 to Sir Heneage Fetherston.[5] H.P. owned an abstract of title (1590–1723), from the title-deeds of the Fetherstonhaugh family, who succeeded to the Fetherstons.[6] From the same source he had Shakespeare's purchase-deed. The

[1] *Eliz. Stage*, ii. 324.   [4] Holdsworth, *Land Law*, 88.
[2] H.P. ii. 36.   [5] H.P. ii. 346.
[3] Lee 488.   [6] *Rarities*, 165.

abstract gave some additional facts, and others are in the suit (c), which is not itself of importance, being only friendly litigation, with the object of covering Mathias Bacon with the authority of the Court of Chancery in handing over the title-deeds of the property and of the larger estate of which it had formed a part.

The earlier history of the house is of interest. I communicated some of the following particulars about it to *The Times* of 23 Apr. 1928. It lay by and over the gate of a 'capital messuage' which had once been the lodging of the Prior of Blackfriars. In 1548, after the Dissolution, this lodging, a house of many chambers to the east of the great cloister and the south of the church choir, was granted, with the convent garden on the south of it, to Sir Francis Bryan. He died in 1550 and the lodging was occupied by Sir Anthony Aucher and Mr. Walsingham. By about 1554 it had passed to Thomas Thirlby, Bishop of Ely, who bought some additional land and buildings from Sir Thomas Cawarden; and from him shortly afterwards to Mr. Blackwell.[1] This was William Blackwell, town clerk of London from *c.* 1538 to his death *c.* 1569.[2] He was a cousin of Thirlby, and married Margaret Campion, a kinswoman of the 'martyr'. Among their children were William Blackwell the younger and Anne Bacon. I do not find Henry Blackwell. The house was left to Margaret, and with her Thirlby, deprived and committed to Lambeth, was given permission to lodge, just before his death in 1570 intervened.[3] In 1577 Katherine Carus, 'with all her pryde and popery', died in 'Bishop Thirlby's chamber' there.[4] In 1584 an examination in connexion with the charge of treason against Henry, eighth Earl of Northumberland, notes that the Countess was to be received at Mrs. Blackwell's house on her coming to town.[5] On 26 Nov. 1585 the sheriff of Sussex reported that, on search being made for Mrs. Margaret Blackwell, it was found that she was residing at Blackfriars. She refused to furnish a light horse, claiming to be no recusant, and furnished certificates of attendance at the church of St. Andrew's, Wardrobe.[6] Shortly afterwards she died, leaving the house to Anne Bacon for three years, after which it was to be divided and the proceeds divided between her and William.[7] Anne's husband was Thomas Bacon, formerly Serjeant of the Acatry to Queen Mary. He belonged to a Norfolk family, only remotely, if at all, related

[1] A. Feuillerat in *M.S.C.* ii. 3, 9, 103; *Eliz. Stage*, ii. 483.

[2] Strype, *Survey of London*, ii. 244.

[3] A. Jessopp, *One Generation of a Norfolk House*[2], 116, 124; H. Hall,

Society in the Eliz. Age, 109.

[4] Wright, ii. 67.

[5] *S.P.D.* clxvii. 13.

[6] *Ibid.* clxxxiv. 46.

[7] Jessopp 126.

to that of the Lord Keeper. Mathias Bacon, of Gray's Inn, was son of Thomas and Anne.[1] About 1586 Richard Frith, himself a dweller in Blackfriars,[2] reported his suspicions of 'One great howse in or adjoyning to the Blackfreres, wherein M[r] Blackwell, the towne clerke, sometyme dwelt '.[3] He says, 'Nowe there dwelleth in it one that is a very inconformable man to her Majesties proceedings. It hath sundry back-dores and bye-wayes, and many secret vaults and corners. It hath bene in tyme past suspected, and searched for papists but no good done for want of good knowledge of the back-dores and bye-wayes and of the dark corners.' He suggests a day-light search. In 1589 Edward Walpole, a Norfolk recusant, was licensed to resort to Mrs. Bacon at the Blackfriars.[4] It was pre-sumably after the division of the property under Margaret Black-well's will that Henry, ninth Earl of Northumberland, himself from time to time suspected of papistry, occupied the 'capital messuage'.

The gate-house came to Mathias Bacon in 1590,[5] and here the tradition of Catholic intrigue continued. I do not know anything of the first tenant named in (a), James Gardyner. The second, John Fortescue, of Lordington, Sussex, was nephew and in 1574 'servant' to Sir John Fortescue, who had his official residence as Master of the Wardrobe on the other side of St. Andrew's Hill. Unlike his uncle, he was a Catholic. His father, Sir Anthony, married a Pole, and was concerned in the conspiracy of 1562. John, who seems to have had a minor place in the Wardrobe, married Ellen, daughter of Ralph Henslowe, a recusant, of Boarhunt, Hants, who was kin to the Earls of Southampton.[6] In 1591 the priests Anthony Tyrrell and John Ballard, who himself used the *alias* of Fortescue, presented John and Ellen with 'such stuff as we brought from Rome'.[7] In 1591 'Fennell the priest doth use to come very muche to M[r] John Fortescue his house'.[8] John and his uncle were warned by Richard Topcliffe, the priest-hunter, of the risk he ran, and on 1 Mar. 1598 the house was searched for hidden priests on a report from William Udall, who described it as having 'many places of secret conveyance in it', apparently communicating with

[1] *Harl. Soc.* xv. 38; *Machyn's Diary,* 300; W. Rye, *Norfolk Families,* 13.
[2] *Eliz. Stage,* ii. 494.
[3] Wright, ii. 249.
[4] *Stiffkey Papers,* 169; H. Foley, *Records of the Society of Jesus,* ii. 235.
[5] *H.P.* ii. 345.
[6] Lord Clermont, *Family of Fortes-*

cue[2], 255, 317, 426; *V.H. Hants,* iii. 145; Foley, v. 960; St. G. K. Hyland, *A Century of Persecution,* 380.
[7] J. Morris, *Troubles of our Catholic Forefathers,* ii. 372.
[8] Foley, i. 380, from *S.P.D. Eliz.* ccxxxviii. 62.

'secret passages towards the water'. Fortescue was away. His wife resisted the searchers, and, according to Udall, one of two priests who were there slipped away with Hugh the butler. An examination of Ellen Fortescue and her daughters Katherine and Elizabeth produced admissions of recusancy, but denial of the presence of priests.[1] John attempted to clear himself in a letter to the Earl of Essex, with whom he claimed cousinship: [2]

> I crave no favor ether of her Mati or of any peere within this Realme, yf any unnaturall or disloyall fact can be proved against me ether in harboringe, maintaininge or abbettinge ether prist or Jesuit, and forbidden by her highnes lawes. And in this serche at my howse (my self beinge in the Countrey) There was nothinge founde within my commande in all my howse, but suche things as my lewde and wretched butler had locked in a desk of his within that office, so farr from my knolledge (on my Salvation) as is heven from yerthe. And nothing, Right honorable, can torment me more, then that her Mati should think me so undutifull, in whose service I have bine imployd thes 21 yers, and never yet tutched with any blott of suche disorder, and not lickly I would bereve my self of that benefytt which hathe maintained my self, my wyfe and children thes many yeres. And in which spaece yf I have retayned my consciens at all, her Mati: hathe bine no looser by yt, nor my self, God knowith, any greate gainer.

Time has its revelations. The autobiography of the Jesuit Oswald Greenway [3] records how, on the day after the raid, he called at the house, which he believed in error to be Sir John's, and was told that there had been priests there, of whom one was Joseph Pollen, but that by God's grace they had got into hiding-places. John Fortescue and his wife, and his 'two little girls, held to be the fairest in London' were confined, and there was fear that John would lose his place in the Wardrobe. Greenway's informant was probably Ellen's brother, Henry Henslowe. In after life, John Fortescue and his wife retired to St. Omer. Their son George was the author of *Feriae Academicae* (1630). Their daughter Katharine married Francis Bedingfield and gave eleven daughters to religion. Their daughter Elizabeth married Sir John Beaumont of Grace Dieu, brother of Francis Beaumont.[4] A curious document bearing upon the Gunpowder Plot is printed by Clermont 433 from a copy once at Douai and now, as I learn by the kindness of Father William Godfrey, at St. Cuthbert's College, Ushaw, Durham.

---

[1] *Hatfield MSS.* vii. 138, misdated in *Cal.*; viii. 74; xiv. 57.
[2] Clermont 435.
[3] Morris, *Troubles*, i. 141.
[4] Foley, i. 682; v. 568, 960; vi. 255; *Catholic Record Soc. Misc.* vi. 240, 423.

Relatio quorumdam Catholicorum de Patre Gerardo Jesuitâ

Narrationem hanc sequentem nos infrascripti accepimus a Viro quodam Catholico et fide digno qui illam nobis narravit partim ex ore perillustris D. Dñi Joannis Fortescue, partim ex ore conjugis ejus Dña⟨e⟩ Helenae Fortescue, qui Audomari diem suum sancte obiêre. Pater Joannes Gerardus Societatis Jesu Sacerdos venit ad domum dicti Domini Joannis Fortescue quae sita erat prope monasterium olim Si Dominici, Londini, vulgò, Black-Fryers, et opportunitatem nactus dum Dñus Fortescue abesset, instanter petiit a Dña Fortescue ut cubiculum aliquod haberet domi suae. At illa, semper mihi gratus est adventus tuus: at ille respondit se velle cubiculum privatum ubi aliqui illum convenirent qui cum illo videri libenter nollent. Illa prudens quidem foemina non bene digerebat illa verba scilicet quosdam illum frequentaturos qui cum illo libenter videri nollent, petiit itaque ab illo quinam illi essent. Respondit ille viros esse praestantes, generosos, atque Catholicos, adhuc vero illâ urgente quinam essent nominavit Catsbeum, Perseum, Vintorum, Digbeum et plures alios conjurationis pulverariae conscios, nec praeter conjuratores nominavit quemquam. Tum Dña Fortescue, quosdam, inquit, ex illis aliquantulum novi, ut Catsbeum, Vintorum. Catsbeum, inquit, nunquam probavi nec mores ejus, cum sit vitae admodum laxae: quare petiit a patre Gerardo ut ignosceret illi quod in absentia mariti sui denegaret accessum horum virorum ad domum suam. Hoc responso accepto abiit Pater Gerardus, descenditque in domum in vicinio positam Domini Doret, ubi tota familia aberat muliere tantum exceptâ quae domûs curam gerebat: cum hac egit et obtinuit Pater Gerardus ut viri illi Nobiles prius nominati, caeterique conjurationis pulverariae participes privatim illum convenirent in illa domo, quod postea publicè probatum est, etiam testibus ipsis pincernis Taberniae adjacentis qui illos omnes quotidie ingredientes et egredientes conspexerant. At patefacta postmodum conjuratione et Patre Gerardo nominatim publicis per totum Regnum edictis proscripto, Pater Gerardus supposi⟨ti⟩tiâ barbâ et capillamento conficto domum Dñi Fortescue adit et de improviso absque ullâ praevia notitia petit a Dño Fortescue ut in domum suam illum reciperet quod plane nesciret ubi absconderet caput suum: quem intuens Dnus Fortescue plenus dolore ait, Neminem habes quem perdas praeter me et meam familiam.

The signatories are not given in the copy, which is dated 1631, in a later hand, probably that of John Kirk (1760–1851), on the information of Alban Butler. I do not find this incident referred to in J. Morris, *Life of Father John Gerard*[3] (1881), or S. R. Gardiner, *What the Gunpowder Plot Was* (1897). It cannot have been before the autumn of 1605, as Digby was only then brought into the plot, and although clearly Fortescue was still in the Blackfriars, it is not clear that he was still in the gate-house. This was sold for £100 by Mathias Bacon in 1604 to Henry Walker[1] and leased by

[1] H.P. ii. 345.

him to William Ireland, haberdasher (*a*), on 12 December of that year. He did not occupy it until later,[1] and possibly Fortescue remained as sub-tenant. On the other hand the priest Richard Dudley was reported on 31 May 1599 to be in Robinson's house, steward to Sir John Foskewe, over against Sir John's door.[2] This looks rather like the gate-house, but was more probably hard by, as a John Robinson was already a Blackfriars resident in 1596.[3] The steward was dead by 1613, and left two sons, of whom one, Edward, entered the English College at Rome.[4] The other is unnamed. He might conceivably be the John Robinson mentioned in Shakespeare's will as his tenant at Blackfriars. William Ireland's lease appears to have been surrendered while the conveyance to Shakespeare was in preparation. But it was he who gave his name to the present Ireland Yard, to the north of and over the entrance to which from St. Andrew's Hill the gate-house probably stood. On the south of the gate represented by this entrance may have been the Porter's Hall theatre built in 1615 and soon suppressed.[5] I think that the house 'near St. Andrew's church' figured in H.P., *1848*, 247, and said to have been occupied until the 19th century by Robinsons, must be another one. St. Andrew's Church is on the other side of the Hill from the Blackfriars, and the entail papers show that by 1639 one Dicks, cordwainer, had succeeded to Robinson's tenancy of the gate-house.]

XXIV. SHAKESPEARE'S WILL

[1616, Mar. 25. The original is preserved in the Principal Probate Registry at Somerset House. There are facsimiles by J. H. Friswell (1864) and in H. Staunton, *Memorials of Shakespeare* (n.d. ⟨1864⟩), *Jahrbuch*, xxiv (1889), S. A. Tannenbaum, *Problems in Shakespeare's Penmanship* (1927). I have also used a recent photograph by R. B. Fleming & Co. The will was found by Joseph Greene, an extract from whose letter of 1747 sending a copy to James West is in H.P., *1848*, 274 from *Lansd. MS.* 721, f. 2. A copy of 1747 by Joseph Greene is noted in H.P., *Rarities*, 114. The first print was in *Biographia Britannica*, vi (1763) 1. 3627 (art. signed 'P'). The writing, in an English hand, covers one side of each of three sheets. The second alone is numbered. When found, the sheets were fastened together by a narrow strip of parchment along the top margins. Now (Lee 520) each sheet has been mended with transparent material, and placed in a separate locked oaken frame between two sheets of glass, to which it is fixed. The first signature has become illegible, and a few other

---

[1] H.P. ii. 346.
[2] *Hatfield MSS.* ix. 186.
[3] *Eliz. Stage*, iv. 320.
[4] Foley, vi. 264.
[5] *Eliz. Stage*, ii. 472.

words are very obscure. There is practically no punctuation; I have added a minimum. The inventory exhibited at probate has not been found. A search of 1881 described by Furnivall in *N.S.S. Trans.* (1880–6) 15† makes it probable that most of the early 17th-century inventories at the P.C.C. perished in the Fire of London.]

⟨*Sheet 1*⟩

Vicesimo Quinto die ~~Januarij~~ **Martij** Anno Regni Domini nostri Jacobi nunc Regis Anglie &c decimo quarto & Scotie xlix° Annoque domini 1616.

T⟨*estamentum*⟩ W⟨*illel*⟩mj Shackspeare.

R⟨*ecognoscatu*⟩r. In the name of god Amen I William Shackspeare of Stratford vpon Avon in the countie of Warr gent in perfect health & memorie god be praysed doe make & Ordayne this my last will & testament in manner & forme followeing. That is to saye ffirst I Comend my Soule into the handes of god my Creator, hoping & assuredlie beleeving through thonelie merittes of Jesus Christe my Saviour to be made partaker of lyfe everlastinge, And my bodye to the Earth whereof yt ys made. Item I Gyve & bequeath vnto my ~~sonne in L~~ daughter Judyth One Hundred & ffyftie poundes of lawfull English money to be paied vnto her in manner & forme followeing; That ys to saye, One Hundred Poundes **in discharge of her marriage porcion** within one yeare after my deceas, with consideracion after the Rate of twoe shillinges in the pound for soe long tyme as the same shalbe vnpaied vnto her after my deceas, & the ffyftie poundes Residewe thereof vpon her Surrendring **of**, or gyving of such sufficient securitie as the overseers of this my will shall like of to Surrender or graunte, All her estate & Right that shall discend or come vnto her after my deceas or **that shee** nowe hath of in or to one Copiehold tenemente with thappurtenaunces lyeing & being in Stratford vpon Avon aforesaied in the saied countie of Warr, being parcell or holden of the mannour of Rowington, vnto my daughter Susanna Hall & her heires for ever. Item I Gyve & bequeath vnto my saied daughter Judith

PLATE XIX

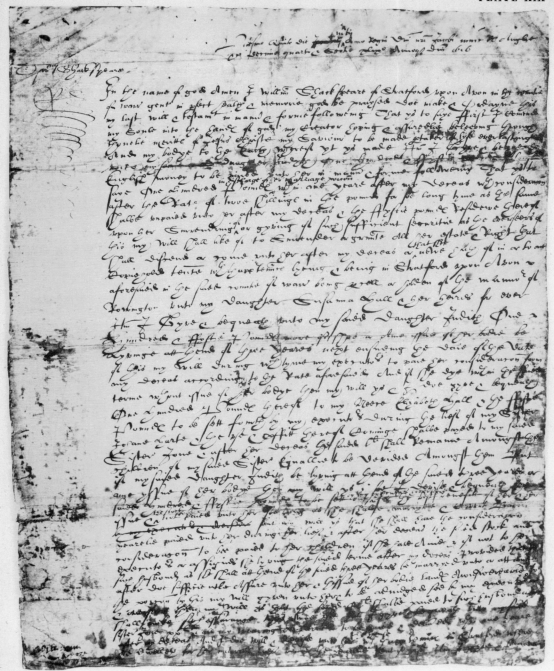

SHAKESPEARE'S WILL (*First Sheet*)

One Hundred & ffyftie Poundes more if shee or Anie
issue of her bodie be Lyvinge att thend of three Yeares
next ensueing the daie of the date of this my will, during
which tyme my executours to paie her consideracion from
my deceas according to the Rate aforesaied. And if she
dye within the saied terme without issue of her bodye then
my will ys & I doe gyve & bequeath One Hundred
Poundes thereof to my Neece Elizabeth Hall & the
ffiftie Poundes to be sett fourth by my executours during
the lief of my Sister Johane Harte & the vse & profitt
thereof Cominge shalbe payed to my saied Sister Jone, &
after her deceas the saied l^{li} shall Remaine Amongst the
children of my saied Sister Equallie to be devided Amongst
them. But if my saied daughter Judith be lyving att thend
of the saied three Yeares or anie yssue of her bodye, then
my will ys & soe I devise & bequeath the saied Hundred
& ffyftie poundes to be sett out **by my executours &
overseers** for the best benefitt of her & her issue & **the
stock** not **to be** paied vnto her soe long as she shalbe
marryed & covert Baron ~~by my executours & overseers,~~
but my will ys that she shall have the consideracion yearelie
paied vnto her during her lief & after her deceas the saied
stock and consideracion to bee paied to her children
if she have Anie & if not to her executours or assignes
she lyving the saied terme after my deceas. Provided
that yf such husbond as she shall att thend of the
saied three Yeares be marryed vnto or attaine after doe
sufficientlie Assure vnto her & thissue of her bodie landes
Awnswereable to the porcion by this my will gyven vnto
her & to be adiudged soe by my executours & over-
seers then my will ys that the said cl^{li} shalbe paied to
such husbond as shall make such assurance to his owne
vse. Item I gyve & bequeath vnto my saied sister
Jone xx^{li} & all my wearing Apparrell to be paied &
deliuered within one yeare after my deceas, And I doe
will & devise vnto her **the house** with thappurtenaunces
in Stratford wherein she dwelleth for her naturall lief
vnder the yearelie Rent of xij^d. Item I gyve and bequeath
⟨(*In left margin now illegible*) William Shakspere⟩

⟨*Sheet 2*⟩

Vnto her three sonns Welliam Harte ⟨*blank*⟩
Hart & Michaell Harte ffyve poundes A peece
to be payed within one Yeare after my deceas.
~~to be sett out for her within one Yeare after my deceas~~
~~by my executours with thadvise & direccions of my~~
~~overseers for her best proffitt vntill her Marriage and then~~
~~the same with the increase thereof to be paied vnto~~
her. Item I gyve & bequeath vnto ~~her~~ the saied Elizabeth
Hall All my Plate (except my brod silver & gilt bole)
that I now have att the date of this my will. Item I gyve
& bequeath vnto the Poore of Stratford aforesaied tenn
poundes, to m^r Thomas Combe my Sword, to Thomas
Russell Esquier ffyve poundes, & to ffrauncis Collins
of the Borough of Warr in the countie of Warr gent
thirteene poundes Sixe shillinges & Eight pence to be paied
within one Yeare after my deceas. Item I gyve & bequeath to ~~m^r Richard Tyler thelder~~ Hamlett Sadler xxvj^s
viij^d to buy him A Ringe, to William Raynoldes gent xxvj^s
viij^d to buy him A Ringe, to my godson William Walker
xx^s in gold, to Anthonye Nashe gent xxvj^s viij^d, & to
Mr John Nashe xxvj^s viij^d ~~in gold~~, & to my ffellowes
John Hemynge Richard Burbage & Henry Cundell xxvj^s
viij^d A peece to buy them Ringes. Item I Gyve Will
bequeath & Devise vnto my daughter Susanna Hall
for better enabling of her to performe this my will &
towardes the performans thereof All that Capitall Messuage or tenemente with thappurtenaunces in Stratford
aforesaied Called the newe place wherein I nowe dwell
& twoe messuages or tenementes with thappurtenaunces
scituat lyeing & being in Henley streete within the borough of Stratford aforesaied, And all my barnes stables
Orchardes gardens landes tenementes & hereditamentes
whatsoever scituat lyeing & being or to be had Receyved
perceyved or taken within the townes Hamlettes villages
ffieldes & groundes of Stratford vpon Avon Oldstratford
Bushopton & Welcombe or in anie of them in the saied
countie of Warr, And alsoe All that Messuage or tene-

PLATE XX

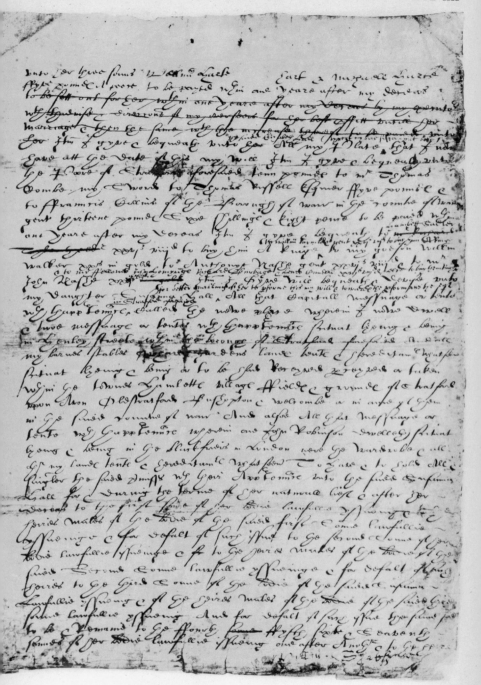

SHAKESPEARE'S WILL (*Second Sheet*)

mente with thappurtenaunces wherein one John Robinson
dwelleth, scituat lyeing & being in the blackfriers in
London nere the Wardrobe, & all other my landes tenementes and hereditamentes whatsoever; To Have & to
hold All & singuler the saied premisses with their
Appurtennaunces vnto the saied Susanna Hall for &
during the terme of her naturall lief, & after her Deceas
to the first sonne of her bodie lawfullie yssueing & to the
heires Males of the bodie of the saied first Sonne lawfullie
yssueing, & for defalt of such issue to the second Sonne
of her bodie lawfullie issueing and ~~so~~ to the heires Males
of the bodie of the saied Second Sonne lawfullie yssueinge,
& for defalt of such heires to the third Sonne of the bodie
of the saied Susanna Lawfullie yssueing and of the heires
Males of the bodie of the saied third sonne lawfullie
yssueing, And for defalt of such issue the same soe to be
& Remaine to the ffourth ~~sonne~~ ffyfth sixte & Seaventh
sonnes of her bodie lawfullie issueing one after Another
& to the heires

2   Willm̃ Shakspere

⟨*Sheet 3*⟩

Males of the bodies of the said fourth fifth Sixte &
Seaventh sonnes lawfullie yssueing, in such manner as
yt ys before Lymitted to be & Remaine to the first second
and third Sonns of her bodie & to their heires Males;
And for defalt of such issue the said premisses to be &
Remaine to my sayed Neece Hall & the heires males of
her bodie Lawfullie yssueing, and for defalt of issue to my
daughter Judith & the heires Males of her bodie lawfullie
yssueing, And for defalt of such issue to the Right heires
of me the saied William Shackspere for ever. **Item I
gyve vnto my wief my second best bed with the furniture**
Item I gyve & bequeath to my saied daughter Judith my
broad silver gilt bole. All the Rest of my goodes chattels
Leases plate Jewels & householde stuffe whatsoever, after
my dettes and Legasies paied & my funerall expences
discharged, I gyve devise & bequeath to my Sonne in
Lawe John Hall gent & my daughter Susanna his wief

whom I ordaine & make executours of this my Last will and testament. And I doe intreat & Appoint **the saied** Thomas Russell Esquier & ffrauncis Collins gent to be overseers hereof. And doe Revoke All former wills & publishe this to be my last will and testament. In witnesse whereof I have hereunto put my ~~Seale~~ **hand** the daie & Yeare first aboue Written.

witnes to the publishing   By me Wılliam Shakspeare.
hereof. Fra: Collyns
Julyus Shawe
John Robinson
Hamnet Sadler
Robert Whattcott

[*Endorsed*] Probatum coram magistro Willielmo Byrde legum doctore Comissario &c xxij^do die mensis Junij Anno domini 1616. Juramento Johannis Hall vnius executoris &c Cui &c de bene &c Jurato. Reservata potestate &c Susanne Hall alteri executori &c cum venerit &c petitura

Inventorium exhibitum

[The structure and terms of the will are considered in H. Staunton, *Memorials of Sh.*; H.P. i. 252; ii. 390; Lee 482, 487; Adams 460; S. A. Tannenbaum, *A New Study of Sh.'s Will*;[1] and incidentally in connexion with the signatures (cf. vol. i, p. 505). I have had the advantage of discussion with Dr. Greg.

The text is probably in the hand of a clerk employed by Francis Collins, a solicitor of Warwick, who no doubt drafted the will; the ink of sheet 1 appears to be slightly lighter than that of the others. The attestation of Collins is presumably in his own hand. The names of the other witnesses are written with the same pen and ink, not that used by Collins; Dr. Greg thinks that each wrote his own name, and Dr. Tannenbaum that this pen and ink were also used by the clerk for the interlineations.

Most of the interlineations and cancellations are such as might naturally be made either in the process of drafting or on reading over a draft will with a view to final settlement of its terms. They correct slips, make the legal terminology more precise, or incor-

[1] 1926; repr. *Problems in Sh.'s Penmanship*, 66.

PLATE XXI

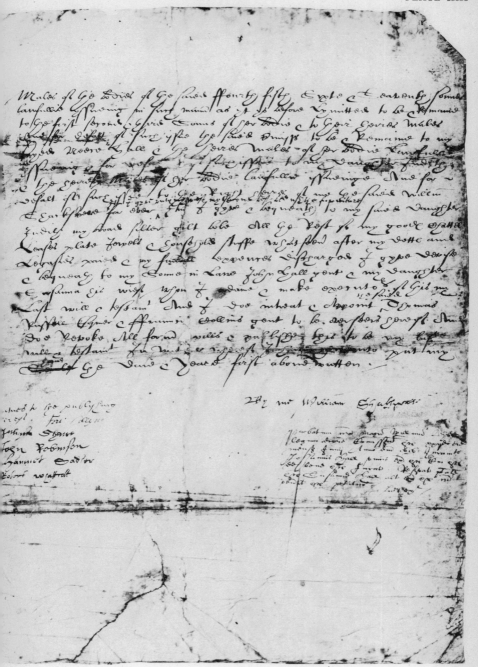

SHAKESPEARE'S WILL (*Third Sheet*)

porate afterthoughts. There are, however, some odd features. At the top of sheet 1 'Martij' has been substituted for a word which Malone and others incorrectly read 'Februarij', which is probably 'Januarij', but which Dr. Greg thinks might conceivably be 'Jacobi', since there is a protuberance above the line, a little to the right of the middle of the word. Alternatively, he thinks, an attempt may at first have been made to correct the word to 'Martij' without cancelling it. The writing at the foot of sheet 1 is cramped and comes very near the bottom margin. That at the top of sheet 2 begins with two lines written higher up than one would expect from a comparison with the other sheets. And these are followed by a cancelled passage, with which they can never have had any sense-connexion. This passage must originally have been the conclusion of something other than what now precedes it, and this something was probably at the foot of a sheet 1. The following hypothesis seems best to fit the facts. In or before a January, probably of 1616, Shakespeare gave instructions for a will. Collins prepared a complete draft for execution in that month. It was not then executed, but on 25 Mar. 1616 Shakespeare sent for Collins. The changes he desired in the opening provisions were so substantial that it was thought best to prepare a new sheet 1. The heading and initial formulas as to health and religious expectation were adapted by the clerk from the old draft. He gave correctly the calendar year which had begun on the very day on which he wrote, and the regnal year which had begun on the day before; and this of itself shows that the present sheet 1 cannot be earlier than 25 Mar. 1616. But he made, and afterwards corrected, the slip of transcribing 'Januarij' from the old draft. Then the opening provisions were dictated afresh with one or two corrections, such as the elimination of 'sonne in L', during the process, and proved so much longer than those they replaced, as to crowd the writing and necessitate the carrying of two lines on to the old sheet 2, where they were inserted before a cancelled passage. The rest of this sheet and sheet 3 were allowed to stand, with some alterations; and in this form it was signed on each sheet by Shakespeare, 'published' by his declaration to the witnesses that it was his will, and signed by them. Sheet 1 is mainly occupied with bequests in favour of Shakespeare's daughter Judith, and it is reasonable to suppose that it was her marriage on 10 Feb. 1616 which determined the principal changes. As the will finally stood, Judith was to receive £100 as her marriage 'porcion', and £50 more contingently on her resignation to her sister of any right in Shakespeare's Rowington copyhold. Of another £150 she was to have the interest. If she died without issue in three years, the capital was to be divided between Shakespeare's grand-daughter Elizabeth Hall, whom he calls his 'neece', and his sister Joan Hart. If not, and if any husband, whom Judith might have at the end of the three years or might thereafter 'attaine', had made a settlement upon her and her issue of lands answerable to her portion, it was to be paid to him. If no such settlement had been made, the sum was to be held in trust for her and her heirs. Palaeographically the word 'attaine' might also be read, and has been read, 'att anie'. But this would involve a *lacuna*, while 'attaine' gives an adequate and complete sense. The scribe of an old copy at the P.C.C., cited by Staunton, wrote 'attayne'. Possibly the elaborate provisions with regard to Judith indicate a lack of confidence in Thomas Quiney. Some students have thought that the will also indicates displeasure with Judith herself, either at her marriage or at its accompanying excommunication, and have suggested that Shakespeare originally left all his plate to Judith, and in the end cut her off with his silver-gilt bowl. This implies that the 'her' in the cancelled passage at the top of sheet 2, and the cancelled 'her' in the next line, which clearly go together, referred in the first draft to Judith. But it is possible that they referred to Elizabeth Hall; and if so the inference may be, not that Judith was less tenderly treated in the revision, but that a trust fund originally meant, wholly or in part for Elizabeth, was transferred to make better provision for Judith, and Elizabeth left with only a reversion. Moreover, the specific bequest of the silver-gilt bowl to Judith is unaltered in sheet 3 from the original draft, and would have been superfluous there if sheet 2 had already given her all the plate. I think that the bulk of the plate was always for Elizabeth, although, curiously enough, an inconsistent mention of 'plate' appears in the residuary bequest to John and Susanna Hall.

And now as to the 'second best bed'. A good deal of sheer nonsense has been written about this. Wills have been ransacked,[1] for cases, none quite analogous, of other bequests of solitary or inferior household articles. And baseless theories of domestic discord or infirmity have been devised to account for the absence of any further provision in the will for Shakespeare's wife. No such provision was needed. If no equivalent jointure had been substituted, as to which there is no evidence, Mrs. Shakespeare would have been entitled by common law [2] to her dower of a life interest in one-third of any of the testator's heritable estates on which dower had not, as in the

---

[1] *Var.* ii. 609; H.P. i. 258; Adams 466; S. O. Addy in *N.Q.* cl. 39, with   letters in *Times*, 18–22 Jan. 1926.
[2] Challis 345.

case of the Blackfriars property (no. xxiii), been legally barred; and
to residence in his principal mansion house. Whether she would
also be entitled to 'free-bench' in copyhold property would depend
on the custom of the manor. The normal Rowington custom [1] was
to admit the widow on payment of 1*d.*; otherwise the estate passed
to sons or daughters according to the rule of primogeniture. It is
doubtful (no. xv) whether this applied to the outlying property in
Stratford, and Mrs. Shakespeare does not appear to have paid her
1*d.* Whether the widow was entitled to a third of personalty
similarly depended upon local custom; the Warwickshire custom is
unknown. Such legal or customary rights are sometimes incorporated in the provisions of wills, sometimes not; they would be
operative in either event. A best bed might naturally be treated, as
by Thomas Combe in his will of 1608 (cf. p. 136), as an heirloom.
To regard the interlineated bequest as a deliberate slight is absurd.
If an explanation is wanted, let us guess that, when the draft will
was read over, Mrs. Shakespeare asked for the bed; it had come
from her old home at Hewland.

Why was the will executed in the form of a much-corrected
draft, unpunctuated and unparagraphed, instead of in a fair copy?
One answer is that such was the practice of Francis Collins. John
Combe's will, made by Collins long before his death, is in the same
condition. Lawyers, indeed, are never fond of relying on punctuation. Elizabethan probate courts were not particular as to the form
of a will, where only personal property was involved. But where
there was real property, the will had to be in writing and evidence
of its publication forthcoming. This ordinarily took the form of
testimony by two or three witnesses to the testator's signature. On
this point Collins was careful enough, and as two of the witnesses
were legatees, whose legacies would be invalidated if they had to
give testimony, he secured five. Even then the rough form of the
will might give rise to legal questions, and Dr. Tannenbaum is
probably right in thinking that a fair copy was dispensed with
because of some need for haste, such as the serious illness of the
testator. It is not inconsistent with this that Shakespeare in fact
lived for nearly a month after his will was signed, or that the pre-
amble describes him as 'in perfect health and memorie'. No doubt
invalid testators are often described as 'sick in body, but of perfect
mind and memory', but the phrase may have been allowed to stand
from the original sheet 1, and would be of little importance, so long
as the testator was mentally of testamentary capacity. Dr. Tannen-

---

[1] Elton 131.

baum finds further evidence of failing powers in the character of Shakespeare's signatures (cf. vol. i, p. 507), and of haste in certain ambiguities in the terms of the bequest to Judith. These are not, I think, very serious, and a court would probably find no great difficulties of interpretation. It is not, perhaps, quite clear whether the 'porcion' to be met by a husband's assurance of 'answerable' lands was the specific marriage 'porcion' of £100 or the whole bequest of £300.

Of Shakespeare's minor legatees, most belonged to families of good standing in Stratford; Hamlet Sadler, the probable godfather of his lost son (no. i); Anthony and John Nash, father and uncle of the Thomas who later married Elizabeth Hall (no. i); Thomas Combe, brother of the encloser and nephew of the usurer (no. xviii); William Reynolds, a connexion by marriage of the Combe family (no. xviii); William Walker, probably son of Henry Walker, mercer, alderman, and bailiff of Stratford. Why a bequest to Richard Tyler, also of Stratford, was cancelled, we do not know; he was still alive. Francis Collins himself came to Stratford to replace Thomas Greene as town clerk in 1616 and died in 1617.[1] London friends are remembered in three of Shakespeare's 'fellows' of the King's men, and possibly in Thomas Russell, if Lee 492 rightly identifies him with a London metallurgist of that name, known to Bacon and Drayton. But an 'overseer' is likely to have been a neighbour, and Thomas may have been one of a family of Russells of Strensham, Worcestershire, who had held Clifford Chambers before the Rainsfords.[2] The witnesses, other than Collins and Sadler, were Julius Shaw, an alderman who lived next door but one to New Place in Chapel St., Robert Whatcott, who had appeared for Susanna Hall in the Consistory case of 1613 (no. i), and John Robinson, presumably not Shakespeare's Blackfriars tenant, but a Stratford man whose baptism is recorded in 1589.

Surprise has been felt that the will contains no mention of books or manuscripts. There was no reason why it should, unless the testator wished to make a special bequest of such articles. A will is a legal instrument for devising property, and not a literary auto-biography. Books and manuscripts may have appeared in the lost inventory. In any case, they would pass to John and Susanna Hall under the residuary bequest of 'goods'. In fact Hall, by his will of 1635,[3] left his 'study of bookes' and his manuscripts to Thomas

[1] H.P., *Cal.* 104.
[2] *Harl. Soc.* xxvii. 119; J. Maclean
in *Bristol and Gloc. Arch. Soc.* xiv. 63.
[3] H.P. ii. 61.

Nash, and under Nash's will of 1642 [1] any that remained probably passed to his wife as his residuary legatee. Whether books belonging to Shakespeare were among them, and whether he kept any manuscripts of his plays, or handed them all to the King's men, we do not know. Bailiffs took some books from the study about 1637.[2]

A word as to the devolution of the entailed estate. Lee 489 is clearly wrong in stating that this included the Rowington copyhold and the interest in tithes. The copyhold followed the custom of the manor and the tenancy possibly ended (no. xv) with Susanna's life. The interest in tithes was a lease for a term of years. It passed to the Halls under the residuary bequest, and they were able to sell, as they did (p. 126) in 1625. Probably Shakespeare had himself parted with his theatrical leases. The entailed estate, although described in very wide terms in the will, seems in fact to have consisted of New Place, the Henley St. houses, the Old Stratford land, and the Blackfriars house, the trustees of which made a conveyance (no. xxiii), on 10 Feb. 1618, to bring its trusts into harmony with those of the entail. But the hopes of the will were doomed to failure. Susanna Hall had no issue, other than Elizabeth. Elizabeth had no issue. Judith Quiney's last child died in February 1639. Steps were taken to bar the entail. A settlement of 'the inheritance of William Shakespeere gent. deceased' was made by Susanna and the Nashs on 27 May 1639, and was followed by fines and a fictitious legal action.[3] Possibly Judith was compensated. Her expectation was small, and in fact she predeceased Elizabeth. The Harts, who had no legal claim, may have had a promise of Henley St. Under the settlement the estate was vested successively in Susanna, Thomas and Elizabeth Nash and the survivor, their joint issue, the issue of Elizabeth, and the heirs and assigns of Thomas. On the strength of this Thomas appears to have thought that he was entitled to dispose of it by will; which he would have been, if the settlement had continued. His will of 26 Aug. 1642 and codicil of 4 Apr. 1647, while making ample provision for Elizabeth out of his own property, left New Place, the Old Stratford land, and the Blackfriars house to his cousin (cf. no. i) Edward Nash, and directed that Edward should settle it on his own son Thomas.[4] On 4 Apr. 1647 the elder Thomas died. Fresh procedure was set on foot to defeat the intention of his will. Presumably the trustees made a surrender to Susanna and Elizabeth. These made a fresh settlement on 2 June 1647 [5] vesting the estate successively in Susanna, Elizabeth, and

---

[1] *Var.* ii. 619.

[2] *Times* (6 May 1930).

[3] B.P. *Cat.* 68, pr. Halliwell, *1848*,

309.

[4] *Var.* ii. 619.

[5] B.P. *Cat.* 69, pr. Halliwell, *1848*,

314.

any issue of Elizabeth, and leaving Elizabeth free to dispose of it in default of issue. A complaint of February 1648 in an action brought by Edward Nash in defence of the will, and apparently compromised, seems to show that means were found to sell the Blackfriars property, probably to Edward Bagley, who resold it in 1667.[1] On 5 June 1649 Elizabeth married John, who became Sir John, Bernard, and her mother's death on 11 July left the Bernards in control of the inheritance. On 20 Oct. 1652 a third settlement of New Place and the Stratford land, but not of Henley St., was made upon the husband and wife in survivorship, with remainder to their issue, or in default as Elizabeth might appoint.[2] On 18 Apr. 1653 she made a deed of appointment, to trustees for sale to the benefit of such persons as she might nominate.[3] And the nomination is in her will of 29 Jan. 1670.[4] After Sir John Bernard's decease New Place and the Old Stratford land were to be offered for sale to Edward Nash 'according to my promise formerly made to him'. If he did not take them, as in fact happened, they were to be sold to her 'kinsman', executor, and residuary legatee, Edward Bagley. There is a legacy to a cousin, Thomas Welles of Carlton, Beds. He was parson of Carlton and Chellington for about seventy years and died aged about 100 on 5 Aug. 1642.[5] We do not know whether Bagley and Welles were father's or mother's kin. Possibly a marriage of 1579 at Barton between Robert Welles and Elizabeth Lambert points to a connexion through the Ardens.[6] Sir John Bernard died on 3 Mar. 1674. On 18 May 1675 the surviving trustee and Bagley, described as 'citizen and pewterer of London', sold the property to Sir Edward Walker for £1,060.[7] The Henley St. houses were left (no. iii) to the Harts. Thus the inheritance of William Shakespeare passed away. Elizabeth's will makes no disposition of personal effects. Presumably these, including any books or manuscripts, remained with Sir John Bernard at Abington after Elizabeth's death in February 1670. His inventory [8] shows 'In the Studdy . . . all the Bookes' worth £29 11s., 'a Rent at Stratford vpon Avon' worth £4, and 'old goods and lumber at Stratford vpon Avon' worth £4. 'Shadows we are and shadows we pursue.']

[1] H.P. ii. 115, 347.
[2] pr. Halliwell, *1848*, 316.
[3] *B.P. Cat.* 70, pr. Halliwell, *1848*, 317.
[4] Probate copy *B.P. Cat.* 71, pr.

Halliwell, *1848*, 318.
[5] *V.H. Beds.* iii. 53.
[6] *Warwick Registers*, iii. 143.
[7] Halliwell, *1848*, 321.
[8] *N.S.S. Trans. 1880–6*, 13†.

XXV. SHAKESPEARE'S EPITAPHS

(*a*) [From gravestone in chancel of Stratford Church, between that of Anne Shakespeare, which is next the north wall bearing the monument, and that of Susanna Hall. The verses are transcribed in substantially, but not orthographically, their present form by Dugdale (1656) 520, from 'a plaine free stone', by Dowdall (1693), and Roberts (1729), and in variant forms by Dobyns (1673) and Hall (1694); cf. App. C, nos. xi, xviii, xix, xxxi. The stone bears no name.]

> GOOD FREND FOR IESVS SAKE FORBEARE,
> TO DIGG THE DVST ENCLOASED HEARE!
> BLESTE BE Y̐ MAN Y̐ SPARES THES STONES,
> AND CVRST BE HE Y̐ MOVES MY BONES·

[Dowdall in 1693 first records a tradition (App. C, nos. xviii, xxxi, xlv) that Shakespeare wrote these lines himself, and says that the curse prevented the opening of the grave for his wife and daughters. Hall in 1694 adds that the grave was seventeen feet deep—most improbable so near the Avon—and that Shakespeare was in fear of a transfer of his bones to the charnel-house. This has now been pulled down, but Halliwell (*1848*) 287 reproduces a drawing of it, and its door remains in the north wall of the chancel. Halliwell, *Wit and Wisdom*, 118, gives an analogy of *c.* 1630 from a *Rawl. MS.*, which I cannot identify.

> *Epitaphe on a Bakere.*
>
> For Jesus Christe his sake forbeare
> To dig the bones under this biere;
> Blessed is hee who loues my duste,
> But damned bee he who moues this cruste!

H.P. i. 269 says that the present stone is not the original one, but was substituted 'about ninety years ago', and that in 1796 an opening in the side of the grave was made in digging a neighbouring vault, but did not lead to an examination. R. Hendrie [1] saw a hole about 1827 made by sinking of the stone, and was told that no workman would meddle with it, because of the curse. There was an intention to put fresh slabs round.]

[1] 1881, July 9, *Athenæum*.

(*b*) [1616◇1623. From tablet in monument on north wall of chancel.]

Ivdicio Pylivm, genio Socratem, arte Maronem:
  Terra tegit, popvlvs mæret, Olympvs habet.

Stay Passenger, why goest thov by so fast?
read if thov canst, whom enviovs Death hath plast,
with in this monvment Shakspeare: with whome,
qvick natvre dide: whose name doth deck y̆ Tombe,
Far more then cost: sieh all, y̆ He hath writt,
Leaves living art, bvt page, to serve his witt.
                    obiit año do¹ 1616
                  Ætatis · 53 die 23 apᴿ.

[The authorship of the lines is unknown. Hall would hardly have
spoken of the burial as 'within this monument'. It was no very
accurate scholar who shortened the first vowel of 'Socratem'.
Steevens conjectured 'Sophoclem', but the stone-cutter, who put
'sieh' for 'sith', would be less capable of the classical substitution.
Elton 233 gives analogies to the imagery, and in particular to the
use of Olympus for Parnassus.

The controversial history of the monument may be studied in
H.P. i. 281; Lee 496, 524; Stopes, *Env.* 104, 346; A. Lang, *Sh.*,
Bacon, and the Great Unknown (1912); G. Greenwood, *Is There a
Sh. Problem?* (1916) and *The Stratford Bust and the Droeshout
Engraving* (1925); M. H. Spielmann, *Sh.'s Portraiture* (1921;
Studies in the First Folio, 1); K. Esdaile, *Sh.'s Monument* (1928,
Aug. 6, *Times*). The best photograph of the bust is in *Sh. Homage*,
4; a coloured chromo-phototype of the whole was issued (1880) by
the N.S.S.

The design is in good Jacobean Renaissance style. A central
niched arch contains the half-length 'bust' of the poet, whose hands
rest with pen and paper on a cushion before him. This is flanked by
Corinthian columns, supporting a cornice. Beneath is a tablet with
the inscription. On the cornice is a square block with the arms, helm,
and crest in relief. It has a pyramidal top, with a skull at the apex,
and is flanked by two small nude figures, on mounds, one with a spade,
the other with a second skull and an inverted torch. They are Rest and
Labour. The main structure is of white marble, with inlaid panels
of black touchstone; the columns are of black marble, with gilt capitals
and bases; two of the supporting brackets are of alabaster, but the
third is an imitation. The bust itself is of a soft Cotswold limestone.

PLATE XXII

SHAKESPEARE'S MONUMENT

The monument existed by 1623, when it is referred to in Digges's F1 lines (App. B, no. lii). A note by Sir W. Dugdale in an almanac of 1653 [1] ascribes the workmanship to 'one Gerard Johnson'. This was Gerard the younger, who with his brothers Nicholas, Bernard, and John carried on the business of their father Gheerart Janssen (ob. 1611), an immigrant (c. 1567) from Amsterdam. The style of the work resembles that of the tomb of Roger Manners, 5th Earl of Rutland, erected by Nicholas at Bottesford in 1619; and in particular the two nude figures are paralleled there, and described by Nicholas in a 'plot' as Labour and Rest.

The carving of the bust lacks detail, and this was no doubt supplied from the beginning by the use of colour. The rigidity of the features has led Sir Francis Chantrey and others to think that they were modelled from a mask. If so, this was not [2] necessarily a death-mask, and in any case it is improbable that it was that found at Mainz in 1849 and conjectured to have come from the family of a Count von Kesselstadt. This differs from the bust in important structural features, notably its receding, instead of perpendicular, forehead. It is championed by P. Wislicenus, *Shs Totenmaske* (1910), and in *J.* xlviii (1912), 116, and by E. Gundolf, *Zur Beurteilung der Darmstädter Sh.-Maske*,[3] and rejected by A. Brandl, *Zu Shs Totenmaske und Ben Jonsons Totenbild*,[4] and by E. Benkard, *Das ewige Antlitz* (1927).

By 1746 the monument had 'through length of years and other accidents become much impaired and decayed'. A company of players under John Ward, grandfather of Mrs. Siddons, gave a benefit performance, which produced £12 10s. For this it was agreed in 1748 that 'Mr. John Hall, Limner', should 'repair and beautify, or have the direction of repairing and beautifying the original monument'. There appears to have been some difference of opinion as to the limits of Hall's commission between Edward Kenwrick, then vicar, and Joseph Greene, from whose memoranda [5] these details are taken. Greene proposed that he should be instructed to 'take care, according to his ability, that the monument shall become as like as possible to what it was, when first erected'; and Kenwrick wanted some further limitation. In the end a paper, unfortunately not now known, was prepared, 'signifying what Mr. Hall was to do, and of what materials to repair the monument'. H.P. i. 283, who seems [6] to have had a collection of documents on

---

[1] W. Hamper, *Life*, 99.
[2] Spielmann 9, 12.
[3] 1928, *J.* lxiv. 132.

[4] 1911, *J.* xlvii. 156.
[5] Stopes, *Env.* 346.
[6] *Rarities*, 42.

the transaction of 1748, says that the bust had lost 'the forefinger of the right hand, a pen and a fragment of the adjoining thumb, all of which were restored at the same time in new material'. No doubt the limner also refreshed the colouring. A character in Garrick's jubilee performance at Drury Lane in 1769 says,[1] 'I saw how it would be when they wouldn't let his Image alone in the Church, but the show-folk from Lunnonshire would paint it over like a popish saint'. Probably this refers to the event of 1748, and not to any further beautifying at Stratford's own jubilee of 1769. Hall himself took occasion to paint a picture of the monument, reproduced by Spielmann 24, which according to an endorsed memorandum by H.P. was done 'before he re-coloured the bust'. It is ill-drawn, but the head, right arm, hand and pen are much as now; the left arm does not emerge from a black shadow. Rest and Labour have much smoother hair, and are differently posed, and each has a torch and skull. H.P. i. 283 is responsible for the statement that the finger and thumb were again replaced by William Roberts of Oxford in 1790, and a quill inserted to represent the pen. On 15 Nov. 1793 Malone wrote to Lord Charlemont[2] that on a visit to Stratford in the foregoing summer he had done 'a public service'. With the permission of James Davenport, the vicar, he had 'brought' the bust 'back to its original state, by painting it a good stone-colour'. Indiscreet man! He deserved the epigram printed in *Gent. Mag.* (1815), i. 390, from an entry of 1810 in a Stratford *Visitors' Book*:

> Stranger, to whom this monument is shewn,
> Invoke the Poet's curse upon Malone;
> Whose meddling zeal his barbarous taste betrays,
> And daubs his tombstone, as he mars his plays!

In 1861 the stone colour was removed by Simon Collins, and the present colours put on. Mr. Spielmann describes them as follows:

'The painted face of the bust shows a glow of health usually to be seen only in sculptured effigies. The hair and beard are auburn; the doublet scarlet; the gown black; the falling-band white; the cushion green above and crimson below; the cord and tassels black. The eyes are hazel gone dark.'

We cannot, through all these metamorphoses, be confident of veracity of coloration; otherwise the scarlet doublet might perhaps be taken to represent the official livery of the King's men.

The controversy, however, is on a more fundamental point. Dugdale made a drawing of the monument, which still exists. This

[1] R. C. Rhodes in *T.L.S.* 7 May 1925.   [2] *H.M.C. Charlemont MSS.* ii. 221.

PLATE XXIII

SHAKESPEARE'S BUST

was engraved, with fair fidelity, by Hollar or his assistant Gaywood for the *Antiquities of Warwickshire* (1656), 520. It differs singularly from the monument as we see it. The architectural proportions are caricatured. Irrelevant leopards' heads are placed over the capitals. The allegorical figures, one with an hour-glass, the other with a spade, are poised at the extreme ends of the cornice, where no Renaissance sculptor would have placed them. The bust itself is elongated; the elbows project angularly; there are no pen and paper; the face is narrow and melancholy, more like that of a tailor than of a humorist; the moustache droops, instead of following a straight line with an uptwist at each end. Two explanations have been given of these discrepancies. One, and the only reasonable one, is that such was the way of conscienceless 17th-century engravers, and that, learned as Dugdale was on tenures, genealogy, and heraldry, there are other monumental illustrations in his book which completely misrepresent the originals. The other explanation we owe to Mrs. Stopes. She thinks that the repairing and beautifying of 1748 amounted to a considerable reconstruction through which the present aspect of the monument replaced that faithfully recorded by Dugdale; and that in the process the position of the allegorical figures was altered, and the worn outline of the bust 'made up somehow to hold the paint, either by skilfully inserted pieces of stone, or by some plastic material'. The restorers 'had no pattern to go by'—although Dugdale's engraving had been reissued in a new edition of the *Antiquities* as recently as 1730. 'Probably the outline of the moustache had been obliterated, and they moulded one after what they thought the best fashion. They would mend the nose, plump out the hollow cheeks and fill up the eyes,' and so forth. 'The result would necessarily be very different from the original.' The technics of all this seem absurd. It would be simpler to accept the alternative suggestion of Sir George Greenwood that another bust was substituted for the original one. But the whole theory seems to me to be a mare's nest. It certainly gets no support from the Stratford documents disinterred by Mrs. Stopes. These show that both Greene and Kenwrick were determined that John Hall should be tied to making the monument 'as like as possible to what it was, when first erected', and that the only question between them was as to whether he had been tied tight enough. It seems to me incredible that the monument should ever have resembled Dugdale's engraving. But it is conceivable that the present Rest and Labour, with the Georgian *chevelure*, may date from 1748.]

APPENDIX B

CONTEMPORARY ALLUSIONS

[*Bibliographical Note.* C. M. Ingleby collected a score of important passages in his *Shakspeare Allusion-Books, Part I* (1874, *N.S.S.*), and a long series in *Shakespeare's Centurie of Prayse* (1874, *N.S.S.*). This was revised and expanded by L. Toulmin Smith (1879) and F. J. Furnivall (1886), and again by J. Munro as *The Shakespeare Allusion Book* (1909). Additions were made by J. Munro, *More Sh. Allusions* (1916, *M.P.* xiii. 497); G. Thorn-Drury, *Sh. Allusions* (1912, *11 N.Q.* vi. 426), *Some Seventeenth Century Allusions to Sh. and his Works* (1920), *More Seventeenth Century Allusions to Sh. and his Works* (1924); H. E. Rollins, *Sh. Allusions* (1922, *12 N.Q.* x. 224). These collections contain many references to individual plays and poems, and many mere echoes, which might be indefinitely multiplied. I have limited myself to passages which make some personal reference to Shakespeare, and excluded some, although not all, in which I do not concur in suspecting a veiled reference.]

I. EDMUND SPENSER (1591, 1595)

(*a*) [From *The Teares of the Muses*, in *Complaints* (1591, S.R. 29 Dec. 1590), as part of a complaint by Thalia of the decadence of comedy. The printer's epistle describes the *Complaints* as 'disperst abroad in sundrie hands', and some of them 'imbeziled and purloyned' from Spenser 'since his departure ouer Sea'. It has been thought that Spenser was not in Ireland between Nov. 1589 and Dec. 1591, and that the reference must be to his original migration of 1580. F. P. Wilson, however, has shown (*R.E.S.* ii. 456) that he was almost certainly there in May 1590. But even this date is too early to make a reference to Shakespeare, as conjectured by Rowe, at all plausible. If Shakespeare had written any comedies by 1590, of which there is no proof and little probability, he was at the beginning of his career and not, in a literary sense, 'dead'. The name Willy is given to Sidney in a poem by A. W. in Davison's *Poetical Rhapsody* (1602), but he had not much to do with Thalia. Some convergent external evidence (cf. *Eliz. Stage*, ii. 343) points to Tarlton (ob. 1588). But from all we know of Tarlton, an antithesis between him and Scurrility would be an odd one. If he is meant, Willy must be distinct from the 'gentle spirit', who is clearly not literally dead. The passage as a whole seems most appropriate to Lyly, whose series of plays for Paul's terminated about 1590.]

> And he the man, whom Nature selfe had made
> To mock her selfe, and Truth to imitate,
> With kindly counter vnder Mimick shade,
> Our pleasant *Willy*, ah is dead of late:
> With whom all ioy and iolly meriment
> Is also deaded, and in dolour drent.

In stead thereof scoffing Scurrilitie,
And scornfull Follie with Contempt is crept,
Rolling in rymes of shameles ribaudrie
Without regard, or due Decorum kept,
Each idle wit at will presumes to make,
And doth the Learneds taske vpon him take.

But that same gentle Spirit, from whose pen
Large streames of honnie and sweete Nectar flowe,
Scorning the boldnes of such base-borne men,
Which dare their follies forth so rashlie throwe;
Doth rather choose to sit in idle Cell,
Than so himselfe to mockerie to sell.

(*b*) [From *Colin Clout's Come Home Againe* (1595), 444–7. The *Epistle*
to this is dated 27 Dec. 1591, and although attempts have been made to
upset this date, the poem was probably written as a whole after a visit to
England ending in 1591. But at least one passage, referring to the death of
Ferdinando, Earl of Derby, on 16 Apr. 1594, must have been added before
1595, and conceivably the Aetion lines may also be an afterthought. They
might, therefore, so far as chronology goes, relate, as suggested by Malone
(*Var.* ii. 273) to Shakespeare; but I do not agree with Lee 150 that the
identification is 'hardly doubtful'. Shakespeare's name is heroic enough, but
Ven. & Ad. and *Lucrece* were not heroic poems, and Spenser is cataloguing
court poets, not dramatists. On the whole I agree with O. Elton, *Michael
Drayton*, 37, in thinking Drayton more likely. He used the heroic pen-
name Rowland in his *Idea* (1593), and had published the historical poems
of *Peirs Gaveston* (1593) and *Matilda* (1594) by 1595, even if his *England's
Heroical Epistles* (1597) was not already circulating in manuscript. A
suggested derivation of Aetion from αἴτιον in the sense of Drayton's ἰδέα
cannot be relied on. Aetion is a Greek proper name, and means 'eaglet';
Spenser should not have scanned it as trisyllabic. Of other conjectures,
Warner wrote *Albion's England* as far back as 1586 and his name is not
heroic; Thomas Edwards (Stopes in *M.L.R.* xvi. 222) had neither heroic
name nor heroic muse; William Stanley, Earl of Derby (A. Lefranc, *Sous
le Masque de W. Sh.* i. 199), bore the eagle in his crest, and would be a
possibility, could he be shown to have written heroic poetry. Even if a
falcon were an eagle, it is not likely that the arms of which Shakespeare's
father had a pattern (App. A, no. ii) were a matter of public knowledge
in 1591 or 1595.]

And there though last not least is *Aetion*,
A gentler shepheard may no where be found:
Whose *Muse* full of high thoughts inuention,
Doth like himselfe Heroically sound.

II. THOMAS NASHE (1592)

[From *Pierce Penilesse his Supplication to the Diuell*, ed. R. B. McKerrow, *Works*, i. 212.]

How would it have ioyed braue *Talbot* (the terror of the French) to thinke that after he had lyne two hundred yeares in his Tombe, hee should triumphe againe on the Stage, and haue his bones newe embalmed with the teares of ten thousand spectators at least, (at seuerall times) who, in the Tragedian that represents his person, imagine they behold him fresh bleeding?

III. ROBERT GREENE (1592)

[From *Greenes Groats-worth of Wit* (1592, S.R. 20 Sept. 1592).]

To those Gentlemen his Quondam acquaintance, that spend their wits in making plaies, R. G. wisheth a better exercise, and wisdome to preuent his extremities. . . .

Base minded men all three of you, if by my miserie you be not warnd: for vnto none of you (like mee) sought those burres to cleaue: those Puppets (I meane) that spake from our mouths, those Anticks garnisht in our colours. Is it not strange, that I, to whom they all haue beene beholding: is it not like that you, to whome they all haue beene beholding, shall (were yee in that case as I am now) bee both at once of them forsaken? Yes trust them not: for there is an vpstart Crow, beautified with our feathers, that with his *Tygers hart wrapt in a Players hyde*, supposes he is as well able to bombast out a blanke verse as the best of you: and beeing an absolute *Iohannes fac totum*, is in his owne conceit the onely Shake-scene in a countrey. O that I might intreat your rare wits to be imploied in more profitable courses: & let those Apes imitate your past excellence, and neuer more acquaint them with your admired inuentions. I knowe the best husband of you all will neuer proue an Usurer, and the kindest of them all will neuer proue a kind nurse: yet, whilest you may, seeke you better Maisters; for it is pittie men of such rare wits, should be subiect to the pleasure of such rude groomes.

In this I might insert two more, that both haue writ against these buckram Gentlemen: but lette their owne workes serue to witnesse against their owne wickednesse, if they perseuere to maintaine any more such peasants. For other new-commers, I leaue them to the mercie of these painted monsters, who (I doubt not) will driue the best minded to despise them: for the rest, it skils not though they make a ieast at them.

IV. HENRY CHETTLE (1592, 1603)

(*a*) [From *Epistle* to *Kind-Harts Dreame* (n.d., S.R. 8 Dec. 1592).]

About three moneths since died M. *Robert Greene*, leauing many papers in sundry Booke sellers hands, among other his Groatsworth of wit, in which a letter written to diuers play-makers, is offensiuely by one or two of them taken; and because on the dead they cannot be auenged, they wilfully forge in their conceites a liuing Author: and after tossing it to and fro, no remedy, but it must light on me. How I haue all the time of my conuersing in printing hindered the bitter inueying against schollers, it hath been very well knowne; and how in that I dealt, I can suffi-ciently prooue. With neither of them that take offence was I acquainted, and with one of them I care not if I neuer be: The other, whome at that time I did not so much spare, as since I wish I had, for that as I haue moderated the heate of liuing writers, and might have vsde my owne discretion (especially in such a case) the Author beeing dead, that I did not, I am as sory as if the originall fault had beene my fault, because my selfe haue seene his demeanor no lesse ciuill than he exelent in the qualitie he professes: Besides, diuers of worship haue reported his uprightnes of dealing, which argues his honesty, and his facetious grace in writting, that aprooues his Art.

(*b*) [From *Englandes Mourning Garment* (n.d., S.R. 25 Apr. 1603).]

Nor doth the siluer tonged *Melicert*,
Drop from his honied muse one sable teare
To mourne her death that graced his desert,
And to his laies opend her Royall eare.
    Shepheard, remember our *Elizabeth*,
    And sing her Rape, done by that *Tarquin*, Death.

V. THOMAS EDWARDES (1593?)

[From *Envoy* to *Narcissus* (ed. W. E. Buckley, 1878). The earliest known ed., containing also *Cephalus and Procris*, is of 1595 and a dedication has an allusion to Chapman's *Shadow of Night* (1594, S.R. 31 Dec. 1593). But *C. and P.* was entered in S.R. 22 Oct. 1593), and this may therefore be the earliest reference to *Ven. & Ad.* Edwardes appears to have had a post at court in 1594; for speculations on him, cf. C. C. Stopes in *M.L.R.* xvi. 209.]

> *Adon* deafly masking thro,
> Stately troupes ⟨tropes?⟩ rich conceited,
> Shew'd he well deserued to,
>   Loues delight on him to gaze
> And had not loue her selfe intreated,
>   Other nymphs had sent him baies.

VI. R. B. (1594)

[From *Greenes Funeralls*. By R. B. Gent. (1594, S.R. 1 Feb.), Sonn. ix (ed. R. B. McKerrow, 81). The identity of the author is uncertain. McKerrow shows that Richard Barnfield (no. xiv) is more likely than Barnabe Rich, but the printer Danter says that the book was published 'contrary to the Authours expectation, for it was his priuate study at idle times', and Barnfield in 1595 repudiates two unnamed books which had been imputed to him.]

> Greene, is the pleasing Obiect of an eie:
> Greene, pleasde the eies of all that lookt vppon him.
> Greene, is the ground of euerie Painters die:
> Greene, gaue the ground, to all that wrote vpon him.
> Nay more the men, that so Eclipst his fame:
> Purloynde his Plumes, can they deny the same?

VII. W. HAR (1594)

[From *Epicedium. A funeral Song, upon . . . the Lady Helen Branch*. This seems to be the first allusion to *Lucrece*. It was assigned by Sir E. Brydges (*Restituta*, iii. 298) to Sir William Harbert of St. Julian's, but he ob. 4 Mar. 1593, and Lady Branch on 10 Apr. 1594 (*Cat. of Cambridge Univ. MSS.* i. 287). One might guess at William Harvey, who later married Mary, Countess of Southampton. A William Harvey was juror at the i.p.m. on Sir John Branch who ob. 1588 (*London i.p.ms.* iii. 132), but this is probably a coincidence.]

> You that haue writ of chaste Lucretia,
> Whose death was witnesse of her spotlesse life:

Or pen'd the praise of sad Cornelia,
Whose blamelesse name hath made her fame so rife,
As noble Pompey's most renoumed wife:
　　Hither vnto your home direct your eies,
　　Whereas, vnthought on, much more matter lies.

VIII. HENRY WILLOBIE (1594)

[From *Willobie his Avisa* (1594, S.R. 3 Sept.), c. xliv. On the relation of
the poem to Shakespeare cf. vol. i, p. 568. I do not quote the verse-dialogue
introduced by this passage, which may be read in the eds. of C. Hughes
(1904) and G. B. Harrison (1926), and gives no further clue beyond a
possible echo of *Tit. Andr.* ii. 1. 83 in the lines:
　　　　　She is no Saynt, She is no Nonne,
　　　　　I thinke in tyme she may be wonne.]

Henrico Willobego.　Italo-Hispalensis.

H. W. being sodenly infected with the contagion of a
fantasticall fit, at the first sight of *A*, pyneth a while in
secret griefe, at length not able any longer to indure the
burning heate of so feruent a humour, bewrayeth the
secresy of his disease vnto his familiar frend W. S. who
not long before had tryed the curtesy of the like passion,
and was now newly recouered of the like infection; yet
finding his frend let bloud in the same vaine, he took
pleasure for a tyme to see him bleed, & in steed of stopping
the issue, he inlargeth the wound, with the sharpe rasor
of a willing conceit, perswading him that he thought it a
matter very easy to be compassed, & no doubt with payne,
diligence & some cost in time to be obtayned. Thus this
miserable comforter comforting his frend with an im-
possibilitie, eyther for that he now would secretly laugh
at his frends folly, that had giuen occasion not long before
vnto others to laugh at his owne, or because he would see
whether an other could play his part better then himselfe,
& in vewing a far off the course of this louing Comedy,
he determined to see whether it would sort to a happier
end for this new actor, then it did for the old player. But
at length this Comedy was like to haue growen to a
Tragedy, by the weake & feeble estate that H. W. was
brought vnto, by a desperate vewe of an impossibility of

obtaining his purpose, til Time & Necessity, being his best Phisitions brought him a plaster, if not to heale, yet in part to ease his maladye. In all which discourse is liuely represented the vnrewly rage of unbrydeled fancy, hauing the raines to roue at liberty, with the dyuers & sundry changes of affections & temptations, which Will, set loose from Reason, can deuise. &c.

IX. ANON (1594)

[From commendatory verses to *Willobie his Avisa* (cf. no. viii), signed 'Contraria Contrarijs: Vigilantius: Dormitanus', in apparent allusion to St. Jerome's *Contra Vigilantium*, in which he calls his opponent Dormitantius.]

Though Collatine *haue deerely bought,*
To high renowne, a lasting life,
And found, that most in vaine haue sought,
To haue a Faire, *and* Constant *wife,*
 Yet Tarquyne *pluckt his glistering grape,*
 And Shake-speare, *paints poore Lucrece rape.*

X. MICHAEL DRAYTON (1594, 1627)

(*a*) [From *Matilda* (1594), st. 6. It does not seem to me clear that the reference is to *Lucrece*. The wording suggests a play. Heywood may possibly have been writing for the stage as early as 1594 (cf. *Eliz. Stage*, iii. 338), but his extant *Rape of Lucrece* was published in 1608.]

Lucrece, of whom proude Rome hath boasted long
Lately reuiu'd to liue another age,
And here ariu'd to tell of *Tarquins* wrong,
Her chast deniall, and the Tyrants rage,
Acting her passions on our stately stage.
 She is remembred, all forgetting me,
 Yet I, as fayre and chast as ere was She.

(*b*) [From *Elegy* 'To my most dearely-loued friend HENERY REYNOLDS Esquire, of *Poets & Poesie*', pr. with *The Battaile of Agincourt* (1627).]

And be it said of thee,
Shakespeare, thou hadst as smooth a Comicke vaine,
Fitting the socke, and in thy naturall braine,
As strong conception, and as Cleere a rage,
As any one that trafiqu'd with the stage.

XI. ROBERT SOUTHWELL (>1595)

[From *Epistle* to *Saint Peters Complaynt* (1595). Supposed echoes of *Ven. & Ad.* and *Love's Lab. Lost*, iv. 3. 302–54 are very doubtful. M. Praz (*M.L.R.* xix. 273) shows that the poem may be earlier than 1585, and that literature is not likely to have reached Southwell in prison from 1592 to his death on 21 Feb. 1595.]

Christ's thorne is sharpe, no head His garland weares;
Stil finest wits are 'stilling Venus' rose . . .
O sacred eyes! the springs of liuing light,
    The earthly heauens where angels ioy to dwell . . .
Sweet volumes, stoard with learning fit for saints,
    Where blissfull quires imparadize their minds;
Wherein eternall studie neuer faints
    Still finding all, yet seeking all it finds:
How endless is your labyrinth of blisse,
Where to be lost the sweetest finding is!

XII. WILLIAM COVELL (1595)

[From tract appended to *Polimanteia, or the Meanes Lawfull and Unlawfull to Judge of the Fall of a Commonwealth*, sign. R2ᵛ, as marginal note to a laudation of Spenser and Daniel. The epistle in most copies is only signed W. C., and the writer has been taken for William Clerke; but a copy formerly owned by Prof. Dowden and now (*S.T.C.* 5884) in New York has 'W. Covell'. Covell (ob. 1614) was a Fellow of Queens', Cambridge.]

All praiseworthy. Lucrecia Sweet Shakspeare. Eloquent Gaveston. Wanton Adonis. Watsons heyre.

XIII. FRANCIS MERES (1598)

[From *Palladis Tamia: Wits Treasury* (S.R. 7 Sept. 1598). F. S. Ferguson (1928, June 7, *T.L.S.*) describes a copy, with preliminary leaves containing a dedication from London on 19 Oct. 1598 to Thomas Eliot of the Middle Temple, Esq., as well as an address 'Candido Lectori'. These are missing from other copies, probably because the address criticizes the 'illiberalem chartae parsimoniam' of the 'bibliopola' Burby, who cut some of Meres's copy. The treatise mentions Edward Guilpin's *Skialetheia*, registered as late as 15 Sept. 1598. I have omitted some of the classical comparisons. Meres (1565–1647) was of Lincolnshire and Pembroke, Cambridge. He was living in London in 1597 and 1598, and seems to have been in touch with literary men. From 1602 he was rector and schoolmaster at Wing, Rutland.]

A comparatiue discourse of our English Poets
with the *Greeke, Latine, and Italian Poets.*

... The English tongue is mightily enriched, and gorgeouslie inuested in rare ornaments and resplendent abiliments by sir *Philip Sidney, Spencer, Daniel, Drayton, Warner, Shakespeare, Marlow* and *Chapman.* ...

As the soule of *Euphorbus* was thought to liue in *Pythagoras:* so the sweete wittie soule of *Ouid* liues in mellifluous & hony-tongued *Shakespeare*, witnes his *Venus* and *Adonis*, his *Lucrece*, his sugred Sonnets among his priuate friends, &c.

As *Plautus* and *Seneca* are accounted the best for Comedy and Tragedy among the Latines: so *Shakespeare* among the English is the most excellent in both kinds for the stage; for Comedy, witnes his *Gentlemen of Verona*, his *Errors*, his *Loue labors lost*, his *Loue labours wonne*, his *Midsummers night dreame*, & his *Merchant of Venice:* for Tragedy his *Richard the 2. Richard* the *3. Henry the 4. King Iohn, Titus Andronicus* and his *Romeo* and *Iuliet.*

As *Epius Stolo* said, that the Muses would speake with *Plautus* tongue, if they would speak Latin: so I say that the Muses would speak with *Shakespeares* fine filed phrase, if they would speake English....

As *Ouid* saith of his worke ... as *Horace* saith of his ... so say I seuerally of sir *Philip Sidneys, Spencers, Daniels, Draytons, Shakespeares,* and *Warners workes;*

> *Non Iouis ira, imbres, Mars, ferrum, flamma, senectus,*
> *Hoc opus vnda, lues, turbo, venena ruent....*

As *Pindarus, Anacreon* and *Callimachus* among the Greekes; and *Horace* and *Catullus* among the Latines are the best Lyrick Poets: so in this faculty the best among our Poets are *Spencer* (who excelleth in all kinds) *Daniel, Drayton, Shakespeare, Bretton....*

These are our best for Tragedie, the Lorde *Buckhurst*, Doctor *Leg* of Cambridge, Doctor *Edes* of Oxforde, maister *Edward Ferris*, the Author of the *Mirrour for Magistrates, Marlow, Peele, Watson, Kid, Shakespeare, Drayton, Chapman, Decker,* and *Beniamin Johnson....*

The best for Comedy amongst us bee, *Edward* Earle of

Oxforde, Doctor *Gager* of Oxforde, Maister *Rowley* once
a rare Scholler of learned Pembrooke Hall in Cambridge,
Maister *Edwardes* one of her Maiesties Chappell, eloquent
and wittie *John Lilly*, *Lodge*, *Gascoyne*, *Greene*, *Shakespeare*,
Thomas Nash, *Thomas Heywood*, *Anthony Mundye* our best
plotter, *Chapman*, *Porter*, *Wilson*, *Hathway*, and *Henry
Chettle*. . . .

These are the most passionate among us to bewaile and
bemoane the perplexities of Loue, *Henrie Howard* Earle
of Surrey, sir *Thomas Wyat* the elder, sir *Francis Brian*,
sir *Philip Sidney*, sir *Walter Rawley*, sir *Edward Dyer*,
Spencer, *Daniel*, *Drayton*, *Shakespeare*, *Whetstone*, *Gascoyne*,
Samuell Page sometimes fellowe of *Corpus Christi* Colledge
in Oxford, *Churchyard*, *Bretton*.

XIV. RICHARD BARNFIELD (1598)

[From *Poems in Divers Humors*, sign. E2ᵛ.]

A Remembrance of some English Poets.

And *Shakespeare* thou, whose hony-flowing Vaine,
(Pleasing the World) thy Praises doth obtaine.
Whose *Venus*, and whose *Lucrece* (sweete, and chaste)
Thy Name in fames immortall Booke haue plac't.
    Liue euer you, at least in Fame liue euer:
    Well may the Bodye dye, but Fame dies neuer.

XV. JOHN MARSTON (1598)

[From *The Scourge of Villanie*, Sat. x. I agree with Munro, i. 32, in
rejecting the conjectures of C. A. Herpich (9 *N.Q.* x. 63) that Shakespeare is the Labeo of Marston's *Metamorphosis of Pigmalion's Image* (1598)
and of J. Hall's *Virgidemiarum* (1597) and of C. S. Harris (9 *N.Q.* ii. 183)
that he is the Castilio of Marston's *Satyres* (1598).]

Luscus, what's playd to day? faith now I know
I set thy lips abroach, from whence doth flow
Naught but pure *Iuliat* and *Romio*.
Say, who acts best? *Drusus* or *Roscio*?

Now I have him, that nere of ought did speake
But when of playes or Plaiers he did treate.
H'ath made a common-place booke out of plaies,
And speakes in print: at least what ere he sayes
Is warranted by Curtaine plaudeties.

XVI. ADAM DYRMONTH? (c. 1598)

[From the *Northumberland MS.* f. 1. I give it in facsimile only (Plates XXIV, XXV) as reproduction in ordinary type is impossible. The MS., reproduced as a whole in F. J. Burgoyne, *Collotype Facsimile and Type Transcript of an Elizabethan MS. at Alnwick Castle* (1904), is imperfect, but still contains some essays and speeches by Francis Bacon, a letter by Sidney, and a copy of *Leicester's Commonwealth*. On f. 1 is the beginning of a list of contents, and the rest of the page has been covered by a second hand with scribbles, which include (*a*) the name of 'M^r ffrauncis Bacon'; (*b*) many repetitions of the whole or part of the name 'William Shakespeare'; (*c*) the titles 'Rychard the second' and 'Rychard the third'; (*d*) an inexact quotation of *Lucrece*, 1086–7; (*e*) the word 'honorificabilitudine' (in *Love's Lab. Lost*, v. 1. 44, 'honorificabilitudinitatibus'); (*f*) the title 'Asmund and Cornelia'; (*g*) references to 'Ile of Dogs frmnt' and 'Thomas Nashe & inferior plaiers'; (*h*) the names 'Dyrmonth' and 'Adam'. On f. 1^v is written 'Anthonie Fitzherbert', the name of a judge and legal writer who died in 1538. A suggestion that the scribbler was Shakespeare is absurd (cf. vol. i. p. 506). I take him to have been Adam Dyrmonth. The name, if distinct from Derman and Durman, is rare. A Henry Dermount was christened at St. Martin-in-the-Fields on 21 May 1601 (*Harl. Soc. Reg.* xxv). The date cannot be earlier than 1597, when Nashe's *Isle of Dogs* was suppressed and *Rich. II* and *Rich. III* printed, and is probably not earlier than 1598 when *Love's Lab. Lost* was printed. Bacon, here 'M^r', was knighted on 23 July 1603.]

XVII. GABRIEL HARVEY (1598⟨ ⟩1601)

[From MS. note in copy of Speght's *Chaucer* (1598), pr. with facs. in G. C. Moore Smith, *Gabriel Harvey's Marginalia*, 232. The volume, owned by Bp. Percy and known to Malone (*Var.* ii. 369) was long supposed to have perished in a fire, but is in the hands of a descendant of Percy. The date of the note remains uncertain; 'gabriel haruey. 1598' on the t.p. can only be taken as that of acquisition. The note itself is on f. 394^v. Most of the books referred to were available to Harvey (ob. 1631) in 1598; a partial translation of Tasso's *Gerusalemme Liberata* by R. Carew (1594) preceded that by E. Fairfax (1600), and there was one of his *Aminta* by Fraunce in 1591. The *Arcadia* (reprinted 1598) and *Faerie Queene* (enlarged 1596) are 'freshest in request'. Spenser (ob. 16 Jan. 1599) is one

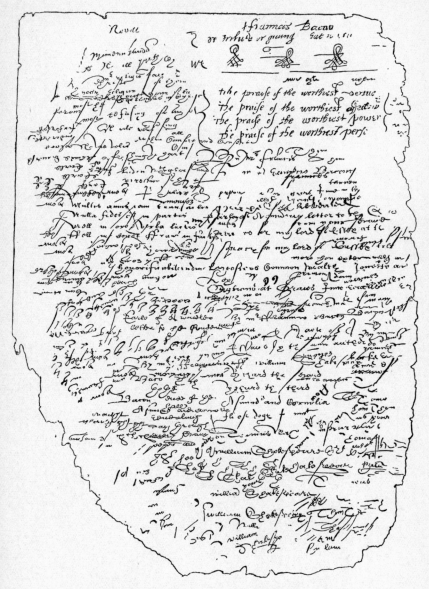

PLATE XXIV

COVER OF THE *NORTHUMBERLAND MS. (Facsimile)*

PLATE XXV

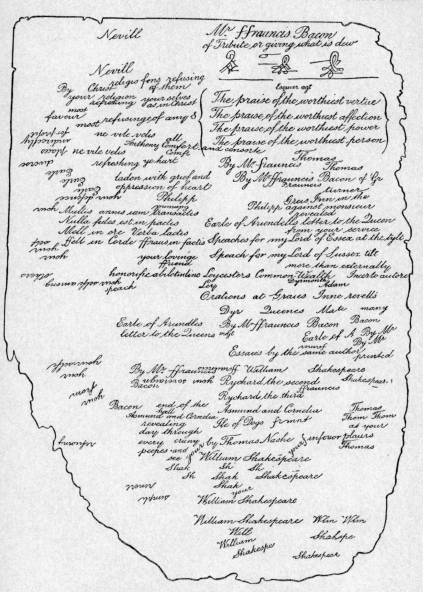

COVER OF THE *NORTHUMBERLAND MS.* (Transcript)

of 'owr florishing metricians'; that this does not prove him alive is shown
by the fact that Thomas Watson (ob. Sept. 1592) is another. There is
much force in Prof. Moore Smith's argument that 'commendes' implies a
date before the death of the 2nd Earl of Essex on 25 Feb. 1601. I find it
even less easy than he does to explain the reference to John Owen's 'new'
Epigrams (1607, S.R. 29 June) as resting upon a knowledge of them in
manuscript. But the reference to 'Lord Mountioy' makes any date later
than his creation as Earl of Devonshire on 21 July 1603 impossible.
H. J. C. Grierson (*M.L.R.* xii. 218) argues for 1598 itself, because Harvey
again refers to his own Axiophilus poems in a letter of this year; and this,
with an 'in or about', is accepted by F. S. Boas, *Sh. and Univ.* 27, 256. Both
suppose the note contemporaneous with another on f. 393ᵛ, which refers
to 'the King of Scotland' and calls Cecil, Speght's dedicatee, 'the new
patron of Chawcer'. I think this is pressing the evidence rather hard,
especially as the two notes repeat each other in places. On the whole, any
date from 1598 to the opening weeks of 1601 seems to me possible.]

Heywoods prouerbs, with His, & Sir Thomas Mores
Epigrams, may serue for sufficient supplies of manie of
theis deuises. And now translated Petrarch, Ariosto,
Tasso, & Bartas himself deserve curious comparison with
Chaucer, Lidgate, & owre best Inglish, auncient &
moderne. Amongst which, the Countesse of Pembrokes
Arcadia, & the Faerie Queene ar now freshest in request:
& Astrophil, & Amyntas ar none of the idlest pastimes
of sum fine humanists. The Earle of Essex much commendes Albions England: and not vnworthily for diuerse
notable pageants, before, & in the Chronicle. Sum Inglish, & other Histories nowhere more sensibly described,
or more inwardly discouered. The Lord Mountioy makes
the like account of Daniels peece of the Chronicle, touching the Vsurpation of Henrie of Bullingbrooke. Which
in deede is a fine, sententious, & politique peece of
Poetrie: as proffitable, as pleasurable. The younger sort
takes much delight in Shakespeares Venus, & Adonis:
but his Lucrece, & his tragedie of Hamlet, Prince of
Denmarke, haue it in them, to please the wiser sort. Or
such poets: or better: or none.

Vilia miretur vulgus: mihi flavus Apollo
Pocula Castaliae plena ministret aquae:
quoth Sir Edward Dier, betwene iest, & earnest.
Whose written deuises farr excell most of the sonets, and

cantos in print. His Amaryllis, & Sir Walter Raleighs Cynthia, how fine & sweet inuentions? Excellent matter of emulation for Spencer, Constable, France, Watson, Daniel, Warner, Chapman, Siluester, Shakespeare, & the rest of owr florishing metricians. I looke for much, as-well in verse, as in prose, from mie two Oxford frends, Doctor Gager, & M. Hackluit: both rarely furnished for the purpose: & I haue a phansie to Owens new Epigrams, as pithie as elegant, as plesant as sharp, & sumtime as weightie as breife: & amongst so manie gentle, noble, & royall spirits meethinkes I see sum heroical thing in the clowdes: mie soueraine hope. Axiophilus shall forgett himself, or will remember to leaue sum memorials behinde him: & to make an vse of so manie rhapsodies, cantos, hymnes, odes, epigrams, sonets, & discourses, as at idle howers, or at flowing fitts he hath compiled. God knows what is good for the world, & fitting for this age.

XVIII. ELIZABETH WRIOTHESLEY, COUNTESS OF SOUTHAMPTON (1599)

[From *Letter* to the Earl of Southampton, printed from *Cecil Papers*, ci. 16, in *H.M.C.* iii. 148, but not in the full Elizabethan calendar of *Hatfield MSS*. The letter is only dated 'Chartley the 8th of July'. But Stopes, *Southampton*, 160, who prints it with a group of related letters, rightly ascribes it to 1599, when the Earl was in Ireland. The clue is in a companion letter of 9 July by Penelope Lady Rich, with whom the Countess was living at Chartley. This refers to a recent head wound of Sir Henry Danvers, which the journal of Sir John Harington (*Nugae Antiquae*, i. 283) puts in June 1599. Lady Southampton's gossip is probably of some acquaintance whom she nicknames Falstaff, rather than of Sh. One would guess at Henry Lord Cobham, but he appears to have had no children.]

Al the nues I can send you that I thinke wil make you mery is that I reade in a letter from London that Sir John Falstaf is by his Mrs Dame Pintpot made father of a godly milers thum, a boye thats all heade and veri litel body; but this is a secrit.

XIX. JOHN WEEVER (1599)

(a) [From *Epigrammes in the oldest Cut, and newest Fashion*, iv. 22 (ed. R. B. McKerrow, 75). Weever (1576–1632) was a Lancashire man, a student of Queens', Cambridge, and an antiquary. C. M. Ingleby (*Sh. Allusion Books*, Part I, 182) assumes an earlier edition of *c.* 1595 in error. Verses to the readers claim that the writer 'twenty twelue months yet did neuer know', but McKerrow shows that, while the earliest epigram may be of 1594, others refer to events of 1598 and 1599.]

Ad Gulielmum Shakespeare.

Honie-tong'd *Shakespeare* when I saw thine issue
I swore *Apollo* got them and none other,
Their rosie-tainted features cloth'd in tissue,
Some heauen born goddesse said to be their mother:
Rose-checkt *Adonis* with his amber tresses,
Faire fire-hot *Venus* charming him to loue her,
Chaste *Lucretia* virgine-like her dresses,
Prowd lust-stung *Tarquine* seeking still to proue her:
Romea Richard; more whose names I know not,
Their sugred tongues, and power attractiue beuty
Say they are Saints althogh that Sts they shew not
For thousands vowes to them subiectiue dutie:
They burn in loue thy children *Shakespear* het them,
Go, wo thy Muse more Nymphish brood beget them.

(b) [From *The Mirror of Martyrs, or The Life and Death of Sir John Oldcastle* (1601), St. 4. The dedication says that the book 'some two yeares agoe was made fit for the Print'.]

The many-headed multitude were drawne
By *Brutus* speach, that *Caesar* was ambitious,
When eloquent *Mark Antonie* had showne
His vertues, who but *Brutus* then was vicious?

XX. ANON (1599?, 1601?)

[From *Parnassus*, ed. W. D. Macray (1886), a series of plays: (1) *The Pilgrimage to Parnassus*, (2) *The Returne from Parnassus*, Part I, (3) *The Returne from Parnassus*, Part II, performed at St. John's, Cambridge, probably at the Christmases of 1598–9, 1599–1600, and 1601–2; cf. *Eliz. Stage*, iv. 38. An early inscription suggests the authorship of J. D., for whom John Day is a very doubtful conjecture.]

(*a*) [From 2 *Parnassus* (1599 ?).]

[iii. 1. 1006–55.] *Gull* ⟨*io* ⟩. Pardon, faire lady, thoughe sicke-thoughted Gullio maks amaine unto thee, and like a bould-faced sutore 'gins to woo thee.

Ingen ⟨*ioso* ⟩. (We shall have nothinge but pure Shakspeare and shreds of poetrie that he hath gathered at the theators !)

Gull. Pardon mee, moy mittressa, ast am a gentleman, the moone in comparison of thy bright hue a meere slutt, Anthonio's Cleopatra a blacke browde milkmaide, Hellen a dowdie.

Ingen. (Marke, Romeo and Juliet! O monstrous theft! I thinke he will runn throughe a whole booke of Samuell Daniell's !)

Gull. Thrise fairer than myselfe (—thus I began—)
The gods faire riches, sweete above compare,
Staine to all nimphes, ⟨m⟩ore lovely the ⟨n⟩ a man.
More white and red than doves and roses are!
Nature that made thee with herselfe had ⟨at⟩ strife,
Saith that the worlde hath ending with thy life.

Ingen. Sweete Mr. Shakspeare! . . .

Ingen. My pen is youre bounden vassall to commande. But what vayne woulde it please you to have them in?

Gull. Not in a vaine veine (prettie, i'faith!): make mee them in two or three divers vayns, in Chaucer's, Gower's and Spencer's and Mr. Shakspeare's. Marry, I thinke I shall entertaine those verses which run like these;
Even as the sunn with purple coloured face
Had tane his laste leave on the weeping morne, &c.
O sweet Mr. Shakspeare! I'le have his picture in my study at the courte.

[iv. 1. 1211–27.] *Gull.*—Let mee heare Mr. Shakspear's veyne.

Ingen. Faire Venus, queene of beutie and of love,
Thy red doth stayne the blushinge of the morne,
Thy snowie necke shameth the milkwhite dove,
Thy presence doth this naked worlde adorne;
Gazinge on thee all other nymphes I scorne.
When ere thou dyest slowe shine that Satterday,
Beutie and grace muste sleepe with thee for aye!

Gull. Noe more! I am one that can judge accordinge to the proverbe, *bovem ex unguibus.* Ey marry, Sir, these have some life in them! Let this duncified worlde esteeme of Spencer and Chaucer, I'le worshipp sweet Mr. Shakspeare, and to honoure him will lay his Venus and Adonis under my pillowe, as wee reade of one (I doe not well remember his name, but I am sure he was a kinge) slept with Homer under his bed's heade.

(*b*) [From *3 Parnassus* (1601 ?).]

[i. 2. 304.] *Ingenioso. . . . William Shakespeare.*

Iudicio. Who loues not *Adons* loue, or *Lucrece* rape?
His sweeter verse contaynes hart trobbing line,
Could but a graver subiect him content,
Without loues foolish lazy languishment.

[iv. 3. 1806–79.] *Kempe.* Few of the vniuersity men pen plaies well, they smell too much of that writer *Ouid,* and that writer *Metamorphosis,* and talke too much of *Proserpina* & *Iuppiter.* Why heres our fellow *Shakespeare* puts them all downe, I and *Ben Ionson* too. O that *Ben Ionson* is a pestilent fellow, he brought vp *Horace* giuing the Poets a pill, but our fellow *Shakespeare* hath giuen him a purge that made him beray his credit:

Burbage. Its a shrewd fellow indeed: I wonder these schollers stay so long, they appointed to be here presently that we might try them: oh, here they come. . . .

Bur. I like your face, and the proportion of your body for *Richard* the 3. I pray, M. *Phil.* let me see you act a little of it.

Philomusus. 'Now is the winter of our discontent,
Made glorious summer by the sonne of Yorke.'

XXI. ANON (1599⟨)

[From MS. notes in two early 17th-century hands (cf. ed. with facs. in *M.S.R.*) cropped by binder on t.p. of the Devonshire copy of *George a Greene* (1599).]

Written by . . . a minister, who ac⟨ted⟩ the pinners part in it himself. Teste W Shakespea⟨re.⟩
Ed Iuby saith that the play was made by Ro. Gree⟨ne.⟩

XXII. BEN JONSON (1599–1637.)

(*a*) 1599. [From *Every Man Out of His Humour*, as printed in Q1 (1600), iii. 1. 2010–47. The date of representation is given in F1 as 1599 (cf. *Eliz. Stage*, iii. 360). Sogliardo's motto seems to glance at Shakespeare's, although the coat does not resemble his, and obviously Sogliardo, described as 'an essential clowne', who 'comes vp euery Tearm to learn to take Tabacco & see new Motions', is not a 'portrait' of Shakespeare. A few lines earlier (1956) comes Jonson's quotation of *Jul. Caes.* iii. 2. 109; cf. vol. i, p. 397.]

Sog⟨liardo⟩. Nay I will haue him, I am resolute for that, by this Parchment Gentlemen, I haue ben so toil'd among the Harrots yonder, you will not beleeue, they doe speake i'the straungest language, and giue a man the hardest termes for his money, that euer you knew.

Carl⟨o⟩. But ha' you armes? ha' your armes?

Sog. Yfaith, I thanke God I can write my selfe Gentleman now, here's my Pattent, it cost me thirtie pound by this breath.

Punt⟨arvolo⟩. A very faire Coat, well charg'd and full of Armorie.

Sog. Nay, it has as much varietie of colours in it, as you haue seene a Coat haue, how like you the Crest Sir?

Punt. I vnderstand it not well, what is't?

Sog. Marry Sir, it is your Bore without a head Rampant.

Punt. A Bore without a head, that's very rare.

Carl. I, and Rampant too: troth I commend the Heralds wit, he has deciphered him well: A Swine without a head, without braine, wit, any thing indeed, Ramping to Gentilitie. You can blazon the rest signior? can you not?

Sog. O I, I haue it in writing here of purpose, it cost me two shillings the tricking.

Carl. Let's heare, Let's heare.

Punt. It is the most vile, foolish, absurd, palpable, and ridiculous Escutcheon that euer this eye survis'd. Saue you good Mounsieur *Fastidius.*

They salute as they meete in the walke.

Carl. Silence good Knight: on, on.

Sog. GYRONY of eight peeces, AZVRE and GVLES, between three plates a CHEV'RON engrailed checkey, OR, VERT and ERMINES; on a cheefe ARGENT between two ANN'-LETS, sables a Bores head PROPER.

Carl. How's that? on a cheefe ARGENT?

Sog. On a cheefe ARGENT, a Bores head PROPER betweene two ANN'LETS sables.

Carl. S'lud, it's a Hogs Cheeke and Puddings in a Peuter field this.

Sog. How like you them signior?

Punt. Let the word be, *Not without mustard*, your Crest is very rare sir.

Carl. A frying pan to the Crest had had no fellow.

(*b*) 1601. [From *Poetaster* (F1), first printed in Q (1602), registered on 21 Dec. 1601. The date of representation is given in F1 as 1601; cf. *Eliz. Stage*, iii. 364.]

(1) [v. 1.99–138. I do not think that Jonson meant Virgil for Shakespeare, or for Chapman or any one but Virgil; the point is well discussed in Herford-Simpson, i. 432.]

CAES[AR]   Say then, lou'd HORACE, thy true thought of
                  VIRGIL.
HORA[CE]   I iudge him of a rectified spirit,
         By many reuolutions of discourse
         (In his bright reason influence) refin'd
         From all the tartarous moodes of common men;
         Bearing the nature, and similitude
         Of a right heauenly bodie; most seuere
         In fashion, and collection of himselfe:
         And then as cleare, and confident, as IOVE.
GALL[US]   And yet so chaste, and tender is his eare,
         In suffering any syllable to passe,
         That, he thinkes, may become the honour'd name
         Of issue to his so examin'd selfe;
         That all the lasting fruits of his full merit
         In his owne *poemes*, he doth still distaste:
         As if his mindes peece, which he stroue to paint,
         Could not with fleshly pencils haue her right.

TIBU[LLUS] But, to approue his workes of soueraigne
   worth,
  This obseruation (me thinkes) more then serues:
  And is not vulgar. That, which he hath writ,
  Is with such iudgement, labour'd, and distill'd
  Through all the needfull vses of our liues,
  That could a man remember but his lines,
  He should not touch at any serious point,
  But he might breathe his spirit out of him.
CAES[AR] You meane, he might repeat part of his workes,
  As fit for any conference, he can vse?
TIBU[LLUS] True, royall CAESAR. CAES[AR]. Worthily
   obseru'd:
  And a most worthie vertue in his workes.
  What thinks materiall HORACE, of his learning?
HORA[CE] His learning labours not the schoole-like
   glosse,
  That most consists in *ecchoing* wordes, and termes,
  And soonest wins a man an empty name:
  Nor any long, or far-fetcht circumstance,
  Wrapt in the curious generalties of artes:
  But a direct, and *analyticke* summe
  Of all the worth and first effects of artes.
  And for his *poesie*, 'tis so ramm'd with life,
  That it shall gather strength of life, with being,
  And liue hereafter, more admir'd, then now.

(2) [From *To the Reader*, 128–39, added to F1, and called by Jonson
'an apologeticall Dialogue: which was only once spoken vpon the stage'.
Shakespeare may be one of the 'better natures'; cf. vol. i, p. 71.]

Now for the Players, it is true, I tax'd 'hem,
And yet, but some; and those so sparingly,
As all the rest might haue sat still, vnquestion'd,
Had they but had the wit, or conscience,
To thinke well of themselues. But, impotent they
Thought each mans vice belong'd to their whole tribe:
And much good doo't 'hem. What th'haue done 'gainst
  me,
I am not mou'd with. If it gaue 'hem meat,

Or got 'hem clothes. 'Tis well. That was their end.
Onely amongst them, I am sorry for
Some better natures, by the rest so drawne,
To run in that vile line.

(*c*) 1605 ? [From *Prologue* to *Every Man In His Humour*, as printed in
F 1 (1616); for the probable date cf. *Eliz. Stage*, iii. 359, and for the
alternative conjecture of 1612, Herford-Simpson, i. 333.]

Though neede make many *Poets*, and some such
As art, and nature haue not betterd much;
Yet ours, for want, hath not so lou'd the stage,
As he dare serue th'ill customes of the age:
Or purchase your delight at such a rate,
As, for it, he himselfe must iustly hate.
To make a child, now swadled, to proceede
Man, and then shoote vp, in one beard, and weede,
Past threescore yeeres: or, with three rustie swords,
And helpe of some few foot-and-halfe-foote words,
Fight ouer *Yorke*, and *Lancasters* long iarres:
And in the tyring-house bring wounds, to scarres.
He rather prayes, you will be pleas'd to see
One such, to day, as other playes should be.
Where neither *Chorus* wafts you ore the seas;
Nor creaking throne comes downe, the boys to please;
Nor nimble squibbe is seene, to make afear'd
The gentlewomen; nor roul'd bullet heard
To say, it thunders; nor tempestuous drumme
Rumbles, to tell you when the storme doth come;
But deedes, and language, such as men doe vse;
And persons, such as *Comœdie* would chuse,
When she would show an Image of the times,
And sport with humane follies, not with crimes.
Except, we make 'hem such by louing still
Our popular errors, when we know th'are ill.
I meane such errors, as you'll all confesse
By laughing at them, they deserue no lesse:
Which when you heartily doe, there's hope left, then,
You, that haue so grac'd monsters, may like men.

(*d*) 1605. [From*Epistle* to Q 1 (1605) of *Sejanus*; cf. *Eliz. Stage*, iii. 368. In the absence of the original (1603) text, it is useless to conjecture whether Shakespeare, or another was the collaborator. It was certainly not Samuel Sheppard. H. E. Rollins (*S.P.* xxiv. 509) shows that he was born after 1623, and that his phrase about dictation to Jonson 'when as Sejanus' fall he writ' is put dramatically in the mouth of Apollo.]

I would informe you, that this Booke, in all numbers, is not the same with that which was acted on the publike Stage, wherein a second Pen had good share: in place of which I haue rather chosen, to put weaker (and no doubt lesse pleasing) of mine own, then to defraud so happy a *Genius* of his right, by my lothed vsurpation.

(*e*) 1614. [From *Induction* to *Bartholomew Fayre* (as printed in 1631); cf. *Eliz. Stage*, iii. 372.]

Hee that will sweare, *Ieronimo*, or *Andronicus* are the best playes, yet, shall passe vnexcepted at, heere, as a man whose Iudgement shewes it is constant, and hath stood still, these fiue and twentie, or thirtie yeeres. . . .

If there bee neuer a *Seruant-monster* i' the Fayre; who can helpe it? he ⟨the Author⟩ sayes; nor a nest of *Antiques*? Hee is loth to make Nature afraid in his *Playes*, like those that beget *Tales*, *Tempests*, and such like *Drolleries*, to mixe his head with other mens heeles; let the concupisence of *Iigges* and *Dances*, raigne as strong as it will amongst you.

(*f*) 1619. [From *Conversations with William Drummond*, during a visit to Hawthornden of *c*. Dec. 1618 to Jan. 1619. I follow the text of Herford-Simpson, i. 132. Variant versions of the second mock epitaph here given are said in *Ashm. MS.* 38 (App. C, no. vi) and by Plume (App. C, no. vii) to have been completed by Shakespeare. H.P. (*1848*) 186 gives a fourth from 'an early MS. commonplace-book' as follows:

> B. *Johnson in Seipsum.*
>
> Heere lies Johnson,
> Who was ones sonne:
> Hee had a little hayre on his chin,
> His name was Benjamin!

A fifth is in the early 17th-century MS. from Eshton Hall which also contains (*Eliz. Stage*, ii. 420) the verses on the Globe fire, but I do not know whether this is ascribed to Shakespeare.]

[l. 17]   His Censure of the English Poets was this . . .
                  That Shaksperr wanted Arte.

[l. 208]   Sheakspear in a play brought in a number of men
                  saying they had suffered Shipwrack in Bohe-
                  mia, wher ther is no Sea neer by some 100 Miles.

[l. 590]   His Epitaph by a companion written is
                  here Lyes Benjamin Johnson dead
                  and hath no more wit than ⟨a⟩ goose in his head,
                  that as he was wont, so doth he still
                  live by his wit, and evermore will.

      Ane other
                  here lyes honest Ben
                  that had not a beard on his chen.

(*g*) 1623. [From first preliminary leaf to F1, placed opposite the portrait
t.p.; cf. vol. i, p. 142.]

To the Reader.

This Figure, that thou here seest put,
    It was for gentle Shakespeare cut;
Wherein the Grauer had a strife
    with Nature, to out-doo the life:
O, could he but haue drawne his wit
    As well in brasse, as he hath hit
His face; the Print would then surpasse
    All, that was euer writ in brasse.
But, since he cannot, Reader, looke
    Not on his Picture, but his Booke.

B. I.

(*h*) 1623. [From fifth preliminary leaf to F1.]

To the memory of my beloued,

The AVTHOR

MR. WILLIAM SHAKESPEARE:

AND

what he hath left vs.

To draw no enuy (Shakespeare) *on thy name,*
    Am I thus ample to thy Booke, and Fame:
While I confesse thy writings to be such,
    As neither Man, *nor* Muse, *can praise too much.*

'Tis true, and all mens suffrage. But these wayes
  Were not the paths I meant vnto thy praise:
For seeliest Ignorance on these may light,
  Which, when it sounds at best, but eccho's right;
Or blinde Affection, which doth ne're aduance
  The truth, but gropes, and vrgeth all by chance;
Or crafty Malice, might pretend this praise,
  And thinke to ruine, where it seem'd to raise.
These are, as some infamous Baud, or Whore,
  Should praise a Matron. What could hurt her more?
But thou art proofe against them, and indeed
  Aboue th' ill fortune of them, or the need.
I, therefore will begin. Soule of the Age!
  The applause! delight! the wonder of our Stage!
My Shakespeare, rise; I will not lodge thee by
  Chaucer, or Spenser, or bid Beaumont lye
A little further, to make thee a roome:
  Thou art a Moniment, without a tombe,
And art aliue still, while thy Booke doth liue,
  And we haue wits to read, and praise to giue.
That I not mixe thee so, my braine excuses;
  I meane with great, but disproportion'd Muses:
For, if I thought my iudgement were of yeeres,
  I should commit thee surely with thy peeres,
And tell, how farre thou didstst our Lily out-shine,
  Or sporting Kid, or Marlowes mighty line.
And though thou hadst small Latine, and lesse Greeke,
  From thence to honour thee, I would not seeke
For names; but call forth thund'ring Æschilus,
  Euripides, and Sophocles to vs,
Paccuuius, Accius, him of Cordoua dead,
  To life againe, to heare thy Buskin tread,
And shake a Stage: Or, when thy Sockes were on,
  Leaue thee alone, for the comparison
Of all, that insolent Greece, or haughtie Rome
  sent forth, or since did from their ashes come.
Triúmph, my Britaine, thou hast one to showe,
  To whom all Scenes of Europe homage owe.

He was not of an age, but for all time!
　And all the Muses *still were in their prime,*
When like Apollo *he came forth to warme*
　Our eares, or like a Mercury *to charme!*
Nature her selfe was proud of his designes,
　And ioy'd to weare the dressing of his lines!
Which were so richly spun, and wouen so fit,
　As, since, she will vouchsafe no other Wit.
The merry Greeke, *tart* Aristophanes,
　Neat Terence, *witty* Plautus, *now not please;*
But antiquated and deserted lye
　As they were not of Natures family.
Yet must I not giue Nature all: Thy Art,
　My gentle Shakespeare, *must enioy a part.*
For though the Poets *matter, Nature be,*
　His Art doth giue the fashion. And, that he,
Who casts to write a liuing line, must sweat,
　(such as thine are) and strike the second heat
Vpon the Muses *anuile: turne the same,*
　(And himselfe with it) that he thinkes to frame;
Or for the lawrell, he may gaine a scorne,
　For a good Poet's *made, as well as borne.*
And such wert thou. Looke how the fathers face
　Liues in his issue, euen so, the race
Of Shakespeares *minde, and manners brightly shines*
　In his well torned, and true filed lines:
In each of which, he seemes to shake a Lance,
　As brandish't at the eyes of Ignorance.
Sweet Swan of Auon! *what a sight it were*
　To see thee in our waters yet appeare,
And make those flights vpon the bankes of Thames,
　That so did take Eliza, *and our* Iames!
But stay, I see thee in the Hemisphere
　Aduanc'd, and made a Constellation there!
Shine forth, thou Starre of Poets, *and with rage,*
　Or influence, chide, or cheere the drooping Stage;
Which, since thy flight frõm hence, hath mourn'd like night,
　And despaires day, but for thy Volumes light.

BEN: IONSON.

(*i*) *c.* 1629. [From *Ode to Himselfe*, written after the failure of *The New Inn* (1629) and printed in Q (1631).]

> No doubt some mouldy tale,
>   Like *Pericles*; and stale
> As the Shrieues crusts, and nasty as his fish-
>   scraps, out [of] euery dish,
> Throwne forth, and rak't into the common tub,
>   May keepe vp the *Play-club:*
> There, sweepings doe as well
>   As the best order'd meale.
> For, who the relish of these ghests will fit,
> Needs set them, but, the almes-basket of wit.

(*k*) 1623◇37. [From *Timber: or, Discoveries; Made upon Men and Matter* (F 2 of 1641), 98; ed. M. Castelain (1906), 35. This appears to be a selection from note-books of Jonson, partly prepared for the press. His earlier note-books perished in a fire of 1623. Probably *Timber*, which contains references to events of 1626 and 1630, is all later.]

De Shakespeare nostrati.   I *remember*, the Players have often mentioned it as an honour to *Shakespeare*, that in his writing, (whatsoever he penn'd) hee never blotted out line. My answer hath beene, would he had blotted a thousand. Which they thought a malevolent speech. I had not told posterity this, but for their ignorance, who choose that circumstance to commend their friend by, wherein he most faulted. And to justifie mine owne candor, (for I lov'd the man, and doe honour his memory (on this side Idolatry) as much as any.) Hee was (indeed) honest, and of an open, and free nature: had an excellent *Phantsie*; brave notions, and gentle expressions: wherein hee flow'd with that facility, that sometime it was necessary he should be stop'd: *Sufflaminandus erat;* as *Augustus* said of *Haterius.* His wit was in his owne power; would the rule of it had beene so too. Many times hee fell into those things, could not escape laughter: As when hee said in the person of *Cæsar*, one speaking to him; *Cæsar thou dost me wrong.* Hee replyed: *Cæsar did never wrong, but with just cause* and such like: which were ridiculous. But hee redeemed his vices, with his vertues. There was ever more in him to be praysed, then to be pardoned.

(*l*)〉1637. [From *Life* (cf. App. C, no. xxv) in Rowe's *Works of Sh.* (1709). Other versions of the utterance by John Hales (1584–1656) are collected in Munro, i. 373, from Dryden (1668), Nahum Tate (1680), and Gildon (1694), but these do not name Jonson as an interlocutor. Gildon names Lord Falkland, and if he was present, the conversation must have been earlier than his death in 1643.]

In a Conversation between Sir *John Suckling*, Sir William *D'Avenant*, *Endymion Porter*, Mr. *Hales of Eaton*, and *Ben Johnson*; Sir *John Suckling*, who was a profess'd admirer of *Shakespear*, had undertaken his Defence against *Ben Johnson* with some warmth; Mr. *Hales*, who had sat still for some time, hearing *Ben* frequently reproaching him with the want of Learning, and Ignorance of the Antients, told him at last, That if Mr. *Shakespear* had not read the Antients, he had likewise not stollen any thing from 'em; (a Fault the other made no Conscience of) and that if he would produce any one Topick finely treated by any of them, he would undertake to shew something upon the same Subject at least as well written by *Shakespear*.

(*m*)〉1637. [From John Dryden's *Essay on the Dramatique Poetry of the Last Age*, appended to *The Conquest of Granada*, Part II (1672). Dryden (1631–1700) cannot have known Jonson personally.]

In reading some bombast speeches of *Macbeth*, which are not to be understood, he 〈Ben. Johnson〉 used to say that it was horrour.

XXIII. JOHN BODENHAM (1600)

[From *Epistle* to *Bel-vedére or The Garden of the Muses*. Commendatory verses by A. M. call Bodenham the 'causer and collectour' of the anthology. Nothing is known of him, except that he had some share in similar books, of which the most important is *England's Helicon* (1600). The only Shakespeare lines traced in *Belvedere* are *Rom. & Jul.* ii. 2. 157–8.]

I haue set down both how, whence, and where these flowres had their first springing, till thus they were drawne together into the *Muses Garden*. . . .

John Marstone.
Christopher Marlow.
Beniamin Johnson.
William Shakspeare. . . .

P 2

Thomas Nash.
·Thomas Kidde.
George Peele.
Robert Greene. . . .

These being Moderne and extant Poets, that haue liu'd togither; from many of their extant workes, and some kept in priuat.

XXIV. JOHN MANNINGHAM (1602)

[From *Diary* in *Harl. MS.* 5353, f. 29ᵛ, printed in full by J. Bruce (1868, C. S.). A facsimile of the entry is in Tannenbaum, *Problems*, 110. The name of Manningham's informant is obscurely written and was read by Collier in 1831 (*H.E.D.P.* i. 322), with a desire to find a King's actor, as Tooly, by Bruce as Touse, by Ingleby (Munro, i. 98) as Curle. Dr. Greg thinks that the reading Curle is sufficiently justified by another citation of that authority on the same page, and that the 'C' and 'u' have been touched up in a different ink, possibly but not probably modern. Edward Curle was a fellow-student with Manningham at the Middle Temple.]

13 March 1601 ⟨1602⟩ . . . Vpon a tyme when Burbidge played Rich. 3. there was a citizen greue soe farr in liking with him, that before shee went from the play shee appointed him to come that night vnto hir by the name of Ri: the 3. Shakespeare overhearing their conclusion went before, was intertained, and at his game ere Burbidge came. Then message being brought that Rich. the 3.ᵈ was at the dore, Shakespeare caused returne to be made that William the Conquerour was before Rich. the 3. Shakespeare's name William. (*Mr. Curle.*)

XXV. ANON (1603)

[From *A Mourneful Dittie, entituled Elizabeths Losse* (n. d.). That an ignorant writer supposed Robert Greene alive, and did not refer to Thomas Greene the actor, as suggested in Munro, i. 124, is clear from I⟨ohn⟩ C⟨ooke⟩'s *Epigrames* (n. d., S.R. 22 May, 1604), xii—

> some other humbly craues
> For helpe of Spirits in their sleeping graues,
> As he that calde to *Shakespeare, Iohnson, Greene,*
> To write of their dead noble Queene.]

You Poets all braue *Shakspeare*, *Johnson*, *Greene*,
Bestow your time to write for Englands Queene.
Lament, lament, lament you English Peeres,
Lament your losse possest so many yeeres.
Returne your songs and Sonnets and your sayes:
To set forth sweet *Elizabeth⟨a⟩s* praise.

XXVI. ROBERT PARSONS (1603)

[From *The Third Part of a Treatise*, *Intituled: of three Conuersions of England: conteyninge An Examen of the Calendar or Catalogue of Protestant Saints . . . by Iohn Fox*. By N. D. *The Last Six Monethes* (1604), p. 31. There was an earlier issue of 1603. That of 1604 is in two volumes. *The Last Six Monethes* (*Bodl. Th. 8° P*. 94, with Epistle dated 1 Nov. 1603) has this passage in a summary of matter already covered, but without any mention of the 'comediants', in *The First Six Monethes* (*Bodl. Th. 8° P*. 95, with Epistle dated 1 June 1603). The passage is answered by Speed (no. xxxiv). N[icholas] D[olman] is a pseudonym of the Jesuit Parsons.]

The second moneth of *February* is more fertile of rubricate Martyrs, then *Ianuary*, for that yt hath 8. in number, two Wickliffians, *Syr Iohn Oldcastle*, a Ruffian-knight as all England knoweth, & commonly brought in by comediants on their stages: he was put to death for robberyes and rebellion vnder the foresaid *K. Henry* the fifth.

XXVII. JOHN DAVIES OF HEREFORD
(1603, 1605, 1610)

(*a*) [From *Microcosmos* (1603), 215.]

Players, I loue yee, and your *Qualitie*,
As ye are Men, that pass time not abus'd:
And some ⟨*in margin*, W. S. R. B.⟩ I love for *painting*,
    poesie,
And say fell *Fortune* cannot be excus'd,
That hath for better *vses* you refus'd:
Wit, *Courage*, *good shape*, *good partes*, and all *good*,
As long as all these *goods* are no *worse* vs'd,
And though the *stage* doth staine pure gentle *bloud*,
Yet generous yee are in *minde* and *moode*.

(*b*) [From *The Civile Warres of Death and Fortune* (1605), st. 76.]

Some followed her by acting ⟨*in margin*, Stage plaiers⟩
    all mens parts,
These on a Stage she rais'd (in scorne) to fall:
And made them Mirrors, by their acting Arts,
Wherin men saw their faults, thogh ne'r so small:
Yet some she guerdond not, to their ⟨*in margin*, W. S.
    R.B.⟩ desarts;
But, othersome, were but ill-Action all:
Who while they acted ill, ill staid behinde,
(By custom of their maners) in their minde.

(*c*) [From *The Scourge of Folly* (n. d.; S.R. 8 Oct. 1610), Epig. 159. The bit about 'companion for a King' is cryptic; possibly (*a*) and (*b*) allude even more obscurely to the same matter. I once fancied that there might have been some talk of making Shakespeare, and perhaps Burbadge, Esquires of the Bath, like Drayton (cf. no. xli), at the coronation of James. But although there are Companions of the Bath now, they were only introduced into the Order in 1815, and do not represent the old Esquires, who were not so called.]

To our English Terence, Mr. Will.
Shake-speare.

Some say (good *Will*) which I, in sport, do sing,
Had'st thou not plaid some Kingly parts in sport,
Thou hadst bin a companion for a *King;*
And, beene a King among the meaner sort.
Some others raile; but, raile as they thinke fit,
Thou hast no rayling, but, a raigning Wit:
    And honesty *thou sow'st, which they do reape;*
    So, to increase their Stocke *which they do keepe.*

XXVIII. ANTHONY SCOLOKER (1604)

[From *Epistle* to *Daiphantus, or the Passions of Love*, sign. E4ᵛ.]

It should be like the *Neuer-too-well read Arcadia*, where the *Prose* and *Verce* (*Matter* and *Words*) are like his *Mistresses* eyes, one still excelling another and without Coriuall: or to come home to the vulgars *Element*, like *Friendly Shakespeare's Tragedies*, where the *Commedian* rides, when the *Tragedian* stands on Tip-toe: Faith it should please all, like Prince *Hamlet*. But in sadnesse, then it were to be feared he would runne mad: Insooth I will not be moone-sicke, to please: nor out of my wits though I displeased all.

XXIX. WILLIAM CAMDEN (1605)

[From *Remaines of a greater Worke concerning Britaine*, Poems 8.]

These may suffice for some Poeticall descriptions of our auncient Poets, if I would come to our time, what a world could I present to you out of Sir *Philipp Sidney*, *Ed. Spencer*, *Samuel Daniel*, *Hugh Holland*, *Ben: Johnson*, *Th. Campion*, *Mich. Drayton*, *George Chapman*, *Iohn Marston*, *William Shakespeare*, & other most pregnant witts of these our times, whom succeeding ages may iustly admire.

XXX. ANON (1605)

[From *Ratseis Ghost, or the Second Part of his Madde Prankes and Robberies* (n.d. S.R. 31 May 1605), sign. B1. The weary player is more likely to be Alleyn than Shakespeare.]

Get thee to London, for if one man were dead, they will haue much neede of such a one as thou art. There would be none in my opinion fitter then thyselfe to play his parts: my conceipt is such of thee, that I durst venture all the mony in my purse on thy head, to play Hamlet with him for a wager. There thou shalt learne to be frugall (for Players were neuer so thriftie as they are now about London) & to feed upon all men, to let none feede upon thee; to make thy hand a stranger to thy pocket, thy hart slow to performe thy tongues promise: and when thou feelest thy purse well lined, buy thee some place or Lordship in the Country, that growing weary of playing, thy mony may there bring thee to dignitie and reputation. . . . Sir, I thanke you (quoth the Player) for this good counsell, I promise you I will make vse of it, for, I haue heard indeede, of some that haue gone to London very meanly, and haue come in time to be exceeding wealthy.

XXXI. WILLIAM BARKSTED (1607)

[From end of *Myrrha, the Mother of Adonis; or Lustes Prodegies*. Barksted was of the Revels and Lady Elizabeth's; cf. *Eliz. Stage*, ii. 301.]

But stay my Muse in thine owne confines keepe,
    & wage not warre with so deere lou'd a neighbor,
But hauing sung thy day song, rest and sleepe
    preserue thy small fame and his greater fauor:
His Song was worthie merrit (*Shakspeare* hee)
sung the faire blossome, thou the withered tree
    Laurell is due to him, his art and wit
    hath purchast it, *Cypres* thy brow will fit.

XXXII. ANON (1609).

[From Cancel (sign. ¶ 2) in second issue of *Troil. & Cres.*]

A neuer writer, to an euer
reader. Newes.

Eternall reader, you haue heere a new play, neuer stal'd with the Stage, neuer clapper-clawd with the palmes of the vulger, and yet passing full of the palme comicall; for it is a birth of your braine, that neuer under-tooke any thing commicall, vainely: And were but the vaine names of commedies changde for the titles of Commodities, or of Playes for Pleas; you should see all those grand censors, that now stile them such vanities, flock to them for the maine grace of their grauities: especially this authors Commedies, that are so fram'd to the life, that they serue for the most common Commentaries, of all the actions of our liues shewing such a dexteritie, and power of witte, that the most displeased with Playes, are pleasd with his Commedies. And all such dull and heauy-witted world-lings, as were neuer capable of the witte of a Commedie, comming by report of them to his representations, haue found that witte there, that they neuer found in them selues, and have parted better wittied then they came: feeling an edge of witte set vpon them, more then euer they dreamd they had braine to grinde it on. So much and such sauored salt of witte is in his Commedies, that

they seeme (for their height of pleasure) to be borne in
that sea that brought forth *Venus*. Amongst all there is
none more witty then this: And had I time I would comment upon it, though I know it needs not, (for so much as
will make you thinke your testerne well bestowd) but for
so much worth, as euen poore I know to be stuft in it.
It deserues such a labour, as well as the best Commedy
in *Terence* or *Plautus*. And beleeue this, that when hee is
gone, and his Commedies out of sale, you will scramble
for them, and set vp a new English Inquisition. Take
this for a warning, and at the perrill of your pleasures losse,
and Iudgements, refuse not, nor like this the lesse, for not
being sullied, with the smoaky breath of the multitude;
but thanke fortune for the scape it hath made amongst
you. Since by the grand possessors wills I beleeue you
should have prayd for them rather then beene prayd.
And so I leaue all such to bee prayd for (for the states of
their wits healths) that will not praise it. Vale.

XXXIII. ANON (1609)

[From *Pimlyco or Runne Red-Cap* (1609), sign C. According to A. H.
Smyth, *Pericles and Apollonius*, 60, Warton said that this was originally
produced in 1596. If so, it was an error; the registration was on 15 Apr.
1609 (Arber, iii. 406).]

> Amazde I stood, to see a Crowd
> Of *Ciuill Throats* stretchd out so lowd;
> (As at a *New-play*) all the Roomes
> Did swarme with *Gentiles* mix'd with *Groomes*,
> So that I truly thought all These
> Came to see *Shore* or *Pericles*.

XXXIV. JOHN SPEED (1611).

[From *History of Great Britaine*, ix. 15; cf. no. xxvi.]

[*In margin*, The reuiew by N.D., p. 31.] That N.D.
author of the three conuersions hath made *Ouldcastle* a
Ruffian, a Robber, and a Rebell, and his authority taken
from the *Stage-plaiers*, is more befitting the pen of his
slanderous report, then the Credit of the iudicious,
being only grounded from this Papist and his Poet, of

like conscience for lies, the one euer faining, and the other euer falsifying the truth . . . I am not ignorant.

XXXV. JOHN WEBSTER (1612)

[From *Epistle* to *The White Devil* (1612); cf. *Eliz. Stage*, iii. 509.]

Detraction is the sworne friend to ignorance: For mine owne part I haue euer truly cherisht my good opinion of other mens worthy Labours, especially of that full and haightned stile of Maister *Chapman*: The labor'd and vnderstanding workes of Maister *Johnson*; The no lesse worthy composures of the both worthily excellent Maister *Beamont* & Maister *Fletcher*: And lastly (without wrong last to be named), the right happy and copious industry of M. *Shake-speare*, M. *Decker*, & M. *Heywood*, wishing what I write may be read by their light: Protesting, that, in the strength of mine owne iudgement, I know them so worthy, that though I rest silent in my owne worke, yet to most of theirs I dare (without flattery) fix that of *Martiall*.
—*non norunt, Hæc monumenta mori.*

XXXVI. THOMAS HEYWOOD (1612, 1635)

(*a*) [From *Epistle* to the printer after *An Apology for Actors* (1612); cf. *Eliz. Stage*, iv. 250. The reference is to the two poems from Heywood's *Troia Britannica* (1609), pr. in the 1612 ed. of *The Passionate Pilgrim*; cf. vol. i, p. 548.]

Here likewise, I must necessarily insert a manifest injury done me in that worke, by taking the two Epistles of *Paris* to *Helen*, and *Helen* to *Paris*, and printing them in a lesse volume, vnder the name of another, which may put the world in opinion I might steale them from him; and hee to doe himselfe right, hath since published them in his owne name: but as I must acknowledge my lines not worthy his patronage, vnder whom he hath publisht them, so the Author I know much offended with M. *Jaggard* that (altogether vnknowne to him) presumed to make so bold with his name.

(*b*) [From *The Hierarchie of the Blessed Angels* (1635), iv, p. 206.]

Our moderne Poets to that passe are driuen,
Those names are curtal'd which they first had giuen;

And, as we wisht to haue their memories drown'd,
We scarcely can afford them halfe their sound. . . .
Mellifluous *Shake-speare*, whose inchanting Quill
Commanded Mirth or Passion, was but *Will*.

XXXVII. RICHARD CAREW (1614)

[From *Epistle* from R. C. of Anthony Esquire to W. C. on *The Excellencie
of the English Tongue*, added to the 2nd ed. (1614) of Camden's *Remaines
of a Greater Worke concerning Britaine*, 36. Carew (1555–1620) was a Ch.
Ch. man and a Cornish antiquary. The names perhaps suggest 16th-century
composition, but I do not know on what authority C. M. Ingleby (*Sh.
Allusion Books*, Part I, 183) gave the date as 'about 1595–6'. Carew's
manuscript (*Cott. Julius* F. xi, f. 265), printed in G. Gregory Smith,
Elizabethan Critical Essays (1904), ii. 285, has no date.]

Adde hereunto, that whatsoeuer grace any other language
carrieth in verse or Prose, in Tropes or Metaphors, in
Ecchoes and Agnominations, they may all bee liuely and
exactly represented in ours: will you haue *Platoes* veine?
reade Sir *Thomas Smith*, the *Ionicke?* Sir *Thomas Moore.
Ciceroes? Ascham*, *Varro? Chaucer*, *Demosthenes?* Sir *Iohn
Cheeke* (who in his treatise to the Rebels, hath com-
prised all the figures of Rhetorick. Will you reade *Virgill?*
take the Earle of Surrey. *Catullus? Shakespheare* and
Barlowes ⟨*Marlows*⟩ fragment, *Ouid? Daniell. Lucan?
Spencer*, *Martial?* Sir *John Dauies* and others: will you
have all in all for Prose and verse? take the miracle of
our age, Sir *Philip Sidney*.

XXXVIII. C. B. (1614)

[From *The Ghost of Richard the Third*, Part II, stt. 1, 2. The initials
appended to the dedication have been generally taken as those of Christopher Brooke (ob. 1628).]

To him that impt my fame with Clio's quill;
Whose magick rais'd me from Obliuion's den;
That writ my storie on the Muses hill;
And with my actions dignifi'd his pen:
He that from Helicon sends many a rill;
Whose nectared veines, are drunke by thirstie men:

Crown'd be his stile with fame; his head, with bayes;
And none detract, but gratulate his praise.

Yet if his scaenes haue not engrost all grace,
The much fam'd action could extend on stage.

XXXIX. THOMAS FREEMAN (1614)

[From *Runne and a Great Cast* (the second part of *Rubbe, and a Great Cast*), Epig. 92. Freeman was of Magdalen, Oxford.]

To Master W. Shakespeare.

Shakespeare, that nimble *Mercury* thy braine,
Lulls many hundred *Argus*-eyes asleepe,
So fit, for all thou fashionest thy vaine,
At th' *horse-foote* fountaine thou hast drunk full deepe,
Vertues or vices theame to thee all one is:
Who loues chaste life, there's *Lucrece* for a Teacher:
Who list read lust there's *Venus* and *Adonis*,
True modell of a most lasciuious leatcher.
Besides in plaies thy wit windes like *Meander*:
Whence needy new-composers borrow more
Then *Terence* doth from *Plautus* or *Menander*.
But to praise thee aright I want thy store:
    Then let thine owne works thine owne worth upraise,
    And help t' adorne thee with deserued Baies.

XL. SIR WILLIAM DRUMMOND (c. 1614)

[From notes appended, without separate heading, to abstract of Drummond's conversations with Jonson (cf. no. xxii) in *Works* (1711), 226. The date is suggested by a citation of Drayton's *Polyolbion* (1613) as 'in this edition 1614'. It was in 1614 that Drummond made the acquaintance of Alexander to whose *Aurora* (1604) as well as Shakespeare's *Sonnets* (1609) he seems to refer.]

Mr *Drummond* gave the following Character of several Authors. The Authors (saith he) I have seen on the Subject of Love, are the Earl of *Surrey*, Sir *Thomas Wyat* (whom, because of their Antiquity, I will not match with our better Times) *Sidney*, *Daniel*, *Drayton*, and *Spencer*. He who writeth the Art of *English* Poesy praiseth much

Rawleigh and *Dyer*; but their Works are so few that are come to my Hands, I cannot well say any thing of them. The last we have are Sir *William Alexander* and *Shakespear*, who have lately published their Works.

XLI. EDMUND HOWES (1615)

[From continuation to 1614 in ed. 5 of John Stow's *Annales*.]

Our moderne, and present excellent Poets which worthely florish in their owne workes, and all of them in my owne knowledge lived togeather in this Queenes raigne, according to their priorities as neere as I could, I have orderly set downe (viz) *George Gascoigne* Esquire, *Thomas Churchyard* Esquire, Sir *Edward Dyer* Knight, *Edmond Spencer* Esquire, Sir *Philip Sidney* Knight, Sir *John Harrington* Knight, Sir *Thomas Challoner* Knight, Sir *Frauncis Bacon* Knight, & Sir *John Davie* Knight, Master *Iohn Lillie* gentleman, Maister *George Chapman* gentleman, M. *W. Warner* gentleman, M. *Willi. Shakespeare* gentleman, *Samuell Daniell* Esquire, *Michaell Draiton* Esquire, of the bath, M. *Christopher Marlo* gen., M. *Benjamine Johnson* gentleman, *Iohn Marston* Esquier, M. *Abraham Frauncis* gen., master *Frauncis Meers* gentle., master *Josua Siluester* gentle., master *Thomas Deckers* gentleman, M. John Flecher gentle., M. *John Webster* gentleman, M. *Thomas Heywood* gentleman, M. *Thomas Middleton* gentleman, M. *George Withers*.

XLII. J. M. (*c.* 1615)

[From *The New Metamorphosis* (*Addl. MSS.* 14824–26), vol. i, pt. ii, p. 96. On this poem, cf. Munro, ii. 480 and J. H. H. Lyon, *A Study of The N. M.* (1919). Lyon makes a good case for the authorship of Gervase ⟨Jervis⟩ Markham (1568 ?–1637). Neither the script nor the style is John Marston's.]

who hath a lovinge wife & loves her not,
he is no better then a witlesse sotte;
Let such have wives to recompense their merite,
even Menelaus forked face inherite.
Is love in wives good, not in husbands too?
why doe men sweare they love then, when they wooe?

it seemes 't is true that W. S. said,
when once he heard one courting of a Mayde,—
Beleve not thou Mens fayned flatteryes,
Lovers will tell a bushell-full of Lyes!

XLIII. THOMAS PORTER (>1615)

[From a book of Latin epigrams in the possession of the Earl of Leicester (*Coke MS*. 436, cent. i. 57), dated at end '12 die Martij Mensis 1614'. A dedication ascribes the epigrams to the writer's days at Cambridge. He was minister at Hempnall, Norfolk, in 1615.]

Gul: Shakespeare Poëtam lepidum.

Quot lepŏres in Atho tot habet tua Musa lepôres
Ingenii vena diuite metra tua.

XLIV. FRANCIS BEAUMONT (c. 1615)

[I give the poem, which has not been printed in full before, from two copies, both in 17th-century manuscript anthologies and not autograph.

(*a*) *Holgate MS*., f. 110. This is now in the Pierpont Morgan Library, New York, to which I owe my gratitude for its use, obtained through the kind offices of Mr. F. S. Ferguson. It was described in *T.L.S.* (1921, Sept. 15) by a former owner W. G. P., who printed a bit on Shakespeare, but stopped at l. 18. I had an opportunity of examining it carefully in 1925. W. G. P. took the poems to be of 1603–26. I doubt whether the collection can have been completed quite so soon. It contains much by Donne, Corbet, and other Jacobean writers, but the latter part also has much by William Strode (*c*. 1601–45). The manuscript was found at Colne Priory, Essex, and is believed to have come from some member of the Holgate family of Saffron Walden, Essex, to whom the priory passed by marriage in the 18th century. Pedigrees are in *Harl. Soc*. xiii. 421; xiv. 666. W. G. P. suggested John Holgate, who was of Caius, Cambridge in 1623 and the Middle Temple in 1626 and died in 1673. An alternative would be his nephew, William Holgate (1618–46) of Great Bardfield, Essex, and of Queens' in 1635 (Venn, ii. 392). Apparently he fell in the Civil War, to judge by lines in *Bodl. Tanner MS*. 306, f. 408, and *Bodl. Rawl. Poet. MS*. f. 12 which are headed 'To the memory of M[r] W[m]: Holgate', begin 'Harke! 'Tis a Kingdome groans. Her hartstrings crack', and end 'Sleepe folded in three dying Nations Armes'. These are ascribed in the *Tanner MS*. to 'Rob. Paman Sen[r]' and in the *Rawlinson MS*. to 'M[r] Paman pater', while the next poem is by 'Cl⟨ement⟩ P⟨aman⟩ fil'. The Pamans were of Chevington, Suffolk. Robert, of Emanuel,

Cambridge (1604), was apparently father of Henry, also of Emanuel (1643) and Public Orator, and also of Clement (1628) of Sidney Sussex (*D.N.B.*; Venn iii. 302; J. Gage, *Hist. of Suffolk*, 328, 333, 335). The *Holgate MS.* itself contains several poems by a W. H., which I have not seen elsewhere. It must be added that its *milieu* seems to be Oxford, rather than Cambridge.

(*b*) *Addl. MS.* 30982, f. 75ᵛ. This is of similar type, in date and contents, to the *Holgate MS.*, and on f. 1ᵛ is written 'Daniel Daye his Booke witnesse William Strode'. The *B. M. Cat.* makes the name 'Leare', but Mr. D. T. B. Wood, to whom I showed it, agreed in reading 'Daye'. Other owners appear to have been Anthony Evans and in 1773 Alexander Croke. The *D.N.B.* has a Daniel Daye (1683–1767), the son of a Southwark brewer, with property in Essex, but he was probably of a later generation.

The *Holgate MS.* is a good text; the *Addl. MS.* much less good, but identical errors in ll. 17, 30 suggest a common origin. In view of the variant initials, one cannot be quite sure of the author. But I see no reason why it should not be Francis Beaumont, who wrote another well-known verse epistle to Jonson, and to whom the theatrical allusions in ll. 28, 30 would be natural. There are some indications of date. Marston's *Fawn* was played *c.* 1604–6 and printed in 1606, Sharpham's *Fleir* played in 1606 and printed in 1607 (*Eliz. Stage*, iii. 432, 490). Beaumont died on 6 Mar. 1616. I think it is possible that 'the post of Douer' and the 'Carriers pist-ling ghost' (ll. 11–12) are allusions respectively to Anthony Nixon's *A Straunge Foot-Post* (1613) which has a woodcut of the Dover postman and was reissued in 1616 as *The Foot-Post of Dover*, and to G⟨ervase⟩ M⟨arkham's⟩ *Hobsons Horse-load of Letters: or A President of Epistles* (1613). Thomas Hobson was a well-known Cambridge carrier. He had not strictly a ghost, however, until 1631. There is no book by Nicholas Breton called *Common Talke*, although the description might serve for many of his compilations, including the *Wits Private Wealth*, of which a new edition appeared in 1613. Beaumont, who was a lawyer, which Jonson was not, might intelligibly refer here to the law-book ascribed to John Breton. It is an analysis of common pleas. But the title of the *c.* 1540 print is simply *Britton*, and *Common Talke* would be a very forced name to give it. If one may take 1613–16 as the limits, there were two Garter installations at Windsor (l. 27) during this period; for Frederick Count Palatine and Count Maurice of Nassau, afterwards Prince of Orange, on 7 Feb. 1613, and for Thomas Erskine, Viscount Fenton, and William Lord Knollys on 22 May 1615. (G. F. Beltz, *Memorials of the Garter*, clxxxv). I do not know whose the white and orange tawny liveries were. One would suppose them a compliment to Maurice of Nassau, but he was only installed by proxy, and presumably with no unusual splendour. John Chamberlain (Birch, *James*, i. 362) records the contention to make the best show between the knights of 1615. Fenton was to be followed by all the Bedchamber, and a hundred of the Guard, of which he was Captain, in 'new rich coats'. James Lord Hay was then a Gentleman of the Bedchamber, and he had tawny liveries on an embassy to France in 1616 (A. Wilson in W. Kennett, *Hist. of England*, ii. 704). He was rich in

royal gifts, but extravagant and sometimes in debt. No doubt he had many
needy followers. On the whole, I think that 1615 is likely to have been
the occasion which Beaumont had in mind.]

To M^r B: J :·

Neither to follow fashion nor to showe
my witt against the State, nor that I knowe
any thing now, with which I am with childe
till I haue tould, nor hopeinge to bee stilde
a good Epist'ler through the towne, with which   ⟨5⟩
I might bee famous, nor with any ytch
like these, wrote I this Letter but to showe
the Loue I carrie and mee thinkes do owe
to you aboue the number, which ⟨can⟩ best
in something which I vse not, be exprest.   ⟨10⟩
to write this I invoake none, but the post
of Douer, or some Carriers pist-ling ghost,
for if this equall but the stile, which men
send Cheese to towne with, and thankes downe agen,
tis all I seeke for: heere I would let slippe   ⟨15⟩
(If I had any in mee) schollershippe,
And from all Learninge keepe these lines as ⟨cl⟩eere
as Shakespeares best are, which our heires shall heare
Preachers apte to their auditors to showe
how farr sometimes a mortall man may goe   ⟨20⟩
by the dimme light of Nature, tis to mee
an helpe to write of nothing; and as free,
As hee, whose text was, god made all that is,
I meane to speake: what do you thinke of his
state, who hath now the last that hee could make   ⟨25⟩
in white and Orrenge tawny on his backe
at Windsor? is not this mans miserie more
then a fallen sharers, that now keepes a doore,

Title] To Ben Jonson. T. B. *A*   6 famous] famoust *A*   7 wrote I]
writ in *A*   8 do owe] dew *A*   9 can] *blank in H:* are *A*   10 I vse
not,] vse not to *A*   12 Douer] Doare *A*   14 downe agen,] dowen *A*
15 for: heere] for here; *A*   17 cleere] deere *H:* deare *A*   18 which]
& *A*   heare] teare *A*   19 apte] apt *A*   21 dimme] diuine *A*   23 whose
text] whoe *A*   24 I meane to speake:] all to (speake) I meane, *A*   26 tawny]
lawny *A*   27 mans] *om. H*   28 keepes] keepe *A*   doore,] doore *H*

hath not his state almost as wretched beene
as ⟨h⟩is, that is ordainde to write the ⟨grinne⟩ ⟨30⟩
after the fawne, and fleere shall bee? as sure
some one there is allotted to endure
that Cross. there are some, I could wish to knowe
to loue, and keepe with, if they woulde not showe
their studdies to me; or I wish to see   ⟨35⟩
their workes to laugh at, if they suffer mee
not to knowe them: And thus I would Commerse
with honest Poets that make scuruie verse.
by this time you perceiue you did a misse
to leaue your worthier studies to see this, ⟨40⟩
which is more tedious to you, then to walke
in a Jews Church, or Bretons Com̃on talke.
but know I write not these lines to the end
to please Ben: Johnson but to please my frend: ffinis: FB:

30 his] is *H, A* is] & *A* write] om *A* grinne] geinne *H*: Crime *A*
31 fleere] feare *A* 37 thus] y^t *A* 38 verse.] verse *H* 40 your] the *A*
worthier] wortier *H*: worthyer *A* see] vse *A* 42 Bretons] Brittans *A*
42 talke.] talke *H* 43 I write] y^t I wrote *A* 44 ffinis: FB:] om *A*

XLV. EDMUND BOLTON (*c.* 1616)

[From *Bodl. Rawl. MS.* D 1, f. 14ᵛ. This is anonymous, but clearly a draft
for the *Hypercritica* of Bolton (1575 ?–1633 ?). The final version (pr.
J. E. Spingarn, *Critical Essays of the Seventeenth Century*, i. 82) was also
left in MS.; it cannot be earlier than 1616 (cf. Munro, i. 213). It contains
no reference to Shakespeare.]

The bookes also out of which wee gather the most warrant-
able English are not many to my Remembrance, of which
in regard they require a particuler and curious tract, I
forbeare to speake at this present. But among the cheife,
or rather the cheife are in my opinion these . . . Shakespere, Mʳ Francis Beamont and innumerable other
writers for the stage and presse tenderly to be vsed in this
Argument.

XLVI. WILLIAM BASSE (1616◊1623)

[From *Lansdowne MS*. 777, f. 67ᵛ. Basse (*c.* 1583–*c.* 1653) was an Oxford student and a retainer of Lord Wenman of Thame. Full accounts of the numerous versions of the elegy are in Munro, i. 287 and R. W. Bond, *Works of Basse* (1893), 113. It was printed as Donne's in his *Poems* of 1633, but omitted from later editions. In Benson's ed. of Shakespeare's *Poems* (1640), sign. K8ᵛ, it has the initials W.B. and six MS. versions ascribe it to Basse. A MS. not identified by Munro is *Bodl. Rawl. Poet.* 60 (*c.* 1640), f. 13ᵛ. Here it is anonymous; the only interesting variant is 'comedian' in l. 12.]

On Mr. Wm. Shakespeare
he dyed in Aprill 1616.

Renowned Spencer, lye a thought more nye
To learned Chaucer, and rare Beaumont lye
A little neerer Spenser to make roome
For Shakespeare in your threefold fowerfold Tombe.
To lodge all fowre in one bed make a shift
Vntill Doomesdaye, for hardly will a fift
Betwixt this day and that by Fate be slayne
For whom your Curtaines may be drawn againe.
If your precedency in death doth barre
A fourth place in your sacred sepulcher,
Vnder this carued marble of thine owne
Sleepe rare Tragœdian Shakespeare, sleep alone,
Thy vnmolested peace, vnshared Caue,
Possesse as Lord not Tenant of thy Graue,
    That vnto us and others it may be
    Honor hereafter to be layde by thee.

                                        Wm. Basse.

XLVII. JOHN TAYLOR (1620)

[From *The Praise of Hemp-seed*, 26.]

In paper, many a Poet now suruiues
Or else their lines had perish'd with their liues.
Old *Chaucer*, *Gower*, and Sir *Thomas More*,
Sir *Philip Sidney*, who the Lawrell wore,
Spencer, and *Shakespeare* did in Art excell,
Sir *Edward Dyer*, *Greene*, *Nash*, *Daniell*.

Siluester, Beumont, Sir *John Harrington,*
Forgetfulnesse their workes would ouer run,
But that in paper they immortally
Doe liue in spight of death, and cannot die.

XLVIII. NICHOLAS RICHARDSON (1620)

[From *Bodl. MS. Eng. Misc.* d. 28, p. 359, col. 705. This is one of several passages from Shakespeare in a commonplace book formerly preserved in the Principal's lodgings at Brasenose, and possibly compiled by Principal Samuel Radcliffe (1614–48). Richardson became a Fellow of Magdalen in 1614 (Munro, ii. 279; *Clarendon Press Periodical* for Dec. 1901; *Cat. Bodl. Shakespeare Exhibition,* 57; W. D. Macray, *Magdalen Register,* iii. 144). The text is a slight variation of *Rom. & Jul.* ii. 2. 177–82. The pagination, as in other extracts in the MS., does not belong to any early Q. Dr. Greg suggests to me that the compiler probably had before him a bound collection of Qq, paginated by hand.]

Tis' almost morning I would haue thee gone
And yet no farther then a wantons bird,
That lets it hop a little from his hand,
Like a poore prisoner, in his twisted gyues,
Then with a silken thread plucks it back againe
So iealous louing of his liberty. Tragedy of
Romeo and Juliet. 4°: pag. 84:
      Said by Juliet: pro eadem.
this Mr Richardson Coll. Magd: inserted hence into his
Sermon, preached it twice at St Maries 1620. 1621.
applying it to gods loue to his Saints either hurt with
sinne, or aduersity neuer forsaking thē.

XLIX. THOMAS WALKLEY (1622)

[From Q 1 of *Oth.,* sign. A 2. Walkley was the publisher.]

The Stationer to the Reader.

To set forth a booke without an Epistle, were like to the
old English prouerbe, A blew coat without a badge, &
the Author being dead, I thought good to take that piece

of worke vpon mee: To commend it, I will not, for that which is good, I hope euery man will commend, without intreaty: and I am the bolder, because the Authors name is sufficient to vent his worke. Thus leauing euery one to the liberty of iudgement: I haue ventered to print this Play, and leaue it to the generall censure.

Yours,
Thomas Walkley.

L. JOHN HEMINGES AND HENRY CONDELL (1623)

(*a*) [*Epistle* to the Earls of Pembroke and Montgomery, on third preliminary leaf of F1; cf. vol. i, p. 142.]

Right Honourable,
Whilst we studie to be thankful in our particular, for the many fauors we have receiued from your L. L we are falne vpon the ill fortune, to mingle two the most diuerse things that can bee, feare, and rashnesse; rashnesse in the enterprize, and feare of the successe. For, when we valew the places your H. H. sustaine, we cannot but know their dignity greater, then to descend to the reading of these trifles: and, while we name them trifles, we haue depriu'd our selues of the defence of our Dedication. But since your L. L. haue beene pleas'd to thinke these trifles something, heeretofore; and haue prosequuted both them, and their Author liuing, with so much fauour: we hope, that (they out-liuing him, and he not hauing the fate, common with some, to be exequutor to his owne writings) you will vse the like indulgence toward them, you haue done vnto their parent. There is a great difference, whether any Booke choose his Patrones, or finde them: This hath done both. For, so much were your L L. likings of the seuerall parts, when they were acted, as before they were published, the Volume ask'd to be yours. We haue but collected them, and done an office to the dead, to procure his Orphanes, Guardians; without ambition either of selfe-profit, or fame: onely to keepe the memory of so worthy a Friend, & Fellow aliue, as was our SHAKESPEARE, by humble offer

of his playes, to your most noble patronage. Wherein, as we haue iustly obserued, no man to come neere your L. L. but with a kind of religious addresse; it hath bin the height of our care, who are the Presenters, to make the present worthy of your H. H. by the perfection. But, there we must also craue our abilities to be considerd, my Lords. We cannot go beyond our owne powers. Country hands reach foorth milke, creame, fruites, or what they haue: and many Nations (we haue heard) that had not gummes & incense, obtained their requests with a leauened Cake. It was no fault to approch their Gods, by what meanes they could: And the most, though meanest, of things are made more precious, when they are dedicated to Temples. In that name therefore, we most humbly consecrate to your H. H. these remaines of your seruant *Shakespeare;* that what delight is in them, may be euer your L. L. the reputation his, & the faults ours, if any be committed, by a payre so carefull to shew their gratitude both to the liuing, and the dead, as is

Your Lordshippes most bounden,
John Heminge.
Henry Condell.

(*b*) [*To the great Variety of Readers,* on fourth preliminary leaf of F1.]

From the most able, to him that can but spell: There you are number'd. We had rather you were weighd. Especially, when the fate of all Bookes depends upon your capacities: and not of your heads alone, but of your purses. Well! it is now publique, & you wil stand for your priuiledges wee know: to read, and censure. Do so, but buy it first. That doth best commend a Booke, the Stationer saies. Then, how odde soeuer your braines be, or your wisedomes, make your licence the same, and spare not. Judge your sixe-pen'orth, your shillings worth, your fiue shillings worth at a time, or higher, so you rise to the iust rates, and welcome. But, what euer you do, Buy. Censure will not driue a Trade, or make the Iacke go. And though you be a Magistrate of wit, and sit on the Stage at *Black-Friers,* or the *Cock-pit,* to arraigne Playes dailie, know, these Playes haue had their triall alreadie, and stood out all Appeales; and do now come forth quitted rather by a Decree of Court, then any purchas'd Letters of commendation.

It had bene a thing, we confesse, worthie to haue bene wished, that the Author himselfe had liu'd to haue set forth, and ouerseen his owne writings; But since it hath bin ordain'd otherwise, and he by death departed from that right, we pray you do not envie his Friends, the office of their care, and paine, to haue collected & publish'd them; and so to haue publish'd them, as where (before) you were abus'd with diuerse stolne, and surreptitious copies, maimed, and deformed by the frauds and stealthes of iniurious impostors, that expos'd them: euen those, are now offer'd to your view cur'd, and perfect of their limbes; and all the rest, absolute in their numbers, as he conceiued them. Who, as he was a happie imitator of Nature, was a most gentle expresser of it. His mind and hand went together: And what he thought, he vttered with that easinesse, that wee haue scarce receiued from him a blot in his papers. But it is not our prouince, who onely gather his works, and giue them you, to praise him. It is yours that reade him. And there we hope, to your diuers capacities, you will finde enough, both to draw, and hold you: for his wit can no more lie hid, then it could be lost. Reade him, therefore; and againe, and againe: And if then you doe not like him, surely you are in some manifest danger, not to vnderstand him. And so we leaue you to other of his Friends, whom if you need, can bee your guides: if you neede them not, you can leade your selues, and others. And such Readers we wish him.

John Heminge.
Henrie Condell.

LI. HUGH HOLLAND (1623)

[From sixth preliminary leaf to F1. Holland (ob. 1633) was a traveller and poet of Trinity, Cambridge.]

Vpon the Lines and Life of the Famous
Scenicke Poet, Master WILLIAM SHAKESPEARE.

Those hands, which you so clapt, go now, and wring
You *Britaines* braue; for done are *Shakespeares* dayes:
His dayes are done, that made the dainty Playes,
Which made the Globe of heau'n and earth to ring.
Dry'de is that veine, dry'd is the *Thespian* Spring,
Turn'd all to teares, and *Phœbus* clouds his rayes:
That corp's, that coffin now besticke those bayes,
Which crown'd him *Poet* first, then *Poets* King.
If *Tragedies* might any *Prologue* haue,
All those he made, would scarse make one to this:
Where *Fame*, now that he gone is to the graue
(Deaths publique tyring-house) the *Nuncius* is.
  For though his line of life went soone about,
  The life yet of his lines shall neuer out.
                                    HVGH HOLLAND.

LII. LEONARD DIGGES (1623, 1640)

(*a*) [From eighth preliminary leaf to F1. Digges (1588–1635) was a translator, of University College, Oxford.]

To THE MEMORIE
of the deceased Authour Maister
W. SHAKESPEARE.

Shake-speare, at length thy pious fellowes giue
The world thy Workes: thy Workes, by which, out-liue
Thy Tombe, thy name must: when that stone is rent,
And Time dissolues thy *Stratford* Moniment,
Here we aliue shall view thee still. This Booke,
When Brasse and Marble fade, shall make thee looke
Fresh to all Ages: when Posteritie
Shall loath what 's new, thinke all is prodegie

That is not *Shake-speares;* eu'ry Line, each Verse,
Here shall reuiue, redeeme thee from thy Herse.
Nor Fire, nor cankring Age, as *Naso* said,
Of his, thy wit-fraught Booke shall once inuade.
Nor shall I e're beleeue, or thinke thee dead
(Though mist) untill our bankrout Stage be sped
(Impossible) with some new strain t' out-do
Passions of *Iuliet,* and her *Romeo;*
Or till I heare a Scene more nobly take,
Then when thy half-Sword parlying *Romans* spake,
Till these, till any of thy Volumes rest
Shall with more fire, more feeling be exprest,
Be sure, our *Shake-speare,* thou canst neuer dye,
But crown'd with Lawrell, liue eternally.

                                        L. Digges.

(*b*) [Commendatory verses to Shakespeare's *Poems* (1640).]

Poets are borne not made, when I would prove
This truth, the glad rememberance I must love
Of never dying *Shakespeare,* who alone,
Is argument enough to make that one.
First, that he was a Poet none would doubt,
That heard th' applause of what he sees set out
Imprinted; where thou hast (I will not say)
Reader his Workes (for to contrive a Play
To him twas none) the patterne of all wit,
Art without Art unparaleld as yet.
Next Nature onely helpt him, for looke thorow
This whole Booke, thou shalt find he doth not borrow,
One phrase from Greekes, nor Latines imitate,
Nor once from vulgar Languages Translate,
Nor Plagiari-like from others gleane,
Nor begges he from each witty friend a Scene
To peece his Acts with, all that he doth write,
Is pure his owne, plot, language exquisite,
But oh! what praise more powerfull can we give
The dead, than that by him the Kings men live,
His Players, which should they but have shar'd the Fate,
All else expir'd within the short Termes date;

How could the Globe have prospered, since through want
Of change, the Plaies and Poems had growne scant.
But happy Verse thou shalt be sung and heard,
When hungry quills shall be such honour bard.
Then vanish upstart Writers to each Stage,
You needy Poetasters of this Age,
Where *Shakespeare* liv'd or spake, Vermine forbeare,
Least with your froth you spot them, come not neere;
But if you needs must write, if poverty
So pinch, that otherwise you starve and die,
On Gods name may the Bull or Cockpit have
Your lame blancke Verse, to keepe you from the grave:
Or let new Fortunes younger brethren see,
What they can picke from your leane industry.
I doe not wonder when you offer at
Blacke-Friers, that you suffer: tis the fate
Of richer veines, prime judgements that have far'd
The worse, with this deceased man compar'd.
So have I seene, when Cesar would appeare,
And on the Stage at halfe-sword parley were,
Brutus and *Cassius*: oh how the Audience,
Were ravish'd, with what wonder they went thence,
When some new day they would not brooke a line,
Of tedious (though well laboured) *Catilines;*
Sejanus too was irkesome, they priz'de more
Honest *Iago*, or the jealous Moore.
And though the Fox and subtill Alchimist,
Long intermitted could not quite be mist,
Though these have sham'd all the Ancients, and might
        raise,
Their Authours merit with a crowne of Bayes.
Yet these sometimes, even at a friend's desire
Acted, have scarce defraied the Seacoale fire
And doore-keepers: when let but *Falstaffe* come,
Hall, Poines, the rest you scarce shall have a roome
All is so pester'd: let but *Beatrice*
And *Benedicke* be seene, loe in a trice
The Cockpit Galleries, Boxes, all are full
To heare *Maluoglio* that crosse garter'd Gull.

Briefe, there is nothing in his wit fraught Booke,
Whose sound we would not heare, on whose worth looke
Like old coynd gold, whose lines in every page,
Shall passe true currant to succeeding age.
But why doe I dead *Sheakspeares* praise recite,
Some second *Shakespeare* must of *Shakespeare* write;
For me tis needlesse, since an host of men,
Will pay to clap his praise, to free my Pen.

LIII. I. M. (1623)

[From the eighth preliminary leaf to F1. Lee 557 says that I. M. was 'perhaps Jasper Mayne', who in 1623 was a boy leaving Westminster for Ch. Ch., Oxford; perhaps he was thinking of the I. M. S. lines in F2. A better guess is James Mabbe (1572–1642), translator, of Magdalen, Oxford, since the same 'tyring house' simile is in his translation of *Guzman de Alfarache* in 1623.]

To the memorie of *M.* W. Shake-speare.

Wee wondred (*Shake-speare*) that thou went'st so soone
From the Worlds-Stage, to the Graues-Tyring-roome.
Wee thought thee dead, but this thy printed worth,
Tels thy Spectators, that thou went'st but forth
To enter with applause. An Actors Art,
Can dye, and liue, to acte a second part.
That's but an *Exit* of Mortalitie;
This, a Re-entrance to a Plaudite.   I. M.

LIV. SIR HENRY SALISBURY? (*c.* 1623)

[From *Nat. Library of Wales MS.* 5390 D, p. 141, pr. with facsimile by I. Gollancz in *Studies in the First Folio*, xxx. The MS. belonged to the family of Salisbury of Llewenny. The poem follows entries of 1622. Gollancz thinks the author likely to be Sir Henry Salisbury, son of the Sir John to whom *Love's Martyr* was dedicated.]

To my good freandes m^r John Hemings & Henry Condall.

To yowe that Joyntly with vndaunted paynes
vowtsafed to Chawnte to vs thease noble straynes,
how mutch yowe merrytt by it is not sedd,
butt yowe haue pleased the lyving, loved the deadd,

Raysede from the woambe of Earth a Ritcher myne
then Curteys Cowlde with all his Castelyne
Associattes, they dydd butt digg for Gowlde,
Butt yowe for Treasure mutch moare manifollde.

LV. JOHN MILTON (1630)

[From *Poems* (1645). I follow this text, as authorized and dated by the
writer. The lines had, however, already appeared (*a*) in the prefatory
matter to F2 (1632), unascribed and headed *An Epitaph on the admirable
Dramaticke Poet, W. Shakespeare*; (*b*) in Shakespeare's *Poems* (1640), sign.
K 8 (cf. vol. i, p. 557), initialled I. M. and headed *An Epitaph on the admirable
Dramaticke Poet, William Sheakespeare*. They reappeared in F 3 (1663–4),
in Milton's *Poems* (1673), and (*pace* Garrod) in F 4 (1685). The
slight variants can be studied in H. W. Garrod, *Milton's Lines on Sh.*
(1926, *Essays and Studies*, xii. 7) and R. M. Smith, *The Variant Issues of
Sh's. F 2 and Milton's First Published English Poem* (1928, *Lehigh Univ.
Publ.* ii. 3). Milton, born in 1608 and a Londoner, might conceivably
have seen Shakespeare. It is only a guess of Warton and independently of
Malone (*Var.* ii. 4) that Milton might have written the short appreciation
in his nephew Edward Phillips's *Theatrum Poetarum* (1675), 194, '*William
Shakespear*, the Glory of the English Stage; whose nativity at *Stratford*
upon *Avon*, is the highest honour that Town can boast of: from an Actor
of Tragedies and Comedies, he became a *Maker*; and such a Maker, that
though some others may perhaps pretend to a more exact *Decorum* and
œconomie, especially in Tragedy, never any express't a more lofty and
Tragic heighth; never any represented nature more purely to the life, and
where the polishments of Art are most wanting, as probably his Learning
was not extraordinary, he pleaseth with a certain wild and native Elegance;
and in all his Writings hath an unvulgar style, as well in his *Venus and
Adonis*, his *Rape of Lucrece* and other various Poems, as in his Dramatics'.]

On *Shakespear*, 1630.

What needs my *Shakespear* for his honour'd Bones,
The labour of an age in piled Stones,
Or that his hallow'd reliques should be hid
Under a Star-ypointing *Pyramid*?
Dear son of memory, great heir of Fame,
What need'st thou such weak witnes of thy name?
Thou in our wonder and astonishment
Hast built thy self a live-long Monument.
For whilst toth' shame of slow-endeavouring art,
Thy easie numbers flow, and that each heart

Hath from the leaves of thy unvalu'd Book,
Those Delphick lines with deep impression took,
Then thou our fancy of it self bereaving,
Dost make us Marble with too much conceaving;
And so Sepulcher'd in such pomp dost lie,
That Kings for such a Tomb would wish to die.

LVI. ANON (1632)

[From preliminary matter to F 2. The unknown author seems to claim personal knowledge of Shakespeare.]

*Upon the Effigies of my worthy
Friend, the Author Master William
Shakespeare, and his Workes.*

Spectator, this Life's Shaddow is; To see
The truer image and a livelier he
Turne Reader. But, observe his Comicke vaine,
Laugh, and proceed next to a Tragicke straine,
Then weepe; So when thou find'st two contraries,
Two different passions from thy rapt soule rise,
Say, (who alone effect such wonders could)
Rare *Shake-speare* to the life thou dost behold.

LVII. SIR WILLIAM DAVENANT (1638)

[Lines printed with *Madagascar* (1638). I give them because they have been regarded as written in 1616, when Davenant was only ten years old (cf. vol. i, p. 573). B. Corney (*3 N.Q.* xii. 3) showed that this was due to an error in A. Chalmers, *General Biographical Dictionary* (1812).]

In Remembrance of
Master *William Shakespeare.*
Ode.

Beware (delighted Poets!) when you sing
To welcome Nature in the early Spring;
Your num'rous Feet not tread
The Banks of Avon; for each Flowre
(As it nere knew a Sunne or Showre)
Hangs there, the pensive head.

Each Tree, whose thick, and spreading growth hath made,
Rather a Night beneath the Boughs, than Shade,
　　(Unwilling now to grow)
Looks like the Plume a Captive weares,
Whose rifled *Falls* are steept i'th teares
　　Which from his last rage flow.

The piteous River wept it selfe away
Long since (Alas!) to such a swift decay;
　　That read the Map; and looke
If you a River there can spie;
And for a River your mock'd Eie,
　　Will find a shallow Brooke.

LVIII. JOHN BENSON (1640)

[*Epistle* to *Poems: Written by Wil. Shake-speare. Gent.* (1640, John Benson).]

To the Reader.

I here presume (under favour) to present to your view, some excellent and sweetely composed Poems, of Master *William Shakespeare*, Which in themselves appeare of the same purity, the Authour himselfe then living avouched; they had not the fortune by reason of their Infancie in his death, to have the due accommodation of proportionable glory, with the rest of his everliving Workes, yet the lines of themselves will afford you a more authentick approbation than my assurance any way can, to invite your allowance, in your perusall you shall finde them *Seren*, cleere and eligantly plaine, such gentle straines as shall recreate and not perplexe your braine, no intricate or cloudy stuffe to puzzell intellect, but perfect eloquence; such as will raise your admiration to his praise: this assurance I know will not differ from your acknowledgement. And certaine I am, my opinion will be seconded by the sufficiency of these ensuing Lines; I have beene some what solicitus to bring this forth to the perfect view of all men; and in so doing, glad to be serviceable for the continuance of glory to the deserved Author in these his Poems.   I. B.

APPENDIX C

THE SHAKESPEARE-MYTHOS

[*Bibliographical Note*. The notices of Shakespeare in Edward Phillips, *Theatrum Poetarum* (1675), William Winstanley, *Lives of the most Famous English Poets* (1687), Gerard Langbaine, *Momus Triumphans* (1688), *An Account of the English Dramatick Poets* (1691), Charles Gildon, *The Lives and Characters of the English Dramatick Poets* (1698), are so meagre as to be now of no biographical value. We may share the regrets of Malone (*Var.*ii. 4) that Thomas Heywood's *Lives of All the Poets* (cf. *Eliz. Stage*, iii. 339) if more than projected, is unknown, that Anthony Wood found no room for Shakespeare in the *Athenae Oxonienses* (1692), and that so many persons of Shakespeare's generation or the next, who lived to the end of the 17th century or the beginning of the 18th, yet died with unconsulted memories, before Nicholas Rowe (no. xxv) made the first attempt at a considered *Life* in 1709. From one of these, indeed, Sir William Bishop of Bridgetown (ob. 1700), isolated statements of no great value found their way to John Roberts (no. xxxi) in 1729 and William Oldys (no. xxxiv) before 1761. They are utilized in the *Variorum* itself, with others, which include those of Thomas Jones of Tardebigge (no. xliv) who died in 1703, Richard Davies of Sapperton (no. xv) who died in 1708, Sir Hugh Clopton (no. xxxiii) who died in 1751 but preserved the traditions of New Place, and the collections of John Aubrey (no. xiii) in 1681. A few other notices, even from the 17th century, have come to light since Malone's day. The most interesting are those of Thomas Plume (no. vii) about 1657 and John Ward (no. ix) about 1662. Many which emerged in the 18th and even the 19th centuries are, of course, of doubtful origin and still more doubtful validity. There are partial collections in H.P. (ii. 69, and illustrative notes, *passim*) and in J. Munro, *Shakespeare Allusion Book*. I have brought together as many as possible in this Appendix, and have attempted to make a discreet use of them in chs. i and iii and elsewhere. It is, I think, possible to underestimate the value of biographical tradition, where it is not inconsistent with other evidence. Provincial memories are long-lived, and so are those of professions which, like that of the stage, are largely recruited as hereditary castes. There is, of course, a tact to be exercised in taking the gist of a statement, without laying too much stress on its details. And it must be admitted that after all there is much here which throws less light upon Shakespeare than upon the mental processes which lead to the development of myths. There are three streams of tradition, deriving respectively from London, from Oxford, and from Stratford. The London tradition is mainly theatrical. Its main channel of transmission seems to have been through Sir William Davenant (1606–68) and his associate Thomas Betterton (*c.* 1635–1710), who also visited Stratford on behalf of Rowe (no. xxv), and from Betterton through Alexander Pope (1688–1744) and his circle, including Spence (no. xxx), Oldys (no. xxxiv), and Johnson (no. xlii). But Oldys also learnt something from John Bowman and Aubrey (no. xiii), from Thomas Shadwell, John Lacy, and William Beeston. Dryden (no. xii), Ravenscroft (no. xiv), and Gildon (no. xxi) drew independently on theatrical sources. In this way we get a few *personalia* of Shakespeare, especially as an actor, something about his relations with Jonson (cf. vol. i, p. 69, and App. B, no. xxii), and stories as to the composition of *Tit. Andr.* (no. xiv), *Rom. & Jul.* (no. xii), *Hen. IV* (nos. i, iv, v, xxxiv), *Merry Wives of W.* (nos. xxiii, xxv), *Ham.* (xxi), *Oth.* (no. xxi), and *Per.* (no. xii). These are not all to be despised, and in the case of *Hen. IV* at least there is bibliographical confirmation. The Oxford tradition only concerns itself with the relations between Shakespeare and the Davenants. It has evidently a local element, but again owes something to Sir William Davenant, if only for tacit acquiescence in a not very reputable version. I discuss it (vol. i, p. 573) in connexion with the *Sonnets.* The Stratford contribution is of a very miscellaneous kind. The nearest approach to a personal reminiscence is Plume's story (no. vii), apparently not free from blunder, of a visit by a member of the Mennis family to John Shakespeare's shop. But Stratford was not unaware of the reputation of its distinguished inhabitant, and became a place of pilgrimage at an early date. A visit is already recorded in *A Banquet of Jeasts* (1630, quoted in Munro, i. 347). It was by an anonym, who, although 'walking in the Church to doe his devotion', noted nothing of its object. It was followed by those of Robert Dobyns (no. xi) in 1673, Dowdall (no. xviii) in 1693, and William Hall (no. xix) in 1694; and the babble of the sexton about Shakespeare's curse on his tomb (App. A, no. xxv) and the epigram on Combe (cf. p. 138), whether there was anything in it or not, shows that the inquisitiveness of tourists was already beginning to meet with its natural response. Similarly, the 'crab-tree' story (nos. xl, xlvi), which is studied in C. F. Green, *The Legend of Shakespeare's Crab-Tree* (1857) probably owes its development to the desire of local guides that visitors should take a remunerative trip. It appears late, and may have been suggested by the analogous story of the deer-stealing. But this, which comes to us in its earliest form (cf. vol. i, p. 18) from two independent sources, is likely to have more substance in it. Its later modifications are clearly affected by a desire to get round the objections of historically minded sceptics. A study is C. H. Bracebridge, *Shakespeare no Deer-stealer* (1862). The interplay of tradition and research is indeed a factor which must be supposed to have affected many statements made from Stratford, especially after some antiquarian knowledge had been brought to bear by Joseph Greene (1712–90), master of the Stratford Grammar School from 1735 and afterwards rector of Welford, and James Davenport, vicar (1787–1841) of Stratford. Greene found (cf. p. 169) Shakespeare's will, and collected information for James West (cf. no. xlvii), once a Secretary to the Treasury, more friendly than some of his coat to learning. Many of Greene's papers passed to H.P. (*Rarities*, 2, 5, 42, 114, 257, 282, 289). H.P. edited *The Correspondence*

of E. Malone and J. Davenport (1864). By the time that we come to
Jordan (no. xlvi) it is very difficult to determine what is due to tradition,
invention, and literary sources respectively. There are various stories (nos.
xxxi, xxxiii, xlvi, li, liii, liv) of lost papers of Shakespeare, but none in which
much credence can be placed. Any which he left are more likely to have
gone to Abington than to have remained at New Place. They may have
passed to Edward Bagley (cf. p. 180) on Lady Bernard's death. Tradition
naturally tends to fortify itself by concrete evidence in the form of tangible
relics. Of many of those which have appeared at Stratford the less said the
better. I do not know whether the bench and mug owned by West (no.
xlvii) were supposed to have come from Wincot (cf. no. viii), or like a
'Shakespeare's chair' now at the Birthplace (*Cat.* 20) from the Falcon
Inn at Bidford. The Birthplace has also a desk from the Grammar School
(*Cat.* 264) alleged to have been Shakespeare's, and a seal ring (*Cat.* 223)
found near Stratford churchyard in 1810. It bears the initials W. S., but
they are separated by a lovers' knot, and may indicate two persons rather
than one. F. H. Fairholt, *The Home of Shakespeare* (1847), 27, figures a
square of painted glass, believed to have come from New Place, which
links W and A and above them S in a lovers' knot, and has the date 1615.
It was afterwards owned by H.P. (*Rarities*, 151). More recently, the
frame of a horn-book, bearing initials, which may be W. S. and may be
W. B., was found in Anne Hathaway's Cottage at Shottery. It was described by F. C. Wellstood in *The Times* for 8 Oct. 1926, and is figured
in *M. A.* iii, f.p. But at the best, such common initials as W. S.
afford little guidance. In 1758 Francis Gastrell cut down a mulberry tree
at New Place, which Sir Hugh Clopton had believed to have been planted
by Shakespeare. Considerable resentment was aroused and the wood of
this tree, and not improbably others, was used in the construction of many
small articles for sale (nos. xxxiii, xl, l, lii; cf. *Var.* ii. 522; H.P. i. 411; Lee
289, 516). There was some planting of mulberries in England about 1609,
but Shakespeare was already familiar with the fruit in *Mid. N. Dr.* Most
of the reputed portraits of Shakespeare can claim no greater authenticity
than the relics. Being inexpert in such matters, I am content to rely on
the learned research of M. H. Spielmann in the *Encyclopaedia Britannica*,
the *Stratford Town Shakespeare* (1904–7), x, the *Connoisseur* (1908–13),
and *Shakespeare's Portraiture* (1923, and in *Studies in F 1*, 1). Earlier
treatises are A. Wivell, *Inquiry into Sh.'s Portraits* (1827), G. Scharf,
On the Principal Portraits of Sh. (1864), J. H. Friswell, *Life Portraits of
Sh.* (1864), W. Page, *Study of Sh.'s Portraits* (1877), J. P. Norris, *The
Portraits of Sh.* (1885). There are also some monographs upon individual
pictures. Apart from the bust (cf. App. A, no. xxv), we can only rely upon
the engraving which forms part of the title-page of F 1. This is by Martin
Droeshout, of the third generation of a family of Flemish artists resident
in London. It exists, so far as F 1 is concerned, in two states. Of the first,
sometimes called a proof, only four examples are known: (*a*) in Malone's
copy (*Bodl. Mal.* 1, now Arch. G. c. 8), mounted upon an 18th-century
reprint of the t.p., (*b*) in a recent B.M. acquisition (C. 39. k. 15), (*c*) in

PLATE XXVI

DROESHOUT ENGRAVING (*First State*)

PLATE XXVII

DROESHOUT ENGRAVING (*Second State*)

the collection of H. C. Folger, removed by H.P. from a copy now in the
Shakespeare Memorial at Stratford, (*d*) in an undivulged American collection. The ordinary impressions differ (cf. Plates XXVI, XXVII) from the
'proof' in several respects. The eyebrows and moustache have been intensi-
fied. The chin is stubbly, instead of smooth. Light has been added at the
edge of the hair and a shadow on the collar. The plate continued to be used
for F2, F3, and F4. It deteriorated considerably, seems to have been more
than once touched up, and was finally restored by 'violent cross-hatching'
for F4. Even in the proof, the presentment is an ungainly one. The head
is too large for the body. The line of the jaw is hard. There is bad drawing
in the hair, eyes, nose, ear, and mouth, which is too much to the right. The
lines of the dress are distorted. The lighting comes from more than one
direction. But the perpendicular forehead and the shape of the skull are
in conformity with those of the bust. Spielmann thinks that the engraver
may have worked from an outline drawing with colour washes, which may
have shown a Shakespeare twenty years younger than the Shakespeare of
the bust. The doublet may be his own addition. It is the rich costume of
a well-placed man. I do not think it need be inferred that Shakespeare
would only have worn it on the stage, or that it is the livery of a groom of
the chamber. The 'Flower' portrait, now in the Stratford Memorial, was
given in 1895, with an unverifiable history of derivation from a descendant
of Shakespeare's family. It bears the date, not necessarily contemporary, of
'1609', and has been claimed as the original of the engraving. Spielmann
has demonstrated that, on the contrary, it is derived from this, some of the
defects of which a fairly competent hand has modified. The convincing
proof is that it agrees with the ordinary impressions, where these deviate
from the first state. The attractive 'Chandos' portrait in the National
Portrait Gallery, traditionally ascribed to the brush of Burbadge, has a
pedigree (Lee 534) taking it back to the ownership of Sir William
Davenant, but in view of its incomplete resemblance to the bust and the
engraving cannot be supposed to be from life. Of the rest, some are
derivative, others depend on mistaken identifications, and many are sheer
frauds.

I. RICHARD JAMES (*c.* 1625)

[From *Epistle* to Sir Harry Bourchier, with a copy of Occleve's *Legend
and Defence of Sir John Oldcastle* (*Bodl. James MS.* 34; *B.M. Grenville
MS.* 35), pr. A. B. Grosart, *Works of R. James* (1880). James (1592–1638)
was of C.C.C. Oxford and librarian to Sir Robert Cotton. Many of his
MSS. are in the Bodleian, and H.P., *On the Character of Sir John Falstaff*
(1841), 19, thought that the *Epistle* was in his script of *c.* 1625. Bourchier
was knighted 9 Nov. 1621.]

A young Gentle Lady of your acquaintance, having read
yᵉ works of Shakespeare, made me this question. How
Sʳ John Falstaffe, or Fastolf, as he is written in yᵉ Statute

book of Maudlin Colledge in Oxford, where everye day
that society were bound to make memorie of his soul,
could be dead in yᵉ time of Harrie yᵉ Fift and again live
in yᵉ time of Harrie yᵉ Sixt to be banished for cowardice:
Whereto I made answear that it was one of those humours
and mistakes for which Plato banisht all poets out of his
commonwealth. That Sʳ John Falstaffe was in those times
a noble valiant souldier, as apeeres by a book in yᵉ Heralds
Office dedicated unto him by a Herald who had binne
with him, if I well remember, for the space of 25 yeeres
in yᵉ French wars; that he seems also to have binne a man
of learning, because, in a Library of Oxford, I find a book
of dedicating Churches sent from him for a present unto
Bishop Wainflete, and inscribed with his own hand. That
in Shakespeares first shew of Harrie the fift, the person
with which he undertook to playe a buffone was not
Falstaffe, but Sir Jhon Oldcastle, and that offence beinge
worthily taken by Personages descended from his title
(as peradventure by many others allso whoe ought to
have him in honourable memorie) the poet was putt to
make an ignorant shifte of abusing Sir Jhon Falstophe,
a man not inferior of Vertue, though not so famous in
pietie as the other, who gave witnesse unto the truth of our
reformation with a constant and resolute Martyrdom, unto
which he was pursued by the Priests, Bishops, Moncks,
and Friers of those days.

II. LIEUTENANT HAMMOND (1634)

[1634, Sept. 9. From *A Relation of a Short Survey of 26 Counties . . . By
a Captaine, a Lieutennant and an Ancient, All three of the Military Company
of Norwich* (*Lansd. MS.* 213, f. 315), pr. L. G. Wickham Legg (1904).
The narrator was evidently the lieutenant, who says that the town-clerk
of Maldon (one Hammond in 1635) was his namesake. He has not been
further identified. The tour began on Monday 11 Aug. 1634, and seems
to have reached Stratford on 9 Sept.]

[p. 77.] In that dayes trauell we came by Stratford vpon
Auon, where in the Church in that Towne there are
some Monuments which Church was built by Archbishop
Stratford; Those worth obseruing and of which wee

tooke notice of were these . . . A neat Monument of that famous English Poet, Mʳ. William Shakespeere; who was borne heere.

And one of an old Gentleman a Batchelor, Mʳ Combe, vpon whose name, the sayd Poet, did merrily fann vp some witty, and facetious verses, which time would nott giue vs leaue to sacke vp.

III. SIR NICHOLAS L'ESTRANGE (1629–55)

[From *Merry Passages and Jeasts* (*Harl. MS.* 6395, f. 2), pr. W. J. Thoms, *Anecdotes and Traditions* (1839, C.S.); Herford-Simpson, *Jonson*, i. 186. The MS. is anonymous, but can be safely ascribed to L'Estrange (ob. 1655), who was of Hunstanton, Norfolk, and as many items are initialed S. N. L. was presumably compiled after he became a baronet in 1629. As authority for this story he gives (f. 89) 'Mʳ Dun:', probably, as suggested in Munro, ii. 8, an abbreviation for 'Mʳ Duncomb', since a Capt. Duncomb is cited elsewhere. It is not likely to mean Dr. Donne.]

Shake-speare was Godfather to one of *Ben: Johnsons* children, and after the christning being in a deepe study, Johnson came to cheere him vp, and askt him why he was so Melancholy? no faith *Ben*: (sayes he) not I, but I haue beene considering a great while what should be the fittest gift for me to bestow vpon my God-child, and I haue resolu'd at last; I pry'the what, sayes he? I faith *Ben*: I'le e'en giue him a douzen good Lattin Spoones, and thou shalt translate them.

IV. GEORGE DANIEL OF BESWICK (1647)

[From *The Raigne of Henrie the Fifth*, in *Trinarchodia* (*Addl. MS.* 19255), pr. Grosart, *Works of G. Daniel*, iv. 113. A longer extract is in Munro, i. 507, where the poem is called in error *Trinachordia*. Oldys (cf. no. xxxiv) had a copy, but there is nothing in the *Addl. MS.* to show this his. The date 7 Nov. 1647 is at the beginning of the poem.]

Here to Evince the Scandall, has bene throwne
Vpon a Name of Honour, (Charactred
From a wrong Person, Coward, and Buffoone;)
Call in your easie faiths, from what y'aue read
    To laugh at Falstaffe, as an humor fram'd
    To grace the Stage, to please the Age, misnam'd.

V. THOMAS FULLER (1643–61)

[Fuller (1608–61) seems to have been collecting material for the *Worthies* as early as 1643. His passage on Shakespeare and Jonson reads like fancy, not tradition.]

(*a*) [From *Church History* (1655), iv, cent. xv, 168.]

Stage-Poets have themselves been very *bold* with, and others very *merry* at, the Memory of S͏ʳ *John Oldcastle*, whom they have fancied a *boon Companion*, a *jovial Royster*, and yet a *Coward* to boot, contrary to the credit of all Chronicles, owning him a *Martial man* of merit. The best is, S͏ʳ *John Falstaffe*, hath relieved the Memory of S͏ʳ *John Oldcastle*, and of late is substituted *Buffoone* in his place; but it matters as little what *petulant Poets*, as what *malicious Papists* have written against him.

(*b*) [From *Worthies of England* (1662), Norfolk, 253.]

J O H N   F A S T O L F E Knight * * the *Stage* hath been overbold with his memory, making him a *Thrasonical Puff*, & emblem of *Mock-valour*.

True it is, *Sir John Oldcastle* did first bear the brunt of the one, being made the *make-sport* in all plays for a *coward*. It is easily known out of what *purse* this black *peny* came. The *Papists* railing on him for a *Heretick*, and therefore he must also be a *coward*, though indeed he was a *man* of *arms*, *every inch of him*, and as valiant as any in his age.

Now as I am glad that *Sir John Oldcastle* is *put out*, so I am sorry that *Sir John Fastolfe* is *put in*, to relieve his memory in this base service, to be the *anvil* for every *dull wit* to strike upon. Nor is our Comedian excusable, by some alteration of his name, writing him *Sir John Falstafe* (and making him the *property* of *pleasure* for King *Henry* the fifth, to abuse) seeing the *vicinity* of sounds intrench on the memory of *that worthy Knight*, and few do heed the *inconsiderable difference* in spelling of their name.

(*c*) [From *Worthies, Warwickshire*, 126.]

W I L L I A M   S H A K E S P E A R E was born at *Stratford* on *Avon* in this County, in whom three eminent Poets may seem in some sort to be compounded.

1. *Martial* in the *Warlike* sound of his Sur-name (whence some may conjecture him of a *Military extraction,*) *Hasti-vibrans,* or *Shake-speare.*

2. *Ovid,* the most *naturall* and *witty* of all Poets, and hence it was that Queen *Elizabeth,* coming into a Grammar-School, made this extemporary verse,

> '*Persius* a Crab-staffe, Bawdy *Martial,*
>   *Ovid* a fine Wag.'

3. *Plautus,* who was an exact Comædian, yet never any Scholar, as our *Shake-speare* (if alive) would confess himself. Adde to all these, that though his Genius generally was *jocular,* and inclining him to *festivity,* yet he could (when so disposed) be *solemn* and *serious,* as appears by his Tragedies, so that *Heraclitus* himself (I mean if secret and unseen) might afford to smile at his Comedies, they were so *merry,* and *Democritus* scarce forbear to sigh at his Tragedies they were so *mournfull.*

He was an eminent instance of the truth of that Rule, *Poeta not fit, sed nascitur,* one is not *made,* but *born* a Poet. Indeed his Learning was very little, so that as *Cornish diamonds* are not polished by any Lapidary, but are pointed and smoothed even as they are taken out of the Earth, so *nature* it self was all the *art* which was used upon him.

Many were the *wit-combates* betwixt him and *Ben Johnson,* which two I behold like a *Spanish great Gallion* and an *English man of War*; Master *Johnson* (like the former) was built far higher in Learning; *Solid,* but *Slow* in his performances. *Shake-spear,* with the *English-man of War,* lesser in *bulk,* but lighter in *sailing,* could turn with all tides, tack about and take advantage of all winds, by the quickness of his Wit and Invention. He died *Anno Domini* 16 . ., and was buried at *Stratford* upon *Avon,* the Town of his Nativity.

VI. ANON (c. 1650)

[From *Bodl. Ashm. MS.* 38, a collection of verses, many of them Caroline, in the hand of Nicholas Burgh, a Poor Knight of Windsor, who was alive in 1661. Black's *Catalogue* dates the MS. 'in the former part of the xvii[th] century'.]

(*a*) [p. 180.]

On John Combe A Coueteous rich man m[r] Wm. Shak-spear wright this att his request while hee was yett Liueing for his Epitaphe

Who Lies In this Tombe
Hough; Quoth the Deuill, Tis my Sonn John A Combe.

finis

but being dead, and making the poore his heiers hee after wrightes this for his Epitaph

How ere he liued Judge not
John Combe shall neuer be forgott
While poor, hath Memmorye, for hee did gather
To make the poore his Issue; hee their father
As record of his tilth and seede
Did Crowne him In his Latter deede.

Finis W: Shak.

(*b*) [p. 181.]

m[r] Ben: Johnson and m[r]. W[m]: Shake-speare Being Merrye att a Tauern, m[r] Jonson haueing begune this for his Epitaph

Here lies Ben Johnson that was once one

he gives ytt to m[r] Shakspear to make vpp who presently wrightes

Who while hee liu'de was a sloe things
and now being dead is Nothinge.

finis

(*c*) [p. 186.]

Another on hym [Sir John Spenser].

Ten In the hundred lies vnder this stone
yttes a hundred to ten to the deuill he's gone.

VII. THOMAS PLUME (*c.* 1657)

[From *Plume MS.* 25 in library at Maldon, Essex, founded by Plume (1630–74), Archdeacon of Rochester. The collection is described by A. Clark in *Essex Review*, xii–xiv. Plume was compiling MS. 25 at various dates from 1657 to 1680 (xiv. 9), but these notes, or at least those of the first pagination, seem to be in his hand of *c.* 1657. I have extended and occasionally capitalized the careful transcripts of Mr. P. Simpson, who printed the Jonsonian ones in Jonson's *Works*, i. 184, and kindly sent me (*c*). Most of the notes were first printed by Furnivall from Clark's transcript in *Westminster Gazette* (31 Oct. 1904) not quite correctly. Thus in (*c*) he reads 'darent' for 'durst', and in (*e*) 'shipwreck' for 'Athyns'. The only Sir John Mennis known was born in Kent on 1 Mar. 1599, and could not have remembered John Shakespeare who died in Sept. 1601. His brother Sir Matthew Mennis, born about 1593, might have, and he, according to Hotson 117, was interested in 1637 in a lease of the site of Gibbons's tennis-court in Clement's Inn Fields, which ultimately became that of the Theatre Royal. Possibly Plume confused the two.]

(*a*) [f. 77.]

Here lies Ben Johnson—who was once one—

*th*is he made of hims*elf*—Shakspe*ar* t*oo*k *th*e pen fr*om* him & made *th*is

Here lies Benjamin—*with* short hair up*on* his Chin— Who w*hil*e he lived was a slow thing—& now he's b*u*r*i*ed is no thing.

(*b*) [f. 161.]

Ben Johnson at *th*e *Ch*ris*t*ning of Shakesp*ear* his child to w*h*ich he w*as* jnvit*ed* g*o*d F*ather* s*a*id to him—now y*o*u exp*ect* a *great* matter—But I w*ill* giue it a Latin spoon & you sh*all* transl*at*e it.

(*c*) [f. 161.]

He was a glovers son—*Sir* John Mennis saw once his old F*ather* in h*is* shop—a merry Cheekd old man—*th*at s*a*id—Will was a g*oo*d Hon*est* Fellow, but he durst h*ave* crackt a jeast w*ith* him at any time.

(*d*) [f. 51 (*bis*).]

Here lies Ben Johnson Who once was one—h*is* own Epit*aph*.

Here lies Benjamin—with little hair up*o*n his chin
Who w*hi*le he liued w*as* a slow th*ing*—& now he is b*u*ri*e*d
Shakespe*ar*. is Noth*ing*.

(*e*) [f. 71 (*bis*).]

One told Ben Johns*o*n—Shakespe*ar* nev*er* studied for
any th*ing* he wrott. B. J. s*ai*d—*th*e mo*r*e to blame He—
s*ai*d—Cesar never punishes any but for a just Cause &
a*no*the*r* time m*ak*es Athyns in Bohemia—So Tom Goff
brings in Etiocles & Polynices disc*ou*rs*ing* of K*in*g
Rich*ard* 2ᵈ.

VIII. SIR ASTON COKAIN (1658)

[From *Small Poems of Divers Sorts* (1658), Epig. ii. 69. Cokain (1608–84)
was of Pooley Hall in Polesworth, Warwickshire. Fisher, afterwards Sir
Clement, Bart., was the son and heir of Robert Fisher of Great Packington,
Warwickshire. The Wincott at which he lived was presumably Wilnecote
in north Warwickshire, adjacent to Polesworth. But I take it that Lee 237
has no other authority than the verses themselves for calling him 'a well-
known resident at Wilnecote', and the manors, according to Dugdale 824,
belonged to other families. Cokain evidently thought that it was at
Wilnecote that 'Marian Hacket, the fat ale-wife of Wincot' (*The Shrew*,
Ind. ii. 22) lived, and this view is taken by A. Gray, *A Chapter in the Early
Life of Shakespeare* (1926), who believes that Shakespeare was brought
up as a page at Polesworth. It is most improbable, since there were two
places called Wincot much nearer Stratford. One of these was Wilmcote,
the home of the Ardens (cf. App. A, nos. ii, iv). Most of this lay in Aston
Cantlow, but there was also a hamlet of Little Wilmcote in Stratford-on-
Avon, just over the boundary between the two parishes. The tithes of
this had belonged to the Gild of Stratford, and were granted to the town
by the Charter of 1553. In local records it is spelt Wylmyncote, Wylmecote, Wilmecote, Wilmicote, Willmcott, Wymcote, Wimcot, Wyncote,
Wincott (Dugdale 616; *Var*. ii. 13; *M.A.* i. 7; iii. 127, 144, 150, 164;
Wheler 22; H.P. ii. 307, *Vestry Book* 88). A second hamlet of Willicote
or Wincot is just south of the Avon in Gloucestershire, partly in
the parish of Clifford Chambers and partly in that of Quinton. It had
been a manor of the Wilcote family. In 1567 a moiety was purchased by
William Barnes, step-father of Sir Henry Rainsford. It is represented now
by two farms in Clifford Chambers, called respectively Willicote and
Wincote (H. Rudder, *Hist. of Gloucestershire*, 374, 616; H.P. ii. 307;
A. Ransford, *Williamscote and Wilcotes* in *N.Q.* cli. 425, *Rainsford Associa-*

tions with Shakespeare, Southampton and Hall in *N.Q.* clii. 311). I do not know which of these hamlets Warton (no. xliii), Capell (no. xliv), and perhaps West (no. xlvii) related to *The Shrew*, although Warton was certain that Wilnecote was not concerned. But that Marian Hacket in fact belonged to Wincot in Gloucestershire is made clear by R. Savage's discovery (Lee 237) of the baptism of Sara, daughter of Robert Hacket, in Quinton church on 21 Nov. 1591.]

To Mr. Clement Fisher *of* Wincott.

Shakspeare your *Wincot*-Ale hath much renownd,
That fo'xd a Beggar so (by chance was found
Sleeping) that there needed not many a word
To make him to believe he was a Lord:
But you affirm (and in it seem most eager)
'Twill make a Lord as drunk as any Beggar.
Bid *Norton* brew such Ale as *Shakspeare* fancies
Did put *Kit Sly* into such Lordly trances:
And let us meet there (for a fit of Gladness)
And drink our selves merry in sober sadness.

IX. JOHN WARD (1661–3)

[From C. Severn, *Diary of John Ward* (1839), 183. The note-books of Ward (1629–81), who was vicar of Stratford (1662–81) came into the possession of the Medical Society of London towards the end of the 18th century. They were sold to Mr. A. S. W. Rosenbach in 1928. The first four extracts are from a book of 1661–3; the fifth Miss Toulmin Smith (Munro, ii. 111) could not trace. But Severn saw seventeen books and there were only sixteen at the time of the sale. Sir D'Arcy Power (*Trans. Medical Soc.* xl, xliii), who also studied the voluminous documents, found no more of direct Shakespearean interest, but showed that Ward had been an ardent student of medicine, before he took orders.]

Shakespear had but 2 daughters, one whereof M. Hall, yᵉ physitian, married, and by her had one daughter, to wit, yᵉ Lady Bernard of Abbingdon. . . .

I have heard yᵗ Mʳ. Shakespeare was a natural wit, without any art at all; hee frequented yᵉ plays all his younger time, but in his elder days lived at Stratford: and supplied yᵉ stage with 2 plays every year, and for yᵗ had an allowance so large, yᵗ hee spent att yᵉ Rate of a 1,000*l.* a year, as I have heard.

Remember to peruse Shakespears plays, and bee versd in *them*, y^t I may not bee ignorant in y^t matter. . . .

Shakespear, Drayton, and Ben Jhonson, had a merry meeting, and itt seems drank too hard, for Shakespear died of a feavour there contracted. . . .

A letter to my brother, to see Mrs. Queeny, to send for Tom Smith for the acknowledgment.

X. DAVID LLOYD (1665)

[From *Statesmen and Favourites of England since the Reformation* (1665), 504. The historical accuracy of Lloyd (1635–92) is discredited by Anthony Wood (*Athenae*, iv. 352), who calls him an 'impudent plagiary' and a 'false writer and meer scribbler'. There seems no particular reason for falsity here. But it is impossible to say what the statement about Shakespeare and Jonson rests on. Greville, in his long life, had many offices. Those in the Navy and Exchequer would not bring him into touch with poets. He was a Gentleman of the Privy Chamber to Elizabeth, but this would not normally give him any special responsibility for plays. He also had important posts under the Council for Wales from as early as 1577. Conceivably he might have found employment for Shakespeare in the Marches when he left Stratford. If so, the fact has eluded research.]

One great argument for his ⟨Fulke Greville, Lord Brooke's⟩ worth, was his respect of the worth of others, desiring to be known to posterity under no other notions than of *Shakespear's* and *Ben Johnson's* Master, Chancellor *Egerton's* Patron, Bishop *Overal's* Lord, and Sir *Philip Sidney's friend*.

XI. ROBERT DOBYNS (1673)

[Printed by B. Dobell in *Athenæum* (19 Jan. 1901) from f. 72 of a MS. in his possession, written mainly between 1679 and 1685, but in part as late as 1710 or thereabouts.]

In 1673 I Robert Dobyns being at Stratford upon Avon & visiting the church there transcribed these two Epitaphs, the first is on William Shakespeare's monument: the other is upon ye monument of a noted usurer.

1. Good friend for Jesu sake forbeare
   To dig the Dust that lyeth incloased here
   Blessed is the man that spareth these stones
   Cursed be he yt moveth these bones.

2. Tenn in the hundred here lyeth engraved
   A hundred to tenn his soule is now saved
   If anny one aske who lyeth in this Tombe
   Oh ho quoth the Divell tis my John a Combe.

Since my being at Stratford the heires of Mr Combe have
caused these verses to be razed, so yt now they are not
legible.

XII. JOHN DRYDEN (1672, 1684)

(*a*) [From *Essay on the Dramatique Poetry of the Last Age*, appended to
The Conquest of Granada, Part ii (1672), 172. For a passage reporting a
criticism by Jonson, cf. App. B, no. xxii.]

Shakespear show'd the best of his skill in his *Mercutio*,
and he said himself, that he was forc'd to kill him in the
third Act, to prevent being kill'd by him. But, for my
part, I cannot find he was so dangerous a person: I see
nothing in him but what was so exceeding harmless, that
he might have liv'd to the end of the Play, and dy'd in
his bed, without offence to any man.

(*b*) [From *An Epilogue* in *Miscellany Poems* (1684), 292. This is a
rewritten form of an epilogue or prologue originally written for Charles
Davenant's *Circe*, produced at Dorset Gardens in March 1677 (Nicoll,
Restoration Drama, 358). The original version, presumably first printed
as a broadside, contains no reference to Shakespeare.]

Your *Ben* and *Fletcher* in their first young flight
Did no *Volpone*, no *Arbaces* write.
But hopp'd about, and short excursions made ⎫
From Bough to Bough, as if they were afraid, ⎬
And each were guilty of some *slighted Maid*. ⎭
Shakespear's own Muse her *Pericles* first bore,
The Prince of *Tyre* was elder than the *Moore*:
'Tis miracle to see a first good Play,
All Hawthorns do not bloom on *Christmas-day*.
A slender Poet must have time to grow,
And spread and burnish as his Brothers do.
Who still looks lean, sure with some Pox is curst,
But no Man can be *Falstaff* fat at first.

XIII. JOHN AUBREY (1681)

[Aubrey (1626–97) collected his *Brief Lives* as material for the *Athenae Oxonienses* of Anthony Wood (cf. no. xvii). They were arranged from the somewhat disordered manuscripts in the edition (1898) of A. Clark, who treats (*a*) as part of a life of William Beeston, a Caroline and Restoration actor, and the son of Christopher Beeston, a Chamberlain's man in 1598. Later discussions (E. K. Chambers in *M.S.C.* i. 341; F. Madan in *Cat. of Bodleian Tercentenary Shakespeare Exhibition*, 95; H. C. Beeching in *Sh. Homage*, 120; all with facss.) show that it relates to Shakespeare, that the part below his name was probably written after the actor John Lacy had advised him to apply for information to Beeston, and the upper part, which seems to be in a different ink, added after an interview with Beeston himself. This was probably about August 1681. Aubrey seems to have made no use of this note in writing the life (*b*). But this also must be later than the interview with Beeston, since he is quoted at the end as the authority for a statement, which does not appear to be a later addition in the manuscript. This statement is not in (*a*), but Aubrey may have seen Beeston more than once before his death about 24 Aug. 1682. Some interesting new information about Beeston and his father is collected by L. Hotson, *The Commonwealth and Restoration Stage* (1928), but does not affect the testimony as to Shakespeare.]

(*a*) [From *Bodl. Aubrey MS.* 8, f. 45ᵛ, a leaf inserted in the third part (*Auctarium Vitarum*) of Aubrey's *Brief Lives*, and containing on the *recto* notes about John Ogilby the dancing-master, and on the *verso*, with that here printed, others about Ogilby, Jonson, and Fletcher; cf. Plate XXVIII.]

the more to be admired q⟨uia⟩ he was not a company
    keeper
lived in Shoreditch, wouldnt be debauched, & if invited to
writ; he was in paine.
W. Shakespeare.

Lacy

q⟨uaere⟩ Mʳ Beeston who knows most of him fr⟨om⟩ Mʳ;
he lives in Shore-ditch. ~~neer Nort~~ at Hoglane
within 6 dores—Norton—folgate.
q⟨uaere⟩ etiam for B. Jonson.

(*b*) [From *Bodl. Aubrey MS.* 6, f. 109 (Part i of Aubrey's *Brief Lives*).]

Mʳ. William Shakespear. [*bay-wreath in margin*] was borne at Stratford vpon Avon, in the County of Warwick; his father was a Butcher, & I have been told heretofore by some of the neighbours, that when he was a boy he exer-

cised his father's Trade, but when he kill'd a Calfe, he
would doe it in a *high style*, & make a Speech. There was
at that time another Butcher's son in this Towne, that was
held not at all inferior to him for a naturall witt, his
acquaintance & coetanean, but dyed young. This Wm.
being inclined naturally to Poetry and acting, came to
London I guesse about 18. and was an Actor at one of the
Play-houses and did act exceedingly well: now B. Johnson was never a good Actor, but an excellent Instructor.
He began early to make essayes at Dramatique Poetry,
which at that time was very lowe; and his Playes tooke
well: He was a handsome well shap't man: very good
company, and of a very readie and pleasant smooth Witt.
The Humour of . . . the Constable in a Midsomersnight's
Dreame, he happened to take at Grendon [*In margin*,
'I thinke it was Midsomer night that he happened to lye
there'.] in Bucks which is the roade from London to
Stratford, and there was living that Constable about 1642
when I first came to Oxon. M^r. Jos. Howe is of that
parish and knew him. Ben Johnson and he did gather
Humours of men dayly where ever they came. One time
as he was at the Tavern at Stratford super Avon, one
Combes an old rich Usurer was to be buryed, he makes
there this extemporary Epitaph

> Ten in the Hundred the Devill allowes
> But *Combes* will have twelve, he sweares & vowes:
> If any one askes who lies in this Tombe:
> Hoh! quoth the Devill, 'Tis my John o' Combe.

He was wont to goe to his native Country once a yeare.
I thinke I have been told that he left 2 or 300^li per annum
there and therabout: to a sister. [*In margin*, 'V. his
Epitaph in Dugdales Warwickshire'.] I have heard
S^r Wm. Davenant and M^r. Thomas Shadwell (who is
counted the best Comœdian we have now) say, that he
had a most prodigious Witt, and did admire his naturall
parts beyond all other Dramaticall writers. He was wont
to say, That he never blotted out a line in his life: sayd
Ben: Johnson, I wish he had blotted out a thousand.

[*In margin*, 'B. Johnsons Underwoods'.] His Comœdies will remaine witt, as long as the English tongue is understood; for that he handles *mores hominum*; now our present writers reflect so much upon particular persons, and coxcombeities, that 20 yeares hence, they will not be understood. Though as Ben: Johnson says of him, that he had but little Latine and lesse Greek, He understood Latine pretty well: for he had been in his younger yeares a Schoolmaster in the Countrey. [*In margin*, 'from M^r ———— Beeston'.]

(*c*) [From *Bodl. Aubrey MS.* 6, f. 46. The passages in square brackets are scored out, perhaps by Anthony Wood.]

Sr William Davenant Knight Poet Laureate was borne in ———— street in the City of Oxford, at the Crowne Taverne (*In margin*, 'V. A. W. Antiq: Oxon:'). His father was John Davenant a Vintner there, a very grave and discreet Citizen: his mother was a very beautifull woman, & of a very good witt and of conversation extremely agreable. . . . Mr William Shakespeare was wont to goe into Warwickshire once a yeare, and did commonly in his journey lye at this house in Oxon: where he was exceedingly respected. [I have heard parson Robert D⟨avenant⟩ say that Mr W. Shakespeare here gave him a hundred kisses.] Now Sr. W^m would sometimes when he was pleasant over a glasse of wine with his most intimate friends e.g. Sam: Butler (author of Hudibras) &c. say, that it seemed to him that he writt with the very spirit that Shakespeare, and was **seemed** contentended enough to be thought his Son: he would tell them the story as above. [in which way his mother had a very light report, whereby she was called a whore.]

XIV. EDWARD RAVENSCROFT (1687)

(*a*) [From *Address* to *Titus Andronicus, or the Rape of Lavinia*, adapted from *Tit. Andr.* by Ravenscroft, and produced, according to the *Address*, 'at the beginning of the pretended Popish Plot', in 1678.]

I think it a greater theft to Rob the dead of their Praise then the Living of their Money. That I may not appear

Guilty of such a Crime, 'tis necessary I should acquaint you, that there is a Play in M^r. *Shakespears* Volume under the name of *Titus Andronicus*, from whence I drew part of this. I have been told by some anciently conversant with the Stage, that it was not Originally his, but brought by a private Authour to be Acted, and he only gave some Master-touches to one or two of the Principal Parts or Characters; this I am apt to believe, because 'tis the most incorrect and indigested piece in all his Works; It seems rather a heap of Rubbish then a Structure.

(*b*) [From G. Langbaine, *English Dramatick Poets* (1691), 465. Presumably this *Prologue*, not in the print of 1687, was for the production at Drury Lane *c*. December 1686 (Nicoll 370). Langbaine has quoted an attack by Thomas Shadwell in his preface to *The Sullen Lovers* (1668) on Ravenscroft as a plagiary. It may be, as suggested by Knight, that both Shadwell and Langbaine meant to discredit the story of a 'private Authour' which they quote; but this is not clear.]

But to make Mr *Ravenscroft* some Reparation, I will here furnish him with part of his Prologue, which he has lost; and if he desire it, send him the whole.

> To day the Poet does not fear your Rage,
> Shakespear *by him reviv'd now treads the Stage;*
> *Under his sacred Lawrels he sits down*
> *Safe, from the blast of any Criticks Frown.*
> *Like other Poets, he'll not proudly scorn*
> *To own, that he but winnow'd* Shakespear's *Corn*;
> *So far he was from robbing him of 's Treasure,*
> *That he did add his own, to make full measure.*

XV. RICHARD DAVIES (1688–1708)

[From *Fulman MS.* xv (*C.C.C. MS.* 309), no. 7, p. 22 in the library of C.C.C. Oxford; cf. Plate XXIX. A note on *C.C.C. MS.* 296 (Coxe, ii. 131) says that these MSS. were given to the college by Mr. Woods, executor of Richard 'Davis', Archdeacon of Lichfield. This is the main source of the notice by Malone (*Var*. ii. 121) who saw the MS. (*Letters to Davenport*, 57) in 1792. He ascribes the additions in a second hand to Davies. This is confirmed by the script of Davies, four signed examples of which I have had the opportunity of examining. One is a letter of 9 June 1693 to Gilbert Burnet, Bishop of Salisbury, the historian (*Bodl. Addl. MS.* D 23, f. 18). A second, kindly shown to me by the Rev. P. G. Latham, is in the register of Sandford-on-Thames, Oxon., of which Davies became curate. Two others are in *C.C.C. MSS.* 301, f. 185 and 319, f. 114. William Fulman, who has nothing himself to tell us about Shakespeare, became a Scholar of C.C.C. in 1648, was expelled in the same year, restored in 1660, and in 1669 took the college living of Maisey-Hampton, Gloucestershire, where he died (A. Wood, *Life and Times*, iii. 270) on 28 June 1688. There is no doubt that his papers passed to Davies. Wood (iii. 408) describes a dispute with 'Mr. Ric. Davies of Sanford' about some of his own letters to Fulman then held by Davies, on 18 Nov. 1692, when 'Mr. Davies look⟨t⟩ red and jolly, as if he had been at a fish dinner at C.C.C., and afterwards drinking—as he had been'. He notes a second meeting at C.C.C. itself on 21 November. In *Athenae Oxonienses*, iv. 240, he complains of his inability to use Fulman's collections, 'All which being afterwards conveyed to C.C. coll. to be, according to his desire, put into the archives of the library of that house, what had it been for those that had the care, to have permitted the author of this work the perusal of them, when they could not otherwise but know that they would have been serviceable to him in the promotion of this work, then almost ready for the press'. I note *pietatis causa* that, although the phrasing is ambiguous, Wood's grievance was clearly against Davies and not the college, to whom the manuscripts did not come until sixteen years after the publication of the *Athenae* in 1691–2. Davies became rector of Sapperton, Gloucestershire, on 5 Mar. 1695 (H.P. *1848*, 328) and Archdeacon of Coventry in the diocese of Lichfield (not Archdeacon of Lichfield) on 26 July 1703 (T. D. Hardy, *Fasti Eccl. Angl.* i. 570). He was buried at Sapperton on 19 June 1708 (H.P. *ut supra*). His earlier history is not so clear. I suppose him to have been a chaplain of C.C.C. who suggested and contributed to the alteration of the chapel *c.* 1675–6 (Fowler 259) and appears in the Buttery Books during 1667–81 (Fowler 424) and, as Dr. J. G. Milne tells me, also in the Manciple's Books during 1667–80. These dates agree with the fact that the hand of the notes seems to make its first appearance in the Sandford register during 1681. The signatures of two Fellows of C.C.C. in the register, Cuthbert Ellison (1704) and Joshua Reynolds (1707), point to relations between the college and the parish. A letter of 16 Jan. 1678 to Fulman (*C.C.C. MS.* 301, f. 86ᵛ), from a distinct 'Ric: Davis', speaks of his 'namesake' of C.C.C. as then at the Bath. Finally some notes of *c.* 1670–1700 by Thomas Baskerville (*O.H.S. Collectanea*, iv. 217) mentions among gentlemen he had known at C.C.C. 'Mr. Davies, now Parson of Sandford in Oxford Shire, who lately did purchase there a good estate of Mr. Dunce of Pissie⟨Pusey ?⟩ in Berks'. Dunce had inherited this from his aunt Mrs. Isham. Davies does not seem to have been a Fellow or undergraduate of C.C.C. The present rector of Sapperton, Mr. W. C. Davies, who is a descendant, tells me that he was of a yeoman family in Pembrokeshire, and built the existing rectory in 1700. The Davies who would best fit him in the University records is a Richard, who matriculated as a servitor of Queen's in 1659, and took his B.A. thence in 1663, and apparently his M.A. from

PLATE XXIX

7. William Shakespeare.

William Shakespeare was born at Stratford
upon Avon in Warwickshire about 1563.4.
much given to all unluckiness in Stealing venison &
Rabbits particularly from Sr ___ Lucy who had him
oft whipt & sometimes Imprisoned & at last made Him
fly, his Native Country to his great Advancemt. but
His reveng was so great that he is his Justice Clodpate
and calls him a great many in his plays for thee luces
in his coat & scandals: rampant for his Arms
From an Actor of Playes, he became a Composer

Ætat. 53.

He dyed Apr. 23. 1616. probably at Stratford,
for there he is buryed, and hath a Monument on
wch he lays a Heavy curse upon any one
who shall remove his bones. He dyed a papist.

buryd.
p. 620.

MEMORANDA OF WILLIAM FULMAN AND RICHARD DAVIES

St. Alban's Hall in 1666 (Foster, *Alumni Oxonienses*). He was a benefactor
to the college library (J. R. Magrath, *Queen's College*, ii. 270). Probably
our Richard Davies, who made gifts to the Bodleian (Macray, *Annals*,
150), was a scholar, although when Mme. Longworth de Chambrun,
Shakespeare: Actor-Poet (1927), 275, says that he 'had participated in the
historical work of Burnet on the Reformation' she is obviously confusing
him with Fulman. It is only one of many blunders. The historical *Collectanea* preserved as his in *C.C.C. MSS.* 317–19 seem to be largely
Fulman's. But the letter to Burnet cited above is in reply to one from
the bishop (f. 16) in which he thanks him for sending a paper of Fulman's,
and says that, although not knowing him personally, 'I look upon you as
one in whom our *Church* has great reason to *Glory*'. Davies in his reply
mentions Fulman, then dead, and his children left in a 'mean Condition'.]

7. William Shakespeare.

William Shakespeare was born at Stratford upon Avon
in Warwickshire about 1563·4.

**much given to all unluckinesse in stealing venison & Rabbits
particularly from S^r   Lucy who had him oft whipt &
sometimes Imprisoned & at last made Him fly his Native
Country to his great Advancem^t. but His reveng was so
great that he is his Justice Clodpate and calls him a great
man & y^t in allusion to his name bore three lowses rampant
for his Arms**

From an Actor of Playes, he became a Composer

Ætat. 53.

He dyed Apr. 23. 1616. probably at Strat-
ford, for there he is buryed, and hath a   Dugd.,
Monument **on w^c He lays a Heavy curse vpon**   p. 520.
**any one who shal remoove his bones He dyed
a papist.**

XVI. JOSHUA BARNES (*c.* 1690)

[From Malone (1790), i. 1. 106; *Var.* ii. 143. I have not been able to
find the MS. referred to. For Chetwood cf. no. xxxvii and App. F.
Barnes (1654–1712) was of Emmanuel, Cambridge.]

In a Manuscript *History of the Stage*, full of forgeries and
falsehoods of various kinds, written (I suspect by William
Chetwood the prompter) some time between April 1727

and October 1730, is the following passage, to which the reader will give just as much credit as he thinks fit:

'Here we shall observe, that the learned Mr Joshua Barnes, late Greek Professor of the University of Cambridge, baiting about forty years ago at an inn in Stratford, and hearing an old woman singing part of the above-said song, such was his respect for Mr Shakespeare's genius, that he gave her a new gown for the two following stanzas in it; and, could she have said it all, he would (as he often said in company, when any discourse has casually arose about him) have given her ten guineas:

> Sir Thomas was too covetous,
>   To covet so much deer,
> When horns enough upon his head
>   Most plainly did appear.
>
> Had not his worship one deer left?
>   What then? He had a wife
> Took pains enough to find him horns
>   Should last him during life.'

XVII. ANTHONY WOOD (1692)

[From *Athenae Oxonienses*, ii. (1692) 292 (ed. Bliss, iii. 802). Wood (1632–95) may have taken this from Aubrey (cf. no. xiii), but was himself a life-long Oxford resident. Langbaine (1691) follows Wood.]

WILLIAM D'AVENANT. . . . His father John Davenant was a sufficient vintner, kept the tavern now known by the name of the Crown (wherein our poet was born) and was mayor of the said city in the year 1621. His mother was a very beautiful woman, of a good wit and conversation, in which she was imitated by none of her children but by this William. The father, who was a very grave and discreet citizen (yet an admirer and lover of plays and play-makers, especially Shakespeare, who frequented his house in his journies between Warwickshire and London) was of a melancholic disposition, and was seldom or never seen to laugh, in which he was imitated by none of his children but by Robert his eldest son, afterwards fellow of St. John's College and a venerable doct. of div.

XVIII. MR. DOWDALL (1693)

[1693, Apr. 10. From *Letter* written at Butler's Marston, Warwickshire, signed 'John at Stiles', addressed to 'Mr Southwell' who is the writer's 'cousin', and endorsed 'From Mr Dowdall'; pr. as *Traditionary Anecdotes of Shakespeare* (1838, T. Rodd), and in extract by H.P. ii. 71; *Life* (1848), 87; facs. in *Folio* (1853), i. 78. The MS. owned by H.P. came from the family papers of Lord de Clifford. Rodd calls Southwell Edward; he might be the Edward (1671–1730) of Merton, afterwards Secretary for Ireland, a son of Sir Robert of King's Weston, Gloucestershire. I do not know why Lee 25, 642, calls Dowdall 'John'. A William Castle was christened at Stratford on 17 July 1614 and another on 10 Aug. 1628. No doubt the earlier was the clerk.]

The 1st Remarkable place in this County y^t I visitted was Stratford super avon, where I saw the Effigies of our English tragedian, m^r Shakspeare, parte of his Epitaph I sent m^r Lowther, and Desired he w^ld Impart it to you, wch I finde by his Last Letter he has Done: but here I send you the whole Inscription.

Just und^r his Effigies in the wall of the Chancell is this written. . . .

Neare the Wall where his monument is Erected Lyeth a plaine free stone, vnderneath wch his bodie is Buried with this Epitaph, made by himselfe a little before his Death.

> Good friend, for Jesus sake forbeare
> To digg the dust inclosed here
> Bles't be the man that spares these stones
> And Curs't be he that moves my bones!

the clarke that shew'd me this Church is aboue 80 y^rs old; he says that this *Shakespear* was formerly in this Towne bound apprentice to a butcher; but that he Run from his master to London, and there was Rec^d Into the playhouse as a serviture, and by this meanes had an oppertunity to be w^t he afterwards prov'd. he was the best of his family but the male Line is extinguished; not one for feare of the Curse aboues^d Dare Touch his Grave Stone, tho his wife and Daughters Did Earnestly Desire to be Layd in the same Graue wth him.

XIX. WILLIAM HALL (1694)

[From *Letter* of W. Hall to Edward Thwaites (*Bodl. Rawl. MS.* D. 377, f. 90), n.d., bound in MS. before letter dated 'Lichfield, Jan. 2ᵈ 9⅘'; pr. H.P. (1884); J. Munro, in *M.P.* xiii. 539; *Bodleian Terc. Cat.* 60, the compiler of which says that nothing is known of Hall. But he was son of a G⟨ul?⟩ Hall, innkeeper of Lichfield, took his B.A. from Queen's, 1694, and became rector of Acton, Middlesex, and prebendary of St. Paul's (Foster, *Alumni*; Elton 340). Thwaites (*D.N.B.*) was also a Queen's man, later an Anglo-Saxon scholar, Regius Professor of Greek, and White's Professor of Moral Philosophy at Oxford.]

Dear Neddy,

I very greedily embraced this occasion of acquainting you with something which I found at Stratford upon Avon. That place I came unto on Thursday night, and yᵉ next day went to visit yᵉ ashes of the Great Shakespear which lye interr'd in that Church. The verses which in his life-time he ordered to be cut upon his tomb-stone (for his Monument have others) are these which follow;

> Reader, for Jesus's Sake forbear
> To dig the dust enclosed here:
> Blessed be he that Spares these Stones,
> And cursed be he that moves my bones.

The little learning these verses contain, would be a very strong argument of yᵉ want of it in the Author; did not they carry something in them which stands in need of a comment. There is in this Church a place which they call the bone-house, a repository for all bones they dig up; which are so many that they would load a great number of waggons. The Poet being willing to preserve his bones unmoved, lays a curse upon him that moves them; and haveing to do with Clarks and Sextons, for yᵉ most part a very ⟨i⟩gnorant sort of people, he descends to yᵉ meanest of their capacitys; and disrobes himself of that art, which none of his Co-temporaryes wore in greater perfection. Nor has the design mist of its effect; for lest they should not onely draw this curse upon themselvs, but also entail it upon their posterity, they have laid him full seven-teen foot deep, deep enough to secure him. And so much for Stratford. . . .

Direct your letter for   Your friend and Servant
Wᵐ. Hall Junʳ. at yᵉ   Wᵐ. Hall.
White-hart in Lichfield.

XX. ANON (17th cent.)

[From 'a MS. note written towards the end of the seventeenth century, which is preserved in a copy of the third folio', pr. H.P. ii. 357. I omit the words of the gravestone as there given.]

In the church of Strattford-uppon-Avon, uppon a stone in the chancell, these words were orderd to be cutt by Mʳ Shackspeare, the town being the place of his birth and buriall.

XXI. CHARLES GILDON (1694–1710)

[Gildon (1665–1724) was a dramatist and booksellers' hack, pilloried by Pope in the *Dunciad*.]

(*a*) [From *Reflections on Rymer's Short View of Tragedy* in *Miscellaneous Letters and Essays, on several Subjects. By several Gentlemen and Ladies* (1694), 88.]

I'm assur'd from very good hands, that the Person that Acted Jago was in much esteem for a Comoedian, which made *Shakespear* put several words, and expressions into his part (perhaps not so agreeable to his Character) to make the Audience laugh, who had not yet learnt to endure to be serious a whole Play.

(*b*) [From *The Lives and Characters of the English Dramatick Poets. First begun by Mʳ Langbain, improv'd and continued down to this Time*, by a *Careful Hand* (n.d.), 126. W. W. Greg (*M.S.C.* i. 334) gives evidence for publication in 1698, and accepts Gildon as general editor, although other hands contributed.]

William Shakespear.

. . . I have been told that he writ the scene of the Ghost in *Hamlet*, at his House which bordered on the Charnel-House and Church-Yard. . . .

(*c*) [From *Remarks on the Plays of Shakespear* in *The Works of M*ʳ *William Shakespear. Volume the Seventh* (1710). This, edited by ⟨Charle⟩S ⟨Gildo⟩N, contains the *Poems*, omitted from Rowe's six vol. edition of 1709, and is uniform in appearance with that edition. It is sometimes regarded as a supplement to it, but the publisher was Curll, while Rowe's was Tonson, who is criticized for including non-Shakespearean plays 'to swell the Volume and the Price' by the editor, 'Mr. *Betterton* having more than once assur'd me, that the first Folio Edition by the Players, contain'd all those, which were truely his'.]

[p. 291.]

The *Fairys* in the fifth Act ⟨of *Merry Wives of W.*⟩ makes a Handsome Complement to the Queen, in her Palace of *Windsor*, who had oblig'd him to write a Play of *Sir John Falstaff* in Love, and which I am very well assured he perform'd in a Fortnight; a prodigious Thing, when all is so well contriv'd, and carry'd on without the least Confusion.

[p. 404.]

The former Scene ⟨*Ham.* i. 4⟩, which as I have been assur'd he wrote in a Charnel House in the midst of the Night.

(*d*) [From Malone, 1790, i. 1. 115; *Var.* ii. 517. I do not find any such statement in Gildon; probably Malone wrote his name by a slip for that of Aubrey (cf. p. 253).]

Gildon, without authority, I believe, says, that our author left behind him an estate of 300ˡ per ann.

XXII. JAMES WRIGHT? (1699)

[From *Historia Histrionica . . . In a Dialogue of Plays and Players*, anonymous, but usually ascribed to Wright (1643–1713), an antiquary and play-collector; (cf. *Eliz. Stage*, iv. 370).]

Lovewit. Pray Sir, what Master Parts can you remember the Old *Black-friers* men to Act, in *Johnson*, *Shakespear*, and *Fletcher's* Plays?

Truman. What I can at present recollect I'll tell you; *Shakespear* (who, as I have heard, was a much better Poet, than Player) *Burbadge*, *Hemmings*, and others of the Older sort, were Dead before I knew the Town.

XXIII. JOHN DENNIS (1702–4)

[Dennis (1657–1734) of Caius and Trinity Hall, Cambridge, was an unsuccessful dramatist, an enemy of Pope, and a critic of some merit.]

(*a*) [From *Epistle* to *The Comicall Gallant* (1702), based on *Merry Wives of W.*]

That this Comedy was not despicable, I guess'd for several Reasons: First, I knew very well, that it had pleas'd one of the greatest Queens that ever was in the World, great not only for her Wisdom in the Arts of Government, but for her knowledge of Polite Learning, and her nice taste of the Drama, for such a taste we may be sure she had, by the relish which she had of the Ancients. This Comedy was written at her Command, and by her direction, and she was so eager to see it Acted, that she commanded it to be finished in fourteen days; and was afterwards, as Tradition tells us, very well pleas'd at the Representation.

(*b*) [From *The Person of Quality's Answer to Mr. Collier's Letter* (1704), 4. This was repr. in *Original Letters, Familiar and Critical* (1721), i. 232, and was a reply to Jeremy Collier's *A Dissuasive from the Play-House* (1703). I owe my knowledge of the original issue, which is not in the B.M. or Bodleian, to the kindness of Mr. P. J. Dobell.]

Nay the poor mistaken Queen her self, encouraged Play-Houses to that degree, that she not only commanded *Shakespear* to write the Comedy of the *Merry Wives*, and to write it in Ten Days time; so eager was she for the wicked Diversion; but ev'n with that Hand that weilded the Scepter descended poorly to Translate a Play that was writ by a *Grecian* Poet.

XXIV. JOHN DOWNES (1708)

[From *Roscius Anglicanus, or, an Historical Review of the Stage*, 21. Downes was a prompter in London theatres from 1662 to 1706. He gives a list of plays acted at Lincoln's Inn Fields during 1662–5. Shakespeare may have instructed Lowin, but hardly Taylor, who joined the King's in 1619.]

The Tragedy of *Hamlet*; *Hamlet* being Perform'd by Mʳ. *Betterton*, Sir *William* ⟨Davenant⟩ (having seen

Mr *Taylor* of the *Black-Fryars* Company Act it, who being Instructed by the Author Mr *Shaksepeur*) taught Mr *Betterton* in every Particle of it. . . .

King *Henry* the 8*th*. . . . The part of the King was so right and justly done by Mr *Betterton*, he being instructed in it by Sir *William*, who had it from Old Mr *Lowen*, that had his Instructions from Mr *Shakespear* himself, that I dare and will aver, none can, or will come near him in this Age, in the performance of that part.

XXV. NICHOLAS ROWE (1709)

[Extracts from *Life* in *Works of Shakespeare* (1709), i. 1. This was reprinted in Rowe's (1674–1718) second ed. of 1714; an abbreviated form is in later eds. from Pope's (1725) to *Var.* i. 436. The full original text is in D. Nichol Smith, *Eighteenth Century Essays on Sh.* (1903). The scepticism of John Bowman, reported by Oldys (cf. no. xxxiv), as to Thomas Betterton's journey to Warwickshire can hardly weigh against Rowe's statement, even though Bowman, who died in 1739, was a colleague of Betterton (*c.* 1635–1710) as an actor from 1688 and married his adopted daughter (*Var.* ii. 120). Malone (*ibid.* 163) says that the journey was in 1708. Evidently Betterton ascribed to John Shakespeare the three children of the corvizer as well as his own (cf. App. A, no. i), but it is not clear how he came to give the poet three daughters.]

. . . He was the Son of M^r. *John Shakespear*, and was Born at *Stratford* upon *Avon*, in *Warwickshire*, in *April* 1564. His Family, as appears by the Register and Publick Writings relating to that Town, were of good Figure and Fashion there, and are mention'd as Gentlemen. His Father, who was a considerable Dealer in Wool, had so large a Family, ten Children in all, that tho' he was his eldest Son, he could give him no better Education than his own Employment. He had bred him, 'tis true, for some time at a Free-School, where 'tis probable he ac-quir'd that little *Latin* he was Master of: But the narrow-ness of his Circumstances, and the want of his assistance at Home, forc'd his Father to withdraw him from thence, and unhappily prevented his further Proficiency in that Language. . . . Upon his leaving School, he seems to have given intirely into that way of Living which his

Father propos'd to him; and in order to settle in the
World after a Family manner, he thought fit to marry
while he was yet very Young. His Wife was the Daughter
of one *Hathaway*, said to have been a substantial Yeoman
in the Neighbourhood of *Stratford*. In this kind of Settlement he continu'd for some time, 'till an Extravagance
that he was guilty of, forc'd him both out of his Country
and that way of Living which he had taken up; and tho'
it seem'd at first to be a Blemish upon his good Manners,
and a Misfortune to him, yet it afterwards happily prov'd
the occasion of exerting one of the greatest *Genius*'s that
ever was known in Dramatick Poetry. He had, by a
Misfortune common enough to young Fellows, fallen
into ill Company; and amongst them, some that made
a frequent practice of Deer-stealing, engag'd him with
them more than once in robbing a Park that belong'd
to Sir *Thomas Lucy* of *Cherlecot*, near *Stratford*. For this
he was prosecuted by that Gentleman, as he thought,
somewhat too severely; and in order to revenge that ill
Usage, he made a Ballad upon him. And tho' this,
probably the first Essay of his Poetry, be lost, yet it is
said to have been so very bitter, that it redoubled the
Prosecution against him to that degree, that he was
oblig'd to leave his Business and Family in *Warwickshire*,
for some time, and shelter himself in *London*.

It is at this Time, and upon this Accident, that he is
said to have made his first Acquaintance in the Play-house.
He was receiv'd into the Company then in being, at
first in a very mean Rank; but his admirable Wit, and
the natural Turn of it to the Stage, soon distinguish'd
him, if not as an extraordinary Actor, yet as an excellent
Writer. His Name is Printed, as the Custom was in
those Times, amongst those of the other Players, before
some old Plays, but without any particular Account of
what sort of Parts he us'd to play; and tho' I have inquir'd,
I could never meet with any further Account of him this
way, than that the top of his Performance was the Ghost
in his own *Hamlet*. . . . Mr *Dryden* seems to think that
Pericles is one of his first Plays; but there is no judgment

to be form'd on that, since there is good Reason to believe that the greatest part of that Play was not written by him; tho' it is own'd, some part of it certainly was, particularly the last Act. . . . Besides the advantages of his Wit, he was in himself a good-natur'd Man, of great sweetness in his Manners, and a most agreeable Companion; so that it is no wonder if with so many good Qualities he made himself acquainted with the best Conversations of those Times. Queen *Elizabeth* had several of his Plays Acted before her, and without doubt gave him many gracious Marks of her Favour: . . . She was so well pleas'd with that admirable Character of *Falstaff*, in the two Parts of *Henry* the Fourth, that she commanded him to continue it for one Play more, and to shew him in Love. This is said to be the Occasion of his Writing *The Merry Wives* of Windsor. How well she was obey'd, the Play it self is an admirable Proof. Upon this Occasion it may not be improper to observe, that this Part of *Falstaff* is said to have been written originally under the Name of *Oldcastle*; some of that Family being then remaining, the Queen was pleas'd to command him to alter it; upon which he made use of *Falstaff*. . . . What Grace soever the Queen confer'd upon him, it was not to her only he ow'd the Fortune which the Reputation of his Wit made. He had the Honour to meet with many great and uncommon Marks of Favour and Friendship from the Earl of *Southampton*, famous in the Histories of that Time for his Friendship to the unfortunate Earl of *Essex*. It was to that Noble Lord that he Dedicated his *Venus* and *Adonis*, the only Piece of his Poetry which he ever publish'd himself, tho' many of his Plays were surrepticiously and lamely Printed in his Life-time. There is one instance so singular in the Magnificence of this Patron of *Shakespear's*, that if I had not been assur'd that the Story was handed down by Sir *William D'Avenant*, who was probably very well acquainted with his Affairs, I should not have ventur'd to have inserted, that my Lord *Southampton*, at one time, gave him a thousand Pounds, to enable him to go through with a Purchase which he heard he had a mind to. A Bounty very great, and very rare at any time, and almost equal to that profuse Generosity the present Age has shewn to *French* Dancers and *Italian* Eunuchs.

What particular Habitude or Friendships he contracted with private Men, I have not been able to learn, more than that every one who had a true Taste of Merit, and could distinguish Men, had generally a just Value and Esteem for him. His exceeding Candor and good Nature must certainly have inclin'd all the gentler Part of the World to love him, as the power of his Wit oblig'd the Men of the most delicate Knowledge and polite Learning to admire him. Amongst these was the incomparable Mr *Edmond Spencer*, who speaks of him in his *Tears of the Muses*, not only with the Praises due to a good Poet, but even lamenting his absence with the tenderness of a Friend. . . . Mr *Dryden* was always of Opinion these Verses were meant of *Shakespear*; and 'tis highly probable they were so, since he was three and thirty Years old at *Spencer's* Death; and his Reputation in Poetry must have been great enough before that Time to have deserv'd what is here said of him. His Acquaintance with *Ben Johnson* began with a remarkable piece of Humanity and good Nature; Mr *Johnson*, who was at that Time altogether unknown to the World, had offer'd one of his Plays to the Players, in order to have it Acted; and the Persons into whose Hands it was put, after having turn'd it carelessly and superciliously over, were just upon returning it to him with an ill-natur'd Answer, that it would be of no service to their Company, when *Shakespear* luckily cast his Eye upon it, and found something so well in it as to engage him first to read it through, and afterwards to recommend Mr *Johnson* and his Writings to the Publick. After this they were profess'd Friends; tho' I don't know whether the other ever made him an equal return of Gentleness and Sincerity. . . .

Falstaff is allow'd by everybody to be a Master-piece; . . . Amongst other Extravagances, in *The Merry Wives of Windsor*, he has made him a Dear-stealer, that he might at the same time remember his *Warwickshire* Prosecutor, under the Name of Justice *Shallow*; he has given him very near the same Coat of Arms which *Dugdale*, in his Antiquities of that County, describes for a Family there, and makes the *Welsh* Parson descant very pleasantly upon 'em. . . .

. . . I cannot leave *Hamlet*, without taking notice of the Advantage with which we have seen this Master-piece of *Shakespear* distinguish it self upon the Stage, by Mr *Betterton's* fine Performance of that Part. A Man who tho' he had no other good Qualities, as he has a great many, must have made his way into the Esteem of all Men of Letters, by this only Excellency. . . . I must own a particular Obligation to him, for the most considerable part of the Passages relating to his Life, which I have here transmitted to the Publick; his Veneration for the Memory of *Shakespear* having engaged him to make a Journey into *Warwickshire*, on purpose to gather up what Remains he could of a Name for which he had so great a Value. . . .

. . . The latter Part of his Life was spent, as all Men of good Sense will wish theirs may be, in Ease, Retirement, and the Conversation of his Friends. He had the good Fortune to gather an Estate equal to his Occasion, and, in that, to his Wish; and is said to have spent some Years before his Death at his native *Stratford*. His pleasurable Wit, and good Nature, engag'd him in the Acquaintance, and entitled him to the Friendship of the Gentlemen of the Neighbourhood. Amongst them, it is a Story almost still remember'd in that Country, that he had a particular Intimacy with Mr *Combe*, an old Gentleman noted thereabouts for his Wealth and Usury: It happen'd, that in a pleasant Conversation amongst their common Friends, Mr *Combe* told *Shakespear* in a laughing manner, that he fancy'd, he intended to write his Epitaph, if he happen'd to out-live him; and since he could not know what might be said of him when he was dead, he desir'd it might be done immediately: Upon which *Shakespear* gave him these four Verses.

> *Ten in the Hundred lies here ingrav'd,*
> *'Tis a Hundred to Ten, his Soul is not sav'd:*
> *If any Man ask, Who lies in this Tomb?*
> *Oh! ho! quoth the Devil, 'tis my* John-a-Combe.

But the Sharpness of the Satyr is said to have stung the Man so severely, that he never forgave it.

He Dy'd in the 53d Year of his Age, and was bury'd on the North side of the Chancel, in the Great Church at *Stratford*, where a Monument, as engrav'd in the Plate, is plac'd in the Wall. On his Grave-Stone underneath is,

> *Good Friend, for Jesus sake, forbear*
> *To dig the Dust inclosed here.*
> *Blest be the Man that spares these Stones,*
> *And Curst be he that moves my Bones.*

He had three Daughters, of which two liv'd to be marry'd; *Judith*, the Elder, to one Mr *Thomas Quiney*, by whom she had three Sons, who all dy'd without Children; and *Susannah*, who was his Favourite, to Dr *John Hall*, a Physician of good Reputation in that Country. She left one Child only, a Daughter, who was marry'd first to *Thomas Nash*, Esq; and afterwards to Sir John *Bernard* of *Abington*, but dy'd likewise without Issue.

This is what I could learn of any Note, either relating to himself or Family: The Character of the man is best seen in his Writings. . . .

XXVI. THOMAS HEARNE (1709)

[From notes at end of diary for June–July 1709, pr. C. E. Doble, *Remarks and Collections of Thomas Hearne* (*O.H.S.*) ii. 228. Hearne (1678–1735) was a lifelong student of antiquities in Oxford.]

'Twas reported by Tradition in Oxford that Shakespear as he us'd to pass from London to Stratford upon Avon, where he liv'd & now lies buried, always spent some time in ye Crown Tavern in Oxford, which was kept by one Davenant who had a handsome Wife, & lov'd witty Company, tho' himself a reserv'd and melancholly Man. He had born to him a Son who was afterwards Christen'd

by yᵉ Name of Wᵐ. who prov'd a very Eminent Poët, and
was knighted (by yᵉ name of Sʳ. William Davenant) and
yᵉ said Mʳ. Shakespear was his God-father & gave him
his name. (In all probability he got him.) 'Tis further
said that one day going from school a grave Doctor in
Divinity met him, and ask'd him, *Child whither art thou
going in such hast?* to wᶜʰ the child reply'd, *O Sir my Godfather is come to Town, & I am going to ask his blessing.* To
wᶜʰ the Dʳ. said, *Hold Child, you must not take the name of
God in vaine.*

XXVII. ANON (c. 1709)

[From *Advertisement* on A 2ᵛ of *A Collection of Poems* . . . By Mʳ. William
Shakespeare, London. Printed for Bernard Lintot, n.d. There seem to
have been several variant issues of this edition, which has not always been
distinguished from Gildon's of 1710. Some have a second vol. containing
the *Sonn.* and *Lov. Compl.* The editor is unknown. The *Advertisement*
refers to a 'late' six vol. ed. of the plays, with a life; obviously Rowe's of
1709. On the identification by Oldys of the 'credible Person' with
⟨John Sheffield⟩ Duke of Buckingham (1648–1721), cf. p. 280.]

I cannot omit inserting a Passage of Mʳ *Shakespeare's*
Life, very much to his Honour, and very remarkable,
which was either unknown, or forgotten by the Writer of it.

That most learn'd Prince, and great Patron of Learning,
King *James* the First, was pleas'd with his own Hand
to write an amicable Letter to Mʳ *Shakespeare*; which
Letter, tho now lost, remain'd long in the Hands of Sir
William D'avenant, as a credible Person now living can
testify.

XXVIII. LEWIS THEOBALD (1727)

[A tradition, cited by him, that Shakespeare had written *Double Falsehood*,
in his retirement from the stage, for the benefit of a natural daughter, is
discussed in ch. x.]

XXIX. ANON (1728)

[From *Essay against too much Reading* (1728), 14. Copies are in *B.M.* 1087,
i. 11 (1), and *Bodl. G. Pamph.* 1309 (2).]

I will give you a short Account of Mʳ *Shakespear's*
Proceeding; and that I had from one of his intimate

Acquaintance. His being imperfect in some Things, was owing to his not being a Scholar, which obliged him to have one of those chuckle-pated Historians for his particular Associate, that could scarce speak a Word but upon that Subject; and he maintain'd him, or he might have starv'd upon his History. And when he wanted anything in his Way, as his plays were all Historical, he sent to him, and took down the Heads of what was for his Purpose in Characters, which were thirty times as quick as running to the Books to read for it: Then with his natural flowing Wit, he work'd it into all Shapes and Forms, as his beautiful Thoughts directed. The other put it into Grammar; and instead of Reading, he stuck close to Writing and Study without Book. How do you think, Reading could have assisted him in such great Thoughts? It would only have lost Time. When he found his Thoughts grow on him so fast, he could have writ for ever, had he liv'd so long.

XXX. JOSEPH SPENCE (1728–43)

[From *Anecdotes, Observations and Characters, of Books and Men. Collected from the Conversation of M*ʳ *Pope, and other eminent Persons of his Time*, ed. S. W. Singer (1820). These notes were left by Spence (1699–1768), of New College, Professor of Poetry and Regius Professor of Modern History at Oxford, and Prebendary of Durham. He became acquainted with Pope about 1726.]

[*Anecdotes of 1728–30.*]

(*a*) [p. 5.] It was a general opinion, that Ben Jonson and Shakspeare lived in enmity against one another. Betterton has assured me often, that there was nothing in it: and that such a supposition was founded only on the two parties, which in their lifetime listed under one, and endeavoured to lessen the character of the other mutually. —Dryden used to think that the verses Jonson made on Shakspeare's death, had something of satire at the bottom; for my part, I can't discover any thing like it in them.—*P[ope]*.

(*b*) [p. 23.] That notion of Sir William Davenant being more than a poetical child only of Shakspeare, was common in town; and Sir William himself seemed fond of having it taken for truth.—*P[ope]*.

[Anecdote of 1742–3.]

(*c*) [p. 269.] Shakspeare, in his frequent journeys between London and his native place, Stratford-upon-Avon, used to lie at Davenant's, the Crown, in Oxford. He was very well acquainted with Mrs Davenant; and her son, (afterwards Sir William), was supposed to be more nearly related to him, than as a godson only.—One day when Shakspeare was just arrived, and the boy sent for from school to him, a head of one of the colleges, (who was pretty well acquainted with the affairs of the family), met the child running home, and asked him, whither he was going in so much haste? The boy said: 'to my Godfather Shakspeare'.—'Fie, child, (says the old gentleman), why are you so superfluous? have you not learned yet that you should not use the name of God in vain?'—*P[ope]*.

XXXI. JOHN ROBERTS (1729)

[From *An Answer to Mr. Pope's Preface to Shakespear . . . By a Strolling Player*, 45, 47, ascribed to John Roberts. Sir William Bishop (1626–1700) was of Bridgetown, a hamlet partly in Stratford. There was in fact a disastrous fire at Warwick in 1694, but certainly no descendant of Shakespeare dwelt there, and French 397 shows no Hart.]

How much is it to be lamented, that *Two* large *Chests* full of this GREAT MAN's *loose Papers* and *Manuscripts*, in the Hands of an ignorant *Baker* of WARWICK, (who married one of the Descendants from *Shakespear*) were carelesly scatter'd and thrown about, as Garret Lumber and Litter, to the particuler Knowledge of the late *Sir William Bishop*, till they were all consum'd in the generall Fire and Destruction of that Town? . . .

> Good Frend for Iesus SAKE forbeare
> To diGG TE Dust EncloAsed HERe
> Blese be THE Man ỹ spares TEs Stones
> And curst be He ỹ moves my Bones.

In Regard of his own Epitaph above (if that were his
Writing, as the Report goes it was) the false Spelling, and
irregular Mixture of Characters could not be his, but the
Workman's.

XXXII. FRANCIS PECK (1740)

[From *Explanatory and Critical Notes on Shakespeare's Plays*, appended
to *New Memoirs of Milton* (1740), 222. Peck (1692–1743) was of Trinity,
Cambridge, a Leicestershire clergyman and prebendary of Lincoln, and a
desultory antiquarian.]

Every body knows *Shakespeare's* epitaph for *John a
Combe*. And I am told he afterwards wrote another for
Tom a Combe, alias *Thin-Beard*, brother of the said *John*;
& that it was never yet printed. It is as follows.

> *Thin* in *beard*, and thick in purse;
> Never man beloved worse:
> He went to th' grave with many a curse:
> The Devil & He had both one nurse.

This is very sour.

XXXIII. CHARLES MACKLIN (1742)

[Macklin (*c.* 1697–1797) was an actor in London and Dublin. In May
1742 (*Var.* ii. 522) he visited Stratford with Garrick, where they were
entertained under the New Place mulberry by Sir Hugh Clopton. The
stories he gathered were probably given orally to Malone. On a fabrication
by Macklin, cf. App. F.]

(*a*) [From Malone (1790, i. 1. 136; *Var.* ii. 623).]

Sir Hugh Clopton, who was born two years after her
death, mentioned to Mʳ Macklin, in the year 1742, an
old tradition that she ⟨Lady Bernard⟩ had carried away
with her from Stratford many of her grandfather's papers.

(*b*) [From Malone (1790, i. 2. 113; *Var.* iii. 133), as note to the lines
in *Tarlton's Jests*, 14—

> Gentlemen, this fellow, with this face of mapple,
> Instead of a pipin, hath thrown me an apple.]

This appears to have been a common sarcasm. There is
a tradition yet preserved in Stratford, of Shakspeare's

comparing the carbuncled face of a drunken blacksmith to a *maple*. The blacksmith accosted him, as he was leaning over a mercer's door, with

'Now, Mr Shakspeare, tell me, if you can,
The difference between a youth and a young man.'

to which our poet immediately replied,

'Thou son of fire, with *thy face like a maple*,
The same difference as between a scalded and a coddled apple.'

This anecdote was related near fifty years ago to a gentleman at Stratford by a person then above eighty years of age, whose father might have been contemporary with Shakspeare.

(*c*) [From 'an unpublished letter, written by Malone in 1788', quoted H.P. (*1848*), 243. But either Macklin or Malone had varied the story, which in (*b*) has nothing to do with Combe.]

Mr Macklin tells but a blind story of Sir Hugh Clopton's having sent for a very old woman, near ninety, who repeated to him a couplet that she remembered to have heard in her youth, and which was said to have been made by Shakspeare on old John Combe, in which he compares his face to a maple.

XXXIV. WILLIAM OLDYS (*c.* 1743–61)

[Oldys was the illegitimate son of William Oldys, chancellor of Lincoln. Born in 1696, he became an antiquarian at an early age. In 1724 he left London for Yorkshire and housed mainly at Wentworth Woodhouse with Thomas Lord Malton, afterwards 1st Marquis of Rockingham. In 1730 he returned to London, sold his literary collections to Edward Harley, 2nd Earl of Oxford, and studied in the Harleian Library. He wrote an elaborate *Life* for Raleigh's *History of the World* (1736), and published his *British Librarian* in 1737. In 1737 he also wrote a life of Sir John Fastolf for T. Birch's *General Dictionary* (1734–41). In 1738 Oxford made him his literary secretary, and he thus became known to Pope and other literary men. Oxford died in 1741, and his library was sold to Thomas Osborne the bookseller, who employed Oldys with Samuel Johnson in compiling the *Harleian Miscellany* (1744–6). During 1747–60 he contributed several lives, including one of Edward Alleyn (1747) and a revised one of Fastolf (1750), to the *Biographia Britannia* (1747–66).

About 1751 he got into debt and the Fleet, but was ultimately befriended by Edward 9th Duke of Norfolk, through whom he was appointed Norroy King-at-Arms in 1755. He lived at the Heralds' College until his death on 15 Apr. 1761. Much material on Oldys is collected in a *Memoir* (1862), anonymous but by J. Yeowell, reprinted from *N.Q.* His library was sold by Thomas Davies on 12 Apr. 1762, and is described in J. Fry's *Biblio-graphical Memoranda* (1816). Among his MSS. in the B. M. are *Addl.* 4240 (Family Memoirs), *Addl.* 22667 (Diary for 1737–9, printed by Yeowell 1), *Addl.* 12522–3 (Collections for a work on Literary Patronage). But many of his notes on English writers were in the form of interlineations and marginalia to printed books. The most important is the Langbaine of 1691 (v. *infra*), and of this he annotated two copies. Of the first he says (C. 28. g. 1, p. 353) that he left it in 1724 among other books in the care of 'Mʳ Burridge's family, with whom I had several years lodged', but on returning in 1730 found this property dispersed, and learnt that the Langbaine had been sold by a bookseller to Thomas Coxeter. 'This', he says, 'must have been of service to him, and he has kept it so carefully from my sight, that I could never have the opportunity of transcribing into this I am now writing in, the notes I had collected in that'. A supplementary note by Thomas Percy (*Addl. MS.* 22594, f. 51ᵛ) adds that the book passed at Coxeter's sale with Coxeter's own notes to Theophilus Cibber, who with others used it 'with their own trash intermixed' for the *Lives of the Poets*. Possibly, therefore, rather than probably, Oldys is the source for no. xxxviii.

The quarto *Life* of Shakespeare which Oldys had written by 1750 must have been in a parchment volume of *Lives* which he also refers to in C. 28. g. 1 as containing a life of Suckling. It does not seem to have been in his sale, and is not now known. One would suppose it to be the manuscript used by Steevens in 1778 (*infra*). But there may have been later additions. A Chalmers, *General Biographical Dictionary* (1815) gives a MS. note of A. C. Ducarel (ob. 1785), 'who knew him well', as authority for the statement that Oldys 'had by him, at the time of his death, some collections towards a Life of Shakespeare, but not digested into any order, as he told the doctor a few days before he died'. A fuller account is given in *Records of my Life* (1832), i. 28, by John Taylor, whose father had been a friend of Oldys in his later years. 'Mʳ Oldys had engaged to furnish a bookseller in the Strand, whose name was Walker, with ten years of the life of Shake-speare unknown to the biographers and commentators, but he died and "made no sign" of the projected work'. The elder Taylor repaid an advance of twenty guineas made by Walker. Some at least of Oldys's manuscripts did not pass at the sale of 1762. Taylor describes them as 'consisting of a few books written in a small hand, and abundantly inter-lined'. They remained long in his father's possession, and were then lent to Thomas Percy, in whose hands they continued some years. The last seen by the younger Taylor had been lent by Richard Heber to William Gifford for a contemplated edition of Shirley. Others were purchased, nearly thirty years after Oldys's death, by T. Cadell for the *Bibliographia*

Britannica. I may add that Gifford's notes on Shirley were used in A. Dyce's edition (1833), and that the 2nd edition of the *Bibliographia Britannica*, edited by A. Kippis (1778–93), never got beyond the letter F. An incomplete further volume perished in a fire of 1808. I. Disraeli, who wrote an account of Oldys, based on information from the elder Taylor, in his *Curiosities of Literature* (2nd series, 1823, iii. 446), ascertained that the material for a continuation was returned to the booksellers G. and J. Robinson, but could not learn what ultimately became of it. Whether Oldys ever added anything to his quarto *Life* must therefore remain doubtful. In any case, it seems probable that Steevens saw all there was to see. I cannot trace the source of the statement in Yeowell xxxvii that Oldys kept his notes 'on slips of paper, which he afterwards classified and reposited in small bags suspended about his room'.

(*a*) [From G. Steevens, *Works of Sh.* (1778) i. 202 (after Rowe's *Life*), 223 (note to *Merry Wives of W.* i. 1. 16); repr. in *Var.* i. 462 (*Additional Anecdotes of the Life of Shakspeare*), ii. 141 and viii. 11. The edition is sometimes ascribed in error to I. Reed. Yeowell 43 includes these among 'Choice Notes' which he describes as from Oldys's 'manuscript Adversaria', and this in Lee 642 becomes 'his manuscript "Adversaria" (now in the British Museum)'. There is no such MS. and Yeowell must have taken them from the *Variorum*, from which he gives Malone's comments as foot-notes. Steevens must have had access to some MS. of Oldys which was not sold with his library, either the quarto *Life* of Shakespeare referred to in the Langbaine (*supra*) or the Heralds' College notes; if, indeed, the two were not the same. Malone (*Var.* ii. 138, 286) conjectures that Oldys's information was derived, like Capell's (no. xliv), through Thomas Jones of Tardebigge. One of the notes points to a tradition through John Bowman and Sir William Bishop (cf. no. xxxi) who died in 1700. But the Lucy verses might have come through Jones. The Harleian volume quoted under (4) has not been identified. C. M. Ingleby (*Ce.* 410) thinks that the jottings on the t.p. of the Langbaine are evidence that Oldys wrote the verses on the basis of Petronius Arbiter, *Fragmenta* (ed. Burmann 673), 'quod fere totus mundus exerceat histrionem', and suggests that Steevens dished them up as Jonson's and Shakespeare's.]

(1) Mʳ Rowe ⟨cf. no. xxv⟩ has told us that he derived the principal anecdotes in his account of Shakspeare, from Betterton the player, whose zeal had induced him to visit Stratford for the sake of procuring all possible intelligence concerning a poet to whose works he might justly think himself under the strongest obligations. Notwithstanding this assertion, in the manuscript papers of the late Mʳ Oldys it is said, that one Bowman (according to Chetwood, p. 144, 'an actor more than half an age on

the London theatres') was unwilling to allow that his
associate and contemporary Betterton had ever undertaken
such a journey. Be this matter as it will, the following
particulars, which I shall give in the words of Oldys, are,
for ought we know to the contrary, as well authenticated
as any of the anecdotes delivered down to us by Rowe.

Mr Oldys had covered several quires of paper with
laborious collections for a regular life of our author. From
these I have made the following extracts, which (however
trivial) contain the only circumstances that wear the least
appearance of novelty or information; the song excepted,
which the reader will find in a note on the first scene of
the *Merry Wives of Windsor* [*vide* (6) *infra*].

(2) If tradition may be trusted, Shakespeare often baited
at the Crown Inn or Tavern in Oxford, in his journey to
and from London. The landlady was a woman of great
beauty and sprightly wit, and her husband, Mr John
Davenant (afterwards mayor of that city,) a grave melancholy man, who as well as his wife used much to delight
in Shakespeare's pleasant company. Their son young
Will Davenant (afterwards Sir William) was then a little
school-boy in the town, of about seven or eight years old,
and so fond also of Shakespeare, that whenever he heard
of his arrival, he would fly from school to see him. One
day an old townsman observing the boy running home-
ward almost out of breath, asked him whither he was
posting in that heat and hurry. He answered, to see his
god-father Shakespeare. There's a good boy, said the
other, but have a care that you don't take *God's* name in
vain. This story Mr Pope told me at the Earl of Oxford's
table, upon occasion of some discourse which arose about
Shakespeare's monument then newly erected in Westminster Abbey; and he quoted Mr Betterton the player
for his authority. I answered, that I thought such a story
might have enriched the variety of those choice fruits of
observation he has presented to us in his preface to the
edition he had published of our poet's works. He replied
—'There might be in the garden of mankind such plants

as would seem to pride themselves more in a regular production of their own native fruits, than in having the repute of bearing a richer kind by grafting; and this was the reason he omitted it.'

(3) One of Shakespeare's younger brothers, who lived to a good old age, even some years, as I compute, after the restoration of *K. Charles II.* would in his younger days come to London to visit his brother *Will*, as he called him, and be a spectator of him as an actor in some of his own plays. This custom, as his brother's fame enlarged, and his dramatic entertainments grew the greatest support of our principal, if not of all our theatres, he continued it seems so long after his brother's death, as even to the latter end of his own life. The curiosity at this time of the most noted actors to learn something from him of his brother, &c. they justly held him in the highest veneration. And it may well be believed, as there was besides a kinsman and descendant of the family, who was then a celebrated actor among them, this opportunity made them greedily inquisitive into every little circumstance, more especially in his dramatick character, which his brother could relate of him. But he, it seems, was so stricken in years, and possibly his memory so weakened with infirmities (which might make him the easier pass for a man of weak intellects) that he could give them but little light into their enquiries; and all that could be recollected from him of his brother *Will*, in that station was, the faint, general, and almost lost ideas he had of having once seen him act a part in one of his own comedies, wherein being to personate a decrepit old man, he wore a long beard, and appeared so weak and drooping and unable to walk, that he was forced to be supported and carried by another person to a table, at which he was seated among some company, who were eating, and one of them sung a song.

(4) 'Verses by Ben Jonson and Shakespeare, occasioned by the motto to the Globe Theatre—*Totus mundus agit histrionem.*

Jonson.

If, but *stage actors*, all the world displays,
Where shall we find *spectators* of their plays?

Shakespeare.

Little, or much, of what we see, we do;
We're all both *actors* and *spectators* too.

Poetical Characteristicks, 8vo. MS. vol. i, some time in
the Harleian Library; which volume was returned to its
owner.

(5) Old Mʳ Bowman the player reported from Sir William Bishop, that some part of Sir John Falstaff's character
was drawn from a townsman of Stratford, who either
faithlessly broke a contract, or spitefully refused to part
with some land for a valuable consideration, adjoining
to Shakespeare's, in or near that town.

(6) There was a very aged gentleman living in the neighbourhood of Stratford, (where he died fifty years since,)
who had not only heard, from several old people in that
town, of Shakespeare's transgression, but could remember
the first stanza of that bitter ballad, which, repeating to
one of his acquaintance, he preserved it in writing; and
here it is, neither better nor worse, but faithfully transcribed from the copy which his relation very curteously
communicated to me.

A parliemente member, a justice of peace,
At home a poor scare-crowe, at London an asse,
If lowsie is Lucy, as some volke miscalle it,
Then Lucy is lowsie whatever befall it:
  He thinks himselfe greate,
  Yet an asse in his state,
We allowe by his ears but with asses to mate.
  If Lucy is lowsie, as some volke miscalle it,
  Sing lowsie Lucy, whatever befall it.

Contemptible as this performance must now appear, at
the time when it was written it might have sufficient power

to irritate a vain, weak, and vindictive magistrate; especially as it was affixed to several of his park-gates, and consequently published among his neighbours.—It may be remarked likewise, that the jingle on which it turns, occurs in the first scene of *The Merry Wives of Windsor.*

(*b*) [From G. Steevens, *Shakespeare* (1778), i. 205; repr. *Var*. i. 468; after a quotation of the statement in the Lintot *Poems* (no. xxvii) as to a letter by James I to Shakespeare. The copy of T. Fuller, *Worthies of England* (1662), annotated by Oldys, is now unknown. A transcript by Steevens of notes both by Oldys and by R. Thoresby is in another copy (*Bodl. Mal.* 3), but this contains no notes on the account of Shakespeare, and I could not find the note here quoted elsewhere in the volume. After searching for it, I found from a letter of Malone to Bp. Percy on 28 Oct. 1802 (*Malone MS.* 26, f. 46) that he too had looked for it in vain, but had some memory of his discussing it with Steevens 'and of his taking down his Fuller for the purpose of showing me this notice'. Probably Steevens had the original, and did not copy the note into *Malone* 3. Oldys himself refers to it in his Langbaine (v. *infra*). The Duke of Buckingham was John Sheffield (1648–1721).]

Mr Oldys, in a MS. note to his copy of Fuller's Worthies, observes, that 'the story came from the duke of Buckingham, who had it from Sir William D'avenant'.

(*c*) [From *marginalia* to copy (*B.M.* C. 28. g. 1) of G. Langbaine, *Account of the English Dramatick Poets* (1691). The t.p. is inscribed 'W. O. 1727'. The note on *Hen. IV* refers to the 1737 and not the 1750 version of Oldys's *Fastolf* article. Another note (p. 469) refers to a statue of Shakespeare set up 'in the year 1740' in Westminster Abbey, and yet another to a book of 1743. A date of 1743◊50 is therefore likely for the annotation. This Langbaine was bought by T. Birch from the bookseller T. Davies at the death of Oldys (Yeowell xlv) and left by him to the B.M. The notes are often quoted from transcripts made, directly or indirectly, from C. 28. g. 1 by various scholars; e.g. T. Percy (*B.M.* 011795. ee. 1), G. Steevens (*B.M. Addl. MSS.* 22592–5), E. Malone (*Bodl. Mal.* 129–32), J. Haslewood (*B.M.* C. 45. d. 14). A list of others is in Yeowell xliii. For the τριναρχοδια, cf. no. iv.]

(1) *Title-page at foot.*

Totus Mundus agit Histrionem

If all the World the *Actor* plays,
Who are *Spectators* of its Plays?

Corrected to—

> If but Stage-Actors all the World displays,
> Who are allowd *Spectators* of their Plays?

In inner margin.

> Little or much, of what we see we Do,
> We are both Actors and Spectators too.

(2) *p. 106, s.v. Davenant.*

The Story of his Visiting Shakspear when a Boy as M^r
Pope told me.

(3) *s.v. Shakespear.*

p. 454. I haue observed in my Fuller and repeat it here
that K. James I honourd Shakespear with an Episto-
lary correspondence and I think Sir W. Davenant had
either seen or was possessed of ~~them~~ **his Maties Letter
to him.** I haue read it in Print and yet all our late Pre-
tenders to the Exaltation of Shakespeares Memory are
quite silent of this particular. Tis very much if Sr William
had them y^t he did not publish them.

p. 455 (app. as note to whole Life). So in my Lyfe of
Shaks Q°.

p. 455. The son of Mr John Shakespeare Wool Stapler
was the eldest of Ten Children born 23 of April 1563
. . . *[The rest is obviously from Rowe].*

p. 455. Tis a Tradition descended frō old Betterton that
he was drawn into a company of deer Stealers & con-
cernd wth y^m. in robbing Sr Thos. Lucy's Park at
Charlecot wch drove him to London so among the Players
where he became the Great Genius we read him in his
Plays.

p. 456, s.v. Hen. IV. See the Censures of him in Verse and
Prose, for this freedom with a famous Name in my Life
of Sir John Fastolf in the General Dictionary. The Verses
quoted from the Three Historical Poems I have in MS.
called τρινιαρχοδια, written 8°. 1650.

p. 457, s.v. Hen. V. Shakespear was not 29 years of age when he wrote his Henry the Fifth: For Tarlton who acted in it died in 1592 or before. [*Against this*]

$$\begin{array}{r} 53 \\ 24 \\ \hline 29 \end{array}$$

p. 459. The Story of Davnants Godfather Shakespeare, as Mr Pope told it me is printed among the Jests of John Taylor the Water Poet in his Works, folio, 1630 ⟨ii. 184⟩, but without their Names and with a seeming fictitious one, of the boys Godfather vizt Goodman Digland the Gardener, I suppose of Oxford, for Taylor tells other Jests y^t he pickd up at Oxford in the same collection.

p. 468. I have now no more to do, but to close up all with an Account of his Death; which was on the 23^d of April, Anno Dom. 1616.

[*So Langbaine. Oldys underlines '23^d of April', and writes what may be 'Q', '&', or '2' in the margin.*]

p. 469. Obiit An. Dom. 1616
      Aet. 53. die 23. Apr.

[*So Langbaine from the monument. Oldys underlines 'die 23. Apr.' writes '53' under '1616' and '1563' in the margin.*]

(*d*) [From *marginalia* to copy (*Bodl. Mal.* 562) of W. Winstanley, *Lives of the Most Famous English Poets* (1687), 133. The t.p. is inscribed 'Willm Oldys' and a fly-leaf 'July 1737', but the note was altered after Oldys's *Biographia Britannica* article of 1750.]

See ye Stanzas ag^t him ⟨Shakespeare⟩ for this Liberty in my old MS Poem on the Three Reigns, calld Trinarchodia 8° 1650 two of which Stanzas are printed in my Lives of Sr John Fastolf in the General Dictionary and again in the Biographia Britannica.

(*e*) [From Malone, *Supplementary Observations* (1780), i. 44; repr. *Var.* iii. 162. I have not traced the MS. cited.]

Oldys, in one of his manuscripts, says that Shakspeare received but *five pounds* for his *Hamlet*; whether from the players who first acted it, or the printer or bookseller who first published it, is not distinguished.

XXXV. JOSEPH WIGHT (*c.* 1744–72)

[From *Letter* of John Taylor of the Sun Office to Malone in August 1810, printed by H.P. ii. 46. A similar account, with Malone's reply, which adds nothing, is in Taylor's *Records of My Life* (1832), ii. 152. Here he names a Mrs. Bembridge with a son in the Army Pay Office as a friend of 'White'. I think he was really 'Wight'. The latest issue (1755) I can find of John Chamberlayne, *Magnae Britanniae Notitia*, ii. 8, gives Joseph Wight as then Assistant Clerk to the Clerk of the Parliaments, and there are letters from him in the correspondence (1697–1768) of the Duke of Newcastle in the B.M.; the last is of 1766 (*Addl. MS.* 32974, f. 125). I have found no trace of the book referred to by Taylor.]

On re-perusing your history of the English stage and your anecdotes of Shakespeare and Davenant, I see no allusion to a story which I copied in early life from a manuscript book, and which, many years afterwards, when I became connected with the public press, I inserted in a newspaper. It is very probable that you have heard the story, though perhaps you did not think it was established on a sufficient tradition for notice in your work. I assure you upon my honour I found it there, and, if this could be doubted, I am ready to make oath of the accuracy of my statement. The manuscript-book was written by Mr White, a very respectable gentleman who was a reading-clerk to the House of Lords. He died about the year 1772, and his property chiefly descended to a Miss Dunwell, his niece. He lived upon Wandsworth Common in a very good house. That house and other property was bequeathed by Miss Dunwell to a Mrs Bodman, a very old acquaintance of my family, and who knew me from my birth. All Mr White's books and manuscripts came into Mrs Bodman's possession, and most of them, I believe, were sold by auction. The book to which I allude consisted chiefly of observations and anecdotes written by Mr White himself, and were gleanings of conversations at which he was present. He was well acquainted with Mr Pope ⟨ob. 1744⟩, and often dined in company with him, and many of the observations and anecdotes had Mr Pope's name at the bottom of them, indicating the source whence Mr White derived them. What became of the book I know not. After all this preface, you will perhaps exclaim, *parturiunt montes, &c*, but, as it relates to Shakespeare, it must be interesting. The story was to the following purport. It was generally supposed or whispered in Oxford that Shakespeare, who was the godfather of Sir William Davenant, was in reality the father. The story mentioned that Shakespeare used to come to London every two years, and always stayed a night or two, going and coming, at the Crown. On such occasions the boy was always sent for from school to pay his respects to Shakespeare. On one of these occasions, as the child was running along the street, he was met by one of the heads of the colleges, who asked where he was going. The child said,—to see my godfather Shakespeare. What! said the gentleman, have they not taught you yet not to use the Lord's name in vain?

XXXVI. ANON (1748)

[From 'a manuscript note preserved in the University Library, Edinburgh, written about the year 1748', pr. H.P. ii. 286.]

Sir William Davenant, who has been call'd a natural son of our author, us'd to tell the following whimsical story of him;—Shakespear, when he first came from the country to the play-house, was not admitted to act; but as it was then the custom for all the people of fashion to come on horseback to entertainments of all kinds, it was Shakespear's employment for a time, with several other poor boys belonging to the company, to hold the horses and take care of them during the representation;—by his dexterity and care he soon got a good deal of business in this way, and was personally known to most of the quality that frequented the house, insomuch that, being obliged, before he was taken into a higher and more honorable employment within doors, to train up boys to assist him, it became long afterwards a usual way among them to recommend themselves by saying that they were Shakespear's boys.

XXXVII. WILLIAM RUFUS CHETWOOD (1749)

[From *A General History of the Stage*, 21. Chetwood (ob. 1766) was prompter at Drury Lane (*c.* 1722–*c.* 1741) and afterwards in Dublin. His ignorance is certain and his *bona fides* improbable (cf. no. xvi and App. F). But this appears to be the first printed reference to the scandal.]

Sir William Davenant was by many, suppos'd the natural Son of Shakespear.

XXXVIII. ROBERT SHIELS (1753)

[From *The Lives of the Poets of Great Britain and Ireland, to the Time of Dean Swift. Compiled from ample Materials scattered in a Variety of Books, and especially from the MS. Notes of the late ingenious Mr. Coxeter and others, collected for this Design.* By Mr. Cibber. In Four Volumes. London: Printed for R. Griffiths, at the Dunciad in St. Paul's Church-Yard, i. 130. In both copies (*Bodl.* and *London Library*) seen by me, there are in fact five vols., and i. 1 is headed 'The Lives of the Poets. The Second Edition'. Johnson, in conversation with Boswell (ed. G. Birkbeck Hill, i. 187; iii. 29), and in his *Life of Hammond* (*Works*, viii. 90), says that the main author was his amanuensis Shiels, whose manuscript he possessed, and that Griffiths paid Theophilus Cibber (1703–58) a fee for the use of the name Cibber, to give an impression that the lives were by his father Colley Cibber (1671–1757). An article in *Monthly Review* (May 1792), owned by Griffiths, which claims that the contribution of T. Cibber was substantial, is hardly a refutation. Malone (*Var.* ii. 159) says that the only new matter was from Thomas Coxeter's notes derived from Oldys (cf. no. xxxiv). Except for this passage, which Shiels is more likely to have got from Johnson (cf. no. xlii) than from Oldys, the only source of the Shakespeare life appears to be Rowe.]

Here I cannot forbear relating a story which Sir William Davenant told Mr Betterton, who communicated it to Mr Rowe; Rowe told it Mr Pope, and Mr Pope told it to Dr. Newton, the late editor of Milton, and from a gentleman, who heard it from him, 'tis here related.

Concerning Shakespear's first appearance in the play-house. When he came to London, he was without money and friends, and being a stranger he knew not to whom to apply, nor by what means to support himself.—At that time coaches not being in use, and as gentlemen were accustomed to ride to the playhouse, Shakespear, driven to the last necessity, went to the playhouse door, and

pick'd up a little money by taking care of the gentlemens
horses who came to the play; he became eminent even in
that profession, and was taken notice of for his diligence
and skill in it; he had soon more business than he himself
could manage, and at last hired boys under him, who were
known by the name of Shakespear's boys: Some of the
players accidentally conversing with him, found him so
acute, and master of so fine a conversation, that struck
therewith, they and ⟨sic⟩ recommended him to the house.

XXXIX. ANON (c. 1760)

[From the *Town Jester*, given H.P. (*1848*), 187. H.P. found the jest
attributed to Ambrose Phillips in another collection, and (244) in a
variant form to Shakespeare in *Shakespeare's Jests, or the Jubilee Jester*
(1769), with other witticisms which only illustrate the 18th-century habit
of hanging tavern 'chestnuts' on Shakespeare's name.]

Ben Johnson and Shakespeare were once at a tavern-club
where there were several lords from the court who went
to hear their wit and conversation; Shakespeare call'd
upon Ben Johnson to give a toast; he nam'd that lord's
wife that sat near him; the nobleman demanded why he
nam'd her: Why not, replied the poet, she has the
qualifications of a toast, being both brown and dry; which
answer made them all laugh, his lordship having been
obliged to marry her against his inclinations.

XL. ANON (1762)

[From *Letter from the Place of Shakespear's Nativity* in *British Magazine
Or Monthly Repository for Gentlemen and Ladies*, iii. 301.]

I . . . put up at the White Lion . . . My chearful landlord
. . . took me to the house where the poet was born and
there I saw a mulberry-tree of that great man's planting,
a piece of which I brought away with me, to make tobacco-
stoppers for our vicar. . . . From thence my landlord was
so complaisant as to go with me to visit two young women,
lineal descendants of our great dramatic poet: they keep
a little ale-house, some small distance from Stratford.

On the road thither, at a place called Bidford, he shewed me in the hedge, a crab-tree, called Shakespear's canopy, because under it our poet slept one night; for he, as well as Ben Johnson, loved a glass for the pleasure of society; and he, having heard much of the men of that village as deep drinkers and merry fellows, one day went over to Bidford, to take a cup with them. He enquired of a shepherd for the Bidford drinkers; who replied they were absent; but the Bidford sippers were at home; and, I suppose, continued the sheepkeeper, they will be sufficient for you: and so, indeed, they were. He was forced to take up his lodging under that tree for some hours.

XLI. BIOGRAPHIA BRITANNICA (1763)

[From *Life* of Shakespeare (vi. 1. 3627), signed 'P'. A MS. note in the Bodl. copy has 'said to be written by Bp. ⟨William⟩ Warburton, and another on the t.p. gives 'P' as the mark of Philip Nichols. The ballad was that on Lucy; the other shaft *Merry Wives of W.*]

This ballad was not the only shaft which he let fly against his persecutor, whose anger drove him to the extreme end of ruin, where he was forced to a very low degree of drudgery for a support;—how long the Knight continued inexorable is not known; but it is certain that Shakespeare owed his release at last to the Queen's kindness.

XLII. SAMUEL JOHNSON (1765)

[From *Works* of Shakespeare (1765), i. clii, where it follows a reprint of Rowe's *Life* and copies of the 1599 grant of arms and the will.]

To the foregoing accounts of Shakespear's life, I have only one passage to add, which Mr Pope related, as communicated to him by Mr Rowe.

In the time of *Elizabeth*, coaches being yet uncommon, and hired coaches not at all in use, those who were too proud, too tender, or too idle to walk, went on horseback to any distant business or diversion. Many came on horse-back to the play, and when *Shakespear* fled to *London* from the terrour of a criminal prosecution, his first expedient was to wait at the door of the play-house, and hold the horses of those that had no servants, that they might be ready again after the performance. In this office he became so conspicuous for his care and readiness, that in a short time every man as he alighted called for *Will. Shakespear*, and scarcely any other waiter was trusted with a horse while *Will. Shakespear* could be had. This was the first dawn of better fortune. *Shakespear* finding more horses put into his hand than he could hold, hired boys to wait under his inspection, who when *Will. Shakespear* was summoned, were immediately to present themselves, *I am* Shakespear's *boy*, *Sir*. In time *Shakespear* found higher employment, but as long as the practice of riding to the play-house continued, the waiters that held the horses retained the appellation of Shakespear's *Boys*.

XLIII. THOMAS WARTON (1770, 1790)

[Warton (1728–90) was of Trinity, Professor of Poetry at Oxford, Poet Laureate, and author of a *History of English Poetry* (1774–81), which never reached a systematic account of Shakespeare.]

(*a*) [From *Glossary* to Sir T. Hanmer's *Works* of Shakespeare (ed. 2), vol. vi (1770), s.v. *Wincote*.]

Wilnecote is a village in *Warwickshire*, with which Shakespeare was well acquainted, near *Stratford*. The house kept by our genial hostess still remains, but is at present a mill.

(*b*) [From letter of 31 Mar. 1790, quoted by H.P., ii. 308. Francis Wise's testimony may not (cf. App. F) be altogether beyond suspicion.]

My note about Wilnecote I had from Mr Wise, Radclivian librarian, a most accurate and inquisitive literary antiquary, who, about fifty years ago, made a journey to Stratford and its environs to pick up anecdotes about Shakespeare, many of which he told me; but which I, being then very young, perhaps heard very carelessly and have long forgott;—this I much regrett, for I am sure he told me many curious things about Shakespeare;—he was an old man when I was a boy in this ⟨Trinity, Oxford⟩ college;—the place is Wylmecote, the mill, or Wilnicote, near Stratford, not Tamworth.

XLIV. EDWARD CAPELL (1774, 1780)

[Capell (1713–81) was of Catharine Hall, Cambridge, and inspector of plays under the Lord Chamberlain. The text of his *Works* of Shakespeare was publ. in 1767–8; the first part of the commentary in 1774, but withdrawn, reprinted with a second part in 1779, and republished, with third and fourth parts printed in 1780, in *Notes and Various Readings to Shakespeare*, 3 vols. (1783).]

(*a*) [*Note* on *As You Like It*, ii. 6, from *Notes* (1774), i. i. 60.]

A traditional story was current some years ago about Stratford,—that a very old man of that place,—of weak intellects, but yet related to Shakespeare,—being ask'd by some of his neighbours, what he remember'd about him; answer'd,—that he saw him once brought on the stage upon another man's back; which answer was apply'd by the hearers, to his having seen him perform in this scene the part of Adam: That he should have done so, is made not unlikely by another constant tradition,—that he was no extraordinary actor, and therefore took no parts upon him but such as this: for which he might also be peculiarly fitted by an accidental lameness, which,— as he himself tells us twice in his '*Sonnets*', v. 37, and 89, —befell him in some part of life; without saying how, or when, of what sort, or in what degree; but his expressions seem to indicate—latterly.

(*b*) [*Note* on *Merry Wives of W.* i. 1, from *Notes* (1780), iii. 75.]

One stanza of it ⟨Rowe's 'lost' ballad; cf. p. 265⟩, which has the appearance of genuine, was put into the editor's hands many years ago by an ingenious gentleman (grandson of it's preserver) with this account of the way in which it descended to him.—Mr Thomas Jones, who dwelt at Tarbick ⟨Tardebigge⟩ a village in Worcestershire a few miles from Stratford on Avon, and dy'd in the year 1703. aged upwards of ninety, remember'd to have heard from several old people at Stratford the story of Shakespeare's

robbing sir Thomas Lucy's park; and their account of it
agreed with Mr Rowe's, with this addition—that the
ballad written against sir Thomas by Shakespeare was
stuck upon his park gate, which exasperated the knight
to apply to a lawyer at Warwick to proceed against him:
Mr Jones had put down in writing the first stanza of this
ballad, which was all he remember'd of it, and Mr Thomas
Wilkes (my grandfather) transmitted it to my father by
memory, who also took it in writing, and his copy is this;
—'*A Parliamente member a Justice of Peace,* | *At Home a*
poore Scarecrow at London an Asse. | *If Lowsie is Lucy as*
some Volke Miscalle it | *Then Lucy is Lowsie whatever befalle*
it | *He thinkes himselfe greate* | *Yet an Asse in his State* |
We allowe by his Eares but with Asses to mate | *If Lucy is*
Lowsie as some Volke miscalle it | *Sing [O] Lowsie Lucy*
whatever befalle it'.—an exact transcript, bating the *O*;
to which is added a note, telling us—that the people of
those parts pronounce 'Lowsie like Lucy':— . . . M^r
Jones, of whom we had it originally, was also the hander-
down of that anecdote which has been given you in a note
upon 'a.y.l.i.' at 40. 4; and of this anecdote, Mr Wilkes
(in the letter that brought the stanza) quotes another
confirmer in the person of Mr Oldys, a late stage-anti-
quarian (cf. p. 279).

(*c*) [*Note* on *The Shrew*, Ind. ii. 23, from *Notes* (1780), ii. iv. 26.]

Wincot is in Stratford's vicinity, where the memory of the
ale-house subsists still: and the tradition goes—that 'twas
often resorted to by Shakespeare for the sake of diverting
himself with a fool who belong'd to a neighbouring mill.

XLV. ANON (1777)

[From account of visit in July 1777 added to 8th ed. (1778) ii. 263 of
Defoe's *Tour through the Island of Great Britain* (1724).]

At the side of the chancel is a charnel house almost filled
with human bones, skulls, &c. The guide said, that
Shakespeare was so much affected by this charnel house,
that he wrote the Epitaph (Good friend, &c) for himself,
to prevent his bones being thrown into it.

XLVI. JOHN JORDAN (1770–90)

[Jordan (1746–1809) was a self-educated wheelwright, born at Tiddington near Stratford. He developed a taste for poetry and antiquities, and published verses on *Welcombe Hills* (1777). He supplied information about 1790 to Malone, who received it critically, but helped him financially. About 1794 he was evidently acting as a *laquai de place* at Stratford, and escorted the elder and younger Ireland (cf. nos. li, liii).]

(*a*) [From 'a manuscript written about the year 1770', pr. H.P. ii. 326. It was in H.P.'s possession (*Rarities*, 175) and previously in that of W. H. Ireland (cf. no. iii), who gives the story from it in *Confessions*, 34. Later versions by Jordan, not materially different, are in his *Collections*, 40, and *Memoirs*, 22, and in *Var.* ii. 500. He was also the source of those in *Gent. Mag.* (1794) and S. Ireland (cf. no. li), *Picturesque Views* (1795), 229.]

The following anecdote of Shakspeare is tho a traditional Story as well authenticated as things of this nature generally are. I shall therefore not hesitate relating it as it was Verbally delivered to me. Our Poet was extremely fond of drinking hearty draughts of English Ale, and glory'd in being thought a person of superior eminence in that proffession if I may be alowed the phrase. In his time, but at what period it is not recorded, There were two companys or fraternitys of Village Yeomanry who used frequently to associate to gether at Bidford a town pleasantly situate on the banks of the Avon about 7 Miles below Stratford, and Who boasted themselves Superior in the Science of drinking to any set of equal number in the Kingdom and hearing the fame of our Bard it was determined to Challenge him and his Companions to a tryal of their skill which the Stratfordians accepted and accordingly repaired to Bidford which place agreeable to both parties was to be the Scene of Contendtion. But when Shakespeare and his Companions arrived at the destined spot, to their disagreeable disapointment they found the Topers were gone to Evesham fair and were told that if they had a mind to try their strenght with the Sippers, they were ther ready for the Contest, Shakesp[r]. and his compainions made a Scoff at their Opponents, but for want of better Company they agreed to the Contest and in a little time our Bard and his Compainions got so intollerable intoxicated that they was not able to Contend any longer and accordingly set out on their return to Stratford But had not got above half a mile on the road e'er the⟨y⟩ found themselves unable to proceed any farther, and was obliged to lie down under a Crabtree which is still growing by the side of the road where they took up their repose till morning when some of the Company roused the poet and intreated him to return to Bidford and renew the Contest he declined it saying I have drunk with

> Piping Pebworth, Dancing Marston,
> Haunted Hillborough, Hungry Grafton,
> Dadgeing Exhall, Papist Wicksford,
> Beggarly Broom, and Drunken Bidford.

(b) [From *Original Collections on Shakespeare and Stratford-on-Avon*, by *John Jordan, Selected from the Original Manuscripts, written about the year 1780*, ed. H.P. (1864). One of the MSS. used is dated by H.P. ii. 287 as about 1783. T. Seccombe (*D.N.B.*) says that Jordan completed a work under this name by 1780, but failed to get it published. Besides the passages here extracted it contains a mention of John Sh.'s 'religious Testament' (cf. p. 380), some historical notes on the hamlets of Stratford, the crab-tree story, versions of the Mercutio and horsekeeping stories, derived from Dryden (no. xii) and Johnson (no. xlii) respectively, and an account of Sh.'s ancestry, which probably contains nothing traditional, but merely inferences from the Stratford Registers and from the heraldic grants of arms, as given in the Johnson-Steevens editions of 1765–78. But it provides him with a great-great-grandfather John, a cousin Anthony, and a father-in-law Hathaway.]

[*p. 50.*] The large barns, built with bricks, still standing in the Gild-pits, by the side of the Birmingham road, and which are now possessed by Mr Peyton, have always been thought to have been built by him ⟨Shakespeare⟩. . . .

[*p. 54.*] There is an improbable tale that two chests full of manuscripts and papers, having been thrown about without the least regard to their merit, came at length into the hands of Sir Will. Bishop, in whose possession they were, when they remained until reduced to ashes in one of the conflagrations that happened in Stratford; but as tradition says that they were at one time in the hands of a baker, a descendant of Shakespear, it shews the falseness of that report, as no descendants of his was of that trade; besides, the last fire in Stratford happened in 1614, two years before the poet's death; nor should it be omitted that his daughter, Susanna, who was extremely well informed, survived her father twenty six years.

(*c*) [From *Original Memoirs and Historical Accounts of the Families of Shakespeare and Hart*, ed. H.P. (1865), based on a copy of the original presented by Jordan to Malone and sold on Boswell's death in 1826 to Mr. Merridew, bookseller at Warwick. Another MS., dated 1790, is in the Birmingham Shakespeare Memorial Library (*Cat.* 2510). As in the *Collections*, the account of Sh.'s family seems to rest on mistaken research rather than tradition. The texts of the alleged ballad on Lucy (*d*) and of John Sh.'s 'will' (cf. p. 380) are given, with an account of the discovery of the latter. The MS. seems to have been sent to Malone while his edition of 1790 was in the press, and a number of letters from Malone inquiring about points in it, but without Jordan's replies, are in *Original Letters from Edmund Malone to John Jordan*, ed. H.P. (1864). The passage on the Combe epigrams is printed in H.P. (*1848*) 242.]

[*p. 11.*] Let us return to the father, who it is said was a considerable dealer in wool; for this we have not only the tradition of Stratford, but also the authority of Mr Rowe.

[*p. 19.*] ⟨Sir Thomas Lucy⟩ had at the time also another park at a place called Fullbroke, two miles distant from the other; and there tradition reports it was that Shakspeare and his companions made a practise of following their favourite diversion; which they did so often, that the knight's resentment was raised, and he commenced a prosecution against them, but desisted upon their making an abject submission; but which so hurt the high spirit of our poet that he could not repress his indignation. A satirical song went abroad, which inflamed Sir Thomas to the utmost pitch, and he renewed the prosecution with redoubled vigour. His power was too great for poor Shakspeare to contend with, and he now saw, perhaps with horror, that his youthful levity obliged him to quit his father, his fond wife, his prattling babes, and his native place.

[*p. 32.*] Mr Combe and the bard of Stratford were intimately acquainted. The former one day in a tavern, said to be the sign of the Bear, in the Bridge street in Stratford, said to the other: 'I suppose you will write my epitaph when I am dead; you may as well do it now, that I may know what you will say of me, when I am gone'. Immediately he replied, 'It shall be this, "Ten in the hundred. . . ." '. The company instantly burst into a loud laugh, perhaps from the justness of the idea, and the hatred all men have to the character of a miser and usurer; the violence of the mirth somewhat subsiding, they desired to hear what he had to say of Mr Thomas Combe, brother of the former gentleman, when he instantly said: 'But thin in beard. . . .'. This brother was remarkable for the thinness of his beard, and no doubt also for his covetous disposition; therefore the poignancy of the sarcasm afforded no small diversion amongst the convivial meeting; but it is said the severity of this satire made so deep an impression upon the two brothers that they never forgave the author of their epitaphs.

(*d*) [From *Variorum*, ii. 565. Jordan's account (*Memoirs*, 20) of its discovery 'in a chest of drawers, that formerly belonged to Mrs. Dorothy Tyler, of Shottery, near Stratford' is given in *Var.* ii. 140, with an expression of Malone's belief that 'one part of this ballad is just as genuine as the other; that is, that the whole is a forgery'. There are slight variants in the text as given in the *Memoirs*, but it is clear from the *Letters* that Jordan had sent the alleged original to Malone, who already knew the fragment given by Oldys and Capell (nos. xxxiv, xliv), which he includes in his condemnation. On 25 Mar. 1790 he wrote to Jordan, 'I . . . have not much faith in it. The handwriting is certainly either of this age or of the latter end of the last century; and there has been much study to give it something of an ancient cast; but in vain'. H.P. ii. 382 cites an unprinted letter by Jordan in March 1790 for another version of the discovery amidst some deeds that had been given to a tailor for conversion into measure-strips.]

Complete Copy of the Verses on Sir Thomas Lucy.

A parliement member, a justice of peace,
At home a poore scarecrowe, in London an asse,
If Lucy is Lowsie as some volke misscall it
Synge Lowsie Lucy whatever befall it.

He thinks hymself greate, yet an asse in hys state
We allowe bye his eares but with asses to mate;
If Lucy is Lowsie as some volke misscall it,
Synge Lowsie Lusy whatever befall it.

He 's a haughty proud insolent knighte of the shire
At home nobodye loves, yet there 's many hym feare.
If Lucy is Lowsie as some volke misscall it
Synge Lowsie Lucy whatever befall it.

To the sessions he went and dyd sorely complain
His parke had been rob'd and his deer they were slain.
This Lucy is Lowsie as some volke misscall it
Synge Lowsie Lucy whatever befall it.

He sayd twas a ryot his men had been beat,
His venson was stole and clandestinely eat.
Soe Lucy is Lowsie as some volke miscall it
Synge Lowsie Lucy whatever befall it.

Soe haughty was he when the fact was confess'd
He sayd 'twas a crime that could not bee redress'd,
Soe Lucy is Lowsie as some volke misscall it
Synge Lowsie Lucy whatever befall it.

Though Lucies a dozen he paints in his coat
His name it shall Lowsie for Lucy bee wrote
For Lucy is Lowsie as some volke misscall it
Synge Lowsie Lucy whatever befall it.

If a iuvenile frolick he cannot forgive
We'll synge Lowsie Lucy as long as we live
And Lucy the Lowsie a libel may call it
We'll synge Lowsie Lucy whatever befall it.

XLVII. GEORGE STEEVENS (1780)

[From note in Malone's *Supplement* (1780), ii. 369. West (*c.* 1704–72) was a Secretary to the Treasury (1741–62), and President of the Royal Society (1768–72). He was from Prior's Marston, Warwickshire, and had a house at Alscot in Gloucestershire, three miles from Stratford.]

The late Mr James West, of the Treasury, assured me, that at his house in Warwickshire he had a wooden bench, once the favourite accommodation of Shakespeare, together with an earthen half-pint mug, out of which he was accustomed to take his draughts of ale at a certain publick house in the neighbourhood of Stratford, every Saturday afternoon.

XLVIII. EDMUND MALONE (1780)

[From *Supplement*, i. 67; *1790*, i. 1. 107 (with the added words here bracketed). The statement is not in *Var*.]

There is a stage tradition that his first office in the theatre was that of [*Call-boy*, or] prompter's attendant; whose employment it is to give the performers notice to be ready to enter, as often as the business of the play requires their appearance on the stage.

XLIX. S. COOPER (1788)

[From H.P. ii. 379. But a farm at Ingon could not possibly be contiguous to Charlecote Park (see Plate II).]

The Rev. S. Cooper, of Loxley, writing to Jordan in 1788, mentions a farm 'at Ingon containing now about two hundred acres of land adjoining to the old park, now deparked, from which it is said William Shakespere stole Mr Lucy's deer' . . . the park herein mentioned unquestionably referring to one at Charlecote.

L. JAMES DAVENPORT (1790)

[From Malone (*1790*), i. 1. 118; *Var*. ii. 523. Davenport was vicar of Stratford from 1787 to 1841 (*B.P. Cat.* 236). Malone (*Var*. i. 252) acknowledges his help in the 1790 ed., and letters of inquiry from him between 1788 and 1805 are in H.P. *The Correspondence of E. Malone and J. Davenport* (1864). H.P. i. 412 traced a Taylor family in a house bordering on the New Place garden, but not quite at the point where the destroyed mulberry appears to have stood. There may have been more than one. He gives several notices which show that the planting was ascribed to Shakespeare at the time of the destruction in 1758; this and no. xxxiii alone seem to carry the tradition farther back. Modern speculation has decided that Shakespeare planted his mulberry in 1609 when James I issued *Instructions* to encourage the growth of them and the breeding of silkworms (*Harleian Miscellany*, ii. 218).]

The Rev. Mr Davenport informs me, that Mr Hugh Taylor, (the father of his clerk,) who is now eighty-five years old, and an alderman of Warwick, where he at present resides, says, he lived when a boy at the next house to New-Place; that his family had inhabited the house for almost three hundred years; that it was transmitted from father to son during the last and the present century, that this tree (of the fruit of which he had often eaten in his younger days, some of its branches hanging over his father's garden,) was planted by Shakspeare; and that till this was planted, there was no mulberry-tree in that neighbourhood. Mr Taylor adds, that he was frequently, when a boy, at New-Place, and that this tradition was preserved in the Clopton family, as well as in his own.

LI. SAMUEL IRELAND (1795)

[From *Picturesque Views on the Warwickshire Avon.* Ireland visited Stratford with his son (no. liii) in 1794; they were shown round by Jordan (no. xlvi).]

[*p. 152.*] It was in this ⟨Fulbrook⟩ park our bard is said to have been, in a youthful frolic, engaged in stealing deer, and thereby to have drawn upon himself a prosecution from the then owner, Sir Thomas Lucy. . . . Within this park is now standing, on a spot called Daisy Hill, a farm house, which was antiently the keeper's lodge. To this lodge it is reported our Shakspeare was conveyed, and there confined at the time of the charge, which is supposed to have been brought against him. This supposition, how slight soever the foundation of it may be, I yet thought sufficient to give an interest to the spot in which it is presumed to have passed, and under that idea I have subjoined a sketch of the present building.

[*p. 189.*] He ⟨Thomas Hart⟩ informed me, that, when a boy, he well remembered having, with other boys, dressed themselves as Scaramouches (such was his phrase) in the wearing apparel of our Shakespeare.

[*p. 204.*] Upon the demolition of New Place above mentioned, all the furniture and papers were removed to the antient mansion of the Clopton family, about one mile distant from Stratford. Amongst those papers I have long imagined that it was very possible some manuscripts of our Shakspeare might have been conveyed. Prompted by a faint hope of this sort, as well as by curiosity, I last summer visited this spot, but without the desired success.

LII. THOMAS SHARP (1799)

[From 'a declaration made upon oath shortly before his death in 1799', given in H.P. i. 412. Sharp had been making and selling as relics articles of mulberry wood since the destruction of the New Place tree in 1758.]

I have often heard the said Sir Hugh Clopton solemnly declare that the mulberry-tree which growed in his garden was planted by Shakespear, and he took pride in shewing it to and entertaining persons of distinction whose curiosity excited them to visit the spot known to be the last residence of the immortal bard.

LIII. WILLIAM HENRY IRELAND (1805)

[From *Confessions*. Ireland visited Stratford with his father in 1794 (cf. no. li). He is not a credible witness (cf. App. F), and the story of burnt papers, repeated from his *Authentic Account* (1796), 5, may be compared with his father's sober account. According to R. B. Wheler (Ingleby, ii. 142) it was 'utterly and entirely without foundation of fact'. Unsuccessful attempts to trace the alleged letters at Knole, built by Thomas, Earl of Dorset (ob. 1608), Lord Treasurer, not Lord Chamberlain, are described by Malone in letters of 28 Oct. and 9 Dec. 1802 to Bp. Percy (*Bodl. Mal. MS.* 26, ff. 46, 50) and in R. B. Wheler, *Guide to Stratford* (1814), 155.]

[*p. 30.*] ⟨Mr. Williams, a gentleman-farmer occupying Clopton House said⟩ 'By G——d, I wish you had arrived a little sooner! Why, it isn't a fortnight since I destroyed several baskets-full of letters and papers, in order to clear a small chamber for some young partridges which I wish to bring up alive: and as to Shakespeare, why there were many bundles with his name wrote upon them. Why it was in this very fire-place I made a roaring bonfire of them.'

[*p. 271.*] It has been stated in the public prints, and I conjecture with truth, that two letters from the pen of

Shakespeare were discovered some time since at Knole in Kent, among the papers of the Dorset family, written by our bard to the then lord-chamberlain upon mere official business relative to theatrical matters.

LIV. SIR RICHARD PHILLIPS (1818)

[From *The Monthly Magazine; or British Register*, xlv. 1. Phillips (1767–1840), a publisher and sheriff of London, who edited the periodical, found descendants of Joan Hart in poverty at Tewkesbury, and was led to pay a visit to Stratford. The mother of J. M. Smith was a Hart (cf. French 403). Mary Hornby was caretaker in Henley St. from 1793 to 1820 (*B.P. Cat.* 1). The eastern house became the Swan and Maidenhead.]

At Stratford, the family maintain that Shakspeare stole Sir Thomas Lucy's buck, to celebrate his wedding-day, and for that purpose only. . . .

Mr J. M. Smith said, he had often heard his mother state that Shakspeare owed his rise in life, and his introduction to the theatre, to his accidentally holding the horse of a gentleman at the door of the theatre, on his first arriving in London. His appearance led to enquiry and subsequent patronage. . . .

The landlord of the Swan and Maidenhead . . . assured the writer, that, when he re-laid the floors of the parlour, the remains of wool, and the refuse of wool-combing, were found under the old flooring, imbedded with the earth of the foundation. . . .

Mrs Hornby shows a very small deep cupboard, in a dark corner of the room in which Shakspeare was born; and relates that a letter was found in it some years since, which had been addressed by Shakspeare from the playhouse in London to his wife. She asserts that this letter was in her possession, and that she used to show it to visitors; that one morning, a few years since, she exhibited it to a company, who went from her house to the church; but presently sent a message to beg that she would send the letter for further inspection at the tomb,—a request with which she complied. She saw nothing further, however, of her letter; but the parties, on leaving Stratford, sent her a shilling, and their thanks! Persons in Stratford doubt the truth of this relation; but the woman persists.

LV. SIR JAMES BLAND BURGESS (1818)

[From *Letter* of 26 June 1818 to James Boswell (*Var.* i. xxviii). The portrait was the Hilliard miniature, not generally thought genuine. An account of the Somervilles of Edstone in Wootton Wawen, Warwickshire, is in Stopes, *Cont.* 68. Sir William Somerville (ob. 1616) was brother of John S. who died while in prison for an attempt to murder Elizabeth in 1583 and involved his father-in-law, Edward Arden of Park Hall, in his fate. A lawsuit shows Sir William in relations with several inhabitants of Stratford.]

Mr Somerville of Edstone, near Stratford upon Avon, ancestor of Somerville, author of the Chace, &, lived in habits of intimacy with Shakspeare, particularly after his retirement from the stage, and had this portrait painted, which, as you will perceive, was richly set, and was carefully preserved by his descendants, till it came to the hands of his great grand-son, the poet, who, dying in 1742, without issue, left his estates to my grand-father, Lord Somerville, and gave this miniature to my mother.

LVI. RICHARD RYAN (1825)

[From *Dramatic Table Talk*, ii. 156, anonymous but ascribed (*D.N.B.*) to the editorship of Richard Ryan (1796–1849), a bookseller.]

It is well known that Queen Elizabeth was a great admirer of the immortal Shakspeare, and used frequently (as was the custom of persons of great rank in those days) to appear upon the stage before the audience, or to sit delighted behind the scenes, when the plays of our bard were performed. One evening, when Shakspeare himself was personating the part of a King, the audience knew of her Majesty being in the house. She crossed the stage when he was performing, and, on receiving the accustomed greeting from the audience, moved politely to the poet, but he did not notice it! When behind the scenes, she caught his eye, and moved again, but still he would not throw off his character, to notice her: this made her Majesty think of some means by which she might know, whether he would depart, or not, from the dignity of his character while on the stage.—Accordingly, as he was about to make his exit, she stepped before him, dropped her glove, and re-crossed the stage, which Shakspeare noticing, took up, with these words, immediately after finishing his speech, and so aptly were they delivered, that they seemed to belong to it:

'And though now bent on this high embassy,
    Yet *stoop* we to take up our *Cousin's* glove!'

He then walked off the stage, and presented the glove to the Queen, who was greatly pleased with his behaviour, and complimented him upon the propriety of it.

LVII. SIR WALTER SCOTT (1828)

[From Diary in Lockhart, *Life of Scott* (1838), vii. 123.]

April 8 . . . Charlecote is in high preservation, and inhabited by Mr Lucy, descendant of the worshipful Sir Thomas. . . . He told me the park from which Shakspeare stole the buck was not that which surrounds Charlecote, but belonged to a mansion at some distance, where Sir Thomas Lucy resided at the time of the trespass. The tradition went that they hid the buck in a barn, part of which was standing a few years ago, but now totally decayed. This park no longer belongs to the Lucys.

LVIII. S. W. FULLOM (1862)

[From *History of William Shakespeare*. The 'note' referred to is not printed as a whole, and the writer's actual account of the deer-stealing episode is in a romantic vein. For his inquiries into the Luddington register, cf. App. A, no. v.]

[*p. iii.*] My best thanks are due to Mrs Lucy, of Charlecote Park, for valuable information, which is a key to the whole history of Shakespeare . . . [p. 130] The proof of the ⟨deer-stealing⟩ story is a note in a manuscript pedigree of the Lucys, made about ninety years ago by an old man named Ward, who derived his information from the family papers then in his hands. This version of the incident has been obligingly communicated to us by Mrs Lucy, of Charlecote. . . . [p. 136] We can now remove all doubt as to the founder of this antique pile, being the Justice Shallow of Shakespeare. The fact is mentioned by Ward, in the manuscript pedigree of the family; and it is worthy of remark, that the only one of Shakespeare's plays of an old date, found at Charlecote, is a copy of the octavo edition of 'The Merry Wives of Windsor', published in 1619, which was lately discovered by Mrs Lucy, among the family records . . . [p. 149] The note by Ward in the manuscript pedigree of the Lucys, informs us that his ⟨Sh.'s⟩ friends interested in his behalf the most important man in Warwickshire, no less a person than Robert, Earl of Leicester; and this great magnate now interceded with Sir Thomas Lucy, and prevailed on him to abandon the prosecution. . . . [p. 152] The note by Ward agrees with Rowe as to the course he ⟨Sh.⟩ pursued. The ballad was nailed on the park-gates at Charlecote . . . [p. 196] The Lucy note reports that the satiric ballad obliged him to quit Stratford —'at least for a time'. . . . [p. 232] The note in the Lucy pedigree affirms that he ⟨Leicester⟩ required Sir Thomas Lucy to adopt his badge of the bear and ragged staff, which he wished to see worn by the servants of all the gentry of Warwickshire, and the Charlecote Knight refused to comply, at the same time calling him an upstart. But it is dangerous to hurl opprobrious names at the friend of a poet. Leicester remembered Justice Shallow, and according to the Lucy note, he now applied to Shakespeare to take up his quarrel, by bringing Sir Thomas Lucy again on the stage.

APPENDIX D

PERFORMANCES OF PLAYS

[*Bibliographical Note*. I give here records of (i) performances from September 1588 to May 1594 by (*a*) Strange's, Derby's or the Alleyn company, (*b*) the Admiral's or the Alleyn company, (*c*) Pembroke's, (*d*) Sussex's (from 1590–1 only), (*e*) Hunsdon's, (*f*) Leicester's, but not, unless in conjunction with other companies, the Queen's (cf. vol. i, p. 33) or Morley's; (ii) performances by the Chamberlain's and King's from June 1594 to 1616; (iii) performances of Shakespeare's plays from 1616 to the closing of the theatres in 1642. The entries for the Rose and Newington Butts are from W. W. Greg, *Henslowe's Diary* (1904–8) and I have adopted Dr. Greg's corrections (ii. 324) of Henslowe's dating. The entries of court payments are from *Eliz. Stage*, iv. 142. I have been able to correct and expand the provincial notices in ch. xiii of that work from new material. For Bath (up to 1603) I now use F. D. Wardle, *The Accounts of the Chamberlains of Bath* (1923, Somerset Record Soc. xxxviii), and for Maidstone, K. S. Martin, *Records of Maidstone* (1926). I have notices for three new places, for Bewdley from J. R. Burton, *History of Bewdley* (1883), for King's Lynn from Lee (1921, May 5, *T.L.S.*), and for Sudbury from E. Stokes and L. Redstone, *Calendar of the Muniments of the Borough of Sudbury* (1909, *Proc. of Suffolk Institute of Archaeology*, xiii. 259). The unreliable character of the Ipswich dates, as given by Murray, ii. 287, from *Hist. MSS.* ix. 1. 248, was noted in *Eliz. Stage*, ii. 2, 106, 209, but there is no disorder, as there suggested, in the records, and Mr. V. B. Redstone has been good enough to send me a complete set of corrected extracts, with many new entries, which will be printed in the Malone Society's *Collections*. Professor E. A. Sonnenschein has also kindly consulted the Bath archives on my behalf, Miss M. Dormer Harris those of Coventry, the Hon. Henry Hannen those of Maidstone, Mr. A. M. Oliver those of Newcastle, the Rev. W. G. D. Fletcher those of Shrewsbury, Dr. J. W. Horrocks those of Southampton, and Miss M. Sellers those of York. Subject to some valuable additions and corrections thus obtained, my other main sources are—for Barnstaple, Bristol, Canterbury, Coventry, Dover, Folkestone, Gloucester, Ludlow, Marlborough, Norwich, Shrewsbury, Southampton, Winchester, and York, J. T. Murray, *English Dramatic Companies* (1910); for Aldeburgh, A. T. Winn, *Extracts from the Aldeburgh Records* (1920, *12 N.Q.* vii. 504), and Stopes, *William Hunnis*, 314; for Cambridge, C. H. Cooper, *Annals of Cambridge*, ii (1843), 476, 518, 538; for Dunwich, *Various Collections* (*Hist. MSS.*), vii. 82; for Faversham, J. M. Cowper, *Notes from the Records of Faversham* (1871, *1 Royal Hist. Soc. Trans.* i. 218); for Leicester, W. Kelly, *Notices Illustrative of the Drama* (1865), and M. Bateson, *Records of the Borough of Leicester*, iii (1905); for Maldon, A. Clark, *Maldon Records and the Drama* (1907, *10 N.Q.* vii. 181, 342, 422; viii. 43); for Newcastle, G. B. Richardson, *Reprints of Rare Tracts*, iii (1848), and R. Welford,

Players and Minstrels at Newcastle upon Tyne (1909, *10 N.Q.* xii. 222); for Nottingham, W. H. Stevenson, *Records of the Borough of Nottingham*, iv (1889); for Oxford, F. S. Boas, *Shakespeare and the Universities* (1923), 14, and H. E. Salter, *Oxford Council Acts* (1928, *O.H.S.*); for Saffron Walden, A. Clark, *Extracts from Saffron Walden Accounts* (1909, *10 N.Q.* xii. 41); for Stafford, T. Pape, *Shakespeare in Staffordshire* (1919, *Trans. North Staffs. Field Club*, liii. 47); for Hythe, New Romney, and Rye, Halliwell-Phillipps, *The Visits of Shakespeare's Company of Actors to the Provincial Cities* (1887). Murray reproduces lists from many of the sources I have used, and H.P. independently collected entries in the book named, in *Notices of Players Acting at Ludlow* (1867), and for Pembroke's in *A Budget of Notes and Memoranda* (1880). The ultimate sources are in all cases civic accounts, which were ordinarily kept by Chamberlains or similar financial officers. In most places the financial year ended on Michaelmas Day; at Coventry and, I think, Maidstone on All Saints' (Nov. 1); at Sudbury about St. Denys's (Oct. 9); at Stafford on St. Luke's (Oct. 18); at Ludlow on SS. Simon and Jude's (Oct. 28); at Bath, I think, about Pentecost up to 1592, and thereafter on Midsummer Day; at Maldon on Epiphany (Jan. 6); at York, I think, on St. Blaize's (Feb. 3). As to Faversham, Folkestone, Hythe, and New Romney I do not know, but treat them as Michaelmas accounts. Accounts were audited some little time after these terms, but it may be assumed that cash payments, such as rewards, were regularly debited to the year in which they were made. The provincial records of plays are, of course, meagre, but their incidence helps to establish the careers of companies, and even to suggest the outlines of their provincial tours. Where there are no precise dates, some recorders, such as Kelly, have attempted to assign approximate ones on the evidence of neighbouring entries. The validity of this depends on whether the accounts follow the chronological order of payments. It is not always so. Some accountants seem to transcribe day-books; others to work from loose vouchers. And rewards are often picked out and put under a separate heading.]

I. PERFORMANCES OF 1588 TO 1594

1588. Provinces.

[Ipswich]. The 14th September to the Earle of Lesiter his plaiers j^{li}.

[This is the latest of many records for this company in 1587–8.]

1588–9. Provinces.

[Maidstone]. P^d to my Lord Chamberlen's ⟨Hunsdon's⟩ playeres 1. 0. 0.

[This seems to be from an intermediate account ending 20 Jan. 1589.]

1588-9. Court.

Dec. 29 〈Richmond〉; Feb. 11 〈Whitehall〉. the Lorde Admyrall his players . . . for twoe Enterludes or playes . . . and for showinge other feates of activity and tumblinge.

[The P.C. Acts give February 9 for the second performance.]

1588-9. Provinces.

[Cambridge]. Item, given to the Lord Admiral's players x[s].

1589. London.

[Nov. 5. Letter of Lord Mayor Harte to Lord Burghley (*Eliz. Stage*, iv. 305).]

My very honourable good L. Where by a lettre of your Lps. directed to m[r] Yonge it appered vnto me, that it was your honours pleasure I sholde geue order for the staie of all playes within the Cittie, in that m[r] Tilney did vtterly mislike the same. According to which your Lps. good pleasure, I presentlye sente for suche players as I coulde here of, so as there appered yesterday before me the L. Admeralles and the L. Straunges players, to whome I speciallie gaue in Charge and required them in her Maiesties name to forbere playinge, vntill further order mighte be geuen for theire allowance in that respecte: Whereupon the L. Admeralles players very dutifullie obeyed, but the others in very Contemptuous manner departing from me, went to the Crosse keys and played that afternoon, to the greate offence of the better sorte that knewe they were prohibited by order from your L. Which as I might not suffer, so I sent for the said Contemptuous persons, who haueing no reason to alleadge for theire Contempt, I coulde do no lesse but this evening Comitt some of them to one of the Compters, and do meane according to your Lps. direction to prohibite all playing, vntill your Lps. pleasure therein be further knowen. And thus resting further to trouble your L., I moste humblie take my leaue. At London the Sixte of Nouember 1589.

1589–90. Court.

Dec. 28 ⟨Richmond⟩. the Servauntes of the Lorde Admirall . . . for shewinge certen feates of activitie.

Mar. 3 ⟨Greenwich⟩. the servauntes of the Lord Admirall . . . for playinge.

1589–90. Provinces.

[Faversham]. Given to my Lord of Leicester's Players 13. 4.

[I suspect an error here. Leicester died on 4 Sept. 1588. The accounts were in bad condition when Cowper saw them.]

[Ipswich]. To my Lord Admeralles players j^{li}.
To my Lord Admerales players the second tyme x^s.

[Maidstone. (Nov. 1 year)]. P^d to my lord Admirals men x^s.

[Winchester]. in reward given to the players of the Lord Admiral of England by order of the mayor this year x^s.

[Marlborough]. Given to the Lord Admirals players at St James tide ⟨July 25⟩ 7^s 4^d.

[Gloucester]. geven to the lorde Admiralls players the xviith of September xx^s.

[Coventry. (Nov. 1 year)]. given to the Lo. Admirals players xx^s.

[Oxford]. to my Lord Admyralls men vi^s viii^d.

1590–1. Court.

Dec. 27 ⟨Richmond⟩; Feb. 16 ⟨Greenwich⟩. George Ottewell and his companye the Lorde Straunge his players for ⟨plays⟩ . . . and for other feates of Activitye then also done by them.

[The P.C. Acts (Dasent, xx. 328) record warrants for these dates to the Admiral's and name no payee.]

1590–1. Provinces.

[Southampton]. pd. on Shrove Sunday ⟨Feb. 14⟩ to the Queenes maiesties & the Earle of Sussex players xxx^s.
p^d to my L. Admiralls players j^{li}.

[Dr. Horrocks puts this *c.* September 1591.]

[Winchester]. given in reward to the players of the Lord
   High Admiral of England by order of the mayor
   this year xxˢ.
[Bath]. paid to my Lord Admiralls players xviˢ iiiᵈ.
   paid to my L. Stranges plaiers xviiˢ.

[An entry of September 6 is between the two payments. The
Pentecost account runs from 24 May 1591 to 14 May 1592, but
as Strange's were at the Rose from February to June 1592, it is
best to treat the payments as belonging to 1591.]

[Gloucester]. to the lord Admiralls players xxxˢ.
   To the Queenes and the Earle of Sussex players xxxˢ.
[Oxford]. geven to the lord Admyralls players xˢ.
[Coventry]. geven to the Quenes players & the Erle of
   Sussex players 24 of Marche xvˢ.
[Faversham]. Given to the Queen's Players and to the
   Earl of Essex's Players 1. 0. 0.

[Possibly Essex's may be a slip for Sussex's. There are other records
about this time for Essex's; they are in fact also separately entered
at Faversham in this year. Sussex's were alone at Norwich on
5 June 1591 and at Leicester on August 11.]

1591–2. Court ⟨Whitehall⟩.

Dec. 27, 28; Jan. 1, 9; Feb. 6, 8. yᵉ seruantes of yᵉ lo:
   Straunge . . . for six severall playes.
Jan. 2. yᵉ servauntes of yᵉ Earle of Sussex.

1592. London.
[From Henslowe, i. 13. The plays were probably at the Rose.]

In the name of god Amen 1591 beg⟨in⟩inge the 19 of
Febreary my lord Stranges mene a⟨s⟩ ffoloweth 1591.

Feb.	19.	Fryer Bacune	xviiˢ iijᵈ.
	20 ⟨21⟩.	Mulomurco	xxixˢ.
	21 ⟨22⟩.	Orlando	xvjˢ vjᵈ.
	23.	Spanes comodye	
		Donne Oracoe	xiijˢ vjᵈ.
	24.	Syr John Mandevell	xijˢ vjᵈ.
	25.	Harey of Cornwell	xxxijˢ.

Feb.	26.		the Jewe of Malltuse	l^{s}.
	28.		Clorys & Orgasto	xviij^{s}.
	29.		Mulamulluco	xxxiiij^{s}.
Mar.	1.		Poope Jone	xv^{s}.
	2.		Matchavell	xiiij^{s}.
	3.	ne	Harey the vj	iij^{li} xvj^{s} 8^{d}.
	4.		Bendo & Richardo	xvj^{s}.
	6.		iiij playes in one	xxxj^{s} vj^{d}.
	7.		Hary vj	iij^{li}.
	8.		the Lookinglasse	vij^{s}.
	9.		Senobia	xxij^{s} vj^{d}.
	10.		the Jewe of Malta	lvj^{s}.
	11.		Hary the vj	xxxxvij^{s} vj^{d}.
	13.		the comodey of Doneoracio	xxviij^{s}.
	14.		Jeronymo	iij^{li} xj^{s}.
	16.		Harey	xxxj^{s} vj^{d}.
	17.		Mulo Mullocco	xxviij^{s} vj^{d}.
	18.		the Jewe of Malta	xxxix^{s}.
	20.		Joronymo	xxxviij^{s}.
	21.		Constantine	xij^{s}.
	22.		Jerusallem	xviij^{s}.
	23.		Harey of Cornwell	xiij^{s} vj^{d}.
	25.		Fryer Bacon	xv^{s} vj^{d}.
	27.		the Lockinglass	lv^{s}.
	28.		Harey the vj	iij^{li} viij^{s}.
	29.		Mulomulucko	iij^{li} ij^{s}.
	30.		Doneoracio	xxxix^{s}.
	31.		Jeronymo	iij^{li}.
Apr.	1.		Mandefell	xxx^{s}.
	3.		Matchevell	xxij^{s}.
	4.		the Jewe of Malta	xxxxiij^{s}.
	5.		Harey the vj	xxxxj^{s}.
	6.		Brandymer	xxij^{s}.
	7.		Jeronymo	xxvj^{s}.
	8.		Mulo Muloco	xxiij^{s}.
	10.		the comodey of Jeronymo	xxviij^{s}.
	11.	ne	Tittus & Vespacia	iij^{li} iiij^{s}.

Apr.	12.	Byndo & Richardo	xxiij^s.
	13.	Harey the vj	xxvj^s.
	14.	Jeronymo	xxxiij^s.
	15.	Mandevell	xxvj^s.
	17.	Mullo Mulluco	xxx^s.
	18.	the Jewe of Mallta	xxxxviij^s vj^d.
	19.	the Lockingglasse	xxiiij^s.
	20.	Tittus & Vespacia	lvj^s.
	21.	Harey the vj	xxxiij^s.
	22.	the comodey Jero-nymo	xvij^s.
	24.	Jeronymo	xxviij^s.
	25.	Jerusalem	xxxxvj^s.
	26.	Fryer Bacon	xxiiij^s.
	27.	Mvlo Mvloco	xxvj^s.
	28. ne	the second parte of Tamber came	iij^{li} iiij^s.
	29.	Harey of Cornwell	xxvj^s.
	30 ⟨May 1⟩.	Mulo Mulluco	lviij^s.
May	2.	Jeronymo	xxxiiij^s.
	3.	Titus & Vespacia	lvij^s vj^d.
	4.	Harey the vj	lvj^s.
	5.	the Jewe of Mallta	xxxxj^s.
	6.	Fryer Bacon	xiiij^s.
	8.	Brandimer	xxiiij^s.
	7 ⟨9⟩.	Harey the vj	xxij^s.
	8 ⟨10⟩.	Tittus & Vespacia	xxx^s.
	9 ⟨11⟩.	Jeronymo	xxvj^s.
	10 ⟨12⟩.	the 2 parte of Tam-bercam	xxxvij^s.
	11 ⟨13⟩.	the Jewe of Mallta	xxxiiij^s.
	13 ⟨15⟩.	Jeronymo	iij^l 4^s.
	14 ⟨16⟩.	Harey the 6	l^s.
	15 ⟨17⟩.	Tittus & Vespacia	iij^{li}.
	16 ⟨18⟩.	Mandevell	xxxx^s.
	17 ⟨19⟩.	Mullomuloco	xxxvj^s vj^d.
	18 ⟨20⟩.	Harey of Cornwell	xxvj^s.
	19 ⟨22⟩.	Harey the vj	xxx^s.
	20 ⟨23⟩.	the Jewe of Mallta	liiij^s.

May 21 ⟨24⟩.		the comodey of Jero-nymo	xxviijˢ.
22 ⟨25⟩.		Jeronymo	xxvijˢ.
23 ⟨26⟩.	ne	the Taner of Den-marke	iijˡⁱ xiijˢ vjᵈ.
24 ⟨27⟩.		Titus & Vespacia	xxxˢ.
25 ⟨29⟩.		Harey the vj	xxiiijˢ.
26 ⟨30⟩.		Tambercame	xxxvjˢ vjᵈ.
27 ⟨31⟩.		Jeronymo	xxiijˢ.
29 ⟨June 1⟩.		Matchevell	xxvjˢ.
30 ⟨June 2⟩.		the Jewe of Malta	xxxiijˢ.
31 ⟨June 3⟩.		Mulemuloco	xxiiijˢ.
June 5.		Bendo & Richardo	xxxijˢ.
6.		Tittus & Vespacia	xxxxijˢ.
7.		the Lockinglasse	xxixˢ.
8.		Tambercame	xxxxˢ.
9.		Jeronymo	xxviiijˢ.
10.	ne	A Knacke to Knowe a Knave	iijˡⁱ xijˢ.
12.		Harey the vj	xxxijˢ.
13.		Mulemuloco	xxˢ.
14.		the Jewe of Malta	xxxviijˢ.
15.		the Knacke to Knowe a Knave	lijˢ.
16.		Mandevell	xxˢ.
18 ⟨19⟩.		Jeronymo	xxiiijˢ.
19 ⟨20⟩.		Harey the vj	xxxjˢ.
20 ⟨21⟩.		the comodey of Jero-nymo	xvˢ.
21 ⟨22⟩.		Tambercame	xxxijˢ.
22 ⟨23⟩.		the Knacke to Knowe a Knave	xxvijˢ.

1591–2. Provinces.

[Canterbury]. Item payd the xiii day of July to the L Straunge his players when they played in the courte halle before Mʳ Lawes maior & other his brethren xxxˢ.

[Aldeburgh]. To my Lorde Admyralls plaiers xˢ.

[It is not quite clear from the extracts by Winn and Stopes whether his visit belongs to 1591–2 or 1592–3.]

[Ipswich]. Payde unto the players of ye Erle of Warwiches as by warrant ye 30 of March xiij^s iiij^d.

[But Warwick had died on 20 Feb. 1590.]

Payd unto therll of Darbys playe⟨r⟩s and to the Lorde admirals players the 7 of August 1592 xx^s.

[Jeaffreson inserts 'the ii amongste' before the amount. It is probably a misreading of 'the 7 of August'. He dates the entry 'March 7', when Strange's were at the Rose. Probably Strange's are meant by 'therll of Darbys' here (cf. vol. i, p. 45). Murray gives a 'Darbyes' company at Shrewsbury in 1591–2, but Mr. W. G. D. Fletcher tells me that the name is plainly Darsyes (Darcy's).]

[Cambridge]. Item, to my Lord Stranges Plaiers 20^s.

[Oxford]. geven to the Lorde Stranges players the vjth of October ⟨1592⟩ vi^s viii^d.

[This is the Michaelmas account for 1592–3 and follows a payment for 25 Feb. 1593. Boas thinks it a payment for 6 Oct. 1593, but I agree with Salter, *O.C.A.* 371, in rejecting this (cf. p. 304).]

[Coventry. (Nov. 1 year)]. given to the Lord Strange players xx^s.

[Gloucester]. Gaue the Lo: Straunge his players x^s.

[Leicester]. Item the 19 of December ⟨1592⟩ geven to the Lord Admiralls Playars more than was gathered viii^s.

1592–3. Court ⟨Hampton Court⟩.

Dec. 26; Jan. 6. the servantes of the Erle of Pembroke.
Dec. 27, 31; Jan. 1. the Servantes of the Lorde Strange.

[The P.C. Acts give December 27, not 26, for Pembroke's.]

1592–3. London.

[From Henslowe, i. 15. The plays were probably at the Rose, and no doubt by the Alleyn company, as a comparison of the titles with those of Henslowe's former list shows.]

In the Name of god Amen 1593 begin⟨i⟩nge the 29 of Desember.

Dec. 29.	Mulomulloco	iij^{li} x^s.
30.	Joronymo	iij^{li} viij^s.
31 ⟨Jan. 1⟩.	the Cnacke	xxx^s.

Jan.	1 ⟨2⟩.		the Jewe	lvjˢ.
	3.		the Cnacke	xxixˢ.
	4.		Mandevell	xijˢ.
	5.	ne	the Gelyous comodey	xxxxiiijˢ.
	6.		Titus	lijˢ.
	8.		Jeronymo	xxijˢ.
	9.		Mulo Mulocko	xxˢ.
	10.		Frier Bacon	xxiiijˢ.
	12 ⟨11⟩.		the comodey of Cosmo	xxxxvijˢ.
	13 ⟨12⟩.		Mandevell	ixˢ.
	14 ⟨13⟩.		the Cnacke	xxiiijˢ.
	15.		Tittus	xxxˢ.
	16.		Harey the 6	xxxxvjˢ.
	17.		Frer Bacon	xxˢ.
	18.		the Jew	iijˡⁱ.
	19.		Tambercam	xxxvjˢ.
	20.		Mulomulco	xxˢ.
	22.		Jeronymo	xxˢ.
	23.		Cossmo	xxxˢ.
	24.		the Knacke	xxxiiijˢ.
	25.		Titus	xxxˢ.
	30 ⟨26⟩.	ne	the tragedey of the Guyes	iijˡⁱ xiiijˢ.
	31 ⟨27⟩.		Mandevell	xiijˢ.
	30 ⟨29?⟩.		Frier Bacon	xijˢ.
	31 ⟨30?⟩.		Harey the vj	xxvjˢ.
Feb.	1 ⟨Jan. 31?⟩.		the Jewe of Malta	xxxvˢ.

1592–3. Provinces.

[The sparsely dated records must be read in the light of the Privy Council warrants (Dasent, xxiv, 209, 212; *Eliz. Stage*, ii. 94, 123) of assistance for (*a*) Sussex's men on 29 Apr. 1593 and (*b*) the Alleyn company on 6 May 1593 and of letters (Greg, *Henslowe Papers*, 34), (*c*) from Alleyn to his wife on 2 May 1593, (*d*) from Henslowe to Alleyn on 5 July, (*e*) from Alleyn to his wife on 1 Aug. ⟨1593⟩, (*f*) from Henslowe to Alleyn on 14 Aug. 1593, (*g*) from Henslowe to Alleyn on 28 Sept. 1593.]

(*a*) An open warrant for the plaiers, servantes to the Erle of Sussex, authorysinge them to excercyse theire qualitie of playinge comedies and tragedies in any county, cittie, towne or corporacion not being within vij^{en} miles of London, where the infection is not, and in places convenient and tymes fitt.

(b) Whereas it was thought meet that during the time of the infection and continewaunce of the sicknes in the citie of London there shold no plaies or enterludes be usd, for th' avoiding of th' assemblies and concourse of people in anie usual place apointed nere the said cittie, and though the bearers hereof, Edward Allen, servaunt to the right honorable the Lord Highe Admiral, William Kemp, Thomas Pope, John Heminges, Augustine Phillipes and Georg Brian, being al one companie, servauntes to our verie good Lord the Lord Strainge, ar restrained their exercize of playing within the said citie and liberties thereof, yet it is not therby ment but that they shal and maie in regard of the service by them don and to be don at the Court exercize their quallitie of playing comodies, tragedies and such like in anie other cities, townes and corporacions where the infection is not, so it be not within seaven miles of London or of the Coort, that they maie be in the better readines hereafter for her Majesty's service whensoever they shalbe therunto called. Theis therfore shalbe to wil and require you that they maie without their lett or contradiccion use their said exercize at their most convenient times and places (the accustomed times of Devine praiers excepted).

(c) I thank god we ar all well & in helth which I pray god to contine⟨w⟩ with us in the contry and with you in London . . . from Chellmsford the 2 of May 1593.

(d) I pray you lyck wise doe my comendations vnto all the reste of your fealowes & I praye god to seand you all that good health that we haue as yet at London which I hoope in god yt will contenew, frome London the 5 of July 1593.

(e) I reseved your letter att Bristo by Richard Couley. . . . I haue sent you by this berer Thomas Popes kinsman my whit wascote . . . If you send any mor letters send to me by the cariers of Shrowsbery or to West Chester or to

York to be keptt till my Lord Stranges players com . . .
from Bristo this Wensday ⟨Aug. 1⟩ after saint Jams his
day being redy to begin the playe of Hary of Cornwall . . .
we shall not com home till Allholland tyd.

(*f*) We hard that you weare very sycke at Bathe & that
one of youre felowes weare fayne to playe youre parte for
you . . . I praye ye sonne comend me harteley to all the
reast of youre fealowes in generall for I growe poore for
lacke of them . . . from London the 14 of Aguste 1593.

(*g*) As for my lord a Penbrockes which you desier to knowe
wheare they be, they ar all at home and hausse ben t⟨his⟩
v or sixe weackes, for they cane not saue ther carges ⟨wi⟩th
trauell as I heare & were fayne to pane the⟨r⟩ parell for
ther carge . . . from London the 28 of September 1593.

[Maidstone. (Nov. 1 year)]. Item to my Lord Strange's
  players xx^s.

[Rye]. To the Earle of Pembrockes plaiers in rewarde
  xiij^s iiij^d.

[H.P. *Budget*, 25, put this in July 1593.]

[Southampton]. 'Accordingly an order (6 May 1593)
  informed the town that a famous company just
  arrived would play at convenient times, hours of
  divine service excepted.'

[This is from J. S. Davies, *History of Southampton* (1883), 217,
citing a *Liber Notationum*, not now known. Dr. Horrocks tells me
that the pages for 1592–3 have been cut out of the *Liber de Finibus*,
which is the only financial record likely to contain a payment for
the year. The date named is of course that of the Privy Council
warrant for the Alleyn company, to which Davies refers immediately before.]

[Bath]. paid to my Lord Penbrookes plaiers xvj^s.
  paid to my Lord Stranges plaiers xvj^s iij^d.
  receaved of my lord of Penbrokes plaiers for a bowe
  that was broken by them ij^s.

[From account for 15 May 1592 to Midsummer 1593.]

  paide and given unto the Lorde Admiralles and the
  Lord Norris players xj^s.

paid and given more to the same players vij^s ix^d.

[From account for Midsummer 1593 to Midsummer 1594. 'Norris' is clear in the manuscript, which Professor Sonnenschein checked for me, but no other record of such a company is known, and a scribal error for 'Morleys' is possible.]

[Ludlow. (Oct. 28 year)]. Item to my Lord Presidentes ⟨Pembroke's⟩ players a quarte of whit wine & suger in the new howse xii^d.

Item, to them for theyre play xx^s.

[Bewdley. 1593]. P^d to my Lord President ⟨Pembroke⟩ his players xx^s.

[Shrewsbury]. Item p^d and geven to my L. Admeralls players x^s.

Item to my lorde prysydents ⟨Pembroke's⟩ players cominge to this towne xl^s.

It^m p^d and geven to my l. Stranges and my l. Admyralls players xl^s.

[The above are from the bundle of accounts for 1592–3.]

The iii of feb: 1592. Bestowed vppo⟨n⟩ the players of my Lorde Admyrall x^s.

[Murray puts this last item under 1591–2. Mr. Fletcher did not find it in the bundle for that year, and the total expenditure on rewards for the year does not leave room for it. It must belong, as it should from its date, to the bundle for 1592–3, and the total for that year suggests that it is a duplicate of the first item.]

[Coventry. (Nov. 1 year)]. Item given to the Lo. Admiralls players xiii^s iiii^d.

And to the Erle of Pembroke players xxx^s.

given to the Lo: of Darbyes players the 2 of December 93 xx^s.

[Sudbury. (Oct. 9 year)]. Gave to the Lord Stranges players 3^s 6^d.

To the Earle of Sussex players 2^s 6^d.

[Ipswich]. To the Earle of Penbrokes players xiij^s viij^d.

Paid to John Fisher one of the sergents for the Lord Admyrals & the Lord Staffords Joyntly together xx^s.

Paide to the Servants of the Right Honnorable the Earle of Sussex being players for ther Rewarde xiij^s iiij^d.

[Norwich]. Paid in Reward geven to the Lorde admiralles players by m^r Mayours comandement xx^s.

[Leicester]. Item geven to the Earle of Pembrucke his playars more than was gaythered xiiij^s.

Item geven to the Erle of Darbyes playors who did playe v^s.

[The first item is from the 1592–3, the second from the 1593–4 account. Kelly puts them respectively in October–December 1592 and October–December 1593.]

[York. 1593–4 (Feb. 3 year)]. Item geven to my L Admirall & my L Morden players in Aprill 1593 xl^s.

Item geven to my L Pembroks players in June xl^s.

Item in Reward to my L of Sussex players in August 1593 xl^s.

[Miss Sellers tells me that 'Morden' is quite clear; it is written over a cancelled word which looks like 'burell'. Lord Borough's men were at York in October 1594. Lord Mordaunt's men were at Coventry in 1585–6 and at Syston in 1602. In view of the Newcastle entry, I suspect that 'Morden' is here an error for 'Morley'.]

[Newcastle]. Maie 1593 The 1 Weike . . . geuen in reward to my l: admiralles plaiers and my l.— Morleis plaiers beinge all in one companye xxx^s.

September 1593 The 1 Weike . . . Paide & geuen in reward to the erle of Sussessx: plaiers xl^s.

September 1593 The 2 Weike . . . Paide to the erle of Sussessx plaiers in full paymente of iij^li for playing a free play com by Mr Maiore xx^s.

[Winchester. 1593–4]. Dec. 7. The same day and year it is agreed that 10^s shall be given by the Chamberlain of the City to the players of the R^t Honorable the Earl of Sussex.

1593–4. London.

[From Henslowe, i. 16. The plays were probably at the Rose.]

In the name of god Amen beg⟨i⟩ninge the 27 ⟨26⟩ of Desember 1593 the earle of Susex his men.

⟨Dec. 26⟩.   Good Spede the Plowghe   iij^{li} j^s.
    28 ⟨27⟩.   Hewen of Burdoche   iij^{li} x^s.
    29 ⟨28⟩.   Gorge a Gren   iij^{li} x^s.
    30 ⟨29⟩.   Buckingam   lj^s.
    31.   Richard the Confeser   xxxviij^s.
Jan. 1.   Buckingam   lviij^s.
    2.   Gorge a Grene   xviij^s.
    3.   Hewen of Burdockes   xiiij^s.
    4.   William the Conkerer   xxij^s.
    5.   God Spead the Plowe   xj^s.
    7.   Frier Frances   iij^{li} j^s.
    8.   the Piner of Wiackefelld   xxiij^s.
    9.   Abram & Lotte   lij^s.
    10.   Buckingam   xxij^s.
    11.   Hewen   v^s.
    12.   the Fayer Mayd of Ytale   ix^s.
    14.   Frier Frances   xxxvj^s.
    15.   Gorge a Grene   xx^s.
    16.   Richard the Confeser   xj^s.
    17.   Abram & Lotte   xxx^s.
    18.   Kinge Lude   xxij^s.
    20 ⟨21⟩.   Frier Frances   xxx^s.
    21 ⟨22⟩.   the Fayer Mayd of Ytaly   xxij^s.
    22 ⟨23⟩.   Gorge a Grene   xxv^s.
    23 ⟨24⟩.   ne   Titus & Ondronicous   iij^{li} viij^s.
    27.   Buckengam   xviij^s.
    28.   Titus & Ondronicous   xxxx^s.
    31.   Abrame & Lotte   xij^s.
Feb. 4.   the Jewe of Malta   l^s.
    6.   Tittus & Ondronicus   xxxx^s.

1594. London.

[From Henslowe, i. 17. The plays were probably at the Rose.]

In the name of God Amen begininge at Easter 1593 the
Quenes men & my lord of Susexe to geather.

Apr. 1.   Frier Bacone   xxxxiij^s.
    2.   the Rangers comodey   iij^{li}.
    3.   the Jewe of Malta   iij^{li}.

Apr.	4.	the Fayer Mayd of Italey	xxiij^s.
	5.	Frier Bacon	xx^s.
	6.	Kinge Leare	xxxviij^s.
	7 ⟨8⟩.	the Jewe of Malta	xxvj^s.
	8 ⟨9⟩.	Kinge Leare	xxvj^s.

1594. Provinces.

[King's Lynn]. Lord Derby's.

[They had 20*s.*, but were not allowed to play. If the payment was late in the year, the company might be William Earl of Derby's.]

[Ipswich]. To the Earle of Darbies players the 8th of Maye xx^s.

[Southampton]. geven to my L. Morleys players and the Earle of Darbyes j^{li}.

[Dr. Horrocks tells me that the dating of the account in 1592–3 by Murray, ii. 398, is an error for 1593–4. The entry comes between others for May 15 and 19. There are many records of separate performances of Morley's in 1591–5 besides those in conjunction with the Admiral's and Derby's here given.]

[Winchester]. May 16. The same day and year it is agreed that there shall be given in reward by the Chamberlain of the City unto the players of the Countess of Derby vi^s viii^d.

[Lord Derby died on 16 Apr. 1594.]

1594. London.

[From Henslowe, i. 17.]

In the name of god Amen begininge the 14 of Maye 1594 by my lord Admeralls men.

May	14.	the Jewe of Malta	xxxxviij^s.
	15.	the Rangers comodey	xxxiij^s.
	16.	Cutlacke	xxxxij^s.

II. PERFORMANCES OF 1594 TO 1616

1594. London.

[From Henslowe, i. 17.]

In the name of god Amen begininge at Newington my Lord Admeralle men & my Lorde Chamberlen men As ffolowethe 1594.

June 3 ⟨5?⟩.		Heaster & Asheweros	viij^s.
4 ⟨6?⟩.		the Jewe of Malta	x^s.
5 ⟨7?⟩.		Andronicous	xij^s.
6 ⟨8?⟩.		Cutlacke	xj^s.
8 ⟨10⟩.	ne	Bellendon	xvij^s.
9 ⟨11⟩.		Hamlet	viij^s.
10 ⟨12⟩.		Heaster	v^s.
11 ⟨13⟩.		the Tamynge of A Shrowe	ix^s.
12 ⟨14⟩.		Andronicous	vij^s.
13 ⟨15⟩.		the Jewe	iiij^s.

1594. Provinces.

[Marlborough. 1593–4]. Paid to him ⟨the Mayor⟩ which he gave to the Lord Chamblyns players 2^s 8^d.

[Murray puts this *c.* September 1594.]

1594. Court ⟨Greenwich⟩.

Dec. 26, 27. William Kempe William Shakespeare & Richarde Burbage seruantes to the Lord Chamberleyne.

[The record gives Innocents' Day, December 28, but an error for 27 is probable, in view of the Gray's Inn record, and of the fact that a payment to the Admiral's for December 28 also appears.]

1594. London.

[Dec. 28. Gray's Inn. From *Gesta Grayorum*, ed. W. W. Greg (*M.S.R.*), 20.]

The next grand Night was intended to be upon *Innocents-Day* at Night. . . . The Ambassador ⟨of the Inner Temple⟩ came . . . about Nine of the Clock at Night . . . there arose such a disordered Tumult and Crowd upon the Stage, that there was no Opportunity to effect that which was intended. . . . The Lord Ambassador and his Train thought that they were not so kindly entertained, as was before expected, and thereupon would not stay any longer at that time, but, in a sort, discontented and displeased. After their Departure the Throngs and Tumults did some-what cease, although so much of them continued, as was able to disorder and confound any good Inventions what-soever. In regard whereof, as also for that the Sports intended were especially for the gracing of the *Templarians*, it was thought good not to offer any thing of Account, saving Dancing and Revelling with Gentle-women; and after such Sports, a Comedy of Errors (like to *Plautus* his *Menechmus*) was played by the Players. So that Night was begun, and continued to the end, in nothing but Confusion and Errors; whereupon, it was ever afterwards called, *The Night of Errors*. . . . We pre-ferred Judgments . . . against a Sorcerer or Conjuror that was supposed to be the Cause of that confused Incon-venience . . . And Lastly, that he had foisted a Company of base and common Fellows, to make up our Disorders with a Play of Errors and Confusions; and that that Night had gained to us Discredit, and itself a Nickname of Errors.

1595. Provinces.

[Cambridge. 1594–5]. Item, to the Lord Chamberlyns players xl^s.

[Ipswich. 1594–5]. To the Lord Chamberlains players xl^s.

[Both visits might be late in 1594, but the Ipswich accounts seem to be chronological and the entry is after one for June 9.]

1595. London.

[Dec. 7. From *Letter* of Sir Edward Hoby, who had a house in Canon Row, Westminster, to Sir Robert Cecil (*Hatfield MSS*. xxxvi. 60), pr. *R.E.S.* i. 75.]

Sir, findinge that you wer not convenientlie to be at London to morrow night I am bold to send to knowe whether Teusdaie ⟨Dec. 9⟩ may be anie more in your grace to visit poore Channon rowe where as late as it shal please

you a gate for your supper shal be open: & K. Richard
present him selfe to your vewe. Pardon my boldnes that
ever love to be honored with your presence nether do I
importune more then your occasions may willingly assent
unto, in the meanetime & ever restinge At your command
Edw. Hoby. [*Endorsed*] 7 Dec. 1595 [*and*] readile.

1595–6. Court ⟨Richmond⟩.

Dec. 26, 27, 28; Jan. 6; Feb. 22. John Hemynge and
    George Bryan servauntes to the late Lorde Chamber-
    layne and now servauntes to the Lorde Hunsdon.

[The 'now' refers to the date of the warrant, 21 Dec. 1596.]

1596–7. Court ⟨Whitehall⟩.

Dec. 26, 27; Jan. 1, 6; Feb. 6, 8. Thomas Pope and John
    Hemynges servauntes to the Lord Chambleyne.

1597. Provinces.

[Faversham. 1596–7]. Item, payde to mye Lorde of
    Hunsdouns players aboute Lamas ⟨August 1⟩ bye
    thappoyntmente of Mr Saker xvi^s.
[Rye]. Paid for a reward given to my Lord Chamberlens
    players at the assignement of M^r. Maior xx^s.
[Dover. 1596–7]. Item then vnto my L. Chamberleynes
    players xiii^s iiii^d.

[Murray puts this between September 3 and 20.]

[Bristol. 1596–7]. 4 qu. 12 wk ⟨September 11–17⟩
    Item paid unto my L Chambrlens plaiers playinge in
    the Guildhall xxx^s.
[Bath. 1596–7 (Mids. year)]. gave unto the Lord
    Chamberlins players xx^s.
[Marlborough. 1596–7]. Item to my lo: Chamberlayns
    players vj^s viij^d.

1597–8. Court ⟨Whitehall⟩.

Dec. 26; Jan. 1, 6; Feb. 26. John Heminges and Thomas
    Pope servauntes to the Lorde Chamberleyne.

1598–9. Court.

Dec. 26; Jan. 1 〈Whitehall〉; Feb. 20 〈Richmond〉. John Heminges and Thomas Pope servantes unto the Lorde Chamberleyne.

1599. London.

[From account of travels of Thomas Platter, ed. G. Binz (*Anglia*, xxii. 456); transl., *Eliz. Stage*, ii. 364.]

Den 21 Septembris nach dem Imbissessen, etwan umb zwey vhren, bin ich mitt meiner geselschaft vber daz wasser gefahren, haben in dem streüwinen Dachhaus die Tragedy vom ersten Keyser Julio Caesare mitt ohngefahr 15 personen sehen gar artlich agieren; zu endt der Comedien dantzeten sie ihrem gebraucht nach gar vberausz zierlich, ye zwen in mannes vndt 2 in weiber kleideren angethan, wunderbahrlich mitt einanderen.

1599–1600. Court 〈Richmond〉.

Dec. 26; Jan. 6; Feb. 3. John Hemynge servaunt to the Lorde Chamberlaine.

1600. London.

[1600, Mar. 6. From *Letter* (March 8) of Rowland Whyte to Sir Robert Sidney (*Sydney Papers*, ii. 175). The play was probably at Hunsdon House, Blackfriars.]

All this Weeke the Lords haue bene in London, and past away the Tyme in Feasting and Plaies; for Vereiken dined vpon Wednesday, with my Lord Treasurer, who made hym a Roiall Dinner; vpon Thursday my Lord Chamberlain feasted hym, and made him very great, and a delicate Dinner, and there in the After Noone his Plaiers acted, before Vereiken, Sir John Old Castell, to his great Contentment.

[1600, July 3. Quoted by C. A. Mills (*Times*, 11 Apr. 1914) as from the travels of 'a foreign nobleman, to be published by J. A. F. Orbaan from a *Vatican MS.*'. But 3 July was not Monday (N.S.) between 1598 and 1609. I suspect 1601 (O.S.). The play was probably at the Globe, but possibly the Rose or Swan, and if so not by the Chamberlain's.]

1600 die Lunae 3 Julii. Audivimus comoediam Anglicam 〈? Anglicanam〉; theatrum ad morem antiquorum Ro-

manorum constructum ex lignis, ita formatum ut omnibus ex partibus spectatores commodissime singula videre
possint. In reditu transivimus pontem magnificis aedificiis ornatum e quibus uni adhuc affixa cernuntur capita
quorundam comitum et nobilium, qui laesae Majestatis rei
supplicio affecti sunt.

1599–1600. Provinces.

[Oxford]. to Baldwyn Hedges to geve the players x^s.

1600–1. Court ⟨Whitehall⟩.

Dec. 26; Jan. 6; Feb. 24. John Hemynges and Richarde
    Cowley servunts to the Lorde Chamberleine.

1601. London.

[1601, Feb. 7. Globe. The performances referred to in (*a*) must date back
to 1595–6. Apparently that of 1601 was arranged on Friday, February 6,
and given on the next day. It was on the same day that Essex received a
summons to appear before the Privy Council. This interrupted his plans
for securing possession of the Queen's person and arresting her ministers,
and precipitated his futile outbreak of February 8.]

(*a*) [1600 ? n.d., but dated in *Cal. S.P.Dom. c.* 24 July 1600, and clearly
before the events of 1601. From Abstract of Evidence in *S.P.Dom. Eliz.*
cclxxv. 33. The document is in tabular form, not preserved here.]

The Erle of Essex is charged with high Treason, namely,
That he plotted and practised with the Pope and king of
Spaine for the disposing and settling to himself Aswell the
Crowne of England, as of the kingdome of Ireland. This
is prooved fyue wayes . . . 5. By the Erle of Essex owne
Actions. In some matters concerning this cause apparantly confirming ye intent of this Treason. His vnderhand permitting of that most treasonous booke of ⟨John
Hayward's⟩ Henry the fourth to be printed and published, being plainly deciphered not onely by the matter,
and by the Epistle itself, for what ende and for whose
behoof it was made, but also the Erle himself being so
often present at the playing thereof, and with great applause giving countenance and lyking to the same. . . .
[*Endorsed.* An Abstract of the Erl of Essex his Treasons.]

(*b*) [1601, Feb. 16. From *Examination* of Sir William Constable (*S.P.Dom. Eliz.* cclxxviii. 72).]

On Saterday the seventh of this present month this examinate together with my L. Mounteagle, Sᵣ Christof. Blunt, Sᵣ Gilly Merick, Sir Charles Percy, Henry Cuffe, Edward Bushell, Ellis Jones, (& Sᵣ John Davies as hee thinketh) at one Gunters howse over against Temple gate, & for ought hee knoweth they met by chaunce; and there they all dined; & after diner Thomas Lee came to the play, where they were all assembled saving Cuffe at the Globe on the bank side. And after the play this examinate & Edward Busshell came to Essex howse, where he supped and lay all night, which hee had never done before.

(*c*) [1601, Feb. 17. From *Examination* of Sir Gelly Meyricke (*S.P.Dom. Eliz.* cclxxviii. 78), pr. Munro, i. 81.]

Sir Gelly Meyricke 17th Feb. 1600.

The Examination of Sᵣ Gelly Merick Knyght taken the xvijᵗʰ of Februarij, 1600. He sayeth that vpon Saterday last was sennyght he dyned at Gunter's in the Company of the L. Monteegle, Sᵣ Christoffer Blont, Sᵣ Charles Percye, Ellys Jones, and Edward Busshell, and who else he remembreth not and after dynner that day & at the mocyon of Sᵣ Charles Percy and the rest they went all together to the Globe over the water wher the L. Chamberlens men vse to play and were ther somwhat before the play began, Sᵣ Charles tellyng them that the play wold be of Harry the iiijᵗʰ. Whether Sᵣ John Davyes were ther or not thys examinate can not tell, but he sayd he wold be ther yf he cold. He can not tell who procured that play to be played at that tyme except yt were Sᵣ Charles Percye, but as he thyncketh yt was Sᵣ Charles Percye. Thenne he was at the same play and Cam in somwhat after yt was begon, and the play was of Kyng Harry the iiijᵗʰ, and of the kyllyng of Kyng Richard the second played by the L. Chamberlen's players

Gelly Meyricke

(*d*) [1601, Feb. 18. From *Examination* of Augustine Phillips (*S.P.Dom. Eliz.* cclxxviii. 85), pr. Munro, i. 82.]

Augustine Phillipps 18 Feb., 1600.

The Examination of Augustyne Phillypps servant vnto the L Chamberlyne and one of hys players taken the xviij[th] of Februarij 1600 vpon hys oth

He sayeth that on Fryday last was sennyght or Thursday S[r] Charles Percy S[r] Josclyne Percy and the L. Montegle with some thre more spak to some of the players in the presans of thys examinate to have the play of the deposyng and kyllyng of Kyng Rychard the second to be played the Saterday next promysyng to gete them xl*s.* more then their ordynary to play yt. Wher thys Examinate and hys fellowes were determyned to have played some other play, holdyng that play of Kyng Richard to be so old & so long out of vse as that they shold have small or no Company at yt. But at their request this Examinate and his fellowes were Content to play yt the Saterday and had their xl*s.* more then their ordynary for yt and so played yt accordyngly

Augustine Phillipps

(*e*) [1601, Feb. 19. From speech of Sir Edward Coke in *Trial* of Earl of Essex, pr. Stopes, *Southampton*, 210, from MS. *penes* Dr. Smedley. A passage, practically identical, is in D. Jardine, *Criminal Trials*, i (1832), 337.]

I protest upon my soul and conscience I doe beleeve she should not have long lived after she had been in your power. Note but the precedents of former ages, how long lived Richard the Second after he was surprised in the same manner? The pretence was alike for the removing of certain counsellors, but yet shortly after it cost him his life.

(*f*) [1601, Mar. 5. From report of *Trial* of Sir Gilly Meyricke and others, pr.⟨S. Emlyn⟩ *State Trials*, vii (1735), 47, from a *Le Neve MS.*]

Against Sir *Gilly Merrick*, M[r] Attorney ⟨Coke⟩ urged . . . And the story of *Henry IV* being set forth in a play, and in that play there being set forth the killing of the King upon a stage; the Friday before, Sir *Gilly Merrick* and some others of the Earl's train having an humour to see a play, they must needs have the play of *Henry IV*. The players told them that was stale, they should get nothing by playing of that, but no play else would serve; and Sir *Gilly Merrick* gives forty shillings to *Philips* the player to play this, besides whatsoever he could get.

(*g*) [1601. From ⟨Francis Bacon's⟩ *A Declaration of the Practises and Treasons . . . by Robert late Earle of Essex.*]

The afternoone before the rebellion, Merricke, with a great company of others, that afterwards were all in the action, had procured to bee played before them, the play of deposing King Richard the second. Neither was it casuall, but a play bespoken by Merrick. And not so onely, but when it was told him by one of the players, that the play was olde, and they should haue losse in playing it, because fewe would come to it: there was fourty shillings extraordinarie giuen to play it, and so thereupon playd it was. So earnest hee was to satisfie his eyes with the sight of that tragedie which hee thought soone after his lord should bring from the stage to the state, but that God turned it vpon their owne heads.

(*h*) [1601, Aug. 4. *Memorandum*, pr. Nichols, *Eliz.* iii. 552, from Lambard family MS. A copy is in the *De la Warr MSS.* (*H.M.C.* iv. 300).]

That which passed from the Excellent Majestie of Queen Elizabeth, in her Privie Chamber at East Greenwich, 4° Augusti 1601, 43° Reg. sui, towards WILLIAM LAMBARDE.

He presented her Majestie with his Pandecta of all her rolls, bundells, membranes, and parcells that be reposed in her Majestie's Tower at London; whereof she had given to him the charge 21st January last past. . . . She proceeded to further pages, and asked where she found cause of stay. . . . He expounded these all according to their original diversities . . . so her Majestie fell upon the reign of King Richard II. saying, 'I am Richard II. know ye not that?'

W. L. 'Such a wicked imagination was determined and attempted by a most unkind Gent. the most adorned creature that ever your Majestie made.'

Her Majestie. 'He that will forget God, will also forget his benefactors; this tragedy was played 40^{tie} times in open streets and houses.'

(*i*) [1615. From W. Camden, *Annales*, 867.]

Mericus accusatur, quod . . . exoletam tragoediam de tragica abdicatione Regis Richardi Secundi in publico theatro coram conjurationis participibus data pecunia agi curasset. Quod ab eo factum interpretati sunt Jurisconsulti, quasi illud pridie in scena agi spectarent, quod postridie in Elizabetha abdicanda agendum.

(*k*) [1615. From *Charge* of Francis Bacon against Oliver St. John in Star Chamber (Spedding, *Works*, v. 145). St. John had opposed benevolences on the ground *inter alia* that they recalled the methods of Richard II.]

For your comparison with Richard II, I see you follow the example of them that brought him upon the stage and into print in Queen Elizabeth's time.

1600–1. Provinces.

[Oxford]. to three companies of players xxx^s.

1601–2. Court ⟨Whitehall⟩.

Dec. 26, 27; Jan. 1; Feb. 14. John Hemyng servaunte
to the Lord Chamberleyne.

1601–2. London.

[1601, Dec. 29. From *Letter* of Dudley Carleton to John Chamberlain (*S.P.Dom. Eliz.* cclxxxii. 48).]

The Q: dined this day priuatly at my Ld Chamberlains; I came euen now from the Blackfriers, where I saw her at the play with all her *candidae auditrices*.

[1602, Feb. 2. Middle Temple. From *Diary* of John Manningham, ed. J. Bruce (C.S.), 18.]

At our feast wee had a play called 'Twelue Night, or

What You Will', much like the Commedy of Errores, or
Menechmi in Plautus, but most like and neere to that in
Italian called *Inganni*. A good practise in it to make the
Steward beleeve his Lady widdowe was in love with him,
by counterfeyting a letter as from his Lady in generall
termes, telling him what shee liked best in him, and pre-
scribing his gesture in smiling, his apparaile, &c., and
then when he came to practise making him beleeue they
tooke him to be mad.

[1602, Sept. 13. Globe ? From *Diary* by Frederic Gerschow of visit by
Philip Julius of Stettin-Pomerania, ed. G. v. Bülow (*2 R. Hist. Soc. Trans.*
vi. 6). The Fortune and Blackfriars were visited on other days, but this
play might have been by Worcester's men at the Rose; cf. *Eliz. Stage*,
ii. 367.]

13. Den 13 ward eine comedia agirt, wie Stuhl-Weissen-
burg erstlich von den Türken hernacher von den Christen
wiederum erobert.

1602–3. Court.

[From *Chamber Account*.]

Dec. 26 ⟨Whitehall⟩; Feb. 2 ⟨Richmond⟩. John Hemynges and the rest of his companie servauntes to the
Lorde Chamberleyne.

1603. Provinces.

[Bath. 1602–3 (Mids. year)]. item givin to the Kinges
players xxx⁵.

[Shrewsbury. 1602–3]. Item geven to the kinges his
Majesties players xx⁵.

[Coventry. 1602–3 (Nov. 1 year)]. to the Kyngs players
xl⁵.

[Ipswich. 1602–3]. To his Majesties players for a reward
xxvj⁵ viij^d.

[This is not the entry given by Jeaffreson and Murray under
30 May 1602 (cf. *Eliz. Stage*, ii. 209), which is rightly dated, but
reads 'hir Majesties Players'.]

[Maldon. 1603–4 (Jan. 6 year)]. 15⁵ to the King's players
this year.

[Oxford. 1603–4]. To Mr Niccolls for the Kinges
    players xx^s.

[Boas puts the visit in May–June 1604, but the entries do not
appear to be chronological.]

1603. Court ⟨*Wilton*⟩.

(*a*) [From *Chamber Account.*]

Dec. 2. John Hemyngs one of his Maiesties players . . .
    for the paynes and expences of himself and the rest
    of the company in comming from Mortelake in the
    countie of Surrie unto the courte aforesaid and there
    presenting before his Maiestie one playe.

(*b*) [1865, Aug. 5. From a journal note of a visit to Wilton House in
F. W. Cornish, *Extracts from the Letters and Journals of William Cory*
(1897), 168. The late Earl of Pembroke and Montgomery wrote to me
on 4 Mar. 1898 that no trace of the letter in question could then be found
at Wilton, and that his mother, Lady Herbert, then not in very good
memory, believed that a copy was at the B.M., or possibly the R.O.
Nothing has since been heard of it. The Court was at Wilton from at
least 24 Oct. to 12 Dec. 1603, and James paid a visit to Salisbury on
1 Nov., and may well have paid others (*Eliz. Stage*, iv. 117). Lee 380,
691, is hardly justified in speaking of the letter 'if it exists, as an ignorant
invention', and an 'alleged tradition, recently promulgated for the first
time by the owners of Wilton'. Cory was a competent historian. But he
does not say that he himself saw the letter.]

The house (Lady Herbert said) is full of interest: above
us is Wolsey's room; we have a letter, never printed, from
Lady Pembroke to her son, telling him to bring James I
from Salisbury to see *As You Like It*; 'we have the man
Shakespeare with us'. She wanted to cajole the King in
Raleigh's behalf—he came.

1603–4. Court.

(*a*) [From *Chamber Account.*]

Dec. 26, 27, 28, 30; Jan. 1 (two plays); Feb. 2 ⟨all
    Hampton Court⟩; Feb. 19 ⟨Whitehall⟩. John
    Hemynges one of his maiesties players.

(*b*) [1604, Jan. 15. From *Letter* of Dudley Carleton to John Chamberlain
(*S.P.Dom. Jac. I*, vi. 21; cf. *Eliz. Stage*, iii. 279).]

On New yeares night we had a play of Robin goode-fellow.

1604. London.

[From *Letter* (Dec. 18) of John Chamberlain to Ralph Winwood (*Memorials*, ii. 41).]

The Tragedy of *Gowry*, with all the Action and Actors hath been twice represented by the King's Players, with exceeding Concourse of all sorts of People. But whether the matter or manner be not well handled, or that it be thought unfit that Princes should be played on the Stage in their Life-time, I hear that some great Councellors are much displeased with it, and so 'tis thought shall be forbidden.

1604–5. Court ⟨Whitehall⟩ and London.

[The argument in favour of the authenticity of (*b*) set out in *Eliz. Stage*, iv. 136, is supplemented by D. T. B. Wood, *The Revels Books: the Writer of the 'Malone Scrap'* and *The Suspected Revels Books* (1925, *R.E.S.* i. 72, 166), with evidence that the abstract in *Bodl. Malone MS.* 29 may well be in the hand of Sir William Musgrave, Commissioner for Auditing the Public Accounts from 1785 to 1800, and if so, antedates any probable forgery. Wood's demonstration of the identity of hands may not be absolutely complete, but obviously Musgrave, who had already told Malone of the Elizabethan *Revels Books*, is the most likely person to have sent him any additional information that became available at the Audit Office. P. Simpson (1925, *Bodleian Quarterly Record*, iv. 178) calls attention to a letter of 2 Dec. 1799 from Musgrave to Malone (*Bodl. Malone MS.* 27, f. 15), 'I enclose a memorandum about a MS. which you have probably met with already—if not it may furnish matter for some of your illustrations of Shakespear'. The memorandum is not now with the letter; it may or may not have been the 'scrap'. This, by the way, is *Malone MS.* 29, f. 19[v] (not f. 69[v], as cited in *Eliz. Stage*, iv. 137). More recently, a renewed attack upon the genuineness of the documents has been made by S. A. Tannenbaum in *Shakespeare Forgeries in the Revels Accounts* (1928). He claims that not the play-lists only, but the whole of the accounts in which they occur, are the handiwork of Collier. In view of the diplomatic correctness of the documents, imperfectly appreciated by Tannenbaum, and the confirmation which they receive from the *Declared Accounts* for the years concerned, it would be impossible even to entertain such a theory, unless it were supported by the strongest palaeographical evidence. It is abundantly clear from Greg's review in *R.E.S.* v. 344 that this is not so, and that Tannenbaum, working from photographs, has misunderstood appearances in the manuscripts which are due to the flaking of ink and other accidents of time, and has ascribed to a forger corrections and touchings up of the scribe's work by contemporary revisers. Tannenbaum regards the 'scrap' as itself a forgery of Musgrave's hand, placed by Collier among the Bodleian papers as a blind. This, already suggested by Mrs. Stopes, is a fantastic notion. Collier's methods had not that subtlety. And the 'scrap' did not come to light through him; it was discovered by H.P. about 1885.

So far as the King's men are concerned, the only discrepancy in the records for 1604-5 between (*a*) and (*b*) is as regards the performance of *Love's Lab. Lost*. It is possible that, although the play was not officially ordered, and therefore not paid for by the Treasurer of the Chamber, the Revels officers attended, in view of the Queen's presence, and that the Clerk or his scribe misdated the performance before Twelfth Night, instead of between January 8 and 15, which is the period suggested by (*d*).

(*a*) [From *Chamber Account*.]

Nov. 1, 4; Dec. 26, 28; Jan. 7, 8; Feb. 2, 3, 10, 11, 12. John Hemynges one of his Maiesties players.

(*b*) [From *Revels Account*.]

The plaiers.		The poets which mayd the plaies.
By the Kings Maiesties plaiers.	Hallamas Day being the first of Nouembar A Play in the Banketinge house att Whit Hall Called The Moor of Venis.	
By his Maiesties plaiers.	The Sunday ffollowinge ⟨Nov. 4⟩ A play of the Merry wiues of winsor.	
By his Maiesties plaiers.	On St Stiuens night in the Hall A play Caled Mesur for Mesur.	Shaxberd.
By his Maiesties plaiers.	On Inosents night The plaie of Errors.	Shaxberd.
By his Maiesties plaiers.	Betwin Newers Day and Twelfe day A play of Loues Labours Lost.	
By his Maiesties plaiers.	On the 7 of January was played the play of Henry the fift.	
By his Maiesties plaiers.	The 8 of January A play Cauled Euery on out of his Vmor.	

By his Maiesties plaiers.	On Candelmas night A playe Euery one In his Vmor. The Sunday ffollowing ⟨Feb. 3⟩ A playe provided And discharged.	
By his Maiesties plaiers.	On Shrousunday ⟨Feb. 10⟩ A play of the Marthant of Venis.	Shaxberd.
By his Maiesties plaiers.	On Shroumonday A Tragidye of The Spanishe Maz.	
By his Maiesties players.	On Shroutusday A play Cauled the Martchant of Venis Againe Commanded By the Kings Maiestie.	Shaxberd.

(*c*) [*Letter* of Sir Walter Cope to Robert Cecil, Lord Cranborne (*H.M.C.* iii. 148 from *Hatfield MSS.*), endorsed '1604'; cf. *Eliz. Stage*, iv. 139.]

I have sent and bene all thys morning huntyng for players Juglers & Such kinde of Creaturs, but fynde them harde to finde, wherfore Leavinge notes for them to seeke me, Burbage ys come, & Sayes ther ys no new playe that the quene hath not seene, but they have Revyved an olde one, Cawled *Loves Labore lost*, which for wytt & mirthe he sayes will please her excedingly. And Thys ys apointed to be playd to Morowe night at my Lord of Sowthamptons, unless yow send a wrytt to Remove the Corpus Cum Causa to your howse in Strande. Burbage ys my messenger Ready attendyng your pleasure.

(*d*) [1605, Jan. 9⟨⟩14. From *Letter* (Jan. 15) of Dudley Carleton to John Chamberlain (*S.P.Dom. Jac. I*, xii. 13); cf. *Eliz. Stage*, iv. 139.]

It seems we shall have Christmas all the yeare and therefore I shall never be owt of matter. The last nights revels were kept at my Lord of Cranbornes, where the Q. with the D. of Holst and a great part of the Court were feasted, and the like two nights before at my Lord of Southamptons. The Temples have both of them done somewhat since Twelftide.

1605. Provinces.

[Oxford]. To ye Kinges players, ye ixth day of October, 1605 x^s.

[Barnstaple. 1604–5]. geven to the Kynges players beyng in Towne this yere x^s.

[Saffron Walden. 1605–6]. Item, given to the Kinges plaiers vj^s viij^d.

[A. Clark (*10 N.Q.* xii. 41) says 'probably autumn 1605'. In this year or in 1606 or 1607, the company must have gone to Cambridge with Jonson's *Volpone* (*Eliz. Stage,* iii. 368).]

1605–6. Court.

Before Mar. 24 ⟨Whitehall⟩. John Hemynges one of his Maiesties players . . . for presenting tenn severall playes or enterludes before his Maiestie in the tyme of Christmas laste and since.

July–Aug. ⟨Greenwich⟩; Aug. 7 ⟨Hampton Court⟩. John Hemynges, one of his Maiesties players . . . for three playes before his Maiestie and the kinge of Denmarke.

1606. Provinces.

[Oxford. 1605–6]. To ye Kinges players xx^s.

[Between entries for July 28 and 31.]

[Leicester. 1605–6]. Item in August given to the Kings Maiesties P⟨l⟩ayars: quer xl^s.

[H.P. says the entry is cancelled and 'quer' added.]

[Marlborough. 1605–6]. Item, to Mr Maior for the Kinges players xxiij^s iiij^d.

[Murray puts the payment after January 17.]

[Dover. 1605–6]. Itm geven to his maiesties players beyng here on Saturday last 2. 0. 0.

[Murray puts the payment between September 6 and 24.]

[Maidstone, 1605–6 (Nov. 2 year)]. Item payd to the Kinges players by Mr Maior and to the trompetters ij^{li} v^s.

1606–7. Court ⟨Whitehall⟩.

Dec. 26, 29; Jan. 4, 6, 8; Feb. 2, 5, 15, 27. John Heminges one of his Maiesties Players.

1607. Provinces.

[Oxford]. Given to the Kinges players, the vii[th] day of September xx[s].

[Barnstaple. 1607]. Given to the King's Majesties players being in towne 20[s].

[Dunwich. 1606–7]. Gratuitie to the King's players vj[s] viij[d].

1607–8. The High Seas.

[From T. Rundall, *Narratives of Voyages towards the North-West* (1849, *Hakluyt Soc.*), 231. I include these entries for convenience, although the performances were not by the King's. They were taken from a journal of William Keeling, captain of the East India Company's ship *Dragon*, bound with the *Hector* (Capt. William Hawkins) and *Consent* to the East Indies. In September 1607 the ships were off Sierra Leone. The 'interpreter' was Lucas Fernandez, a converted negro, brother-in-law of the local king Borea. The third entry was dated in Rundall's print September 31, but corrected, probably by him, in the India Office copy. Lee 649 treats the document as a forgery, because only the first leaf of Keeling's journal is now traceable at the India Office, and the 'modern phrasing gives an impression of spuriousness'. Its authenticity seems to me fully established by W. Foster (*9 N.Q.* vi. 41) and F. S. Boas, *Sh. and the Universities*, 84. Lee's view originally rested on a statement of C. R. Markham, *Voyages of Sir James Lancaster* (1877, *Hakluyt Soc.*), ix, that the pages for 1607–8 had been cut out of the manuscript. This was a confusion with another journal of the same voyage. Rundall appears to have been allowed to take documents home from the office, and probably Keeling's journal, except its first leaf, was so removed and never returned. Other extracts had been printed in Purchas, *Pilgrims*, i. iii. 188, and Boas points out that the phrasing of Rundall's—in which I see nothing particularly 'modern'—is there paralleled.]

1607, Sept. 5. I sent the interpreter, according to his desier, abord the Hector whear he brooke fast, and after came abord mee, wher we gaue the tragedie of Hamlett.

30. Captain Hawkins dined with me, wher my companions acted Kinge Richard the Second.

⟨1608, Mar. 31⟩. I envited Captain Hawkins to a ffishe dinner, and had Hamlet acted abord me: which I permitt to keepe my people from idlenes and unlawful games, or sleepe.

1607–8. Court ⟨Whitehall⟩.

Dec. 26, 27, 28; Jan. 2, 6 (two plays), 7, 9, 17 (two plays), 26; Feb. 2, 7. John Hemynges one of his Maiesties Players.

1608. Provinces.

[Marlborough. 1607–8]. Item, to the Kinges players xx^s.
[Coventry]. Paid to the Kinges players the 29th of October xx^s.

1608? London.

[Extract from evidence of Odoardo Guatz, interpreter, on 18 Apr. 1617, for the trial of Antonio Foscarini at Venice (*V.P.* xiv. 600); cf. *Eliz. Stage*, i. 25, 264; T. S. Graves, *On the Date and Significance of Pericles* (*M.P.* xiii. 545). Zorzi (Giorgio) Giustinian was in England as Venetian ambassador from 5 Jan. 1606 to 23 Nov. 1608 (*V.P.* xi. 193); Antoine de la Boderie, French ambassador, from 16 May 1606 to 1611, with his wife from at least April 1607; Lotto, agent of the Duke of Tuscany, from before May 1606 to 4 Mar. 1608 or later.]

All the ambassadors, who have come to England have gone to the play more or less. Giustinian went with the French ambassador and his wife to a play called *Pericles*, which cost Giustinian more than 20 crowns. He also took the Secretary of Florence.

1608–9. Court ⟨Whitehall⟩.

[From *Chamber Account*, before April 5.]

John Hemynges one of his Maiesties plaiers . . . for twelue plaies by him and the reste of his company presented before the King, Queene, Prince, and Duke of Yorke at severall tymes in Christmas 1608.

1609. Provinces.

[Ipswich]. 9 May. To the Kinges Majesties players xxvj^s viij^d.

[Hythe]. Item, paid to the Kynges players 16 of Maye last xxˢ.

[New Romney]. May 17, item gyven to the Kinges players xxˢ.

1609–10. Court ⟨*Whitehall*⟩.

[From *Chamber Account*, before March 2.]

John Heminges one of the Kinges Maiesties players . . . in the behalfe of himselfe and the reste of his fellowes for presenting thirteene playes before his Maiestie the Queenes Maiestie the Prince the Duke and the Ladie Elizabeth befor Christmas Anno predicto 1609 and in the tyme of the holidayes and afterwardes.

1610. London.

[Globe. From *Relation* by Hans Jacob Wurmsser von Vendenheym of travels of Prince Lewis Frederick of Württemberg (Rye 61).]

1610, April. Lundi, 30. S. E. alla au Globe, lieu ordinaire ou l'on joue les Commedies, y fut representé l'histoire du More de Venise.

1610. Provinces.

[Dover]. Item then paid which was gyven to yᵉ kinges players for a gratuitye o. 10. o.

[Murray puts this between July 6 and August 4. A 'gratuity' probably implies that no performance was allowed (*Eliz. Stage*, i. 339).]

[Oxford. 1609–10]. paid to ⟨Mayor⟩ for the Kinges players xˢ.

[Shrewsbury. 1609–10]. Paid which was geven to the Kings Majesties Players & . . other . . Players this yere iiiˡⁱ xvˢ viiiᵈ.

[Stafford. 1609–10 (Oct. 18 year)]. Item to the King's Majesty's players 10. 0.

[Sudbury. 1609–10 (Oct. 9 year)]. Paid to the Kinge's players 5ˢ.

1610–11. Court ⟨*Whitehall*⟩.

[From *Chamber Account*, before February 12.]

John Hemynges one of the kinges players for presentinge xvᵉⁿ playes before the kinge the quene and the prince.

1611. London.

[From Simon Forman's *Booke of Plaies* (*Bodl. Ashm. MS.* 208, ff. 200–13). The manuscript is composite and Mr. Strickland Gibson kindly ascertained for me from the Bodleian binder that Forman's book is a separate section of seven folio sheets, folded into a single gathering. On f. 200 is the title 'The Booke of plaies and Notes hereof & formans for Common pollicie'; the vº is blank. The notes on *Rich. II* and *Wint. Tale* successively occupy 201 to 202; the vº of 202 and 203, 204, 205 are blank. The note on *Cymb.* occupies 206 as bound and the vº is blank. That on *Macb.* occupies 207 and 207ᵛ. But Liddell showed in his edition of the play that April 20 was not a Saturday in 1610. It was in 1611, and Forman must have written '1610' in error. I think that the sheet forming ff. 206 and 207 has clearly been folded the wrong way round, and that *Cymb.*, which begins 'Remember also', must have been written after *Macb.* Presumably also this sheet, which contains the earliest notes made, was gathered inside the others later. The remaining leaves are blank, except that on 213ᵛ 'On mund' appears inverted at the bottom right-hand corner. This was presumably the beginning of an abandoned entry, and the sheet has been turned the other way up, to serve as a cover. Forman died on 12 Sept. 1611, possibly (cf. F. L. Lucas in *T.L.S.* for 7 Apr. 1927) by suicide, as he had foretold the day.]

(*a*) In Mackbeth at the Glob, 1610 ⟨1611⟩, the 20 of Aprill ♄ ⟨Saturday⟩, ther was to be obserued, firste, howe Mackbeth and Bancko, 2 noble men of Scotland, Ridinge thorowe a wod, the ⟨r⟩ stode before them 3 women feiries or Nimphes, And saluted Mackbeth, sayinge, 3 tyms vnto him, haille Mackbeth, king of Codon; for thou shalt be a kinge, but shalt beget No kinges, &c. Then said Bancko, What all to Mackbeth And nothing to me. Yes, said the nimphes, haille to thee Bancko, thou shalt beget kinges, yet be no kinge. And so they departed & cam to the Courte of Scotland to Dunkin king of Scotes, and yt was in the dais of Edward the Confessor. And Dunkin bad them both kindly wellcome, And made Mackbeth forth with Prince of Northumberland, and sent him hom to his own castell, and appointed Mackbeth to prouid for him, for he would sup with him the next dai at night, & did soe. And Mackebeth contriued to kill Dunkin, & thorowe the persuasion of his wife did that night Murder the kinge in his own Castell, beinge his guest. And ther were many prodigies seen that night & the dai before. And when

Mack Beth had murdred the kinge, the blod on his handes could not be washed of by Any meanes, nor from his wiues handes, which handled the bloddi daggers in hiding them, By which means they became both moch amazed & Affronted. The murder being knowen, Dunkins 2 sonns fled, the on to England, the ⟨other to⟩ Walles, to saue them selues, they being fled, they were supposed guilty of the murder of their father, which was nothinge so. Then was Mackbeth crowned kinge, and then he for feare of Banko, his old companion, that he should beget kinges but be no kinge him selfe, he contriued the death of Banko, and caused him to be Murdred on the way as he Rode. The next night, beinge at supper with his noble men whom he had bid to a feaste to the which also Banco should haue com, he began to speake of Noble Banco, and to wish that he wer ther. And as he thus did, standing vp to drincke a Carouse to him, the ghoste of Banco came and sate down in his cheier behind him. And he turninge About to sit down Again sawe the goste of Banco, which fronted him so, that he fell into a great passion of fear and fury, Vtterynge many wordes about his murder, by which, when they hard that Banco was Murdred they Suspected Mackbet.

Then MackDove fled to England to the kinges sonn, And soe they Raised an Army, And cam into Scotland, and at Dunston Anyse overthrue Mackbet. In the mean-tyme whille Macdouee was in England, Mackbet slewe Mackdoues wife & children, and after in the battelle Mackdoue slewe Mackbet.

Obserue Also howe Mackbetes quen did Rise in the night in her slepe, & walke and talked and confessed all, & the docter noted her wordes.

(b)   Of Cimbalin king of England.

Remember also the storri of Cymbalin king of England, in Lucius tyme, howe Lucius Cam from Octauus Cesar for Tribut, and being denied, after sent Lucius with a greate Arme of Souldiars who landed at Milford hauen, and Affter wer vanquished by Cimbalin, and Lucius taken

prisoner, and all by means of 3 outlawes, of the which
2 of them were the sonns of Cimbalim, stolen from him
when they were but 2 yers old by an old man whom
Cymbalin banished, and he kept them as his own sonns
20 yers with him in A cave. And howe ⟨one⟩ of them
slewe Clotan, that was the quens sonn, goinge to Milford
hauen to sek the loue of Innogen the kinges daughter,
whom he had banished also for louinge his daughter, and
howe the Italian that cam from her loue conveied him
selfe into A Cheste, and said yt was a chest of plate sent
from her loue & others, to be presented to the kinge.
And in the depest of the night, she being aslepe, he opened
the cheste, & cam forth of yt, And vewed her in her bed,
and the markes of her body, & toke awai her braslet, &
after Accused her of adultery to her loue, &c. And in
thend howe he came with the Romains into England &
was taken prisoner, and after Reueled to Innogen, Who
had turned her self into mans apparrell & fled to mete her
loue at Milford hauen, & chanchsed to fall on the Caue
in the wodes wher her 2 brothers were, & howe by eating
a sleping Dram they thought she had bin deed, & laid her
in the wodes, & the body of Cloten by her, in her loues
apparrell that he left behind him, & howe she was found
by Lucius, &c.

(*c*) In Richard the 2 At the Glob 1611 the 30 of Aprill
♂ ⟨Tuesday⟩.

Remember therin howe Jack Straw by his overmoch boldnes, not being pollitick nor suspecting Anye thinge: was
Soddenly at Smithfeld Bars stabbed by Walworth the
major of London, & soe he and his wholle Army was
overthrowen. Therfore in such a case or the like, never
admit any party, without a bar betwen, for A man cannot
be to wise, nor kepe him selfe to safe.

   Also remember howe the duke of Gloster, The Erell of
Arundell, Oxford and others, crossing the kinge in his
humor, about the duke of Erland and Bushy, wer glad to
fly and Raise an hoste of men, and beinge in his Castell,
howe the d. of Erland cam by nighte to betray him with

300 men, but hauing pryuie warninge thereof kept his gates faste, And wold not suffer the Enimie to Enter, which went back Again with a flie in his eare, and after was slainte by the Errell of Arundell in the battell.

Remember also, when the duke and Arundell cam to London with their Army, king Richard came forth to them and met them and gaue them fair wordes, and promised them pardon and that all should be well yf they wold discharge their Army, vpon whose promises and faier Speaches they did yt, and Affter the king byd them all to A banket and soe betraid them And Cut of their heades, &c, because they had not his pardon vnder his hand & sealle before but his worde.

Remember therin Also howe the ducke of Lankaster pryuily contryued all villany, to set them all together by the ears, and to make the nobilyty to Envy the kinge and mislyke of him and his gouernmentes, by which meanes he made his own sonn king, which was Henry Bullinbrocke.

Remember also howe the duke of Lankaster asked A wise man, wher him self should ever be kinge, And he told him no, but his sonn should be a kinge. And when he had told him, he hanged him vp for his labor, because he should not brute yt abrod or speke therof to others. This was a pollicie in the common wealthes opinion. But I sai yt was a villaines parte, and a Judas kisse to hange the man for telling him the truth. Beware by this Example of noble men, and of their fair wordes, & sai lyttell to them, lest they doe the like by thee for thy good will.

(d) In the Winters Talle at the glob 1611 the 15 of maye ☿ ⟨Wednesday⟩.

Obserue ther howe Lyontes the kinge of Cicillia was overcom with Jelosy of his wife with the kinge of Bohemia his frind that came to see him, and howe he contriued his death and wold haue had his cup berer to haue poisoned, who gaue the king of Bohemia warning therof & fled with him to Bohemia.

Remember also howe he sent to the Orakell of Appollo & the Annswer of Apollo, that she was giltles and that the

king was jelouse &c. and howe Except the child was
found Again that was loste the kinge should die without
yssue, for the child was caried into Bohemia & ther laid
in a forrest & brought vp by a sheppard And the kinge
of Bohemia his sonn maried that wentch & howe they fled
into Cicillia to Leontes, and the sheppard hauing showed
the letter of the nobleman by whom Leontes sent a was
⟨away?⟩ that child and the jewells found about her, she
was knowen to be Leontes daughter and was then 16
yers old.

Remember also the Rog that cam in all tottered like
coll pixci and howe he feyned him sicke & to haue bin
Robbed of all that he had and howe he cosened the por
man of all his money, and after cam to the shep sher with
a pedlers packe & ther cosened them Again of all their
money And howe he changed apparrell with the kinge of
Bomia his sonn, and then howe he turned Courtier &c.
Beware of trustinge feined beggars or fawninge fellouss.

1611. Provinces.

[Shrewsbury. 1610–11]. Paid which was geven to the
      Kings, Queens, Princes and other noblemens players
      this yere . . . xxˢ.

[The amount suggests that this was a common-form heading and
is not evidence for any particular visit.   It may be so in other years.]

1611–12. Court ⟨Whitehall and Greenwich⟩.

[The authenticity of (*b*), which I accept, must stand or fall with that of
the corresponding account for 1604–5 (cf. *supra*). But there are considerable discrepancies between (*a*) and (*b*), which are set out in *Eliz. Stage*,
iv. 140. So far as the King's are concerned, there is agreement on Nov. 1
and 5, Dec. 26, and Feb. 23. But (*b*) omits Oct. 31, and gives a Queen's
Revels play for Jan. 5. On the other hand (*a*) omits Jan. 1 and Jan. 13,
unless it is the undated play of the second payment, and gives Jan. 12 to the
Duke of York's. Presumably the Revels officers did not attend a number
of plays before the royal children covered by (*a*).]

(*a*) [From *Chamber Account.*]

Oct. 31; Nov. 1, 5; Dec. 26; Jan. 5; Feb. 23. John
      Heminges . . . for the Kinges Maiesties servauntes
      and players.

Nov. 9, 19; Dec. 16, 31; Jan. 7, 15; Feb. 19, 20, 28;
    Apr. 3, 16; [n. d.]. the sayd John Heminges.
Feb. 9, 20; Mar. 28; Apr. 26. the sayd John Heminges.

(*b*) [From *Revels Account*.]

By the Kings players:	Hallomas nyght was presented att Whithall before ye kinges Maiestie a play Called the Tempest.
The Kings players:	The 5th of nouember A play Called y^e winters nightes Tayle.
The Kings players:	On St Stiuenes night A play called A King & no king.
The Kings players.	On neweres night A play Called the Twinnes Tragedie.
By the Queens players and the Kings men.	The Sunday following ⟨after Twelfth Night = Jan. 12⟩ att Grinwidg before the Queen and the Prince was playd The Siluer Aiedg: and y^e next night following Lucre⟨ce⟩.
By the Kings players.	Shroue Sunday ⟨Feb. 23⟩ A play Called the Noblman.

1612. Provinces.

[New Romney]. April 21, item, paid to Mr Maior to geve
    to the Kinges players xx^s.
[Winchester. 1611–12]. To the players of our Lord the
    King xx^s.

1612–13. Court ⟨Whitehall⟩.

(*a*) [From *The Magnificent Marriage of the Two Great Princes Frederick Count Palatine and the Lady Elizabeth* (1613).]

Much expectation was made of a stage play to be acted
⟨Feb. 16⟩ in the Great Hall by the King's players, where
many hundred of people stood attending the same; but it
lapsed contrarie, for greater pleasures ⟨the entry of a
mask⟩ were preparing.

(*b*) [From *Chamber Account.*]

Item paid to John Heminges upon the Cowncells warrant dated att Whitehall xx° die Maij 1613, for presentinge before the Princes Highnes the Lady Elizabeth and the Prince Pallatyne Elector fowerteene severall playes, viz: one playe called Filaster, One other called the Knott of Fooles, One other Much Adoe abowte Nothinge, The Mayeds Tragedy, The Merye Dyvell of Edmonton, The Tempest, A Kinge and no Kinge, The Twins Tragedie, The Winters Tale, Sir John Falstaffe, The Moore of Venice, The Nobleman, Caesars Tragedye, And one other called Love lyes a bleedinge, All which Playes weare played with-in the tyme of this Accompte, viz: paid the some of iiij^{xx} xiij^{li} vj^s viij^d.

Item paid to the said John Heminges vppon the lyke warrant, dated att Whitehall xx° die Maij 1613, for presentinge sixe severall playes, viz: one playe called A badd begininge makes a good endinge, One other called the Capteyne, One other the Alcumist, One other Cardenno, One other The Hotspur, And one other called Benedicte and Betteris, All played within the tyme of this Accompte viz: paid Fortie powndes, And by waye of his Majesties rewarde twentie powndes, In all lx^{li}.

1613. Court ⟨Greenwich⟩.

Item paid to John Heminges vppon lyke warrant, dated att Whitehall ix° die Julij 1613 for himself and the rest of his fellowes his Majesties servauntes and Players for presentinge a playe before the Duke of Savoyes Embassadour on the viijth daye of June, 1613, called Cardenna, the some of vj^{li}, xiij^s iiij^d.

1613. London.

[1613, June 29. Globe. From *Letter* (2 July) of Sir Henry Wotton to Sir Edmund Bacon (L. Pearsall Smith, *Letters of Wotton*, ii. 32). This is the most detailed account of the play. I have added several others in *Eliz. Stage*, ii. 419. Two speak of 'the play of Henry VIII'; one names 'Burbidge', 'Henry Condye', and 'old stuttering Heminges', as present.]

Now, to let matters of state sleep, I will entertain you at the present with what has happened this week at the

Bank's side. The King's players had a new play, called *All is True*, representing some principal pieces of the reign of Henry VIII, which was set forth with many extraordinary circumstances of pomp and majesty, even to the matting of the stage; the Knights of the Order with their Georges and garters, the Guards with their embroidered coats, and the like: sufficient in truth within a while to make greatness very familiar, if not ridiculous. Now, King Henry making a masque at the Cardinal Wolsey's house, and certain chambers being shot off at his entry, some of the paper, or other stuff, wherewith one of them was stopped, did light on the thatch, where being thought at first but an idle smoke, and their eyes more attentive to the show, it kindled inwardly, and ran round like a train, consuming within less than an hour the whole house to the very grounds. This was the fatal period of that virtuous fabric, wherein yet nothing did perish but wood and straw, and a few forsaken cloaks; only one man had his breeches set on fire, that would perhaps have broiled him, if he had not by the benefit of a provident wit put it out with bottle ale.

1613. Provinces.

[Folkestone. 1612–13]. Item, gyven to the Kinges players ij^s.

[Murray found the record, given by H.P., untraceable.]

[Oxford. 1612–13]. paid to Mr Niccolls for the Kinges players, given by Mr Mayor x^s.

[Stafford. 1612–13 (Oct. 18 year)]. Given to the Kyngs players 10^s.

[Shrewsbury. 1612–13]. Paid which was bestowed upon the Kyngs maiesties & Lady Elizabethes players xx^s.

1613–14. Court ⟨Whitehall⟩.

To John Heminges and the rest of his fellowes his Maiesties servaunts the Players upon warrant dated 21 June 1614 for presentinge seaven severall playes before the Princes highnes viz on the 4th of Novr the 16th of Novr the 10th of January the 4th of February the 8th the 10th and the 18th of the same moneth 1614 xlvj^{li} xiij^s.

To the said John Heminges and the rest of his fellowes upon a like warraunt of a lyke date for presenting before his Maiesty nyne severall playes viz on the first v^{th} & xv^{th} of November 1614 ⟨1613⟩ on the xxvij^{th} of December the first and fourth of Januar the second of February following and the vj^{th} & viij^{th} of March followinge 1614—iiij x^l.

[The play of February 4 may have been that given for the Lord Mayor and Aldermen at Somerset House (Nichols, *James*, ii. 754).]

1614. Provinces.

[Coventry. 1613–14 (Nov. 1 year)]. Given to the kings players as appeareth by a bill vnder Mr Maiours hand xl^s.

1614–15. Court ⟨Whitehall⟩.

To John Hemynges uppon the Lorde Chamberleynes warrant dated xix^{no} Maii 1615 in the behalfe of himself and his fellowes the Kings Maiesties players for eighte severall plaies before his Maiestie iiij^l.

1615. Provinces.

[Nottingham]. April. Item geven in reward to the Kinges players xiii^s iiij^d.

1615–16. Court (⟨Whitehall and⟩ Somerset House).

[From *Chamber Account* and *Account* of Queen Anne.]

Nov. 1 to Apr. 1. John Heminges and the rest of his fellowes the Kings Maiesties Players ⟨14 plays⟩.
Dec. 21. John Heminge one of the Kinge Maiesties plaiers for so much paid vnto him in the behalfe of himselfe and the reste of his fellowes of that companie for one plaie acted before her Maiestie at Queenes Court.

1616. Provinces.

[Oxford. 1615–16 (Vice-Chancellor's accounts).]
Solutum Histrionibus Domini Regis xl^s.

III. PERFORMANCES OF 1616 TO 1642

[1618, Apr. 6, 7. From entry in *Original Chamber Account*, pr. Cunningham, xlv.]

To John Heminges . . . upon a warrant dated 20 April 1618 for presenting two severall Playes before his Maiesty, on Easter Monday Twelfte night the play soe called and on Easter Tuesday the Winter's Tale xx^{li}.

[1619, May 20. From *Letter* (May 24) of Sir Gerrard Herbert to Sir Dudley Carleton (*S.P.Dom.Jac.I*, cix. 46) pr. Halliwell, *A Copy of a Letter* (1865); Munro, i. 276.]

The Marquise Trenell ⟨La Tremoile⟩ on Thursday last tooke leaue of the Kinge: that night was feasted at White hall, by the Duke of Lennox in the Queenes greate chamber . . . In the kinges greate Chamber they went to see the play of Pirrocles, Prince of Tyre, which lasted till 2 aclocke. After two actes, the players ceased till the French all refreshed them with sweetmeates brought on Chinay voiders, & wyne & ale in bottells, after the players begann anewe.

[*c.* 1619–20. Court? From lists of plays on backs of slips added to *Cott. MS. Tiberius*, E. X. of *History of Richard III* by Sir George Buck, Master of the Revels (1610–22), pr. with facs. F. Marcham, *The King's Office of the Revels*, 1610–22 (1925). The original MS. is dated 1619. The slips appear to be waste paper from the Revels Office, and the lists may represent plays considered for performances at Court; cf. my review in *R.E.S.* i. 479. The last two entries cannot be assumed to be Shakespearean.]

[f. 70^v]   The Winters Tale.
            The 2. Noble Kinesmen.
[f. 197^v]   The Tradgedy of Ham⟨let⟩ . . .
[f. 211^v]   ⟨Seco⟩nd part of Falstaff
            ⟨not p⟩laid theis 7. yeres.
[f. 247]   Henrye the vna⟨   ⟩ . . .
            Titus, and Vespatian.

[1623, Feb. 2. Court. From *Office Book* (*Var.*iii. 147; Adams, *Herbert*, 50).]

At Candlemas Malvolio was acted at court, by the kings servants.

[1623, Aug. 19. From *Office Book* of Sir Henry Herbert, Master of the Revels. This is now lost, but was in 1790 in the house of Francis Ingram at Ribbesford, Worcestershire, which had belonged to Herbert. It was 'damaged, and in a very mouldering condition'. It is now lost, but many extracts were made by E. Malone in his *Shakespeare* (1790) and repeated in *Var.* (1821), and by G. Chalmers, *S.A.* (1799). These are conveniently collected in J. Q. Adams, *Dramatic Records of Sir Henry Herbert* (1917). W. J. Lawrence (*T.L.S.* 29 Nov. 1923) quotes a record from Malone's annotated Langbaine that he had made a copy of the *Office Book* by 22 June 1789, and gives a few additional extracts copied into other books once owned by him. The present entry is from *Var.* iii. 229; Adams, *Herbert*, 18, 25.]

For the king's players. An olde playe called Winter's Tale, formerly allowed of by Sir George Bucke, and likewyse by mee on Mr Hemmings his worde that there was nothing profane added or reformed, thogh the allowed booke was missinge; and therefore I returned it without a fee, this 19 of August, 1623.

[1624, Jan. 18. Court. From *Office Book* (*Var.* iii. 228; Adams, *Herbert*, 51).]

To the Duchess of Richmond, in the king's absence, was given The Winters Tale, by the K. company, the 18 Janu. 1623. Att Whitehall.

[1625, Jan. 1. Court. From *Office Book* (*Var.* iii. 228; Adams, *Herbert*, 52).]

Upon New-years night, the prince only being there, The First Part of Sir John Falstaff, by the kings company. Att Whitehall, 1624.

[1627, Apr. 11. From *Office Book* (*Var.* iii. 229; Adams, *Herbert*, 64).]

From Mr Hemming, in their company's name, to forbid the playing of Shakespeare's plays, to the Red Bull Company, this 11 of April, 1627.—5^l. o. o.

[1628, July 29. Globe.]

(*a*) [From *Newsletter* (Aug. 1) among *Isham MSS.* at Lamport Hall, pr. G. Bullen (*Athenæum*, 18, 25 Oct. 1879); Munro, i. 338.]

On Teusday his Grace ⟨the Duke of Buckingham⟩ was present at ye acting of King Henry 8 at ye Globe, a play bespoken of purpose by himselfe, whereat he stayed till ye Duke of Buckingham was beheaded & then departed. . . .

Another Dicto . . .

On Teusday was a play at ye Globe of ye downfall of ye great Duke of Buckingham, whereunto ye Savoian Ambassadour, ye Duke, Earle of Hollande & others came, yet stayed only ye disgracing not ye beheading of ye great Duke of Buck.

(*b*) [From *Letter* (Aug. 9) of Robert Gell to Sir Martyn Stuteville (*Harl. MS.* 383, f. 65), pr. Halliwell (1845, *Sh. Soc. Papers*, ii. 151); Munro, i. 337.]

On Teusday his Grace was present at ye acting of K. Hen. 8 at ye Globe, a play bespoken of purpose by himself; whereat he stayd till ye Duke of Buckingham was beheaded, & then departed. Some say, he should rather have seen ye fall of Cardinall Woolsey, who was a more lively type of himself, having governed this kingdom 18 yeares, as he hath done 14.

[1629, Nov. 22. Blackfriars? From *Office Book* (*Var.* iii. 177; Adams, *Herbert*, 44).]

The benefitt of the winters day from the kinges company being brought me by ⟨William⟩ Blagrave ⟨deputy to Herbert⟩ upon the play of The Moor of Venise, comes, this 22 of Nov. 1629, unto—9^l. 16^s. 0^d.

[1631, June 10. Globe. From *Office Book* (*Var.* iii. 177; Adams, *Herbert*, 64).]

Received of Mr Benfielde, in the name of the kings company, for a gratuity for ther liberty gaind unto them of playinge, upon the cessation of the plague, this 10 of June, 1631,—£3^l. 10^s. 0^d. This was taken upon Pericles at the Globe.

[1631, June 12. Globe. From *Office Book* (*Var.* iii. 177; Adams, *Herbert*, 44).]

Received of Mr Shanke, in the name of the kings company, for the benefitt of their summer day, upon ye second daye of Richard ye Seconde, at the Globe, this 12 of June, 1631,—5^l. 6^s. 6^d.

[?1631. The date of the performance is not quite certain. Spencer's letters were written in November 1631, but September 27 was not in that year a Sunday. It was in 1629. Either the day given in (*a*) should have been September 29, or the protest was belated. John Williams, Bishop of

Lincoln (1621–41), although no puritan, was opposed to the extreme ecclesiastical policy of Laud. A Star-chamber prosecution of 1628 for betraying Privy Council secrets seems to have led to an accumulation of charges, serious and trivial, against him. The performance described in Spencer's controversial gambollings no doubt took place at his house of Buckden in Huntingdonshire. It is not so clear that it was of *Mid. N. Dr.*, although this is fairly probable, even apart from the words in the margin of (*a*), of which L. Toulmin Smith (Munro, i. 352) says, 'These are evidently the work of a later hand and have been written over an erasure: they are not in the hand of either Laud, Lincoln, or Spencer, or of the endorser of the paper, but look like a bad imitation of old writing'. The performers were not professional actors, but 'Mr Wilson' might be either the Jack Wilson of the F1 text of *Much Ado*, or the court musician John Wilson (1595–1674), if indeed the two are distinct. But perhaps it is more likely that he is the Harry Wilson of *Believe As You List*, played by the King's men in this same year 1631.]

(*a*) [1631, Nov. 10. Extract from *Letter* of John Spencer to an un-named lady, printed in full by Collier, i. 460, from *Lambeth MS*. 1030. 5, a collection endorsed by Abp. Laud 'These papers concerning the Bp. of Lincoln ⟨John Williams⟩ wear delivered to me bye his Majesty's command'. The lady may be the wife of Sir Sidney Montagu of Hinchin-brooke or of Sir Thomas Headsey; cf. (*b*).]

Good Madame . . . Soe, I trust, your noble harte will tell you; though you were drawne with the Bishopps coach to his house to heare such excellent musicke, such rare conceits, and to see such curious actors, and such a number of people to behold the same, yett all was but vanity and vexation of spiritt; and the more vanity, the more vexation of speritt, because it was upon the Lords-day, which should have been taken upp with better meditations, and contemplations of heaven and heavenly things. And therefore, that this maye not prove a precedente unto others, I beseeche you submitt your selfe to this censure that is passed against you . . . John Spencer. November 10, 1631.

[Appended on the second leaf of the sheet.]

A COPIE OF THE ORDER, OR DECREE (*ex officio Comisarii generalis*).

JOHN SPENCER.

Forasmuch as this Courte hath beene informed, by Mr Comisary general, of a greate misdemenor committed in the house of the right honorable Lo. Bishopp of Lincolne, by entertaining into his house divers Knights and Ladyes, with many other householders servants, uppon the 27th Septembris, being the Saboth day, to see a playe or tragidie there acted; which began aboute tenn of the clocke at night, and ended about two or three of the clocke in the morning:

Wee do therefore order, and decree, that the R^t honorable John, Lord Bishopp of Lincolne, shall, for his offence, erect a free schoole in Eaton, or else at Greate Staughton, and endowe the same with 20^l. per ann. for the maintenance of the schoolmaster for ever.

Likewise wee doe order, that Sr Sydney Mountagu, Knight, for his offence, shall give to the poore of Huntingdon 5^l; and his lady, for her offence, five blacke gownes to 5 poore widdowes, uppon Newyeares day next.

Likewise wee doe order, that Sir Thomas Headsey, Knight, for his offence, shall give unto the poore of Brampton 5^l; and his lady, for her offence, black cloath gownes to 5 poore, uppon Newyeares day nexte.

Likewise wee doe order that Mr Williams, Mr Trye, Mr Harding, Mr Hazarde, and Mr Hulton shall eche one of them give a blacke coate, and 5^s in money, unto 5 poore in Bugden, uppon newyeares day nexte.

Likewise wee doe order, that Mr Wilson, because hee was a speciall plotter and contriver of this business, and did in such a brutishe manner acte the same with an Asses head [*in margin, in another hand*, 'The playe, *M. Nights Dr*']; and therefore hee shall, uppon Tuisday next, from 6 of the clocke in the morning till six of the clocke at night, sitt in the Porters Lodge at my Lords Bishopps House, with his feete in the stocks, and attyred with his asse head, and a bottle of hay sett before him, and this subscription on his breast:

> Good people I have played the beast,
>   And brought ill things to passe:
> I was a man, but thus have made
>   My selfe a silly Asse.

[*Endorsed*. John Spencer presents the Lord Byshop of

Lincolne for having a play that night in his house, being the Lord's Day.]

(b) [1641. Extract from John Spencer, *Discourse of Divers Petitions of High Concernment*, 18. This is preceded by a letter of 4 Nov. 1631 from Spencer to the Bishop, which repeats much of the language used to the lady, but gives no new facts, and by an account of a chaffing promise of Williams to make Spencer his Commissary General. It introduces a summary of Spencer's burlesque 'presentment', and his subsequent 'censure' when the Bishop did not appear in court. But here there is nothing of the penalty suggested for Wilson.]

Well I thanked his Lorp. & shortly after made more use of my Office than he would have had me: for one M*ʳ Wilson* a cunning Musition having contrived a curious Comodie, and plotted it so, that he must needs have it acted upon the Sunday night, for he was to go the next day toward the Court; the Bishop put it off till nine of the clock at night: a while after, the Commissarie, Doctor *Morrison*, kept a Court at *Huntington*, and I came thither and went into the seat with the Commissarie, and put on my hat: the Doctors and Divines stood with hats off, and gave their attendance; then some offered their presentment, but I told Master Commissarie, that I had a presentment, and that must be the first, and so he took it, and read it, the tennour was thus: ... So when Master Commissarie had read it, he was somewhat amazed at it, and asked me who was the Commissarie Generall. I bade him ask my Lord of *Lincolne* who was Commissary Generall. ...

(c) [1659. Extract from P. Heylyn, *Examen Historicum*, i. 243.]

The Peoples turn he serv'd next, in the condemning and recanting of some points about the Sabbath, though therein he ran cross to his former practice. Who had been not long since so far from those Sabbatarian rigors (which now he would fain be thought to countenance) that he caus'd a Comedy to be acted before him at his house at *Bugden*, not only on a Sunday in the afternoon, but upon such a Sunday also on which he had publickly given sacred Orders both to Priests and Deacons. And to this Comedy he invited the Earl of *Manchester* ⟨Henry Montagu⟩, and divers of the neighbouring Gentry.

(*d*) [1693. Extract from J. Hacket, *Scrinia Reserata*, ii. 37.]

I have not done with the Governance of this Family. Which was the worse thought of by some strict Censurers, because the Bishop ⟨Williams⟩ admitted in his publick Hall a Comedy once or twice to be presented before him, exhibited by his own Servants for an Evening Recreation. . . . No Man more wise, or more serious than Arch-Bishop *Bancroft*, the Atlas of our Clergy in his time: and he that writes this hath seen an Enterlude, well presented before him at *Lambeth*, by his own Gentlemen, when I was one of the youngest Spectators.

[1633–4. Court. From *Office Book* (*Var.* iii. 233; Adams, *Herbert*, 53).]

On Saterday, the 17th ⟨16th⟩ of Novemb. being the Queens birthday, Richarde the Thirde was acted by the K. players at St James, wher the king and queene were present, it being the first play the queene sawe since her Maiestys delivery of the Duke of York. 1633.

On Tusday night at Saint James, the 26 of Novemb. 1633, was acted before the Kinge and Queene, The Taminge of the Shrewe. Likt.

On Wensday night the first of January, 1633, Cymbeline was acted at court by the Kings players. Well likte by the kinge.

The Winters Tale was acted on Thursday night at Court, the 16 Janua. 1633, by the K. players, and likt.

[1635, May 6. Blackfriars. From *Diary* of Sir Humphrey Mildmay of Danbury (*Harl. MS.* 454, f. 10ᵛ), pr. Collier, ii. 5; Munro, i. 397.]

1635 . . . Maij . . . 6: not farre from home all day att yᵉ bla: ffryers & a play yⁱˢ day called yᵉ More of Venice.

[1636–7. Court.]

(*a*) [From *Schedule* of plays (*R.O. Audit Office, Accounts Various, Revels*, 3, 908), pr. Cunningham, xxiv; Adams, *Herbert*, 75; E. Law, *More About Shakespeare Forgeries* (1913), 39 (facs.). Cunningham removed the document and sold it to a bookseller, from whom it was recovered by the R.O. and classified as above. It must, however, have come originally to the Audit Office as a subsidiary document to an account, not of the Revels Office, but of the Treasurer of the Chamber. Presumably it was attached to the Lord Chamberlain's warrant for payment to the King's men (pr. Law 71), with which its total number of plays agrees (cf. *Eliz. Stage*, i. 219). Its authenticity is defended by Law, and Tannenbaum, *Shakespeare Forgeries*, 58, does not succeed (cf. Greg in *R.E.S.* v. 356) in showing anything 'necessarily suspicious' about it. One or two discrepancies with (*b*), which, for example, omits *Ham*. and assigns to Jan. 24 *Rollo*, put by (*a*) on Jan. 17, are perhaps due to slips in Malone's transcription from the *Office Book*. Malone gives no entries before Dec. 26; it does not follow that there was none for Dec. 8 in the *Book*. Nor can it weigh much against (*a*) that a news-letter of 17 Jan. 1637 by ⟨Capt.⟩ E⟨dmund⟩ R⟨ossingham⟩ printed from one of Birch's transcripts in R. F. Williams, *The Court and Times of Charles I*, ii. 266, states an intention of the King and Queen to remove from Hampton Court on Jan. 18. Such royal resolves were often altered.]

Playes acted before the kinge and Queene this present
        yeare of the lord. 1636.

... The 8th of December at Hampton Court. the Moore
        of Venice ...

The 24th of January at Hampton Court—Hamlett. ...

The 31th of January at St James. the tragedie of Cesar.

(*b*) [From *Office Book* (*Var.* iii. 239; Adams, *Herbert*, 57).]

Julius Caesar, at St James, the 31 Janu. 1636.

[1638–9. Court. From *Bill*, evidently submitted by the King's as a basis for the Lord Chamberlain's warrant for payment, pr. with facs. G. R. Wright, in *Brit. Arch. Ass. Journal*, xvi (1860), 275, 340, and in his *Archaeologic and Historic Fragments* (1887); Herbert 76. Tannenbaum, *Shakespeare Forgeries*, 60, believes the document to be fabricated. The original is not available for comparison, but Greg (*R.E.S.* v. 356) shows that there is no ground for suspicion in the letter forms, and that the substance is consistent with the Treasurer of the Chamber's *Declared Account* for 1638–9.]

... At the Cocpit the 29th of May the princes berthnyght
        —ould Castel ...

At the Cocpit the 13th of November—Ceaser.

At the Cocpit the 15th of November—The mery wifes
        of winsor.

APPENDIX E

THE NAME SHAKESPEARE

[*Bibliographical Note*. Records of the name Shakespeare are collected in *Variorum*, ii. 15; J. Hunter, *New Illustrations of Sh.* (1845); G. R. French, *Shakespeareana Genealogica* (1869); J. P. Yeatman, *The Gentle Shakspeare* (⟨1896⟩; 1904, 1906, with additions; here cited as Y.); C. C. Stopes, *Sh.'s Family* (1901). Many have been contributed to *Notes and Queries*. Of particular value for the northern villages of Warwickshire are W. B. Bickley, *Register of the Guild of Knowle* (1894, cited as G. of K.); J. W. Ryland, *Records of Rowington* (vol. i ⟨1896⟩, vol. ii, 1922, cited as R.R.), *Records of Wroxall Abbey and Manor* (1903, cited as R.W.), *Parish Registers of Wroxall* (1903). I have attempted to give all notices known to me up to the end of the 15th century, and in Warwickshire, counties contiguous to Warwickshire, and London up to about the end of the 16th century. I give the recorded spellings of the name where my sources permit, and elsewhere substitute 'Sh.']

I. NOTICES BEFORE THE FIFTEENTH CENTURY

1248 (Gloucestershire). William Sakspere, of Clopton in Kiftesgate Hundred, was hanged for robbery.[1]—1250 (Essex). Simon Sakesper was a verderer in the half hundred of Waltham.[2]—1261 (Gloucestershire). By then Simon Shakespeye, royal *valettus*, had transferred land at Pruslbury ⟨Prestbury⟩.[3]—1268 (Surrey). Geoffrey Sh. was a juryman in the hundred of Brixton.[4]—1279 (Kent). John Shakespere was a plaintiff at Canterbury.[5]—1318 (Staffordshire). William Shakespere was surety in a suit by the Prior of Trentham. In 1324 Simon Shakespere was himself sued by the Prior. In 1327 Simon Schakespere of Penkhull in Stoke upon Trent was on the subsidy roll. The name is traceable at Penkhull and at Shelton, also in Stoke, to 1417. The form Schacosper occurs in 1374.[6]—

[1] Lee 1, from *Assize Roll*, 32 Hen. III, r. 274.

[2] W. R. Fisher, *Forest of Essex*, 374, prob. from *Cotton Roll*, xiii. 5.

[3] 5 *N.Q.* ii. 146, from *Coram Rege Roll*, 45 Hen. III, m. 13, no. 117.

[4] Stopes 4, from *Coram Rege Roll*, 52–3 Hen. III, 139, m. 1.

[5] W. H. Hart in *1 N.Q.* xi. 122, from *Placita Coronae*, 7 Ed. I, Kent.

[6] T. Pape, in *Trans. North Staffs. Field Club*, liii. 47, from *Plea Rolls* and manorial rolls of Newcastle under Lyme.

1348–9 (Cheshire). Rolyn Shakespere was a tenant on the manor of Harden in Stockport.[1]—1349 (Cumberland). From this year to 1357 Henry Shakespere withheld a payment due to the hospital of St. Nicholas, Carlisle.[2]— 1357 (Nottingham). John Shakespere was in a law-suit, and again in 1360.[3]—1359 (Warwickshire). The bailiffs of Coventry account for the property of Thomas Sh. a felon who had fled the country.[4]—1359–89 (Warwickshire). See (II) s.vv. Balsall, Baddesley Clinton.—1375 (Ireland). Thomas Shakespeare was connected with the port of Youghal, where he was appointed collector of customs in 1377.[5]—1378–9 (Yorkshire). Robert Schackspere, cooper, and his wife Emma paid poll-tax at Pontefract.[6]—1378–9 (Essex). Walter Shakespere had been recently a prisoner in Colchester Castle, whither also John Shakspere went for breach of peace on 3 Mar. 1381.[7]—1398 (Cumberland). William Shakespere witnessed a transfer of land at Penrith, next to that of Alan Shakespere.[8]

II. NOTICES OF THE FIFTEENTH AND LATER CENTURIES

(a) *Warwickshire.*

(1) *Balsall.* Adam of Oldediche, a farm in B., was father of Adam of Baddesley Clinton (1389).[9] Richard and Alice Shakspere de Woldiche of the G. of K. died *c.* 1457. Thomas and Alice Shakspere joined the G. in 1486. Alice joined the G. in 1511–12 and paid for the soul of Thomas. John of Wroxall (1575) had a cousin Laurence Shaxper of B. Thomas of Warwick (1577) left a copyhold on the

---

[1] J. A. Swettenham in *T.L.S.* for 27 Apr. 1916, from *Macclesfield Court Rolls*, Pfo. 155, no. 85.

[2] *2 N.Q.* x. 122.

[3] W. Stevenson, *Records of N.* i. 166, 176.

[4] Stopes 5, from J. Hunter's *Addl. MS.* 24, 484, art. 246.

[5] Halliwell-Phillipps, *Folio Sh.* i. 4;

Cal. Irish Close Rolls, i. 1. 996.

[6] *Yorks. Arch. Journal,* vi. 3, from *Lay Subsidies,* 206, 49.

[7] F. J. Furnivall in 5 *N.Q.* i. 25, from *Controlment Roll,* 2 Rich. II; 7 *N.Q.* ii. 318, from *Close Roll,* 4 Rich. II.

[8] *6 N.Q.* iv. 126.

[9] H. Norris in *8 N.Q.* viii. 501.

manor to his wife Agnes. A John hanged himself in his house 23 July 1579.[1]

(2) *Baddesley Clinton*. Adam Shakespere, son and heir of Adam of Oldediche, held, and probably then acquired, land on the manor by military service in 1389. He ob. 1414, leaving a widow Alice and son John, a minor, who held the land in 1425 and 1441. Probably his sons were Ralph and Richard, who held Great Chedwyns in 1465. Ralph's wife was Joanna. He was alive on 17 Apr. 1493 but dead by 14 Apr. 1496, when his land was divided between Robert Huddespit and Robert Rakley, husbands of his daughters Elizabeth and Isolda. On 14 Dec. 1506 Elizabeth was a widow, and held some of the land which was Adam's in 1389.[2] Johanna Schakespere joined the G. of K. in 1464 and the next enrolment is of Ralph and Isabella Schakespeire, who paid for Johanna's soul. These entries give no place of abode, but the date fits for Ralph of B. C.

(3) *Wroxall*. Almost the next G. of K. entry in 1464 to Ralph's is for Richard and Margery Schakespeire of W., probably Ralph's brother. In 1503–4 is the entry 'Orate pro anima Isabella Shakspere quondam priorissa de Wraxale'. There may be some error of date, since manor courts were held for Isabella on 17 Apr. 1501 and 3 Nov. 1507.[3] She may very well be the widow of Ralph of Baddesley Clinton. Dugdale, *Mon.*, iv. 89, names no prioress between Isabella Asteley (ob. 1431) and Jocosa Brome (resigned 1524). The earliest Sh. on the manor records is Elizabeth Shakspere, whose copyhold was forfeited for irregular alienation in 1417.[4] Richard and Margery alone bridge a gap to 1504–5 when land late of Robert Hutsped of Hatton (cf. s.v. Baddesley Clinton) was conveyed by William Shakespere of W. and John Shakespere of Rowington to charity trustees for W.[5] They were probably executors of Hutsped, and possibly sons of Richard and Margery. In 1515, on the other hand, a conveyance was taken for Wroxall charities by William Sh.

---

[1] Stopes, *Env.* 43, from *Ancient Indictments*, 650.

[2] H. Norris in *8 N.Q.* viii. 501.

[3] R.W. 90, 95.

[4] R.W. 71.

[5] R.W. 91.

of Rowington and others.[1] Evidently the two places
were closely connected. A William Shakespere, not necessarily the same as in 1504–5, with a wife Agnes and a son
whose name is lost, took a copyhold for their three lives
in 1530.[2] William is traceable, sometimes as Shakesepere,
on this holding to 1542. He is an archer in a muster roll
of 1536–7, and is on the subsidy rolls for 1542–4
(Schakespere) and (Shaxespere) as late as 10 Mar. 1546.[3]
It is reasonable to identify him and his wife with the
William and Agnes Shakspere, who joined the G. of K.
in 1526–7. This is one of a continuous group of unlocated Shakspere entries. The others are Richard and Alice,
and John and Johanna. They are followed by Richard
and Agnes Wodham and Richard and Anna Saunders.
Some family connexion is likely, and may extend to an
earlier entry in the same year for 'Domina Jane Shakspere'.
She was sub-prioress of Wroxall in 1525,[4] and is traceable
after the dissolution at Hatton. There were at least two
early Johns at W. John Shakspere took a copyhol l with
his wife Ellen and son Anthony in 1507.[5] He was dead
by 1530, when Ellen, then Cockes, and Anthony surrendered it.[6] Another John Shakespere died between
1532 and 1534, when a different holding reverted to the
lord for lack of a tenant.[7] One of these may have been the
John who once held land, belonging to the manor of
Hatton which was a 'member' of Wroxall, but situated
in Haseley (q. v.), and held after him by Richard Sh. and
Richard Wodham, under a twenty-year lease of 1 June
1523. I take it they were John's son and son-in-law, and
the two Richards of the 1526–7 G. of K. entries. This
John might be one of the Johns of Rowington (q. v.), holding land in both parishes, and the John of the same entries.
But it is also quite possible that he was a distinct John,
since Richard Schakespere is already on the subsidy roll for
18 Jan. 1525, which suggests that his father was then dead.[8]

---

[1] R.W. 149.   [2] R.W. 94.   [6] R.W. 94; cf. p. 18.
[3] R.W. 104, 107, 115, 116, 117,   [7] R.W. 95, 98.
118, 184; Brewer, xvii. 261; Y. 137.   [8] R.W. 92.
[4] R.W. 92.   [5] R.W. 95.

Richard was on manor juries in 1530 and 1532.[1] He was bailiff of the manor in 1534–5, but a successor was appointed on 4 Jan. 1535.[2] He was not, however, dead. He had in 1535–6 a copyhold at W., as well as his share in the Hatton lease, and is traceable on this to 1542.[3] He was a billman in 1536–7,[4] and a feoffee of the W. charities in 1539.[5] In 1539 he witnessed a will as Richard Shakyspear.[6] Yeatman 239 sqq. suggests that his wife Alice was the Alys Shakespere named as a sister in the will (1546) of Francis Griffin of Braybrook, Northants, and also (cf. App. A, no. ii) that he was the poet's grandfather. But Griffin does not say that his brother-in-law was a Richard or of Warwickshire, although there were Griffins in that county. And the ex-bailiff clearly ended his days, not at Snitterfield, but at Haseley (q. v.). Records of W. are sparse between the sale of the manor (other than Hatton) to the Burgoynes in 1542 to the beginning of the parish registers in 1586. A Robert Shackspeare was charity feoffee in 1559[7] and died in 1565, naming in his will (Shaxpere, Shaxspere) a wife Joan, son Nicholas, daughters Frances and Margaret, brothers-in-law Lone and Richard Yeman. A William Sh. prized his goods.[8] Both might be sons of the elder William. A John Shaxper, possibly a third son, died in 1575, naming in his will a son Edward, daughter Alice Windmills, brothers William and Nicolas, cousin Laurence of Balsall, brother-in-law James Woodham.[9] A Nicholas was charity feoffee in 1582 and 1592.[10] A Nicholas married Alice Edmunds in 1592, and had (Shaxper, Shaxpere, Saxper) several children, including a Peter, whose baptism is recorded at Hatton or Haseley, as well as at W. Elizabeth, wife of William, died in 1595. William made his will in 1609 and died by 1613.[11] It is not worth while giving full details of those later Shs. of W. who are traceable to 1665, and whose name was alive as that of a tenement in 1714.

[1] R.W. 93, 95.
[2] R.W. 103; Y. 134.
[3] R.W. 104, 107, 115, 117, 184; Brewer, xvii. 261.
[4] Y. 137.   [5] R.W. 150.
[6] R.W. 224.   [7] R.W. 152.
[8] R.W. 226; Y. 152.
[9] *Var.* ii. 18; Y. 153.
[10] R.W. 151, 152.
[11] *Var.* ii. 18; Y. 156.

(4) *Rowington*. John and Alice Shakespeyre joined the
G. of K. about 1460 and Thomas and Christiana Chacsper
in 1476. Richard Shakespeare surrendered a copyhold in
1467.[1] The William Sh. who was a feoffee for Wroxall
in 1515 is not traceable at Rowington itself, unless he is
one who had a 2*d.* cottage in 1548, which had passed to
another occupier by 1561. The commonest name is John.
A John Shakespere was a feoffee for Rowington charities
in 1485 and witnessed a deed in 1496.[2] He might be the
gildsman and Hutsped's executor (cf. Wroxall) of 1504–
5. On the other hand, the executor, but hardly the gildsman, might be a John Shaxpere 'the elder', who was on
the subsidy roll for 1523–4. That for 1524–5 shows a
John Shakespere and a John Schakespere the younger.
There is no Sh. on that for 1540.[3] But a John Shakespere
'the yong' was a charity feoffee in 1541.[4] The subsidy roll
for 1543 shows John, Thomas, Richard, and Lawrence;[5]
that for 1546 John Shaxespere only.[6] As at Wroxall,
the multiplicity of Johns is puzzling. But I think that one
of those in 1524–5 is the John who joined the gild (cf.
Wroxall) in 1526–7 with his wife Johanna, and that he
was the father of a younger John, who died in 1546. The
latter's will shows that two wives were dead and a mother
still alive.[7] A son John gets the residue, Nicolas land at
Bawdy Shorts (Beaudesert); Thomas is left to the care of
Thomas Cryar and his wife. There are three unnamed
daughters. Debts of a brother Nicolas Shaxspere and of
a Richard Sh., not said to be a brother, are forgiven. There
are legacies to Jane Shaxspere and to 'all the rest of my
brothers and sisters', after which is excised 'of Hatton'.
Nicholas Bird was an overseer, and a debt was owing by
Richard Bird. Now begins a series of surveys and rentals
which, with the aid of parochial documents and wills,
makes it possible to distinguish the descendants of this
John from other Sh. families in Rowington. They are of

[1] R.R. i. 45.
[2] R.R. i. 17, 22.
[3] R.R. i. 138, 139, 143.
[4] R.R. i. 27.

[5] Y. 142.
[6] R.R. i. 144.
[7] Y. (1906) 2.

28 Mar. 1548,[1] 10 Sept. 1561,[2] 6 Oct. 1590,[3] 24 Oct. 1604,[4] August 1606.[5] I give a conjectural pedigree:

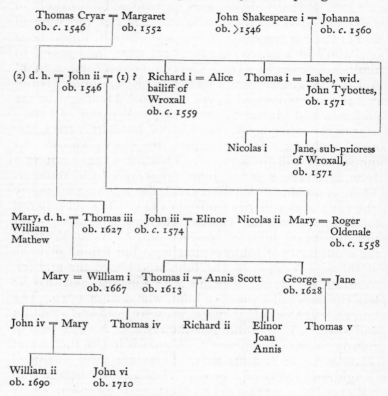

Most of this, but not the connexion with Richard the bailiff (cf. Wroxall, Haseley), is, I believe, fairly certain, although the reconstruction in Fripp, *Haunts*, 68, does not quite agree with mine. The family was of Mousley End. Here a copyhold called the Hill, with some forty acres of land, rented at 10s. 4d., formerly belonging to a John Shakyspere, was left by Roger Oldenale in 1557 or 1558 to his widow Mary, probably a daughter of John ii.[6] There

[1] R.R. i. 146.
[2] R.R. i. 151.
[3] Bellew, *New Place*, 98.

[4] R.R. i. 176, misdated 1605.
[5] H.P. *W. and W.* 143.
[6] R.R. i. 205, 221 ; Y. 145.

seems to have been a mortgage to William Bird, but the holding was recovered by John iii about 1562–3 by payment of a fine of 10s. 4d. and a heriot due on Bird's death.[1] A will of Mary Oldenale is said to have been sold with Sir T. Phillipps's manuscripts.[2] Her husband was a brother of John Oldenale, bailiff and lessee of the manor, whose son-in-law William Skinner, as owner of the tithes, became involved in disputes with John iii and other tenants. I only note this because John Sh. of Stratford served on a jury at Warwick in a resultant suit of 1569.[3] The Hill passed to Thomas ii, a mealman, who added land to it, and with his descendants it remained to the 18th century. With it went a small copyhold of a croft and seven acres, rented at 2s., in Lowston End, which John iii had in 1548 and had apparently transferred to Thomas ii by 1561. Another tenant at Mousley End in 1548 was Joan Shaxspere widow, occupying two copyholds, one rented at 3s. 8d., and a smaller one, called the Long Croft, at 2s. She had also a lease for her life of some land rented at 6s. 8d., called Lyance.[4] This belonged to a Rowington charity, but was in Hatton, which explains the reference to that place in the will of John ii. I take Joan to have been the widow of John i and mother of John ii, and the Johanna who, with a husband John, joined the G. of K. (cf. Wroxall) in 1526–7. She made a will, once at Worcester, but now lost, in 1557,[5] and probably died a little later, as her son Thomas i continued to pay rent for Lyance up to 1559–60. Thereafter it was held by John iii and his widow Elinor to 1578–9, when it went out of Sh. hands.[6] The 3s. 8d. copyhold had also gone by 1561. John iii had then Long Croft, and it passed to his younger son George, who had it in 1590 and 1604–6, and then to Thomas v. With it went a freehold called Madge Wattons in Shrewley (v. infra) left to George by the will of John iii in 1574.[7] John iii, as early as 1554, had taken a twenty-one-year

[1] R.R. i. 160.
[2] R.W. xxv.
[3] R.R. i. 41 ; Fripp, *Haunts*, 69.
[4] R.R. i. 28.
[5] Y. 143.
[6] R.R. ii, *passim*.
[7] R.R. i. 210.

lease of Rowington charity land known as Harvey's. This was renewed for another twenty-one years to his widow Elinor in 1576, and held after 1577–8 by Thomas ii.[1]

Long Croft, alone of the holdings of this family, is described in 1606 as 'Shackspeares ex antiquo'. Probably this does not mean much, as it is also said in 1561 to have been William Goodman's. I suspect that the family came from Wroxall and prospered in Rowington. They certainly acquired one property, more important than any yet mentioned. This was the only Sh. freehold in Rowington, a virgate called Brookfurlong at Lowston End, rented at 10s. 10d. It had been held under a charter of 1522 by Thomas Cryar, who with his wife Margaret joined the G. of K. in 1506. It is put down to John ii in 1548. He was in fact dead, but his executors may still have been in possession. It did not come to John iii, but to the son Thomas iii, left to the charge of the Cryars in John ii's will. Presumably John ii acquired it by a second marriage with their daughter, late in life. Thomas iii, unless a step is missing, held it in 1561, 1590, 1604, and 1606, and up to his death in 1627. If so, he must have been younger than his half-nephew Thomas ii, who is called 'senior' in 1606. By marriage with another heiress, Mary Mathew, he also acquired property in Claverdon, Shrewley, and Pinley. He is the Thomas Shaxpere of the list of Warwickshire freeholders in 1580,[2] and probably the Thomas Shaxspere, Shackespeare, and Schackspear of subsidy rolls for 1594, 1598, and 1599.[3] Fripp, *Haunts*, 78, describes his battle with Thomas Holt in 1601 about common rights at Bushwood in Lapworth.

Two other households, not obviously linked to those of Mousley End, can be traced from 1548. In Rowington or Wood End, a cottage and half-virgate was held, at 6s. 10d. and afterwards 6s. 8d., by John Shaxspere in 1548, John Shakisspere in 1561, Richard Shackspere in 1590, and John Shakespere or Shackspere in 1604–6. It is said to be 'Shacksperes ex antiquo', but had once belonged to Spencers. Richard was a turner, who died

[1] R.R. i. 30, 42; ii, *passim*.   [2] M.A. iii. 63.   [3] R.R. i. 169, 171.

in 1591–2, being then 'the elder', and naming in his will his wife Joan, sons John, Roger, Thomas, and William, grandson Thomas by John, daughter Dorothy Jenks, and sister Turner.[1] The widow Joan made her will in 1599.[2] A house and half-virgate in Back Lane at Church End, called Le Hilles, was held at 14s. in 1548 by another Richard Shaxspere, a weaver. He also leased from 1551–2 an acre of charity meadow known as Les Tyings. He appears in several wills, as Shax'spere, Shakspere, Shakysspere, and made his own and died in 1560, naming sons William and Richard, and brothers-in-law John and William Reve.[3] Fripp, *Haunts*, 68, gives his wife's name as Alice. The son Richard succeeded both to the copyhold and the lease, and held the former (Shakisspere, Shackespere, Shakespere, Schackspeare) in 1561, 1590, and 1604–6. This also was 'Schackspeares ex antiquo'. He made his will in 1613[4] and his widow Elizabeth hers in 1614,[5] and their sons William and John, the latter still a weaver, disputed the inheritance.[6]

A few early Shs. remain unattached. The Laurence of the 1543 subsidy roll was of Lowston End about 1559. He was fined for burdening the commons at a court of about 1562–3, and from 1554–62 leased at 4s. charity land known as the Hill Close, in which a Thomas followed him to 1587–8.[7] This was not one of the Mousley End family, but an 'old Thomas', traceable, apparently as a labourer, in 1585–6.[8] A Robert Shakespere was fined as a common brewer at a court of 1562–3.[9] The 17th-century Shs. of R. become too complicated to be worth disentangling. A William, who was a trained soldier in 1605, and who was identified by W. J. Thoms, *Three Notelets on Sh.* 113, with the poet, might be the son of Thomas iii of Brookfurlong, or the son of Richard the turner of Rowington End, or the son of Richard of Church End, or another.[10]

[1] Y. 156; *Var.* ii. 16.
[2] *Worcester Wills*, i. 408.
[3] R.R. i. 206, 209, 210; ii, *passim*; Y. (1906) 11.
[4] *Var.* ii. 16; Y. 156.
[5] *Worcester Wills*, ii. 62.
[6] Stopes, *Env.* 94.
[7] R.R. i. 160; ii. 4, 24, and *passim*.
[8] R.R. ii. 90, 91.
[9] R.R. i. 160.
[10] *Cal. S.P.D. Jac. I* (1603–10), 234.

(5) *Haseley*. The register (from 1538) now at Hatton seems to be common to that place, with its hamlets Beausale and Shrewley, and Haseley. Extracts are in Yeatman 168 and Stopes 124. Yeatman 287 says that he has given earlier in the book the will (temp. Hen. VIII) of Richard Sh., weaver of H., whom he supposes related to the Shs. of Tachbrook (q.v.). But he has not given it. The holding at Haseley of Richard of Wroxall (q. v.) did not pass to the Burgoynes, and Richard still held it with Richard Wodham in 1546–7, although the twenty-year lease of 1523 had expired.[1] He was on the jury for Hatton manor in 1551.[2] On 5 Oct. 1556[3] Nicholas Edwards, probably of Hatton, where a Richard Edwards is traceable before 1515,[4] wrote in reply to an inquiry from royal commissioners as to the bells of Wroxall Priory, that 'one Richard Shaxpeir, my neighbar and one of the tenants of Wroxall' had been instructed *c.* 1536 by the receiver and auditor to carry them to Studley. In 1559 was buried Roger Shakspere, and the will of 'Sur Roger Sadspere priest' dated 17 Feb. 1559 is witnessed by Richard Sadspere.[5] Roger had been a monk of Bordesley Abbey, Worcestershire, received a pension (Shaxsper) of 100*s.* at the dissolution, and became on 2 May 1549 incumbent (Shadspere) of Flyford Flavel, Worcestershire, where the next presentation was on 15 May 1560.[6] It is not likely that Richard the bailiff, traceable at Haseley to 1559, was, as Yeatman thinks, the Richard, traceable at Snitterfield (cf. App. A, no. ii) from 1528–9 to 1561, who was the poet's grandfather. In 1589 William Sh. married Barbara Stiffe, and the baptisms of children are in the register. William is described as 'gentleman'. His death is not recorded, but his wife's is in 1610. He was of Haseley, where a cottage in which he had dwelt was granted to another tenant in 1597.[7] He might be a son, or more likely grandson, of Richard.

---

[1] *Monastic Estates*, 20.
[2] Y. 144.
[3] R.W. 122.
[4] R.W. 149.

[5] Y. (1906) 8; *Worcester Wills*, i. 57.
[6] Nash, *Worc.* i. 456; ii. 407; French 356; Y. 192; Stopes 14.
[7] Stopes 122.

(6) *Hatton*. Shs. from Rowington (q.v.) held Lyance, now the Moat Farm, here from 1547 to 1578; and several entries in the register may be of this family. One can be sure of that for 21 Oct. 1571, 'mortua et sepulta erat Domina Jana aliquando una monicarum Wraxall'. Possibly Thomas i is the Thomas whose wife Isabel, formerly wife of John Tybotes, was buried on 4 Apr. 1570. Possibly his brother is the Nicolas whose daughter Katharine was baptized on 5 Nov. 1570. There were Nicolases of Wroxall (q.v.), however, about this date, who had some connexion with either Hatton or Haseley. But Nicolas and Elizabeth, whose son Thomas was baptized on 8 Sept. 1593, were buried in 1607 and 1608 as of Beausale in Hatton.

(7) *Shrewley*, in Hatton. (8) *Pinley*. (9) *Beaudesert*. (10) *Claverdon*. For S. holdings in these places, cf. Rowington. (11) *Budbrooke, with Hampton Corley*; cf. App. A.

(12) *Warwick*. There are no early notices. Thomas Shaxper, shoemaker, died in 1577. His will leaves his widow Agnes freebench in a copyhold on the manor of Balsall, and names sons William, Thomas, John, and a daughter Joan, wife of Francis Ley.[1] Conceivably he might be Thomas i of the family at Mousley End, Rowington, to whose brother John ii a Roger Ley was executor. Joan Ley died in 1577.[2] Probably all the remaining Warwick notices belong to his sons. On 6 June 1579 'sepultus fuet Gulielmus Saxspere, qui demersus fuet in rivulo aquae qui vel quae vocatur Avona'.[3] John and Thomas were assessed for poor rate in 1582.[4] Thomas took a copyhold in Smith St. in 1585.[5] He bought other property in Warwick in 1597, married Elizabeth Letherbarrow, daughter of the mayor of Coventry, in 1598, and was bailiff of Warwick in 1612.[6] In 1601–2 he acquired land in Bishop's Tachbrook.[7] He is described as a butcher in the record of his son John's apprenticeship to William Jaggard the London stationer, which extended from

---

[1] *Var.* ii. 19; Hunter, i. 14; *Worcester Wills*, i. 248.

[2] Stopes 131.

[3] H.P., *1848*, 5, from register of St. Nicholas; *Worcester Wills*, i. 259.

[4] T. Kemp, *Book of John Fisher*, 81.

[5] Bellew 97, misdescribed as in Stratford.

[6] Stopes 131.   [7] *Var.* ii. 19.

March 1610 to 22 May 1617.[1] John does not seem to have printed or published for himself. Thomas Shakespeare, gent., is a principal burgess of Warwick in the *Visitation*[2] of 1619, and made his will in 1632.[3]

(13) *Bishop's Tachbrook*. Roger Shakesspere had a son Roger in 1557 and buried a daughter Alice in 1559. He married Agnes Steward of Haseley in the same year and had a daughter Anne in 1560 and a son John born and buried (Shaskespeare) in 1574. He had also (Shaxpere) a daughter Isabel, who married Thomas Turner in 1593. He was buried (Shakespeare) as a weaver in 1592 and his widow, here Anne, in 1599. His son Roger Shaxpear married Isabel Parkins in 1592 and (Shaxpere) Alice Higgins in 1595, by whom he had a son John in 1596, alive when Roger made his will in 1605.[4] No connexion with Thomas of Warwick (q.v.) is apparent.

(14) *Lapworth*. William Shorte married Alice Shackespere in 1564. George Sh. had a daughter Anne in 1586 and a son Richard in 1590. John Shackespere had a daughter Elizabeth in 1595.[5]

(15) *Packwood*. Christopher and Isabella Shakespere joined the G. of K. in 1511–12. Christopher Shakspeyre is mentioned in a document of 1528. Petters, in his tenure and that of his sons William and John, was granted to William Sheldon in 1544. He is on the subsidy rolls for 1548–9 and 1549–50, and died *c.* 1558. A will of 1551 leaves his copyhold Hancoxe to William, and names his wife Isabel, other sons Richard, Roger, Christopher, and John, daughters Alice and Agnes, and son-in-law William Featherstone.[6]

(16) *Tanworth*. Christopher Shakespeare held charity lands in 1553.[7]

(17) *Knowle*. A manorial rental of 22 Sept. 1612 shows Elizabeth Shaksper a copyholder.[8] I note here for con-

---

[1] *Var.* ii. 73; Arber, iii. 684.
[2] *Harl. Soc.* xii. 183.
[3] *Worcester Wills*, ii. 146.
[4] E. T. Codd in *3 N.Q.* viii. 185; Y. 161, from *Lichfield Wills*.
[5] *Var.* ii. 17; Hudson, *Lapworth*, 140, 146.
[6] H.P. *Rarities*, 246; Brewer, xix. 1. 77; Y. 161; Miller, i. 148.
[7] *C.P.R. Ed. VI*, v. 29.
[8] *Greville Papers* 4612 at Warwick Castle.

venience two unlocated entries of payments for the souls of Thomas Schakspere and Thomas Shakspere to the G. of K. in 1486.

(18) *Barston*. Ralph Shakespere was a juror for Barston in 1547. He had a wife Bridget, who surrendered a meadow with a daughter Elizabeth Buttrey. He is on the subsidy roll for Barston and Ascote in 1546–7.[1]

(19) *Berkswell*. A Ralph Shakspere is on the subsidy roll for 1524–5 and a Ralph, not necessarily the same, in 1570–1. A Ralph is also on the manor jury in 1550–1.[2] The same family may have held at Barston and Berkswell.

(20) *Hampton in Arden*. Elizabeth, widow of Roger Sh. of Chesset Wood, was his administratrix in 1597.[3]

(21) *Coventry*. Cf. p. 355 for an early record of 1359. In 1416 William Sturdy of C. slew a Richard Shakspere there.[4] A Robert Shakespier was of the Corpus Christi gild in 1489.[5] A Richard Shakespere had a legacy from John Dwale in 1500.[6] Henry, William, and John Shs. are traceable during 1583–1606. William made his will in 1606 as a shoemaker.[7]

(22) *Alcester*. Thomas Shakspere is on the subsidy roll for 1522–3. He was manor bailiff in 1530–1 and appears in rolls for 1531–2 and 1532–3.[8] He may be the Thomas Sikestaffe, billman, of a muster roll for 1536–7.[9] He made his will in 1539, naming a father Richard and mother Margaret, both alive, a wife Margaret with a son Alexander Fox, and a son William.[10] Hunter made this Richard the poet's grandfather.

(b) *Cambridgeshire*.

Alice Langham of Snailwell left legacies to William Shakespere 'pauperi' of S. and his wife Agnes by a will of 1449.[11]

---

[1] R.W. 230; Y. 160.

[2] Y. 160.

[3] C. Hopper in *Herald and Genealogist*, i. 265, from *P.C.C.*

[4] *N.Q.* cxlvii. 188, from *Coram Rege Roll* 655, m. 116.

[5] M. D. Harris in *Trans. Bristol and Glouc. Arch. Soc.* xxxvii. 190.

[6] Stopes 8, from *P.C.C.*

[7] M. D. Harris in *11 N.Q.* v. 24, 104, 406; Stopes 125, from *Lichfield Wills*.

[8] J. H. Bloom, *Ancient Warw. Deeds*, from *Greville Rolls*, 208, 209, 210b.   [9] Y. 192.

[10] Hunter, i. 9; *Worcester Wills*, i. 96, proved at Stratford-on-Avon.

[11] C.S. *Bury Wills*, 12.

(c) *Derbyshire.*

John Shakespere was of Derby in 1544–5 [1] and Elizabeth of St. Werberg's, Derby, in a will of 1558, names a sister Grace and cousins Alice Shepherd and Jane Firebrace.[2]

(d) *Gloucestershire.*

A Thomas Shakespeir, Shakespeire, Schaftspere, Sheftspere, Shafftespere occurs in several Bristol wills about 1501. In one he is Sir Thomas and a curate.[3] James Sh. was buried at Bisley on 13 Mar. 1570. The Shs. of Dursley (cf. vol. i, p. 25) are not traceable before 3 Mar. 1678, when Thomas, a weaver, married Joan Turner. They had children Edward, Mary (two), and Thomas, and Shs. were still at Dursley to 1754. In 1848 there was a 'Shakespeare's Walk' at Dursley, and a 'tradition' of the poet's residence. Shs. are also traceable at Beverston in the 17th century, and at Newington Bagpath, where a John made his will in 1624, and there were freeholders of the name in 1848 who claimed kinship with the poet.[4]

(e) *Leicestershire.*

William Shakespare of Walton on the Wolds is on the subsidy roll for 1544–5 and William of Waltham on the Wolds, a distinct place, is husbandman in a deed of 1553.[5] Thomas Sh. was of Lutterworth in 1597 and of Staple Inn in 1604 and 1607. He is named in a letter about the affairs of Newark Hospital in Leicester as 'of Lutterworth gent' in 1611, and wrote to the mayor of Leicester to protest against visitors to Lutterworth from plague-stricken Leicester in 1609–11. In 1613 he was deputy-steward of Lutterworth.[6]

(f) *Nottinghamshire.*

Robert Shakespeyr was licensed to trade at Nottingham in 1414–15, and Robert Shakesper had a suit for the price

[1] Hunter, i. 9.
[2] Y. 161.
[3] T. P. Wadley, *Notes on Bristol Wills* (Bristol and Glouc. Arch. Soc.).
[4] 1848, R. W. Huntley, *Glossary of the Cotswold Dialect*; 1877, J. H. Blunt, *Dursley and its Neighbourhood.*
[5] 11 *N.Q.* vi. 228, 429.
[6] French 542; H. Stocks, *Records of Leicester*, iii. 111, 119; Stopes, *Ind.* 270.

of wood sold for making arrows in 1443.[1] Sir Thomas
Chaworth of Wiverton, by his will of 16 Jan. 1459 in
Testamenta Eboracensia (Surtees Soc.), ii. 228, directed his
feoffees to manumit Margery Shakesper among other
'bandmen and whamen' who had done him long service,
and left her six marks towards her marriage. George
Shakspere sued for two rosaries at Nottingham in 1533.[2]
Richard Shakesper was of Mansfield early in the reign of
Hen. VIII, and Peter Schakespeyr in 1544–5.[3] A Peter
Shakespur was a trained soldier there in 1596–7.[4]

(g) *Yorkshire.*

The will, dated 31 Oct. 1433, of John Shakespere, chapman, of Doncaster, with a wife Johanna is in *Testamenta
Eboracensia (Surtees Soc.)*, ii. 32.

(h) *Ireland.*

Thomas Shakespere is on a muster roll of troops under
Henry Lord Grey taken near Conway on 27 Aug. 1478.[5]

(i) *London.*

William Schakesper by a will of 1413 desired burial in
the Hospital of St. John.[6] Peter Shakespeare witnessed
a Southwark deed in 1484.[7] John Shakesper, also Shakespers, had a lease in the sanctuary at Westminster shortly
before 1506.[8] William Shakespert was buried at St.
Margaret's, Westminster, on 30 Apr. 1539. A later hand
in the register comments, 'Query if this be the poet or
not'![9] Roger Schackespere was appointed yeoman of the
guard in 1547 and is traceable to 1555–6.[10] Thomas Sh.,
minister, of St. Mildred's, Bread St., received a grant of 100s.
a year in 1548. He made a will (Shackespere) in 1557,

[1] W. Stevenson, *Records of N.* ii.
102, 180.
[2] Stevenson iii, 188.
[3] Hunter, i. 9.
[4] Stevenson, iii. 188; iv. 244.
[5] French 350, from *Misc. of Receipt
of Exchequer*, 39. 18.
[6] Stopes 9, from *Commissary Court*

of London Wills, ii, f. 12.
[7] French 356, from deed at Cord-
wainers' Hall.
[8] E. J. L. Scott in 1900 *Athenæum*,
i. 219, from *Sacrist Rolls*.
[9] A. M. Burke, *Registers*, 373.
[10] Brewer, xxii. 2. 406; Stopes, *Ind.*
271.

being then a priest living in Jesus Commons, Dowgate Hill, Essex, and names brothers Robert, Harry Willson, John Cooke, and sisters Joan, Grace Starke, and Cecily Richardson. A later will of 1559 names sisters Joan, Thomasina Cooke, Grace Stourton, Anne Willson.[1] Matthew Shakspere married Isabel Peelle of Christ Church, Newgate, possibly a relative of the dramatist, on 5 Feb. 1569. Presumably this is the Matthew, the births and deaths of whose children occur in the register of St. James's, Clerkenwell, from 18 Jan. 1570 to 7 Apr. 1583.[2] Thomas Shakspere (also Shakespare) is traceable as a Messenger of the Chamber from 1571 to 1577.[3] John Shackspere married Dorothea Dodde at St. Martin-in-the-Fields on 22 Jan. 1590. A daughter Maria was christened in 1593. Dorothea died in 1608. John is long traceable as a leading parishioner, and may be a John buried in 1646.[4] John Shakspear married Mary Godtheridg in St. Clement Danes on 3 Feb. 1605 and had a long family there. The variation of spelling in the registers is notable. Shaxbee, Shaksbye, Shakesby, Shasper, Shakespeer, Shakspeer, Shackspeer occur as well as more normal forms. An entry of the burial of Jane daughter of William on 8 Aug. 1609 is probably a slip, as John had a daughter Jane a year before. John was buried in 1633 as 'the King's Bitmaker'. Many payments to him for bits and spurs are found in royal and private accounts from 1617 onwards. Here he even appears as Shasspeere and Sashpierre.[5] There are no obvious links between any one of these London families and another, or between any of them and the poet. It is a mere guess by Mrs. Stopes that the bitmaker was the son of Thomas of Snitterfield (App. A, no. i). She also suggests that it was the bitmaker and not the poet who furnished Rutland's *impresa* of 1613 (App. A, no. xxii). Edmund

[1] Stopes 139, from *Auditors' Patent Books*, vi, and *P.C.C.* 40, Chayney; A.C. Veley in *Trans. Essex Arch. Soc.* iii. 70.

[2] *Harl. Soc. Registers*; 2 *Gen.* xii. 223.

[3] Halliwell-Phillipps, *Marriage of Wit and Wisdom*, 118; *Archaeologia*, xiii. 403; Stopes 144.

[4] *Harl. Soc. Registers*; Stopes 145.

[5] Collier, i. 469; Stopes 146, *Env.* 229, *Ind.* 272; Halliwell-Phillipps, *Marriage of Wit and Wisdom*, 120; H. Southam in *N.Q.* cxlvii. 334.

Shakespeare of Southwark and probably of Cripplegate was the poet's brother (App. A, no. i) and John of Warwick (p. 365) was apprenticed in London.

III. SPELLING AND SIGNIFICANCE
OF THE NAME

The notices collected in this and other appendixes and in the records of John Shakespeare [1] yield eighty-three spellings of the name. They may be classified as follows:

Shakespeare, Shakespear, Shakespere, Shakesspere, Shakesper, Shakespers, Shakespeer, Shakespeyre, Shakespeire, Shakespeyr, Shakespeir, Shakespeye, Shakespare, Shakesepere, Shakespheare, Shakespur, Shakespert, Shakesby.

Shakspeare, Shakspear, Shakspere, Shaksper, Shaksperr, Shakspeer, Shakspeyre, Shakspeyr, Shakkespere, Shakispere, Shakisspere, Shakyspear, Shakysspere, Shakysper, Shakyspeyr, Shaksbye.

Shackespeare, Shackespear, Shackespere, Shackesper, Shackspere, Shacksper, Shackspeere, Shackspeer.

Schakespere, Schakesper, Schakespeire, Schakespeyr, Schakspere, Schacosper.

Schackspear, Schackspere.

Shaxpeare, Shaxpear, Shaxpere, Shaxper, Shaxpeir, Shaxbere, Shaxberd, Shaxspere, Shaxsper, Shax'spere, Shaxespere, Shaxver, Shaxbee.

Shexpere, Shexspere, Shexsper.

Sakesper, Sakspere, Saxpere, Saxper, Saxspere.

Shaskespeare, Sheakspear, Shagspere, Shasper, Shasspeere, Sashpierre.

Shadspere, Sadspere.

Schaftspere, Shafftespere, Sheftspere.

Chacsper.

A few others, which are late or need verification, are

given by French 348 and Ingleby, i. 6. Some of the forms
may be merely scribal eccentricities or may rest on misreadings. Thus the Shaxberd of the Revels account (App.
D) for 1604–5 may derive from Shaxbere, which is found
for John S. in a deed of 1573.[1] The Shagspere of the
poet's marriage bond (App. A, no. v) is rare. The Shaksperr and Sheakspear of the Scottish Drummond or his
18th-century transcribers (App. B, no. xxii) are abnor-
malities. Shakespear, dear to the 18th century, is not yet
common. Forms without 'h' in the first member are
unusual, but occur among the earliest records. Those
in Shack-, Schak-, Shax- are nearly as common as
those in Shake- and Shak-. In the Sadspere and Shadspere of the monk of Bordesley, who is, however, also Shaxsper, in the Schaftspere and similar alternatives for Sir
Thomas of Bristol, and in the -bye, -bee variants of St.
Clement Danes, to which there are analogous forms in
17th-century Essex,[2] we almost see distinct names bud-
ding off. And there is even a more curious permutation
much earlier, since Richard Shakespeare clearly appears
also in the Snitterfield court rolls as both Shakeschafte and
Shakstaff (App. A, no. ii). Similarly an Alcester Shakespeare seems to appear as Sikestaffe. Shakeshaft is not an
uncommon name. I have noted examples in several parts
of the country from 1423 to 1545.[3] In the last of these
a Shakeschaft and a Shakestaff hold land together in
Shropshire. A John Shakeshaft is at Balsall in 1543–
9.[4] The variants are clearly not a matter of differing
family usage. To take a brief example (App. A, no. i),
Margaret Sakspere, wife of Henry Shakspere, is buried
at Snitterfield in 1597, and Henry is also Shakespeare,
Shakespere, Shakesper, Shaxper, Shaxspere, Saxspere,
Shagspere. Indeed the same man's name is often variously
spelt in a single document. But an accustomed scribe
sometimes has his own preference. John Shakespeare gets
at least a score of the forms. There is an appearance of

---

[1] H.P. ii. 232.
[2] Stopes 140.
[3] R. R. Sharpe, *London Letterbooks*,

K 29; Brewer, ii. 1. 51; iv. 2. 2227;
v. 628; xix. 2. 420; xx. 2. 456, 542.
[4] Yeatman 160.

a fairly uniform Shakspere in the register, but this, up to
1600, is a transcript in a single hand. One town official,
Richard Symons, nearly always makes him Shakspeyr;
another, Henry Rogers, is less uniform, but tends to Shaxpeare. Unfortunately John was a marksman, and we do not
know how he spelt his own name. The poet's own spelling
(cf. vol. i, p. 504) seems to have been usually Shakspere,
sometimes in an abbreviated form, but the main signature
to the will is Shakspeare. The epistles to *Ven. & Ad.* and
Lucrece are subscribed Shakespeare, and this is the form used
in F 1 and in nearly all the Qq. Occasionally it is hyphenated
Shake-speare. *Love's Lab. Lost* (Q1) has Shakespere,
K. Lear (Q1) Shak-speare, *Yorkshire Tragedy* (Q1) and
T.N.K. Shakspeare. In literary references and in official
documents written in London, Shakespeare is also pre-
dominant, although by no means invariable. In documents
of Stratford origin it is otherwise. Here the forms in Shack-
and Shax- rather markedly prevail. The poet's cousin,
Thomas Greene, however, writes (App. A, no. xix) Shakspeare, and this is the form on the monument. On those
of his wife, daughter, and son-in-law it is Shakespeare.

Shakespeare's admirers, like the heralds in devising his
arms, no doubt gave the name a heroic significance.
Camden, *Remaines* (1605), 111, says that men derived
names 'from that which they commonly carried, as Palmer,
that is, Pilgrime, for that they carried Palme when they
returned from Hierusalem, Long-sword, Broad-speare,
Fortescu, that is, Strong-shield, and in some such respect,
Breake-speare, Shake-Speare, Shotbolt, Wagstaffe'. He is
followed by Richard Verstegan, *Restitution of Decayed Intelligence* (1605), 294, John Done, *Polydoron* (1631), 9, and
in special relation to the poet by Thomas Fuller, *Worthies*
(1662), *Warwick*, 126, who compares him to Martial, 'in
the *Warlike* sound of his Sur-name (whence some may
conjecture him of a *Military extraction*,) *Hasti-vibrans*, or
Shake-speare'. Jonson's verses pun on 'break a lance', and
Thomas Bancroft, *Epigrammes* (1639), cxix writes:

> Thou so hast us'd thy Pen, (or shocke thy Speare)
> That Poets startle, nor thy wit come neare.

It must not be assumed that every mention of shaking a spear in Elizabethan literature is a covert allusion to Shakespeare. The phrase is common in Spenser. Camden's philology may not be sound, although the name Fewterspere affords an analogy. Some rather absurd guesses at alternative derivations have been made, which it is not necessary to record. Adams 3 argues for an origin in the Norman Sakeespée, which he finds in the English forms Sakespeie, Sakespey, Syakespeye, Saxpey, Shakespeie from 1260 onwards. If he is right, the Simon Shakespeye of Gloucestershire in 1261 is a link. But a misspelling here for Shakespeyre is also possible, and in any case Adams is hardly justified in identifying this Simon with the contemporary Simon Sakesper of Essex. A. F. Heintz suggests that the name originated by translation from that of Levelaunce or Lyvelaunce, which he finds in Warwickshire from the 12th to the 14th century, and that Shakelaunce, which appears on the Hundred Rolls for Northants in 1274–5, may be an intermediate form.[1] And he notes as analogous the occurrence of Briselaunce and Breakspear together on Herts. subsidy rolls in 1325–6. He believes Lyvelaunces to have lived at Lyance in Hatton. This, however, would not help his argument, as the Shakespeares found there clearly came in the 16th century from a neighbouring village. On the other hand, the Shakespeares, so far as the records go, show no obvious signs of belonging to the spear-using class. The only ones known to have held land by military tenure are Adam and his kin of Baddesley Clinton, and that probably not from an earlier date than 1389. Mostly they are copyholders; some freeholders. There are hints of serfdom. Henry Bradley proposed a more humble derivation from the A.S. personal name Seaxberht, and compared Winfarthing from Wineferhth and Allfarthing from Ealhferhth.[2] If so, Shaxberd, although probably only by an accident, becomes the nearest representative of the original form. But I owe to Mr. K. Sisam the criticisms that (*a*) West Saxon *seax* would not, as a rule and in wide

[1] 1916, Apr. 20, *T.L.S.*   [2] 1887, Feb. 5, *Academy.*

areas, yield *Sh-*, and (*b*) *-berht* would not yield *-bere* and still less *-pere*, and probably would yield dental forms, such as *-bright*, *-brith*, which do not appear. The Shack-, Shax-forms suggest that the original short vowel of an imperative *scac* may have often been retained in pronunciation.

IV. THE CASE OF HUGH SAUNDER

Attention was called to this case by G. C. Brodrick, *Memorials of Merton College* (1885, *O.H.S.*), 242. The facts are fully given in H. E. Salter, *Registrum Annalium Collegii Mertonensis* (1923, *O.H.S.*), xxxiv, xliii, 96, 98, 334, 370. There was an election of Fellows on 8 Apr. 1487, 'In qua electione electi sunt . . . dominus Hugo Shakspere, Wigorniensis diocesis'. On 23 June 1487, 'Admissi sunt in communas collegii sex baccallarii nouiter electi, scilicet . . . Hugo Sawnder alias dictus Shakspere, sed mutatum est istud nomen eius, quia vile reputatum est'. Saunder became M.A. in 1490 and D.D. in 1501. He held many college offices and was *Rex Fabarum* for the Christmas of 1501–2, when he resigned his Fellowship on taking the vicarship of Meopham in Kent.[1] In April 1507 he was rector of Mixbury in Oxfordshire. In 1507 and again in 1508 he was one of three named to the Archbishop of Canterbury as suitable for the Wardenship of Merton, but was not chosen. In March 1513 he became rector of St. Mary's, Whitechapel, and was also rector of Gestingthorpe in Essex. He became Canon of St. Paul's on 25 Nov. 1517 and died before 3 Nov. 1537. A will is at Somerset House. In the Bishop of London's *Register* he appears as 'Saunder alias Shakespere alias Brakespere'. The Brakespere is unexplained. It seems (cf. *supra*) to have been a distinct name from Shakespeare. The name Saunders, variously spelt, is common in the records of Rowington, Wroxall, and the neighbourhood. The Gild of Knowle register gives many examples from 1460 to 1527. One follows a group of related Shakespeare entries.[2] I do not find a Hugh. The worthy Fellow perhaps did not know the

---

[1] Cf. *Med. Stage*, i. 260, 407.   [2] Cf. p. 357.

variant Saunder-Knaue, which is in a Tamworth subsidy list of 1332.

There are other examples of such changes of name in the Merton records. One who had been elected Fellow as Robert Barbour in 1484 became Robert Dale during 1488–9. Here there is no comment in the *Register*. Robert Dykke was elected Fellow in June 1492 and on 28 October was received into commons as 'Robertus Dykke, alias dictus Robertus Hyll, et ita appellatus in collegio'.[1] A possible explanation of the 'vile nomen' may be that Hugh Shakespeare was, like Margery of Wiverton, of a bondman family, and had fled his village or had been manumitted on taking orders. On 21 Sept. 1312 Richard de Kellawe, Bishop of Durham, manumitted Walter de Heghington, clerk, because 'ascribi desideras militiae clericali', and there is a note in the register that on the same day 'habuit magister Robertus de Heghington, Scolaris Aulae de Merton in Oxoniis, quandam literam libertatis sub eadem formula'.[2] Robert de Hegynton was a Fellow of Merton by 1310.[3]

[1] Salter, xliii. 159, 167.
[2] J. Raine, *Depositions and other Ecclesiastical Proceedings from the*
Courts of Durham (1845, Surtees Soc.), 5.
[3] Brodrick 192.

APPENDIX F

SHAKESPEAREAN FABRICATIONS

A list of forgeries, certain or suspected, will be useful. Most of them have long been exposed, but some occasionally still appear in the writings of persons whose historical equipment is imperfect. The list is limited, in the main, to those directly concerned with Shakespeare or his company and theatres. A few others are referred to in *Eliz. Stage*, i. 59; ii. 79, 159, 229, 515; iii. 247, 252, 266, 267, 273, 292, 421, 423, 425, 426, 428, 434, 512; iv. 1.

I. LEWIS THEOBALD (1688–1744)

Theobald is sometimes thought to have fabricated his ascription to Shakespeare of *The Double Falsehood* (1727), which he claimed to have revised from manuscript versions. The play is discussed in Chapter X.

II. CHARLES MACKLIN (*c.* 1697–1797)

In April 1748, Macklin communicated to the *General Advertiser* some anecdotes on Shakespeare, Ben Jonson, and Ford, as from a Caroline pamphlet which he had lost on a voyage from Ireland. These were accepted by Steevens,[1] but Malone[2] showed them to be a fabrication.

III. WILLIAM RUFUS CHETWOOD (ob. 1766)

Chetwood first appears as a bookseller in 1720. He became prompter about 1722 at Drury Lane, and wrote several plays, of which A. Nicoll, *Early Eighteenth Century Drama*, 306, gives a list. About 1741 he became prompter at the Smock Alley Theatre, Dublin, got into financial difficulties, and was a prisoner for debt in the King's Bench (1741), and at Dublin (1760). His *General History*

---

[1] 1778, i. 219.   [2] 1790, i. 1. 387; *Var.* i. 402.

of the Stage (Dublin, 1749) is chiefly concerned with the
Irish stage, but contains (cf. App. C, no. xxxvii) the first
specific statement that Sir William Davenant was supposed to be Shakespeare's son. His *British Theatre* (Dublin, 1750, London, 1752) has a life of Shakespeare. It is
mainly based on Rowe, but gives, as from the dialogue
between a groom and a country girl at the beginning of
R. Armin's *Two Maids of Moreclacke*,[1] fabricated lines in
which the groom says that he was

> born where late our Swan of Avon sung
> In Avon's Streams, we both of us have lave'd.

The life is followed by a bibliography of Shakespeare's
plays, which includes many imaginary early editions of
impossible dates and bearing long descriptive sub-titles.
These editions, Chetwood says, 'from the reputed Modesty
of Shakespear, we may suppose had pompous titles given
to them by the editors'. The list, with a life reduced to
three lines, is reproduced in *Theatrical Records* (1756), of
which a copy is in the Bodleian, and also, according to
Greg,[2] who calls it 'a work of abundant fancy and some
humour', in *An Apology for the Life of Colley Cibber* (4th ed.
1756) and in *The Playhouse Pocket Companion* (1779).

Malone conjectured (cf. App. C, no. xvi) that Chetwood
was also the author of a manuscript history of the stage,
written between April 1727 and October 1730, and 'full
of forgeries and falsehoods of various kinds'. The manuscript is not now known.

IV. GEORGE STEEVENS (1736–1800)

The contributions of Steevens to Shakespearean learning
were substantial and valuable. But he had a devil of per-
versity, which sufficiently accounts for Gifford's description of him as 'the Puck of commentators'. He is said to
have ascribed his notes on the more indecent passages of
Shakespeare to two clergymen, Richard Amner and John
Collins, who had offended him. Nor do I think that he
can have been altogether serious when he wrote on the

---

[1] *Eliz. Stage*, iii. 210.   [2] *M.S.C.* i. 337.

'parish top' in *Twelfth Night*, i. 3. 44, to be solemnly followed by later annotators down to the *Arden* edition, 'This is one of the old customs now laid aside. A large top was formerly kept in every village, to be whipped in frosty weather, that the peasants may be kept warm by exercise, and out of mischief, while they could not work.' Whether he was ever responsible for a deliberate fabrication is less clear. Some of the dupes of the Ireland forgeries seem to have accused him of being behind them; and Collier hinted that he had had opportunities of tampering with the Bridgewater documents.[1] But these are the wild charges of entrapped persons. Three points need closer consideration.

(*a*) Lee [2] ascribes to Steevens, following I. Disraeli, *Curiosities of Literature*, vi (1823), 39, a fabricated letter from Peele to 'Henrie Marle', with an account of a discussion of *Hamlet* between Shakespeare and Alleyn at the Globe. This first appeared in an anonymous life of Alleyn in the *Theatrical Review* (1763), i. 61. Here the writer says, 'A gentleman of honour and veracity, in the commission of the peace for Middlesex, has shown us a letter dated in the year 1600, which he assures us has been in the possession of his family, by the mother's side, for a long series of years, and which bears all the marks of antiquity'. The letter was reproduced in the *Annual Register* (1770), in John Berkenhout's *Biographia Literaria* (1777), 399, and many times thereafter. The *Biographia Literaria* omits the date 1600 and has the note, 'Whence I copied this letter, I do not recollect; but I remember that at the time of transcribing it, I had no doubt of its authenticity'. Disraeli ascribes this note, and with it the authorship of the letter, to Steevens, and assumes that he suppressed the date, because he had discovered that Peele had died before 1600. But why should the note be by Steevens, rather than by Berkenhout himself? It is true that in his preface Berkenhout acknowledges indebtedness to Steevens for 'several manuscript notes on the lives of our poets'. But

---

[1] D. T. B. Wood in *R.E.S.* i. 172.   in *Sh. and the Modern Stage*, 188; *Life*,
[2] *A Peril of Shakespearean Research*   646.

he certainly does not ascribe all the numerous notes in the *Biographia* to him. And is not Steevens likely to have known in 1763 that Marlowe, if he is meant, was dead in 1600?

(*b*) C. M. Ingleby, *Centurie of Praise*, 410, suggested that Steevens had fabricated the lines by Shakespeare and Jonson which he gave from a manuscript by Oldys (cf. App. C, no. xxxiv). There is no obvious ground for this.

(*c*) According to Steevens, the names Othello and Iago occur in the Argument to the Eighth History in John Reynolds's *God's Revenge Against Adultery*, and may have come to both Shakespeare and Reynolds from a lost tale.[1] This work was an appendix to Reynolds's *God's Revenge against Murder* (1621), and was added to the sixth edition of 1679 by Samuel Pordage. A failure to find the names in an altered version of 1708, or in the work of Reynolds himself, has led to the suggestion of a fabrication.[2]

V. FRANCIS WISE (1695–1767)

Wise was under-keeper of the Bodleian (1719), keeper of the archives (1726), and Radcliffe librarian (1748). He contributed material to Thomas Warton's *Life of Sir Thomas Pope* (1772), which rests upon fabrications, although it is not clear that they were his own.[3] Perhaps, therefore, his Shakespearean communications to Warton (App. C, no. xliii) may not have been altogether trust-worthy.

VI. JOHN JORDAN (1770–90)

Jordan was a self-educated man of literary tendencies. He probably embroidered the crab-tree story, and was responsible for the enlarged form of the Lucy ballad (App. C, no. xlvi). But there is no reason to believe him capable of any fabrication which required scholarly knowledge, and I cannot believe that he was responsible for the text of John Shakespeare's 'spiritual will'. Much of our informa-

---

[1] *Var*. ix. 214.
[2] E. Engel in *J*. xxxv. 272.
[3] H. E. D. Blakiston in *E.H.R.* xi. 282.

tion as to this, however, comes through him, and extracts from his letters and Malone's on the subject are conveniently given in H.P. ii. 399. On 14 June 1784 he sent a copy to the *Gentleman's Magazine*, which was not printed. About 1789 the original, of which the first leaf was missing, was sent to Malone by Mr. Payton of Shottery, an alderman of Stratford, through James Davenport, the vicar. It had been found, some twenty years before, by Joseph Mosely, a master bricklayer, in retiling the western house in Henley St., then occupied by Thomas Hart, and was given by him to Payton. Mosely was dead, but both his daughter and Hart remembered the discovery. Malone accepted the fragment as genuine and printed it (1790 ed., i. 2. 161). Before the book was printed off, he was able to add (i. 2. 330) the contents of the first leaf from a copy ascribed to Mosely. Presumably this was sent him by Jordan (cf. p. 293). Malone, however, was not altogether satisfied, and made further inquiries of Jordan, who said that the copy of the first leaf was made by him, and that the original of this bore the date of Mosely's discovery on 29 Apr. 1757. Mosely had expressed an intention of giving this also to Payton. There are some slight discrepancies in Jordan's letters from other statements about the document, but nothing to throw any doubt on his bona fides. I think that this correspondence was after Malone had printed the additional fragment. In his *Inquiry* (1796), 195, Malone rejected the will, not apparently as a forgery, but as connected with Shakespeare, saying, 'I have since obtained documents that clearly prove it could not have been the composition of any one of our poet's family, as will be fully shewn in his Life'. In *Var.* ii. 517 this is substantially repeated, but Boswell adds in a note that he could not discover the documentary evidence referred to in the *Inquiry*, but thought that Malone might have had the identification of John the shoemaker in mind. Yeatman 193 reprints Jordan's complete copy of the document from the *Original Memoirs*, with variants from some other copy, probably also by Jordan. Obviously these are of less authority than Malone's version, taken largely from the original, which is not now known. Halliwell-Phillipps assumed a forgery, probably by Jordan, and Lee 647 ascribes it confidently to Jordan. But it is most unlikely that Jordan or any one else in 18th-century Stratford would reproduce the language of what certainly reads like the devotional exercise of a professing Catholic. H. S. Bowden, *The Religion of Shakespeare*, 85, says the practice of making spiritual testaments was common, and cites examples from the Sarum *Horae* of 1508 in W. Maskell, *Monumenta Ritualia* (1846), ii. 262, and from Jasper Loarte, *The Exercise of a Christian Life* (1579), 155, 218. These last references are not quite correct. Loarte recommends making a profession of faith in mortal sickness (266), and gives a formula (377). Neither this nor those in the *Horae* are in testamentary form, but the tone is much that of the will. Even if the will is genuine, it does not quite follow that Shakespeare's father wrote it, although the discovery in his house points to this. If he did, it must have been in comparatively early life, as the writer refers to his 'parents'. He names as a patron St. Winifred, whose well at Holywell in Flintshire was a famous resort for pilgrims.

VII. WILLIAM HENRY IRELAND (1777–1835)

Ireland's forgeries deceive nobody now. He was a conveyancer's clerk, and had access to old deeds, in imitation of which he began in 1794 to produce others purporting to be signed by Shakespeare, together with bogus manuscripts of plays and inscriptions on the title-pages of many books. These he palmed off on his father, Samuel Ireland the antiquary (cf. App. C, no. li), with a story of a gentleman who preferred to remain anonymous, and whose ancestor had saved Shakespeare from drowning and received these documents in reward. Samuel Ireland exhibited the forgeries at his house in 1795 and reproduced a collection of them in *Miscellaneous Papers and Legal Instruments under the Hand and Seal of William Shakespeare* (1796). Here are a letter and verses from Shakespeare to

'Anna Hatherrewaye', letters to the Earl of Southampton and Richard Cowley, letters from Southampton and Queen Elizabeth, deeds between Shakespeare and John Heminges, Henry Condell, and John Lowin, a Profession of Faith by Shakespeare, and many minor things. The collection included manuscripts of *K. Lear* and part of *Ham.*, but not two complete plays, *Vortigern and Rowena*, given unsuccessfully at Drury Lane in 1796 and printed in 1799, and *Henry II*, also printed in 1799. Many scholars became victims, among others Joseph Warton, James Boaden, and George Chalmers; but not Steevens, and not Malone, who demonstrated the fraud in his *Inquiry into the Authenticity of Certain Miscellaneous Papers and Legal Instruments* (1796). Ireland acknowledged the imposture in *An Authentic Account of the Shaksperian Manuscripts* (1796), and in the later and very readable *Confessions of William Henry Ireland* (1805). He absolved his father of complicity. Samuel made his own case in *A Vindication of his Conduct* (1796), which receives confirmation from his correspondence in *Addl. MSS.* 30349–53. Chalmers, in *An Apology for the Believers in the Shakespeare-Papers* (1797) and *A Supplemental Apology for the Believers in the Shakspeare-Papers* (1799), abandoned the documents, did his best to defend the scholarship of their dupes from Malone's strictures, and incidentally made some useful contributions to stage history. Summaries of the controversy are in Ingleby, ii. 142 and in Lee's *D.N.B.* account of Samuel Ireland. Some of the original forgeries are in the British Museum and other collections, and many of the unauthentic signatures of Shakespeare (cf. vol. i, p. 506) derive from Ireland.

VIII. F. G. WALDRON (1744–1818)

One of Ireland's forgeries refers to an 'Interlude called ye Virgin Queene'. Waldron printed some passages as from such a play in his *Free Reflections on Miscellaneous Papers and Legal Instruments* (1796), and a complete play under the name in 1797. It is obvious from the way in which he speaks of it that no deception was intended.

IX. RICHARD FENTON (1746–1821)

In his anonymous *Tour in Quest of Genealogy* (1811), 187, Fenton describes his purchase at a sale in Carmarthen of 'a curious journal of Shakespeare, an account of many of his plays, and memoirs of his life by himself'. He says that it was a copy of an old manuscript in the hand of Mrs. Shakespeare, found at the house of a Welsh gentleman who had married a Hathaway, and from it he prints several extracts. Ingleby, ii. 145, thinks that Fenton was hoaxed by Ireland manuscripts, but the whole thing reads to me like a *jeu d'esprit*. There is nothing about it in Fenton's original notes of his Welsh tours, printed by J. Fisher in 1917 for the Cambrian Archaeological Association, from manuscripts in the Cardiff Free Library.

X. GEORGE AMBROSE RHODES (1830)

C. F. Tucker Brooke, *Shakespeare Apocrypha*, xi, treats as a forgery *The Fifth of November, or, The Gunpowder Plot* (1830). This anonymous play is attributed to Rhodes by a cutting from a sale-catalogue in the Bodleian copy. The t.p. describes it as 'supposed to be written by William Shakespeare' and an 'Advertisement' says 'The reasons of it not being published in his lifetime are sufficiently obvious'. I see no attempt at fabrication.

XI. JOHN PAYNE COLLIER (1789–1883)

Collier began life as a barrister and journalist. He acted as parliamentary reporter to *The Times*, and in that capacity was taken into custody and reprimanded for misreporting a speech of 1819. His main interest was in literary history, and although his work was ill-arranged and sometimes inaccurate, he produced valuable materials in his *History of English Dramatic Poetry and Annals of the Stage* (1831), and in many publications for the Camden, Percy, and Shakespeare Societies. He became librarian to William, 6th Duke of Devonshire (1790–1858), and obtained access to the Bridgewater Library, containing the papers of Thomas Egerton, Lord Ellesmere (*c.* 1540–1617), which had passed on the failure of the direct line to Lord Francis Leveson-Gower (1800–57), who took the name of Egerton, and was created Earl of Ellesmere in 1846. At an early date he took to diversifying his studies by fabrication. Mr. D. T. B. Wood called attention to a sonnet on Sidney, said by Collier to have been inserted on a blank leaf of Thomas Churchyard's *A True Discourse Historicall of the Succeeding Gouernours in the Netherlands* (1602), of which he found a copy annotated and corrected by Collier himself, with alterations amounting to 'little less than a complete re-writing, impossible to any one but the author'.[1] Mr. Wood did not give full details. But Collier's statement was in 5 *Critical Review*, iii (1816), 636, and the rewriting in a collection of articles cut from that journal, once in Collier's possession, and now *B.M.* 836, f. 26. There is no insertion in the B.M. or Bodl. copies of *A True Discourse*, although pp. 91–2, missing from the B.M. copy, have some printed epitaphs on Sidney. I have not seen that published by Churchyard in 1587,[2] of which the only copy is said by Bullen [3] to have been once in the Bodleian, but is now in the Huntington collection. Some of Collier's fabrications appeared in print only, but in support of others he forged manuscript evidence in the Bridgewater and Dulwich archives, and in the State Paper (now Record) Office. Suspicion fell upon him in 1853, after the publication of the readings from the 'Perkins' Folio, and a controversy arose, which may be studied in S. W. Singer, *The Text of Shakespeare Vindicated* (1853); ⟨A. E. Brae⟩ *Literary Cookery* (1855), *Collier, Coleridge, and Shakespeare* (1860); C. M. Ingleby, *The Shakspeare Fabrications* (1859), *Complete View of the Shakspeare Controversy* (1861); N. E. S. A. Hamilton, *Inquiry into the Genuineness of the Manuscript Corrections in Mr. J. Payne Collier's Annotated Shakespeare, etc.* (1860); J. P. Collier, *Reply to Mr. N. E. S. A. Hamilton's Inquiry* (1860); H. B. Wheatley, *Notes on the Life of John Payne*

[1] 1925, *R.E.S.* i. 73.   [2] *S.T.C.* 5228.   [3] *D.N.B.*

Collier (1884); G. F. Warner, *Catalogue of the Manuscripts at Dulwich College* (1881), *John Payne Collier* (1887, *D.N.B.*). Collier died impenitent, but left clear evidence behind him in a transcript of *Alleyn's Diary* (now *Dulwich MS.* ix) containing drafts for the forged interlineations in the original, which were certainly not written concurrently with the main text of the transcript. His forged volume of ballads is now *Addl. MS.* 32380, and *Addl. MS.* 32381 is a transcript of it. *Egerton MS.* 2623 is a miscellaneous collection of theatrical documents, some of which are genuine, while others are or contain forgeries. Thus at the end of a play fragment (f. 37) have been added the words 'and to one hee knowes will shake his tayl'.

(*a*) *History of English Dramatic Poetry* (1831).

The fabrications in this stand unabashed in the later edition of 1879, to which the second references relate.

(1) Insertion (i. 180; i. 176) of 'played' after 'Julyus Sesar' in Machyn's account of a mask on 1 Feb. 1562. The word is probably forged in *Cotton MS. Vitellius*, F.v. Cf. J. G. Nichols, *Machyn's Diary* (1848), 276.

(2) Petition (i. 297; i. 288) of the Chamberlain's men, including Shakespeare, against closing of the Blackfriars in 1596. A forged copy is in *S.P.D. Eliz.* cclx. 117. The petition of the inhabitants of the Blackfriars, to which this professes to be a reply, is *S.P.D. Eliz.* cclx. 116, and seems to be genuine. Collier cites it, but also prints it earlier in the book (i. 227; i. 219) as of 1576. Cf. Ingleby 289; *Eliz. Stage*, ii. 195, 508; iv. 319.

(3) Ballad (i. 402; i. 386) on the Cockpit riot of 4 Mar. 1617, with a reference to Troilus and Cressida. No source is cited and none is known.

(4) The reading 'Tooly' in Manningham's *Diary* (App. B, no. xxiv) may be a mere error.

(5) Marginal reference (ii. 31; i. 460) to '*Mid. N. Dr.*' on a letter of John Spencer. This appears to be a modern addition in the manuscript (cf. App. D, s.a. 1631).

(6) Marginal note (ii. 42; i. 469) 'No player now'

against a payment of 31 May 1633 to John Shake-speare, bitmaker (cf. p. 370), noted in Sir Humphrey Mildmay's *Diary*.[1] This seems to me a clear forgery.

(b) New Facts Regarding the Life of Shakespeare (1835).

(1) Note (9) of opinion of the Chief Justices on city juris-diction in the Blackfriars. This, dated 27 Jan. 1580, is in the Bridgewater collection, and is probably genuine. Cf. Ingleby 250; *Eliz. Stage*, ii. 478.

(2) Privy Council Order (9) of 23 Dec. 1579 for tolera-tion of Leicester's men at the Blackfriars. This, for which no source is cited, must be a fabrication. Cf. *Eliz. Stage*, ii. 479, 496.

(3) Certificate (11) of November 1589, with list, in-cluding Shakespeare, of Queen's men as sharers in the Blackfriars. A forged copy is in the Bridgewater collec-tion. Cf. Ingleby 249; *Eliz. Stage*, ii. 108, 496; iii. 459.

(4) Report (16) of the Lord Mayor to the Privy Council in 1605 on plays against aldermen by Kempe, Armin, and others at the Blackfriars. No source is cited and none can be traced. Cf. Lee, *D.N.B.* (s.v. Kempe); *Eliz. Stage*, ii. 229, 510.

(5) Statement (22), assigned by Collier to 1608, of interests of Shakespeare and others in the Blackfriars. A forged copy is in the Bridgewater collection. Cf. Ingleby 246; *Eliz. Stage*, ii. 480.

(6) Certificate (27; *H.E.D.P.*[2] i. 477) of Middlesex justices as to the value of the Blackfriars on 20 Nov. 1633. Collier says he owned this. It passed to Halliwell-Phillipps (*Rarities*, 198). Ingleby 304 doubted it, but it is probably genuine. Cf. *Eliz. Stage*, ii. 512; *M.S.C.* i. 386.

(7) Letter (32) from H. S., presumably the Earl of Southampton, to Lord Ellesmere, in favour of the King's men at the Blackfriars, with descriptions of Shakespeare and Burbadge, assigned by Collier to 1608. A forged copy is in the Bridgewater collection. Cf. Ingleby 256; *Eliz. Stage*, ii. 480.

(8) Warrant (41) by James I, dated 4 Jan. 1610, ap-

[1] *Harl. MS.* 454, f. 180.

pointing Shakespeare and others to provide Children of
the Queen's Revels at the Blackfriars, with marginal lists
of theatres (45) and plays (53). A forged copy is in the
Bridgewater collection. Cf. Ingleby 252; *Eliz. Stage*,
ii. 56.

(9) Letter (48) from Samuel Daniel to Sir Thomas
Egerton, criticizing Shakespeare's claim to the Mastership
of the Queen's Revels, assigned by Collier to 1603. A
forged copy is in the Bridgewater collection. Cf. Ingleby
247; *Eliz. Stage*, iii. 273.

(c) *New Particulars Regarding the Works of Shakespeare*
    (1836).

(1) Notes (6) of Simon Forman. These have been questioned, but are genuine. Cf. App. D, s.a. 1611.

(2) Extracts (27) from versions of an elegy, possibly by
Fletcher, upon Burbadge, naming Shakespearean parts as
played by him. Cf. (h) (1).

(3) Ballad (49) on Othello, from a MS. of 'about the
date of the Protectorate', with a list of the contents of the
MS. This, which Collier had already cited for a jig not
concerned with Shakespeare in *New Facts*, 18, is the
forged *Addl. MS.* 32380.

(4) Insertion (58) referring to a performance of *Oth.*
in Sir Thomas Egerton's accounts for Elizabeth's visit of
31 July to 2 Aug. 1602 to Harefield. A forged page is
in the Bridgewater collection, and was printed as a whole
by Collier in the *Egerton Papers* (1840, *C.S.*), 343. Cf.
Ingleby 261; *Eliz. Stage*, iv. 68.

(d) *Farther Particulars Regarding Shakespeare and his*
    Works (1839).

Ballad (54) of *The Inchanted Island*, with a plot resembling
that of *Temp.* It is from the forged *Addl. MS.* 32380.

(e) *Memoirs of Edward Alleyn* (1841).

(1) Verses (13) on Alleyn, referring to 'Willes newe playe'
and several of the Globe actors. A forged copy is *Dulwich
MS*. i. 7. Cf. Ingleby 267; Warner 4.

(2) Insertions (19) of references to *K. Lear, Rom. & Jul.*,

Oth., and *Per.* in an Admiral's wardrobe inventory, probably of 1598. These are forged in *Dulwich MS.* i. 30.
Cf. Warner 21; Greg, *Henslowe Papers*, 52.

(3) Insertion (63) of a reference to 'Mr Shakespeare of
the globe' in a letter of 20 Oct. 1603 from Joan to Edward
Alleyn. The passage in *Dulwich MS.* i. 38 is lost owing to
decay of the paper. A version of the incident in *Prospective
Review*, ix (1853), 446, is probably based on Collier,
although it contains a further reference to Heminges.
Cf. Ingleby 279; Warner 26; Greg, *Henslowe Papers*, 59.

(4) List (68) of King's men, including Shakespeare, on
the margin of a copy of the Privy Council warrant for
playing of 9 Apr. 1604.[1] This is from a forged insertion
in *Dulwich MS.* i. 39. Cf. Ingleby 269; Warner 27;
Greg, *Henslowe Papers*, 61.

(5) Insertion (92) of 'Mr Shakespeare vj^d' in an assessment list of 6 Apr. 1609 for the Clink. The insertion is
forged in *Dulwich MS.* i. 49, and with it is a copy of the
altered list, forged throughout. A copy on the back of a
letter addressed to Malone is also inserted at p. 210 of
the example of Malone's *Enquiry* (1796) formerly owned
by Collier (B.M. C. 45, e. 23), and referred to by marks
against the passage (p. 215) in which Shakespeare's residence in Southwark (App. A, no. ix) is discussed. The
copy is not in Malone's hand, but Collier in his *Reply* (53)
to Hamilton refers to it as evidence that Malone knew the
list before his time. Cf. Ingleby 276; Warner 30; D. T. B.
Wood in *R.E.S.* i. 73.

(6) Memorandum (105) of April 1612 by Edward
Alleyn of sums paid for a lease in the Blackfriars, used
by Collier in support of a suggestion that Alleyn acquired
Shakespeare's share in the theatre. No MS. copy is
known. Alleyn did in fact lease property in Blackfriars,
but not until 1617, and at some distance from the
theatre. In this connexion Collier also forged insertions
to entries in Alleyn's *Diary*[2] for 27 July and 28 Aug.
1618, but made no use in print of these insertions, or of
others in entries for 9 Apr. 1618 and 30 Oct. 1619,

[1] *Eliz. Stage*, iv. 336.   [2] *Dulwich MS.* ix.

intended to suggest that performances at the Fortune on
those dates were of *As You Like It* and *Rom. & Jul.* respectively. Cf. Warner xliv, 170, 172, 174, 175, 271.

(7) Insertion (174) in draft letter of *c.* 1625 from Alleyn
to John Donne of 'as the plaie howse theare' after a reference to the Blackfriars tenements. The words are forged
in *Dulwich MS.* iii. 102. Cf. Warner 115.

(*f*) *Works of Shakespeare* (1842–4).

(1) Letter (1844, I. clvi; *H.E.D.P.*[2] i. 290) from Richard
Veale on behalf of the Master of the Revels, dated 3 May
1596, giving the Privy Council's allowance to the Chamberlain's men at the Blackfriars; cf. (*a*) (2). A forged
copy is *Dulwich MS.* i. 19. Cf. Warner 13.

(2) List (I. clviii) of Southwark residents in 1596, including Shakespeare and Phillips. A forged copy is
Dulwich MS. i. 20. Cf. Ingleby 274; Warner 13.

(3) Emendation (1843, viii. 574) of *Passionate Pilgrim*
from a 'manuscript in our possession'; cf. (*i*).

(4) Various emendations from *marginalia* 'probably as
old as the reign of Charles I' on a copy of F 1 in the Bridgewater Library. These are forgeries, written over pencilled
outlines. Cf. Ingleby 13.

(*g*) *The Diary of Philip Henslowe* (1845).

Collier's forgeries in this do not directly concern Shakespeare. On one that does indirectly, cf. (*m*) *infra*. T. Eich-
hoff, *Der Weg zu Sh.* (1902), suggested that they included
the marking of plays as 'ne'. But this was known to
Malone. Cf. Greg, *Henslowe*, I. xlv.

(*h*) *Memoirs of the Principal Actors in the Plays of Shakespeare* (1846).

(1) Full text (52; *H.E.D.P.*[2] iii. 299) of the enlarged
elegy on Burbadge; cf. (*c*) (2). Collier cites as the source
a MS. formerly belonging to Richard Heber. Ingleby said
in 1881 that it was supposed to be at Cheltenham, pre-

sumably in the collection of Sir Thomas Phillipps's MSS. at Thirlestane House. Cf. Ingleby, *Shakespeare; the Man and the Book*, ii. 169; *Eliz. Stage*, ii. 309.

(2) Epigram (220; *H.E.D.P.*[2] iii. 437) on Nathan Field, with the title *De Agello et Othello*. Of this also a MS. of Heber is cited as the source, and it would be dangerous to regard it as genuine.

(*i*) *Extracts from the Registers of the Stationers' Company* (1848, 1849).

Here Collier gives many extracts from ballads in the MS. used for (*f*) (3), of which two (ii. 189, 200) refer respectively to the Timon and Romeo and Juliet stories. He says that the MS. is in two or three hands, beginning *c.* 1600 and going on to after the Restoration, and contains entire poems by Shakespeare and quotations from the plays. He gives (II. viii) a list of the ballads. The MS. was clearly distinct from B. H. Bright's (now *Addl. MS.* 15225), which he also used, and from *Addl. MS.* 32380. It may be one of similar type to the latter, which Sir E. M. Thompson mentioned in 1885 as then in America.[1] In *An Old Man's Diary* (1871), i. 39, Collier says that he bought a MS. Elizabethan and Jacobean anthology on 7 Mar. 1832.

(*k*) *Notes and Emendations to the Text of Shakespeare's Plays* (1852).

Emendations from *marginalia* on a copy of F 2 inscribed 'Tho Perkins, his booke'. These are forgeries, many of them written over outlines pencilled in a modern hand. Collier claimed to have bought the volume in 1849. He presented it to the Duke of Devonshire, and it is now in the Huntington Library. Cf. Ingleby 27.

(*l*) *Works of Shakespeare* (1858).

Extract (v. 382) from *Stationers' Register*, purporting to show that Thomas Millington was fined for irregular publication of ballads on *The Shrew* and *Macb.* (qq.v.). S. A. Tannenbaum[2] claims the whole as a forgery, as it

---

[1] *Academy*, xxvii. 170.   [2] 1929, *M.L.N.* xliv. 13.

could not be found among the registration entries. It is in fact among the *Decrees and Ordinances*,[1] and part of it, which is genuine, was cited in W. Herbert, *Typographical Antiquities*, iii (1790), 1379. It is on 27 Aug. 1596, and runs:

'Thomas Myllington is likewise fyned at ij^s. vj^d for printinge of a ballad contrarye to order wch he alsoe presently paid.

~~Md the ballad intuled The taminge of a shrewe Also~~ ~~one oth Ballad of Macdobeth.~~'

The last word may be 'Macedbeth'. W. W. Greg says that the cancelled part is in a different hand from the rest, and has little doubt that it is a modern fabrication.[2]

(m) The Trevelyan Papers (1863).

Items (ii. 98) in the accounts of a servant of John Willoughby of Payhembury during 1595 include:

For peyrce Pennyles	vj^d
For Tarlton's Jests	vj^d
Robin Goodfelow	vj^d
Hamblett's historie	vj^d.

This looks like a fabrication, intended to support conjectures as to the existence of earlier editions of the last three pamphlets than those now known. I have not seen the MS. Collier had already forged entries in Henslowe's *Diary* purporting to show that Chettle, as well as Shakespeare, wrote a play on the Robin Goodfellow theme.[3] For a non-Shakespearean forgery by Collier in the *Trevelyan Papers*, cf. *Eliz. Stage*, i. 59.

(n) Bibliographical and Critical Account of the Rarest Books in English (1865).

Notice (i. 95) of a copy of *Locrine*, with an ascription of the authorship to Charles Tilney. I was sceptical of this in *Eliz. Stage*, iv. 27, but the copy exists and the manuscript note on it appears to be genuine. Cf. vol. i, p. 536.

---

[1] *Register B*, f. 462ª.   xlv. 141.
[2] *4 Library*, viii. 418 and *M.L.N.*   [3] Henslowe, I. xliv.

(*o*) *Twenty-five Old Ballads and Songs from Manuscripts in the Possession of John Payne Collier* (1869).

A Ballad of his Mistresse (30), with a reference to 'our Will' among other poets, agrees in title with an item in the MS. used for (*f*) (3) and (*i*).

XII. PETER CUNNINGHAM (1816–69)

The authenticity of the lists of Shakespearean performances at court during the winters of 1604–5 and 1611–12, published by Cunningham in *Extracts from the Accounts of the Revels at Court*,[1] is discussed in App. D.

XIII. THOMAS RUNDALL (1849)

Some notices of Shakespearean performances at sea in 1607–8 printed by Rundall in *Narratives of Voyages towards the North-West*[2] have been regarded as fabrications, but are now (cf. App. D) rehabilitated.

[1] 1842, *Shakespeare Soc.*   [2] 1849, *Hakluyt Soc.*

TABLE OF QUARTOS

['Bad' Quartos are in square brackets. *T* denotes a transfer.
Only Quartos before 1623 are given.]

Years	S.R. Entries	Original Editions	Reprints
1594	6 Feb. *T.A.* (Danter) 12 Mar. *2 Hen. VI* (Millington)	*T.A.* Q1 (Danter) [*2 Hen. VI.* Q1 (Millington)]	
1595		[*3 Hen. VI.* Q1 (Millington)]	
1597	29 Aug. *Rich. II* (Wise) 20 Oct. *Rich. III* (Wise)	*Rich. II.* Q1 (Wise) *Rich. III.* Q1 (Wise) [*R.J.* Q1 (Danter)]	
1598	25 Feb. *1 Hen. IV* (Wise) 22 July. *M.V.* (Roberts)	*1 Hen. IV.* Q1 (Wise) *L.L.L.* Q1 (Burby)	*Rich. II.* Q2, Q3 (Wise) *Rich. III.* Q2 (Wise)
1599		*R.J.* Q2 (Burby)	*1 Hen. IV.* Q2 (Wise)
1600	4 Aug. *A.Y.L.* *Hen. V* }'staied' *M.A.* 14 Aug. *Hen. V* (T. to Pavier) 23 Aug. *2 Hen. IV* (Wise and Aspley) 23 Aug. *M.A.* (Wise and Aspley) 8 Oct. *M.N.D.* (Fisher) 28 Oct. *M.V.* (T. Roberts to T. Heyes)	[*Hen. V.* Q1 (Millington and Busby)] *2 Hen. IV.* Q (Wise and Aspley) *M.A.* Q (Wise and Aspley) *M.N.D.* Q1 (Fisher) *M.V.* Q1 (T. Heyes)	[*2 Hen. VI.* Q2 (Millington)] [*3 Hen. VI.* Q2 (Millington)] *T.A.* Q2 (E. White)

Years	S.R. Entries	Original Editions	Reprints
1602	18 Jan. *M.W.* (Busby. T. Busby to Johnson) 19 Apr. *2 Hen. VI* ⎫ (T. Millington *3 Hen. VI* ⎬ lington *T.A.* ⎭ to Pavier) 26 July. *Ham.* (Roberts)	[*M.W.* Q1 (Johnson)]	*Rich. III.* Q3 (Wise) [*Hen. V.* Q2 (Pavier)]
1603	7 Feb. *T.C.* (Roberts) 25 June. *Rich. II* ⎫ (T. Wise *Rich. III* ⎬ to Law) *1 Hen. IV* ⎭	[*Ham.* Q1 (Ling and Trundell)]	
1604		*Ham.* Q2 (Ling)	*1 Hen. IV.* Q3 (Law)
1605			*Rich. III.* Q4 (Law) *Ham.* Reissue of Q2 (Ling)
1607	22 Jan. *L.L.L.* ⎫ (T. Burby *R.J.* ⎬ to Ling) 19 Nov. *L.L.L.* ⎫ *R.J.* ⎬ (T. Ling to *Ham.* ⎭ Smethwick) 26 Nov. *Lear* (Butter and Busby)		
1608	20 May. *A.C.* (Blount) 20 May. *Per.* (Blount)	*Lear.* Q1 (Butter)	*Rich. II.* Q4 (Law) *1 Hen. IV.* Q4 (Law)
1609	28 Jan. *T.C.* (Bonian and Walley)	*T.C.* Q1, two issues (Bonian and Walley) *Per.* Q1, Q2 (Gosson)	*R.J.* Q3 (Smethwick)

Years	S.R. Entries	Original Editions	Reprints
1611			*T.A.* Q3 (E. White) *Ham.* Q3 (Smethwick) *Per.* Q3 (pr. Stafford)
1612			*Rich. III.* Q5 (Law)
1613			*1 Hen. IV.* Q5 (Law)
1615			*Rich. II.* Q5 (Law)
1619	8 July. *M.V.* (T. T. to L. Heyes)		[Jaggard's Reprints] [*2 Hen. VI.* Q3 (Pavier)] [*3 Hen. VI.* Q3 (Pavier)] [*Per.* Q4 (Pavier)] [*M.W.* Q2 (Johnson)] *M.V.* Q2 (Jaggard?) *Lear.* Q2 (Butter) [*Hen. V.* Q3 (Pavier)] *M.N.D.* Q2 (Jaggard?)
1621	6 Oct. *Oth.* (Walkley)		
1622		*Oth.* Q (Walkley)	*Rich. III.* Q6 (Law) *1 Hen. IV.* Q6 (Law)
n. d. 1611 ⟨⟩37			*R.J.* Q4 (Smethwick) *Ham.* Q4 (Smethwick)

APPENDIX H
METRICAL TABLES

[*Bibliographical Note.* I give here a selection of tables, from various sources, which seem of value as a check upon the chronology of the plays. The principal dissertations bearing directly upon Shakespearean metre, as distinct from discussions of the fundamental nature of verse-rhythm, are: R. Roderick, *On the Metre of Hen. VIII*, in T. Edwards, *Canons of Criticism* (6th ed. 1758); S. Hickson, *The Shares of Sh. and Fletcher in T.N.K.* (1847, *Westminster and Foreign Quarterly*; 1874, *N.S.S. Trans.* 25*, with discussion); J. Spedding, *Who Wrote Sh.'s Hen. VIII?* (1850, *Gent. Mag.* 115; 1874, *N.S.S. Trans.* 1*, with discussion), *On the Pause-Test* (1874, *N.S.S. Trans.* 26); ⟨C. Bathurst⟩ *Remarks on the Differences in Sh.'s Versification in Different Periods of his Life* (1857); E. A. Abbott, *A Shn. Grammar* (1869, 1870, etc.); W. Hertzberg, *Introduction* to *Cy.* (1871, *Schlegel-Tieck Sh.*), *Metrisches, Grammatisches, Chronologisches zu Shs Dramen* (1878, *J.* xiii. 248); F. J. Furnivall, *The 'Stopped Line' Test* (1873, *N.S.S. Prospectus; Leopold Sh.* xx); F. G. Fleay, *On Metrical Tests as Applied to Dramatic Poetry* (1874, *N.S.S.* 1, with discussion; *Sh. Manual*, 121), *On Two Plays of Sh.* (1874, *N.S.S. Trans.* 339, with discussion), *Metrical Tests Applied to Sh.* (1881, C. M. Ingleby, *Sh., the Man and the Book*, ii. 50, with revised tables); J. K. Ingram, *On the 'Weak Endings' of Sh.* (1874, *N.S.S. Trans.* 442); F. S. Pulling, *The 'Speech-Ending' Test Applied to Twenty of Sh.'s Plays* (1879, *N.S.S. Trans.* 457); J. Harrison, J. Goodlet, and R. Boyle, *Report of the Tests Committee of the St. Petersburg Sh. Circle* (1880, *E.S.* iii. 473); J. Schipper, *Englische Metrik* (1882–9); J. B. Mayor, *Chapters on English Metre* (1886); G. König, *Der Vers in Shs Dramen* (1888); M. M. A. Schröer, *Über T.A.* (1891); J. Heuser, *Der Coupletreim in Shs Dramen* (1893–4, *J.* xxviii. 177; xxix. 235); H. Conrad, *Metrische Untersuchungen zur Feststellung der Abfassungzeit von Shs Dramen* (1895, *J.* xxxi. 318), *J.C., Ham.* (1905, *Shs Ausgewählte Dichtungen*), *Mac.* (1907), *Shs Timon* (1909, *Z.f. vergleichende Literatur-geschichte*, N.F. xvii. 337); *Eine neue Methode der chronologischen Sh-Forschung* (1909, *Germ. Rom. Monatschrift*, i. 232, 307); B. A. P. van Dam and C. Stoffel, *William Sh., Prosody and Text* (1900); D. L. Chambers, *The Metre of Mac.* (1903); A. C. Bradley, *Shn. Tragedy* (1904); W. Viëtor, *Sh.'s Pronunciation* (1906); G. Saintsbury, *History of English Prosody* (1906–10); A. Kerrl, *Die Metrischen Unterschiede von Shs K.J. und J.C.* (1913); H. Norpoth, *Metrisch-chronologische Untersuchung von Shs T.G.* (1916); M. A. Bayfield, *A Study of Sh.'s Versification* (1920).]

[TABLES I–V. NORMAL PLAYS]

TABLE I. SUMMARY

	(1) External	(2) Prose	(3) Rhyme	(4) Blank	(5) Total
2 Hen. VI . .		551	96	2515	3162
3 Hen. VI . .		3	128	2773	2904
Rich. III . .		83	152	3384	3619
C.E. . . .		244	378	1155	1777
T.G. . . .		654	128	1510	2292
L.L.L. . .		1051	1150	584	2785
R.J. . . .	28	455	466	2101	3050
Rich. II . .		0	529	2228	2757
M.N.D. . .	160	470	798	746	2174
John . . .		0	132	2438	2570
M.V. . . .		633	142	1883	2658
1 Hen. IV . .		1493	76	1607	3176
2 Hen. IV . .	141	1813	72	1420	3446
M.A. . . .		2105	76	644	2825
Hen. V . . .	379	1440	58	1504	3381
J.C. . . .		176	32	2269	2477
A.Y.L. . .	54	1659	217	926	2856
T.N. . . .		1752	176	762	2690
Ham. . . .	139	1211	135	2444	3929
M.W. . . .	114	2664	26	214	3018
T.C. . . .	57	1188	186	2065	3496
A.W. . . .	6	1478	279	1203	2966
M.M. . . .		1154	89	1577	2820
Oth. . . .		685	103	2528	3316
Lear . . .		925	169	2234	3328
Mac. . . .	148	158	108	1692	2106
A.C. . . .		287	40	2732	3059
Cor. . . .		829	28	2549	3406
Cy. . . .	84	526	122	2607	3339
W.T. . . .	32	876	59	2107	3074
Tp. . . .	89	464	64	1445	2062

TABLE II. RHYME

	(1) Heroic	(2) Other 5 foot	(3) Short	(4) Dog-gerel	(5) Total (2)–(5)	(6) %
			(Fleay, corrected)			
2 Hen. VI	96	0	0	0	96	3
3 Hen. VI	128	0	0	0	128	3
Rich. III	152	0	0	0	152	4
C.E.	216	64	0	98	378	19
T.G.	76	19	15	18	128	7
L.L.L.	548	272	102	228	1150	62
R.J.	414	42	10	0	466	17
Rich. II	525	4	0	0	529	19
M.N.D.	564	35	199	0	798	43
John	116	16	0	0	132	5
M.V.	86	4	48	4	142	5
1 Hen. IV	74	0	0	2	76	3
2 Hen. IV	50	0	22	0	72	3
M.A.	18	22	36	0	76	5
Hen. V	48	0	10	0	58	3
J.C.	32	0	0	0	32	1
A.Y.L.	58	10	147	2	217	6
T.N.	108	0	68	0	176	14
Ham.	64	0	71	0	135	3
M.W.	16	0	10	0	26	6
T.C.	170	0	16	0	186	9
A.W.	245	22	12	0	279	19
M.M.	61	0	28	0	89	4
Oth.	78	0	25	0	103	3
Lear	70	0	97	2	169	3
Mac.	108	0	0	0	108	6
A.C.	34	0	6	0	40	1
Cor.	28	0	0	0	28	1
Cy.	90	0	32	0	122	3
W.T.	2	0	57	0	59	0
Tp.	4	0	60	0	64	0·1

TABLE III. BLANK VERSE: LENGTH AND SYLLABIC VARIATION

	(1) Short Lines	(2) Alexandrines (6 foot)	(3) Normal (5 foot)	(4) Feminine Endings	(5) (4) as % (König)	(6) (4) as % (Hertzberg)	(7) Extra Mid-line Syllables
2 Hen. VI	52	15	2448	332	14	11	13
3 Hen. VI	37	9	2727	366	14	12	9
Rich. III	100	10	3274	638	20	18	11
C.E.	17	8	1130	198	17	12	0
T.G.	74	6	1430	269	18	15	5
L.L.L.	18	4	562	26	8	4	0
R.J.	47	9	2045	168	8	7	12
Rich. II	74	54	2100	258	11	11	17
M.N.D.	5	0	741	59	7	6	1
John	15	5	2418	151	6	6	13
M.V.	49	14	1820	325	18	15	32
1 Hen. IV	65	8	1534	92	5	5	19
2 Hen. IV	31	8	1381	221	16	15	21
M.A.	26	7	611	145	23	21	11
Hen. V	33	13	1458	336	21	18	25
J.C.	108	21	2140	413	20	18	35
A.Y.L.	41	8	877	230	26	23	22
T.N.	55	9	698	167	26	20	28
Ham.	154	43	2247	528	23	25	78
M.W.	7	3	204	54	27	21	8
T.C.	147	42	1876	463	24	21	104
A.W.	68	18	1117	349	29	21	66
M.M.	117	65	1395	377	26	22	98
Oth.	166	73	2289	679	28	26	208
Lear	191	64	1979	580	29	27	131
Mac.	97	35	1560	420	26	23	78
A.C.	143	47	2542	666	27	26	120
Cor.	136	43	2370	710	28	28	120
Cy.	70	43	2494	799	31	32	90
W.T.	58	63	1986	675	33	33	60
Tp.	67	19	1359	472	35	32	33

TABLE IV. BLANK VERSE: PAUSE-VARIATION

	(1) Overflows as % (König)	(2) (Conrad)	(3) Light	(4) Weak	(5) Verse Speeches	(6) Broken Ends	(7) (6) as % (Pulling)	(8) (König)	(9) Split Lines as %
2 Hen. VI	11		2	1				1	
3 Hen. VI	10		3	0				1	
Rich. III	13		4	0				3	
C.E.	13	6	0	0	488	6	1	1	
T.G.	12	9	0	0	517	24	5	6	7
L.L.L.	18		3	0				10	12
R.J.	14		6	1	634	71	11	15	
Rich. II	20		4	0	554	38	7	7	
M.N.D.	13		0	1				17	
John	18		7	0	548	46	8	12	
M.V.	22	20	6	1	464	79	17	22	17
1 Hen. IV	23	19	5	2				14	13
2 Hen. IV	21		1	0				17	
M.A.	19	13	1	1				21	
Hen. V	22		2	0	261	43	16	18	
J.C.	19	15	10	0	698	107	15	20	21
A.Y.L.	17		2	0	239	44	19	22	
T.N.	15		3	1	250	56	22	36	
Ham.	23		8	0	679	205	30	52	
M.W.	20		1	0				21	19
T.C.	27		6	0				31	
A.W.	28		11	2	418	164	39	74	
M.M.	23	23	7	0	479	169	35	51	33
Oth.	20	16	2	0	935	245	26	41	30
Lear	29	24	5	1	742	290	39	61	35
Mac.	37	30	21	2				77	43
A.C.	43	35	71	28				78	45
Cor.	46	37	60	44	817	365		79	48
Cy.	46		78	52	651	391		85	
W.T.	38	39	57	43	508	340	67	88	68
Tp.	42	37	42	25	409	253	61	85	56

TABLE V. BLANK VERSE: PAUSE-VARIATION (*continued*)

	(1) Full Lines (5 +6 foot)	(2) Split	(3) Unsplit	(4) Unsplit, with Pauses	(5) (4) as % of (3)
2 Hen. VI	2463	13	2450	270	11
3 Hen. VI	2736	8	2728	340	12
Rich. III	3284	66	3218	423	13
C.E.	1138	8	1130	171	15
T.G.	1436	43	1393	174	12
L.L.L.	566	11	555	79	14
R.J.	2054	71	1983	496	25
Rich. II	2154	34	2120	293	13
M.N.D.	741	28	713	131	18
John	2423	64	2359	357	15
M.V.	1834	79	1755	369	21
1 Hen. IV	1542	43	1499	235	16
2 Hen. IV	1389	43	1346	208	15
M.A.	618	35	583	126	21
Hen. V	1471	31	1440	219	14
J.C.	2161	129	2132	437	20
A.Y.L.	885	34	851	177	21
T.N.	707	44	663	164	25
Ham.	2290	194	2096	552	26
M.W.	207	9	198	41	21
T.C.	1918	133	1785	439	25
A.W.	1135	138	997	316	32
M.M.	1460	148	1312	398	30
Oth.	2362	268	2094	694	33
Lear	2043	243	1800	691	38
Mac.	1595	246	1349	494	37
A.C.	2589	470	2119	935	44
Cor.	2413	394	2019	749	37
Cy.	2537	393	2144	1027	48
W.T.	2049	330	1719	699	41
Tp.	1378	227	1151	481	42

[TABLES VI–VIII. ABNORMAL PLAYS]

TABLE VI. SUMMARY

	(1) External	(2) Prose	(3) Rhyme	(4) Blank	(5) Total
1 Hen. VI . . .		2	318	2357	2677
T.A. . . .		41	130	2352	2523
T.S. { (Sh.) . .		321	38	1084	1443
(Non-Sh.) .		304	113	787	1204
(Whole) . .		625	151	1871	2647
Edw. III (Sh.) . .		0	128	615	743
Tim. . . .		701	160	1513	2374
Per. { (Sh.) . .		337	22	781	1140
(Non-Sh.) .	311	140	197	605	1253
Hen. VIII { (Sh.) .		7	6	1154	1167
(Non-Sh.)	46	74	20	1512	1652
T.N.K. { Sh.) . .		57	24	1050	1131
(Non-Sh.) .	98	102	44	1442	1686

TABLE VII. BLANK VERSE: LENGTH AND SYLLABIC VARIATION

	(1) Short Lines	(2) Alex- andrines (6 foot)	(3) Nor- mal (5 foot)	(4) Full (5 & 6 foot)	(5) Feminine Endings	(6) (5) as %	(7) Extra Mid-line Syllables
1 Hen. VI . .	21	8	2328	2336	191	8	3
T.A. . . .	36	17	2299	2316	200	9	12
T.S. { (Sh.) . .	36	16	1032	1048	208	19	13
(Non-Sh.) .	31	15	741	756	135	17	7
(Whole) . .	67	31	1773	1804	371	20	20
Edw. III (Sh.) . .	22	5	588	593	74	12	0
Tim. . . .	171	57	1285	1342	334	22	50
Per. { (Sh.) . .	133	8	640	648	171	22	28
(Non-Sh.) .	62	6	537	543	91	15	0
Hen. VIII { (Sh.) .	25	24	1105	1129	374	32	34
(Non-Sh.) .	30	4	1478	1482	892	59	3
T.N.K. { (Sh.) . .	41	2	1007	1009	312	30	30
(Non-Sh.) .	48	19	1375	1394	780	54	4

TABLE VIII. BLANK VERSE: PAUSE-VARIATION

	(1) Over-flows as %	(2) Light	(3) Weak	(4) Full Lines Split	(5) Full Lines Unsplit	(6) Unsplit with Pauses	(7) (6) as % of (5)
1 Hen. VI	10	3	1	17	2319	233	10
T.A.	12	5	0	17	2299	303	13
T.S. (Sh.)				21	1027	194	19
(Non-Sh.)				16	740	122	16
(Whole)	8	1	1	37	1767	316	18
Edw. III (Sh.)				8	585	57	10
Tim.	33	16	5	145	1197	404	34
Per. (Sh.)	25	15	5	84	564	209	37
(Non-Sh.)	12			18	525	58	11
Hen. VIII (Sh.)	39	45	37	179	950	437	46
(Non-Sh.)	24	7	1	210	1272	437	35
T.N.K. (Sh.)	30	50	34	124	885	401	45
(Non-Sh.)	13	3	1	294	1100	478	43

NOTES
General.

In all percentage-tables I turn decimal figures into the nearest integers, treating 0·5 as 1. The use of decimals gives a specious appearance of scientific precision, warranted neither by the nature of the material, nor the legitimate inferences to be drawn from the figures arrived at.

Table I.

This is based upon Fleay's figures, scene by scene, in Ingleby, ii. 99. But many corrections have been necessary. Fleay adds up wrongly, puts figures in the wrong columns, misses bits of prose, omits a whole scene in *T.C.*, and the like. I think I have traced all the main errors and brought the totals into reasonable agreement with the computation of lines by T. R. Smith and F. J. Furnivall in *N.S.S. Trans.* (1880–6) 3†. The maximum divergence is by not more than six lines. Fleay probably differed as to the unity of a few lines from the editors of the *Globe*, upon which he worked, and which is not itself always accurate. I have not attempted to revise Fleay's counts systematically, or to vary his judgement as to whether particular lines are prose or short verse, or whether particular rhymes are deliberate or accidental. There is often room for difference of opinion. But I have substituted my own figures for *M.N.D.*, *M.V.*, and *T.C.* which I had occasion to count, although I am not sure that my treatment of accidental rhymes has been uniform. I now prefer to include them, and thus avoid subjectivity. And I have placed in the column headed 'External' all prologues, epilogues, and choruses, the interludes and masks in *M.N.D.*, *A.Y.L.*, *Ham.*, *M.W.*, *Mac.*, *Cy.*, and *Tp.*, the player's speech in *Ham.*, and the bombastic lines of Pistol in *2 Hen. IV*, *Hen. V*, and *M.W.* The metrical quality of these is naturally distinct from that of the plays to which they are related. The mask-matter in *L.L.L.* did not prove detachable from the surrounding dialogue, but is mainly in rhyme, and barely affects the figures for blank verse.

Table II.

Cols. (1)–(5). From Fleay's figures, as revised for Table I.

Col. (6). From König 131. The proportion is of rhymed five-foot lines to all five-foot lines. Rhymes judged by König as accidental are excluded, and those in prologues and epilogues, interludes, and love-poems, but alternate as well as heroic rhymes seem to be included.

I do not print the table in Conrad, *Macbeth*, xxxiii. It claims to give the proportion of all rhymed lines to blank-verse lines, but figures of 302 per cent. for *L.L.L.* and 210 per cent. for *M.N.D.* cannot be accurate.

Table III.

Col. (1). From Fleay in Ingleby, ii. 99.   ·

Col. (2). From Fleay in Ingleby, ii. 71. Fleay would himself eliminate many of these by textual emendation or slurring. By Alexandrines he means six-foot lines with six stresses; other six-foot lines he treats as having triple, instead of double, endings, and includes in col. (4). Conrad, *Macbeth*, xxviii, has a proportion table of Alexandrines, which includes all six-foot lines, but the figures are too low to make it of value.

Col. (3). By deduction of cols. (1) and (2) from col. (4) of Table I. The sum of cols. (2) and (3) is in col. (1) of Table V.

Col. (4). From Fleay in Ingleby, ii. 99. The counts differ so materially from those in *Sh. Manual*, 135, that Fleay must have altered his treatment of words capable (cf. vol. i, p. 260) of either a monosyllabic or a disyllabic pronunciation. My own counts, based on the disyllabic alternative, for a few plays do not differ much from Fleay's later ones.

Col. (5). From König 132. As he prefers the monosyllabic basis, I do not understand why his percentages are sometimes as high as those calculated by D. L. Chambers 43 from Fleay's later figures. The percentages for a few plays in Conrad, *Macbeth*, xxxiv, run slightly lower than König's.

Col. (6). From *J.* xiii. 252.

Col. (7). From Fleay in Ingleby, ii. 99. Conrad, *Macbeth*, xxvii, has a proportion table, but the figures are too low to make it of value.

Table IV.

Col. (1). From König 133.

Col. (2). From Conrad, *Macbeth*, xxvii.

My conception of overflow is stricter (cf. vol. i, p. 262) than that of either of these counters. For *M.V.* I only reckon 13 per cent. against König's 22 per cent. and Conrad's 20 per cent.

Cols. (3) *and* (4). From *N.S.S. Trans.* (1874), 450. Ingram adds some percentages for the later plays, but even here the numbers are too low to make them of value.

Cols. (5) *to* (7). From *N.S.S. Trans.* (1877–9), 457. The proportion in (7) is to all verse speeches, however short.

Col. (8). From König 134. Here the proportion is only to the number of verse speeches of more than a line in length and not ending with rhyme-tags.

Col. (9). From Conrad, *Macbeth*, xxvi. The proportion is of lines divided between two or more speeches, or split by a long pause for action, to all verse speeches.

Table V.

This is the only table which I have myself constructed. It rests upon a rather rough count, and checking would probably vary the figures in cols. (2)–(4), but not the round percentages in col. (5).

Col. (1) is by deduction of the short lines in Table III, col. (1), from the totals for blank verse in Table I, col. (4).

Col. (2) includes all full blank-verse lines divided between two or more speakers. It differs from Table IV, col. (6), because it does not include short lines ending a speech and not completed by the next speaker, and, on the other hand, does include lines in which a short speech is begun and ended, and which are then completed. It differs from the count underlying Table IV, col. (9), because it does not include lines which contain pauses for action, since the incidence and length of these can only be judged subjectively.

Col. (4). I take as the evidence for a pause, which is of course strictly a matter of degree, the use of a period, colon, semicolon, interrogation mark or exclamation mark in the *Eversley* text. There is subjectivity in this also, but it is not mine.

Tables VI to VIII.

I only give a selection of figures for the abnormal plays. Some of the sources used for the earlier tables do not take account of divided authorship, and in fact such cases really require scene-by-scene figures. The scansion of *Tim.* and *Per.* is often very doubtful.

Table VI.

I use my own counts, except for 1 *Hen. VI, T.A., Hen. VIII*, which are from Fleay, corrected as for Table I. The texts of *Edw. III* and *T.N.K.* used are those in the *Temple Dramatists*.

Table VII.

Cols. (1) *and* (2). The counts are as in Table VI.

Cols. (5) *and* (7). The counts are Fleay's, except in (5) for the divided parts of *T.S.* where Fleay divides differently. His total is slightly above mine. He works on his own text of *Per.*, not on the Globe-Eversley text, as I do.

Col. (6). Calculated by me from col. (5). The figures are fairly consonant with those in König 132 for the complete plays.

Table VIII.

Col. (1). The figures for complete plays are from König 133. Those for divided parts are adapted from Boyle's tables for *Per.* in *E.S.* v. 363, for *Hen. VIII* in *N.S.S. Trans.* (1885) 487, for *T.N.K.* in *E.S.* iv. 39. But Boyle's conception of an overflow is more restricted than König's, and the two sets of figures are therefore not comparable. Boyle includes rhymed lines in his accounts. For *Per.* he works on Fleay's text for Shakespeare's part, and takes no account of the brothel scenes.

Cols. (2) *and* (3). From *N.S.S. Trans.* (1874) 450.

Cols. (4)–(7). These figures are arrived at as in Table V.

LIST OF BOOKS

[This list is mainly intended to elucidate the foot-note references. But I have included the titles of some general surveys, largely critical, which there was no occasion to cite in the *Bibliographical Notes*. A list of the chief editions of the plays, some of which contain biographies, is in that to Chapter IX. For books on stage-history in general, I must refer readers to *The Elizabethan Stage*. I have not attempted any complete bibliography of Shakespeare, which indeed would have had to cover much that falls outside the scope of these volumes. I am glad to learn that one is in prospect from other hands. The older attempts have now lost what value they ever had. But current literature is well recorded in the *Shakespeare-Jahrbuch*, the *Annual Bibliography of English Language and Literature* (Modern Humanities Research Association), *The Year's Work in English Studies* (English Association), and for periodicals, *The Review of English Studies*. This book went to the printers in the autumn of 1929, and there are already important contributions, such as Professor Wilson's editions of *All's Well* and *Twelfth Night*, and Mr. Alexander's full study of *Henry VI* and *Richard III*, which I have not been able to take into account.]

ABBOTT. A Shakespearean Grammar. By E. A. Abbott. 1869, &c.
ABERCROMBIE. A Plea for the Liberty of Interpreting. By Lascelles Abercrombie. 1930. [*British Academy*.]
Academy. The Academy. A Weekly Review of Literature, Science, and Art. Vols. i–lv, 1869–98.
ACHESON. Shakespeare and the Rival Poet. By A. Acheson. 1903.
ACHESON. Mistress Davenant. 1913.
ACHESON. Shakespeare's Lost Years in London. 1920.
ACHESON. Shakespeare's Sonnet Story. 1922.
ADAMS. Shakespearean Playhouses. By J. Q. Adams. 1917.
ADAMS. A Life of William Shakespeare. 1923.
    See HERBERT.
ALDEN. Shakespeare. By R. M. Alden. 1922.
ALLEN. Notes on the Shakespeare-Bacon Question. By C. Allen. 1900.
ANDERS. Shakespeare's Books. By H. Anders. 1904.
Anglia. Zeitschrift für englische Philologie. Vols. i–liv. 1878–1930. [In progress.]
ARBER. Transcript of the Registers of the Company of Stationers, 1554–1640. Edited by E. Arber. 5 vols., 1875–94.
ARBUTHNOT. Guide to the Collegiate Church of Stratford-on-Avon. By G. Arbuthnot. [*c.* 1895.]
ARBUTHNOT. The Vestry Minute Book of Stratford-on-Avon. 1899.
Arch. Archaeologia, or, Miscellaneous Tracts Relating to Antiquity. Vols. i–lxxix, 1773–1929. [*Society of Antiquaries of London.* In progress.]

Archiv. Archiv für das Studium der neueren Sprachen und Literaturen. Vols. i–clvii, 1848–1930. [Known as *Herrig's Archiv*. In progress.]

Athen. The Athenæum. Journal of Literature, Science, the Fine Arts, Music, and the Drama. 1828–1921.

BAB. Shakespeare. Wesen und Werke. Von J. Bab. 1925.

BAKER. The Development of Shakespeare as a Dramatist. By G. P. Baker. 1907.

BALDWIN. The Organization and Personnel of the Shakespearean Company. By T. W. Baldwin. 1927.

BARNARD. New Links with Shakespeare. By E. A. B. Barnard. 1930.

BARTLETT, H. C. Mr. William Shakespeare. Original and Early Editions of his Quartos and Folios, his Source Books and those containing Contemporary Notices. By H. C. Bartlett. 1922.

BARTLETT-POLLARD. A Census of Shakespeare's Plays in Quarto. By H. C. Bartlett and A. W. Pollard. 1916.

BARTLETT, J. A New and Complete Concordance of the Dramatic Works and Poems of Shakespeare. By J. Bartlett. 1894.

BARTON. Shakespeare's Links with the Law. By D. P. Barton. 1929.

BAYNES. Shakespeare Studies. By T. S. Baynes. 1894.

BEECHING. William Shakespeare, Player, Playmaker, and Poet. By H. C. Beeching. 1908.

BELLEW. Shakespeare's Home at New Place. By J. C. M. Bellew. 1863.

Bibl. Soc. Trans. Transactions of the Bibliographical Society. 15 vols., 1893–1919. [Amalgamated from 1920 with *Library* (q.v.).]

BICKLEY. The Register of the Guild at Knowle. By W. B. Bickley. 1894.

BIRCH, *Eliz.* Memoirs of the Reign of Queen Elizabeth from the year 1581 till her Death. By T. Birch. 2 vols., 1754.

BIRCH, *James*. The Court and Times of James the First. Edited [from collections of T. Birch] by the Author of 'Memoirs of Sophia Dorothea'. 2 vols., 1848.

BLADES. Shakespeare and Typography. By W. Blades. 1872.

BLOOM. Shakespeare's Church. By J. H. Bloom. 1902.

BLOOM. The Register of the Gild of Holy Cross at Stratford-on-Avon. 1907.

BLOOM, *Top. Notes*. Topographical Notes on Stratford-on-Avon. 3 vols., 1903–5.

BOAS. Shakspere and his Predecessors. By F. S. Boas. 1896.

BOAS. University Drama in the Tudor Age. 1914.

BOAS. Shakespeare and the Universities. 1923.

Bodleian. A Catalogue of the Shakespeare Exhibition held in the Bodleian Library to Commemorate the Death of Shakespeare. 1916.

Bodleian. Specimens of Shakespeareana in the Bodleian Library at Oxford. 1927.

BOSWELL-STONE. Shakespeare's Holinshed. By W. G. Boswell-Stone. 1896.

BOWDEN. The Religion of Shakespeare. By H. S. Bowden. 1899.

B. P. Cat. Catalogue of the Books, Manuscripts, &c., in Shakespeare's Birthplace. By F. C. Wellstood. 1925.

BRACEBRIDGE. Shakespeare no Deer Stealer. By C. H. Bracebridge. 1862.

BRADLEY. Shakespearean Tragedy. By A. C. Bradley. 1904.

BRADLEY. Oxford Lectures in Poetry. 1909.

BRADLEY. A Miscellany. 1929.

BRANDES. William Shakespeare. By George Brandes. Translated from Copenhagen edition by W. Archer and others. 2 vols., 1898.

BRANDL. Shakespeare. Leben, Umwelt, Kunst. Von A. Brandl. 1922, ed. 4. 1929.

BRASSINGTON. Shakespeare's Homeland. By W. S. Brassington. 1903.

BREWER. Letters and Papers, Foreign and Domestic, of the Reign of Henry VIII. Arranged and catalogued by J. S. Brewer [and afterwards J. Gairdner and R. H. Brodie]. 21 vols., 1862–1910; vol. i, ed. 2, 1920; Addenda, vol. i, 1929. [*Calendars of State Papers.*]

British Academy. Annual Shakespeare Lectures, 1911–30, in *Transactions of the British Academy.* 13 vols., 1903–27. [In progress.]

BROOKE, S. A. On Ten Plays of Shakespeare. By Stopford A. Brooke. 1905.

BROOKE, S. A. Ten More Plays of Shakespeare. 1913.

BROOKE, T. The Shakespeare Apocrypha. Edited by C. F. Tucker Brooke. 1908.

BROOKE. Shakespeare of Stratford. 1926. [*Yale Shakespeare.*]

BUCKNILL. The Medical Knowledge of Shakespeare. By J. C. Bucknill. 1860.

BUCKNILL. The Mad Folk of Shakespeare. 1867.

CAMPBELL. Shakespeare's Legal Acquirements. By John Lord Campbell. 1859.

CARTER. Shakespeare, Puritan and Recusant. By T. Carter. 1897.

CARTER. Shakespeare and Holy Scripture. 1905.

C. H. The Cambridge History of English Literature. Edited by A. W. Ward and A. R. Waller. 14 vols., 1907–16.

CHALLIS. The Law of Real Property. By H. W. Challis. 1885; 3rd ed. 1911.

CHALMERS. An Apology for the Believers in the Shakspeare-Papers. [By G. Chalmers.] 1797.

CHALMERS, *S. A.* A Supplemental Apology for the Believers in the Shakspeare-Papers. 1799.

CHAMBERS. The Mediaeval Stage. By E. K. Chambers. 2 vols., 1903.

CHAMBERS. Notes on the History of the Revels Office under the Tudors. 1906.

CHAMBERS. The Elizabethan Stage. 4 vols., 1923.

CHAMBERS. The Disintegration of Shakespeare. 1924. [*British Academy.*]

CHAMBERS. Shakespeare: A Survey. 1925.

CHAMBRUN. Shakespeare Acteur-Poète. Par C. Longworth de Chambrun. 1926. English Translation, 1927.

CHEYNEY. A History of England, from the Defeat of the Armada to the Death of Elizabeth. By E. P. Cheyney. 2 vols., 1914, 1926.

COHN. Shakespeare in Germany in the Sixteenth and Seventeenth Centuries. By A. Cohn. 1865.

COLERIDGE. Notes and Lectures upon Shakespeare and Some of the Old Poets and Dramatists. By S. T. Coleridge. Edited by Mrs. H. N. Coleridge. 2 vols., 1849.

COLERIDGE. Lectures and Notes on Shakspere and other English Poets. Collected by T. Ashe. 1883. [Includes some reports of doubtful authenticity, published by J. P. Collier in 1856.]

COLLIER, *H.E.D.P.* The History of English Dramatic Poetry to the Time of Shakespeare: and Annals of the Stage to the Restoration. By J. P. Collier. 3 vols., 1831; new ed., 3 vols., 1879.

COLLIER, *N. F.* New Facts regarding the Life of Shakespeare. 1835.

COLLIER, *N. P.* New Particulars regarding the Works of Shakespeare. 1836.

COLLIER, *F. P.* Further Particulars regarding Shakespeare and his Works. 1839.

COLLIER, *M. A.* Memoirs of Edward Alleyn. 1841. [*Shakespeare Society.*]

COLLIER, *A. P.* Alleyn Papers: Original Documents illustrative of the Life of Edward Alleyn, and of the Early Stage. 1843. [*Shakespeare Society.*]

COLLIER, *Henslowe.* The Diary of Philip Henslowe. 1845. [*Shakespeare Society.*]

COLLIER, *Actors.* Memoirs of the Principal Actors in the Plays of Shakespeare. 1846; new ed. in *H. E. D. P.*, 1879.

COLLIER, *S. R.* Extracts from the Registers of the Stationers' Company. 1848-9. [*Shakespeare Society.*]

COLLINS. Studies in Shakespeare. By J. Churton Collins. 1904.

Columbia Sh. Studies. Shaksperian Studies by the Members of the Department of English and Comparative Literature in Columbia University. Edited by B. Matthews and A. H. Thorndike. 1916.

CONNES. Le Mystère Shakespearien. Par G. Connes. 1926.

CONRAD (formerly Isaac). Shaksperes Selbstbekenntnisse. Von H. Conrad. 1897.

CORNEY. Argument on the Assumed Birthday of Shakespeare. By B. Corney. 1864.

CREIZENACH. Schauspiele der englischen Komödianten. Von W. Creizenach. 1889.

CREIZENACH. Geschichte des neueren Dramas. Vols. i, 1893 (2nd ed. 1911); ii, 1901; iii, 1903; iv, 1909; v, 1916.

CREIZENACH. The English Drama in the Age of Shakespeare. Translated from vol. iv of *Geschichte des neueren Dramas.* 1916.

CROCE. Ariosto, Shakespeare and Corneille. By B. Croce. 1920.

C. S. Camden Society, now incorporated with Royal Historical Society.

CUNLIFFE. A New Shakespearean Dictionary. By R. J. Cunliffe. 1910

CUNNINGHAM. Extracts from the Accounts of the Revels at Court, in the Reigns of Queen Elizabeth and King James. By P. Cunningham. 1842. [*Shakespeare Society.*]

DASENT. Acts of the Privy Council of England. New Series, by J. R. Dasent. 32 vols., 1890–1907.

DELIUS. Abhandlungen zu Shakspere. Von N. Delius. 2 vols., 1878, 1888.

DEVECMON. In re Shakespeare's Legal Acquirements. By W. C. Devecmon. 1899.

D. N. B. Dictionary of National Biography. Edited by L. Stephen and S. Lee. Re-issue, with Supplement, 22 vols., 1908–9. Second Supplement, Index, and Epitome, 1913.

DOWDEN. Shakspere: A Critical Study of his Mind and Art. By E. Dowden. 1875.

DOWDEN. Shakspere. 1877. [*Literature Primers.*]

DOWDEN. Introduction to Shakespeare. 1893.

DRAKE. Shakspeare and his Times. By N. Drake. 2 vols., 1817; 2nd ed., 1 vol., 1838.

DUGDALE. Antiquities of Warwickshire. By W. Dugdale. 1 vol., 1656; ed. W. Thomas, 2 vols., 1718.

ECKHARDT. Das englische Drama im Zeitalter der Reformation und der Hochrenaissance. Vorstufen, Shakespeare und Seine Zeit. Von E. Eckhardt. 1928.

E. H. R. The English Historical Review. Vols. i–xlv, 1886–1930. [In progress.]

ELLACOMBE. Shakespeare as an Angler. By H. N. Ellacombe. 1883.

ELLACOMBE. The Plant-Lore and Garden-Craft of Shakespeare. Ed. 3, 1896.

ELTON. William Shakespeare: His Family and Friends. By C. I. Elton. 1904.

ELZE. William Shakespeare. Von K. Elze. 1876. English translation by L. D. Schmitz. 1888.

ELZE. Abhandlungen zu Shakespeare. 1877. English Translation by L. D. Schmitz. 1874.

E. S. Englische Studien: Organ für englische Philologie. Vols. i–lxv, 1877–1930. [In progress.]

Essays and Studies. Essays and Studies by Members of the English Association. 15 vols., 1910–30.

EYRE. A Transcript of the Registers of the Worshipful Company of Stationers, 1640–1708. Edited by G. E. B. Eyre. 3 vols., 1913–14. [*Roxburghe Club.*]

FARMER. An Essay on the Learning of Shakespeare. By Richard Farmer. 1767. [*Variorum,* i. 300.]

FEUILLERAT, *Eliz.* Documents relating to the Office of the Revels in the Time of Queen Elizabeth. Edited by A. Feuillerat. 1908. [*Materialien,* xxi.]

FIGGIS. Shakespeare. A Study. By D. Figgis. 1911.

FLEAY, *Manual.* Shakespeare Manual. By F. G. Fleay. 1876, new ed. 1878.

FLEAY, *L. W.* A Chronicle History of the Life and Work of William Shakespeare. 1886.

FLEAY, *C. H.* A Chronicle History of the London Stage, 1559–1642. 1890.

FLEAY, *B. C.* A Biographical Chronicle of the English Drama, 1559–1642. 2 vols., 1891. *See* INGLEBY.

FORREST. The Old Houses of Stratford-on-Avon. By H. E. Forrest. 1925.

FRANZ. Shakespeare-Grammatik. By W. Franz. 1900, 1924.

FRENCH. Shakespeareana Genealogica. By G. R. French. 1869.

FRIPP, *Quyny.* Master Richard Quyny. By E. I. Fripp. 1924.

FRIPP, *S. S.* Shakespeare's Stratford. 1928.

FRIPP, *Haunts.* Shakespeare's Haunts near Stratford. 1929.

FRIPP. Shakespeare Studies. 1930.

FROUDE. A History of England from the Fall of Wolsey to the Defeat of the Armada. By J. A. Froude. 12 vols., 1856–70; new ed., 12 vols., 1881, &c.

FULLOM. The History of William Shakespeare. By S. W. Fullom. 1862.

FURNIVALL-MUNRO. Life and Work of Shakespeare. By F. J. Furnivall and J. Munro. 1908. [*Century Shakespeare.*]

G. of K. See BICKLEY.

GARDINER. History of England from the Accession of James I to the Outbreak of the Civil War. By S. R. Gardiner. 1863–84, &c.

GEIKIE. The Birds of Shakespeare. By A. Geikie. 1916.

GERVINUS. Shakespeare. Von G. G. Gervinus. 4 vols., 1849–50. English translation, as Shakespeare Commentaries, by F. E. Bunnètt. 1863, 1883 (with introduction by F. J. Furnivall).

GILDERSLEEVE. Government Regulation of the Elizabethan Drama. By V. C. Gildersleeve. 1908. [*Columbia Univ. Studies in English.*]

Gloucestershire Wills. Edited by W. P. W. Phillimore and others. 2 vols. [*Index Library of British Record Society*, xii, xxxiv.]

GORDON. Shakespeare's English. By G. S. Gordon. 1928.

GRANVILLE-BARKER. Prefaces to Shakespeare. By H. Granville-Barker. 2 series. 1927, 1930.

GRAY, A. A Chapter in the Early Life of Shakespeare. By A. Gray. 1926.

GRAY, A. How Shakespeare 'Purged' Jonson. 1928.

GRAY, J. W. Shakespeare's marriage and Departure from Stratford. By J. W. Gray. 1905.

GREEN, C. F. The Legend of Shakespeare's Crab-Tree. By C. F. Green. 1857, 1862.

GREEN, H. Shakespeare and the Emblem-Writers. By H. Green. 1870.

GREENWOOD. The Shakespeare Problem Re-stated. By George Greenwood. 1908.

GREENWOOD. Is There a Shakespeare Problem? 1916.

GREENWOOD. Shakespeare's Law and Latin. 1916.

GREENWOOD. Shakespeare's Law. 1920.

GREENWOOD. Shakespeare's Handwriting. 1920.

GREENWOOD. Ben Jonson and Shakespeare. 1921.
GREENWOOD. Lee, Shakespeare and a Tertium Quid. 1923.
GREENWOOD. The Shakespere Signatures and Sir Thomas More. 1924.
GREENWOOD. The Stratford Bust and the Droeshout Engraving. 1925.
GREG, *Plays*. A List of English Plays written before 1643 and printed before 1700. By W. W. Greg. 1900. [*Bibliographical Society*.]
GREG, *Masques*. A List of Masques, Pageants, &c., Supplementary to a List of English Plays. 1902. [*Bibliographical Society*.]
GREG. Catalogue of the Books Presented by Edward Capell to the Library of Trinity College in Cambridge. 1903.
GREG. A Descriptive Catalogue of the Early Editions of the Works of Shakespeare Preserved in the Library of Eton College. 1909.
GREG. Two Elizabethan Stage Arrangements: The Battle of Alcazar and Orlando Furioso. An Essay in Critical Bibliography. 1923.
GREG. English Literary Autographs. Part 1, Dramatists; Part 2, Poets. 1925, 1928.
GREG. Principles of Emendation in Shakespeare. 1928. [*British Academy*.]
See HENSLOWE, *M. S. R.*
GUNDOLF. Shakespeare. Sein Wesen und Werk. Von F. Gundolf. 2 vols., 1928, 1929.
HABINGTON. A Survey of Worcestershire. By T. Habington. Edited by J. Amphlett. [*Worcestershire Hist. Soc.*]
HALES. Notes and Essays on Shakespeare. By J. W. Hales. 1884.
H.P. J. O. Halliwell, afterwards Halliwell-Phillipps.
H.P., *W. W.* The Marriage of Wit and Wisdom: to which are added Illustrations of Shakespeare and the Early English Drama. 1846. [*Shakespeare Society*.]
H.P. 1848. Life of William Shakespeare. 1848.
H.P. *New Boke*. A New Boke about Shakespeare and Stratford-on-Avon. 1850.
H.P., *Reliques*. Some Account of the . . . Reliques, Illustrative of . . . Shakespeare, in the Possession of J. O. Halliwell. 1852.
H.P., *Folio*. The Works of William Shakespeare. 16 vols., 1853–65. [With revised *Life*, 1853.]
H.P., *Cal*. Descriptive Calendar of the Ancient Manuscripts and Records . . . of the Corporation of Stratford-upon-Avon. 1863. [Index, 1865.]
H.P., *Facs*. Shakespearian Facsimiles. 1863.
H.P., *New Place*. An Historical Account of New Place. 1864.
H.P., *Subsidies*. Extracts from the Subsidy Rolls, Stratford-on-Avon. 1864.
H.P., *Council Books*. Extracts from the Council Books of Stratford-on-Avon. 1864.
H.P., *Vestry-Book*. Extracts from the Vestry Book of Stratford-on-Avon. 1865.
H.P. The Chamberlains' Accounts of Stratford-on-Avon, 1590–7. 1866.

H.P. Extracts from the Chamberlains' Accounts of Stratford-on-Avon. 1866–7.

H.P., *Court of Record*. Extracts from the Registry of the Court of Record of Stratford-on-Avon. 1867.

H.P. Notices of Players Acting at Ludlow. 1867.

H.P., *Dramatic Records*. A Collection of Ancient Documents respecting the Office of Master of the Revels. 1870.

H.P., *Illustrations*. Illustrations of the Life of Shakespeare. Part 1. 1874.

H.P., *Budget*. A Budget of Notes and Memoranda. 1880.

H.P. Outlines of the Life of Shakespeare. 1881, &c.; eds. from 1887 stereotyped. [*Cited as* H. P.]

H.P., *Visits*. The Visits of Shakespeare's Company of Actors to the Provincial Cities. 1887.

H.P., *Rarities*. A Calendar of the Shakespeare Rarities . . . at Hollingbury Copse. 1887; ed. by E. E. Baker, 1891.

See JORDAN, MALONE.

Harl. Soc. The Publications of the Harleian Society. Vols. i–lxxxii, 1869–1930. [In progress; mainly Visitations.] Registers (a separate series), vols. i–lix, 1877–1929.

HARRIS. The Man Shakespeare and his Tragic Life Story. By F. Harris. 1909.

Hatfield MSS. Calendar of the Manuscripts of the Marquis of Salisbury at Hatfield House, Hertfordshire. Parts i–xv, 1883–1930. [*Hist. MSS.*; also known as *Cecil Papers*.]

HAZLITT, W. Characters of Shakespeare's Plays. By William Hazlitt. 1817.

HAZLITT, W. C. A Manual for the Collector and Amateur of Old English Plays. By W. C. Hazlitt. 1892.

HAZLITT, W. C. Shakespear. Himself and his Work. Ed. 4. 1912.

HAZLITT, S. L. Shakespeare's Library. 2nd ed. by W. C. Hazlitt. 6 vols., 1875.

HAZLITT-WARTON. History of English Poetry, from the Twelfth to the close of the Sixteenth Century. By T. Warton. Edited by W. C. Hazlitt. 4 vols., 1871.

HENSLOWE. Henslowe's Diary. Edited by W. W. Greg. 2 vols., 1904–8.

Henslowe Papers. Henslowe Papers : being Documents supplementary to Henslowe's Diary. Edited by W. W. Greg. 1907.

HERBERT. The Dramatic Records of Sir Henry Herbert. Edited by J. Q. Adams. 1917.

HERFORD. A Sketch of Recent Shakespearean Investigation. By C. H. Herford. 1923.

HERFORD-SIMPSON. Ben Jonson. Edited by C. H. Herford and P. Simpson. Vols. i–iii, 1925–7. [In progress.]

HERZ. Englische Schauspieler und englisches Schauspiel zur Zeit Shakespeares in Deutschland. Von E. Herz. 1903.

Hist. MSS. Reports of the Historical Manuscripts Commission, 1870–

1930. [In progress. The earlier Reports on individual collections were mostly issued as Appendices to General Reports; those since about 1899 as separate publications.]

HOLDSWORTH. A History of English Law. 9 vols. By W. S. Holdsworth. 1922–6.

HOLDSWORTH. An Historical Introduction to the Land Law. 1927.

HOLINSHED. Chronicles of England, Scotland, and Ireland. By R. Holinshed. 1577, 1587; reprint, 6 vols., 1807–8.

HOPWOOD. A Calendar of the Middle Temple Records. By C. H. Hopwood. 4 vols., 1901–5.

HOTSON. The Commonwealth and Restoration Stage. By J. L. Hotson. 1928.

HUDSON. Shakespeare, his Life, Art and Characters. By H. N. Hudson. 2 vols., 1872, new ed. 1895.

HUNTER. New Illustrations of Shakespeare. By J. Hunter. 2 vols. 1845.

INGLEBY. A complete View of the Shakspere Controversy concerning the Genuineness of the Manuscript Matter published by Collier. By C. M. Ingleby. 1861.

INGLEBY, *Allusion-Books*. Shakspere Allusion-Books. Part I. 1874. [*N. S. S.*]

INGLEBY. Shakespeare, The Man and the Book. 2 vols. 1877, 1881. [With a paper on Metrical Tests Applied to Shakespeare, by F. G. Fleay.]

INGLEBY. Shakespeare and the Enclosure of Common Fields at Welcombe. 1885.

IRELAND, S. Miscellaneous Papers and Legal Instruments under the Hand and Seal of William Shakespeare. Edited by Samuel Ireland. 1796.

IRELAND, S. A Vindication of His Conduct. 1796.

IRELAND, W. H. An Authentic Account of the Shakespearian Manuscripts. By W. H. Ireland. 1796.

IRELAND, W. H. Confessions of William Henry Ireland. 1805, 1874 (N.Y.).

JAGGARD. Shakespeare Bibliography: A Dictionary of every Known Issue of the Writings of our National Poet and of Recorded Opinion thereon in the English Language. By W. Jaggard. 1911.

Jahrbuch. Jahrbuch der Deutschen Shakespeare-Gesellschaft. Vols i–lxv, 1865–1929. [In progress.]

JAMESON. Shakespeare's Heroines; Characteristics of Women. By A. B. Jameson. 1832.

J. E. G. P. The Journal of Germanic Philology [afterwards The Journal of English and Germanic Philology.] Vols. i–xxix, 1897–1930. [In progress.]

JENTE. The Proverbs of Shakespeare. By R. Jente. 1926.

JORDAN. Original Collections on Shakespeare and Stratford-on-Avon. By J. Jordan. Edited by J. O. Halliwell-Phillipps. 1864.

JORDAN. Original Memoirs and Accounts of the Families of Shakespeare and Hart. Edited by J. O. Halliwell-Phillipps. 1865.

See MALONE.

KELLNER. Restoring Shakespeare. A Critical Analysis of the Misreadings in Shakespeare's Works. By L. Kellner. 1925.

KÖNIG. Der Vers in Shakespeares Dramen. Von G. König. 1888.

KOEPPEL. Studien über Shakespeare's Wirkung auf zeitgenössische Dramatiker. Von E. Koeppel. 1905. [*Materialien*, ix.]

KOHLER. Shakespeare vor dem Forum der Jurisprudenz. Von J. Kohler. 1883–4, 1919.

KREYSSIG. Vorlesungen über Shakespeare. Von F. A. T. Kreyssig. 3 vols. 1858–60.

LAMBERT. Cartae Shakespeareanae. By D. H. Lambert. 1904.

LANG. Shakespeare, Bacon and the Great Unknown. By A. Lang. 1912.

LAW. Shakespeare as a Groom of the Chamber. By E. Law. 1910.

LAW. Some Supposed Shakespeare Forgeries. 1911.

LAW. More about Shakespeare 'Forgeries'. 1913.

LAWRENCE. Pre-Restoration Stage Studies. By W. J. Lawrence. 1927.

LAWRENCE. Shakespeare's Workshop. 1928.

LEACH. English Schools at the Reformation. By A. F. Leach. 1896.

LEE. Stratford-on-Avon from the Earliest Times to the Death of Shakespeare. By S. Lee. 1885, 1906.

LEE. A Life of William Shakespeare. 1898; new ed. 1925.

LEE. Shakespeare and the Modern Stage. 1906.

LEE. Elizabethan and other Essays. 1929.

LEE-CHAMBERS. A Shakespeare Reference Library. By S. Lee and E. K. Chambers. 2nd ed. 1925. [*English Association*, Pamphlet 61.]

LEFRANC. Sous le Masque de William Shakespeare. Par A. Lefranc. 2 vols. 1919.

LEO. Four Chapters of North's Plutarch. Edited by F. A. Leo. 1878.

Library. The Library: a Quarterly Review of Bibliography and Library Lore. 1st Series, 10 vols., 1889–98; 2nd Series, 10 vols. 1900–9; 3rd Series, 10 vols., 1910–19; 4th Series, vols. i–x, 1920–30. [In progress. See *Bibl. Trans.*]

LODGE. Illustrations of British History, Biography, and Manners in the Reigns of Henry VIII, Edward VI, Mary, Elizabeth, and James I. By E. Lodge. 3 vols., 1791; 2nd [3rd] ed., 3 vols., 1838.

LOOTEN. Shakespeare et la Religion. By C. Looten. 1924.

LOUNSBURY. Shakespeare as a Dramatic Artist. By T. R. Lounsbury. 1902.

LOUNSBURY. The First Editors of Shakespeare. 1906.

LUCE. Handbook to Shakespeare's Works. By M. Luce. 1906.

M. A. Minutes and Accounts of the Corporation of Stratford-on-Avon and other Records. Transcribed by R. Savage, with Introduction and Notes by E. I. Fripp. 4 vols., 1921–30. [*Dugdale Society*, in progress.]

MACHYN. The Diary of Henry Machyn, Citizen and Merchant-Taylor of London, 1550–63. Edited by J. G. Nichols. 1848. [*C. S.* xlii.]

MACKENZIE. The Women in Shakespeare's Plays. By A. M. Mackenzie. 1924.

MADDEN. The Diary of Master William Silence. By D. H. Madden. 1897, new ed. 1907.

MADDEN. Shakespeare and his Fellows. 1916.

MALONE. Supplement to the Edition of Shakespeare's Plays Published in 1778 by Samuel Johnson and George Steevens. By Edmond Malone. 2 vols. 1780. [With second appendix, 1783.]

MALONE, *Inquiry*. An Inquiry into the Authenticity of Certain Miscellaneous Papers and Legal Instruments. 1796.

MALONE. Letters to John Jordan, the Poet. Edited by H.P. 1864.

MALONE. Correspondence with the Rev. J. Davenport. Edited by H. P. 1864.

See *Variorum*.

Manly Studies. The [J. M.] Manly Anniversary Studies in Language and Literature. 1923.

MARRIOTT. English History in Shakespeare. By J. A. R. Marriott. 1918.

MARTIN. On Some of Shakespeare's Female Characters. By Helena Lady Martin. 1885.

MASEFIELD. William Shakespeare. By John Masefield. 1911. [*Home University Library.*]

MASSON. Shakespeare Personally. By D. Masson. 1914.

Materialien. Materialien zur Kunde des älteren englischen Dramas. Begründet und herausgegeben von W. Bang. Louvain. 44 vols., 1902–14.

MATHEW. An Image of Shakespeare. By F. Mathew. 1920.

McCALLUM. Shakespeare's Roman Plays and their Background. By M. W. McCallum. 1910.

McKERROW, *Dict.* A Dictionary of Printers and Booksellers, 1557–1640. By R. B. McKerrow and others. 1910. [*Bibl. Soc.*]

McKERROW, *Devices.* Printers' and Publishers' Devices, 1455–1640. 1913. [*Bibl. Soc.*]

McKERROW. An Introduction to Bibliography for Literary Students, 1927. See NASHE.

M. H. R. A. Bibl. Annual Bibliography of English Language and Literature. Edited by A. C. Paues, and later D. Everett, A. Seaton, M. S. Serjeantson. Vols. i–ix, for 1920–8. [*Modern Humanities Research Association.* In progress.]

Michigan Studies. Studies in Shakespeare, Milton and Donne. 1925. [*Univ. of Michigan.*]

Misc. Documents. Records of the Borough of Stratford-on-Avon, preserved at Shakespeare's Birth-place. [In *MS.*; cf. *B. P. Cat.*; H.P., *Cal.*]

M. L. N. Modern Language Notes. Vols. i–l, 1886–1930. [In progress.]

M. L. R. The Modern Language Review. Vols. i–xxv, 1905–30. [In progress.]

Monastic Estates. Abstract of the Bailiffs' Accounts of Monastic and Other Estates in the County of Warwick. Translated by W. B. Bickley. 1923. [*Dugdale Soc.*]

MORGAN. Mrs. Shakespeare's Second Marriage. By A. Morgan. 1926.

MOULTON. Shakespeare as a Dramatic Artist. By R. G. Moulton. 1885, 1897.

MOULTON. The Moral System of Shakespeare. 1903. 2nd ed. as Shakespeare as a Dramatic Thinker. 1907.

MOYES. Medicine and Kindred Arts in the Plays of Shakespeare. By I. Moyes. 1896.

M. P. Modern Philology: a Quarterly Journal devoted to Research in Modern Languages and Literatures. Vols. i–xxvii, 1903–30. [In progress].

M. S. C. Collections of the Malone Society. Vol. i, 1907–11; Vol. ii, pts. 1, 2, 1913–23. [In progress.]

M. S. R. The Malone Society Reprints. Edited by W. W. Greg and others. 62 vols., 1907–29. [In progress.]

MUNRO. The Shakespeare Allusion-Book, 1591–1700. Revised with Introduction by J. Munro. 2 vols., 1909.

MURRAY. English Dramatic Companies, 1558–1642. By J. T. Murray. 2 vols., 1910.

NASH. Collections for the History of Worcestershire. By T. R. Nash. 2nd ed., 2 vols., 1799.

NASHE. The Works of Thomas Nashe. Edited by R. B. McKerrow. 5 vols. 1904–10.

NEILSON-THORNDIKE. The Facts about Shakespeare. By W. A. Neilson and A. H. Thorndike. 1913.

NICHOL SMITH. Eighteenth-Century Essays on Shakespeare. Edited by D. Nichol Smith. 1903.

NICHOL SMITH. Shakespeare Criticism. A Selection. 1916.

NICHOL SMITH. Shakespeare in the Eighteenth Century. 1928.

NICHOLS, *Eliz.* The Progresses and Public Processions of Queen Elizabeth. By J. Nichols. 3 vols., 1788–1807; 2nd ed. 3 vols., 1823.

NICHOLS, *James.* The Progresses, Processions, and Magnificent Festivities of King James the First. 4 vols., 1828.

NICHOLS. Six Old Plays. 1779.

NICOLL. A History of Restoration Drama, 1660–1700. By Allardyce Nicoll. 1923.

NICOLL. Studies in Shakespeare. 1927.

NICOLL. Holinshed's Chronicles as Used in Shakespeare's Plays. Edited by A. and J. Nicoll. 1927.

NOBLE. Shakespeare's Use of Song. By R. S. H. Noble. 1923.

Noctes Shakespearianae. Papers by Members of the Winchester Shakespeare Society. Edited by C. H. Hawkins. 1887.

N. Q. Notes and Queries: a Medium of Intercommunication for Literary Men and General Readers. 13 Series, vols. i–clviii, 1850–1930. [In progress.]

N. S. S. New Shakspere Society.

N. S. S. Trans. Transactions of the New Shakspere Society, 1874, 1875–6, 1877–9, 1880–6, 1887–92.

NUNGEZER. A Dictionary of Actors and other Persons Associated with the Public Representation of Plays in England before 1642. By E. Nungezer. 1929.

N. U. S. Nebraska University Studies. Vols. i–xiii, [1888]–1913.

OLIPHANT. The Plays of Beaumont and Fletcher. By E. H. C. Oliphant. 1927.

ONIONS. A Shakespeare Glossary. By C. T. Onions. New ed. 1922.

Oxf. Bibl. Soc. Proceedings and Papers of the Oxford Bibliographical Society. Vols. i, ii, pts. 1–3, 1923–9. [In progress.]

PENNIMAN. The War of the Theatres. By J. H. Penniman. 1897.

PLOMER, Dict. A Dictionary of Booksellers and Printers, 1641–67. By H. R. Plomer. 1907. [Bibl. Soc.]

P. M. L. A. Publications of the Modern Language Association of America. Vols. i–xlv, 1886–1930. [In progress.]

POLLARD, F. Q. Shakespeare Folios and Quartos: a Study in the Bibliography of Shakespeare's Plays, 1594–1685. By A. W. Pollard. 1909.

POLLARD, S. F. Shakespeare's Fight with the Pirates and the Problems of the Transmission of his Text. 1917, 1920.

POLLARD. The Foundations of Shakespeare's Text. 1923. [British Academy.]
    See Sh.'s Hand, S. T. C.

Procl. Bibliography of Royal Proclamations, 1485–1714; with Historical Essay by R. Steele. 2 vols., 1910–11. [Bibliotheca Lindesiana, v, vi.]

QUILLER-COUCH. Shakespeare's Workmanship. By A. T. Quiller-Couch. 1918.

RALEIGH. Shakespeare. By Walter Raleigh. 1907. [English Men of Letters.]

Register. See SAVAGE.

R. E. S. The Review of English Studies. A Quarterly Journal of English Literature and the English Language. Vols. i–vi, 1925–30. [In progress.]

RHODES. Shakespeare's First Folio. By R. C. Rhodes. 1923.

R. H. S. Trans. Transactions of the Royal Historical Society. Four Series, 1873–1929. [In progress.]

RIBTON-TURNER. Shakespeare's Land. By C. J. Ribton-Turner. 1893.

ROBERTSON. Montaigne and Shakespeare. By J. M. Robertson. 1909.

ROBERTSON. The Baconian Heresy. A Confutation. 1913.

ROBERTSON. Shakespeare and Chapman. 1917.

ROBERTSON. The Shakespeare Canon. Parts i–iv. 1922–30.

ROBERTSON. Did Shakespeare Write Titus Andronicus? 1905. Revised as An Introduction to the Study of the Shakespeare Canon. 1924.

ROBERTSON. The Genuine in Shakespeare. 1930.

ROLFE. Life of Shakespeare. By W. J. Rolfe. 1904.

ROOT. Classical Mythology in Shakespeare. By R. K. Root. 1903.

RUDDER. A New History of Gloucestershire. By S. Rudder. 1779.

RUSHTON. Shakespeare a Lawyer. By W. L. Rushton. 1858.

RUSHTON. Shakespeare's Legal Maxims. 1859, 1907.

RUSHTON. Shakespeare's Testamentary Language. 1869.

RUSHTON. Shakespeare Illustrated by the Lex Scripta. 1870.

RUSHTON. Shakespeare an Archer. 1897.

RYE. England as seen by Foreigners in the Days of Elizabeth and James the First. By W. B. Rye. 1865.

RYLAND. Records of Rowington. By J. W. Ryland. 2 vols. 1896, 1922.

RYLAND. Records of Wroxall Abbey and Manor. 1903.

RYLAND. Parish Registers of Wroxall. 1903.

SACK. Darstellerzahl und Rollenverteilung bei Shakespeare. Von M. Sack. 1928.

SARRAZIN. William Shakespeares Lehrjahre. Von G. Sarrazin. 1897.

SARRAZIN. Aus Shakespeares Meisterwerkstatt. 1906.

SARRAZIN. Kleine Shakespeare-Studien. 1902.
    See SCHMIDT.

SAVAGE, F. G. The Flora and Folk-Lore of Shakespeare. By F. G. Savage. 1923.

SAVAGE, R. Edward Pudsey's Book. By R. Savage. 1888.

SAVAGE, R. The Parish Registers of Stratford-on-Avon. 3 vols., 1897–1905. [*Parish Register Society*.]

SCHELLING. Elizabethan Drama, 1558–1642. By F. E. Schelling. 2 vols., 1908.

SCHMIDT. Shakespeare-Lexicon. By Alexander Schmidt. 2 vols., 1874–5; 3rd ed. by G. Sarrazin, 1902.

SCHÜCKING. Die Charakterprobleme bei Shakespeare. Von L. L. Schücking. 1919. English Translation. 1922.

Sh. Association. Studies in the First Folio. By M. H. Spielmann, T. Dover Wilson, Sir Sidney Lee, R. C. Rhodes, W. W. Greg, Allardyce Nicoll, with an Introduction by Sir I. Gollancz. 1924.

Sh. Association. A Series of Papers on Shakespeare and the Theatre. By members of the Shakespeare Association. 1927.

Sh. Eng. Shakespeare's England. An Account of the Life and Manners of his Age. [By various writers.] 2 vols., 1916, 1926.

Sh. Homage. A Book of Homage to Shakespeare. Edited by I. Gollancz. 1916.

Sh. Q. Shakespeare Quarto Facsimiles. Issued under the Superintendence of F. J. Furnivall. 43 vols., 1880–9.

Sh. Soc. The Shakespeare Society. 1841–53.

Sh. Soc. P. The Shakespeare Society's Papers. 4 vols., 1844, 1845, 1847, 1849.

Sh.'s Hand. Shakespeare's Hand in the Play of Sir Thomas More. By A. W. Pollard, W. W. Greg, E. M. Thompson, J. D. Wilson, and R. W. Chambers. 1923.

SHAW, A. C. An Index to the Shakespeare Memorial Library. By A. C. Shaw. 3 Parts, 1900–3. [*Birmingham Free Libraries*.]

SHAW, W. A. The Knights of England. By W. A. Shaw. 2 vols., 1906.

SIMPSON, P. Shakespearian Punctuation. By P. Simpson. 1911.

SIMPSON, R. The School of Shakespeare. Edited by R. Simpson. 2 vols., 1878.

SIMROCK. Die Quellen des Shakespeare in Novellen, Märchen und Sagen. Von K. Simrock, etc. 1831, 1870.

SKEAT. Shakespeare's Plutarch. Edited by W. W. Skeat. 1875.

SMALL. The Stage-Quarrel between Ben Jonson and the So-called Poetasters. By R. A. Small. 1899.

SMART. Shakespeare Truth and Tradition. By J. S. Smart. 1928.

S. P. Studies in Philology. Vols. xii–xxvii, 1915–30. [*University of North Carolina.* In progress.]

S. P. D. Calendar of State Papers: Domestic Series, of the Reigns of Edward VI, Mary, Elizabeth, and James I. Edited by R. Lemon [and later, M. A. E. Green]. 12 vols., 1856–72.

SPENS. An Essay on Shakespeare's Relation to Tradition. By J. Spens. 1916.

SPURGEON. Leading Motives in the Imagery of Shakespeare's Tragedies. By C. F. E. Spurgeon. 1930. [*Shakespeare Association.*]

S. R. Stationers' Register. *See* ARBER; EYRE.

STAPFER. Shakespeare and Classical Antiquity. By P. Stapfer. 1880.

STAUNTON. Memorials of Shakespeare. By H. Staunton. [1864.]

S. T. C. A Short-Title Catalogue of Books Printed in England, Scotland, and Ireland, and of English Books Printed Abroad, 1475–1640. Compiled by A. W. Pollard and G. R. Redgrave. 1926. [*Bibl. Soc.*]

STEELE. Plays and Masques at Court during the Reigns of Elizabeth, James and Charles. By M. S. Steele. 1926.

STOKES, F. G. A Dictionary of the Characters and Proper Names in the Works of Shakespeare. By F. G. Stokes. 1924.

STOKES, H. P. An Attempt to Determine the Chronological Order of Shakespeare's Plays. By H. P. Stokes. 1878.

STOLL. Shakespeare Studies. By E. E. Stoll. 1927.

STOPES. Shakespeare's Family. By C. C. Stopes. 1901.

STOPES. Shakespeare's Warwickshire Contemporaries. 1907.

STOPES. Burbage and Shakespeare's Stage. 1913.

STOPES. Shakespeare's Environment. 1914, 1918.

STOPES. Shakespeare's Industry. 1916.

STOPES. The Life of Henry, Third Earl of Southampton. 1922.

STOW. Annales, or, a General Chronicle of England. Begun by J. Stow. Continued and Augmented unto 1631 by E. Howes. 1580, 1592, 1605, 1615, 1631.

STOW, *Survey.* A Survey of London. By John Stow, 1598, &c. Edited by C. L. Kingsford. 2 vols., 1908.

STRATFORD-ON-AVON. The Grammar School of King Edward VI. A Tercentenary Volume. 1853. See *B. P. Cat.*, FRIPP, H. P., LEE, *M. A.*, *Misc. Docts.*, SAVAGE, WHELER, &c.

SUGDEN. A Topographical Dictionary to the Works of Shakespeare and his Fellow Dramatists. By E. H. Sugden. 1925.

SWINBURNE. A Study of Shakespeare. By A. C. Swinburne. 1880.

Sydney Papers. Letters and Memorials of State. Written and Collected by Sir Henry Sydney, Sir Philip Sydney, Sir Robert Sydney, &c. By A. Collins. 2 vols., 1746.

SYKES. Sidelights on Shakespeare. By H. D. Sykes. 1919.

SYKES. Sidelights on Elizabethan Drama. 1924.

SYMONS. Studies in the Elizabethan Drama. By A. Symons. 1920.

TANNENBAUM. The Shakespeare Coat of Arms. By S. A. Tannenbaum. 1908.

TANNENBAUM. Problems in Shakespeare's Penmanship, including a Study of the Poet's Will. 1927.

TANNENBAUM. Shakespeare Forgeries in the Revels Accounts. 1928.

TAYLOR. Shakespeare's Debt to Montaigne. By G. C. Taylor. 1925.

TEN BRINK. Five Lectures on Shakespeare. By B. ten Brink. Translated by J. Franklin. 1895.

Texas Studies. A Memorial Volume to Shakespeare and Harvey. 1916. [*Univ. of Texas.*]

THOMPSON. Shakespeare's Handwriting. By E. M. Thompson. 1916.

THOMS. Three Notelets on Shakespeare. By W. J. Thoms. 1865.

THORNDIKE. The Influence of Beaumont and Fletcher on Shakespeare. By A. H. Thorndike. 1901.

THORNDIKE. Shakespeare's Theatre. 1916.

T. L. S. The Times Literary Supplement. 1902–30. [In progress.]

TOLMAN. The Views about Hamlet, and other Essays. By A. H. Tolman. 1904.

ULRICI. Shakespeares dramatische Kunst. Von H. Ulrici. 1839. English Translation by L. D. Schmitz. 2 vols., 1876.

VAN DAM-STOFFEL. William Shakespeare, Prosody and Text. By B. A. P. van Dam and C. Stoffel. 1900.

VAN DAM-STOFFEL. Chapters on English Printing, Prosody, and Pronunciation, 1559–1700. 1902.

Variorum. The Plays and Poems of William Shakespeare. With a Life of the Poet and an Enlarged History of the Stage. By the late E. Malone. Edited by J. Boswell. 21 vols., 1821. [Vol. iii also contains Chalmers's *Account of the English Stage.*]

V. H. The Victorian History of the Counties of England. Edited by W. Page and others. [In progress. Vols. i, ii only issued for Warwickshire, 1904, 1908. Complete for Worcestershire, 4 vols., 1901–24.]

VIËTOR. Shakespeare's Pronunciation. By W. Viëtor. 2 vols., 1906.

WALLACE. Advance Sheets from Shakespeare, the Globe, and Blackfriars. By C. W. Wallace. 1909. [Privately printed.]

WARD, A. W. History of English Dramatic Literature to the Death of Queen Anne. By A. W. Ward. 2 vols., 1875; 2nd ed., 3 vols., 1899.

WARD, H. S., C. W. Shakespeare's Town and Times. By H. S. and C. W. Ward. 1896, 1905.

WARNER. Catalogue of the Manuscripts and Muniments at Dulwich. [Vol. i.] By G. F. Warner. 1881.

WENDELL. William Shakespeare. A Study in Elizabethan Literature. By Barrett Wendell. 1894.

WETZ. Die Lebensnachrichten über Sh. mit dem Versuch einer Jugend- und Bildungsgeschichte des Dichters. Von W. Wetz. 1912.

WHELER. History and Antiquities of Stratford-on-Avon. By R. B. Wheler. 1806.

WHELER. Historical Account of the Birthplace of Shakespeare. 1824, 1863.

Wheler MSS. Collections of R. B. Wheler, preserved at Shakespeare's Birthplace. [In *MS.*; cf. *B. P. Cat.*]

WILSON, J. D. The Copy for Hamlet, 1603, and the Hamlet Transcript, 1593. By J. D. Wilson. 1918.

WILSON, J. D. The Elizabethan Shakespeare. 1929. [*British Academy.*]

WILSON, F. P. The Plague in Shakespeare's London. By F. P. Wilson. 1927.

WINDLE. Shakespeare's Country. By B. C. A. Windle. 1899.

WINWOOD. Memorials of Affairs of State in the Reigns of Queen Elizabeth and King James I. Collected (chiefly) from the Original Papers of the Right Honourable Sir Ralph Winwood. By E. Sawyer. 3 vols., 1725.

Wisconsin Studies. Shakespeare Studies by Members of the Department of English of the University of Wisconsin. 1916.

WISE. Shakespeare, his Birthplace and its Neighbourhood. By J. R. Wise. 1861.

WISLICENUS. Shakespeares Totenmaske. By P. Wislicenus. 1910.

WOLFF. Shakespeare, Der Dichter und sein Werk. Von M. J. Wolff. 2 vols., 1907. Ed. 6. 1926.

Worcester Wills. Calendar of Wills and Administrations in the Consistory Court of the Bishop of Worcester. Edited by E. A. Fry. 2 vols., 1904, 1910. [*Index Library* of *British Record Society*, xxxi, xxxix.]

WORDSWORTH. Shakespeare's Knowledge and Use of the Bible. By C. Wordsworth, 1864; ed. 4, 1892.

WRIGHT. Queen Elizabeth and her Times. A Series of Original Letters. Edited by T. Wright. 2 vols., 1838.

WYLD. A History of Modern Colloquial English. By H. C. Wyld. 1920, 1925.

Year's Work. The Year's Work in English Studies. Edited by Sidney Lee, and later F. S. Boas and C. H. Herford. Vols. i–ix, for 1920–8. [*English Association.* In progress.]

YEATMAN. The Gentle Shakspeare. By J. P. Yeatman. [1896]; ed. 4, 1906.

YOUNG. The History of Dulwich College, with a Life of the Founder, Edward Alleyn, and an Accurate Transcript of his Diary, 1617–22. By W. Young. 2 vols., 1889.

SUBJECT-INDEX

[This index is selective, not exhaustive. In particular, many topics in chh. iv–viii find further unindexed illustration in chh. ix, x. The more important excursuses and extracts are distinguished by thick type. The titles of non-extant plays are in inverted commas.]

I. PLAYS.

What You Will. See *Twelfth Night.*
When You See Me, You Know Me, i. 498.
Winter's Tale, i. 70, 102, 104, 151, 154, 197, 233, 485, **487–90**; ii. 207, 248, 340, 342, 343, 346, 347, 352.

Wisdom of Dr. Dodipoll, i. 397.
'*Wise Man of West Chester*', i. 510.
Witch, i. 92, 125, 472.
Woman in the Moon, i. 490.

Yorkshire Tragedy, i. 134, **535.**

II. PERSONS.

Accolti, Bernardo, i. 452.
Adams, John, player, i. 53.
Addenbroke, John, i. 84; ii. 114–18.
Adlington, W., i. 362.
Adorno, Prospero, i. 494.
Aldus Manutius, i. 190.
Alençon, Francois, duc de, i. 337.
Allde, Edward, stationer, i. 169.
Alleyn, Edward, player, i. 38, 39, 45, 48, 51, 54, 55; ii. 215, 274, 312–14, 379, 386, 389.
Alleyn, John, player, i. 39, 41, 48, 51, 52, 513.
Amyot, Jacques, i. 401.
Anne, queen, i. 414; ii. 332.
Antonio of Portugal, i. 372.
Appian, i. 401, 478.
Apuleius, i. 362, 487.
Archer, Edward, stationer, i. 538.
Arden family, i. 12; ii. **28–32,** 39.
Arden, Robert, i. 11, 12; ii. **18–32,** **35–41.**
Arden, Thomas, ii. 30–2.
Ariosto, Ludovico, i. 388.
Aristotle, i. 444.
Armin, Robert, player, i. 79, 83, 411; ii. 73–9.
Ashborne, Edward, player, ii. 81.
Ashley, Sir John, i. 99, 100, 130.
Aspley, William, stationer, i. 131, 138.
Attewell. *See* Ottewell.
Aubrey, John, i. 12 *sqq.*; ii. **252.**
Aumont, Maréchal de, i. 338.
Ayrer, Jacob, i. 388, 493.

B., C. (1614), ii. **219.**
B, R. (1594), ii. **190.**
'b. Samme', player, i. 44, 52.
Bacon, Anne, ii. 160–6.
Bacon, Sir Francis, i. 444; ii. 196, 327.
Bacon, Mathias, ii. 159–69.
Bagley, Edward, ii. 7, 164, 180, 240.

Baker, Daniel, ii. 103–5, 122.
Bales, Peter, i. 161.
Bancroft, Thomas, ii. 373.
Bandello, Matteo, i. 346, 387, 407, 518.
Banks, John, i. 335.
Barber, Thomas, ii. 143, 149.
Bardolfe, George, i. 25, 396.
Barker family, ii. 118–27.
Barksted, William, i. 453; ii. **216.**
Barnes, Barnabe, i. 561, 568.
Barnes, Joshua, i. 20; ii. **257.**
Barnfield, Richard, i. 548; ii. 190, **195.**
Basse, William, i. 557; ii. **226.**
Beauchamp family, ii. 26, 29, 32.
Beaumont, Francis, i. 70, 210, 219, 221, 399, 486, 492, 532, 542, 557; ii. **222.**
Beeston, Christopher, player, i. 80, 136, 147; ii. 71–82, 252.
Beeston, William, player, i. 22, 85, 90, 101, 149; ii. 252.
Belleforest, F. de, i. 387, 407, 423.
Bellenden, John, i. 475.
Belott, Stephen, ii. 90–5.
Belt, T., player, i. 44.
Bendish, Sir Thomas, ii. 159–65.
Benfield, Robert, player, i. 80; ii. 65–77, 348.
Benson, John, stationer, i. 557; ii. **237.**
Bentley, Thomas, ii. 98.
Berkeley, Sir Thomas, i. 358, 567.
Bernard, Sir John, i. 90; ii. 13, 180, 269.
Betterton, Thomas, player, i. 16, 107; ii. 262, 263, 264, 268, 271, 276, 277, 281, 540.
Bettie, W., i. 363.
Bevis, player, i. 50, 288; ii. 80.
Bindon, Thomas Howard, viscount, i. 571.
Birch, George, player, ii. 78.

F f

III. GENERAL

i. 161, 350, 465, 521; purpose of, i.
158, 289, 327. *See* Quartos, Textual
corruption.
Reprints, i. 133, 136, 175, 185.
Revels Accounts, i. 206; ii. **330, 341**.
'Revises', i. 173.
Revision of plays, i. 211–35.
Revivals of plays, i. 211, 235–42; ii.
329–53.
'Rhetoric' in typography, i. 191–6.
Rhyme, i. 256, 258, 267, 444, 455.
Rose theatre, i. 37, 43, 293; ii. 307,
311, 316, 317.
Rowington, ii. 111–13; Shakespeares
of, ii. 28, 359–63.
'Run-on' lines. *See* Overflows.

Scansion. *See* Metre.
Scenari, i. 493.
Scene-divisions, i. 118, 124, 155, 199.
Scenes, new or altered, at revivals, i.
212–14, 285, 291, 321, 361.
'Schallanalyse', i. 467.
'Scrolls', i. 124, 198, 370.
'Servitors', i. 108. *See* Hired men.
'Sharers', i. 78; ii. **68–71, 77–80**,
224.
Short lines, i. 229, 258.
Shorthand, i. 147, 159–62, 350, 391,
465, 521.
Shottery, ii. 47–51, 101.
'Signatures', i. 172.
'Slurred' syllables, i. 262.
Snitterfield, i. 5, 11, 12, 14; ii. 5, 14,
26–8, 31, 39–41; Shakespeares of, ii.
14.
Social criticism in plays, i. 102, 116,
238, 467.
Songs, i. 235, 402, 405, 455, 460, 462,
472.
Sources, as evidence of date, i. 245.
'Spear-shaking', i. 84, 443.
Spectacle, interpolation of, i. 235, 302,
404, 472, 486, 493.
Speech-endings in mid-line, i. 230,
265; table of, ii. 401.
Speech-prefixes, i. 113, 118, 203, 236,
307, 315, 326, 370, 510.
Speech-rules, i. 113, 123, 204.
Split lines, i. 184, 459, 477. *See* Pause-
variation.
Spondaic feet, i. 259.

Stafford's men, i. 45; ii. 315.
Stage, early history of, i. 27; regula-
tion of, i. 28; opposition to, i. 29.
Stage-adaptation of plays, i. 98, 108–
12, 117–22, 153, 158, 164, 235–7,
284, 298, 380, 416. *See* Book-
keepers.
Stage-directions, i. 113, 118–22, 154,
157, 181, 201–3, 236, 283, 300, 306,
323, 341, 416, 491.
Stage-keepers, i. 108.
Stage-right, i. 147, 208.
Stationers' Company, i. 128, 136.
Stationers' Register, i. 128, 145, 245.
'Staying' of plays, i. 145.
Stenography, i. 161.
Strange's men, i. 38, 39–41; ii. 305.
See Alleyn company.
Strange's tumblers, i. 32, 33, 39, 41.
Stratford-on-Avon, i. 3–11; manor, i.
4, 5, 6, 75; ii. 147; charters, i. 7, 8;
corporation, i. 7; court of record,
ii. 25, **113–18**; charnel-house, ii. 261,
290; gild, i. 5, 7; ii. 130; college, i.
6, 7; ii. 125, 132, 135; grammar
school, i. 5, 6, 9, 22; 'pastoral' at,
i. 9; decay, i. 8; ii. 99–101; extracts
from registers, ii. **1–13**.
Stress-variation, i. 259.
Style, percipience of, i. 219; analysis
of, i. 220, 253; in early drama, i.
223, 317; as evidence of authorship, i.
220–3; as evidence of date, i. 254–
69. *See* Shakespeare.
'Stylistic' revision of plays, i. 213, 215,
218, 234, 282, 298.
Subsidies, ii. 87–90, 105.
'Supernumeraries', i. 120, 236.
'Surreptitious' play-prints, i. 55, 143,
147, 156, 162, 225, 298. *See* Quartos,
'Reported' plays.
Sussex's men, i. 28, 36, 37, 46, 47, 54,
60, 315–21; ii. 306–18.
Swan theatre, i. 411.
Syllabic variation, i. 260; tables of, ii.
400, 404.

Tables, of metre, ii. 397; of play-dates,
i. 246, 270; of quartos, ii. 394.
Temple Grafton, ii. 45, 51.
Tenancy, 'joint' and 'in common', i.
82; ii. 66.

PRINTED IN GREAT BRITAIN AT THE UNIVERSITY PRESS, OXFORD
BY JOHN JOHNSON, PRINTER TO THE UNIVERSITY